W9-BMZ-944

Praise for the
Barefoot Bay series!

"Lovely, lush, and layered—this story took my breath away. Rich, believable characters, multilayered plot, gorgeous setting, and a smokin' hot romance. One of the best books I've read all year."

—Kristan Higgins, *New York Times*
bestselling author

"Pack this one in your beach bag and get ready for nonstop fun."

—Susan Mallery, *New York Times*
bestselling author

"An all-around knockout and soul-satisfying read. I loved everything about this book...Roxanne St. Claire writes with warmth and heart, and the community she's built in Barefoot Bay is one I want to revisit again and again and again."

—Mariah Stewart, *New York Times*
bestselling author

"St. Claire writes books that keep the reader engrossed in the story from cover to cover."

—*Booklist*

"Readers will be delighted."

—*Library Journal*

"4½ Stars! St. Claire, as always, brings a scorching tear-up-the-sheets romance combined with a great story: dealing with real issues starring memorable characters in vivid scenes."

—*RT Book Reviews*

meet me in barefoot bay

Also by Roxanne St. Claire

Guardian Angelinos Series
Edge of Sight
Shiver of Fear
Face of Danger

Barefoot Bay Series
Barefoot in the Sand
Barefoot in the Rain
Barefoot in the Sun
Barefoot by the Sea

meet me in barefoot bay

Two Complete Novels:
Barefoot in the Sand and
Barefoot in the Rain

Roxanne St. Claire

FOREVER

NEW YORK   BOSTON

This book is a work of fiction. Names, characters, places, and incidents are the product of the author's imagination or are used fictitiously. Any resemblance to actual events, locales, or persons, living or dead, is coincidental.

Copyright © 2021 by Roxanne St. Claire
Barefoot in the Rain copyright © 2012 by Roxanne St. Claire
Barefoot in the Sand copyright © 2012 by Roxanne St. Claire

Cover design by Daniela Medina. Cover images © Shutterstock.
Cover copyright © 2021 by Hachette Book Group, Inc.

Hachette Book Group supports the right to free expression and the value of copyright. The purpose of copyright is to encourage writers and artists to produce the creative works that enrich our culture.

The scanning, uploading, and distribution of this book without permission is a theft of the author's intellectual property. If you would like permission to use material from the book (other than for review purposes), please contact permissions@hbgusa.com. Thank you for your support of the author's rights.

Forever
Hachette Book Group
1290 Avenue of the Americas, New York, NY 10104
read-forever.com
twitter.com/readforeverpub

Barefoot in the Rain originally published in mass market by Hachette Book Group in 2012.
Barefoot in the Sand originally published in mass market by Hachette Book Group in 2012.

First Edition: March 2021

Forever is an imprint of Grand Central Publishing. The Forever name and logo are trademarks of Hachette Book Group, Inc.

The publisher is not responsible for websites (or their content) that are not owned by the publisher.

The Hachette Speakers Bureau provides a wide range of authors for speaking events. To find out more, go to www.hachettespeakersbureau.com or call (866) 376-6591.

Library of Congress Cataloging-in-Publication Data has been applied for.

ISBNs: 978-1-5387-5406-1 (trade paperback); 978-1-5387-3798-9 (ebook)

Printed in the United States of America

LSC-C

Printing 1, 2021

Contents

Barefoot in the Sand

For Deborah Brooks,
my sister, my friend, my blessing.

Chapter One

ᴄᴄ

The kitchen windows shot out like cannons, one right after another, followed by the ear-splitting crash of the antique breakfront nose-diving to the tile floor.

Shit. Granny Dot's entire Old Country Rose service for twelve was in there.

Lacey pressed against the closet door, eyes closed, body braced, mind reeling. This was it. Everything she owned—a meager baking business, a fifty-year-old hand-me-down house, and a few antiques she'd collected over the years—was about to be destroyed, demolished, and dumped into Barefoot Bay by the hand of Hurricane Damien.

She stole a glance over her shoulder. Everything she owned, but not everything she *had*. No matter what happened to the house, she had to save her daughter.

"We need to get in the bathtub and under a mattress!"

Lacey screamed over the train-like howl of one-hundred-and-ten-mile-per-hour winds.

Ashley cowered deeper into the corner of the closet, a stuffed unicorn clutched in one hand, her cell phone in the other. "I told you we should have evacuated!"

Only a fourteen-year-old would argue at a moment like this. "I can't get the mattress into the bathroom alone."

The storm was inside now, tearing the chandelier out of the dining room ceiling, clattering crystal everywhere. Pictures ripped off their hooks with vicious thuds and furniture skated across the oak floor. Overhead, half-century-old roof trusses moaned in a last-ditch effort to cling to the eaves.

They had minutes left.

"We have to hurry, Ash. On the count of—"

"I'm not leaving here," Ashley cried. "I'm too scared. I'm not going out there."

Lacey corralled every last shred of control. "We are. Together."

"We'll die out there, Mom!"

"No, but we'll die in here." At Ashley's wail, Lacey kneeled in front of her, sacrificing precious seconds. "Honey, I've lived on this island my whole life and this isn't the first hurricane." Just the worst. "We have to get in the tub and under the mattress. *Now.*"

Taking a firm grip, she pulled Ashley to her feet, the cell-phone screen spotlighting a tear-stained face. God, Lacey wanted to tumble into Ashley's nest of hastily grabbed treasures and cry with her daughter.

But then she'd die with her daughter.

Ashley bunched the unicorn under her chin. "How could those weather people be so wrong?"

Good damn question. All day long, and into the night, the storm had been headed north to the Panhandle, not expected to do more than bring heavy rain and wind to the west coast of Florida. Until a few hours ago, when Hurricane Damien had jumped from a cat-three to a cat-four and veered to the east, making a much closer pass to the barrier island of Mimosa Key.

In the space of hours, ten thousand residents, including Lacey and Ashley, had been forced to make a rapid run-or-hide decision. A few tourists managed to haul butt over the causeway to the mainland, but most of the hurricane-experienced islanders were looking for mattress cover and porcelain protection about now. And praying. Hard.

Lacey cupped her hands on Ashley's cheeks. "We have to do this, Ashley. We can't panic, okay?"

Ashley nodded over and over again. "Okay, Mom. Okay."

"On the count of three. One, two—"

Three was drowned out by the gut-wrenching sound of the carport roof tearing away.

Lacey pushed open the closet door. Her bedroom was pitch black, but she moved on instinct, grateful the storm hadn't breached these walls yet.

"Get around to the other side of the bed," she ordered, already throwing back the comforter, searching wildly for a grip. "I'll pull, you push."

Ashley rallied and obeyed, sending a jolt of love and appreciation through Lacey. "Atta girl. A little more."

Right then the freight train of wind roared down the back hall, hurtling an antique mirror and shattering it against the bedroom door.

"It's coming!" Ashley screamed, freezing in fear.

Yes, it was. Like a monster, the storm would tear these old walls right down to the foundation Lacey's grandfather had laid when he'd arrived on Mimosa Key in the 1940s.

"Push the damn mattress, Ashley!"

Ashley gave it all she had and the mattress slid enough for Lacey to get a good grip. Grunting, she got the whole thing off the bed and dragged it toward the bathroom. They struggled to shove it through the door just as the wind knocked out one of the bedroom windows, showering glass and wood behind them.

"Oh my God, Mom. This is it!"

"No, this isn't *it*," Lacey hissed, trying to heave the mattress. "Get in!" She pushed Ashley toward the thousand-pound cast-iron claw-foot tub that had just transformed from last year's lavish expenditure into their sole means of survival.

In the shadows Lacey could see Ashley scramble into the tub, but the mattress was stuck on something in the door. She turned to maneuver the beast when the other window ruptured with a stunning crash.

Ducking from the flying debris, Lacey saw what had the mattress jammed.

Ashley's unicorn.

Window blinds came sailing in behind her. No time. No time for unicorns.

"Hurry, Mom!"

With a Herculean thrust, she freed the mattress, the force propelling her toward the tub, but in her mind all she could see was the goddamn unicorn.

The one Zoe brought to the hospital when Ashley

was born and Ashley slept with every night until she was almost ten. In minutes Aunt Zoe's uni would be a memory, like everything else they owned.

From inside the tub Ashley reached up and pulled at Lacey's arm. "Get in!"

This time Lacey froze, the mattress pressing down with the full weight of what they were losing. Everything. Every picture, every gift, every book, every Christmas ornament, every—

"Mom!"

The bathroom door slammed shut behind her, caught in a crosswind, making the room eerily quiet for a second.

In that instant of suspended time, Lacey dove for the unicorn, scooping it up with one hand while managing to brace the mattress with the other.

"What are you doing?" Ashley hollered.

"Saving something." She leaped into the tub on top of her shrieking daughter, dropping the stuffed animal so she could hoist the mattress over and seal them in a new kind of darkness.

The door shot back open, the little window over the toilet gave way, and tornado-strength winds whipped through the room. Under her, Lacey could hear her daughter sobbing, feel her quivering with fright, her coltish legs squeezing for dear life.

And life *was* dear. Troubled, stressful, messy, not everything she dreamed it would be, but dear. Lacey Armstrong was not about to give it up to Mother Nature's temper tantrum.

"Reach around me and help me hold this thing down," Lacey demanded, her fingernails breaking as she dug into the quilted tufts, desperate for a grip.

Her arms screaming with the effort, she clung to the mattress, closed her eyes, and listened to the sounds of that dear life literally falling apart around her.

It wasn't much, this old house she'd inherited from her grandparents, built with big dreams and little money, but it was all she had.

No, it wasn't, she reminded herself again. All she had was quivering and crying underneath her. Everything else was just stuff. Wet, ruined, storm-tattered *stuff.* They were alive and they had each other and their wits and dreams and hopes.

"This is a nightmare, Mom." Ashley's sob silenced Lacey's inner litany of life-support platitudes.

"Just hold on, Ash. We'll make it. I've been through worse." Hadn't she?

Wasn't it worse to return to Mimosa Key a pregnant college dropout, facing her mother's bitter and brutal disappointment? Wasn't it worse to stare into David Fox's dreamy, distant eyes and say "I'm going to keep this baby," only for him to announce he was on his way to a sheep farm in Patagonia?

Pata-frickin'-gonia. It still ticked her off, fourteen years later.

She was *not* going to die, damn it. And neither was Ashley. She stole a look over her shoulder, meeting her daughter's petrified gaze.

"Listen to me," Lacey demanded through gritted teeth. "I'm not going to let anything happen to you."

Ashley managed a nod.

They just had to hang on and...pray. Because most people would be cutting some sweet deals with God at a time like this. But Lacey wasn't most people, and she didn't make deals with anybody. She made plans. Lots of plans that never—

A strong gust lifted the mattress, pulling a scream from her throat as rain and wind and debris whipped over them, and then part of the ceiling thudded down on the mattress. With the weight of saturated drywall and insulation holding their makeshift roof in place, Lacey could let go of the mattress. Relieved, she worked a space on the edge where the tub curved down to give them some air and finally let her body squeeze in next to Ashley.

Now Lacey could think of something else besides survival.

After survival, comes…what? Facing the stark truth that everything was gone. What was she going to do with no home, no clothes, no struggling cake-baking business, and maybe no customers remaining on Mimosa Key to buy her cookies and cupcakes?

The answer was the thunderous roar of the rest of the second floor being ripped away as if an imaginary giant had plucked a weed from his garden. Instantly rain dumped on them.

Once the roof was gone the vacuum dissipated, and, except for the drumbeat of rain on the mattress, it was almost quiet.

"Is this the eye of the storm?" Ashley asked.

Lacey adjusted her position again to curl around Ashley's slender frame. "I don't know, honey. Hey, look what I brought you."

She fished out the unicorn from behind her and laid it on Ashley's chest. Even in the darkness she could see Ashley smile, her eyes bright with tears.

"Aunt Zoe's uni. Thank you, Mommy."

Mommy just about folded her heart in half.

"Shhh." She stroked Ashley's hair, trying to be grateful for the rare moment when her daughter didn't roll her eyes or whip out her cell phone to text a friend. "We're gonna be fine, angel. I promise."

But could she keep that promise? When the storm passed, the home her grandfather had christened Blue Horizon House would be little more than a memory sitting on a stretch of pristine beach known as Barefoot Bay.

But Mimosa Key would still be here. Nothing could wipe away this barrier island or the people who called this strip of land home. Like Lacey, most of the residents were the children and grandchildren of the first group of twentieth-century pioneers who'd built a rickety wooden causeway to take them to an island haven in the Gulf of Mexico.

And nothing could rid Mimosa Key of its natural resources, like magical Barefoot Bay with its peach-toned sunsets or the fluffy red flowers that exploded like fireworks every spring, giving the island its name. Nothing could stop the reliable blue moon that sparkled like diamonds on the black velvet Gulf every night.

If Mimosa Key survived, so would Lacey.

And there is such a thing as insurance, a pragmatic voice insisted.

Insurance would cover the value of the house, and she owned the land, so Lacey could rebuild. Maybe this was her chance to finally turn the big old beach cottage into a B and B, a dream she'd nurtured for years, one she'd promised both her grandparents she'd pursue when they'd left her the house and all the land around it.

But life had gotten in the way of that promise. And now she had nothing.

Instead of wallowing in that reality, she let the B and B idea settle over her heart once again, the idea of finally, *finally* seeing one of her dreams come true carrying her through the rest of the storm while Ashley drifted off into a fitful sleep.

By the time the howling had softened to a low moan and the rain had slowed to a steady drizzle, the first silver threads of dawn were weaving through the air space she'd made. It was time to face the aftermath of the storm. Using all the strength she had left, Lacey managed to push the soaked mattress to the floor.

"Oh my God." Ashley's voice cracked with whispered disbelief as she emerged. "It's all gone."

Yes, it was. A dilapidated old house that was more trouble than it was ever worth had been washed away by Hurricane Damien's clean-up campaign. Lacey's heart was oddly light in the face of the devastation. Buoyed, in fact, with possibilities.

"Don't worry," she said, gingerly navigating the debris, peering into the early morning light. "It's not the end of the world." It was the beginning.

"How can you say that, Mom? There's nothing left!"

A few drops of warm tropical rain splattered her face, but Lacey wiped the water from her cheek and stepped over broken wall studs wrapped in shredded, sopping-wet attic insulation.

"We have insurance, Ashley."

"Mom! Our house is gone!"

"No, the *building's* gone. The beach is here. The sun will shine. The palm fronds will grow back."

Her imagination stirred again, nudged alive by the reality of what she saw around her. She could do this.

This land—and the insurance money—could be used to make a dream come true.

Beside her Ashley sniffed, wiping a fresh set of tears. "How can you talk about palm fronds? We don't even have a—oh!" She dropped to her knees to retrieve a muddy video-game remote. "My Wii!"

"Ashley." Lacey reached for her, pulling her up to hold her close. "Baby, we have each other. We're alive, which is pretty much a miracle."

Ashley just squeezed her eyes shut and nodded, working so hard to be strong and brave.

"I know it hurts, Ashley, but this"—she took the broken remote and pitched it—"is just *stuff*. We'll get more, better stuff. What matters is that we've made it through and, you know, I'm starting to think this hurricane was the best thing that ever happened to us."

Ashley's eyes popped open with an incredulous look. "Are you nuts?"

Maybe she was, but insane optimism was all she had right now.

"Think about it, Ash. We can do anything with this property now. We don't have to pay to remodel a sixty-year-old house; we can start from scratch and make it amazing." Her voice rose as the idea sprouted to life and took hold of her heart. "You know I've always dreamed of opening an inn or B and B, something all mine that would be an oasis, a destination."

Ashley just closed her eyes as if she couldn't even compute an *oasis* right then. "But if you couldn't figure out a way to make it happen when you had an actual house, how can you now?"

The truth stung, but Lacey ignored the pain. This time

she wouldn't make excuses, that was how. She wouldn't be scared of not finishing what she started and she wouldn't let anyone's disapproval make her doubt herself. Not anymore.

"Old Mother Nature just handed us a 'get out of jail free' pass, kiddo," she said, giving Ashley's shoulder a squeeze. "And you know what? We're taking it."

Chapter Two

⌒

Six Weeks Later

He's probably at lunch.
He wouldn't take a job this small.
He might refuse to come to Florida in August.

Lacey had plenty of reasons why she shouldn't press the Call button and ask to speak with Clayton Walker, president and CEO of Walker Architecture and Design. A trickle of sweat meandered down her back and trailed into the waistband of the cutoffs Ashley had pronounced too short for a mom to wear.

Too short? Too bad. She could walk around Barefoot Bay naked if she wanted to. Ever since the storm had ravaged the north hook of the island, she and Ashley had been alone out here at the beach. The insurance adjusters had come and gone, promising the rebuilding money, and the bulldozers had already leveled the storm-damaged house. Lacey's two neighbors, one to the north and one to the south and neither very close by, had bailed after settling their claims and promising to sell her their lots for a song.

The next step in her ambitious scheme didn't require age-appropriate attire, anyway. Her sweaty finger streaked the smooth glass of her phone, but before she dialed, she set the phone on the picnic table, one of the few items she'd salvaged from the storm.

What was stopping her from calling the architect?

Fear of rejection? Of course, an architect with Clayton Walker's outstanding credentials, reputation, and portfolio of glorious hotels and resorts might not want to design her beachfront bed-and-breakfast.

But he *had* responded to her e-mail personally. And he *had* said, "Call when you have the insurance money and I'll take a look at the property."

She swiped beads of sweat from her upper lip and scooted the bench closer to the table, trying to slide into the one slice of shade formed by the trunk of a royal poinciana that had survived the storm. Peering through humidity-drenched curls, she studied her daughter at the water's edge a few hundred feet of burning sand away. Madly texting, something she'd been doing more and more of lately, Ashley seemed oblivious to the squawking seagulls fluttering around her.

Ashley had rebounded remarkably after the storm, moving into Lacey's parents' house with a fairly positive attitude, probably since living down on the south end of the island put her closer to more kids she'd be going to Mimosa High with in a few weeks.

Most of the twelve-mile-long barrier island hadn't fared

quite as poorly as the northern end, where Barefoot Bay was located. South of Center Street they'd lost only screens and roof tiles, and a few windows. Businesses were all open in town and life was nearly back to normal down there. Even still, Lacey's parents had decided to stay longer up north with her brother, giving Lacey and Ashley a place to live.

Good thing, because if Marie Armstrong were breathing down Lacey's neck right now, harping on the complete impossibility of these plans, Lacey would never have the nerve to make this call.

She angled the phone and eyed the architect's name, imagining the conversation with a man she considered a legend. She'd seen his picture on the company Web site and on the Internet. The guy looked like Colonel Sanders with all that white hair and a Southern-gentleman bow tie. How scary could he be?

Okay. It was time. She turned so the sight of Ashley wouldn't distract her, and put her finger on the phone.

Wait.

Should she call him Mr. Walker? His e-mail seemed so casual, at least for an architectural genius. So maybe he wouldn't want—

A voice floated up from the beach. A male voice.

Lacey glanced over her shoulder, inhaling a quick breath at the sight of a man five feet away from Ashley. A half-naked man, wearing nothing but low-hanging board shorts and sockless sneakers. Shaggy hair, big muscles, and, dear God, was that a tattoo on his arm?

Was he a tourist? A surfer? More likely one of the many debris scavengers who'd popped up all over the island since they'd reopened the causeway, ready to make a buck off the misfortune of others.

Ashley laughed at something he said, and he turned just enough for Lacey to get an eyeful of sweat-glistening chest and abs and—wow.

Ashley flipped her hair and the man took a step closer.

Okay, stop right there, buddy. Lacey launched forward, driven by primal instinct, forgetting the call and ignoring the fiery sand singeing her bare feet.

"Excuse me."

They both turned at her words, Ashley's body language screaming disgust as she rolled her eyes. But Lacey barely saw her. Her gaze was locked on the predator, preparing her counterattack in full mother-lioness mode, quickly assessing his danger level.

His danger level was... hot.

Ridiculously so.

He stunned her with a blinding smile. He disarmed her with a shake of his honey-colored locks, revealing a handsome, tanned face and a tiny gold hoop in one ear. Then he stopped her in her tracks by stretching out his hand.

"I'm Clay Walker."

What?

"Are you Lacey Armstrong?"

"No. I mean, yes. But..." She froze, completely thrown, her brain short-circuiting at his words.

Colonel Sanders he was not.

He looked nothing like his picture. No white hair, no bow tie—no shirt! He absolutely couldn't be Clayton Walker because, well, he was gorgeous.

"What are you doing here?" she demanded, not caring that she was a sweaty mess of venom-spewing, short-short-wearing, almost-thirty-seven-year-old mom staring at his washboard abs. Or that she still held the phone that she was just about to use to call him. Well, not him. Colonel Sanders.

"I told you I'd check out the property."

"Oh, I expected someone..." *Older. Dressed. Not gorgeous.* "...after I called."

"I didn't want to wait," he said. He kept his hand out and she had no choice but to take it, her hand instantly lost in big, calloused, masculine fingers. "I was too intrigued by the idea of building here."

"So am I." Intrigued, that was. Intrigued and wary.

"I hope you don't mind." He gave a cursory glance to his naked torso. "It's hot as hell here."

"It's no problem," she lied, extracting her hand and forcing her eyes off his body and onto his face. Like that was any less stupefying. "But there's been a mistake."

Dark brows shot up, revealing eyes just about the color of the water behind him. "A mistake?" he asked.

"You're not Clayton Walker."

"I go by Clay." He smiled, kind of a half-grin that crinkled his eyes and revealed straight white teeth. "Got ID in my truck if you want me to get it."

The hint of a drawl fit him as well as the shorts that hung off narrow hips. "That's not necessary because I've been to the Web site and I've seen Clayton Walker, and he's not..." *Sexy.* "You."

"Don't tell me." The smile turned wry. "You were expecting Clayton Walker *Senior?*"

Senior? Like his *father?* "I was expecting the owner of the firm." The man who designed some of the most stunning hotels in the world, who probably didn't have hair to his shoulders or an earring or a tattoo of a flame-encircled star on a sizable bicep. "*The* Clayton Walker. That's who I e-mailed."

"Actually, you e-mailed me," he said simply.

"I got the contact off the Web site."

He shrugged a brawny shoulder. "I guess my name's still there. It wouldn't be the first time someone's made the mistake."

"Do you work for him?"

"No, I don't have anything to do with my father's business anymore."

"Oh. That's a shame." Disappointment dribbled in her stomach and mixed with some other unfamiliar tightness down there.

"But I am a contractor," he said, an edge taking some of the smoothness out of his voice. "And a builder."

"But you aren't *the* Clayton Walker."

He laughed softly, a rumbly, gritty, sensual sound that reverberated through Lacey's chest down to her toes. "Look, I've been checking out this property for a couple of days and, based on that e-mail you sent, I'm totally capable of doing this job for you."

Except he wasn't capable because he was too young and too inexperienced and too...shirtless. "Are you an architect?"

"Technically, it depends on how you define architect. I am, but not completely licensed, so not officially." He fried her with another smile, taking a step closer, giving her a better look at his really remarkable blue eyes. Not that she was looking for remarkable eyes on her architect. Which, by the way, he wasn't. Not *officially*.

"Why don't we take a look at the site and go over some ideas I have?" he suggested.

"How could you have ideas when I haven't even told you exactly what I want?" She didn't mean to sound snippy, but she couldn't possibly trust this young man with her dream. She'd have to get rid of him and find out how to get to the real Clayton Walker.

"Maybe we want the same thing." His gaze dropped ever so quickly over her, a stark reminder that she wore far too little today. And it was hot out here.

Oh, no. No no *no*. Don't you dare go there, brainless hormones. This guy was twenty-nine on a good day, at least six or seven years younger than she was. The *son* of the man she wanted, not *a man* she wanted.

"When were you here?" she asked. Since the storm she'd been up here almost every day. "I haven't seen you." Because she sure as hell wouldn't have missed him.

"A few days ago." He finally tore his mesmerizing gaze from her and focused on the property behind her. "This is a truly legit location for a resort."

Legit? He sounded like Ashley's friends. Maybe he was even younger than she'd thought. "No resort," she corrected. "Just a little B and B is all I have in mind."

"Really? I'd dream bigger than that, Miss..." He inched imperceptibly closer, a smile lifting the corner of his mouth. "It is 'Miss,' isn't it?"

Was he hitting on her? "Miz," she said, a little edge in her voice. "And this isn't a dream, it's a plan for my— our—future. My *daughter's* and mine." Did he get the emphasis? "I have very specific plans." *But they don't include you.* "And I was hoping to meet—"

"My dad, I got that. He's not who you want for this, trust me."

Trust him? Not likely. "Your father's a legend in his field."

"But he's in North Carolina, and I'm here," he drawled with one more brain-numbing smile. "And I already have a couple of ideas for the kind of place you could put here."

"Well, I have ideas, too. A . . . vision, actually." And a bedroom-eyed, not-yet-thirty not-officially-an-architect wasn't part of it.

"God, Mom, just give him a chance."

Ashley's voice startled her. She'd forgotten her daughter was there, taking in the whole exchange, and, of course, having an opinion. "Honey, this isn't your concern. And, Mr. Walker—"

"Clay. The younger one."

"I have to be honest with you," she said with a sigh of resignation. "This is obviously a huge commitment for me, and I had my heart set on the man who designed Crystal Springs and French Hills, which, as you probably know, were built by Clayton Walker. *The* Clayton Walker. I'm sure you're very good at what you do, but I want someone with more experience."

His expression grew tight and cool. "Sometimes experience can work against you and what you need is"—he ran a hand through sixteen different shades of caramel hair, leaving it just a little more tousled, a lock falling to one eye—"a fresh perspective."

Behind him, Ashley was staring at his *backside* perspective.

No. Yeah. Wow. This guy had to go. "I'm really sorry, but I don't think there's any reason to pursue this. Good-bye."

He half laughed in disbelief. "Good-bye?"

"And thank you."

He took one step backward. "I'd say you're welcome, but I have a feeling you don't really mean that."

"Well, I do mean good-bye."

With his head at a cocky angle that somehow managed to say "You will regret this," without saying a word, he tipped a nod to Ashley and turned to jog off in the opposite direction.

"Mom!" Ashley choked with exasperation. "You were such a b-word to him."

"I didn't mean to be rude, it's just that he's not the person I want to hire. He's not Clayton; he's not the man I wanted."

"But he's obviously the man you e-mailed."

She fired a look at Ashley. "In error." Or was it? "Or maybe he hijacks his father's e-mail or something, looking for lonely women." Not that she was lonely.

"Well, I bet he finds them."

"Dear God, he's twice your age."

"Is that why you sent him away?"

"No. He's too young."

"You just said he was too old."

Frustration zinged through her. "Too old for you to ogle, too young to build my dream." *And for me to ogle.*

Ashley pulled out her phone and thumbed the screen. "Great excuse, Mom."

Chapter Three

I had my heart set on the man who designed Crystal Springs and French Hills.

Well, you had him, darlin', right in your silky little paw. Of course if she called Clayton Walker Architecture and Design, she'd get a different answer.

He ran hard, each jolt of packed sand fueling his determination. He wanted this job. He needed this job. And he had to close the deal before she hooked up with the legend who would squeeze out any competition, including his very own son.

Especially his very own son.

Damn it. He wasn't about to let C-dub near this one. It was a matter of pride. Hell, it was a matter of survival.

And all that stood between him and what he wanted was a closed-minded, uptight, opinionated, voluptuous strawberry blonde. How could he change her mind?

From the minute he'd heard of the hurricane grazing Mimosa Key, he'd known it was the perfect solution. Remote, untouched, and off the competitive radar,
he could get the soup-to-nuts job he needed to reinstate
himself professionally. Post-disaster rebuilding wasn't his
favorite thing, but people in this situation tended to move
fast and not take months to bid out work to competitive
firms.

There had to be a way to win her over.

Well, there was the obvious. She *had* been pretty busy
eyeing his personal landscape. While the idea of spending
a long, hot summer night convincing her he was the man
for the job had definite appeal, using sex to get the job
was flat-out cheesy. It was bad enough that she thought
he'd stolen the lead from his father—an understandable
mistake since his sister refused to take his name off the
Walker Architecture and Design Web site contacts. He
wasn't going to try to screw the work out of her, too.

Of course, she'd have the old man on the phone before
Clay got back to his truck. The thought made him run
faster, hurdling a fallen tree to get to the clearing in the
road where he'd parked.

*So call him, Strawberry. There's nothin' I love more
than a challenge.*

He opened the door to climb into the truck, glancing
in the back cab at the sketches he'd brought. Bet she'd
change her mind if she saw his ideas.

But maybe not. She might not have that much imagination if all she wanted to build on that gem of a property
was "just a little B and B." She'd go traditional. Cookie-
cutter. Dull as dirt. Come to think of it, Dad would be perfect for her job. Reaching back, he grabbed the sketches.

After his first drive to this beach, he'd raced back to the rental unit to draw page after page of thumbnails. Nothing too detailed, just his gut-level reaction to the pristine, tropical hideaway of Barefoot Bay. It had all come together, too, looking like the success he needed so he could give the finger to his father and take the first step to rebuilding a reputation.

But Lacey Armstrong wanted the legend. The legend who would slap down a four-story stucco box, adorn it with Palladian windows, and pronounce it La Bella Vista at the Sea.

Damn stupid woman with her sexy thighs and preconceived notions.

He slid the rubber band off one sketch and studied what he'd drawn. How the hell could he convince her to look at these? And if he did, would it be enough to stop her from calling his father?

Just as he was about to toss them back, an engine rumbled from around the bend, and a muscular, roofless, high-end Jeep Rubicon accelerated toward him, a woman at the wheel, another next to her, and one in the back. Bass-fueled rock music blared from the speakers.

He was checking out the wild blonde hair, sunglasses, and tanned skin of the driver when one of the others yelled, "Stop, Zoe! Ask that guy!"

Tourists, no doubt. The Jeep came to a screeching stop fifteen feet away from him. The driver threw it into Reverse, fishtailing as she backed up to him.

"Excuse me!" she called, turning down the music. She glanced over her shoulder to say something to the other two as he came around the truck to get closer.

The one in the back didn't look like a tourist, more

lady exec with black hair secured in a ponytail and a crisp white shirt. She didn't reply to what the driver said, but the woman in the passenger seat laughed softly, leaning forward to look at him, dishwater-brown locks falling over an angular face.

Blondie slid her sunglasses into her mane. "We're trying to find Barefoot Bay, but the roads aren't marked at all up here. Do you know if we can get through this way?"

Some time to come for vacation, ladies. "The beach is right there." He pointed behind him. "Your best bet is to park here and walk down, or drive a little farther that way. You can get through, but there's a lot of storm damage and the road gets pretty dicey."

"Let's go straight through," the business-like one in the back said. Probably the Realtor helping them snag a cheap lot, he mused. Good luck with the bitchy property owner. "Once we get closer," she added, "I'll recognize Lacey's place."

Oh? Friends of Strawberry's?

"Thank you," the blonde said to him, adding a dazzling smile. "I really appreciate it. Looks like you've been to the beach."

"Zoe," the passenger said, giving the driver a nudge. "Do you have to flirt with every man?"

"Only the good ones," she teased with a laugh.

"'S okay," Clay assured her. "Yeah, I've been up there."

"Is it a complete wreck?"

He gave in to a wry smile. "Complete."

"Oh, man, what a shame." She swiped her hand through her hair, sharing a look with her friends, then beamed another thousand-watter with dimples at him.

"Well, thanks again. Is that your truck? Do you need a ride or anything?"

Oh, yes, he needed something. He couldn't help smiling, because sometimes it seemed that whenever he faced a wall, the universe handed him a ladder.

"As a matter of fact, did I hear you say you're headed up to see Ms. Armstrong?"

"Yes, we are," Crispy said from the back. "Why?"

"Well, if it's not too much trouble, could you give her these?"

"Of course." The driver reached out and he met her halfway, handing off his ideas, which were immediately flipped into the backseat. "Are your name *and* number on there?"

"Tell her they're from Clay Walker. *The* Clay Walker."

Lacey had wasted way too much energy worrying about how to talk to Clayton Walker—Senior. He was unavailable at the moment. That was all Lacey could get from his arctic assistant, even after Lacey told her exactly why she was calling and how much she needed an architect for her inn at Barefoot Bay. She got to leave sketchy details of the land and job, which she doubted Miss Ice Cube was writing down, and only got a promise that Mr. Walker would call when he had a moment.

Which might be never, the bitch managed to imply.

Don't let this be the excuse that stops you, Lacey chided herself as she and Ashley climbed into her mud-covered VW Passat. She'd call again to—

"Someone's coming up the road," Ashley said, holding up a finger to indicate the not-so-distant sound of a car engine.

Oh, God. Maybe he was coming back.

The thought gave Lacey's heart a jump so unnatural and infuriating she twisted the key with a jerk just as a huge white 4x4 rolled over some debris and hit the horn loud and long enough to block out everything else.

"What the—"

"It's Aunt Zoe!" Ashley shouted, throwing off her seat belt.

"Not just Zoe!" Lacey slapped her hand over her mouth, sucking in a shocked gasp. "They're all here!" Tessa and Jocelyn waved and hollered from the roofless vehicle.

Zoe squealed the Jeep to a stop and all three of them scrambled out, running and dancing toward Ashley and Lacey, arms outstretched.

In an instant it was a huddle of hugs. Even Ashley joined in, jumping up and down as they squeezed and shrieked and an avalanche of explanations came pouring out.

"We wanted to surprise you!"

"We're here to cheer you up!"

"We've been planning this since the hurricane but knew you'd tell us not to come!"

Lacey reeled, holding each dear friend in her arms, choking on laughter and disbelief and joy. Finally the eruption ended and she managed to get her head around the fact that her best friends had come to help her pick up the pieces of her storm-shattered life.

They'd come from across the country and, in Tessa's case, the world.

"Tessa Fontaine!" She put her hands on clean, fresh cheeks, as always unadorned by makeup but so naturally pretty. "I didn't know you were back in the States."

"I just got back while you were dealing with this," Tessa

said, her voice as soft and earthy as her hair, shadows of
sadness making her deep brown eyes so serious. "And,
by the way, it's Galloway again. I've officially dropped
Fontaine."

"Oh, Tess." The divorce, of course, must be final.
"Sucks."

"Tessa lives with me now," Zoe announced.

"You do?"

"Not forever." Tessa shrugged a shoulder, which was
toned from hours of farmwork in dozens of distant countries. "I went to Flagstaff to hang out with Zoe for the past
month, but we didn't bother you with any of that, since
you've had your hands full."

"We decided we just had to get out here and lift your
spirits." Zoe squeezed Lacey's hand, her other arm
already hooked over Ashley's shoulder with casual affection. "And see our group goddaughter, who is getting way
too grown-up and gorgeous."

Ashley beamed a mouthful of hot-pink-banded braces
at her. "Thanks, Aunt Zoe."

Lacey turned her attention to Jocelyn, the only person
on earth who could ride in a 4x4 down a beach road and
not have a hair out of place.

"And it only took an act of God to get Jocelyn Bloom
back to Mimosa Key," Lacey exclaimed. "There must be
a dozen L.A. movie stars who are paralyzed right now
without their life coach."

Jocelyn flicked off the comment with dismissive fingertips. "All I need is a phone and Internet and I can work
from here for a while. You've always been there for each
of us, so it was our time to come to you."

"I'm sorry it took so long," Zoe said, her green eyes

sparkling with the joy that always seemed to light her from inside. "My job took off, so to speak."

They all laughed at that, and Lacey could feel the pressure that had crushed her for all these weeks lift as easily as one of the hot air balloons Zoe piloted for a living.

"I already feel better just looking at you three," Lacey said. "I can't even remember the last time we were all together."

"Tessa's wedding," Jocelyn said, probably able to tell them the date and what each of them wore.

"Uh-oh," Tessa moaned. "This adventure better turn out more successful than that one."

"Tess, c'mere." Lacey reached to give her a hug. "You've been through hell this year."

She took the squeeze, but not for long. "Hell is living through a hurricane. Zoe told me you stayed alive in a bathtub! Is that true?" she asked Ashley.

"Totally true," Ashley confirmed. "Mom was incredible. If it weren't for her, we'd have died in her bedroom closet."

"Ohhh!" The outcry was in unison and came with more hugs, but the tears in Lacey's eyes burned from the sweetness of Ashley's unexpected compliment.

"Hey, Ashley propped me up a few times, trust me."

"Lacey's always been our fearless leader," Zoe said. "The RA who kept us out of trouble for our entire freshman year of college."

"Like anyone can keep you out of trouble, Zoe," Tessa said.

They laughed again, but Jocelyn broke away to look around in disbelief at the bare trees, the piles of debris, and what once was a lovely beachfront property.

"God, Lace," she said, turning slowly. "It's like Bare-foot Bay was demolished."

"We got creamed up here," Lacey agreed.

"Almost everything is gone," Ashley said, an under-standable whine rising in her voice. "Mom managed to save like five things of mine but everything else is bull-dozed or blown away."

Tessa gave her a sympathetic look. "That has to be tough on you, honey."

"I'm telling you, sugar"—Zoe leaned into Ashley's ear—"shopping op!"

"And you guys are living with your parents, Lace?" Tessa asked.

"In their house on the other end of the island, but they're staying up in New York with Adam."

"They don't want to come back and help?" Jocelyn gave Lacey a look. "I know your mom likes to, you know, have opinions."

Lacey bit back a laugh. "My dad offered, but honestly, the last thing I want…" *Is to deal with Mother at a time like this.* But she wouldn't admit that in front of Ashley. "Is for them to have to put up with all the construction. But there's plenty of room for you guys," she added. "We'll squeeze in."

"Actually, I'll stay over the causeway in a hotel," Joce-lyn said quickly.

"Like hell you will," Zoe shot back.

"There's plenty of space and we'd love the company. Right, Ash?"

"Oh my God, totally," Ashley agreed, still holding on to her beloved Aunt Zoe. "You have to stay with us."

Jocelyn shook her head. "Nope, sorry. I'm still on the

clock with at least six clients and I've got to be available to them. I booked a room over at the Ritz in Naples, so I'll stay there and come and go with you guys when I can."

"La-dee-dah at the Ritz," Zoe teased, lifting her nose into the air. "We'll be having slumber parties and drinking wine all night." She eyed Ashley. "Not you, of course. Show me the beach, doll face."

Zoe dragged Ashley away and they ran arm in arm toward the sand.

Lacey let out a slow breath, watching them, then turned to Tessa and Jocelyn. "I can't believe you guys are here."

Tessa wrapped an arm around Lacey and tugged her toward the gutted foundation. "I can't believe you lost everything."

"Everything," Lacey confirmed. "Baby pictures and memories, keepsakes and—oh, every day we think of something else."

They tsked and sighed in sympathy.

"But, really, getting wiped out like this teaches you those material things aren't important. What matters is that we survived, and are moving on."

"To think I could charge a client three hundred an hour for doling out that advice," Jocelyn said wryly. "And you figured it all out by yourself."

"I figured a lot out while I was holed up in a bathtub and the world was falling apart around me."

They walked as a threesome, arm in arm. "Like what?" Tessa asked.

"Like it's time to use that three-quarters of a degree in hospitality I have. And I don't mean a shoestring cake-baking business I run from my kitchen."

"That inn full of antiques you've talked about since

college?" Tessa stooped to pluck a stray orange flower that somehow had survived, rolling it in her fingers and giving it a sniff.

"Exactly."

"And how's that working out for you?"

"It's not yet," Lacey admitted sadly. "I thought I had an architect, but I don't think I can get the one I want."

"So you're giving up?" Tessa's voice had a familiar edge of frustration in it. "The world is full of architects, Lacey."

"I need one with the right vision and credentials."

The other two women leaned forward to share a look. "I smell a full-blown Lacey Armstrong rationalization coming on," Jocelyn teased.

"No, no. I want to do this and I have the insurance money, which is enough for a really nice B and B, even a little more if I could swing it, which"—she gave a soft, self-deprecating laugh—"is always the question with me."

"Now you know why we're here," Tessa said softly.

"Why?"

"To stop you from coming up with reasons why you can't build this place and build it right."

"You guys have always been good to me that way." Lacey looked from one to the other. "What do you mean by 'right'?"

"Finished," Jocelyn said. "Up and running and making money."

"I don't know if I can..." Her voice trailed off at their stern expressions, and she laughed. "Okay, okay. And I'm going to need that money because my business is completely shut down now, and I'm living off savings."

Jocelyn settled on the edge of the picnic table. "You want money, you gotta pamper the clients."

"Clients? I can't even get the architect I want to agree to come down."

"You need a spa," Jocelyn said, ignoring her comment. "I can send half of L.A. here if you offer a lava shell massage."

"How about gardens?" Tessa rounded the table. "You have to grow your own food."

"That would be awesome, Tess, but as you can see, we're a long way from a crop of gourmet greens."

Tessa waved a little flower she still held. "But you've got a live *Ixora* 'Nora Grant,' which, I guarantee you, is edible when properly cooked, and quite healthy." She grinned when the other women rolled their eyes. "You'll be back in bloom before long. I was in Borneo after a rough storm and we had an organic farm up and running by the next growing season."

"Oh, definitely go homegrown organic," Jocelyn agreed. "You can totally overcharge for that."

"I love that you guys are planning the spa treatments and menu items and I don't even have building plans yet."

"Lacey." Tessa squeezed her, pulling her to a stand. "Quit finding a reason to say no to everything."

Just then Zoe and Ashley came tearing up from the beach, sand flying in the wake of their happy feet. "Ashley hasn't laughed like that since before the storm."

"Why do you think we put up with Zoe? She's comic relief."

"And she's managed to stay planted in Flagstaff for, what, three years?" Lacey asked. "That's some kind of record for our tumbleweed."

"Her great-aunt Pasha keeps her there, I've discovered," Tessa said. "Or she'd be gone with the next phase of the moon."

"Are you talking about me?" Zoe accused, breathless from the run. "Because I know when that little coven of yours gathers the topic is, What are we going to do with Zoe?"

"Not this time," Tessa said smoothly. "The topic is, What are we going to do with Lacey?"

Zoe fanned herself and cupped her hand over her eyes. "Can we discuss it somewhere shady? Preferably with cocktails? It's hotter here than Arizona and you've got a flippin' beach."

"It's Florida in August, Zoe," Jocelyn said. "That's why they invented air-conditioning."

"Which we didn't have at Nana's house for almost three weeks," Ashley told them. "But we do now."

"Thank God," Zoe said. "Or I would be at the Ritz with Jocelyn, because I don't sweat." She nudged Ashley. "I glisten and glow."

The banter continued as they walked to the cars, but Lacey held back, her arm still around Tessa. "I didn't know how much I needed you," she whispered, her throat suddenly thick with emotion. "Thank you so much for coming, Tess. I know this has been a positively horrific year for you, waiting for the divorce to be final."

"Not horrific for Billy. He's got a girlfriend."

"The bastard."

"She's pregnant."

Lacey froze like ice water had been poured on them. "You have *got* to be kidding me."

"Would I kid about something like that? Five years

I've traipsed around foreign countries to build that organic-farms business with him, growing every seed but the one I wanted."

"Oh, honey." Lacey took both of Tessa's hands.

"He's all smug, too, like he's a real man now that he's finally made a baby." Her voice cracked a little, like it always did on this subject. "He just texted the other day, and she's only like three weeks pregnant."

"I'm so glad you're here now," Lacey said.

"It really was Zoe's idea. But I was on it in a heartbeat."

"And, miracle of miracles, you got Jocelyn to set foot on Mimosa Key again."

"Yeah, sort of." Tessa eyed Jocelyn and shook her head. "Of course you can't get anything out of her she doesn't want to give, but one thing is clear: She won't go south of that road that cuts across the middle of the island."

Where her dad still lived, Lacey thought. "Hey, she's here, Tessa. We'll work around her issues."

"Like that control freak would give us a chance to do otherwise. And, speaking of issues, have you heard from David lately?"

"Oh, Lord, please. Last I heard he was on an icing expedition in Antarctica or maybe he was trekking in Tibet. I lose track."

Tessa rolled her eyes as they reached the Jeep. "So he's still Peter Pan."

"He sends money and Christmas cards," Lacey said, the odd urge to defend Ashley's father and her former boyfriend rising up.

"Hardly enough."

"Enough for me."

"Anybody at all in the romance picture?" Tessa asked.

Lacey just snorted. "What picture? I've dated the few single men on Mimosa Key and I don't feel like bar hopping in Fort Myers with a teenage daughter at home."

"Maybe we can join an online dating service together."

"Get real, Tess." Although Lacey had certainly considered it when she'd looked at the calendar and faced facts. She was going to be thirty-seven, and if she were ever to have another baby... No way she'd bring that up with Tessa now.

Thankfully, Jocelyn ended the conversation by waving her phone. "I need to check into the hotel," she announced. "Client emergency. Why don't you guys put your bags in Lacey's car and ride with her? I'll take the rental."

Next to her, Lacey could feel Tessa tense for an argument, so Lacey jumped in, unwilling to ruin this perfect reunion. "Do what you need to, Joss. I'm just glad you'll be close by."

"Oh my God, Lacey, I was supposed to give you these." Hanging over the driver's seat of the Jeep, Zoe held up a few long cylinders. "They better have Hot Surfer Dude's phone number on them."

Lacey's heart hitched as she took the tubes of paper. "What hot surfer dude?"

"Somebody named Clay Walker."

She almost dropped the rolls. "You saw him?"

"Zoe practically ate him," Tessa said.

"Like you wouldn't have taken a bite," Zoe shot back.

"He was the guy Mom totally dissed on the beach," Ashley said.

"I didn't dis him." Lacey swallowed, the paper sticking to her damp palms. "What did he say?"

"Nothing," Zoe said. "He just gave us those to deliver to you and told us to tell you they were from Clay Walker."

"No," Jocelyn corrected her. "He said *the* Clay Walker, the sign of a massive ego."

"He should have an ego, 'cause that dude was smokin' hot." Zoe elbowed Ashley. "And kinda nekkid, too. I'd like to take a ride on those shoulders."

Tessa covered Ashley's ears. "Nice in front of the kid."

"I'm fourteen, Aunt Tessa."

"I don't give a damn about his shoulders." Lacey snapped the band holding the papers together so hard it broke. "He came here under false pretenses, probably some kind of impostor who hacks e-mail to get work."

Zoe choked. "Yeah, there's a lot of that on the Internet. Like he couldn't get work as a male pros—model."

Lacey spread open one of the rolls on the hood of her car. "We're going to get a lot of con men down here after the storm...so..." *Good God in heaven.* "We should be..."

"We should be what, Mom?"

A slow, prickly chill climbed up her arms, raising the hair on her neck.

"We should be careful," she whispered, staring at the simple ink sketch that took everything she couldn't imagine but felt in her heart and brought it to black-and-white life.

"Careful of what, Mom?"

"Jumping to the wrong conclusion." She stepped back, her hand to her mouth, her breath captured in her lungs, her legs a little wobbly. "Like I just did."

"Wow." Jocelyn leaned over her shoulder. "What do you need to do to get him to build that? 'Cause I'm pretty sure Zoe will do it for you."

"I need..." *An architect with vision.* "A second chance."

Chapter Four

⌁

Hey." Lacey tapped and pushed open the door to her childhood bedroom to find Ashley curled on the bed over her brand-new laptop. The one that had been deemed a "necessity replacement" days after the storm.

Ashley instantly lowered the screen, looking up with surprisingly bright eyes.

"You okay?" Lacey had to fight the urge to launch forward, arms out, maternal instinct at the ready.

"Fine." With one finger she gingerly snapped the computer closed, shutting down whatever she'd been doing.

Lacey ran through a list of possibilities. Nine times out of ten, it was teen-girl drama that brought color to Ashley's cheeks and fire to her eyes.

"You still want to go over to Meagan's tonight?" Lacey asked, walking that fine line between privacy and parenting. Most of the time privacy won, because if anyone knew firsthand what a meddlesome mother could do to a teenage girl, it was Lacey.

"Oh, yeah."

"What's going on, then?" And sometimes parenting won.

"Nothing, Mom. I'm just Facebooking." Evidently, that was a verb now.

"Anyone special?"

"No." She scooted off the bed. "They're waiting for me at Meagan's. Can we go now?"

"Absolutely." Lacey jangled her keys. "Zoe and Tessa and I are going to drop you off and go out to dinner."

"Not Jocelyn?"

"She wanted to stay at the hotel."

As Ashley scooped up a turquoise Hollister tote bag— another post-storm necessity—and grabbed a pillow from the bed, she threw a dubious look at Lacey. "Why does she come all the way across the country to see you and hole up at some hotel?"

Good question. "You've seen the Ritz in Naples. Hardly 'some' hotel."

"But, Mom, I don't get it."

Neither do we, Lacey thought. "You know she grew up here and her mom died a while ago, so she has sad memories of this island." Before a more elaborate explanation was required, Ashley's cell phone vibrated and took her attention.

She read, and shrieked. "Oh my freaking Gawd!" Her fingers flew over the screen.

"Ashley, don't talk like that."

"Tiffany says Matt's breaking up with Cami Stanford! It's totally over!" She clicked more, the text winning over an explanation.

"Tiffany? Tiffany Osborne?" The one who was caught with pot in her locker in eighth grade? "Is she going to be at Meagan's tonight? I didn't think they were friends."

"Maybe I have a chance with Matt now."

Lacey tensed. "Have I met Matt?

Ashley put away her phone and gave Lacey a look that said it all. *Back off, Mom.* And because her own mother never had, Lacey let the conversation go as they piled into Lacey's car and headed toward Meagan's house.

"Would you look at that?" Zoe mused as they cruised through town.

"Look at what?" Lacey asked.

"Interesting," Zoe said, sliding a look to Tessa that Lacey didn't quite get.

"What's interesting?" Lacey pressed.

"Just that little place with the drunk-looking bird on the front. It's cute. Let's have dinner there."

"The Toasted Pelican?" Lacey shook her head. "No way we're going there. They have sucky bar food. I think we should either go to South of the Border for Mexican or see—"

"I want to go to the Toasted Pelican," Zoe said. "It looks like fun."

"It is, if you want to get drunk and meet locals who live, breathe, and sleep fishing."

"Maybe you'll meet a nice guy, so I want to go there."

"Mom doesn't date, Aunt Zoe," Ashley told her. "But if you go to South of the Border will you please get me a doggie bag of enchiladas? They rock."

"Why doesn't Mom date?" Zoe asked pointedly, turning around in the passenger seat to look at Ashley.

"Because she—"

"Because she isn't interested in any of the men on this island," Lacey interjected, watching the yellow light at Center Street, ready to roll through it. "And my nonexistent dating life is not of any interest to my daughter."

"Mom doesn't date because she'll never find a man like my dad."

Lacey's foot jammed on the brake in shock, jerking them all forward into their seat belts. "Sorry, the light was..." Her gaze shifted to Ashley in the rearview mirror. "Honey, where on earth did that come from?"

"Truth hurts, Mom."

Lacey searched her daughter's pale green eyes, exactly the color of David's.

"That's not why I don't date," Lacey said after a long, awkward pause. "I just haven't met anyone interesting."

"Which is why we're going to the Toasted Pelican for dinner."

"Zoe!" Lacey switched her attention to the other wayward child in the car. "I'm telling you, the food, the atmosphere—it's not our kind of place."

Zoe just lifted one eyebrow. "You might change your mind."

Lacey was still too shaken by Ashley's comment about David—which had happened a few other times recently—to argue over where they were eating. Silent, she took the next left and made her way to Meagan's house, where three teenage girls were hanging out in the front, waiting for Ashley.

"Who are those other girls, Ashley?"

"Meagan's friends."

Lacey took a breath. "I mean, what are their names?"

"Oh my God, Mom. You've known Meagan since I

was, like, in preschool. Bye, you guys. Have fun!" She was out before another question could be asked.

Lacey eyed the group but Tessa gave her shoulder a tap. "She's fine, Mom. Anyway, they remind me of us at Tolbert Hall."

"That's the problem," Lacey said. "I know what we did in college."

"She's in ninth grade. Don't worry." The girls were headed toward the house, heads close, giggling. "Nothing like a foursome," Tessa added wistfully.

Lacey glanced over her shoulder. "Hey, you want to drive to the mainland and surprise Jocelyn? I hate that she's alone tonight."

"She doesn't," Tessa said. "You know solitude is like air to Jocelyn. She needs it to survive."

"Anyway, we're going to the Toasted Pelican now," Zoe said again, this time with little humor and plenty of determination.

"What is with you?" Lacey demanded. "That place is a dive, the food is greasy, and the wine is watered down."

"And an extremely sexy architect who may or may not be officially licensed but definitely appears to have some kind of magic drafting tool just walked in the front door. So move your ass, Armstrong. You got work to do."

Lacey's jaw dropped. She'd told her friends about meeting Clay on the beach and the story he'd given about his experience in the field, but clearly they weren't dismayed by his lack of qualifications.

Tessa gave Lacey's shoulder a nudge from the backseat. "C'mon, Lace. You know you want to."

"That's not how I want to talk to him, in some bar. I'll...call him. After I hear back from his father. And check out his credentials. I don't know anything about him and ..."

Her voice faded, met by dead silence and "get real" stares.

"C'mon, you guys. Tonight's for us. This is our reunion, a chance to catch up and talk, not worry about him and—"

"Lacey." The warning came in unison and hit a bull's-eye. They were right, damn it.

"You know, girls, sometimes nothing beats a watered-down wine."

Zoe held up her fist for celebratory knuckles. "That's what I'm talkin' about."

Clay looked from one woman to the other, still having a hard time remembering who was Gloria and who was Grace.

The two had flanked him fairly quickly at the bar. They were not-unattractive MILF-y types, late thirties or early forties. Both looked vaguely familiar, but Mimosa Key was small enough that even in his few days here he'd gotten to know some local faces.

Gloria was the dark-haired one, with thick bangs and big brown eyes, a little younger and more reserved than the other. Grace had frosted hair, a spray-on tan—which struck him as odd in Florida—and, despite the thick gold band on her left ring finger, seemed far more physically aggressive.

Grace's first question was where was he staying.

"Hibiscus Court near the harbor," he replied, sipping a lukewarm draft and fighting the urge to check out the bar for anyone else he might recognize. Not that he expected Lacey Armstrong to show up in a place like this. He'd come to grill the locals and find out what he could about her, so he forced himself to focus on the women who'd zeroed in on him as soon as he'd arrived.

"You planning to stay awhile?" Grace asked. "That's a furnished rental, but I know Chuck Mueller wouldn't let you sign less than a three-month lease."

"I'm still deciding, but I wanted to keep my options open." He'd signed that three-month lease, but he was optimistic like that. "And there aren't a lot of other places to stay around here unless I go to the mainland."

Grace's smile widened as she exchanged a look with Gloria. "You just aren't talking to the right people, hon. I'm the owner of the Fourway Motel."

"There was no vacancy."

She lifted an eyebrow and gave him a deliberate once-over. "Then my husband must have been working the front desk, and he's easily intimidated by big, handsome men."

He laughed off the compliment. "The Fourway, huh? Interesting name."

"If you're in Mimosa Key long enough, you'll know what a Fourway is." She gave him a teasing wink. "My cousin, Gloria, and I will teach you."

"You're going to scare the life out of him, Grace," the other woman said, giving a dismissive wave. "The Fourway is the intersection of Center Street and Harbor Drive, the historic site of the first traffic light on the island." She added a shy smile. "There's a long history on Mimosa Key, you know. Our mothers are the daughters of the first pastor when the island was founded back in the 1940s."

"Which explains your names."

"And theirs," Gloria said. "My mother is Charity and Grace's mom is Patience, and they own the Shell Gas Station and Super Mini Mart Convenience Store, also known as the Super Min, located at—"

"The Fourway," he finished for her.

"You're catching on," Grace said as she leaned in close. "There might be a town council, a mayor, and few influential big mouths on this island, but the fact is, we practically run the place." She trailed a long, white-tipped nail over his knuckles and held his gaze. "So you'd be smart to keep us on your good side if you're looking for business." Her finger continued to his bicep. "I assume you're in construction."

"Are you?" Gloria asked. "Because Beachside Beauty, where I work, lost a few windows and the guy who was supposed to install them never showed."

"I don't do windows. I do full buildings." At their questioning look he added, "I'm an architect."

"Whoa." Grace backed up an inch. "Who's hiring an architect?"

No one yet. "Some of the places in Barefoot Bay were demolished and need a full rebuild."

"Like what places?" Grace asked. "It's mostly wilderness, scrub, and mangroves up there and only a couple of old houses."

Here was the perfect opening to get some information on Lacey Armstrong. "Maybe not for long," he told her. "Could be a bed-and-breakfast going up."

Grace's jaw dropped and all the friendliness went out of her eyes. "I don't fucking think so."

Clay blinked at the unexpected profanity. "Why's that?"

"Zoning ordinances," she said, shifting her gaze to her cousin to share silent communication. "Nobody can build a hotel, motel, inn, resort, B and B, nothing. Won't happen. Better look for work elsewhere, Frank Lloyd Wright."

Everything in her body language changed; her back stiffened, her nostrils flared, and she downed half a glass of wine in a single gulp. Then she stared at him, all the friendliness gone.

"Who's building it?" she asked.

As much as he wanted to know more about Lacey, instinct told him to keep her name out of it. "One of the residents up there."

"Everham? Tomlinson? Who?" Grace asked, her brows knitting as she thought about it. "Surely Lacey Armstrong isn't going to try to put me—try and build some kind of motel."

"But why wouldn't she?"

"I just told you." Grace moved in to make her point, a whiff of bitter Chardonnay on her breath. "Ordinances. Changing them would require approval from the town council, which is controlled by the mayor." She angled her head and gave him a smug smile. "Who is controlled by my mother."

"Really?" Ah, the intricacies of small-town politics.

"Really." Grace signaled the bartender. "Need my bill, Ronny."

"I'll take care of it," Clay said.

But the woman's look was cold. "Trying to bribe me?"

"Trying to buy a lady a drink."

"We're done here, Glo," she said, standing up. "Let's book."

"I'm not ready to leave, Grace." Gloria gave her some not-so-subtle wide eyes.

"Yes, you are."

Gloria smiled apologetically at Clay. "Listen, if you do stick around and you ever need a haircut, stop by Beach-side Beauty. We do men." She laughed self-consciously at the double entendre. "You know what I mean. Anyway,

I'll cut your hair, but"—she reached up to flutter a lock on his neck—"it'd be kind of a shame to cut this off."

Just as she tugged some of the hair he hadn't cut since the day he'd quit working for his dad, the front door opened.

Gloria leaned over and whispered in his ear, "Don't get on Grace's bad side."

At the door, three women walked in, one with copper curls cascading to bare shoulders and a yellow dress cut low enough to steal a man's breath.

Well, holy hell. Look what the wind blew in.

Then all the sounds and smells and sights of the neighborhood bar faded into gray silence as Lacey's and Clay's eyes connected for the space of four, five, six rapid heartbeats.

It took a nudge from the blonde he recognized as the Jeep driver, but Lacey slowly made her way toward him. God-*damn*, she looked good. Shiny, curvy, bright, and beautiful.

When she reached him she bit her lower lip hard enough to wear away the gloss and leave a little white spot and took a breath deep enough to strain some soft flesh against the scooped neck of her sundress.

He let his gaze drop there for just a moment before standing and reaching out a hand. "Of all the gin joints in all Mimosa Key..."

Her glossy lips lifted in a smile that rivaled the blistering sun he'd spent the day under. "You walk into mine," she finished.

Oh, man. He'd just met his match.

Chapter Five

⌒

Lacey couldn't let go of his hand. Not just because his fingers were strong and calloused, or because just the sight of him made her knees a little wobbly, but because . . .

Of all the gin joints.

He'd quoted her number-one all-time favorite movie. *Her* movie. "You've seen *Casablanca*?"

"A dozen times." He guided her to the stool next to him, empty now that Gloria Vail had scooted away.

"Really?" She glanced over her shoulder, but Zoe and Tessa had found a table on the other side of the bar, as planned. Lacey was only supposed to get the drinks and casually "bump into" Clay Walker.

Not sit on a bar stool next to him exchanging movie quotes.

"Why are you surprised? It's a great movie." His leg brushed hers as he sat down and settled too close, sending an electric jolt through her. "At least it would be if they'd changed the ending."

"Change the ending? Of *Casablanca*? Why ruin perfection?"

"Perfection?" Bone-meltingly blue eyes lingered one more time on the sweetheart neckline of her dress, which seemed summery and safe for a night out with the girls but suddenly felt really sexy.

"The wrong guy gets the girl," he said softly. "So that's not perfection."

"The wrong guy?"

"Rick gave up too easily, if you ask me." Almost imperceptibly, he moved closer. "I would never give up that easily."

For a world-tilting second she forgot what they were talking about. Forgot why she'd come to the bar or what she wanted to say to him. Might have forgotten her own name.

"So, this is a really nice surprise," he said. "You a regular here?"

"I just popped in with some friends." *To tell you I love your sketches.*

"Can you forgive me?" he asked.

Forgive him? She was the one who'd kicked him off the beach. "For what?"

"For not liking the ending of *Casablanca*." He gave her a slow, easy smile, all deadly and dreamy at the same time. "And for not being my father."

She had to do this. Had to. No excuse in the world could stop her from jumping through the opening he'd just made. *I like your ideas.* Very simple, very honest. A little crow as an appetizer.

But they just looked at each other, waiting for the other to move first, until the bartender arrived and broke the moment. "What can I get you, miss?"

"Wine...three white wines."

Clay leaned into the bar. "Ronny, put those on my tab."

"That's not necessary."

He held up a hand to stave off her argument. "And take two of them to those lovely young ladies by the window. Miz Armstrong will have hers here." Somehow, he combined that southern drawl with easy authority.

Ronny splashed some yellow liquid into a cheap wineglass and slid it toward her.

"One drink," she agreed, settling on the bar stool.

"That's all I need," he replied.

"To do what?"

He held up a half-empty glass of beer. "Here's lookin' at you, kid."

"Oh, now you're not playing fair." She touched his glass anyway and sipped hers, making a face. "Now that's a fine-tasting nail-polish remover."

He laughed. "So why'd you come in here if you don't like the booze?"

Carefully placing the stemmed glass on a cocktail napkin, she flipped through a bunch of possible, plausible answers. None was the truth.

"I came in here because we spotted you walking in."

His brows raised.

"I'm not a stalker," she assured him. "I just wanted to say..." She took a steadying breath. "I really loved your sketches and—wow, where did you get the idea for that overhang in the front, because it was...*spectacular.*"

"You know what?" He leaned closer and took one

ringlet of her hair, pulled it, and let it bounce back to a natural curl, making blue-white sparks snap at her nerve endings. "So are you, Strawberry."

Oh, he was good. Young, gorgeous, sinfully good. And even nail-polish-remover-tasting wine could take away a woman's inhibitions. She took another drink and gathered more courage.

"Actually, Clay, I think I'm the one who should ask if I'm forgiven for being a total bitch on the beach today."

"I might forgive you," he teased. "What else did you like about the sketches?"

She closed her eyes, picturing the way he'd tucked the building under foliage that wasn't even there anymore, and the way he'd captured the essence of what was meant to be built in Barefoot Bay. "I didn't like the sketches," she said, getting a surprised look. "I *loved* them."

He grinned. "Then you're forgiven."

She tried to back away but couldn't. The guy was a damn human magnet. "Although what you drew looks like a much, much bigger place than anything I want to build."

"Why not go big?"

"Why? Because I can't afford a *resort*, just a little inn."

"Get investors."

"I've never even run a B and B, so I'd be totally in over my head."

"Hire people."

"Hey, don't bulldoze my excuses," she said on a laugh. "I'm trying to tell you all I have is a foundation and..." *A dream.* "An insurance check."

"You have an architect. That is, if I get the job."

Oh, Lord, it would be easy to say yes to this man, yes

to a lot of things, some of which had nothing to do with buildings or dreams. Well, maybe some dreams.

"Do I have it?"

She laughed. "I thought southern gentlemen were supposed to be slow. You move like a bullet train."

"Why waste time?" He leaned a little closer, a whiff of something woodsy and pure shooting right into her brain and directly to her sex hormones. "When something's right, it's right."

"This is right?" She tried to make it a question, but that smell, that hair, those eyes; her voice cracked in the face of it all.

"You know it is."

"But we have a lot to talk about first." Like fees and plans and ideas and when they would—kiss. No, *start.* "I'll grant you a job interview. How's that?"

"I thought that's what this was."

Laughing, she took a sip of lousy wine, which, somehow when shared with the company of this man, didn't taste so bad. "You don't have a resume with you."

"You saw the sketches. What else do I need?"

"Credentials. Education. Experience."

"I've got 'em all, ma'am."

She cringed. "Ouch, I've been ma'amed."

"Southern habit, I swear. And aren't my drawings creds enough?"

Oh, he was good. And evasive. "You said you weren't 'officially' an architect," she said. "What does that mean?"

"That I don't have a piece of paper that doesn't amount to"—he winked—"a hill of beans."

"Don't do that." She pointed a warning finger at him. "Don't toss *Casablanca* quotes. That won't get you the job.

And, honestly, that stuff makes a damn big hill of beans' difference to me. I wouldn't go to a lawyer who wasn't licensed to practice law or a doctor who wasn't board certified. Why would I hire an architect who isn't officially approved by... whoever officially approves architects."

"The AIA and the NCARB," he said.

"No alphabet soup, either. Spell it out in English that a thirty... something-year-old mother of one can understand."

"You're sensitive about your age, aren't you?"

"I just think you might be too young for—"

"Hush." He placed two fingers on her lips. "I'm twenty-nine, not too young for anything." He fluttered his fingers in front of his face. "I knew I smelled strawberry," he said with a smile. "It's your lip gloss, not your hair."

"I don't know what kind of architect you are, but you sure are proficient at changing the subject."

"I'm proficient at a lot of things, Lacey."

He said her name like... sex. Hell, every time he breathed it was like sex. "I'm only interested in your architectural credentials, Mr. Clayton Walker. *Junior.*"

"Ouch. Okay, we're even for the 'ma'am' now." He inched away, sipped his beer, gave her just enough space to make her want him to come back. "I finished a five-year architecture program at the University of North Carolina."

"I thought you said you weren't an architect."

"I *am* an architect and I'm completely capable of designing any kind of structure or facility you want, and contracting the right people to build it."

"Are you licensed and board certified?"

"Pretty much."

"Pretty much?" She choked softly.

He shrugged one shoulder. "It's just that there's some more, you know, *stuff* to getting licensed in North Carolina."

"Stuff such as…"

"A two-year internship, which I completed at Clayton Walker Architecture and Design, Inc."

"I thought you said you have nothing to do with him or his business."

"I'm on my own now," he said simply. "I learned a lot from working with my father's company, paid my dues, and sat for one of the licensing exams. Then…" Another way-too-casual shrug. "Anyway, the exam was in planning and design, which, you have to admit, is a great place for us to start. Listen, Strawberry—"

"Did you just call me Strawberry?"

He smiled and plucked another curl. "My favorite fruit. I'm telling you, tests don't make you an architect."

She tried to take a breath but got a lungful of man again, the smell of someone who did not take no for an answer. And called her *Strawberry*.

"Life gives you enough tests," he said.

Like how long could she sit here, inches from the sexiest man she could remember meeting in her life, and not kiss him? That right there was a real test.

"True success comes from meeting and beating every one of the challenges you're thrown." He inched a little bit closer with every word.

Words that, she realized as she stopped inhaling and admiring and started listening, were as hot as he was. *If* he meant what he said and wasn't just handing her a load of BS.

"Let me ask you something, Clay."

"Anything."

"Do you always get everything you want?"

Something flickered over his features. A memory, maybe. But it was gone in an instant. "Everything," he assured her. "Even if I have to change what it is that I want."

She smiled, totally understanding that.

"Here's all you have to know about me, Lacey." He brushed her knuckles with his fingertips, ostensibly to underscore the point he was about to make, but the touch sent chills over her skin and made her curl her toes around the bar stool just for something to hang on to. "I don't believe in obstacles, brick walls, barriers, roadblocks, or anything else that says I can't. There's a way around everything and everyone, and I find it. I get what I want and I don't quit until I have it. I give you my word on that. Now, can I have the job to design and build your resort?"

Oh, boy. *Casablanca* was a turn-on, but someone who didn't quit? Didn't give up? Didn't find excuses? Wasn't that exactly what she needed?

"I suppose we could meet at the property."

He put one finger under her chin and tilted her face toward his. "Just say yes."

Like a living, breathing human female could say anything else. "After you've come up with some ideas. Right now I can't—"

"Let's agree not to use the word *can't*. Ever. Let's just call it a four-letter word we don't use."

She smiled. "I can't." Then laughed. "You don't know me. I'm…cautious."

He ran his thumb across her bottom lip, a move that, seriously, just ought to be outlawed. "If you were cautious, you wouldn't have followed me in here."

"My friends talked me into it," she admitted.

"Then send them the finest bottle of nail-polish remover. When do we start?"

When do they start what? That was the question. Come on, Lacey.

"We'll finish this interview tomorrow morning at ten o'clock at Barefoot Bay," she said, searching for the strength to escape his lethal touch and coming up with nothing. "Bring your drawings and your imagination, samples of your work, and references." *And, for the love of God, don't bring that thumb that's turning me into a puddle of hormones.*

For one more suspended second, they stayed two inches from each other, sparks and heat arcing between their mouths. If he had kissed her, she'd have kissed him right back.

But somehow, she found the strength to walk away.

Chapter Six

⌒

Lacey pulled into the Super Min wishing she could fill her tank without having to go inside. The Sisters of the Holy Super Min, as Charity Grambling and Patience Vail were known around town, would surely both be working this morning. But Charity refused to install credit-card-accepting pumps in the only gas station in this part of the island, so Lacey had no choice.

Now that their daughters, cousins Grace and Gloria, had met Clay, it was only a matter of time until Lacey's plans were public. Would there be pushback against leveling her grandparents' ancient house to build a bed and breakfast? Probably. Definitely.

With Clay's definition of "true success" still ringing in her ears—and his sexy scent still torturing her memory—Lacey squared her shoulders and entered the Super Min.

A bell tinkled with an old-fashioned preciousness as the door opened, just as Charity shoved the cash-register drawer closed and dismissed a customer with a tight smile. The bell was the only thing "precious" about the Super Min or its owners.

"Well, it's about time somebody got dressed up around here," Charity remarked.

"Not exactly up, but dressed." Lacey paused in the heavenly rush of cool air. "I have a meeting."

A construction worker passed Lacey on his way out, giving her a once-over and zeroing in on her chest.

So much for the "too professional" blouse Zoe had mocked and Lacey thought underplayed her boobs. Those suckers did not underplay easily.

Clay Walker was already a professional risk; she didn't want to encourage a personal one as well. So she kept telling herself that if he got the job, if he proved himself to her, and if they had to work side by side for a year or more, she would just ignore the fact that he turned her into a quivering bowl of Jell-O.

"Bet I know who you're meeting with." Charity situated her bony backside on her stool, smug and cocky.

"I wouldn't be surprised if you did, Char." There were two forms of news delivery on this island: the *Mimosa Gazette* and Charity Grambling. "Forty dollars of regular unleaded," she said, holding out her money.

Charity took the cash and lifted partway off the stool to peer over the counter and get the full view of the white slacks Lacey had switched to when Zoe had called her other choice mom jeans.

"You're going up to that mess in white pants?"

News *and* editorial.

"Yep." Lacey met Charity's judgmental gaze.

The door to the back office flipped open and Patience Vail, who only answered to the nickname Patti, ambled into the room.

"Lacey's got a meeting," Charity said, pressing way too much emphasis on the word. "With *someone*."

Patti lifted her dark brows. "That same someone you were practically licking down at the Pelican last night?"

Oh, boy. This actually could be fun if it weren't true. "There was no licking, Patti." Lacey gave an obviously impatient look at the cash register. "You know, until you press that button, I can't pump the gas."

"I know." Charity situated herself on the stool. "I gotta tell your mama, Lacey. You know that, don't you?"

Lacey rolled her eyes and almost laughed at the warning, like she was a teenager caught shoplifting in the Super Min or something. "My mother's up in New York at my brother's place, Charity."

"I know where she is. We're Facebook friends."

"Well, no need to report anything, Charity, because last time I checked, I was thirty-six years old." About to be thirty-seven, but no need to give them that ammo.

Patti and Charity shared a look. "He isn't," they said simultaneously. "Bet he isn't thirty yet."

Now she couldn't help laughing. "Did you girls get a picture? 'Cause then you can post that on Facebook, too." She started to back away, but Charity's inch-long crimson nails lingered over the computer key, holding Lacey captive. "Any minute now, Charity. I'm kind of in a hurry."

But Patti put a hand on Charity's arm, further stalling things. "Maybe she *is* the one."

What one?

Charity considered the question, eyed Lacey suspiciously, then shook her head. "Nah, she'd never do something that stupid."

"You're right, she wouldn't," Patti said, like they weren't talking about her in the third person.

Lacey refused to take the bait, though.

"'Course not, Pat," Charity continued. "Lacey wouldn't do anything *stupid* with that old house from her grandfather, who was one of our daddy's *dearest friends* and, of course, one of *the founders of Mimosa Key*." She practically breathed fire on the last words. "Or did you forget that your grandparents were pioneers who had a vision for this place? A vision, Lacey. And it included some ironclad rules of the road. Do you know what they are?"

Lacey shifted from one foot to the other, the pressure of being late for a ten o'clock meeting in Barefoot Bay almost as weighty as her curiosity, and a growing concern. What was the issue here? "Not sure where you're going with this, Charity, but I would really appreciate if you'd free the gas pump so I'm not late for my meeting."

"With an architect?" Charity prompted.

She looked from one to the other, knowing that a lie would be discovered and the truth would be broadcast to the next thirty customers. "Yes."

"Uh-huh." Charity nodded, slowly, her lips curled in an "I knew it" smirk. "My Gracie said she met an architect in the Pelican last night, and when she and Glo left, you all but fell into his lap."

"Not exactly." She pointed to the register. "Please?"

Patti, a much bigger woman than her sister, worked her girth around the counter to give Lacey a hard look. "He said he might be building an inn of some kind."

Lacey just stared at her, saying nothing, reality dawning. Grace and Ron Hartgrave owned the Fourway Motel, and no one in the extended family run by these two matriarchs would like the competition. But they couldn't stop it.

Could they?

She cleared her throat and met Patti's beady gaze. "Nothing is set in concrete," she said. "I'm looking at all the possibilities." Damn, she wanted to have more conviction than that, but these two, they were not to be messed with.

"Well, look at this possibility." Charity whipped out a binder and slapped it on the counter. *The Building Code and Bylaws of Mimosa Key* was typed across the top. Literally typed. By a typewriter. Probably before Lacey was born.

Charity flipped open the cover and pointed to a page already marked with a bright pink Post-it note. "Says right here that no structure that contains more than five bedrooms can be built on Mimosa Key."

Lacey almost choked. "That code was written in the 1950s, Charity. It—"

"Still holds true," Patti interjected. "You don't see any six-bedroom houses on this island."

"Which is the problem," Lacey shot back.

"What do you mean?"

"Well, if we would let some people build big houses, we could be the next Jupiter Island or take some of the money that gets poured into Naples' real estate. Mimosa Key is ripe for big money, and I can't imagine who on the town council would be opposed to having more tourist dollars on this island."

They both stared at her, but it was Charity whose eyes narrowed. "So it's true. You're trying to ruin this island."

She fought an exasperated sigh. "No, Charity. I'm

looking for ways to expand it, make it better, bring in jobs, and—"

"We don't need any more jobs," Patti insisted. "We want it just like it is, young lady."

"Oh, now I'm young. A minute ago I was too old for the man I was talking to last night."

"Don't you get snippy," Charity warned.

"That's right," Patti chimed in. "Because your Granny Dot and her dear Theodore would roll over in their graves if they knew what you were planning to do with that beautiful old home they built for you when they founded this island."

She didn't even know what she was planning to do, how could Granny?

"And that home is gone," Lacey said softly, hating that the loss she felt could be heard in her voice. "And so are my grandparents."

"Then you should respect their memory," Charity said.

But Granny Dot always wanted a B and B. She'd been the one who'd planted the idea in Lacey's head years ago. But Lacey wasn't about to share that with these two old witches.

"You don't have your facts straight, Patti," Lacey said. "And you're jumping the gun. I'm not sure at all what I'm going to build on my property. For the most part, I'm just happy Ashley and I survived."

Charity sniffed. Patti crossed her arms. So much for the sense of community and helpfulness that had arisen after the storm. But for one minute, in the face of expressions that looked a lot like her mother's most disapproving scowl, Lacey considered changing her mind.

Was this dream worth getting the doyens of Mimosa

Key riled up and ready to wreck her life? Was it worth fighting for?

Behind her, the bell dinged with a new customer and all Lacey could do was exhale with relief. At least now she could pump her gas.

"Mornin', Strawberry."

The words went into her ear, down her spine, spun through her belly, and gave her knees a little push.

"Strawberry?" Charity choked.

"It is you, isn't it?" He put two strong and solid hands on her shoulders and slowly turned her around. "Yeah, I'd recognize that hair anywhere." He closed his eyes and sniffed. "And the scent."

Oh, Charity ought to have a field day with that. "What are you doing here?"

"I'm addicted to gas-station coffee, so I thought I'd get us some."

Us.

"Introduce your friend, Lacey." Charity tapped impatiently on the counter. "As if we don't already know who he is."

Lacey gave him a secret eye roll and silent warning. "Clay, this is Charity Grambling and Patti Vail, sisters and owners of the Shell Gas Station and Super Mini Mart Convenince Store, also known as the Super Min. Ladies, this is Clay Walker."

"The architect," Patti said. "We've heard *all* about you." She threw a smile at Lacey that gave the distinct impression that *all* they'd heard came right from Lacey herself.

"Mornin', ladies."

Charity's gaze wandered up and down Clay's T-shirt and jeans. "You don't look like an architect."

"Looks are deceiving," he said, stepping toward the coffee station. "Man, that smells good."

"So are you rebuilding Blue Horizon?"

He gave Lacey a questioning look.

"That's what my grandfather called the house," she said, even though she suspected his unspoken question was more along the lines of *Am* I rebuilding it?

"If you are, you better familiarize yourself with this very important piece of historical documentation." Charity lifted the binder. "We have rules against certain-sized buildings and nothing can be, you know, gaudy." Charity dragged out the word and wiggled her fingers. Like those talons weren't the gaudiest things that ever came out of Beachside Beauty.

"I'm not building anything gaudy," Clay said as he filled two large cups.

Patti stepped forward. "'Course you couldn't build that big a place. Your land isn't that sizable, after all. Unless you're planning to buy Everham's and that plot on the other side of yours."

The Tomlinsons'. Yep, that was exactly what Lacey was planning to do. But she just gave a noncommittal shrug.

"That'd be quite a piece of land if you pulled that off," Patti said, proving that speculation was all she needed to turn something into fact.

At the coffee machine, Clay glanced at Lacey. "How do you take your coffee?" he asked, their eyes connecting in silent communication.

"Cream and sugar." She could kiss him for not responding to Patti. Oh, she could kiss him just for standing there like a golden, gorgeous, glorious god, too, but mostly she loved that he didn't take the bait these two were throwing out.

"We're just counting on our Lacey to do the right thing," Charity said. "Seeing as she's part of the very special family of people who built this island for the distinct reason that they wanted to avoid the hellhole of high-rises over in Naples. We want things to stay just the way they've always been."

"Change is good," Clay said, giving Lacey one of the coffees and placing a twenty-dollar bill on the counter. "Can I have some?"

Charity didn't move. "Change isn't good for Mimosa Key and we don't need some big-time architects building eyesores on Barefoot Bay."

"I'm not big-time, and I'm not building an eyesore," he said, putting a hand on the book. "But if you'd like, I'd be happy to give you some ideas about how you could make the elevation of this little convenience store even more attractive, and then when the nice people come to stay at Lacey's new place, they'll all stop here on their way in and out to buy your"—he sipped the coffee and nodded approvingly—"fantastic coffee."

Charity yanked the book away and pushed his twenty back. "The coffee's on the house."

"Much obliged." He toasted her with the cup. "For the coffee and the history lesson."

He shouldered open the door, holding it for Lacey, who walked into the sunshine and let out a long, slow breath.

Clay dipped his head and whispered in her ear as the door closed behind them, "You gonna let those two be a roadblock?"

"No." Maybe. He didn't know how much power they wielded on this island.

"Good." He put his arm around her, pulling her into rock solid muscle in a dizzyingly casual and intimate move. "Now, let's go look at your property and see how many more people we can piss off."

Chapter Seven

⌒

The first thing Jocelyn heard when the elevator doors opened to the Ritz lobby was the ring of Zoe's laughter echoing through the cavern of marble and glass. The sound made her realize how much fun she'd missed the night before. Still, no amount of fun was worth the risk of seeing...someone she did *not* want to see. She'd stay here for Lacey as long as she could, but nothing could make her venture south on Mimosa Key.

Which is why she loved that Zoe, Tessa, and Ashley had sweetly agreed to come to the Ritz for lunch today while Lacey met with her architect. Of course, without Lacey to run interference, they might press her a little about coming over to the island, but she could always manufacture a client crisis. Considering she'd just spent the last half hour on the phone with a weeping Coco Kirkman, there wouldn't be too much manufacturing involved.

The three of them stood outside a high-end boutique, Zoe's arm draped over Ashley's shoulder, their heads close as they discussed the bathing-suited mannequin in the window. As she approached, Tessa turned and brightened at the sight of Jocelyn.

"I never thought I'd utter these words to you, Jocelyn Bloom: You're late."

"Client crisis."

"We were forced to window-shop at the overpriced hotel stores." Zoe tugged Ashley closer. "And decided you might have to buy us all one of those adorable bikinis in different colors."

Jocelyn hugged them all, an extra squeeze for Ashley. "I just might do that after lunch. Ashley, you're a doll to give up your day and hang out with us."

"It's cool," Ashley said, her eyes dancing with youthful happiness. Had Jocelyn's eyes ever danced at that age, she wondered idly. No. Not once. Not ever. Which was why she had to stand her ground and stay off the south end of Mimosa Key.

"I'm really having fun," Ashley added.

"Mom's ignoring our texts while she makes out with the smokin'-hot architect boy," Zoe added. "So we can do whatever we want, including buy skimpy bikinis. Right, Ash?"

The light in Ashley's eyes dimmed. "She's not making out with him."

"A figure of speech," Zoe assured her, leaning behind Ashley to share a secret look with Jocelyn. "She almost did last night," she mouthed.

As they crossed the lobby to the terrace restaurant, Ashley fell a few steps behind, reading her phone.

"C'mon, Ash," Jocelyn prodded, waiting for her.

Ashley quickly covered her phone.

"I'm not going to read your texts," Jocelyn teased.

"I know, but it's private."

"A boy?" Jocelyn asked in a whisper.

Color burst on her cheeks. "No."

Her tone was indignant enough for Jocelyn to let it ride. They followed a maitre d' to a window table with a perfect view of the pool and beach. As soon as they were settled in with iced tea and sodas, Tessa gestured toward the vista.

"I could get used to this," she said. "It beats planting organic gardens in Sri Lanka."

"You love planting," Jocelyn said.

"Not in Sri Lanka."

Out of the corner of her eye Jocelyn noticed Ashley pulling out her phone, but she kept her focus on Tessa. "I thought you loved globe-trotting."

Tessa lifted a shoulder. "My ex-husband loved it more than I did."

Next to Zoe, Ashley flicked her finger across the screen and Tessa reached over and put her hand on the phone. "Hey, no texting at the table," she chided.

"I'm not texting," Ashley shot back.

"Then no e-mail at the table."

Ashley rolled her eyes. "E-mail is so last century, Aunt Tessa."

"Then no doing whatever the heck you're doing. It's rude."

"Facebooking. Sorry."

Just the thought of what would have happened to her if she'd used that tone at the table put an ache in Jocelyn's stomach. "Let her go, Tess. It's no big deal."

"But she's right, Ash," Zoe chimed in. "Cell phones

are not cool at the table. Especially in zee Ritz-Carlton, dahling."

Instead of joining the joke Ashley narrowed her eyes at Zoe. "I'm not your daughter."

Whoa. Something inside Jocelyn twisted. Instantly, she put a gentle hand on Ashley's arm. "But you're our god-daughter, honey, and we don't see you that often. So what do you think of your mom's idea for a B and B?"

Ashley shrugged, obviously unhappy about putting down the phone. "'It's cool if she really does it. She's been talking about it forever."

"This time is different," Tessa said. "I think she can really make it happen."

Ashley's phone vibrated and she sneaked a peek, then let out a soft cry. "Oh, he wrote back."

He. Tessa started to say something, but Jocelyn shook her head quickly, sensing that they had to let go of this one.

"So, have you ever stayed at this hotel, Ashley?" she asked. "Maybe you could spend a night here at the hotel with me sometime. Maybe you all could."

That earned her a big, bright smile. "That'd be cool."

"Perfect timing, too," Zoe said. "We could give Lacey a night alone to play with Clay." She grinned. "He'll be putty in her hands. Hah! I'm so punny."

Ashley's tell-all expression shifted right back to the other side of the pendulum. "That's just gross, Aunt Zoe. The guy's not much older than me."

"Oh, yes he is," Tessa corrected. "I'm guessing thirty, which makes him perfectly acceptable as a builder, archi-tect, contractor, and anything else your mother wants."

Ashley squished up her face. "She doesn't date."

"So you've said." Zoe pulled her straw out of her iced

tea and tapped it, then used it to point at Ashley. "And that might be half her problem."

"She doesn't have a problem." Ashley sneaked a peek at the phone.

"You have an issue with her dating, Ash?" Tessa asked.

"No, no, of course not."

"You don't sound too convincing," Zoe prodded. "She's gone out with a few guys. Did you not like any of them?"

She shrugged. "Nobody was right for her."

"Maybe she ought to be the one to decide that," Jocelyn suggested.

"Well, what if my dad wanted to get back with her?"

The question silenced all of them. Jocelyn knew that Lacey did her best not to paint a negative picture of the absentee father, and it sure wasn't her place, or any of their places, to hit Ashley with the truth. Her dad was a thrill-seeking, adrenaline-junkie, trust-funded, part-time cook. He wasn't ever getting "back" with Lacey.

But Jocelyn took a deep breath and went for a technique that worked with some of the more stubborn clients who hired her as a life coach. "Ashley, do you really think that's possible?"

"Of course I do. They don't... hate each other. They're not divorced; they never even got married." Her voice rose, along with a little color on her cheeks. "Things happen like that, you know."

"In books and movies," Tessa said. "Not so much in real life."

"I don't think that's going to happen," Jocelyn agreed, sensing that Ashley was harboring some serious delusions. "There's a lot of water under that bridge."

"And then he burned that bridge," Tessa added.

"After he bungee jumped off it." Zoe grinned at their surprised faces. "You know I'm right."

But every ray of light disappeared from Ashley's face as teenage frustration pulled at her brows. "None of you know what you're talking about."

"Actually," Jocelyn replied, keeping her voice calm. "We do know what we're talking about, Ashley. But you know what? That's not what's important. What matters is that your mom is happy, right?"

"Well, some creepy guy with a tattoo isn't going to make her happy."

"You told me you thought he was cute," Zoe said.

"And your mom thinks he might be the right architect for her project," Tessa added. "You do know how important this dream is to her, Ashley, don't you?"

"She ought to be building a house," Ashley muttered.

"Excuse me?" Tessa leaned closer.

"I said she ought to be building a place for us to live, not for people to come and have us wait on them."

Is that how she viewed her mother's plans? "Honey, you're not going to wait on them, and I'm sure you'll have a place to live."

"Really? In a bedroom in some inn where strangers are walking around in their bathrobes?" Her voice hitched a little. "Isn't it bad enough I've lived in a dump up in Barefoot Bay for all these years while my friends are, like, normal? And now..." She shook her head, fighting to control her emotions.

"I hate to break the news to you," Jocelyn said. "But some of those so-called normal people aren't nearly as happy as you are. They don't all have moms who dote on them."

"But they have dads."

"Oh, honey, sometimes no father is better than—" The words trapped in her throat and she felt all eyes boring through her. Jesus. Now what? "Than a father who—"

Ashley's phone rang with a rap tune. "I have a text."

Thank God.

"It's Mom." She tapped the phone, letting her hair fall over her face to cover her expression.

They all looked at each other, this time with well-deserved guilt. They'd ganged up on her. While Ashley read, the salads were served, giving the three women a chance to exchange a silent agreement to lay off and give Ashley space.

"So, what did she say?" Zoe asked when the waiter left.

"She said we can meet her at the beach later, in a few hours when she's done with her meeting," Ashley said.

Jocelyn stabbed a cherry tomato. "Can't. Sorry."

"She just wants us to bring a cooler and suits and stuff to Barefoot Bay," Ashley said. "She thought you'd be okay with that, Aunt Jocelyn."

Was she? If she didn't have to go too far south, she'd love a day at the beach. "I guess I could do that."

"We just have to go back to Lacey's and get suits and stuff," Tessa said.

"Hey, I have a better idea." The words were out before Jocelyn could stop herself, and even before she really did have a better idea. But she needed one, fast, because there was no way she was driving to Lacey's parents' house. It was too close for comfort.

"Yeah?"

"We…" She snapped her fingers and pointed to Zoe, who'd be all over this idea. "We shop for everything we need, including new bathing suits, even one for Lacey, right here at the hotel. My treat."

Ashley and Zoe gave each other high fives and whoops, the tension of the last few minutes forgotten. Money might not be able to buy happiness, but sometimes it bought distance.

An hour and a half later they left the Ritz dressed in new suits and cover-ups. The girls had driven up in Lacey's father's van, which they'd parked in the lot, but while they waited for the valet to bring the rented Rubicon for Jocelyn to drive, the discussion was all about the logistics of who was going in which car.

"I want to go in that car," Zoe joked to Jocelyn, pointing to a gorgeous red Porsche that pulled up to the hotel. As a man climbed out of the driver's seat, though, Zoe's expression froze.

"Oh my God," she whispered.

"What is it?" Jocelyn asked.

Zoe didn't speak. In fact, she didn't breathe.

"Someone you know?"

"It can't be him."

Jocelyn squinted at the man as he gave his hand to a beautiful brunette gliding out of the car with preternatural grace and poise. "It can't be who?"

"He's a doctor. In Chicago."

"There's an oncology conference here this week," Jocelyn said, eyeing the man, who was as good looking as his woman and his car. He looked to be six-two or -three, with clipped dark hair, great features, and an even better build. "Is whoever he is an oncologist?"

"Maybe." Zoe suddenly looked left and right. "But I don't want to see him. I don't want to talk to him."

"Why?" Tessa asked, stepping closer to Zoe when she sensed something was up. "How do you know him?"

Jocelyn stepped right in front of Zoe to block her from his view, the instinct to help her friend overriding any questions. Just at that moment the valet drove the giant white Jeep Rubicon up to where they waited.

"Get in," Jocelyn ordered Zoe, ending the discussion.

Muttering thanks, Zoe climbed up to the passenger seat the second the valet opened her door. The man and woman walked right in front of the Jeep as another man approached them.

"Oliver!" the second man exclaimed, reaching out a hand to the man Zoe was avoiding. "So happy you could make it."

Jocelyn slowed her step to hear his response.

"Happy to be here, Michael. You remember my wife, Adele."

"Of course."

Jocelyn missed the rest of the conversation when the valet ushered her into the Jeep.

In the passenger seat, Zoe bent over as though she were getting something off the floor, hiding completely. In all their years of friendship Jocelyn had never seen Zoe shy away from anyone.

Jocelyn pulled away, waving to Tessa as she and Ashley got into the van behind them. "Coast is clear, hon."

Zoe rose and took one more look as the man walked toward the hotel.

Jocelyn waited, but Zoe was uncharacteristically quiet. No jokes, no snide remarks.

"You okay, Zoe?" Jocelyn asked, putting a gentle hand on her friend's leg. "Who was he?"

"Don't ask."

"But I never—"

Zoe turned to her, her green eyes narrowed to slits, all

humor and joy and Zoe-ness gone. "We're not asking you about certain things, so...please. Don't ask, don't tell."

She couldn't argue with that philosophy, Jocelyn thought as she drove toward Mimosa Key. But she had to wonder: How many secrets should there be between best friends?

Chapter Eight

⌒

The noon sun pressed like a blow torch, burning Lacey's skin and leaving a fine sheen of perspiration that probably smeared her makeup and surely curled her hair. But Lacey wasn't thinking about her hair or her makeup as she and Clay slowly circled the perimeter of her property and the land adjacent to it.

She wasn't even thinking about the attractive man who walked a few steps in front of her, giving her a perfect view of a T-shirt molded to ripped muscles and jeans that curved over his backside and down the length of long, strong thighs.

The truth was, he was as skilled verbally as he was physically, and his words were painting a picture so vivid and alluring that Lacey felt as though she'd stepped into his imagination.

And his imagination, it seemed, included villas. The

idea was so out there, so creative, and so perfect that she almost didn't want to let it get too comfortable in her head. But she couldn't stop thinking about it.

"You really think we could do villas?" she asked.

"Why not? Lots of resorts have cabins and separate structures."

"This isn't a resort."

"It ought to be."

She knew that. Deep in her heart, she knew that was what Barefoot Bay needed. But did she dare think that big?

"I don't know," she said quietly.

"Look." He pointed to the slight rise in the Everham property, where a small house had once stood but now only the foundation and some studs remained. "Right there. Picture individual, private villas with cozy patios and intimate rooms. Sleek African mahogany floors and sheer netting over every bed."

Cozy. Intimate. Sleek. Sheer.

Bed.

His words were as hot as the sun, and the images he conjured had her dreaming of a lot more than profit potential.

"Sure, you can have a few rooms or suites in the main building," he continued. "That's where the lobby and restaurant and offices will be, maybe a spa. But the thing that you can do with this virgin area is give people an oasis. High-end, expensive, one-of-a-kind villas that offer a vacation experience unlike—"

"Unlike a bed-and-breakfast, which is all I was prepared to undertake."

He smiled down at her. "You're not letting those two bags of wind at the Super Min scare you off, are you? I'm sure we can find a way around some ancient zoning ord.

Especially with villas, if there's a limit to the number of bedrooms you could have."

He was right about that. But still. "Clay, I don't have the money for what you're talking about. Insurance will barely cover a four- or five-bedroom inn."

"Building a place like this requires investors. We'll get money, Lacey."

"Will *we*?" she asked. "This is still a job interview, you know. I haven't agreed to become a 'we' yet."

"You will." He took her hand, the touch as thrilling as his confidence. "C'mon, let's go look at the view of the beach from that spot. Let's see this place the way your guests will."

So positive. So confident. So attractive. Of course she followed him. Yeah, this was some tough job interview. Who was she kidding? He had the job. Because with every imaginative suggestion, with every "just out of the box enough to be brilliant" idea, with every demonstration of a keen working knowledge of design and building, Lacey was more certain she'd found her man.

His fingers tightened around hers and a thousand butterflies took flight in her stomach. *Easy, Lacey.*

"You certain you can buy this lot?" he asked.

"This one and the one on the other side. I've been in touch with both neighbors and they jumped on my verbal offer. They're just waiting for final paperwork from their insurance company so they can have access to the house deeds at the bank." She'd only planned to buy the lots to make sure no one built too close to her B and B, but the idea of villas had just changed everything.

"How many villas do you think?" she asked. "How big? How . . . much?"

"You're not asking the right questions, Lacey." At the

top of the slight rise he paused, turned her toward the Gulf. He put his hands on her shoulders, pulling her a little too close to him. She could feel the warmth of his body against her back, the power of his muscles, the length of his legs.

For a few minutes they stood very still, nothing but heat and sun and humidity pressing down.

"Ask yourself this question," he finally whispered into her ear. "What would someone pay to wake up to this view, in a private villa, with coffee brewing and a tray of home-grown fruits waiting on their patio? Someone—two some-ones, probably—who would roll out of bed and bask in the sunshine just like we're doing now?"

Roll out of bed . . . oh. Did he *have* to say that?

"They'd stare at that gorgeous blue horizon all day, romp in the waves, roll in the sand, and appreciate this magical place until the sun kissed the water and turned the sky pink gold. Then they'd uncork a bottle of wine and cozy up on a chaise to watch the moon rise and dapple the water."

She closed her eyes, awash in peace, serenity, even hope. Could she create a place like that? It was so much more than she'd ever imagined. It was terrifying and thrilling and daunting and *fabulous*.

And way out of her price range and capabilities. "I can't—"

He squeezed her shoulders. "Hey."

Laughing softly, she dug for a better way to use the banned word. "I *can't* imagine how amazing that would be."

Another squeeze, this one more affectionate and ten-der, his thumbs on the nape of her neck, buried in her hair. The move was intimate but completely natural and noth-ing in heaven or earth could get her to step away from this man or this moment.

"Do you know how rare and valuable this land is, Lacey?" he asked. "You can get loans and investors just based on the value of the property."

"True, if I want to go deep into debt and make promises I might not be able to keep."

"You'd keep them. And you wouldn't be in debt long, not if the resort was like no other around here."

There was that word again. "Resort."

"Doesn't that sound better than bed-and-breakfast?"

"It sounds...big." *And better than a bed-and-breakfast.*

"Big and bold and beautiful." He threaded his fingers deeper into her hair and pulled her body closer. "Go big or go home, I say. And, come on, it would be a crime not to build something unforgettable here. There aren't many beaches like this left in America."

"All the more reason to keep it pristine."

"You sound like Charity."

"I just want to build something that belongs here. It has to be true to the land."

"I promise I will," he said softly, the words pouring over her like the sunshine. "But in the process you can make Mimosa Key the next St. Simons or Tybee or Cumberland."

She snorted softly. "Patience and Charity would love that."

"They just need to see you as a source of income and not competition. You could single-handedly turn this island around."

The thought made her dizzy. Or maybe that was his hands, his chest, his hard body behind hers. His seductive voice and even more seductive ideas.

David.

David? What the hell made her think of David at a time like this?

Maybe the seductive voice and ideas. David had had both, and it had cost her.

"I don't know," she said on a sigh. "I just wanted a little inn."

"And a little in-come," he said wryly. "Why settle for that?"

"Because...because..." There was no reason. She was just scared. She'd never tried anything so big. What if she failed? "I just can't—sorry, but I can*not*—figure out a way to afford that."

He didn't say anything for a moment, but stayed very still. Had she disappointed him? For some reason she didn't want to let him down. She wanted to impress him, to appeal to him, to think as big and wild as he did. But—

"What if your architect was free?"

This time she stilled, and he eased her even closer, taking away all space between them, nestling her head under his chin like it was the most natural place in the world for her to be.

"You would do this job for nothing?" she asked.

"I'd get something out of it."

Could he mean..."What, if not payment?"

"Credentials." He whispered the word, making it sound like pure gold to him. Maybe it was. Maybe becoming "official" mattered more than cash.

"So, you want to work for free." She reached up to close her hands around his so she could uncloak herself from his arms, but he just gripped her tighter.

"I want to work for you," he said, honey over gravel in

his voice. "I won't take a dime until your resort is profitable. How does that sound?"

Very, very slowly she managed to turn in his arms, brushing his body as she did, painfully aware of every masculine inch, every hard bump, every relentless angle, but forcing herself not to let the amazing sensation cloud her brain. He wasn't asking for sex; he was asking to work on spec, for the experience.

"It sounds tempting." Like everything else about him. "But I need you to be perfectly straight with me. Why would you do that?"

"I need this project in order to prove to the Arch Board that I can sit for the exams," he explained. "So it's a win-win for everyone."

"Why couldn't you just take the exams? How can they stop you?"

He stabbed his fingers in his hair, hesitating as he considered his reply. "I need one significant project under my belt," he said slowly. "I left my dad's firm before I got it. After seeing this place and what could be done here, I know that this is the project I not only want to do, but I'd love to do. Enough that I'd do it for free. And that solves some of your money problems."

Some, not all. "It also makes me wonder if I'm getting a good enough architect."

"Fair enough. You can fire me at any time and keep all the work I've done to date. I need the project and you need a partner who can give life to your vision."

She gave him a slow smile. "Except sometime in the last ten minutes, it became your vision."

"It could be our vision, Lacey."

"It could be," she agreed. She did want a partner. She

did want a vision. She did want something as big and bold as he described, especially if she didn't have to attack that challenge alone.

"I guess it's possible."

"Anything is possible, Strawberry."

Right then, with this man holding her in the sunshine, giving her strength and ideas and throwing reason and excuses out to sea, she actually believed that.

"C'mon, I want to show you something." He took her hand again and pulled her back down the hill, toward her property, while she dug for a reason why she shouldn't follow him.

For once in her life, she couldn't think of a single excuse.

Clay almost ran down the sandy slope, light from the weight that had just left his shoulders. When the idea to work pro bono hit him, he didn't even have to think about it. This was the perfect solution to his problem. He needed a significant project to take to the board, exactly like the one he visualized. No one could claim nepotism, no one could suggest that anything untoward had happened, and no one could deny him the chance to get the licenses he needed to move forward.

Lacey Armstrong offered a way out of the Catch-22 he'd been caught up in, and he wanted it. Okay, he hadn't told her everything, but he'd told her enough. And he would give her the whole ugly story, but only after they'd established a level of trust and a deeper connection. Which felt inevitable.

But now he had to close this deal. And he knew exactly how to do that.

He'd left his tools on the picnic table at the edge of her property, situated in the small bit of shade from a tree too stubborn to give in to the storm. Sitting on top of the table, he took out his pencils and pad and gestured for her to sit across from him on the tabletop while he worked.

"I'm going to draw, Lacey," he said. "And you can ask me anything you want. This'll be that job interview you wanted so much."

"Can I watch you work?" She leaned up to look over his sketch pad.

"No." He moved the pad away, out of sight. "I'll show you when we're done. And then you tell me if I can be your architect or not."

Leaning back on her hands, she just watched him for a few moments, quiet.

"No questions?" he asked. "I expected an ambush."

"All right. Why don't you work for your father anymore?"

He feathered a few pencil strokes, starting where he always did, with the first of the two vanishing points, where the horizontal lines would come together if the structure were long enough.

"My father," *speaking of vanishing points*, "is very competitive, and remarkably insecure. We just couldn't work together anymore, so I left."

"On good terms?"

"We talk." *When absolutely necessary, which would be almost never.* He looked up to see her surprised expression. "You were expecting something else?"

"I guess," she admitted. "Something like your ideas are too avant-garde and his old-school approach makes you crazy. Something more...cliché."

What had happened with Dad was a cliché, all right. Right out of a soap-opera script. "He loves my ideas," he said in response. "Steals them all the time, as a matter of fact. Like your favorites, French Hills and Crystal Springs."

"Those are your designs?"

"While I was an intern, so no real credit." But they were his ideas.

He sketched some basic triangles, rounding them off like the buildings he'd been looking at online last night. Almost immediately the bones of the structure started to appear.

"Any siblings?"

"A sister, Darcie, who's a year younger than I am and still works at the firm."

"She's an architect, too?"

"No, a numbers person. Accountant, Web site maintenance, marketing, handles a lot of real estate and contract issues."

"Are you close to her?"

"Yep." He paused at the first window. Arched or square? He went for a soft arch and decided she should know he had more family than just Darcie. "I also have a brother, Elliott."

"Oh, older or younger?"

He smiled. "He just turned one."

"You have a one-year-old brother?"

"Half-. My dad remarried, and they have a child." He congratulated himself on keeping the darkness and anger out of his voice. Maybe he was over it after all.

"And your mother?"

"She's . . ." *Coping.* "Funny line of questioning for a job interview, Strawberry."

Lacey laughed, lifting up her hair to get some air on her neck, looking so sexy and sweet he wanted to put down the sketch pad and kiss her. No, he wanted to sketch her. Just like that, hair up, guard down, eyes bright, smile even brighter.

"I'm just trying to get to know you. You give everyone a nickname?"

"Only if I really like them."

Color darkened her cheeks. "You don't even know me."

"I like what I know of you so far. I know you're a good mother, and I like that."

"How would you know what kind of mother I am?"

He turned the pad to deepen the perspective of one wall. "You'da killed me if I'd gotten any closer to your daughter yesterday. How long have you been a single mom?"

She didn't answer right away, just turned her profile to him. He stopped drawing to study the shape of her nose. Not perfect in a classical sense, but really perfect for her face.

"I've never not been a single mom," she answered, still not turning to him as if the confession embarrassed her. "I didn't marry Ashley's father. I've raised her alone from day one."

It did embarrass her; he could tell by the note of defiance in her voice. "You've done a great job," he said simply. "I'm sure it's been tough."

"My parents are local, and they've helped, but, yeah, it's a challenge. Especially now because she has an opinion on *everything*."

"Did she have an opinion on me?"

She just laughed. "All of us had an opinion on you."

"You mean your friends that were in the bar last night? What did they tell you to do? Run as fast as you can, Lacey; he's got an earring and a tattoo?"

"No, that'll be my mother when she gets back from New

York. Of course, that's not saying much because I've pretty much made a second career out of disappointing my mother. But my friends? They totally encouraged me to give you a chance." She grinned. "Especially Zoe."

"The blonde?"

"The pretty blonde," she added.

He started to outline the balustrade, the vision so clear in his head he wasn't even thinking as his pencil worked. "She's not my type," he said.

"What is?"

He glanced up. "Job interview question?"

"Curious woman question."

"You're my type, Lacey."

"Oh, please. You've already said you'd work for nothing. You don't have to throw in gratuitous praise to get the job."

He stopped drawing and looked directly at her. "You are my type," he repeated.

"I'm older than you are."

He shrugged. "Wouldn't have noticed if you weren't obsessing over it. Ma'am."

Laughing, she shook her head. "So you like well-endowed redheads who use the word *can't* and have teen-age daughters with too many opinions? Why do I find this hard to believe?"

"I like curvy, sexy, gorgeous strawberry blondes who are willing to take risks when something is important enough." The fact that she was a single mother spoke volumes about what kind of woman she was, whether she realized it or not. "I also happen to think we're more alike than you realize."

He finished the balustrade, and considered showing her the drawing, but something was missing.

"Why are you frowning?" she asked.

"I'm not done yet and I can't decide what I've left out."

She leaned forward. "Can I look yet?"

"No. But..." He wanted to ask her to hold perfectly still, just like she was, with dappled sun turning her hair to spun gold and highlighting each little freckle on her nose.

"All right. I got it. Just keep talking. Tell me more about your mother who you constantly disappoint."

She laughed. "You picked that up, huh? No. I'll tell you about my dad, though. He's the only person in my immediate family I've told about the B and B. I wanted to clear the idea of leveling the house with him because his parents built it, as you know, and my dad was born on the kitchen table."

"Really?" He looked up, surprised. "That's a cool piece of history."

"I know, but the kitchen table"—she turned toward the water and closed her eyes—"is gone."

"Must be awful to lose everything."

She nodded. "I go through some bad nights, remembering things, and then I say, Hey, we survived. That's all that matters."

"But you lost your home."

"I'm building a new one," she said with false brightness. "We'll live in the, uh, *resort* someone wants me to build."

He smiled. "I like that."

"And, honestly, I don't want you to think we lost some amazing architectural wonder. My grandparents never did anything to improve the house, then they willed it to me, and it was, honestly, on its last..."

"Support beams?"

"Precisely. Or it might have survived that storm. But

for the years I lived there, all I could really do was piece-
meal repairs. I wanted to do more, promised my Granny
Dot I'd do more, but I always had..."

"A reason not to," he finished for her as he took out a
package of colored pencils and began the job of adding
blues to the water and browns to the building and just the
right colors to capture his vision.

"Bingo." She pointed at him. "I have a daughter and a
small business. Life in general was plenty of reason not to
take a huge risk like this. Then the hurricane came and I...
faced death."

"Whoa." He stopped shading and studied her. "Seriously?"

"Yep. I climbed into a bathtub that is now in a storage facility in Fort Myers, and used a mattress to keep
my daughter alive." Her voice wobbled a little. "After you
go through something like that, it seems stupid to worry
about antique tables and even stupider not to take some
chances."

The look in her eyes said that chance was on him. And
right there, at that angle with the blue-on-blue horizon
cutting a perfect plumb line behind her and determination
setting her jaw at a defiant angle, Lacey Armstrong was
completely lovely, strong, and sexy.

He slid his pencil across the page, a power moving his
fingers like he had no control. But he had plenty of control, and he used it.

"You're drawing so fast."

"I'm inspired by you." Low in his belly, a slow burn
started. Natural, being this close to a woman he found
attractive, but surprising, too. Intimate. Hungry. Hot. "In
fact, when I'm finished, we should go skinny-dipping."

Her jaw dropped in pure shock, then she let out a pretty laugh. "You do? Well, I don't think that's part of the job interview. Unless..." Her voice trailed off, but he didn't take his eyes off the page. The drawing was going too perfectly.

"Unless what, Lacey?"

"Unless you think you're applying for a completely different job."

"One for the day, one for the night." He smiled but kept his head down, his pencil flying. Couldn't stop now, not even to flirt with her.

"That would be..."

He waited for her to finish. *Crazy. Impossible. Unthinkable.* What would it be? When she didn't say anything else, he tore his gaze from the work and met hers.

"That would be what, Lacey?"

"Something new for me."

"How's that? No men in your life, ever?"

"Not many, not recently. I just don't have the time or interest." She didn't sound convincing.

"Ashley's father?"

"I haven't seen him since she was a baby, and he's not in the picture."

"Good, then maybe I could talk you into, you know, my special Architect with Benefits program."

She laughed. "Pro bono and benefits? I'm starting to wonder if I won the lottery."

"You like the idea?" Because he did. A lot.

"Maybe." She brushed a hair off her face; the golden red curl caught in her fingers like her voice caught in her throat. "I'm not going to lie and act like..."

"Like you haven't thought about it."

For a long, heavy moment, neither spoke. Then she whispered, "I've thought about it."

"Me, too," he said, setting down the pencil and slowly turning the pad toward her. "See? I'm thinking about it right now."

The look on her face was priceless and every bit as beautiful as he'd drawn her.

Chapter Nine

O h." It was the best Lacey could do. Just *oh*.

There was so much to take in. So much to absorb. A tiny structure with a sloping roof and cozy patio faced the Gulf, the beach scene beautifully rendered. But the villa and the water were not the focal point of his drawing, just an exotic backdrop for her. "That's me."

Drawn completely and utterly naked, she was stepping from the villa to the sand. He'd captured her copper curls, the shape of her face, the slope of her neck, and, of course, her voluptuous breasts. But it wasn't just the nude body that mesmerized Lacey. This woman exuded power. With squared shoulders and outstretched hands, a confident stride and a fearless look in her eyes, she was the woman Lacey wanted to be.

"That's how you see me?"

"That's how…" His words faded as he touched the

picture, his long, lean finger following the lines of her body, the effect as thrilling as if he were touching her skin.

"Yes?" she prompted.

"You know how some people draw from memory? Or maybe they use an object to copy? I draw from my imagination or, rather, my fantasy." His finger lingered on the two-dimensional drawing of her breast.

"That's quite a talent." Which might be the understatement of the century. "How did you do that?"

"I draw moments that I'd like to see. That's how I design buildings, something I'd like to walk out on the street and see. This villa"—he gestured toward the structure in the sketch—"is something I'd like to walk onto the beach and see."

"Is there a villa in this picture?" she joked. "I can't get past the naked lady."

He laughed. "Look at the building, Lacey. Really. What does it remind you of?"

She studied the villa for a few seconds, then it hit her. "*Casablanca.*"

"I was inspired when I watched the movie last night."

"You watched it last night?" That gave her a little jolt as sexual as his drawing of her.

"When I came home from the bar, I found it on the Internet and watched the whole thing. I still think the wrong guy gets the girl," he said quickly, "But it totally inspired me for your property. What do you think?"

"I love the shape and design of that villa." She'd never seen anything like it, certainly not on Mimosa Key and maybe not in Florida. Instead of the standard Palladian windows and faux Spanish style, this was earthier, cozier.

"I kind of see an all-Morocco-themed architecture,"

he said, excitement making him talk a little faster and get a little closer. "White stucco walls and dark wood floors, the curved windows and low-slung archways. I know it's different, but the buildings are made for intense heat, so it would really fit in around here."

He was right. God, he was a genius.

"Kind of a waterfront paradise without the tacky, typical, tropical feel," she said, tearing her attention from the page to look at its creator. "I love it, Clay."

He beamed a smile at her. "I even have a name for it."

"I was going to keep Blue Horizon House as, you know, an homage to my grandparents."

"And I'm sure they'd love that, but we're not building an assisted-living facility, Strawberry." He was so close their faces almost touched, but neither made a move to back away.

She laughed softly. "So what are *we* building, Clay?"

"You already said it. Casablanca. But I suggest two words. Casa Blanca."

"Spanish for 'white house.'" She sighed, closing her eyes, leaning her head back just to let the beauty of the idea wash over her. "That's perfect."

And so was the kiss he placed on her mouth.

The pressure of his lips was so soft at first that she wasn't sure if the kiss was really happening. Her eyes fluttered open as a breath flickered between their mouths. He slid a hand around her neck, his fingers delving into her hair again. His other hand cupped her jaw and held her face just to make the angles of their lips fit perfectly.

A soft moan escaped her throat as she opened her mouth to him, letting their tongues dance at first, then coil more comfortably, then slide against each other. Lifting her hands to his shoulders, she pulled him closer and made absolutely no effort to stop. It felt too good.

She kept her eyes closed and he kissed her cheek, like a little finishing touch on something that was already flawless.

"You like my ideas, don't you?" he whispered into her mouth.

Oh, she liked more than his ideas. "I like your hands."

That made him chuckle and tunnel deeper into her hair. "How they draw?"

"How they . . ." She closed her eyes and let her forehead fall against his, their noses lined up, their mouths close enough for him to feel the warmth of her breath. "Feel."

He kissed her again, getting their bodies closer on the picnic table, building heat that could rival the tropical air around them. Cicadas buzzed and waves lapped, but all Lacey could hear was the thrum of sex and desire shooting off to every nerve in her body—and the intrusive vibration of her cell phone. The interruption jerked them apart.

"I bet it's Ashley," she said. "She's with my friends and was supposed to call when they're five minutes away."

"Oh, there go all my skinny-dipping plans." He kissed her again, longer, open mouthed, pulling her closer to him on the tabletop. "I was really starting to like this job interview."

"I was really starting to forget this *was* a job interview."

He backed away, holding her face tenderly. "Ms. Armstrong, can we please make this official?"

A crazy thrill electrified her, the question so like a proposal. His eyes were sincere, his mouth still parted from the last kiss, a lock of his hair falling over a brow and making her brush it away.

"I have to think about it," she said. *A lot. For hours.*

Like all she wanted to think about was him and this and Casa Blanca. "How about I tell you tonight?"

He just kissed her again, another clash of tongues, until the phone vibrated one more time. She broke away and pulled it out to read the text.

"They're on their way."

He dragged his hands down her bare arms, letting his fingers brush the sides of her breasts. Like he'd touched a magic switch, her nipples budded through the cotton. "Then I'll see you tonight. I think we should watch *Casablanca*."

She laughed softly. "You watched it last night."

"It inspired me." He kissed her mouth. Her nose. Her forehead. "Who knows what could happen if we watched it together?"

Uh, she knew exactly what would happen.

"I'll call you tonight, okay?" he whispered. "We can watch at my place."

Yep. They both knew where this was headed.

"Oh, I forgot." He tore off the picture and handed it to her. "Here's my resume."

She laughed softly, the drawing stealing her attention again. Good heavens, could she do this? Could she let him have the job, talk her into a resort much bigger than anything she'd imagined, and also—

He started to laugh.

"What's funny?" she asked.

"I can see you rooting around for some reason to say no and you can't find one."

It was true. He was right. "Call me around seven and we'll see if I found a reason to say no."

"Don't look too hard. This is right, and you know it."

She just sat there holding his "resume" until she heard his truck rumble away, taking all her excuses with it.

"Mom!"

Lacey jumped off the picnic table, completely unaware how long she'd been sitting there mooning over Clay Walker.

Long enough for the girls to arrive in two cars, which meant they'd brought Jocelyn, who could practically read minds and body language. Would they notice that the "job interview" had shifted into a little make-out session?

Ashley didn't need to know the details, but she'd tell the girls everything about Clay, from his fabulous ideas to his even more fabulous kisses. This new development was too much fun not to share.

"We got you a bathing suit!" Climbing out of the van, Ashley held a colorful shopping bag in the air. With the other hand she lifted her T-shirt. "I got one, too! It's a push-up!"

Oh. *Thanks, Zoe.*

Behind her, Tessa and Jocelyn hoisted a Styrofoam cooler and Zoe jumped out with arms full of towels and two beach umbrellas.

"You bought me a bikini?"

"You're going to hate it," Tessa predicted.

"She's going to love it." Zoe dropped the umbrellas on the sand.

Lacey looked to Jocelyn for the tie-breaker. She just shrugged. "It was two against two. Zoe's exuberance won, as usual."

Ashley shoved the bag at Lacey. "Don't worry, Mom, yours isn't a push-up."

"A minor miracle." She didn't know whether to laugh

or throw the bag at Zoe, who pushed her sunglasses into her hair so Lacey could get a good look at her why-the-hell-not expression.

"For God's sake, Lacey, you're in your mid-thirties and you are not a nun."

No kidding. *You should have seen me ten minutes ago.*

"Yeah, but you know how I feel about my boobs. They're too big."

"Your boobs are gorgeous. Own them." Zoe trotted off toward the beach without waiting for a response.

Her boobs *were* gorgeous...the way Clay Walker drew them.

"Oh, Mom, you'll love it," Ashley insisted. "Aunt Jocelyn bought us all new suits and, oh my God, they all cost—"

Jocelyn slammed her hand over Ashley's mouth. "Not important."

"Jocelyn," Lacey said, shaking her head. "That wasn't necessary."

"Expediency is very valuable."

"Expediency?" She must have wanted to avoid south Mimosa Key.

"I couldn't wait to get to the beach. Where should we put this?"

"Let's go down by the water." Lacey took in their haul. "God, look at all this stuff. What, no blow-up tubes and rafts?"

"They're in the car," Zoe said on her way back up from testing the water. "Don't worry; we didn't forget sunscreen. Walgreens had everything the Ritz didn't."

Ashley ripped off her T-shirt to expose a minuscule lime green halter bikini with plenty of padding, and tore off for the gentle swells of the Gulf.

"My suit better be bigger than that," Lacey said to Zoe.

"Not much," Zoe replied. Then she leaned in to whisper, "How'd it go with the big stud? That's an architectural term, you know."

"Really good. We made so much progress."

"Really?"

"He has all these amazing ideas, I mean you can't believe his vision for this place. So, so much bigger than anything I've ever dreamed of."

Tessa and Jocelyn came closer, carrying a cooler between them. "Really? Like what?"

"Like villas! Individual, adorable villas. And the style! So beautiful, all Moroccan and *Casablanca*-inspired."

"Ooooh," Jocelyn cooed. "Your favorite movie."

"I know, right? We're going to watch it tonight for more inspiration."

Zoe choked softly. "Is that what you kids are calling it these days? Hah." She turned to the water and reached out her arms. "Here I come, ocean!"

"It's the Gulf!" Lacey called to her, getting a "whatever" wave in response.

Jocelyn looked skyward. "Ignore her. If you want to meet with him tonight...." She frowned at Lacey. "She's right, isn't she?"

Lacey couldn't hide the smile. "I gotta say, there is some smokin'-hot chemistry between us."

"That could complicate things," Tessa said.

"It already has," Lacey agreed. "But you know what else? He wants to do the work for free. So he can...What?"

"For free?" Jocelyn almost choked. "Why would he do that?"

"He needs the creds. And with his ideas, I need to save

money. I can't afford what he wants, but, oh, God, I want to. I'll tell you all about it later. How's Ashley been?"

"She's fine," Tessa said. "Just a little cell-phone-aholic."

"She is that," Lacey agreed. "Sorry. I'll talk to her about it."

"You might have to talk to her about more than that," Jocelyn said as they walked across the sand.

"What do you mean?"

"She thinks you're going to get back together with David."

Jocelyn's words brought Lacey to a dead stop. "*What?*"

"It's true," Tessa said. "I drove over here with her and she dropped enough hints that I am certain she thinks this storm is bringing him home."

"Home?" Lacey had to laugh. "He's been here one time, when she was a year old. Twice if you count meeting my parents when we were dating. Mimosa Key has never been his home. And you know that man couldn't be less interested in being a father." She heard her voice rise and didn't care. "And just for the record, I couldn't be less interested in ever seeing him again."

"Shhh. Don't let her hear you," Jocelyn said, giving up the cooler to put her hands on Lacey's shoulders.

"But doesn't she know that he's had every opportunity to visit and has done nothing but send money?" Little bits of anger and resentment, sharp as nails, pressed against the inside of her chest. How long had Ashley been harboring these ideas? "What started this, the hurricane? Having her home blown away? Facing death at a young age?"

"Maybe all of those things, but…" Jocelyn shook her head. "My guess is it's a pretty natural thing for a fourteen-year-old to have Daddy fantasies."

Daddy fantasies? "Whoa, those are worse than the fantasies I've been having all day."

"She's not happy about you lusting after the architect, either," Tessa added.

"I'm not." She closed her eyes, not about to lie to her best friends. "Okay, I'm lusting. I mean, like whoa and damn, yes, he's so freaking hot I could jump his holy bones. But—"

"Oh my God, don't let Zoe hear you," Tessa warned. "She'll be buying condoms on our next stop at Walgreens."

"Maybe she should."

"I like the sound of this," Jocelyn said. "Go change into your suit in your dad's van. We'll wait for you. I want to hear about these big ideas of his."

Lacey dug into the bag and pulled out something fuchsia, about the size of a Band-Aid. "There better be a cover-up in here, too."

"Ashley said you have a ton of them."

"At home."

"No one's here, Lace," Jocelyn assured her. "Go. We'll set up camp."

Jogging up to the van they'd borrowed from her dad, Lacey squeezed into the back, stripping down and tsking over the price of the suit that barely covered her breasts and bottom. It was cute, but still.

She glanced down at her cleavage, and the rest of her. And all she could think of was the way Clay had drawn her. Did she really look that beautiful to him? That strong and capable? There were no words for how much she wanted to be the woman in that drawing.

The drawing! She had to go snag it before Ashley did. She'd tuck it away somewhere safe so she could pull out it out whenever she felt weak and insecure. Those times when she'd want to be reminded that a gorgeous, smart, funny, kiss-you-crazy man saw her exactly as the woman she wanted to be.

She rolled up her clothes and let her mind drift back to Ashley. Why this sudden preoccupation with David? Was it because she thought Lacey might be truly attracted to another man? Did she sense that Clay Walker was somehow different from the men she'd dated in the past.

Because he was.

She'd talk to Ashley tonight, before she spent another minute with Clay. They needed to be open and honest about this. And about Ashley's father, who was never, ever coming to Mimosa Key.

Opening the back door slowly, she squinted into the bright sunshine as she climbed out.

"Wow. Pink is definitely your color."

At the sound of a male voice, she gasped, spinning around to see a man silhouetted in the sunlight. She was vaguely aware that he held a paper. The sketch, her sketch, but that was not what short-circuited her brain. Oh, no. It was the complete impossibility of what she was seeing.

All she could do was croak his name. "David?"

Chapter Ten

I t's Fox."

Lacey just stared, and tried to breathe despite the six-hundred-pound boulder that had just landed on her chest.

"I go by Fox now." He took a step closer, the world behind and around him fading into black and white as David Fox, a man she had once loved with every fiber of her being and more, stood bathed in sunlight, a dark-haired, green-eyed devil.

"You look fantastic, Lacey." He held out the drawing. "Self-portrait?"

She snatched away the paper, her heart wrenching as a corner tore in her hand. "What are you doing here?"

"I came to see Ashley. And you, of course. And...wow." He angled his head and openly admired her. "As good in three dimensions as"—he nodded to the drawing—"two."

She covered her chest with the paper, painfully aware

that she was in nothing but bright pink strips of silk that barely covered breasts that David had once suggested she have reduced.

"So how are you?" he asked with a wide smile that showed masculine dimples in hollowed cheeks with a hint of whiskers. A linen shirt hung over his lean body, and despite the trousers he wore, he didn't show a bead of perspiration anywhere. In ninety-two degrees.

"I'm…" *Dizzy. Stunned. Hoping to wake up any second.* "You might have warned me you were coming."

He gave her a look of disbelief. "Didn't Ashley tell you?"

Ashley?

She thinks you're going to get back together with David. "Have you talked to her?"

"Not exactly," he said, turning to look at Ashley in the water, offering his classic, handsome profile to her. "We've been communicating online. Today, in fact. She told me you'd be here."

He was chatting online with her daughter?

"Is it safe for her to be out that far?" he asked.

Lacey took a few steps to see over the rise to the water. "She's just past the sandbar. The water's still shallow there, but it drops off after that."

"I don't know. It looks far."

Irritation fired through her. "She's with my friends. She'll be fine, David."

"Fox," he said. "I really don't answer to David anymore. Are your friends CPR trained?"

She choked a little. "Seriously? After thirteen years of doing a complete disappearing act, you're going to show up here and question my parenting skills?"

"I'm not questioning them." He squinted at Ashley. "She seems well adjusted enough."

Seems? He'd determined that from "communicating online" with her and seeing her from three hundred feet?

"She is," Lacey said. "But this is going to throw her for a loop."

"Are those the same women from the dorm you RA'd in college?"

"Yes." She wasn't surprised he remembered them. The year David and Lacey had been together, she'd spent every other minute with her three best friends.

"David, why don't we go somewhere and talk?"

"I want to see Ashley."

Her heart sank. "Just let me..." *Get my head around this*. "Talk to you. Privately. So you can tell me why you're here and how long you're staying."

"I told you why I'm here. And I'm staying for a while."

A while? What was a while? Five minutes was too long a while. "You'll find it pretty boring here, believe me. No cliffs to scale, no rapids to navigate, no icebergs to climb."

"But one very beautiful woman to thaw." He did the head-tilt thing again, letting his gaze roll over her as slowly and sensually as the waves on the sand. "If she'd just relax and say hello." He held out his arms.

Instantly she backed away, toward the van. Feeling silly, she turned and lifted the hatch door, tucking the drawing away safely and grabbing the shirt she'd just taken off.

"I can't believe she was e-mailing you," she said.

"Not e-mail, exactly. We message on Facebook."

"You're her Facebook friend?" Why, oh why, had she stopped looking at Ashley's Facebook page? Because it was a bunch of "you've been tagged" photos and silly middle-school jokes and Farmville announcements. There'd been no *David Steven Fox* when she'd last checked Ashley's page.

"She friended me."

"Of course. You'd never seek her out."

He made her jump by putting a hand on her shoulder. "I'm here, aren't I? Can't I get some credit?"

Actually, no. "Look," she said, letting out a breath as she stabbed her arms into her shirtsleeves and buttoned up with maddeningly unsteady hands. "This has really thrown me, David."

"Please call me Fox. I have a new career now and, as part of that, I legally dropped David from my name."

"A new career? I didn't know you had an old one."

"I've been studying with some of the greatest chefs in the world. What started out as a new adventure became my passion. You know I love to cook, and now I'm formally trained."

"That's great. Congratulations." She still didn't see why he'd change his name, but it didn't matter. What mattered was that he was here and Ashley—

Surely Ashley wouldn't go running into his arms after being ignored her whole life? She glanced again at the beach. Ashley was still swimming, just past the sandbar but visible.

"Let's go over by the table and talk."

He started to follow her through the reeds of sea oats. "You can't keep me from her forever," he said softly.

"David—er, Fox. You can't just spring yourself on a fourteen-year-old who's been through a trauma."

"Ashley told me you spent the storm in the bathtub."

Resentment coiled through her and knotted deep in

her gut. It was bad enough that Ashley had told him about their ordeal and forgotten to mention that she was on Facebook with her father who hadn't seen her since she was a baby. But the slight reprimand in his tone really irked.

"There really wasn't time to evacuate safely," she said. "And I kept her alive."

"She shouldn't have been here." Nothing slight about that accusation.

"Oh, right, David, like you would have been a better parent. Like you wouldn't have her hiking into African villages for an evening of body piercing."

"She should see Africa. Once you've slept in the mud houses of the Bamako, you see life differently."

"She sees life fine." Lacey leaned against the trunk of the poinciana for support. "I don't know how your appearance is going to affect her."

"I'm her father. And it's a reunion, not a return from the dead."

"Reunion?" She had to laugh softly. "You haven't seen her since the week of her first birthday." When he'd stayed exactly forty-eight hours. She could only hope history repeated itself.

"I've sent her cards and presents."

"And she saved every one," she assured him. "But Hurricane Damien stole them, along with a lot of stability. So I'm just really worried about... *this*."

"And the money?"

Was he accusing her of taking it? "Ashley has an account with every dime you've ever sent her. You are free to audit that. I'm saving it to pay for college and whatever else she needs. She knows you've sent it and appreciates it."

But the truth was that every check seemed to make

Ashley sad, and Lacey's heart had broken for her daughter, who deserved to be loved, not bought.

"You owned this house outright, didn't you?" He gestured toward the exposed foundation.

Just how much had Ashley shared with him? "Granny Dot left it to me when she died, about a year after my grandfather died. Ashley and I'd been living in an apartment, so it was a blessing. Without any rent or mortgage, I was able to start a small baking business, mostly cakes for weddings and functions."

His eyes lit. "So we're both in the food industry."

"No. I'm . . . doing something different."

"What's that?"

She took a deep breath and jumped. "I'm building a resort." Ooh, that sounded nice. "As a matter of fact I just hired the architect."

He nodded, gave a slight smile. "I saw his, um, blueprint."

Heat burned her cheeks. "You have no idea what you saw, David. But none of that concerns you."

"Everything about Ashley's life concerns me."

She reared back as if he'd hit her. "Really? Is that a fact? Is that why you've been completely missing from her life even though I told you you could see her anytime?"

"I understand you might be bitter, but I really hope that we're all mature enough to co-exist, and maybe even forgive."

Could she forgive him? His choice to leave her had hurt Lacey, but his decision to stay away had hurt Ashley. And that was unforgivable to a mother.

"I forgave you long ago," she said brusquely, not wanting to get into it with him now or ever.

He was looking around at the post-hurricane mess,

his brows knit. "How on earth are you going to afford to build a resort, Lacey? Don't you think you should start with something a little more modest?"

Exactly the opposite of what Clay thought she should do. That gave her a boost of confidence. "Insurance. Investors. Loans." She tilted her head up, smiling. Clay had done that for her, she thought fleetingly. In one morning, he'd given her confidence. "I have a plan."

"A plan, huh? Not always your strong suit." He tempered the tease with a smile and leveled her with that magnificent green gaze that had melted the clothes right off her about forty-eight hours after he'd guest-lectured in one of her college classes.

"I've changed," she announced.

"You have." When his eyes crinkled she could see his lashes were still thick, and the tiny crow's-feet just made him great looking instead of merely good looking. "And you look terrific, Lacey, considering what you've been through."

"Fourteen years of single parenthood?"

"I meant the hurricane," he said. "But I don't imagine either one was easy." There was an apology in there, she could sense it, and the tone brought her resentment down a notch.

"Thanks, David. Fox. You look good, too." He was thirty-nine now, a full ten years older than the man she'd been with all morning. Ten years and ten million miles apart, she mused. Clay Walker was light, bright, sexy, easy, sunny brilliance. David Fox was dark, threatening, difficult, a sliver of cloud-covered moon impossible to follow and even more impossible to hold.

Reminding her that regardless of his latest career

move, David's next trip to Timbuktu couldn't be much farther than his next breath. That's how he rolled. Away.

"Can I stay with you at your parents' place?" he asked.

What *hadn't* Ashley told him? She tried to think of a good, reasonable explanation for saying no, but none came. Except that she was kind of planning to have sex with her architect.

"Yes, of course you can. For a few…" *Minutes*. "Days. I'm very busy with my building proj—"

The scream from the beach made them both whip around, startled.

"Ashley! There's a shark!"

"Oh my God!" Lacey leaped forward.

"Hellllllllllp!"

All three women stood on the beach screaming at Ashley, who was frozen on the sandbar, the Gulf waters splashing at her thighs. She looked to her left, the horror on her face visible even this far away.

The fin popped up not twenty feet from her, between her and the beach.

Lacey ran, shells stabbing her feet, a scream caught in her throat. Before she'd even reached the girls David tore past her, his long legs eating up the sand, kicking it in his wake, his arms outstretched. Fully clothed, he bounded into the shallow waters, headed directly for Ashley, who kept screaming.

The four women followed, running toward the water, gasping and calling in horror.

The fin popped up again, directly between David and Ashley, making her wail.

"Don't move, Ash!" David called to her, and she froze, staring at him now.

Once again the shark emerged and David lunged in the opposite direction, forcing the creature's attention to focus on him, making it leap and turn toward him, the white teeth of a tiger bared for a horrifying split second.

"Run, Ashley!" David yelled before throwing himself in the water, drawing the shark farther away.

Ashley screamed again and followed the order, her skinny arms flailing as she stumbled through the waist-high water. Lacey ran toward her just as David made a loud noise and—dear God, had he punched the shark? Kicked it?

The fin disappeared, then popped up again, fifteen feet away and headed out into the Gulf.

Instantly David dove into the shallow water toward Ashley, popping up in front of her just as Lacey reached them both.

She threw her arms out to grab Ashley, but her daughter turned and fell into David's embrace.

"Daddy!"

"Baby girl." He kissed her head and hugged her like . . . like he actually cared about the child he'd demanded Lacey abort.

"Daddy, you saved my life."

"No, sweetheart, you saved mine."

Crumbling into the water, an adrenaline dump and cold reality bit Lacey harder than the rare tiger shark in the Gulf of Mexico ever could. Silhouetted in the sunshine, Ashley and David hugged like there was no tomorrow.

But there was, only now it included a man with the totally apt name of Fox.

Chapter Eleven

ᴄ~

After dinner, Lacey could hear David and Ashley laughing in the living room, a bittersweet sound to a mother's ears. She loved to hear Ashley happy, with a giggle that was quick, easy, and joyous. Despite the history, the absence, and a lot of unanswered questions, Ashley had just seamlessly accepted David into her life.

It was shocking, really, that she didn't harbor more of a grudge. Was the loss of her home and all her stuff enough to make her realize what was important in life? At fourteen? If so, Lacey could learn a lot about maturity from her teenage daughter.

Then again, David had a gift. He wielded that irrepressible charm like a razor-sharp blade, slicing away anything that got in the way of people liking him. Somehow, when he teased Ashley he made the empty years disappear, and when he enthralled her with a colorful story about diving with crocodiles in Botswana, Lacey could see her daughter's eyes fill with awe and forgiveness.

Ashley could forgive David, so why couldn't Lacey?

Because she didn't have to. They had made an arrangement many years ago. David held no paternal rights to Ashley, and any gifts and money he gave her were out of concern and care. No strings attached. In return, Lacey had told him he could see Ashley whenever he wanted.

She just hadn't thought he'd ever want to.

She pushed the faucet handle, making the water run louder into the sink, scrubbing the pan with vicious swipes, drowning out the sound of all that happiness in the living room.

Her hands itched to do something other than clean. She eyed her mother's pantry, knowing it was stocked well enough now that she could knock out something simple for dessert. A cobbler, maybe. Or tropical napoleon, which she'd been testing before the storm. He'd be impressed with that.

She grunted softly and whipped the wet sponge. Why should she impress him?

Although he'd certainly impressed them with his cooking skills, making a remarkably good country-style chicken and not letting any of the girls lift a finger.

How could she not invite him to stay here, sending Tessa and Zoe to the Ritz to bunk with Jocelyn for a few days? Lord, she hoped it was a few days. Or less.

Yes, the invitation made sense; the house was too crowded and the decision to move everyone around to accommodate David had seemed smart when adrenaline was soaring and arms were hugging and rational thinking took a backseat to dramatic life-saving dives.

A few minutes ago, when she had a moment to say good-bye to the girls, Zoe had whispered, "Bet he planted the shark."

Zoe meant it as a joke, but part of Lacey—the dark, nasty, resentful, unforgiving part—wondered exactly what David Fox was capable of doing just so he could redeem himself in his daughter's eyes.

"We're going over the causeway!" Ashley burst into the kitchen, practically vibrating with excitement. She hadn't brushed her hair after swimming, so it was a wild mess, and she still wore the bikini Jocelyn had bought her, with a tiny pair of gym shorts rolled down nearly to her pelvic bone. She looked like a delicate flower, lithe, tan, reedy, and blown by the exciting winds of life. No, David Fox wasn't a wind. He was a cat-five hurricane and, damn it, she'd already weathered one of those.

"Now?" Lacey asked.

"We have to get some games! Grandma doesn't have any."

Of course not; they never played games in this house. Unless you call "count Lacey's faults" a game.

"Okay, you can take my car." Because the alternative, the motorcycle David had arrived on, was not up for negotiation.

"Mom, we're riding bikes."

"You're not going on his—"

"Bicycles." David popped in behind Ashley, a glint in eyes that were so identical to his daughter's that the sight took Lacey's breath away. "Relax, Mama. Ashley says you have a couple of beach cruisers, and I saw a Wal-Mart right in Fort Myers. It'll be no problem."

"Over the causeway?" Yes, she sounded lame, but Lacey had never let Ashley ride that far, even if there was a bike lane. "It'll be dark before nine and the tires need air and—"

"It's only six-thirty, Lace," he said, putting a possessive hand on Ashley's shoulder. "We'll pump the tires at a gas station and I'll take good care of her. I can't believe she's never ridden bikes over the causeway. That's the first thing I'd do if I lived here."

"No, you'd dive off it."

He grinned, clearly delighted with the comment. "We'll work up to that."

Lacey glared at him. "Not funny."

"Chill, Mama."

She gritted her teeth to keep from demanding he stop calling her that.

"I already saved her once today," he said.

Ashley turned to look up at him, adoration in her gaze. "He's my hero."

Oh, puh*lease*. "Can't you just stay on the island tonight? Maybe take a drive over the causeway tomorrow? We have a deck of cards, that I'm sure of."

"See, this is why we never made it, Lace."

"Excuse me?" He was going there now? In front of Ashley?

"You're so risk averse. You can't live like that."

"Actually, you can live longer like that." She resisted the urge to snap the dish towel at him. Instead she dried the pot, maybe a little more furiously than necessary.

"And, sorry, but I'm a parent, David. With that title comes certain responsibilities. Like keeping your child safe."

"Mom! He freaking tore into a shark with his bare hands to save me today."

"Not exactly."

"Exactly!" Ashley stood next to David, metaphorically and literally aligning herself with him. "And I totally trust him and, seriously, like everyone I know rides bikes over the causeway, so we're going. Let's go, Fox."

"You can call me Dad."

Cripes, pick a name already. And not *Dad.*

"Dad." Ashley couldn't keep the smile out of her voice. "We'll be back before it gets dark, Mom."

"Wait a sec, Ash." David stepped closer, taking the towel from Lacey's hands. "I'd be happy to forgo a bike ride if you'd come with us."

She swallowed hard. "I'm going to bake you guys something. A surprise."

He nodded knowingly. "So you still head to the flour and sugar when you're strung out, huh?"

"I'm not—"

"Mom, he so knows you!" Ashley exclaimed, delighted. "Mom always stress bakes. It's awesome." She stopped, realizing what she said. "I mean, not that you're stressed, just that we get to eat your amazing cakes and stuff."

"It relaxes her," David said knowingly, that insider info just irritating Lacey more. "Then I'm ordering something light and delicious. Oh, Lace, remember that French apple tart you made once at my apartment?" He slapped his hand to his chest. "Mother of God, I think that's when I knew I loved you."

She just stared at him, numbed by the comment. "I lost my tart pan in the storm," she said softly. "How about meringue cookies?"

"Perfect." For a minute she thought he was going to kiss her good-bye. And it seemed so natural. But he didn't, instead backing away and gesturing to Ashley. "Let's go, kiddo."

They were out the door before Lacey could think of any reason to make them stay, any reason that wouldn't make her sound like a petulant child or a big old jealous meanie.

Anything like *Ashley, he's going to leave and break your heart again. That's what he does, baby.*

She walked to the door, watching them round the yard toward the garage.

"Ashley!" Lacey called, and even as she did she couldn't think of a thing to say. She had no parting shot, no special warning. She just had to see her daughter's face.

"What?" But Ashley didn't turn.

I love you. "Do you have your phone?"

"Don't need it."

Since when could she not be tethered to that damn phone? Since David-Fox-Dad showed up.

And they disappeared, with more happy laughter in their wake.

Back in the kitchen, she headed to the oven to flip the dial and preheat just as her cell phone rang. And she remembered Clay.

She stood stone still, long enough to debate what to say to him. And long enough to let the call go to voice mail, the technology most adored by chickens.

Of course David's appearance shouldn't and wouldn't change a thing as far as Clay, but it was a wrinkle she didn't know how to smooth out yet.

Clay would think she'd made up an excuse. But she certainly couldn't slip out on a "date" tonight to watch *Casablanca* at his apartment. Instead, she listened to his message, enjoying the tenor of his voice as he promised to call later if he didn't hear from her. Maybe she'd answer that call, but she wasn't seeing him tonight.

With a sigh she opened the pantry, stared at the pathetic baking shelf. Mother hated to bake, but there was probably enough to—

I think that's when I knew I loved you.

She slammed the door closed, biting her lip as if that could stop the sting behind her eyes that had started when Ashley first called him Dad.

Had he forgotten? Had he blocked out that conversation in Gainesville, the day he'd told her a child "doesn't fit my lifestyle"? Well, at that age it hadn't fit her lifestyle, either. And she'd had to deal with her parents. Her mother. The face of disapproval.

Not that she'd been mad that Lacey had gotten pregnant. Oh, no. What upset Marie Armstrong was that Lacey didn't have what it took to get David to marry her.

She abandoned the pantry and the kitchen altogether to change the sheets on the guest bed. Passing the den, she glanced at the bookcase, her gaze drawn to photo albums that filled one shelf. There, in the middle, stood an album neatly labeled 1996–1997.

Kind of a wonder Mother didn't call that the Year of David.

She pulled out the album and tucked it under her arm, heading to the backyard to curl up in what had become her favorite getaway lately, the hammock her dad had hung between two queen palms.

Cocooning into the canvas, she opened the photo album and started turning the thick, plastic-covered pages, stepping back in time to the red brick buildings and moss-covered oak trees of the University of Florida. Those were happy days in Gainesville, especially the year she RA'd at Tolbert—and had met David.

She'd finally settled on a hospitality major after trying and quitting at least three others. So even though that deci sion was going to cost her an extra year, she was certain she'd found something to see through to completion. And, of course, she'd made great friends on the fourth floor.

She paused on a picture of the dorm on Halloween night, smiling at Zoe channeling her inner Posh Spice. And Tessa dressed to climb Mount Everest. Jocelyn hadn't gotten into costume that night, but even if she had it wouldn't have hidden the sadness around her eyes that remained there almost the whole year.

And there was Lacey, beaming behind her girls, and bone skinny, damn it. She went as Little Red Riding Hood in a scarlet leotard and boots. The Big Bad Wolf showed up just a few weeks later when she'd gone to hear a guest lecturer speak for her Asian Cultures class, a world traveler doing a slide show on his near-death experience hiking Mount Huashan.

To this day, she couldn't remember a thing David Fox had said about his brush with Huashan Death, but she could describe the shades of green in his eyes, the music of his easy laugh, the strength of his hands, the shape of his lips. By the end of the lecture, she was fantasizing about marrying him.

And he, she learned later, was fantasizing about something else with her.

He got his way, and they were lovers by their second date.

She flipped to the back of the book to spring of that year, the weekend she'd brought David Fox home to meet her parents. It was Easter, and she was two weeks pregnant but had no idea. She was also as in love as a woman could be, and would have given anything to spend her life with David.

Anything but the child she carried inside of her, and that was what David wanted her to sacrifice in order to travel the world with him. Not only did she not want to travel the world; she wanted that baby.

That baby, and more, to be honest. But that was not the life David envisioned.

She rocked the hammock, leaving the book resting on her knees, open to the picture. David's hair had been black and long, curling over his collar, reminding her a little of someone else.

Clay.

The realization hit her hard, making her heart squeeze. Sexy, seductive, so good at talking her into things. Charming, smart, and completely compelling. Look what he'd done already.

In the space of two hours she'd agreed to let him work for her without proper credentials, to build an over-the-top five-star resort that would tax her professionally, financially, and emotionally, and she'd all but made a date to sleep with him.

He'd done that with one scintillating conversation, a sexy drawing, and a few hot kisses.

She pushed the hammock from side to side with all the resentment and second-guessing that was building inside her. What was *wrong* with her? Hadn't she learned anything from her experience with David? Sure, she'd been careful with men for the last fourteen years, maybe too careful. But Clay Walker was David Fox all over again and she wasn't going to make the same mistake twice.

Tears stung and she blinked against them. Damn it, why did David have to show up now and make her realize exactly how wrong Clay was? Just when she was about to have some fun? She *never* had fun, not the kind this young, hot, carefree guy was offering.

All she did was scrape together a living baking cakes and trying to drum up business, then she gave every ounce of remaining energy to drive Ashley around and make sure her daughter had everything she wanted and needed. In her spare time she'd held that old house together with duct tape and hope. She'd had exactly six dates in the last five years and not one of those men had made a single cell in her body tingle.

And then she'd met Clay and, well, forget tingling. He made her feel like she'd sucked her finger and stuck it into a light socket.

But that's how you get electrocuted, Lacey.

A lump of confusion mixed with bitter self-pity filled her throat, sending a teardrop down her cheek. She swiped it. She had no time for this kind of wallowing. She had to be focused and serious about building a new life, not dreaming about sex with the architect she'd hired to do it.

Screw that up and what would happen? She'd quit, like always.

No, she couldn't have the complication of sex with Clay. That was the one thing that had to go. If she didn't sleep with Clay, then she wouldn't be making the same mistake twice and she wouldn't be risking her heart along with her building project.

The minute she saw him again she'd tell him she couldn't—

"So, I'm guessing you dug deep enough to find an excuse to blow me off."

She turned suddenly, the album tumbling off her stomach. She lurched to grab it and rolled right out of the hammock onto the grass, staring up at the most gorgeous man she'd seen since, well, since that morning.

And, damn it, all she wanted to do was reach up and kiss him. Just for *fun*.

Chapter Twelve

Clay kneeled next to Lacey, setting down the six-pack of beer he held in one hand and the DVD from the other. She didn't move right away, looking up at him, her hair spilling everywhere, a tear streaking her cheek.

"Are you crying?"

"I'm fine." She let him help her sit up, and just the contact with her bare shoulders made his hands itch for more.

"Really? 'Cause you don't look fine." He couldn't fight the urge to brush a wayward curl from her forehead, getting a flash of gold in her eyes in response. "Is this why you didn't answer my call?"

She tried to swallow, and it looked like it took a monumental effort. "Something came up."

He gave her a wary smile and lifted the six-pack of Mich he'd grabbed on the way to her house. "Better watch it. I brought Excuse Juice. Every time you make one, you gotta drink. I should have you good and loaded if you're starting off with 'something came up.'"

She laughed softly, pushing herself up and making another quick swipe at her eyes. "I'll take one of those. How'd you find my—never mind. You went to the Super Min, didn't you?"

He smiled. "Gloria was covering the register, and she told me where your parents' house is."

He eased her back into the hammock, which swung under their combined weight and pushed their hips right next to each other. "You all alone out here, Lacey?"

Pulling a bottle out of the carton, he kept his gaze on her while he twisted it open. "Where are your girlfriends? Where's Ashley?"

"My friends are staying on the mainland. Ashley is..." She hesitated, then finished with, "She's out."

"What's going on?" He handed her the bottle and she took it, puffing out a long breath and nodding thanks.

"I'm just thinking."

"About what? Never mind, I know. You're having second thoughts about what we discussed today."

She lifted one corner of her lips in a wry smile. "I'm past second and rounding fifteenth."

"Let me guess." He took his own beer out of the carton and uncapped it but didn't drink. "You think I'm some kind of lunatic stalker serial killer who draws naked women and works for free."

A smile threatened. "Possibly."

"And all you wanted to do was build a little five-room inn—in keeping with zoning code, I might add—with frilly bedspreads and antique water pitchers, but I planted visions of Moroccan villas with imported hardwood floors in your head."

This time she nodded slowly and started to talk, but he silenced her with a finger to her lips.

"Wait, wait. I'm not done. Just to make things worse, the first thing we did when we were alone together was make out like a couple of teenagers and practically agree that we'd end the night in the sack. And you're freaked out about that."

"And you're a mind reader."

"No, but I can read your expression and what I see is a woman who is not only trying to decide how far to run but how fast and how soon. So you decided to blow me off tonight." He held out his bottle for a toast. "You're easy to read, Strawberry."

She dinged the glass. "All of that may be true, but there's more to it." His gaze shifted to the book or whatever it was—a photo album?—that had fallen to the ground. It was closed, but he could see someone had handwritten 1996–1997 on the spine.

Simple math told him that would be close to the year her daughter was born. So maybe she'd had an argument with Ashley. Maybe the teenager had stomped out and left Mom crying. Maybe this had nothing to do with him and what she needed was a friend to talk to.

"Then tell me," he said, finally taking a sip. "What else is bothering you tonight?"

"What isn't bothering me tonight is a better question," she said on a quick laugh. "It's kind of complicated and personal."

"I can do complicated and personal." He situated himself on the hammock, carefully sliding one leg around so she had no choice but to lean back next to him. The canvas was wide and comfortable, and easily accommodated two.

She didn't lean back, though. Instead, she gave him a wary look. "I think this is a bad idea."

"I just want to talk."

"And he gives me the oldest line in the book."

"Okay, I don't just want to talk, but since you stood me up and I found you weeping alone in the backyard, I figure talking's all that's on the agenda tonight." He eased her closer. "C'mon."

"I'm not weeping. I'm just emotional."

"Whatever you want to call it." He searched her face, looking past the dusting of freckles and the soft lashes around big eyes. "I can see fear in your eyes."

"You are right that I'm a little scared of... what you proposed today. It's more than I bargained for."

He wasn't sure if she meant the resort or the invitation for sex, but they were probably both more than she bargained for.

"Well, I have good news," he said, turning so that she had to lean into him or fall out of the hammock again. She chose him. "I've been working on blueprints of Casa Blanca, making some calls about resort zoning, and I even started the ED—that's the environmental determination paperwork—and ordered an auto-CAD system to—"

"Stop, Clay."

"Why?"

"I'm not... I can't—"

"Hey, we had a deal. No *can't*-ing."

"No, please." She curled her legs up into the hammock, tucking them under her, making herself into a ball like she wanted to protect herself and not fall into him or his ideas. "This is happening too fast."

"There's no other way for it to happen. You don't want to sit around for months and think about building some thing, do you?"

The look on her face said she wanted to do just that. "A project this size takes a lot of time and money and—" She closed her eyes. "When you add the complication of our attraction..."

He laughed softly. "The 'complication of our attraction'? Well, gee, when you put it that way, it's *really* sexy."

"You know what I mean." She elbowed him. "You scare me."

"Why?"

"Because...you're...scary."

He took her beer bottle and carefully set it back in the cardboard six-pack along with his. Then he eased back and she had nowhere to go but next to him. Once they were side by side, pressed together in the hammock, he curled a hand into her hair and forced her to look at him. "You're not scared of me. You're scared of sex."

"No, I'm not. I'm scared of...involvement."

"Then we're good. Because with me there's no involvement, other than our business arrangement. All you need to do is relax and have fun."

She smiled, tilting her head so her soft curls brushed his hand. "I was just thinking that I don't have enough fun in my life."

"Then I'm your man." He leaned toward her a little more, the curve of the hammock forcing her a little closer. He tangled his hand in her hair and brought her face closer to his.

"I bet you're a lot of women's man."

"Not really."

"No one in your life? No one up in North Carolina thinking you're just down here on business, not fun?"

"No one at all."

"Why not?"

He dropped back, looking into the purple twilight sky, thinking of the twenty different ways he could answer that question. Hadn't met the right girl. Too busy with work. Standards so high they're rarely met. All true, but none the real reason there was no girlfriend or wife up in North Carolina.

"I had a bad experience," he finally said.

"How bad?"

"Disgustingly bad. Scarred-for-life bad. Keep-all-my-relationships-superficial bad." He didn't turn to look at her. In fact, he closed his eyes and braced for the nasty job of telling his ugly story.

"Are you going to tell me what happened?"

"Only if you're prepared to lose respect for someone you have on a pedestal."

"Someone *I* have on a pedestal?" She sat up a little. "Who?"

"*The* Clayton Walker."

"Your father? You said he was remarried and had a…" Her voice trailed off. "How does that affect your love life?"

It had ended his love life. "Well…" He let a few seconds drag out. "The woman he married was my girlfriend."

He didn't have to look. He knew her jaw must be open, her eyes wide, her breath sucked in with shock. He'd seen the expression on every face, every time he told the story. Which wasn't often.

"Oh. Wow."

"Yeah." That would be the typical response. "So, I'm

pretty much sworn off anything beyond fun, therefore you have nothing to fear from scary me."

"How did it happen? I mean, if you don't mind telling me."

He minded. A lot. But he'd told the story before and survived, so he could do it again. "Jayna was my dad's admin at the firm. When I interned there, we...were together. She's a few years older than I am." He caught her little wince and instantly took her hand. "Trust me, that's where the similarities end."

She nodded, waiting for more.

"We were pretty tight." *Like she was picking rings.* "It was pretty serious." *Like every weekend and most nights were spent in the same bed.* "I was pretty..." Gone.

"Doesn't sound pretty to me."

He smiled. "I admit, I kind of broke it off first. I got gun shy 'cause things were going fast. I'd just finished school and was really serious about training and learning this business. You have to understand that I've been in and around architecture my whole life. I've been working in some capacity at my dad's firm since I was fifteen and I finally had my degree and was interning, really doing some amazing work."

She searched his face. "Like the French Hills."

He barely nodded, turning to face the sky again to corral his emotions. Damn, when would this wound stop festering?

"Anyway, I got some majorly cold feet. I wasn't sure if she was right for me. I wasn't sure if I was ready. I took off for a summer in Europe to just look at the architecture and get my head together. She—Jayna—read that as a permanent breakup. And..."

"And she moved on to *your dad*?" She asked the question like anyone would: with complete disbelief and disgust.

"I think it was the other way around." His throat desert dry, he reached for his beer, slugging the bitter brew quickly, making the hammock sway. "Hey, if you think I'm persuasive with the opposite sex, you ain't seen nothin' till you meet C-dub." Which she never would. Ever.

"C-dub. For Clayton Walker. And they got married?"

"She got pregnant while I was in Europe, so, yeah. He divorced my mom and hopped on a charter to Vegas to make Jayna the next Mrs. Clayton Walker."

She dropped back onto the hammock as it all sank in. "And that's why you left the company?"

Actually, no. But now he was getting into some dangerous territory. Telling her any more tonight, when she was feeling this emotional? Bad idea.

"More or less," he said vaguely.

"What kind of relationship do you have with them?" she asked after a minute.

"My dad and Jayna? I'm not gonna lie. I can't stand the sight of either one of them and I don't feel like taking the high road." Plus, Dad wasn't even done ruining his life, trying to make himself look good and Clay look like a criminal. "I see my half-brother when my sister, Darcie, babysits him. I don't do holidays or birthdays or happy family reunions. Jayna got what she wanted: a husband. And Dad got what he wanted."

"A trophy wife?"

Dad got what belonged to Clay. "My dad's a small-minded, jealous, insecure son of a bitch who resented everything I had because he didn't have it."

"That's not very...fatherly."

He snorted softly. "That fucker doesn't know the first thing about being a father. Pardon my French, but he..." *Brings out the worst.*

"Sounds like he earned that."

"He did."

She didn't say anything for a long time, the only sound the crickets in the trees and some traffic in the distance. Then, "So that's why you want a no-strings-attached sexual relationship?"

"Honestly, Lacey?" He turned to her. "I don't ever plan on putting myself in the line of fire again, no. I want to do my job really well and use my gifts. I want to fix my—build my own reputation in this business, make top dollar, and... avoid anything that tears you to shreds when it ends." He looked hard at her. "But that doesn't mean I can't enjoy myself. It doesn't mean we can't enjoy each other, if you're comfortable with that."

"You know, five minutes before you arrived, I was swearing off sex and now you're basically offering just that."

Just that. "Dumb thing to swear off." He kissed her nose, her eyes, and her mouth again, letting the hammock rock itself so he could use his free hand to trail a finger path down her neck and into the V of her top. "Damn, I thought about you all day."

Color and goose bumps rose on her creamy skin. "What did you think?" she sounded as if she were afraid to ask.

"Well, I didn't think you'd stand me up," he said, faking a frown. "I thought I could get you to my apartment and we could watch your favorite movie from under the covers."

Her eyes widened.

"And we could argue about how the wrong guy gets the girl," he continued. "In between, we could…" His finger reached the rise of her abundant breast, and his mouth nearly followed. "Would you like that?"

She let out a shuddering sigh, rolling her body even closer to his. "Of course I'd like that, but we can't."

"That's funny, Lacey. I could have sworn I heard you use the C-word." He underscored the tease by dragging his finger lower, into the lace of her bra, and leaning forward to kiss the flesh of her cleavage.

"I might have." The confession was buried in a sweet moan of helpless pleasure.

"You like that, too?" he asked, his body reacting as it had been all afternoon: on the brink of an erection.

"I do, but…"

"Sounds like someone needs some Excuse Juice."

"No, I don't. I need"—she stabbed her fingers into his hair, guiding his mouth lower—"this."

"Told you." He rolled so that he could press himself against her hip, hard enough now that she could feel exactly what her body was doing to his.

"Clay," she said, easing away. "We really can't. Not here, not now."

"Okay." He eased off the next kiss. "Your daughter's coming home?"

"Well, yeah, but there's someone—something—else. This afternoon—"

"Mom, where are you?" Ashley's voice cut her off and they both bolted upright, making the hammock sway so hard they almost fell out.

Clay was still processing Lacey's last words. Had she said there was some*one* else?

Lacey face was more panicked than he'd have expected, considering they weren't doing anything.

"I'm out here," she called as they got to their feet. "I didn't get a chance to tell you."

"'Tell me what'?"

The sliding door to the house opened and instead of the sandy-haired teenager he expected, a man walked out. Tall, dark, commanding, and instantly focused on Clay.

Yep. She'd said some*one* else. Damn it.

"Mom, did you start the cookies yet?" Now the teenager charged out, a smile that could light the universe on her youthful face. It disappeared the instant she saw Clay. "What are you doing here?"

"Ashley," Lacey reprimanded. "That's rude. Mr. Walker is here to discuss the building project."

The man crossed the grass with an easy grace, lanky, tall, and confident, reminding Clay of someone but he couldn't quite grasp who.

"I'm Fox," he said to Clay, extending his hand. "Ashley's father."

Ashley's *father*? Clay shook his hand, meeting green eyes the precise color of Lacey's daughter's eyes. "Clay Walker," he said, returning the shake.

"I understand you have some outrageous ideas for our—for Lacey's property."

"Don't know if I'd call anything outrageous," Clay replied, his brain spinning through what he knew about Ashley's father. Hadn't Lacey said he was out of the picture? Like, seriously, gone for the past fourteen years?

Ashley muscled into the middle of the group holding up two bags. "Dad found you a tart pan and Masterson's was open, so we got apples. He got the clear glass kind, like you want. He knew you can't stand to bake with metal or dark glass, so now you can bake the tart that made Dad fall in love with you."

Fox chuckled, putting a warm, fatherly hand on Ashley's shoulder, eyeing the six-pack on the ground. "It looks like your mama's a little busy now, Ash."

Ashley lowered the bags, disappointment making her expression fall.

"No, we were just... meeting," Lacey said quickly.

"And we're just about done," Clay added. "So y'all can bake your, uh, tart."

"Southern boy, are you?" Fox stooped over and picked up the DVD Clay had brought over. "And look at this. Lacey's all-time favorite way to lose two hours. Can we watch it after we bake the tart?"

"It's all yours," Clay said. "I brought it over for Lacey."

"Oh, I'm sure she has a copy, but this is a digital remaster. Ever seen this, Ashley?"

"Mom's tried to make me watch it but, whoa, boring." She rolled her eyes and sang the last word.

"I'll make you love it," Fox said, putting an arm around Ashley and nodding to Clay. "Nice to meet you, Clay. Lace, just come on in when you're done with your meeting. Ashley and I'll start the dough and we can watch the movie while it chills."

They disappeared into the house and Lacey stayed perfectly still, watching them, silent until they'd closed the door. "I wanted to tell you he showed up quite unexpectedly this afternoon and that's why I didn't take your call. I'm sorry."

"No apologies necessary." But he didn't want to hang around and hear the gory details about their reunion. And go through pictures of their life together. "I'll keep working on the blueprints and sketches. And I'll call you in a few days."

Some storm clouds passed her eyes. "Clay, I—"

"Mommy, hurry up! We can't do this without you!"

Lacey closed her eyes. "I don't want to watch that movie with them."

"Of course you do," Clay said. "You love that movie. Even the end."

She looked up at him and smiled. "When the wrong guy gets the girl?"

He laughed softly and backed away toward the gate. "Yep." And wasn't that the story of his life?

Chapter Thirteen

Lacey had backed out of the baking and the movie, claiming exhaustion and the need for a long bath. True enough, as excuses went, so she spent most of the evening in her room—well, her parents' room because she didn't even have a room anymore—in the tub and then on her laptop, digging up resort-management sites and thinking about Clay.

Around ten, David tapped on her door. "Lacey, Ashley's gone to bed. Any chance you want to take an evening stroll down to the beach?"

She closed her computer and rolled off the bed to open the door. He was in sleep pants, his bare torso lean and fit. She refused even to look at a single hair on his chest, meeting his eyes instead, with one hand on her half-opened door. "Ashley went to bed? It's so early." And she hadn't said good night.

He gave a slow, sly smile. "I think she wants us to have some alone time."

Oh, God. "Well, I have no desire to go to the beach," she said.

"That's too bad, because I need to get out."

After a few hours? Really, how long could this man last on Mimosa Key? She nodded toward his bare chest. "Better put a shirt on or the Mimosa Key sheriff'll haul you in for indecent exposure. They're tough like that here. Excuse me." She brushed by him, walking down the hall to Ashley's room.

The door was closed, so she tapped and pushed it open, expecting to find Ashley crouched over her computer or on her phone.

But the room was dark, except for a beam of moonlight that highlighted some clothes on the floor. That mess would normally be the source of a conversation, but, whoa, Lacey had bigger problems than keeping the house clean.

"You really asleep, Ash?"

"Almost," she said groggily, sliding around in the bed. "You and Dad going for a walk?"

"Ashley, do you have to call him that?"

She sat up with a loud tsk. "He's my father, Mom. Why are you so determined to keep us apart?"

Lacey squeezed her fists and let the wave of fury pass. "I am not determined to keep you apart. I've let him stay here."

"Well, where else would he stay?"

A hotel. On another continent. Where he's been for fourteen years. "Did you like the movie?"

"We watched *Rio* instead."

For some reason she was relieved. *Casablanca* was her movie.

"Are you two going to take a walk?" Ashley asked again, hope in her voice.

"I think he is, but I don't feel like it."

"You should go, Mom. I'll be fine here alone."

"I know you will. I just..." She sighed into the darkness. "I don't want you to get too attached to him."

Ashley reached over and snapped on the light, her eyes blazing. "Why not?"

"Because you don't know him. He'll just—"

"Why can't you just accept that people change, Mom?" Her hands clutched the comforter in frustration. "People grow. He has. He'll tell you. I think he's amazing."

"I'm sure he is, but—"

"But what? What is with you?" She gave her big put-upon huff of breath. "I mean, most moms in this situation would be thrilled that their daughter wanted to have a relationship with her dad. I could hate him, you know?"

"Yes, I know."

"I could push him away and say 'no way, you've been missing for my whole damn life, so screw you.'"

"Ashley, don't talk like—"

"I could! But I'm not and I think that's very mature of me."

"Yes, honey, it is mature." And instead of sounding like her own mother and finding fault with Ashley, Lacey knew she should be congratulating her daughter on her behavior. But she couldn't. "It's also dangerous."

"Dangerous?" She practically sputtered. "He wouldn't hurt a fly."

"Not intentionally." How could she warn her daughter

that loving this man could mean deep and profound hurt? "But he hurt me."

"Mom, that was fourteen years ago."

"But it shows you that he's the kind of man who can, and does, leave when something more exciting comes along."

"Oh, that's just a lame excuse so I don't get close to him." She sank back on her pillow. "I think you're jealous."

"I think you're…" *Absolutely right.* "A little out of line talking to me that way."

Ashley made a pouty face but withheld an apology.

"Don't you see, honey?" Lacey sat on the edge of the bed to get closer and make her point. "I'm terrified that he'll get you all wrapped up in a father-daughter relationship and then, you'll see. He'll get a call from a friend in Madagascar to go zebra hunting or rock climbing or jungle hopping and, wham, you're all alone."

"He said he's done with all that travel, Mom. He's a chef now. He wants to open a restaurant." She leaned forward, grabbing Lacey's hand. "Ohmigod, Mom, what if he opened one here on Mimosa Key?" Her voice jumped an octave in excitement.

"Honey, please don't start harboring those fantasies."

"It's not a fantasy. He likes it here. And, Mom, he still cares about you. I could tell when he picked your tart pan."

"It takes a lot more than a tart pan to demonstrate love," Lacey said. It took trust and sticking it out through tough times and it took a commitment. Nothing Lacey'd ever gotten from any man, least of all David Fox.

Ashley grinned, looking suddenly much younger than fourteen. "Mom, haven't you seen the way he looks at you?"

"At me?" She waited for the expected impact of those words, but there was none. No feeling, no happiness, no excitement. "You're always imagining things, Ash."

"Aunt Zoe noticed, too."

"She's *always* imagining things, too."

"Maybe you're just too busy making out with that architect on the hammock to notice the guy who really matters."

Was she? "We weren't making out. Okay, a little."

"Ewww, Mom. He's too young for you!"

"No, he's not."

"Won't you even give Dad a chance? It would be so awesome if you two got back together."

Lacey just shook her head, very slowly. "I gave him a chance, a long time ago."

Ashley leaned forward, taking both of Lacey's hands. "Don't you feel anything for him? Just a little gooey inside when you look at him?" The sheer desperation in her voice almost broke Lacey's heart.

"No," she said honestly.

"Well, can't you try? For me? So we could have a family? He could buy us a house and, and, we could get all the stuff we lost and—"

"Oh, Ashley, please don't put that on me. I don't want your happiness to be contingent on this...this fantasy you have about David and me getting back together." Because it was almost impossible for Lacey to say no to her daughter.

"Just give him a chance, Mom."

"He's staying with us for a few days. That's enough of a chance."

"A step in the right direction." She gave a secret smile.

"And I promise I won't check to see if the guest room's been used."

"Ashley!" Lacey flicked her fingers on the blanket, tapping Ashley's leg. "Don't even *think* about that."

"Why not? You were thinking about it with that Clay guy."

Lacey reached over and switched off the light, her only defense against a rising blush. "End of conversation."

Ashley just tunneled into the covers and turned over. "It's okay, Mom. Clay's cute and he obviously wants to get into your pants."

"Ashley Marie Armstrong, you cannot talk like that. Go to sleep and stop having opinions."

Ashley laughed softly at the admonition. "Only if you stop flirting with boys and give my father a chance."

"Good night, Ash." Lacey closed the door on her way out, ready to warn David to quit planting these stupid fantasies in Ashley's head.

The rest of the house was quiet, so David must have gone for his walk alone. Relieved, Lacey went into the kitchen to make some tea, stopping to examine the tart pan on the counter. The bag of apples sat untouched next to it.

The gesture had been sweet, she admitted to herself. Fingering the pan, she pictured the blossoming rosette of apple slices covering a sweet compote and buttery crust.

Without giving it much thought, she preheated the oven, loaded up the counter with flour, salt, butter, and some ice water, and mentally calculated some recipe amounts that would kick up the flakiness, which made this tart so divine.

She'd like to use her mixer with the paddle, but...

Don't think about what you've lost, Lacey. But the

homey scents of flour and salt alternately soothed and tortured her, reminding her of all that was gone.

Would she bake at Casa Blanca? she wondered. The resort name still felt unfamiliar and awkward in her mind, so new that she couldn't imagine that it might ever exist, let alone become a place for her to live and bake. Was that possible? Or would she and Ashley find an apartment when Mother and Dad came back?

The thought made her dig deeper into the coarse and crumbly dough, the simple action sending a soothing, sweet numbness up her arms. Of course she'd bake wherever she lived. She'd need to, because—

The back door opened as David walked in, looking with surprise at the counter.

"A walk would have de-stressed you, too, Lace. It's a gorgeous night out there."

She wiped a hair away with the back of a floury hand. "Thanks for the tart pan," she said. "It's a nice one."

"You're welcome. Here, I brought you this." He held up a bright pink bougainvillea blossom, then sniffed it. "Smells like Indonesia."

"I wouldn't know what Indonesia smells like, David."

He chuckled. "Okay, you can call me David. But only you. Is Ashley asleep?" He came closer, laying the flower on the counter while her gaze flitted over his loose-fitting T-shirt and cargo shorts.

"No. But she's having dreams."

He looked at her, a frown making him no less attractive in the soft kitchen light. "How's that?"

She shook her head, not quite ready to start that conversation and kill the mellow happiness of making dough. "When were you in Indonesia?" she asked instead.

"When I got serious about cooking, as part of my internship with the Aman Resorts, a corporation that owns some of the most amazing luxury hotels in the world."

She stilled her fingers. "You worked for a resort company?"

"Don't be so surprised. I am capable of holding down a job," he said, grabbing the bag of apples and dumping them in the sink. "I know you think I'm a trust-fund slacker."

"You *are* a trust-fund slacker."

"I'm not a slacker and the trust fund is well invested. I can't just hop from one adventure to the next, Lacey. A man's got to settle down at some point. Where's the peeler?"

She nodded toward a drawer. "Should be in there. What did you do for this company?"

"I started as a busboy and worked my way up to chef. There's not a kitchen in the Aman organization where I haven't worked, and that includes Cambodia, Laos, Thailand, French Polynesia, Montenegro, Turkey, Morocco—"

"Morocco?"

"Yes, and, trust me, it's nothing like your movie."

Her movie. "I understand you went with *Rio* instead," she said, lifting the dough ball out of the bowl to turn it on the counter. "Good choice."

"And, believe me, that cartoon was no more realistic a depiction of Rio de Janeiro than *Casablanca* is of Morocco."

Morocco. Even the word reminded her of Clay and how much she would have liked to have watched their movie together.

Oh, now *her* movie was *their* movie. "Did you like Morocco?"

He shrugged, starting to expertly peel a Granny Smith. "What I saw of it. Mostly I worked."

"That's not like you. Usually you trek."

"I still do now and then," he admitted. "Once I finished my time with Aman, I took a year to hit a few of my favorite haunts, like Kuala Lumpur and, of course, Chile and Argentina."

"Of course." She knew what was down there in Chile and Argentina. "You've always had a soft spot for Patagonia."

He had the apple peeled and cored in a matter of seconds, his hands smooth as silk and lightning fast. "That didn't take too long."

"The apple?"

"The Patagonia dig."

She smiled, shaking her head and giving the dough another fold. "This has to chill for a while," she said. "I can finish the apples."

"Let's do them together," he said. "Do you prefer to peel or slice?"

She wrapped the dough in plastic, then opened the fridge. "You look like you're pretty handy with the peeler. I'll slice."

They worked in silence for a few minutes, the only sounds the sweep of his peeler and the slide of her knife as she made the paper-thin slices. When she started on the second apple, she took a breath and decided to attempt the more serious conversation.

"So, David. What exactly are you doing here?"

The peeler slowed infinitesimally. "Does my being here upset you that much, Lacey?"

"What upsets me is the ideas that are being planted in Ashley's brain. Ideas that will never happen."

"You never know what's going to happen."

"But I know what *isn't* going to happen: You and I are

not getting back together to live happily ever after as Ashley Armstrong's married parents."

"Married?" he choked softly. "You know I don't believe in marriage."

Oh, yes. That she knew for sure and certain. "I know you don't believe in marriage," she replied. "I think that's why we're in this situation to begin with. I *do* believe in marriage."

"Then why aren't you married?"

She should have seen that coming. "Because I haven't met a man I think would be an ideal partner, a perfect father to Ashley, and a great husband."

He finished an apple and put it on her cutting board, the sweet smell making her want a bite of one of her slices. "Maybe you've already found that man."

She looked up at him. "Clay?"

He let out a sharp laugh. "I meant me."

"You?" A thousand responses warred for air time, but she glommed on to the easiest one. "You just said you don't believe in marriage."

"And you think that twenty-something longhair with a tattoo does?"

"Now you sound like a parent."

"Well, I am a parent, and my daughter's well-being is at stake."

What was he saying? "You think Clay could hurt her?"

"I think Clay could hurt you. It's obvious what he wants, drawing naked pictures, bringing beer over to your house, rolling around on the hammock."

It was so obvious she couldn't argue the point. "He's going to work for me. He's doing the work pro bono."

"Oh, he'll get paid all right."

She turned to him, lifting the knife from the apple just

enough to make her point. "Watch it," she said. "You're over the line."

He held up both hands and took a step back. "You're right. I'm sorry. I'm just jealous."

Jealous? "All right, then, color me confused. I mean, how can you be jealous? Why? You've been gone for a lifetime. Suddenly you care who I'm involved with? About Ashley's well-being?"

"I've always cared about Ashley's well-being."

She focused on the blade, sliding it through the apple and letting it thunk to the board. "Then you had a lousy way of showing it," she said. "Or are we supposed to just erase the years, like your absence didn't hurt her?"

There was no answer from him as he worked his magic on one more apple, flipping the fruit like a seasoned pro baseball player handling the game ball.

"I screwed up," he finally said.

The apology didn't feel good, but it didn't hurt, either. In fact, when Lacey looked up at him, met the eyes that had once melted her, she felt...nothing at all.

Well, maybe a little relief *because* she felt nothing. But she wasn't inclined to let him off the hook that easily.

"Yes, you screwed up, David. There were too many Christmases and birthdays with not even a phone call."

"But I could make it up to you," he said. "If you'd let me."

"No, thanks."

"Lacey, I screwed up the past. Let me change our future."

"*We* don't have a future," she said. "There is no 'our' in our future, David. There is a daughter, yes, and I have never, ever tried to deny you the opportunity to know her. Not doing so has been your choice."

"I know—"

"From the beginning," she interjected, dark emotions building inside of her, words she'd wanted to say for years finally getting a voice. "You made that choice from the day I told you I was pregnant, as I recall."

Again, silence.

"And we both know what you wanted me to do." *Take care of it, Lace. It's legal.* She could still hear his voice.

"That would have been a grievous error," he said.

"No shit, Sherlock." She spat the cliché, not caring if it made her sound more like Ashley than a rational adult.

"And you've done a marvelous job with her."

"Don't patronize me," she said. "I've done all I could and it hasn't been easy."

"She's a lovely young lady."

Lacey snorted softly. "Most of the time, yes. But she's also a teenage hormone factory at the moment, given to drama and self-absorption. More than anything, she's a girl searching to fill a great big hole in her life that happens when you are raised by a single parent."

"Which brings us right back to why I'm here."

Suddenly she suspected she knew exactly why he was there. "Is it possible, David, that you're here to fill a hole in your life, not hers?"

"Anything's possible, Lace," he said as he gave her the last apple, then nudged her out of the way. "Let me." He took the knife, gave his shoulders a little flex and started slicing like a human food processor.

"Holy shit," Lacey murmured, rearing back in surprise. "Where'd you learn to do that?"

He grinned at her. "All over the world."

She leaned over, propped her chin on her elbows, and

watched him work, unable to hide her admiration. David Fox was once the man of her dreams and she'd loved him with everything she had.

And he'd crushed that love with a hiking boot.

But the act of baking late at night, talking and sharing and not being alone, the comfort of it, pulled at her heart. Not that she wanted David Fox to fill that role, but, Lord, she wanted someone.

And her most recent find had just hours ago admitted that he'd been so burned by love he only wanted sex. *Lacey, girl, you sure can pick 'em.*

"I'll start the compote," she said, pushing off to grab a bowl and the sugar.

"You know, Lacey," he said, letting her take over and start sugaring the apples. "One of the reasons I'm here is because I had an epiphany a while ago."

She looked up from the bowl, some sugary apples slipping through her fingers. "An epiphany?"

He leaned back against the edge of the counter, crossing his arms, his expression distant. "I was in Bolivia hiking the salt flats. We left late in the day and ended up having to spend the night in this little village, if you can even call it that, across the border in Chile. There was no hotel, no nothing. We stayed with locals, in a hut. They cooked the most amazing food, and the stars that night? You've never seen anything like it."

No, she hadn't, and probably never would. Bolivia held no interest for her. Which was why they were so wrong for each other.

"The next morning," he continued, "just before sunrise, I saw the woman who lived in our hut—a girl, really, barely twenty—outside nursing her baby." He gave her an expectant stare, like she should react to the monumental power of his story.

She didn't. "And?"

"The moment was suspended in time, like God's tableau. A young mother, her black hair falling over her face, her breast giving sustenance to an infant who clung to her with two tiny hands." He held up his own hands as though clutching a breast, which struck her as melodramatic and bizarre, but Lacey just listened.

"And it hit me, Lacey. This girl was just about your age when you had Ashley. That thought just speared me in the gut like nothing I've ever felt before."

She layered the apple mixture over the baking pan, furious that her hands shook a little. But how could they not? It had taken him fourteen years to figure all this out?

"What exactly got you, David? The fact that you ditched me for sheep in Argentina or the fact that the last time you saw your own daughter she was a year old?"

Putting his hands on her shoulders, he turned her from the apples to face him. "The raw power of procreation."

She wiggled out of his touch, an old fury bubbling up. *Little late to figure that out, Daddio.* "It is powerful."

"No, no, Lacey, it's *everything*. It's all that matters. It's the reason we are alive, not to see the seven or seven*ty* wonders of the world. Every single person on this earth is a wonder, and what we need to do—what *I* need to do—is…is…" He balled up his fists like he was grabbing something. "Seize the life we made. That's why I came here."

"To seize Ashley?" Her heart skipped. "You can't take her."

"I don't want to take her, Lace," he assured her, putting his hands on her shoulders again, too tight for her to escape. "I want to be with her, near her, to have a father-daughter relationship with her. You never said I couldn't."

No, she hadn't. But she never thought there was a remote possibility of it happening, either.

"When I looked at that young mother, so connected and alive because of the life she created, I knew that what I'm doing with my life is meaningless. Even the chef's work, which I love, doesn't fill a hole in me. Everything is meaningless without that connection to another human that is part of you."

"I was just thinking that," she admitted. "Although not quite so eloquently."

"Of course you were, because family *is all there is*, Lacey." He pounded his fist on the counter with each word, making the pronouncement like he'd invented the concept. "Nothing else matters. Nothing."

So now he wanted her family? No, not happening. "Family is important," she said, choosing each word carefully. "So why don't you go see yours in New York? They matter, too." *Plus, added benefit, they're a thousand miles away.*

He gripped her shoulders again, doing his damnedest to inch her closer. "Anyway, I'm not talking about that family. I'm talking about our family."

Our. That word again. "We don't have a family, David. We have a child and two separate lives."

"But why?"

"Why?" Was he serious? "Because you had to go to Patagonia. And Namibia. And Botswana. And—"

"Shhh." He put his fingers over her lips, another intimate breach of personal space.

"Don't shush me," she ordered. *And don't touch lips that hours ago were kissing another man.*

"Then don't say things that don't matter anymore. I went. I'm done. I'm back. Why can't it be that simple?"

"Because it isn't simple at all. For one thing, you can't come 'back' to a place where you've never lived or spent more than a week. This is my home, not yours. And she's…"
My daughter.

But she couldn't say that. She was his daughter, too. Biologically, anyway.

"I had another epiphany in that little village, watching that girl."

Watching that girl's breast, more likely. "Which was?"

"I'm still in love with you." His voice was husky. "In fact I never stopped—"

"Well, stop now." She put up both hands in the international sign for shut-the-hell-up. "You aren't in love with me. You don't even know me anymore."

He gave her a patient smile. "And I'm here to rectify that. And I know this: I loved you once." The words, a direct hit at her heart, left her speechless. "And I think—I *think*—I could love you again."

She stared at him. He reached for her, but she grabbed the baking sheet and whipped around to the oven.

He was next to her in a second, opening the oven door for her. "I believe that deep down, in your heart of hearts, you feel the same."

She stuffed the sheet onto the rack. "Then you'd be wrong."

"Now I am, maybe. But if I'm here long enough, you might change your mind."

How he could he not get this? She felt nothing for him. But there was no way to convince him of that right now. Instead, she closed the oven door and stepped away from him.

"However long you're here, David, I don't want you to make promises to Ashley. Do you understand? I will not have her getting hurt."

"And what about promises to you?"

"You can't hurt me anymore, David," she said simply. "But I admit you can annoy the hell out of me."

"That's a start."

How could he be so dense? No, he wasn't dense. He was David. And he'd never had any trouble with her in the past; she'd gone along with his every idea except that she terminate her pregnancy. That one, thank God, she'd stood her ground on.

And she would with this, too.

"Look, this is my life and my family and my dreams, and, I'm sorry, but you are fourteen years too late and not invited to be part of it. Can I make myself any clearer, *Fox*?"

"You're clear," he said with a soft chuckle. "Perhaps you're forgetting how I love a challenge. I live for a challenge. I can climb Kilimanjaro and I can change your mind."

No, he couldn't. She started to wipe the counter with long, sure swipes. "I'm going to read while the dough chills and these apples cook."

"We could watch the movie," he suggested.

No, they couldn't. "I'll pass. You should go to bed. Surely you have jet lag or something."

He just laughed. "All right. But I have to tell you one more thing because I believe in total honesty and having all my cards showing."

She gathered a palmful of crumbs. "Yes?"

"Lacey, I want to have another baby."

A baby? He didn't want the child he had. "Well, good luck with that."

"I want to have another baby with you."

Tiny little flour crumblets slipped through her fingers and fluttered to the floor. She stared at the dusting on the tile, unable even to look at him. "Why would you even say something like that?"

"Because you're a wonderful mother, a lifelong friend, and we make beautiful children together."

She brushed off her hands, let more crumbs hit the floor, and finally lifted her head to check the clock. Because never in her life had she needed to beat out her misery with a rolling pin more.

Of course she'd always wanted another child. Just not with him.

Chapter Fourteen

～

Another baby?" Zoe actually spewed her coffee, splattering a few drops on the glass table at the Ritz-Carlton poolside restaurant.

Tessa and Jocelyn's response was slightly more in keeping with the posh surroundings: silent, gaping mouths of utter disbelief.

"What did you tell him?" Tessa finally asked.

"I told him he's crazy." Lacey picked up her napkin and dabbed at the coffee droplets.

"You don't want another baby?" Tessa asked, a little accusation in her voice. Tessa and Lacey had talked about this, and Lacey had long ago admitted she'd like another baby someday.

Lacey looked up and met her friend's eyes, seeing the battle scars of Tessa's long fight with infertility. "Not bad enough to hook up with David Fox," she said. "I do, but I haven't met the right guy." A thought of Clay flit through her mind. "Definitely haven't met the right guy."

Jocelyn leaned forward. "David's an alpha dog, Lacey. Always has been, always wanted control over you. When he couldn't control you, and force you to have an abortion, he ran. He sees you as a mountain he couldn't climb, a thrill he couldn't conquer."

"Easy, Sigmund," Tessa said. "I suppose there is a possibility the guy's legit."

"And maybe pigs can get airborne," Zoe shot back.

Lacey was definitely on Zoe's side. "Still," she told them. "He did say he worked in the kitchen of this huge five-star resort corporation. He knows how to run the kitchen of a resort. If I go with this idea of Clay's, I'm going to need to talk to someone who's done that."

"Talking to someone is not bearing their child," Zoe said.

"A lot of people have worked in resort kitchens," Jocelyn added quickly. "And they aren't the father of your child or the man who broke your heart."

All three of them looked at her to underscore the warning.

"You guys, I am not interested in him, honestly." In her purse her phone vibrated and she pulled it out, unable to avoid having Tessa read the name on the caller ID.

"Clay Walker texting," Tessa said. "Aren't you going to read it?"

"Later." But she was itching to read what he'd written.

"C'mon," Zoe said with a nudge. "Let's hear what the hottie has to say."

"I heard plenty last night." Lacey folded her napkin

and placed it on the table, over the phone, aware of their curious looks. "He showed up and laid his cards out on the table. Well, the hammock."

"You were on the hammock with him?" Zoe sat up. "Did he lay anything else out?"

"A very ugly story," Lacey said, and they all automatically leaned in closer.

She told them everything about the girlfriend who married the father, and got the expected responses. Tessa was disgusted. Jocelyn quoted Jungian psychology. Zoe said the old man must be hung like a horse.

They spent a good ten minutes imagining how something like that could have happened, how it felt, and what it did to a family.

"I don't know about his family, but Clay's scarred pretty badly," Lacey said. "He's not even going to pretend a relationship could be for any other reason but sex."

"At least he's honest," Zoe said dryly. "'Cause some guys would take you for a major ride, believe me."

"So what are you going to do?" Jocelyn asked.

Lacey shrugged. "I don't know. I have one guy I don't feel a thing for asking to share his life and have his baby, and one I've got the hots so bad for that I can't think straight around him and all he wants is to get laid. What's a girl to do?"

All three of them looked at her like she'd grown another head.

"What?" she asked. "You think I should? Get laid?"

"Why not?" Jocelyn asked.

Lacey frowned at her. "You're not usually the one pushing casual sex, Joss."

"Yeah, that's my job," Zoe said, dinging her spoon

against her glass. "But thanks for the support. So let me repeat: Why the hell not, Lace?"

Lacey looked at Tessa, hoping for the voice of reason but getting a shrug. "I saw the guy. Put me in the why-the-hell-not camp."

"Are you guys serious?" Lacey could barely keep her jaw from hitting the table. "You guys think I should..."

"*Yes*." They answered in unison.

Lacey didn't know whether to laugh or talk them out of this lunacy.

"Without any kind of relationship? Or, worse, *with* a working one? What if we have some messy breakup and have to—"

"You can't technically break up if there are no strings attached," Jocelyn said. "So I don't see that as a problem."

"What about the example I set for my daughter? Do you see that as a problem?"

Tessa took that one. "She's not a baby, Lace. She wants you to be happy. You can be cool and not all in her face about it. You'll be working with the guy. Working *nights*."

"She wants me to be with David," Lacey replied, each excuse sounding weaker even to her ears.

"You can't let her control you like your mother did."

"Whoa," Zoe held up her hand for a high five to Jocelyn. "Sigmund's on fire today."

Jocelyn tapped palms, but her attention was directed to Lacey. "I'm serious, Lace. Maybe Ashley doesn't spend every breath telling you what you're doing wrong like your mom, but she does use her behavior to get you do what she wants you to do. It's time to not give her that power."

Lacey just blinked at her. "Well, then, I guess I..." *Am running out of reasons why this affair was a bad idea.*

"Are you out of excuses?" Tessa asked.

"Seriously, Lace," Jocelyn said. "When was the last time you did something just for fun? For you? For the pure pleasure of feeling..."

"His magic drafting tool," Zoe said, getting a loud burst of laughter that drew a few harsh looks from the other Ritz patrons.

Jocelyn slid the leather bill folder to the side of the table. "Let's take this inside or down to the beach, ladies," she said. "I don't think the Ritz can handle the Fearsome Foursome of Tolbert Hall."

"Ah, the good ol' days," Zoe said as they pushed back their chairs and gathered their bags. "When we had nothing but a few finals and frat boys to worry about."

"You had frat boys," Tessa said. "I had agriculture-major nerds."

"And I had the good luck to meet David Fox."

Zoe put an arm around Lacey. "I believe I tried to talk you out of Asian Cultures that semester."

"No, you tried to talk me into a linguistic class on Elvish."

"I was in my *Lord of the Rings* phase." She squeezed Lacey's shoulder and indicated the phone. "I'm dying here. Read the text, Lacey."

"All right."

"Out loud," Zoe insisted.

Lacey clicked on Clay's name, really wishing that simple act didn't make her heart ratchet up. But it did. "Heard there's a secret Mexican restaurant on this island. Need a local to get a table. Dinner tonight? I have something I want to tell you."

"Mexican?" Zoe did a little dance, shouldering Lacey

across the lobby into the apothecary shop. "Someone's getting the whole enchilada."

"Stop it, Zoe," Lacey said, but nothing could stop the smile that had started just by reading his name on her phone.

"We'll get you all ready," Zoe said, ignoring the order. "Clothes, hair, makeup." She snapped her fingers as if a light bulb had gone on in her head. "And I do believe I saw a condom display in that cute little apothecary in the lobby." She grinned, delighted. "We'll pop right in there and pick something perfect."

She pulled Lacey toward the shop. "Lacey needs to grab something in here," she said to the others. "We'll meet you up in the room, okay? And, Joss, can you throw your weight around and get my friend here an appointment for a wax? I'm thinking the whole shebang, huh?"

"Absolutely," Jocelyn said. "How about a pedicure, too?"

"You guys." But Lacey knew her protests were falling on deaf ears.

"What are you wearing?" Tessa asked.

"Whatever Zoe picks for me," she said, any chance of a fight gone. Besides, she didn't want to go home and dress for a date with Clay while David and Ashley looked on.

"Tell him yes," Zoe prodded, pointing to the phone. "C'mon, before you find some reason not to."

Lacy looked at the phone, typed "Sure," and hit Send before she could do exactly that. "Done."

"Safety first." Zoe guided Lacey into the store, past displays of gifts and toiletries, all the way to the back. "Really, you should see the selection."

"When I was younger, there was only one brand," Lacey said. "Trojan."

"In three sizes. There was Color Me Happy Large, This Will Have to Do Medium, and Oh Isn't That Thing Cute Small. Here we go." They arrived at the condom rack.

Lacey grabbed the first one she saw. "What's this? A warming condom?"

"Oh, they're nice," Zoe said. "Thinner and they get kind of hot. I like these, too, the Pleasure Shaped."

"Do you know all of this from firsthand experience?"

"I read a lot." Zoe flipped the box over. "Stimulates nerve endings and heightens sensitivity. Oooh. Lovely."

"Put that back," Lacey said, giving a nervous glance as a couple entered the little store. "My nerve endings are stimulated enough just by being in the same room with Clay. Are you sure I need these? I think we're jumping the—"

"Here's Durex Tingling Pleasure with a spearmint lubricant." She slipped the box off the wire hook. "Tasty *and* safe."

"Shhh," Lacey warned. "Just pick one. Large. No, extra large."

Zoe gave a soft whoop of approval, flipping through some more boxes. "Oh, my God, French ticklers!" She struggled to get the box off the hook as the man separated from the woman, looking at them, then taking a few steps closer.

"Zoe, quiet."

"These have the most amazing little nodules." She yanked the box and suddenly the whole top row of the display popped off, hooks and all, sending a shower of condom boxes everywhere.

"Oh, shit!" Zoe shrieked a laugh, hands out, missing more than she caught.

The man kept coming toward them, so Lacey gave

Zoe a nudge to start picking up the mess. As she crouched down, Zoe was laughing so hard she lost her balance and tipped onto her backside, letting out a howl as she landed in a sea of condom boxes.

She whipped one out from under her butt holding it up like a prize just as the man walked up behind her. "And the winner is...Kiss of Mint non lubricated, safe for oral—"

"Zoe."

"—sex with a reservoir tip for heightened—"

"Zoe Tamarin?"

"—male..." The arm waving the box overhead froze, but Zoe didn't look up. "...sensation."

"Is that you, Zoe?"

She didn't move. Not a single muscle so much as twitched on a woman who couldn't do "still" with a gun to her head.

"I recognized your laugh," he said.

Dead silent, she put her hand on the floor and started to push up. Instantly, he reached down to help her, and she wrenched her hand out of his, standing on her own.

Lacey was vaguely aware that he was tall and dark-haired, a striking figure with bold features and broad shoulders. But she didn't do a close inspection because she was more concerned with Zoe, who seemed almost unable to face him.

Zoe, who didn't know the meaning of shy with strangers and especially not with great-looking men who already knew her name. When she turned, her fair complexion had gone bone pale, her green eyes as flat and dimmed as if someone had reached inside and turned off her switch.

"Hello, Oliver." And she didn't seem the least bit surprised to see this man, whoever he was.

"Zoe." He said her name on a long, soft sigh, breaking into a huge smile, searching her face like a starving man being dragged past a banquet. "What are you doing here?"

She held up the condom box and attempted a funny face. "Stocking up."

He barely smiled, giving her with a look so intense even Lacey could feel its power. "I mean, in this hotel?"

"Visiting a friend." She gave him a tight smile and tapped the green Kiss of Mint box on her cheek. "Obviously, a good one."

"Obviously."

"Oliver!" The woman he'd come in with called from the front. "I'm ready."

He held up a single finger to the woman without taking his eyes from Zoe. He looked like he wanted to say something but no matter how deep he dug, the right words eluded him.

"Your wife is waiting," Zoe said in a voice that was no louder than a whisper.

"Zoe…"

"As I recall, she doesn't like to wait."

He closed his eyes like she'd kicked him in the stomach. "It was…I can't believe—"

"Oliver, I told the limo driver we'd be right there. Hurry, sweetheart."

"Bye!" Zoe said with completely false brightness, using the condom box to give a stupid little wave.

"I'm sorry," he whispered, the words so soft Lacey wasn't sure she heard right. "I'm so sorry."

Zoe's brightness flickered for a second, but that wasn't joy. It was hate. "Go. I have nothing to say to you."

Without so much as a glance at Lacey he pivoted and returned to the front, where the woman grabbed his arm and nudged him toward the door. "What were you doing back there where they keep the sex toys, you animal?"

Zoe stood transfixed, watching them leave.

"Who was that?" Lacey asked.

Zoe just closed her eyes and collapsed into a heap of fallen condoms, no doubt preparing a punch line she'd deliver with impeccable timing and sarcasm.

Instead, she quietly started to cry.

Chapter Fifteen

Clay only half listened to his sister's account of her latest dating debacle as he strolled through the waters of Barefoot Bay. His other ear was trained on the road that led to the beach, hoping the sound of Lacey's little VW would be the next he heard.

"Do I have a loser magnet hanging around my neck, Clay?" Darcie asked. "I mean, is it me or is it just that all men are assholes who only want sex and games, with no strings attached?"

A little guilt tweaked him, but he shoved it away. "It's all men."

"Not you."

Yes, him. Now, anyway. "Just be careful, use protection, and don't get your hopes up. It's hell out there."

"Great advice, oh cynical brother. Aren't you ever going to get over your heartbreak?"

He snorted. "First of all, I'm honest, not cynical. Second of all, nothing broke except my career. And third, I'm over her, Darcie. I was over it long before the day they got married."

Darcie was quiet for a minute. "He's actually been really good with little Elliott."

"Nice to hear. Change the subject or I'm hanging up."

He heard her sigh softly. "How's it going down there? Getting what you want?"

"Working on it," he said with another glance at the road. "I was right about the job; it could be big. It looks like I'm going to get it from planning to finish, which would be exactly what I need to take to the AIA for certification." He waited a beat, debating how much to tell her. "The owner's nice, too."

"Nice? What do you mean, nice? Like he won't go looking for references or digging up dirt?"

"I mean nice, like *she's* pretty hot and we have good chemistry."

"Ohhhh." She dragged the single syllable out to a full chorus of multiple notes. "Well, use protection and don't get your hopes up."

"Touché."

"And be careful, Clay."

"Don't worry. I'm not going to get hurt again." He wasn't that stupid.

"I mean professionally," Darcie said. "If Dad finds out—"

"He won't," he assured her. "This place is completely remote. I'm not going to file anything official with my name on it that could get on the Internet. Once I finish the job, I'll claim it with the board and fight for a chance to sit for those exams. No one can stop me if I've finished designing and building and have all the personnel here, and the property owner, to support me."

"Are you going to tell her everything?"

"I actually asked her to dinner tonight for that very reason. I'm going to tell her the whole miserable story."

Darcie was quiet too long.

"Darcie, can you think of a better way out of this? Dad has tied my hands and threatened to cut them off."

"No, I think you're being very smart and strategic, but maybe you should try talking to Dad first."

"And throw myself at his feet? No, thanks." He was the prick who moved in on his own son's girlfriend. And she was the one who—

Let it go, Clay.

"I came up with a way to save my own ass, and Lacey Armstrong is the ticket."

"Pretty name. What's she like?" Darcie asked.

"Pretty lady, too. Smart, funny." There was so much more to Lacey he didn't even know what to focus on. "Good mother." Why had he picked *that* out of the hat?

"She has a kid?" Darcie sounded shocked.

"A daughter, fourteen." And an ex, but before he could tell that to his sister, he heard the sound of a motor, too loud to be the Passat but definitely coming this way. "Hey, I gotta go, Darcie. I'll call you in a few days."

"Okay, Clay, but please . . ."

The motor had his attention, but so did the little note of sadness in his sister's voice. "Hey, Darce, you'll find the right guy. Don't worry."

"That's not it. I want you to . . . maybe think about . . ."

He knew where this was going. With Darcie, the family

peacemaker, it was always the same. "I'm not going to forgive him, so drop it."

"Life's short, Clay."

"He should have thought about that when he banged my girlfriend. Bye." He hung up without waiting to hear Darcie's reply, standing still to identify the engine he heard.

A motorcycle. He made his way up the beach to Lacey's property, lingering far enough off the road so he could see who it was without being spotted. The rider was helmetless and Clay instantly recognized Lacey's ex, Fox, perched on an expensive BMW bike.

Fox rolled up to the foundation and cinder-block base of the old house, a good fifty feet away from Clay, shut off the bike, and pulled out a phone. Clay had run here and his truck was parked two miles away, so Fox probably thought he was completely alone. But just as Clay was about to call out to him, Fox spoke into the phone.

"Mr. Tomlinson?" His deep voice carried across the open space, loud, like a man who liked to be heard. "I'm here. Are you on your way?" He was silent for a beat, then, "Well, please hurry. I'd like to get this done as soon as possible."

He shoved the phone into his pants pocket, taking a minute to survey the property.

Clay cleared his throat, instantly getting Fox's attention.

"I didn't see you there," Fox said, accusation in his voice. "What are you doing out here?"

"Working," Clay said. "And you?"

"Same." He walked toward Clay with purpose, his gaze direct, a hand extended when he got close enough. "Good to see you."

Was it? Clay shook his hand. "Working on what?" Clay asked.

"A surprise for Lacey." He smiled and slid his hands into the pockets of crisp khaki pants, then took an expansive look around. "Kind of a magical place, don't you think?"

Once again, something about the guy seemed familiar, or at least he reminded Clay of someone. "Absolutely magical," Clay agreed.

"I saw some of your sketches and it sure looks like you captured the possibilities of the place."

She'd shown him the sketches? For some reason that bugged him. "There are plenty of possibilities," he said vaguely. "I'm sure it'll be beautiful when we're done."

The other man snorted softly.

"You don't agree?" Clay had to ask.

"You obviously don't know Lacey." He shook his head, amused. "She's big on plans. Not so big on finishing things."

"Maybe she's changed. I get the impression you've been more or less gone most of the last fourteen years."

"I've been gone, but she hasn't changed." Fox walked toward the water, gazing out. "But I'll give her the benefit of the doubt on this idea. And I want to help her."

Clay said nothing, the sensation that he knew this guy still nagging. "How do you plan to do that?"

A big fat investment? Lacey could use that when it came time to break ground.

Fox just shrugged. "Oh, I'm working on some plans." He kicked a shell and put his hands on his hips, looking around like he owned the place. And the woman who came with it. "Fact is, Lacey and I have a connection."

Yep, definitely the woman who came with it. "You have a daughter," Clay corrected.

"Indeed we do, and that's a connection in and of itself. But—" He lifted his brows. "We also have a *history*," he said. "A long, emotional, passionate history."

What was his point? Throwing down a gauntlet? Warning Clay off?

"History means it's over," Clay said. "Is it?"

"At the moment," Fox acknowledged. "Is anything going on with you and Lacey?"

Clay refused to react to the bluntness of the question. "We're working on a building project."

"Looked to me like you were working on more than that."

"I don't think that's any of your business."

"I'm making it my business." He turned to face Clay, his expression sheer determination. "I'm putting my broken family back together again."

Clay just looked at him, a lot of different responses in his head, but all he heard was the echo of his sister's words. *Life's short.*

He wanted Lacey, no question. And he wanted this business. But he sure as hell didn't want to be in the middle of another broken family.

"Lacey's a grown woman," Clay said. "Old enough to decide what she wants."

"Absolutely," Fox agreed. "And what she says she wants is this pipe dream."

Clay laughed softly. "I think it's a little more than a pipe dream." *It sure as hell better be.*

"You do? Well, here's where my long-term knowledge of Lacey Armstrong and your short-term attraction to her comes into play. As I told you, she's big on starting, big on planning, big on hoping and dreaming and talking. That's a large part of what took us apart. She just couldn't—" He shook his head, a little condescending, a little bemused. "Just wait until the first or second obstacle. She'll stop cold, give up, and start on her next dream. Believe me, I know her."

"Yeah, but you don't know me."

That earned him a look of surprise. "Maybe I don't, Clayton."

"Clay." God, he hated to be called Clayton.

That's who he reminded Clay of…his father. The thought made him a little sick.

"And I know what she needs," Fox said. "And, even more important, I know what Ashley needs."

"How could you?"

He gave Clay a wry smile. "I take it you don't have any children."

"None."

"And probably don't want them."

He didn't take the bait, but shrugged silently.

"So you cannot even imagine what I feel for that girl, and, by virtue of the way nature works, what I feel for her mother."

That stopped him cold. He was right, damn it. He couldn't imagine how this guy felt about a daughter, even one he hadn't bothered to see for more than a decade.

"More critical," Fox continued, "you cannot imagine how much Ashley needs to be part of a strong, loving, solid family again."

Actually, he could. "I'm sure that's a universal desire," he said.

"Indeed it is. And you're getting in the way of it."

"By helping Lacey build a resort and giving her a way to show Ashley how to go from disaster to a success?" How was that getting in the way?

"So you've really bought into Lacey's fairy tale."

"Hell yeah, I have. And I'm going to help her realize it." Wasn't he? Or was he going to use her to get out of his own professional jam?

"Very noble of you, Clay."

Okay, maybe not so noble.

"On the other hand," Fox said, "I'm going to help her make another dream come true and teach Ashley another important lesson. I'm going to be a father to our daughter, a partner to my former lover, and a presence in her life. I can provide her with stability, family, and"—he tilted his head in acknowledgment—"quite a bit of money."

Holy shit, no wonder the guy reminded him of his old man. He was more like Dad than Dad was. And Clay'd had this conversation once before, and lost.

"And I agree with you." Fox took a few steps closer, leveling Clay with a cold look. "It *will* be up to Lacey to decide if she wants stability, family, security, and love or"—he gestured toward Clay—"the thrill of the younger man. Which, I don't deny, is probably making her feel very girlish and giddy. She certainly sounded giddy with you."

A car engine on the road denied Clay the chance to reply.

"Ah, there's the person I'm meeting. Do you mind? I need some privacy."

Yeah, he minded, a lot. Right now he minded everything. Mostly he minded that he hadn't been completely straight with Lacey, and before they went one step farther toward the bedroom, he needed to tell her exactly why he was there.

If he lost the job, or a chance with her, or if that sent her into the arms of this guy, then she wasn't the right partner for Clay. Partner... of any kind.

Chapter Sixteen

Lacey had assured Clay that he'd never find the place the locals called the SOB, since South of the Border had no sign, no written menu, no bar, no reservations, and very few tables. So they'd agreed to meet in the parking lot of the Super Min and walk to the restaurant.

Problem was, he couldn't find a damn parking spot. He finally pulled into the lot of the Fourway Motel across the street and, just as he climbed out of his truck, two familiar faces cruised by in a Mustang convertible that slowed down when the driver recognized him.

The G-girls. From behind the wheel, the frosted blonde, Grace, if he remembered correctly, gave him a long, slow once-over. Gloria was in the passenger seat.

"Gotta admit I didn't think I'd see you here tonight," Grace called out, turning down her car radio. "Hate to break the news to you, but this is a private party."

So what? He couldn't park in the motel lot? "I'm meeting someone," he said.

Next to her, the other woman leaned forward, her dark eyes much less predatory than her cousin's. "Don't tell me Lacey's going to be here?"

Okay, he wouldn't.

"She better not be," Grace said, all playfulness gone from her voice as she answered before Clay could. "Like I said, private party."

"I'll move the truck," he said, not sure what to make of the woman or what she was implying. "No worries."

Grace narrowed her eyes at him. "I'm not worried about your truck, honey. Believe me." With that, she hit the accelerator and drove off, disappearing around the corner.

"What the hell was that all about?" he asked out loud.

"That, my friend, is the Wicked Witch of Mimosa Key riding her red broomstick."

He turned at the sound of Lacey's voice, and any comeback caught in his throat as he checked her out. And checked her *out*. Whoa.

She crossed the street, high heels clicking to a rhythm that suddenly matched his heart as he drank in the tight black tank top, short jeans skirt, and some very sexy, strappy sandals with red toes peeking out.

"And you must be the Blistering Hot Witch." He reached out both hands, drinking in the sight of her. "Dressed to turn heads and break hearts."

Her reddish blonde curls had been straightened to a sleek and sexy sheen. She wore more makeup than he'd seen her wear before, including something really shiny on her lips that he just wanted to lick.

"This isn't a business meeting?" There was just enough tease in her voice to make him give in to the urge to put his arms around her and pull her close. When he did, woman's curves pressed against him top to bottom, and he closed his eyes and inhaled.

"Strawberry."

"I'm starting to get used to that nickname."

"I smell it."

"Not my idea, I have to admit."

"I like it." He nuzzled her in and took another whiff, letting his lips brush the ultrasmooth hair. "And this no-curl look is pretty, too." He inched back, grinning. "Did you get all dolled up for me?"

"I spent the day with my girlfriends at the Ritz and they were all about doing a shopping and beauty day, so I had a little pampering." She gave him a flirtatious wink. "The strawberry body splash was on the house."

"Then I love that house." He took her hand, her fingers silky from all that pampering, and started walking. "It's a good thing one of us spent the day working since the other was at the spa."

"I was working," she insisted, matching his steps. "Resort research. You mentioned that Casa Blanca really could use a good spa. The girls and I were dreaming up ideas. Jocelyn assures me we could make a mint, especially if we go organic. What did you do all day?"

"I did not get a strawberry pampering or"—he leaned down to look at her feet—"a bright red toe job."

She laughed, a feminine, sexy sound that did stupid things low in his belly. "Then what did you do?"

"Set up a CAD system in my apartment and did the first blueprint for a villa."

"Oh, really? That's..." Her voice trailed as her gaze slipped past him to a group of people across the street, and she frowned. "What's going on tonight?"

"I don't know, but G and G said it was a private party."

Her frown deepened as she surveyed the cars in the lot. "Why are all those are town council members going into the back of the Super Min?"

"Big run on milk?"

She shook her head. "I didn't read about any emergency sessions and, even if there were, they'd be in town hall. What did Grace and Gloria say?"

"Just that whatever it was, it was private. And they seemed surprised you'd be here."

"Grace Hartgrave is all talk," she said. "If you came anywhere near her, her husband, Ron, would sit on you and, trust me, you'd be crushed. She's a lot like her mother, Charity, a major busybody with too many opinions, but Glo, Gloria Vail, her cousin, is pretty cool."

"She seemed a little more laid-back," he agreed.

"I always liked Gloria." Her attention focused in on the group outside the convenience store. "What the heck are they doing?"

"I don't know, but I'm starving. Let's—"

"Lacey!" A woman called in a hushed whisper. "Lacey, come here."

Lacey turned, and they both spied a petite woman ducking behind a van in the Fourway parking lot. "Speaking of Gloria," she said. "What the..."

The woman looked terrified, gesturing wildly for Lacey to come closer while she looked left and right as if she would be caught any second. Lacey headed toward her and Clay followed, curious and on alert.

"What are you doing, Glo?" Lacey asked.

The other woman reached out and pulled Lacey closer, her big brown eyes wide. "Probably getting myself disowned, that's what. Listen, Lacey, I have to tell you something."

"What's up?"

"You are about to get screwed, that's what's up. And my family—my cousin and my aunt, especially—are holding the screwdriver. I hate that they're doing this to you, and behind your back, like cowards."

"What are they doing?" Lacey asked.

The woman looked pained, like she'd already said enough. "You just need to..." Gloria blew out a breath, then took another look around. "They're in the back of the Super Min having a totally off-the-books secret town council meeting. Well, not really a meeting, because then it wouldn't be off the books."

"To do what?" Lacey asked.

"To make sure you don't build a B and B, for one thing. A couple other people are getting stopped from building, too, but your plans are front and center."

"Why?" Clay asked. "What's the basis for the opposition?"

"Competition," she said. "My cousin and her husband, Ron, don't want any competition for the Fourway, and Aunt Charity wants Mimosa Key to stay firmly in the 1950s where, as you know, it is."

"Which is just stupid," Lacey said.

"Well, not to her. My Aunt Charity gets all kinds of tax revenue through all these loopholes. She's doctored up that bylaw book so bad it's like a novel she's written." The woman practically spat in disgust. "I'm the only one in the family who doesn't own a business, since I just work at Beachside Beauty, but I talk to a lot of people and they're sick of my aunt's hold on this place. She knows it, she's scared, and she's trying to make the town council work for her."

"What can she make them do?" Lacey asked.

"Tonight, she's making them read the bylaws and understand how it applies to zoning, then convincing them they need to have an emergency zoning meeting tomorrow that will uphold the five-bedroom maximum. The Fourway Motel, of course, is exempted because it existed before zoning regulations went into effect, and therefore remains the only hotel or motel on the island. There's a few long-term rentals, but not enough to make a dent in Charity or her kids' business."

Lacey looked at Clay, concern in her eyes. "What can we do?"

"Crash the meeting," he said.

"You have to," Glo agreed. "You have to get in there and fight my Aunt Charity or she is going to make all kinds of promises to the council that you can't possibly counter."

Clay snorted, understanding immediately. "Graft and corruption are the lifeblood of the building industry, I'm sorry to say. She wouldn't be the first business owner to throw money, booze, or votes at the people who make zoning decisions."

"So we just walk in and say she can't?" Lacey shook her head. "You don't know Charity Grambling."

"I know this business," he said. "If we go in there and point out the discrepancies in the bylaw book—"

"How can we do that tonight? We don't have that book."

Clay gave her arm a squeeze. "I have a copy in my

truck. I got it out of the Mimosa Key Library right after our first meeting. If the one she has doesn't match what was on record, that'll take some of the teeth out of her bite."

Glo beamed at him. "That's exactly what you need to do. But Lacey has to do the talking because this is Mimosa Key and strangers count for nothing."

"I will." Lacey reached over and gave Glo a quick hug. "Thanks for this." Then she turned to Clay. "Guess we better get those bylaws and kick some town council ass."

As they walked away, he put his arm around her shoulder and nestled her closer. "I like your new attitude, Strawberry. Is it the shoes?"

"And the company."

Lacey didn't let go of Clay's hand all the way back to the truck. She had no idea how to kick town council ass, but when he looked at her like that, she was ready to use these heels for more than making him notice her legs.

So what if the good ol' boys and girls of Mimosa Key were not her favorite people? Not all of the current town council members were in that clique. She and Clay would have to focus on the newer members and hope for the best. Surely she'd baked for some of them over the past few years. Didn't that count for something?

"All you need to remember, Lacey," Clay said as they crossed the Fourway Motel parking lot after retrieving his copy of the bylaws, "is that we have one single objective."

"To build?"

He laughed softly. "We are so far from building it isn't funny. There are about six thousand pieces of paper we need first, and the most important one from this group is a zoning permit. But we aren't ready to get that yet."

"Will we be by tomorrow?"

"No," he said, making her heart slip a little.

"But if they call an emergency meeting—"

"Page fourteen, section three." He held up the binder. "Nothing can be decided in an emergency session of the council that impacts the bylaws without a written notice that is posted a full two weeks in advance."

"You memorized the bylaws?" She couldn't believe it. "I've never even looked at them."

"You should. They're fascinating and totally old school. Of course I read the bylaws regarding building. Oh, and there is no such thing as a secret council meeting. In fact, according to page four, section five-A, if all five members of the town council are in a room together, any citizen of Mimosa Key has the right to call order and take notes, then publish those notes in the *Mimosa Gazette* the next day."

"Seriously?" She slowed her step, looking up at him, knowing there was awe on her face and not caring.

"What?" He laughed. "Did you think I wasn't a legit architect just because I didn't take some stinkin' exams? I'm doing my job. Although I like when you look at me like that. It's hot."

"Yeah? So are you."

He took the time to share a sexy smile with her. "Hold that thought for later. Now we have to concentrate on our goal."

"And you still haven't told me what it is."

"Buy two more weeks. If they want to call an emergency meeting tomorrow, they can. But our little book here says that they can't do anything in that meeting except set an agenda for another meeting two weeks later. We need those two weeks to find a loophole in the law that lets us build whatever we want. Which"—he squeezed her arm and reached for the door—"I think I've found."

"Really?"

He didn't answer because about ten sets of eyes greeted them on the other side of the door. The small group sat in an informal circle of chairs, as innocent as a church meeting but with a lot more guilt on their faces.

"Lacey!" Charity stood up, her arms planted on her narrow hips, her long nails crimson like blood drops against ill-fitting white pants. "This is a private meeting."

"No such thing," Lacey said, her voice cracking as she felt the weight of so many gazes on her. For a moment she had a flash of walking into the kitchen to greet her mother and getting a different version of the same comment every day.

You're wearing that *to school?*

And then she'd start to back down. Change her clothes. Question her decision. Doubt herself.

She cleared her throat. "I came to take notes that will be published in the next issue of the *Gazette*."

"What?" Three people asked the question at the same time.

She glanced around to do a quick count of council members in the gathering. Sam Lennox, the mayor; George Masterson, one of his cronies; a woman named Paula, who was a former neighbor of Lacey's; and that new guy with the heavy New York accent. That was four. Only four?

"Would you care to explain that, Lacey?" asked Sam

Lennox, a fairly reasonable mayor despite Charity's claim to have him in her back pocket.

But Lacey was still doing the math. If there were only four present, the plan wouldn't work. They couldn't threaten to take notes and publish them. They couldn't—

Her gaze fell on the face of Nora Alvarez, who headed up the Fourway Motel cleaning crew. Yes! She had been voted onto the council last month, no doubt through strings Charity and Grace pulled.

"It's in the bylaws," she said authoritatively. "It's on page..."

"Four," Clay supplied.

"Section..."

"Five-A," he finished.

Lacey threw him a grateful look. "I'm a citizen and resident of Mimosa Key and I have the right and privilege to attend any function where all five members of the town council are present and take notes." She beamed a smile right at Charity. "Our forefathers and -mothers were so smart and careful like that."

"I don't remember seeing that rule," Nora said, sliding a look to Charity.

Mayor Lennox stood. "Actually, Lacey's right. Come on in, Lacey. And bring your friend."

"This is Clay Walker. He's the architect I've hired to rebuild my property in Barefoot Bay." Just saying the words made it real and right. They'd never signed a contract, but Lacey didn't care.

They took two empty chairs slightly outside of the main circle of people and, after an awkward moment and some very dirty looks from Charity, talk continued.

Lacey tried to focus, but found herself returning the

glances of her neighbors. Glo avoided eye contact altogether, but Gracie stared her down, and so did several
others.

Charity remained standing as she spoke, her back to
Lacey and Clay. "As I was saying before we were so rudely
interrupted, in light of recent events we should have a brief
meeting—"

"Excuse me, Charity." Lacey interrupted and Charity
turned very slowly, her dark eyes tapering.

"Yes, Miss Armstrong?" she asked with the exaggerated patience of a kindergarten teacher who doesn't want
questions. "Would you like the full spelling of my name
for your report in the paper?"

"What recent events are you referring to?"

"The hurricane. Do you remember it?"

Several people laughed, but not the dark-haired young
man whose name Lacey didn't remember. "Aren't you the
one who rode it out in your bathtub with your little girl?"
he asked, that nasal Bronx sounding so out of place here.

"I am," Lacey said.

A few more mumbles and Charity's back grew stiffer.
"May I continue? As I was saying, we need to have an
emergency town council meeting tomorrow to review the
existing zoning restrictions as they will apply to multiple
new buildings that are proposed to—"

"Excuse me, Charity."

This interruption got a sigh of disgust that Ashley
would envy. "What is it, Lacey?"

Next to her, Clay gave a little nudge with the binder he
held. Taking his cue, Lacey stood. "You can't have an emergency town council meeting that affects zoning without two
weeks' written notice."

Charity stared at her, then tilted her head. "You're wrong."

"I'm right," Lacey replied. "I have the bylaws right here."

Charity reached under her seat and pulled out her heavily tagged binder. "Trust me, I know them. My father wrote them."

"With my grandfather," Lacey reminded them. She took the book from Clay, letting their fingers brush, which gave her a surprising kick of confidence. "I'd ask you to please look at..."

"Page fourteen, section three," Clay prompted.

A few people chuckled, but not Charity. She flipped open her book and ruffled pages with slightly shaky hands.

"There is no section three on page fourteen, Lacey. Perhaps you have an outdated version."

Was that possible? Did the library have an old version and she was about to look like a total fool? "I-I..."

"This book was notarized last year as the latest version of bylaws," Clay said, standing next to Lacey. "I was shown the paperwork by a lady by the name of Marian."

"Marian the Librarian," someone said. "She's never wrong."

Under thick powder blush, pink circles of frustration darkened Charity's cheeks. "Well, my version, which isn't notarized but is quite accurate, contains no such pronouncements, Lacey, and I—"

"Let me see it," Sam said, reaching for her book.

She held it. "No, Sam, this has been in my family for years. Only Vails and Gramblings handle this. It's like a Bible to us."

"Then open it and let me see it, Charity," Sam said. "And Lacey, bring that book here."

Lacey went forward, holding the binder open on page fourteen, her finger on section three, her heart hammering with every step. God, if Clay was wrong...

"Nice shoes, Lacey," Grace said as she passed. "You know what they're called, don't you?"

Lacey ignored her.

"Fuck-me pumps," Grace whispered under her breath, getting a laugh from the two people around her.

Sam took her book and placed it next to Charity's, frowning. For a long, quiet minute, no one said a word. Then Sam looked up and handed the book back to Lacey.

"This is for official record," he said to Nora. "So, as the secretary, I want you to note that for some reason these bylaws don't match. However, we will err on the side of caution and post a two-week notice before holding a zoning meeting."

A small murmur of voices filled the room as Lacey turned to give Clay a victorious smile.

"But in the interest of fairness and expediency," he added, "we'll meet tomorrow to set the agenda for that meeting. The town council can approve an agenda and if a citizen fails to get on that agenda, they can wait up to a year for the next zoning meeting."

A year? "How do I get on?" Lacey asked.

George Masterson stepped forward. "Any property owner who wants to have a structure approved that requires rezoning will have to appear at that meeting with preliminary plans detailed enough for the council to agree to put them on the agenda two weeks later."

Preliminary plans by tomorrow? Lacey swallowed. "How detailed?"

"Very detailed," Charity said.

"Define 'very.'" Everyone turned when Clay spoke, including Lacey. He stood now, and, like a lion ambling across the plains, he walked to the center of the circle, in complete control.

And poor Charity was his prey.

"Because, ma'am, if you'll turn to page twenty-five, section eight, and read real carefully and slow..." Clay drawled out the last word enough to send a little flutter through Lacey and maybe a slight sigh among a few other females in the crowd. "You'll see that getting on a zoning meeting agenda requires the property owner only to give a verbal description of the proposed structure, a timeline for building, a general budget estimate, and a declaration of intent to improve quality of life on Mimosa Key."

That was all? Lacey could have kissed him.

Charity, on the other hand, looked like she wanted to sucker-punch him. "That's correct, young man. And anyone"—she lifted a brow in Lacey's direction—"anyone who thinks they can cavalierly change the status quo of this island will find that last little item very hard to get by my, er, this council."

"What the heck do you mean?" Sam asked Charity.

"I mean, Sam, that quality of life is subjective and I expect this town council to recognize that fact no matter what smoke and mirrors and ridiculous promises Lacey or this tattooed man think they can throw at us tomorrow."

Clay bit back a smile. "We're up for that challenge, ma'am." He took the book from Sam's hand and nodded to Lacey for them to leave. "We have some work to do, Lacey."

He reached for her hand to walk her out. As they passed by Grace, Clay leaned down and whispered, "Actually, they're called fuck-me-*senseless* shoes. They're my favorite."

Chapter Seventeen

⌒

Lacey practically fell against the door when they closed it behind them. "I can't believe we did that."

"We did that," Clay said, pulling her into him for a hug. "You were awesome."

The compliment warmed like a straight shot of whiskey, and the embrace was like a full-body all-muscle chaser that made her dizzy with joy.

"*You* were awesome." She held on to his biceps as he lifted her. "With the pages and the sections and the big save at the end! It was like a movie!"

He laughed, spinning her around, and, when her feet hit the ground, he kissed her. A celebratory kiss that didn't last long enough. She wanted more. She wanted so much more.

But he quickly turned them toward the car, wrapping an arm around her. "You still hungry?" he asked.

Not for dinner. "Maybe we should do takeout." *At your apartment.* "We have a lot of work to do tonight."

"Oookay." He drew out the word.

"What does that mean?"

"It means we might not get enough work done. We might get senseless."

She leaned close and lowered her voice to a whisper. "I can do senseless."

"Really." Very slowly, he turned so they were facing each other. "You're full of surprises, Lacey Armstrong, you know that? You rose to the occasion, headed into the lion's den, beat the crap out of your opponent, and now you want to..."

"I want to." Oh, God, she wanted to more than she wanted to breathe, eat, sleep, or live. She wanted him.

"You're sure?"

The question threw her. Wasn't he sure? Hadn't he just told Grace that was exactly what he wanted, or had she misread him?

"Or," she replied cautiously, "we could go to dinner and discuss preliminary building plans." Which wouldn't do a thing to quell the little sparks of need exploding all over her body. "That would be sensible."

"I like your idea better." He dipped his head close to her mouth, then fooled her by sliding his lips to her ear. "Strawberry," he whispered, sending sex-charged chills over every cell in her body.

The girls were right. This would be *fun.*

At the truck, he opened the passenger door for her. "Once we head down that path," he said, "you know there's no going back."

She put her foot up to climb in, the position forcing her

skirt way up her thigh. *Way* up. He stared at the skin the move revealed, then placed one hand right on her thigh, making her muscle tense in his palm.

She looked up at him, ready to hoist herself into the truck, but she stayed perfectly still. "I don't want to go back," she said softly, her gaze dropping to his mouth. "I want to go home with you."

He closed his eyes and stroked her thigh before letting go, the softest sigh in his throat. "Yeah," he said, leaning close to her face. "Yeah."

She closed her fingers around his neck, pulling him in for a kiss. His mouth opened instantly, her tongue delving against his. He returned the kiss as fire licked her lower half and his hand inched higher and higher until his finger grazed a slippery piece of silk between her legs.

"Go, Lacey," he murmured, giving her a gentle shove into the truck. "Hurry. Or this is going to get senseless right here in the street."

During the short drive they hardly spoke, which just made the tension thicker and the anticipation more palpable.

"So what changed your mind?" he finally asked, breaking the silence with a question she wasn't sure she could answer.

"My friends told me I should have more fun."

He laughed a little. "And they dressed you for tonight?"

She nodded.

"They aren't rooting for the ex?"

"I told you on the phone today what's going on there. I don't have feelings for David." Certainly nothing like the fluttery, twisting, rollercoaster things going on inside her right now. "I doubt he'll be here very long."

"I saw him at Barefoot Bay today."

She turned to him, surprised. "You did? What was he doing up there?"

"Walking around. Talking on the phone to arrange a meeting with someone. Warning me to stay away from you."

Who would he be meeting? But Clay's last statement was the one that got her attention. "He really has no right to say that to you. None at all. Other than his being Ashley's father, he and I have no connection."

"That's a pretty powerful connection." He pulled into the rental complex, finally letting go of her leg to shut off the ignition. After a second, he turned to her, all humor gone from his eyes. "Family is the most powerful pull, you know."

There was just enough hurt in his voice to remind her that his family had caused some deep pain. "I know, but he's not my family."

"He wants to be."

She touched his jaw, trailing a finger over the hint of whiskers. "One more word about David and the mood will officially be killed."

He angled his head, got his mouth on her palm, and kissed. "You look pretty with the sunset behind you," he said. "I could draw you like this."

"I'd rather you kiss me like this," she said, closing the space to take what she wanted. This kiss was softer, easier, slower than any other. When they parted, neither spoke, but opened their doors and climbed out of the truck. She waited by her side, unsure of where to go until he came around and led her toward the one-story stucco building.

"You want to walk on the beach first?" he asked.

"No."

He put his key in the door. "You want to order pizza?"

She almost laughed. "No."

"You want to start working on the presentation?"

"Absolutely not." She stepped inside the darkened apartment and he followed, closing the door. "Do you?"

He paused, something unreadable in his eyes.

"Didn't you say you wanted to tell me something?" she asked. "When you texted about dinner?"

"Later." He locked the door behind him. "Right now I just want to be one hundred and fifty percent certain you know exactly what you're doing."

"I know what I'm doing."

He put his hands on her waist, very carefully, like she was made of glass. "What I want to avoid is any miscommunication. You know where I stand, right?"

No commitments, no relationships, no women who might break his heart. "I do." She slid her hands around his back, pulled him into her body, and stood on the tips of her sexy shoes to whisper in his ear. "You know what's wrong with you, Clay Walker?"

"What?"

"You have too much sense for me and my senseless shoes."

He didn't need to hear another word, devouring her mouth and dragging her into the golden shadows of sunset that warmed the apartment.

He crushed her lips with a kiss she couldn't have stopped if she'd wanted to, tongues clashing with purpose instead of play. Heat licked up her belly like an electrical current, sending fire everywhere he touched.

Everywhere. Down her back, over her rear, up the sides, and—oh, then he cupped her breasts with strong, capable, determined hands.

She cried softly at the touch, arching her back to force her stomach against his hard-on until he backed her against the wall.

"Bedroom?" she murmured.

"Too far." He pushed against her and she rocked right back, driving her hips into a hard-on that strained his zipper, already moving the way they were meant to move, already gripping his backside and holding him right where she wanted him to be.

He dragged her T-shirt up, revealing a lacy black bra that brought a soft moan of appreciation from his throat. Not bothering to take off her shirt, he palmed the flimsy lingerie, her nipple straining against the satin cup.

He tweaked and stroked, whispered her name, and trailed kisses into her cleavage. Hot, wet, hungry kisses that made her worship his mouth and what it could do to her. She bowed her back so he could undo her bra with one hand. Together, they pulled the shirt and bra over her head, sending all of it down to the floor and leaving her breasts naked and exposed, raw and achy.

"Let me look at you," he said gruffly, bracing on one hand as she closed her eyes and flattened her arms to the wall, giving him a full view and complete access.

Which he took, greedily, bending his knees to get to her breasts, his mouth seeking a connection, hungry to taste her, pulling more whimpers and sighs and soft, soft cries of delight from her.

She grabbed him by the hair, the shoulders, pushing him down to a kneel. That mouth. That mouth. She wanted him on her, wanted to touch his long, soft hair and guide his lips between her legs.

He caressed her thighs, pushing her skirt up around her waist to reveal her black lace panties.

He looked up with a smile. "Those girls know how to dress you for a date."

"Zoe," she said.

"I like her."

"She tried to get me to buy edible."

He laughed as he kissed her thigh, his tongue already slipping into the edge of the black silk. "I like her even more."

"Clay..." She could barely speak, her legs and arms splayed against the wall, her fingers digging in so hard she could peel the paint. "Kiss me there."

"I plan on it." He used one finger to tug the silk away from her, inhaling deeply, appreciatively, making her feel so ridiculously feminine she wanted to sob.

He kissed the swollen spot and she closed her eyes, focused on the incredible sweetness of his mouth. Then he licked, very slowly, dragging the tip of his tongue over her until she thought her legs would buckle and her head would explode and the breath she held would come whooshing out when she cried for mercy.

"Clay," she cried. "Don't stop. Please, *please*."

"Not a chance." He tugged at the panties, pulling them down, helping her step out of them. As soon as they were gone he kissed his way back up her thighs, back to where she wanted him most. There.

Curling his tongue like a ribbon around her skin, he sucked her juices, and she reveled in every sensation and sound, in the blood coursing through her with each powerful slide of his tongue. Lights exploded behind her eyes and her pulse hammered and she felt like she was floating through air, utterly lost. Nothing in the world mattered but the need to roll against his mouth and feel each sensation ripple through her, closer and closer to release.

"Oh my gawd, oh my gawd, oh…my…there." She writhed against the wall, his name on her lips, completely surrendering to his tongue and fingers. A sharp twist of pressure, a sweet twinge of tension, then a peak of delicious pain and pleasure so powerful it was almost unbearable.

She rocked into an orgasm, abandoned and wild, her breath nothing but shallow desperation as she moved against his mouth.

Then there were just tender aftershocks and ragged breaths, and the impossible heavy ache in her legs that made them wobble as she started to slide down the wall.

"Now I know," she whispered.

"Now you know what?"

"Why this is so much fun." She hit the floor with a soft thud, her head hanging to the side like a drunk.

"We just got started having fun, darlin'."

But when she looked at him, something swelled up in her chest, and it wasn't laughter. Something squeezed at her heart and clutched her whole body and made her want to reach out to this beautiful, sexy, amazing man and, dear God, it wasn't *fun*.

It kind of hurt inside. And there was nothing *fun* about that at all.

"Lacey, what's wrong?"

"Oh, shit, Clay. I might have made a mistake."

Big, big mistake. God*damn* it. Clay should have known better.

"There's a reason they call it senseless," he said softly, stroking some hair that had fallen in her face. "Because there's no common sense involved. And now you're sorry, aren't you?"

"Not exactly sorry." She gave him a sheepish smile. "Just a little overwhelmed. That's scary."

Damn it. "You don't have to be scared, Lacey. I won't . . ." What wouldn't he do? Use her and leave?

Yes he would. He'd use her for a job he wanted more than anything, and sex he wanted just as badly. But, Jesus, he did not want a good woman with a nice kid and a decent life and a heart of gold, because all of that stuff came with too much potential for disaster. He'd had enough family for one lifetime, thank you very much.

"Wow, you look like you're in pain, Clay."

He used the obvious excuse and looked down. "A little."

She reached to the tent of his jeans, her fingers tentative. For a second he did nothing, the need for her to touch him way bigger than anything he felt in his head or heart. But then he closed his hand over her wrist.

"Reciprocation isn't necessary, Lacey."

"I want to."

"You just said you made a mistake."

"I thought sex would be fun."

He gave a rueful laugh. "Sorry to disappoint."

"No, no, that's not what I mean. I thought that's *all* it would be."

He slowly pushed up, still holding her hand and bringing her with him. "I know you did. So what happened?"

"I like you."

"Yep, big mistake."

"Is it?" She sounded hopeful. So damn hopeful. "I just want to work with you. And, you know, *sleep* with you. Only not much sleeping since I have to be home at night."

Of course she did, because she had a family. A daughter who needed her. An ex who wanted her.

She swiped her hand through her hair, frowning as though she wasn't used to the straight locks, and suddenly realizing she was naked from the waist up. "Shit, what a mess."

"You're not a mess, Lacey. You're beautiful. But here, get comfortable." He scooped up her top and handed it to her, helping her slip it over her head, then tugged her skirt back down. Her bra and panties were still on the floor, and neither of them made a move to get them.

But not because they'd be coming right back off. He knew that. "You want something to drink?" he asked. "Water? Soda? Beer?"

"Water." She followed him through the living area, past the drafting table he'd set up, to the galley kitchen. While he got the water, she stood at the sliders that led out to a small deck that faced the indigo water, nearly the same color as the late evening sky.

He handed her a bottle. "I have some fruit and stuff for a sandwich, if you're hungry."

She shook her head and opened the water bottle. "No, thanks."

That look in her eyes fisted his chest again, so he got behind her, sharing the view, letting their bodies touch front to back because, hell, it seemed he couldn't be in the same room without making contact.

"It's going to be one tough resort to build," he said after taking a sip of water.

"Because of the zoning restrictions?"

"Your zone. My restrictions."

"I think I just proved I have no restrictions." She let her

head fall back against his chest, resignation in her sigh. "And you sure know your way around my zone."

There went his damn erection again. "You talk dirty, little lady, and I'm going to start getting senseless again."

She didn't say anything, but the silence and her steady breathing only made him harder against her. One more minute and he would be reaching up to get a handful of soft, gorgeous breast. One more minute and he could turn her around and have that skirt hiked all the way up again. One more minute and he'd lose this fight.

"You're upset with me," she said.

"I'm not upset. I might not be walking normally in the meeting tomorrow, but I'm getting used to the fact that Barefoot Bay sits squarely in the state of arousal."

Half turning, she looked up at him. "Really?"

"You turn me on," he admitted. "You have since the moment I met you on the beach."

"I was a bitch."

"A bitch with a smokin'-hot body and a smart mouth. And, man, that hair."

She shook her head. "I don't have a smokin'-hot body! I need to lose at least ten pounds."

"Not in any of the places I just handled you don't." He took a slide over her hip, just to make the point. Perfect.

"I'm older than you are. By . . ." She hesitated. "Seven years."

"You worry about numbers too much." He took a drink of his water to wet his throat, which was getting more parched with her ass planted against his poor aching hard-on. "Face it, Lacey, you're just not a roll-in-the-hay-and-walk-away kind of girl."

"I'm not a girl, Clay. I'm a woman."

"I know, I know. Seven years. I heard you. But you—"

She turned. "You're just as afraid," she said, pointing a finger in his face. "You use your bad experience as an excuse, and you're scared to death of failing at a relationship, so you don't try. You know, we're more alike than I realized."

He scratched his chin and thought about all the different ways he could respond, but maybe she was right. "Look, Lacey, I don't want to get so tight with anyone that I get tangled and strangled. Maybe you do, and maybe you ought to give that guy who wants you back another shot."

"I don't want to give him another shot," she said vehemently. "I want—"

Don't say it. Don't say it.

"You."

Shit.

"For sex and fun," she added quickly. "And to stand by my side when I kick more town council ass tomorrow and to help me win the zoning fight and to build this resort. You know, the one *you've* convinced me to build. That's what I want, Clay. You in?"

He smiled slowly. "I like when you get all worked up."

"I'll take that as a yes."

"Yes, but I want to add one stipulation to this verbal contract." He closed his hands over her cheeks and held her face, forcing her to look straight into his eyes, knowing that this was the perfect time to tell her the real reason he'd left his father's firm.

No. Not tonight. It would be way too much for her on top of this, and the unexpected meeting tomorrow. Lacey would lunge at an excuse like that and everything would stop.

In fact, tomorrow he might even be able to go over to

the mainland and get some paperwork that would explain it all to her.

Or was he the one making excuses now?

"You're scaring me, Clay. Why are you thinking so hard about this stipulation?"

"Just trying to get the right words." He took a breath, pulled her closer. "Just listen to me. If at any time this thing, this *us,* doesn't work for you on any level, either professional or personal or physical, just let me know and we stop."

"This us?" she laughed. "When you put it that way . . ."

"I'm serious, Lacey. Will you agree to that?"

"You know what you're doing, Clay?"

God, no. That was the problem. "What?"

"You're giving an easy way out to a woman who loves to find an easy way out."

He leaned forward and kissed her forehead. "I know what I'm doing." At least, he hoped he did.

Chapter Eighteen

And that is why the proposed structure being built by property owner Lacey Armstrong of Barefoot Bay should be added to the agenda of the next Mimosa Key zoning meeting." Lacey took a deep breath and closed her eyes, so grateful to be done. "Thank you for your time, ladies and—ladies."

Three sets of hands clapped loudly and vigorously from the audience lounging around Jocelyn's suite at the Ritz-Carlton.

"You are going to rock, Lacey," Zoe exclaimed.

"I hope so." Lacey straightened the two presentation boards she'd picked up at Clay's apartment that morning, trying not to think about how dead sexy he'd looked when he answered the door wearing nothing but boxers.

He'd worked all night on some preliminary drawings, focused exclusively on the main building. He'd gone to

Fort Myers to get county permit information he thought they might need, so Lacey had decided to use the time before the meeting to rehearse for her friends.

"Aren't you going to talk about the villa concept?" Tessa asked. "That's what really sets this resort apart."

"We want to hold back as much as we can and drop that bomb in the actual zoning meeting. The only thing that matters today is getting on the agenda. I think this is enough, don't you?"

"Absolutely," Jocelyn agreed. "But it will be bigger, won't it?"

Lacey sighed, curling up on the sofa next to Tessa. "Right now, everything's a pipe dream. First I have to close on the two properties next to mine, and then I have to figure out how much insurance money is left. I know Clay is 'free' at this point, but once we break ground, I am going to need some serious cash." She let her head fall back. "It's so daunting to even think about how to get that money."

"Hey." Tessa tapped her leg. "Don't look at the obstacles. You'll trip."

Lacey smiled. "I'm trying."

When none of them said anything for a second, Lacey opened her eyes just in time to catch some silent communication among the three of them.

"What?" she demanded.

Tessa and Jocelyn shared a long look, but Zoe blew out a breath. "Oh, for crying out loud, tell her now. Don't wait until after the stupid meeting."

"Tell me what?"

"No," Jocelyn said. "I'm still ironing out some details."

"But she should know," Zoe insisted.

"It would help her during today's presentation."

Lacey sat up slowly. "What are you guys talking about?"

Three not-so-innocent faces stared back at her and finally, Jocelyn nodded to Tessa.

"We want to invest."

Lacey blinked at her. "Invest?" For a moment Lacey could only stare. And work to keep her jaw from dropping. "You guys want to invest in Casa Blanca?"

"They do," Zoe said, true sadness in her expression. "I can't afford to give you anything but moral support."

"But we can give you actual cash," Jocelyn said. "And we want to. We really do."

A whole new set of chills danced over her while her eyes filled with grateful tears. "You would do that for me? How can you do that?"

Tessa shrugged. "Billy and I weren't running a non-profit company to create organic farms, you know. And the divorce settlement was generous." She leaned closer. "I want to do something extraordinary with that money and, Lacey, I believe in you. As long as we can make everything as organic as possible."

Lacey nodded. "I can do organic."

"And," Tessa added, "gardens where you grow your own food. Or…" She dragged out the last word and added a meaningful look. "Where *I* grow your food."

It took a second to sink in. "You grow it?"

"I want to stay and help you, Lacey." Tessa put her hand on Lacey's to underscore the message. "I want to stay here and create a completely natural, all-organic farm that feeds your resort."

"Which means she leaves Arizona," Zoe said glumly.

"And moves here." The idea wrapped around Lacey's

heart so tightly it threatened to stop her pulse. Tessa here, with her. "Oh my God, Tess. That would be heaven."

"You know I'm going to be a pain about pesticides and processed foods, don't you?"

"I will swear off both of them," Lacey promised.

"And if you want to open in a year, preliminary soil preparation should start, like, almost immediately. In a few months at the latest."

The hope squeezed her chest, making her breathless. "Can you come to the meeting tonight? The organic gardens should be part of the plan we present. I think it would go a long way to showing exactly what kind of resort we're building."

"Of course I can."

Lacey turned to Jocelyn. "And you want to invest, too?"

"Silently. I'm not growing anything or making grand appearances anywhere. But, yes." She added her hand to Lacey's and Tessa's. "I'm working on getting you a cash infusion that should help you really get rolling on the building and gardens."

Words just couldn't form. Not adequate ones, anyway. "You are the most amazing friends." Lacey's voice broke.

"I just suck in general," Zoe said. "I don't have a dime and can't leave my aunt Pasha."

"Zoe, just you being here is more than enough," Lacey said. "Will you all come with me this afternoon?"

Jocelyn's smile faded. "Not me."

"Just meet at the town hall," Lacey said quickly. "Please."

Finally, she nodded. "For you. To the town hall."

"Oh my God!" Lacey shrieked softly. "I have partners!"

"Lots of them," Zoe said. "Silent Jocelyn, organic Tessa, and don't forget the man with the magic drafting tool."

"That's just the problem," she confessed on a sigh. "I can't forget him for one minute."

"So when do we get details on last night?" Zoe asked.

"Let's just put it this way: He liked your choice of underwear." And, because they were her best friends *and* partners, she told them everything. Well, *almost* everything.

Word must have gotten out about the meeting. A few dozen people peppered the community meeting room in Mimosa Key's town hall, with Charity and Patience seated in the front, surrounded by supporters. A handful of other familiar faces filled the front row of folding chairs, while others sat in small groups of two and three, and some people stood in the back at a coffee station.

The low buzz of conversation stopped when Lacey entered with Jocelyn, Tessa, and Zoe. Clay had texted that he'd meet them here but hadn't arrived yet, making Lacey taut with nerves and a vague sense of disappointment.

She squashed any doubts. He'd *be* there.

"Where's the one who tipped you off?" Zoe whispered.

Lacey glanced around but couldn't find Gloria Vail. "Not here."

"She's probably swimming in the bottom of the bay."

Lacey bit back a laugh. "They're not that bad." She hoped. Charity was sending some dagger-like looks Lacey's way, and her sister, Patti, offered a cool, but less deadly, nod.

The long council table remained empty as no members were seated yet, so Lacey led her friends to some seats in the audience. She kept glancing at the door for Clay, but instead saw another man with a familiar face that had graced front pages of the *Mimosa Gazette* for much of Lacey's teenage years.

Will Palmer had been the island's golden boy, blazing through the minor leagues and on his way to the pros, last she'd heard. But in the past few years—

"Oh, shit." Next to Lacey, Jocelyn murmured the curse as color drained from her face.

"What's the matter?"

"My phone's vibrating," she said, stabbing her hand into her bag, lowering her head, hiding her face.

"Jocelyn?" Will approached slowly, but Jocelyn popped up to climb over Lacey to get out of the row.

"I have to take this call."

"Jocelyn," Will called. "Please, wait."

She froze, giving Lacey a pleading look. Then she suddenly composed herself and faced him.

"Hello." She reached out a hand. "How are you, Will?"

His eyes flickered with surprise. "Fine. And you?"

"Great. Oh"—she wiggled the phone—"'scuze me for a second." She walked out, leaving him slightly slack-jawed.

"Hi," Lacey said, trying to cover the awkward moment, looking up at the sizable athlete. "I don't know if you remember me. I'm Lacey Armstrong."

"Hello." He shook her hand, but his attention was still on Jocelyn, giving Lacey a chance to take in how time had changed him. He wasn't as boyishly cute as he had been in his baseball heyday, but he was still seriously tall, dark, and handsome.

"I didn't know you were back in Mimosa Key," she said. "Are you visiting or are you here for good?"

"I'm back," he said. "As a matter of fact, I'm picking

up some work with all the construction going on. That's why I came by today."

Construction? That was a huge step down from major league baseball. "What kind of work? I'll hopefully be looking for some people."

"I've been sort of specializing in carpentry and wood-work, but, really I can do anything. Stucco, drywall, you name it."

"I'll remember that," she said as the council began to take their seats.

Once again Lacey turned to the door, willing Clay to show. Where was he? He'd texted a few hours ago that he was still in Fort Myers but he'd be here on time.

"Where did Jocelyn go?" Tessa asked when she and Zoe came back from a stop in the ladies' room, sliding in right behind Lacey. "She just blew by us in a big fat hurry."

"She's taking a call," Lacey told them.

The slam of Mayor Sam Lennox's gavel silenced the conversation. Lacey once again checked the door for Clay, flinching a little when David entered instead, with Ashley close to his side.

Wouldn't there be enough tension without David look-ing judgmental and Ashley frowning in disapproval at Clay?

If Clay ever got there.

Ashley spotted her and waved, but David guided them to seats across the aisle with a wink to Lacey. "Go get 'em, Tiger," he mouthed.

"Good luck, Mommy," Ashley added. "I love you."

Oh. Her heart turned upside down, tumbled, and landed somewhere in her shoes. Because at the end of the day, Ashley was the one who mattered the most. And, honestly, when was the last time her daughter had said *I love you*?

Was that David's influence?

"Where the hell is Clay?" Tessa asked.

"Good question." Lacey tried to focus, but her mind was whirring. If she had to do this alone, would she?

If Clay didn't show, then she had a good reason—

"Call to order an emergency meeting of the Mimosa Key Town Council!" The gavel slammed a second time, and Lacey scanned the front table for a friendly face.

The mayor was a longtime resident of the island, possibly opposed to changing zoning laws. A political beast who loved the role of heading the town council, he could totally be corrupted by Charity but swayed by re-election votes. Nora Alvarez was on Charity's payroll, but something about her seemed fair and smart. Plus, wouldn't she want to expand her cleaning business to do work for Lacey, too?

"Who's the escapee from *The Sopranos*?" Zoe leaned forward to ask in Lacey's ear.

"New guy from New York," Lacey whispered back. "Rocco something."

"Friend or foe?"

"Don't know."

"And the bald eagle?"

Lacey eyed George Masterson and remembered how he'd jumped to help Charity last night. "I think he's in bed with Charity."

"Ewww. Thanks for that lovely visual that will never leave my brain."

Lacey shushed her as the mayor covered some housekeeping details. When given the floor, George Masterson moved to set the agenda for the September fifteenth meeting, calling to the floor anyone who wanted to present at that time.

Lacey swallowed and gave one last look toward the door, her heart sinking. If no one asked a question that only an architect could answer, she could do this. But she wanted him there. The fact that he wasn't just hurt.

"Hey." Tessa touched her shoulder. "Stop looking for reasons not to get up there."

"I'm not," Lacey whispered. "I just…"

Scanning the room, her gaze fell on Ashley, who gave her a wide, warm smile, her eyes filled with admiration and expectation.

She might have reasons to chicken out, but right there sat the reason to walk up to that council and make her demands. She had to show Ashley how to be strong and independent, had to show her daughter how to get what you want in life, even if your partner lets you down. *Especially* if your partner lets you down.

Slowly rising to her feet, she felt Tessa give her a nudge and heard Zoe whisper, "Knock 'em dead, Lace."

She stepped into the aisle along with a few other people petitioning for something they wanted but might not get. Change was never easy in Mimosa Key, and the knowledge of that was plain to see on her neighbors' faces.

"Let's do this alphabetically," Mayor Lennox suggested. "That'd make you first, Lacey."

"All right," she agreed brightly, carrying the two presentation boards to the podium while the other speakers sat in the second row. Unzipping the case with remarkably steady fingers, she set her typed-up comments in front of her and pulled the first board, Clay's blue-line of the site overview.

They needed only a verbal description according to

the bylaws, but she and Clay both felt that this would be more powerful and sway any council members sitting on the fence.

She and Clay. Except now it was just her.

"Good afternoon," she said, her voice echoing and causing a siren-like feedback on the mike. She backed away and refused to let it throw her. "My name is Lacey Armstrong and I'm here to request a slot on the—"

"I object." Charity stood and stared hard at the mayor. "Save our time, Sam, and let's move to the next person."

A soft murmur rolled through the crowd.

"Excuse me, Charity," Lacey said, "but I haven't even had a chance to show you what I'm building."

"Don't have to. I'm not objecting to your building."

"Then what are you objecting to?" Sam Lennox asked.

"Who's building it."

"What are you talking about?" Lacey asked. "How do you even know who's building it?"

"Because everyone on this island knows you're working, among other things, with that man named Clayton Walker."

"Clay Walker," she corrected, feeling heat rise and wishing to God that Ashley wasn't in this room. "And I fail to see how that has any relevance." His name wasn't even on this presentation. He'd insisted on that.

And he *wasn't even in this room.*

For the first time, a vine of bad, bad feeling slithered up her chest.

"Me too," Paula Reddick chimed in from the front table. "I, for one, would like to see the plans, so zip it, Charity."

The older woman's eyes flew open. "I will not zip it

and I will not allow anything to be built on this island by someone who is not qualified to build."

Oh, *that's* what this was about. His licensing. The tendril of worry loosened as she checked the door again, but no one had entered the room, not even Jocelyn.

She had to do this on her own, straightforward and unafraid.

"Charity, if you're referring to Mr. Walker's licenses, they are not required by any law in any state in order for him to design—"

"I'm talking about his…his…" She gestured to Patti, who shoved some papers closer. Then Charity adjusted her reading glasses and cleared her throat. "His indictment by the FBI for providing fraudulent documents and attempting to obstruct justice in a case against a North Carolina chancellor of secondary education."

Lacey gripped the podium, because her legs couldn't be trusted to hold her upright.

"What?" She barely whispered the question because there were too many other words swimming in her head. *Indictment. FBI. Fraudulent. Obstruct justice.*

"What exactly are you talking about?" Sam demanded. "What do you have on this Clayton Walker?"

"Clay," Lacey said softly. "His name is Clay." Or at least she thought it was. Come to think of it, she'd never seen a driver's license, let alone an architectural license. She'd never called a reference or seen a resume.

All she'd done was let him melt her brain and body and hand him the job. And now he wasn't even here to face the music. And the tune was pretty ugly.

"I'm talking about *this.*" Gripping pages of computer printouts, Charity marched to the front, her sneakers squeaking on the linoleum like Nurse Ratched on her way to stick a needle in someone.

The audience murmured and mumbled, and Lacey stole a look at David, who whispered something to Ashley, then he got up and hustled out of the room. Shame and shock prickled at Lacey's skin, a fine sheen of perspiration tickling the nape of her neck.

Toward the back, Tessa and Zoe held hands, leaning forward like they'd been driven to the edge of their seats. Grace Hartgrave looked smug, and a lot of familiar faces of neighbors, friends, and even some of her baking customers looked confused.

And Clay Walker, or whoever the hell he claimed to be, was suspiciously absent.

Meanwhile, Charity slapped her papers in front of the town council, a copy for each of them, with the officiousness of a teacher handing out failed tests. "I just printed these off today, from the state attorney's office in North Carolina." She turned to Lacey. "Of course, maybe you were too blinded by his good looks to do any of your own homework."

Was that possible? She had Googled him. There was plenty about his father, but no mention of Clay, or the FBI. Her heart slipped down a few notches, like her wet palms on the warm wood of the podium.

Sam rifled through the papers. "Have you seen this, Lacey? Says here Clayton Walker of Clayton Walker Architecture and Design has been indicted—"

"It's his father!" The explanation suddenly seemed so clear she practically barked it into the microphone, shutting up Sam and the audience. "They must be talking about his father, Clayton Walker," she added quickly. "It's a common mistake because of the names and the similar work, but they are two very different men and my architect no longer works for Clayton Walker. Those papers, whatever you have, are not about the same man who's been helping me."

"Actually, they are." Clay's voice came from the back of the room, the door he'd just burst through still open. "Those articles are about me."

Chapter Nineteen

⌐

For a second Lacey felt nothing but numb. Blank brain, deadened heart, no sensation. Just shocked and speechless as she watched the man she'd let take her to an orgasm with nothing but his mouth bound up the aisle of the meeting room, his long hair fluttering around his handsome face, his broad shoulders braced as if he were going into battle, his summer-sky blue eyes locked on her.

Charity was right. She'd been taken by his good looks. How could she be such a fool?

"However, every charge was dropped," he continued as he strode toward the front. "That information is out of date and invalid, erased from all records, and I have an affidavit to prove that, notarized just one hour ago by the Lee County clerk of court."

"Just one minute," Charity said.

"Excuse me," Mayor Lennox interjected.

"I will explain everything," Clay insisted.

"No way!" Charity all but stomped her foot. "Page three, section three, subsection B of the Mimosa Key bylaws—and don't you dare try to contradict me, young man—says that unless you're a resident of Mimosa Key, you're not allowed to address this council without prior approval. You don't have it, so sit down."

He kept coming, his eyes on Lacey. Eyes loaded with apology, regret, and no small amount of anger. "Damn stupidest law I ever heard, so I'm going to speak anyway."

"Oh, no you are not." Charity was beet red and nearly choking now. "Everything you say is inadmissible—"

"This isn't a court!" Lacey hollered over the sound of the crowd. "Let him talk, for God's sake."

"It's the way we run our town, Lacey," the mayor said.

"I need to know." She breathed the words, but the microphone picked them up and amplified her heartache all through the room.

Lacey searched his face, looking for the truth, for an explanation, for some sign that he hadn't lied to her all this time.

No need to sign a contract.

No need to put my name on the boards.

No need to contact my father's company. Just let me tell you how ruthless he is.

Had she been played, or what?

"Sorry, son," Mayor Lennox said. "We can't change the rules. I assume Lacey knows all this and she can speak on your behalf."

"I will speak on my behalf." Clay parked himself right in front of the council table. "That account is old and false."

"Were you indicted?" Lacey asked.

"No, but there was an investigation, and every single charge was dropped."

"See?" Charity said, leaping forward and poking a bony finger at Clay as though he'd just confessed murder. "Lacey doesn't even know who she's working with. She doesn't have a clue who this man is and we're going to let him slap down some kind of monstrosity on Barefoot Bay and ruin the unspoiled beauty of the last perfect place on earth? I don't think so."

Charity's dramatic words rang through the meeting room, causing another rumble of response.

"You cannot speak to this council, sir," Mayor Lennox said. "If you don't leave, we will have to get Security to escort you."

Oh, that would be just perfect. Let's bring Officer Garrison in here and cuff Lacey's lover in front of her daughter and the friends who'd just vowed their belief in her. Really, could the day get any better?

"What do you have to say, Lacey?" Charity demanded.

She just swallowed and dug for words of defense, but there were none.

She knew virtually nothing about Clay Walker, and yet she'd opened her business, her project, her heart, and, oh hell, *her legs* to him. Stupid, stupid, *stupid*.

"Let the guy talk, for crying out loud!" Zoe called from the back. "What is this, the Salem Witch Trials?"

That got a small reaction of laughter, but Clay held up his hand. "I'll leave, but, please, the false allegations have nothing to do with Lacey Armstrong's proposed property getting on your September fifteenth agenda. I won't say anything now, but let her speak." He finally looked at Lacey, a world of sorry in his eyes that reached right down her throat and seized her heart. "You don't need me to do this. You can do this. You *can*."

The emphasis on the last word wasn't lost on her as he took a slow step backward, like the move was the hardest thing he'd ever done. How could she know? How could she know anything he'd told her was true, and why hadn't he told her earlier about this part of his past?

Had he even told her the truth about his father and the woman who'd broken Clay's heart? Or was that an elaborate tale to cover the real reason he didn't work for his dad anymore? The real reason he hadn't put his name on any of the presentation boards and no doubt the *truth* about why he didn't have those seven licenses he needed?

He pivoted and walked out, the entire room staring after him. Including Ashley.

Oh, Lord. Ashley had witnessed the whole thing. And now she'd witness her mother crumbling and quitting and buckling under the weight of the oldest excuse of all.

I was duped by a sexy guy.

"You may speak now, Lacey," Mayor Lennox said.

But everything in Lacey screamed not to.

C'mon, Lacey, you can't do this now. Give up, go home, settle for less than you deserve.

Shut the hell up, demons.

Taking a deep breath, she dug for something she knew she had to have, with or without Clay Walker. Resolve. Tenacity. Dogged stubbornness not to let Charity Grambling win and leave Lacey Armstrong with one big *excuse*.

"This information is entirely irrelevant to what I'm asking for today," she said, gesturing to the newspaper that was still being passed among the council members. "First of all, if you look closely at my presentation, there is no specific architectural firm attached to the plans and nothing has yet been filed with the state or county. All I want is to be on the agenda for September fifteenth, which will give me time to address these issues."

"Not enough time," Charity insisted.

Lacey closed her eyes, still mining inner strength. "That's all the time I need," she said.

"Is this man your architect and builder, Lacey?" George Masterson asked, his lip curled as he read the paper.

"I'm not sure who my architect is going to be," she said firmly. "But it's a moot point as far as the upcoming agenda."

"I agree," Paula said quickly. "Let's put her on the agenda and move on."

"I second that," Rocco chimed in. "That account lifted off the Internet is questionable at best. Let her present, let her make her plea, and let her use who she wants and prepare to defend him on the fifteenth." He drummed the table in front of him. "Let's move it. There's a Yankees game on in twenty minutes."

"Sorry, but this newspaper clipping is enough for me to say no," Masterson said.

"Please hear me out," Lacey said, earning instant silence and all their attention. She searched her brain for her opening lines, for what she'd planned to say about her resort and all the jobs it could create and Mimosa Key's need to get into the next century.

But she couldn't think of anything. Except Ashley still sitting in the seat where David had left her.

Ashley.

All the feasibility notes, the town codes, and the target marketing points she'd made for this presentation just evaporated from her brain. None of them mattered, really.

"Six weeks ago, my home and business were wiped away in one storm," she said quietly. "As many of you know, I stayed alive and kept my daughter safe in a bathtub with a mattress over our heads."

A soft mumbling rolled through the room.

Yes, she did.

That's a fact.

She was hit hard up there at Barefoot Bay.

Buoyed by the tiny bit of support, she kept talking. "The only thing that kept me going that night was the chance to realize a dream that I believe could be a long-term and positive change for my family and for this island. All I am asking for is a slot on your next meeting agenda to prove that to you. At that time, I assure you, I will have an architect, builder, contractor, and subcontractors who will all meet with the council's approval. All I'm asking for is a chance."

Every one of the council members stared at her.

"Let's vote," Sam finally said. "Raise your hand if you want to give Lacey Armstrong a slot on the September fifteenth agenda."

All but George Masterson raised their hands. She only needed a majority, and she'd just gotten it.

"Thank you." She gathered her portfolio and resisted the urge to gloat at Charity, nodding when Sam handed her the paper Clay had brought in to clear himself. She didn't even look at it but walked down the aisle.

"Good work, Mom!" Ashley high-fived her when she reached them.

"Way to go, Lace!" Zoe called from the other side of the room. Tessa gave her two thumbs-up.

"Thanks." She closed her fingers over Ashley's hand and gave a squeeze. "I'll be right back."

Because she sure as hell wasn't going to let Clay Walker slink away without a damn fine explanation. Then he could get the hell out of her life, thank you very much.

Chapter Twenty

⸌⸍

God, Clay hated the taste of regret. And he was choking on the stuff right now.

He stuck his hands in his hair, cursing his stupidity. Across the parking lot, he saw David Fox talking to a guy in a business suit in the shade of palm trees. Clay ducked around the side of the building to have his moment of self-loathing in private.

Son of a bitch! He should have just told her and not worried that an inaccurate record of history could cost him the tentative assignment. He should've gone with his original intention of telling her last night, regardless of the town council meeting. She could have handled the facts. Why had he doubted her? And if he'd been straight she wouldn't have been blindsided. So now he had the affidavit to back up his story but she'd been publicly humiliated and no doubt wanted to drop-kick him off the nearest dock.

He'd been scared to lose her. That was why he hadn't told her the truth; he'd been scared she'd walk. And now she surely would.

The door of the town hall slammed against the stucco wall with enough force that he had no doubt who'd flung it open and what she wanted.

"Where are you?" Lacey demanded.

He stepped around the corner to face her but wished he didn't have to see the abject misery in her expression. "I'm right here, Lacey."

"How could you not tell me?" She snapped the affidavit he'd risked life and a speeding ticket to have back here in time for the meeting.

"I made a mistake."

Her eyes blazed. "No shit. Let me put it another way: *When* were you going to tell me?"

"At first, but then you were so unsure of me, so I planned to tell you last night, but when this agenda-setting meeting came up—"

"Along with a few other things, conveniently."

Ouch. "This has nothing to do with . . . that."

"No? Oldest trick in the book, Clay. Screw a woman *senseless*, so she can't—"

"Stop it." He reached out to her shoulders, but she dodged his touch. "That's why I went to Fort Myers today, Lacey. I wanted the affidavit in my hand before I told you. And I thought it might throw you and give you an excuse to—"

"Speaking of excuses!" she hissed. "You're as bad as I am. Worse. I may stop when I hit a brick wall, but I don't *lie* my way through it."

"A lie of omission, and not intentional."

She puffed out a breath of sheer disgust. "Oh, please. Was *this* why your dad kicked you out of the firm?"

"Not exactly."

"Then what was it, *exactly*?" She took a step closer, venom in her eyes. And pain. Pain he'd put there, damn it.

This was why he didn't want a relationship. This: the pain in her eyes.

"I want the truth," she demanded, her voice low and steady. "The whole truth, Clay. No more vague explanations buried in flirting and kissing and drawing. The truth. What happened?"

"I did something to help someone I...cared about. To protect my family and my father, but it cost me a brief investigation, from which I was completely cleared."

She considered that, frowning, thinking, and definitely not buying. "Not specific enough."

He closed his eyes and nodded. "I took the fall when my ex-girlfriend used my father's name on some documents she shouldn't have had. She made a gross error in judgment, and I helped her out of a jam."

Her eyes flickered. "Why?"

"Because..." Not because he cared about Jayna, that was for sure. Probably because he cared about his father, which was the greatest irony of all. "At the time, it seemed like the right thing to do. She was eight months pregnant and extremely sorry for making a really dumb mistake that she thought would never be discovered. It was, and she came to me asking for help, and I gave it and got into a shitload of trouble for the effort. My father assumed the worst about me." *Naturally.*

Because what better way to get rid of his own guilty conscience than to see Clay as a criminal?

"Why didn't you tell him the truth?"

"Because I thought he'd leave Jayna if he found out what she did, and I was worried about that kid. When I was cleared of everything, my father continued to believe I was guilty."

"Why?"

That was one question he could answer without hesitation. "Because it made him feel less guilty about sleeping with my girlfriend."

She searched his face, clearly having trouble with it all.

"This is the truth, Lacey."

"Are you still in love with her?"

The question didn't surprise him, but the little note of hurt or worry in her voice stunned the shit out of him. "No," he said quietly. "I'm not sure I ever really was."

"Then why risk your career and family for her?"

In truth, he'd helped his family by protecting the business. "She forged his name on documents and I let the authorities believe I'd signed my name, to protect my dad's reputation. If his business collapsed, a lot of people I really care about would be out of work. So I took the blame, hired an attorney, and got the charges dismissed."

She shook her head. "Then who took the blame when you were exonerated?"

"The company who'd filed the original complaint went bankrupt and everything was dropped. No one was charged and..." *Jayna came out smelling like a rose.* "I left my dad's firm."

"He didn't believe you even after you were cleared? Your own father? That's preposterous."

"You've never met him," he said quietly, hearing the hate and anger in the undertones of his words and making no effort to hide those emotions. They were too real. "As long as I was the bad guy, everything he did in the past was excused. He even convinced some cronies on the Arch Board to ban me from getting a license and deny me permission to sit for the rest of the exams."

She leaned against one of the white columns of the building. "Is this why you've kept your name off everything? Won't sign a contract? Haven't filed anything formal yet?"

"I will do all that, but I wanted to convince you first of how right I am for the job."

"Why? Why is it so important?"

"If I complete a full project on this scale, I can sit for my exams, get my licenses, and start my own business." He gave her a direct gaze, as truthful as what he was telling her.

"Were you trying to win me over or convince me to hire you by using sex?"

"No," he insisted. "That just happened."

"Not yet it didn't."

"Whether you believe me or not, my plan was to tell you over dinner, but then they made this decision to have this impromptu meeting and I really didn't want to give you an excuse to quit. Plus"—he tapped the affidavit rolled in her hand—"I wanted to get some concrete proof that I'm telling the truth."

She closed her eyes like he'd hit her, saying nothing.

"What happened when I left?" he asked.

"I got on the agenda." The words were barely a whisper, as soft as the sea breeze that lifted a curl of her hair.

"I knew you could do it." He had to fight the urge to touch her. "That's great, Lacey."

She finally opened her eyes, none of the misery gone from their topaz depths. "Why weren't you straight from day one, Clay? Why didn't you tell me that this job could make or break your career? Maybe I would have been sympathetic."

More regret gnawed at him. Why, indeed? "When we met on the beach, you were so certain I was coming at this through the back door," he admitted. "I thought it was smart to prove to you what I could do first."

"Like last night? What you could do up against a wall?"

The words punched a hole in his chest. "No, Lacey."

"How can I possibly believe you didn't just use sex to sweeten the deal and make sure I was too far gone to send you packing?"

He waited a beat, then asked the obvious. "Are you?"

"Am I what?"

"Too far gone to send me packing?"

She didn't answer.

"Excuse me, do either of you know Ms. Lacey Armstrong?" The voice came from the parking lot, making them both turn.

A man came forward. He was heavyset, and thin gray strands of hair lifted as he hustled toward her. Clay immediately recognized him, mostly by his out-of-place suit, as the person David Fox had been talking to earlier.

"I'm Lacey Armstrong."

His face brightened, already pink and sweaty. "Oh, that's fortunate." He reached out his hand. "I'm Ira Howell with Wells Fargo Bank in Fort Myers. Have you presented your plans to rebuild on the Barefoot Bay property?"

Lacey stole a glance at Clay before answering. "I didn't present much," she said. "Why?"

"Do your plans include building on the Everham and Tomlinson properties adjacent to your lot?"

She tensed a little, and nodded. "Yes, they do. Why?"

"You don't own those properties, ma'am."

"I'm in the process of purchasing both lots. I've made offers and am waiting for the paperwork."

"Not anymore you're not. My client closed sales this afternoon on both properties. Your plans will have to be scaled back. Or canceled."

"The Everham and Tomlinson properties sold? That's not possible." Lacey choked softly, stepping back as if the guy had hit her, while a little bell dinged in Clay's head. "Who bought them?"

Clay knew, instantly. David Fox had been talking to this guy and, when Clay saw him at the beach, he'd heard Fox use the name Tomlinson on the phone.

"Can't say, ma'am, but both neighbors closed this afternoon," the banker said.

The bastard had stolen the land right out from under her. Clay was next to Lacey in a flash, his hand on her back.

"That's not possible. I haven't been informed—"

"I'm informing you now." He pulled an envelope from his breast pocket. "The owners have asked me to return your deposit on both lots, along with my client's apologies for the inconvenience."

"Who is your client, Mr. Howell?" Clay demanded. As if he didn't know.

"The buyer prefers to maintain anonymity." He handed Lacey the envelope, added a nod good-bye, and headed back to the parking lot, as efficient as a process server.

"Lacey," Clay said, gripping her arm. "I know who did this to you."

She looked up at him. "Who?"

"David Fox."

She just shook her head. "I can't believe anything you say anymore."

"Well, you better believe this, because I'm right. He had a meeting with Tomlinson at Barefoot Bay. I was there, I heard the conversation, I heard him use the name Tomlinson. And I just saw him talking to this banker guy in the parking lot less than ten minutes ago." He took her hand, pulling her around the corner to see if he could spot Fox again, but he'd disappeared. "Your ex is the client Howell is protecting. He has the money, the motivation, the need to control you."

She held up her hands to stop him, the check in one fist, the affidavit in the other, and an expression of pure distrust on her face. "Please, Clay. Just leave."

"Lacey, I heard him say 'Mr. Tomlinson' on the phone, and I just saw him talking to Ira Howell. I swear I did, Lacey."

"Mommy! Are you out here?"

Lacey's face registered a flash of horror. "I want you to leave," she said in a soft whisper.

"Leave? The island? No, Lacey, I'm not."

"Lace? You out here?" a woman called.

"Leave!" She gave him a little push. "I need to be with my family."

"Meet me at Barefoot Bay tonight, Lacey."

Her jaw dropped. "You have *got* to be kidding."

"I'm not kidding. And I'm not leaving this island. I've

never walked away from any challenge, and I'm not about to start with a woman I care about as much as you."

"A woman or a job?"

Both. "Meet me tonight at the beach at Barefoot Bay. We're not done, Lacey."

But the look in her eyes said they were.

Chapter Twenty-one

Seriously, Lacey? You're going to believe the accusation of a known criminal over the father of your child? A man who claims to have heard me use a name on the phone twenty feet away?" David lifted his feet onto the ottoman and locked his hands behind his head. "I think you have bigger problems than trying to pin that deal on me."

Lacey glanced at the kitchen, where Tessa and Zoe were making food with Ashley, giving Lacey the quiet moment she'd been waiting for since they'd returned from the town hall. Jocelyn had texted that she was going back to the hotel for a "client emergency," so Tessa and Zoe had returned to the house with Lacey.

"Clay heard you say his name."

"But he didn't actually see me talking to anyone."

"Why would he lie about this?"

David let out a hearty laugh. "Why *wouldn't* he lie is a

better question. Lacey, I really hope you have this cougar fantasy out of your head now."

Irritation stung at the words. "Well, you're not a liar, David, and I notice you haven't directly answered the question. Did you or did you not meet with Mr. Tomlinson at the beach when you ran into Clay?"

He let out a long, slow, put-upon sigh that sounded so much like Ashley when she was trapped and in trouble. "I did meet with him, that's true."

"Why?"

"I thought I could help you."

"How could meeting with Mr. Tomlinson possibly help me?"

Another sigh of resignation. "By buying the property for you—"

"So you did?"

"—as a gift. To save you the added expense and show you how much I care and want to be involved in your life and your project."

Why did every word that came out of his mouth sound like bullshit? Because so often it was. "If that's true, then I can buy the property back directly from you." That might delay things, but at least—

"No, I didn't buy it, Lacey, that's what I'm trying to tell you."

Lacey perched on the edge of the sofa, her hands clasped tightly enough to turn her knuckles white. "Then who did?"

"I don't know. Tomlinson said he had another rock-solid offer that he simply couldn't ignore. Of course, I assumed it was you."

"Did you ask him who the offer was from?"

"I did, because I thought I could go to that buyer. But he said it was anonymous through his bank. So I just let it go as a bad idea and decided to look for other ways to convince you that I care." His face was set in the most sincere expression, his eyes dark with just the right amount of contrition and hope.

God, he was good. Believable. Direct. In some ways, more real than Clay.

Forget Clay, Lacey. But that was the problem. She couldn't forget Clay.

"Why wouldn't you talk to me about it? Why wouldn't you just ask to be an investor? Why go behind my back?"

"I wanted to surprise you. I wanted to show you, and Ashley, that I'm serious about wanting to be a family. Because, Lacey, I *am* serious."

She dropped her head into her hands, grateful that Zoe and Tessa were in the kitchen with Ashley; at least she hoped they weren't listening to this.

"I have never lied to you, Lacey." He stood, the words somehow having far more impact that way.

"I know," she conceded. He was a lot of things— adrenaline junkie, absentee father, even a bit of an actor— but she couldn't remember David lying to her. In fact, when she'd told him she was pregnant he'd been honest in his reaction. She'd hated what he said, but he'd been honest.

Which was more than she could say for Clay Walker.

"I tried to tell you. I wanted to." He took a step forward, looming over her now, making her feel small and helpless. "But you were so preoccupied."

"Don't," she said, pointing a finger at him. "Don't tell me circumstances stopped you from being straight with me. I've had enough of that for one day."

"Then you're over him?"

"I was never under him," she said defiantly. "Whether you want to believe that or not, it's true."

"Of course, I believe it." With no warning David was on his knee in front of her, shifting from his power stance to a proposal pose.

"Listen to me," he said, his voice low and pleading, his gaze soft and so damn credible. "I did not purchase that land. Why would I do that and keep it from you? I don't want to stop you from building this inn or resort or whatever you want it to be. I want to be part of it with you."

"And with me." Ashley burst in from the kitchen, Zoe practically running behind her.

"Ashley, I'm trying to have a private conversation with David."

"His name is Fox." Ashley folded herself on the floor right next to David.

"You know the old joke, Ash," David said, giving her hair a ruffle. "She can call me anything she wants, as long as she calls me."

Ashley giggled and, for a moment, for one suspended, stupid, insane moment, Lacey felt like they were a family. Dad trying to tease a smile out of Mom through an inside joke with Child.

An ache she didn't recognize at first welled up inside her. The ache for a real family. A whole family. A happy family. David had stolen that from her with a one-way ticket to Patagonia. But they probably wouldn't have made it anyway.

"Mommy, you're crying!"

Oh, geez. Was she?

"Ash, remember what we talked about." David put a

gentle arm on Ashley's shoulder. "You have to be sensitive to the stress your mom is under."

He was giving their daughter life lectures now? Maybe he was trying to be a real family. But it was too little too late. And not what she wanted. What she wanted was...

Clay.

"When did you talk about that?" Lacey asked, sounding as wretched and bitter as she felt.

"When we played chess last night," Ashley said. "When you went out to dinner."

Of course. While Lacey was out on a date with a man who was keeping secrets and trying to talk her into commitment-free sex that they could keep entirely separate from their project, a project he had no right going after.

Guilt strangled her. She should have been home teaching Ashley life lessons, not flirting and kissing and offering sympathy for his sad, sad story about his father and the ex-girlfriend.

"Dad and I talk a lot," Ashley said, pride in her voice as she looked at him. "And I'm really trying to work on my attitude, Daddy."

She was clearly possessed by spirits—or the proper parent. The guilt knife cut a fresh wound.

"The thing is, Mom—and don't get mad at me for listening—but Dad didn't try to screw you out of that property and I think he really does want a second chance at love."

"Don't say 'screw,'" David said.

"Don't say 'love,'" Lacey shot back.

On the sofa, Lacey's phone vibrated softly with a text. "That could be Jocelyn," she said, picking it up.

Clay Walker: I'll wait at Barefoot Bay.

She couldn't do anything but close her eyes against the words, feeling a tornado of emotions swirling right down to her toes. A maelstrom of longing and loss, shockingly strong, and remarkably real. Loss? For a man who'd deceived her? Used her?

But had he? His explanation for not telling her made sense, and he hadn't used her. He'd taken what she offered. And she'd offered it because there was something about him. Something different. Something extraordinary.

"Mom?"

"Lacey?"

Their voices pulled her back, forcing her attention away to the two people who were right here, asking her to be a family. The family she wanted. One of them she loved more than anyone or anything. *Unconditionally.* The other she didn't love, but did he deserve a second chance?

And yet there was Clay. And all this unresolved feeling whirling around like one of the mini-tornadoes that had ripped her home to shreds. Was he going to do the same thing to her heart?

Dear God, she *had to know.*

"What did Jocelyn say, Lacey?" Tessa and Zoe stood in the kitchen door, so close they'd no doubt heard the whole preceding conversation.

"Don't tell me she got on a plane and went back to L.A.," Zoe said. "'Cause she is so dead to me if she did."

"It's not, she's not..." She shook the lie out of her head before she said it. "That wasn't Jocelyn." She slid her finger over the screen and deleted the text, shifting back to Ashley. "Honey, there's a lot more to this than you are old enough to understand. But..." She staved off the argument with a flat palm. "*But* I realize how important it is

that David and I are friends. I hope you see that we are."
And that's all we are.

"Does that mean you guys will stop fighting?"

"We're not fighting," David said quickly, unable to keep the appreciative smile off his face as he reached for Lacey's hand. "It's called discussing. Do you believe me now?"

"I don't know," she said honestly. "Who else would have the money or motivation to step in and buy those parcels out from underneath me?"

"I don't know about money, but motivation? I'd start with that skinny bitch who should be named Uncharitable."

Ashley giggled.

"If I find out, will you believe me then?" he asked.

"I suppose."

That seemed to satisfy him. "All right." He put a fatherly arm around Ashley. "Who's up for a game of Monopoly?"

"I am!" Ashley leaped to her feet, sharing a knuckle tap with David.

"Gonna buy me some Boardwalk, baby!" David exclaimed.

Behind them Zoe stuck her finger in her mouth and fake-gagged.

"Listen, Lace. Jocelyn's not answering her cell," Tessa said, "and she took our rental car. You think you could give us a lift to the hotel?"

Lacey gave her a grateful smile. "Of course."

"They can stay here," David said. "No need for you to go out so late alone."

"Or they can take Grandpa's van," Ashley suggested, suddenly the voice of reason and maturity.

No, Lacey had to get away from this house and talk

privately with her friends, even if just for the forty-five minutes it would take to drive to the mainland and back. "Their stuff is at the hotel and, honestly, David, I want to see Jocelyn. I'm worried about her." None of that was a lie.

Her phone vibrated again and she ignored it, throwing it into her purse without looking at the screen.

"It won't take long," she promised, giving Ashley a kiss. In her purse she felt the vibration of another text. She didn't need to look; she knew it was from Clay Walker, the man who always got what he wanted.

"How long will you be gone?" Ashley asked.

If she went to the beach to talk to Clay one more time? "An hour or two, tops."

Not that she'd even consider something so mind-numbingly dumb.

"David is relentless," Tessa said the minute they were alone.

"I know." Lacey cranked the AC to full blast and whipped out of the driveway. "Do you believe him? Do either of you believe Clay?"

Tessa didn't answer, shifting in the passenger seat to adjust her long, lean frame, and let out a sigh. "I'm the wrong man-hater to ask, I'm afraid."

Zoe picked up Lacey's bag. "Mind if I see if Jocelyn was texting you?"

"You can look, but I think it was Clay. He wants to meet me at Barefoot Bay."

Neither one of them said a word.

"I'm thinking about going."

Still no response.

"Are either of you going to talk me out of it?"

Silence.

"Okay," Lacey said with a soft laugh. "You're not advising me because you know that some decisions a person just has to make on her own."

They shared a look, but not a word.

"Or," Lacey said, "meeting Clay at Barefoot Bay tonight is so flipping stupid the idea has left you two speechless."

Zoe leaned forward and quietly set the cell phone in the console. "Bingo."

"Well, what do you think I should do?" Lacey demanded. "Just let it go? Not talk to him more about why he wasn't honest?"

"They lie once, they'll lie again." Zoe turned to the window, crossing her arms, her expression drawn.

"And you know this from experience?" Tessa said, not the least bit of challenge or sarcasm in her voice.

Zoe was silent. They'd all tried to pry out the story of why the doctor they'd seen at the hotel had made her cry, but she was uncharacteristically quiet on the subject. Just like Jocelyn, who was hiding hurt the size of a small country but refusing to talk about it.

"Damn it, are we friends or not?" Lacey demanded. "Don't friends tell each other everything?"

Zoe finally tore her gaze from the street to meet Lacey's in the rearview mirror. "Friends don't let friends have booty calls with liars."

"I am not talking about Clay. I'm talking about you and that married doctor."

Her eyes flashed. "I'm not considering meeting that 'married doctor' at the beach, Lacey. And, Jesus Christ, can't a person have a single drop of privacy around here?"

Her words echoed into the confined space of the car,

Lacey's heartbeat keeping time with the wheels on the causeway bumps. They never fought, but some things had to be aired out. Didn't they?

"I don't get the secrets," Tessa finally said, a little frustration in her voice. "Maybe we could help you, Zoe. You guys knew every time I got my period and how much it hurt to know I wasn't pregnant. Lacey's told us everything about Clay." She hesitated. "Haven't you?"

"Pretty much. I may have left out a hot kiss or two, but you know everything."

"Well, I for one think you ought to go to the beach," Tessa said. At Lacey's surprised look, she added, "To talk to him. You can't just end this without a conversation. That's why he's waiting there."

"That is *so* not why he's waiting there," Zoe said.

"You're both right," Lacey said. "And I think I should go for a completely different reason. There is something about him that makes me feel wonderful."

Zoe snorted. "Dude, that wonderful feeling is your lady bits getting all fired up. A couple more lies will douse the flames, trust me."

"How can we trust you?" Tessa shot back at Zoe. "You won't tell us anything."

Lacey shook her head, glancing out at the causeway lights dancing on the water as they crossed. "Anyway, it really is more than sex."

"That's what I—" Zoe caught herself and laughed. "That's what all women think, Lace."

"I know," Lacey agreed. "Of course there's a sexual attraction. Shit, it's off the charts. But, I also really connect with him." She took a hand off the wheel to stop the jokes or argument before they started. "I mean I see a fundamental goodness in him. And it makes me hope that..." *He's the one*. "He's really a good guy."

Zoe didn't answer, but Tessa put her hand on Lacey's shoulder. "I happen to agree with you. I think you should meet him."

Lacey looked in the rearview mirror at Zoe. "What's your vote?"

"I think you should make him sweat and dangle a little more."

Lacey smiled. "I hate to break it to you, Zoe, but that magic drafting tool doesn't dangle. But let's let Jocelyn cast the tie-breaking vote. I'll do what she thinks is right."

"Fine," Zoe said, turning back to the window.

"Zoe?" Tessa asked softly. "You sure you don't want to talk about it?"

"There's nothing to talk about. I knew the guy in another life. He screwed me over. It's so not interesting. Let it go."

Because they always gave each other what they wanted, Lacey and Tessa let it go. Zoe didn't say another word until they walked into the suite and found Jocelyn in the bedroom, her clothes piled on the bed like neat little mountains of neutral colors, two half-packed suitcases on the floor.

"What are you doing?" Zoe demanded, grabbing a white cotton shirt and yanking it from the suitcase. "You can't leave!"

"I have a client emergency." She took the blouse out of Zoe's hands and laid it on the bed, smoothing the sleeves.

"What client emergency?" Tessa asked. "That crackpot Coco Kirkman?"

"Or did something happen at the meeting this afternoon that freaked you out?"

At Lacey's question Jocelyn's hands froze. She closed her eyes, then silently folded the crisp pleating on the blouse to a precise right angle, her fingers shaking but her breathing calm and steady.

"The only person freaked out is, as Tessa accurately guessed, my client, Coco. And since she pays me an outrageous sum of money to be her sounding board and voice of reason, I'm going back to work."

"Really?" Tessa asked. "You have to go back?"

They both looked at Lacey, expecting her to chime in with agreement. Or maybe acceptance, because wasn't that what they did? Support each other and whatever decisions they made, dumb or not?

Lacey, about to be queen of the dumb decisions, didn't say a word. After an awkward beat, Jocelyn continued packing.

"I know what you want to hear from me," Lacey finally said. "You expect me to say, 'Oh, what a shame, we'll miss you, but do what you have to do, Joss,' right?" They all looked at her, waiting for the *but* to be added. "But I want to ask you a question instead."

Jocelyn's slim fingers hesitated on the next article of clothing. "Go ahead."

"Why'd you leave the meeting?" Lacey asked.

Three, four, five long seconds ticked by before Jocelyn finally said, "Coco called and that took forever, then I got back here and made my reservations."

She wasn't telling them everything, but how far to push? How much does a friend have to know? Where did they draw the line between friendship and privacy?

"Maybe," Lacey said softly, "you should ignore this plea from a client and face down the things that are making you unhappy."

Jocelyn wet her lips. "And maybe you should solve your own problems before tackling my imaginary ones."

That would be the line Lacey just crossed.

"Oh, shit," Zoe mumbled. "We've had a tough day. Can we just drop all the interrogating of friends and let everyone just do what she wants to do?"

"Because that's not what friends do," Tessa said, sitting next to Lacey in a show of support. "Are you telling us the truth, Jocelyn? Is Coco Kirkman really why you're leaving?"

Jocelyn took a deep breath, pain and angst painted on every delicate feature. "Yes. But I will admit she's a convenience, because I want to go."

Lacey leaned forward. "Is it Will Palmer?"

"Who is Will Palmer?" Zoe asked, sitting up. "That hot guy sitting in Lacey's row? I noticed him. Big dude."

"No, it's not Will Palmer," Jocelyn said with so much conviction Lacey believed her. Jocelyn's pain was never about a guy. Not that guy, anyway.

But her father...

"My issues have nothing to do with him, honestly." Jocelyn dropped onto the bed, letting some clothes tumble. "Listen, you guys. I'm not asking you to just feed me a line of bull and say you understand. I'm not asking any of you to do that. All I'm asking for is some space. I need space."

She always wanted space, and, like good friends, they'd given it to her. Maybe that was the wrong thing to do. Maybe it was the absolute right thing to do. Lacey surely didn't know.

Jocelyn stood and shook her head in dismay. "Now I've wrecked my color-coded packing system."

Zoe grabbed a cream-colored T-shirt. "Someone needs to teach you that black, beige, white, and gray are not colors."

Jocelyn just shook her head and her eyes got watery. "'Scuze me." She dashed into the bathroom, leaving them in shocked silence. Then Zoe put up her hand as if she'd had enough and couldn't bear another word.

Tessa sighed heavily and put an arm around Lacey. "Do you see a pattern here? Our two best friends are not telling us everything."

"Should they?" she asked. "Do we owe each other completely bare souls?"

Tessa shrugged, Zoe shook her head, and Lacey just stared at the door of the bathroom where Jocelyn had gone for her precious space.

"Who's the Will Palmer guy?" Tessa asked.

"It's not about him," Lacey said. "At least I don't think so. Remember how weird she was with her father at her mother's funeral all those years ago? This has to do with him and, honestly, I just don't know how much we should push."

"Thank you," Zoe said, blowing out an exasperated breath. "She'll tell us what she wants us to know when she's ready."

And so, Lacey assumed, would Zoe. "Then maybe that's what friends really do for other friends," she said, leaning her head on Tessa's shoulder.

"What's that?" Tessa asked.

"They wait for each other."

The bathroom door popped open and Jocelyn emerged, her face completely empty of the pain she'd worn when she'd gone in there. Her dark eyes were clear and her color was normal.

"By the way," Zoe said. "We need you to break a tie for us, Joss. We're voting on whether or not Lacey should go to the beach to meet the building stud."

"Do you know what happened?" Lacey asked Jocelyn. She nodded. "They texted me. Why would you go?"

She closed her eyes. Did they have to know everything? Only if they could really help her decide, and, face it, she'd made the decision a while ago. Now she just needed to rationalize it. "I feel like there's a chance for something different with him." Zoe rolled her eyes, but Lacey ignored her. "And I've never wanted anything so much in my whole life. I really care about him."

At their silence, she laughed softly. "I'm making excuses to do something. Is that the same as making excuses not to do something?"

Jocelyn didn't answer at first, but started straightening clothes, methodically folding already crisply ironed khaki shorts. "I think," she finally said, "that you should do whatever you want and not worry about what we think."

"But I need your opinion."

"You need our blessing," Jocelyn continued. "Which you know you'll get for whatever you decide to do. But what's really important is that whatever you decide to do, we'll be there to cheer you on or pick up the pieces." She smiled at the others, a hint of tears in her eyes. "That's what friends do for each other. Even when they don't understand everything."

No one argued with that.

"So," Tessa asked, "what are you going to do?"

"I'm going. And when I get there, I'm going to . . ." She let her voice trail off.

"Do something that starts with an *f* and has four letters," Zoe said.

"Right," Jocelyn said. "Fire him."

Lacey just laughed. "One way or the other, somebody's going to get burned."

Chapter Twenty-two

Clay lay flat on the hard-packed sand, close enough to the water that the occasional wave passed under him, soaking his clothes and digging a sinkhole for his body.

A sinkhole. The perfect metaphor for this mess.

He'd been out here long enough that his eyes had completely adjusted to the darkness, allowing him to see the Milky Way in all its celestial glory. A nearly full moon hung in a cloudless sky, cutting a river of silver over the calm waters of the Gulf. Nothing but the sound of the steady surf and the distant buzz of cicadas interrupted his miserable thoughts.

Thoughts that had turned dark, cynical, and circular as each moment passed and he accepted that Lacey wasn't going to show.

A warm wave punctuated the realization, seeping around

his body again, leaving him wet and chilled, sucking him deeper into the sand.

Who could blame her? He'd lied, even if it was a lie of omission. Sure, he had plenty of reasons—she'd back out, he wanted the affidavit, the allegations were false, the charges dropped—but that didn't change the truth.

And he'd given *her* a hard time for having excuses.

Who could blame her for blowing him off tonight? For staying with her friends and family, or letting her ex-boyfriend work his magic and convince her that he could be a real father to Ashley? Because Clay sure as hell didn't want that job. Did he?

He slapped his hands on the wet sand and pushed up, wanting to wash away the thoughts *and* the sticky muck that had turned his skin and clothes into forty-grit sandpaper.

Popping open his button-down shirt, he shimmied free of the wet sleeves and threw the shirt on the sand. Then he stripped off his sopping wet pants and boxers and tossed them on the pile with the shoes he'd long ago abandoned.

Naked, he strode into the surf, instantly relieved of the sand but not of the agony in his chest. He dove underwater and stayed down; his lungs ached. He popped up and sucked in a mouthful of salty night air, wiping the water from his eyes just as headlights cut a swath across Lacey's property.

Holy shit. She came.

She killed the lights, then the engine, and slammed the car door. He heard footsteps on the cement foundation, imagined Lacey walking around her property looking for him.

Why didn't he move? He couldn't. If she came to him, if she forgave him, if she *joined* him in this water and let him do all the things their bodies wanted and needed to do, he'd say things he'd regret in the morning.

Things like *This isn't casual*.

When, exactly, had that happened? Probably when he'd walked into that town hall and seen the heartbreak on her face—and felt it right in his own gut. She mattered, damn it. She mattered to him *already*.

He caught a glimpse of her hair in the moonlight, and the peach-colored dress she'd worn that afternoon. She stood still by the picnic table, looking around, probably trying to get her own eyes to adjust.

After a few seconds she climbed up on the picnic table, wrapped her arms around her legs, and rested her chin on her knees. In a matter of minutes her eyes would adjust and the moonlight would reveal his pile of clothes or his truck parked near the bushes.

But she put her head down and started to sob. Chest-tearing, throat-ripping, nose-sniveling sobs of bone-deep pain.

Oh, man.

Way to go, asshole. Way to crush the spirit of the most spirited woman he'd met in years. Maybe ever.

God*damn* it. He strode forward, unable to stop, scooping up his pants in one move as he walked, barely stopping as he stepped into them, ignoring how wet they were. She didn't hear him over the bawling that already had her shuddering.

He didn't want to scare her, so when he got about fifteen feet away he started to whistle softly. The six notes he often whistled, a favorite song, a simple sentiment, the music from *her* movie.

A kiss is still a kiss.

She stopped crying, but she didn't lift her head.

He whistled the next bar.

Very slowly, she looked up and met his gaze. With each step closer, the moonlight emphasized more clearly her swollen, red eyes, the streaks of makeup and tears, the tremble of her lip.

"Of all the sandy beaches in all the world…"

She shook her head at the lame attempt at humor. "Don't."

He stopped a foot away, aching to reach out and take away all that pain. He went for the obvious instead. "I'm sorry this happened, Lacey."

"Not as sorry as I am." She wiped her face, but that just made her makeup smear worse, and punched his gut a little harder.

For the time it took for two, then three, waves to break on the sand, they just stared at each other.

"Did you talk to David?" he finally asked.

"David didn't buy the properties," she said. "He did meet with Tomlinson, but he said it was to try and buy them as a gift for me, but Tomlinson said an offer was already on the table, which must be the one through the bank. David backed off."

He didn't think that was true, not for one second, but it seemed like a lousy time to try to crucify her ex. "Any theories, then?"

She shook her head. "He's going to try and find out who bought the lots."

"I'll find out."

"How?" she asked.

"How's he going to do it?" he countered.

"The way he does everything: by throwing money around. What's your plan?"

"My sister knows a million mortgage brokers," he said. "She can get information like that."

"Is that legal?" she asked, plenty of disdain in her voice.

"Yes, Lacey, it's legal. I've never done anything illegal in my life. Stupid, short-sighted, chicken-shit cowardly, and badly motivated, yeah. Guilty as charged. I haven't lied to you, except by not telling you everything straightaway, and I haven't broken the law." He blew out a breath but wanted to finish the speech. "I have made some of the biggest mistakes in the name of love and loyalty that a person can make."

She stared at him, still holding tightly to her legs, the skirt slipping down in the awkward position, but he didn't steal a peek at her bare thighs. He was too busy searching for forgiveness in her eyes.

"And I'm still the right man for..." *You.* "The job."

She swallowed, her eyes welling up as she tried to speak. "I know you don't want to hear this, but...I... can't..." Her voice cracked with a sob.

"Forgive me?"

She shook her head. "I can't..."

Again, the word wouldn't come out. "Give me a second chance?"

"I can't..."

"Trust me? I understand all those things, Lacey. I underst—"

"I can't stop *wanting* you."

Oh. "Is that why you're crying?"

"I'm crying because..." She took a deep breath and let out a wry laugh as she exhaled. "Because I thought you left and I felt like a love-sick idiot for coming here."

He came closer, reaching out to her. "We're both idiots, then."

She sniffed and inched back, but only a little. "My friends didn't all agree with this, you know."

"I'm sure they didn't." He sat next to her and she didn't leap away.

"Especially Zoe. And she's been your biggest cheerleader. I didn't want to come here. No, I didn't want to *want* to come here. Does that make sense? Of course it doesn't," she rushed, answering her own questions, barely taking a breath. "Then I got here and I thought you were gone and I can't believe how much that hurt me."

"Shit, I've done a bang-up job with you today."

"I know, right? And still...God, how bad do I have it for you?"

"Bad." He kissed her forehead, then wiped the tears.

"It's like you have some kind of hold, some spell over me, and it's really scary."

"It shouldn't be scary." But were those thoughts that far off from the ones he'd just had? "We're both just cautious," he said softly.

"Cautious means you're scared," she said. "Are you scared?"

To death. "I'm not sure what I'm getting into," he admitted.

She searched his face, practically begging for him to say more. But he was in no position to tell her how he felt for her. He didn't know what he felt for her. Just that he did.

She closed her eyes and leaned her forehead against him. "I'm not a lousy judge of character, usually. I mean, I can spot a bad guy from miles away, and, honestly, I'm not one of those women with a string of loser boyfriends. My heart says you are not a bad guy."

"I'm not."

"And my body..."

"I'm pretty sure I know what your body says."

"But my friends say that I should fire you."

"Want to know what I say?" He cupped her face, holding her gently as she nodded.

He didn't answer his question until he'd eased her all the way back on the table and settled so close he was just about on top of her.

"Fire me later," he whispered into a soft, airy, sweet kiss that wasn't anything like the fury and frantic connection he imagined they'd have the first time they made love.

He let her get used to the weight of his body against hers, the sensation of their tongues doing their favorite dance, the pleasure of his erection rising against her stomach.

She gripped his arms like she might fall without their support, squeezing his muscles and sliding her hands over his back and rear end.

"You're covered in sand and you're wet."

"Mmm." He nibbled his way down the V-neck of her dress, which buttoned from her cleavage to the bottom. "I was in the water."

"You were?"

"But first I was lying on the sand." He got the first few buttons of her dress open with little more than a flick, spreading the cotton to reveal a white lace bra. And the swells of her gorgeous breasts beneath it.

"What were you doing in the sand?"

He kissed her creamy skin, thumbed the nipple, earned a whimper of delight. "Thinking about you."

"Thinking about this?"

The next three buttons were just as easy, and then the dress fell all the way open. He kissed her cleavage, down her stomach, then opened another button. "No, I wasn't thinking about sex."

"You are now."

"True, but..." The last three buttons left her bare but for white lace panties. He completely spread the dress open, kissing his way down to his destination. "I was..." He licked her belly button. "Thinking about..." He put his mouth over the silk. "How much I want to..."

She squeezed his shoulders, lifted her hips, let out another groan as he pulled down her panties. The sight of her shot fire and agony and need to his every cell.

"To what?"

He sat up slowly, drawing away from her skin but knowing he'd be back.

"C'mon." He slipped her dress over her shoulders, unhooked her bra, and scooped her naked body into his arms to carry her across the sand to the water.

Halfway there, she let her head drop back, an act of complete surrender.

At the water's edge he put her on her feet and stood back to look at her, bathed in moonlight and glowing from arousal. "God, you're gorgeous, Lacey."

She just smiled. "You know what I think, Clay Walker?"

"What?"

"That nothing you do is casual, even sex."

The water lapped his ankles and, as it ebbed away, the

sand disappeared, leaving him in a sinkhole again. Once again he was digging himself deeper and deeper, but he just couldn't seem to stop.

"You might be right, Strawberry."

When they reached the sandbar, Clay pulled Lacey into his chest, crushing her mouth with a kiss and then leaning her back so that the moonlight poured over her body and her hair skimmed the water.

Every sense was alive and sparking, her hands desperate to feel every amazing inch of him, her mouth greedy for more of his lips and tongue. She felt light-headed from the scent of sex and salt and the sounds of his sexy words and helpless groans.

But another sense sparked, too, an undercurrent of awareness that had nothing to do with sex but everything to do with emotion.

Standing, embracing, entwining, they kissed, the water lapping waist-high, invading her most private parts as his tongue invaded her mouth. His hands were everywhere, on her breasts, down her back, under her thighs so he could hoist her higher. The tide took her right where she wanted to be, up against the shockingly hard length of him, already sheathed with a condom he'd put on before they got in the water.

That strange awareness, that sense of something familiar, teased her again, then disappeared when he turned her around so her backside was tucked into his hips. Nothing was familiar about that.

He positioned himself between her legs, closing his hands over her breasts, stealing her sanity as he caressed her budded nipples and glided his shaft along the super-sensitive skin between her legs.

Waves of déjà vu rolled over her.

How was that possible? Even if she could remember the last time she'd been intimate with a lover, there had been no water, no full-body assault of pleasure from a man who'd positioned himself behind her. Because she wouldn't have forgotten that.

So why did it feel *familiar*?

The question tickled like his lips on her ear. "Do you like that, Lacey? Does that feel good?"

"Yes, I like it. I like this. I like—oh, that. I like *you*." The admission felt good on her lips. Almost as good as his fingertips on her nipples.

"And this? Do you like this?" He dragged his hands down and cupped her backside, holding it firmly as he stroked from underneath with a granite-like erection.

"Oh my God, I like that *so* much." She moaned as the swollen head rolled over her most tender spot, his hips grinding into her backside.

"And that?"

His body was a relentless, unstoppable assault on her senses, making her weak and helpless and lost, still reminding her of something so powerful she couldn't stop it, something scary and huge and life-changing. But what?

She pushed away the thoughts and gave in to the building tension, the twisting, squeezing, aching knot developing low in her belly as his erection slid between her legs, from the back to the front, right over the knot that was about to unravel.

"Clay, if you keep doing that I'm going to..." She lost the last word as he bent his knees so she could sit on his lap, forcing his erection directly and mercilessly over her clitoris. She cried out a little, wild with pleasure when he reached down and used his hand to intensify the sensation, slipping one finger inside her.

"Are you ready, Strawberry?"

So ready. She nodded, unable to speak.

"Do you want me inside you?"

"Yes. Now. Please, now."

"Now." He echoed her thoughts and then turned her around to face him, the buoyancy of the water bringing her to his eye level. "This is it."

For one breath of a suspended moment, they were eye to eye, mouth to mouth, chest to chest, then he lowered her right onto him...and they were body to body. This is it. *This is it.* The words had an eerie echo of the past, a warning and a threat as well as a promise.

Without closing his eyes or kissing or saying a word, he slid all the way inside, as deep as he could go. His breath caught as he plunged deeper, held still, then began to stroke in and out.

Everything faded. Every deliciously intense feeling and thrill faded to nothing but that one place where they were joined. His hands stilled, his kisses halted, even their tattered, frantic breathing suspended into near silence as they both focused completely on the connection of their bodies.

She dropped her head on his shoulder and gave in to the rhythm. Each stroke took her closer to the edge, each thrust shoved her a little past sane, each splash of water between their hips and thighs and mouths and chests nudged her closer to a climax.

Until he froze completely, all the way inside her, looking right into her eyes, and time completely stopped.

Everything was silent. Motionless. Hovering like the calm before...

"Lacey."

"Clay."

"You can..."

"I know. I'm about to."

Closing the space between their mouths, he kissed her and started up again, thrusting over and over, deeper and deeper, faster and faster until everything shattered and exploded and roared in her head.

And then she remembered when she'd felt this way before. Exactly this way. Torn and destroyed, then lifted up with anticipation and optimism. The only other time in her life when something so powerful crashed through her world and changed it forever. When a force of nature had stolen everything she thought she cared about and left her with nothing but hope.

The hurricane.

Only this time she had no insurance against the damage to her heart.

Chapter Twenty-three

It was barely seven when Lacey's phone buzzed with a text, pulling her out of a watery dream. Clay. It had to be him texting. He'd followed her home from the beach to make sure she arrived safely, which was sweet and had given them another half hour to make out on the porch. When she climbed into bed at almost two, he'd texted one last good night.

She fully expected to see "Good morning, Strawberry" on her phone when she blinked the sleep away to read the message.

Zoe Tamarin: Meet us at airport to say good-bye to J. That is if you are not in use as human canvas for his MDT

Oh, his drafting tool was magic, all right. Smiling, Lacey sat up and texted back. *On my way.*

Fifteen minutes later she tiptoed into Ashley's room

to leave a note, taking one minute to gaze at her sleeping daughter. Why were kids always heartbreakingly beautiful when sound asleep, their needs met, their angelic faces so perfect you'd do absolutely anything for them? God was sneaky that way.

Lacey's fingers itched to touch her child's cheek.

And she *was* still a child, despite the outline of a young woman's body under the sheets and the slow shift in Ashley's features to a heart-shaped face that looked so adult despite a few blemishes every month.

What had happened to her baby? Secure in the knowledge that a freight train could roll through the room and not wake her daughter, Lacey brushed a honey-colored lock from Ashley's face, grazing the cheek she'd kissed a million times.

A mighty ache gripped her heart and closed her throat. Now, this sensation was familiar, a love she'd known since before Ashley was born. A love unlike anything she'd ever felt for anyone or ever would feel. She'd never felt this way about David in their happiest of halcyon days, never looked at either of her parents and felt weak with love, never hugged any girlfriend with the sense of helpless wonder.

This was pure and whole, and so unconditional. When the easy thing to do would have been to give her up or follow David's advice and terminate, Lacey had held on to her princess.

"Princess Pot-Pie," she whispered, the ancient nickname rising up from memories of post-bath cuddles in the rocking chair and early morning walks through town with Ashley still in a stroller. She'd had a million names for her baby, but that was her secret favorite.

The shelf built into the headboard was mostly empty, except for the brand-new iPod Lacey's mother had sent to replace the one lost in the storm. A few hair ties, a *Glamour* magazine Zoe bought her when they'd been at Walgreens the other day. But no well-loved copy of the first Harry Potter book, no pictures from camp last summer, no movie-ticket stubs or eighth-grade yearbook.

The storm had stolen those memories, and Lacey had to remember that the loss couldn't be easy for Ashley. Lacey knew that life went on, and that memories were stored in your heart, but Ashley's world was upside down. They had no home, no stuff, and no way of being sure it would ever come back.

On the corner of the bed Lacey spied Aunt Zoe's uni, awash with gratitude that she'd taken the risk to save it.

But now they were in the middle of another emotional storm and more things were at risk. If a man came into Lacey's life, what would that do to her relationship with Ashley? Would David's reappearance destroy the delicate balance Lacey had cobbled together with her daughter? And what about Clay? Could he ever fit into this tiny family?

An unexpected jolt of desire hit her. She *wanted* Clay to fit into this family.

But by staying close to him, was she distancing herself from her daughter?

Unexpected tears burned and Lacey blinked them away. Had she ever cried this much before?

Ashley turned and let out a quiet sigh and Lacey stroked her head one more time.

"Little Princess Pot-Pie. You know I'll always love you the most." She leaned over and placed the softest kiss on

Ashley's head, loving the smell, the feel, the very being of—

"Did you just call me Princess Pot-Pie?"

Lacey laughed and finished the kiss noisily. "I did."

Expecting mockery, Lacey's tears turned to a smile when two slender arms reached up and wrapped around her neck, pulling her closer. "I love you, Mommy."

She almost folded in half. Instead, she choked a little, mostly because the lump in her throat was strangling her. "I love you, too."

"Oh my God, are you crying again?" Ashley pushed her back to see. "Why are you so weepy all of a sudden?"

"I don't know." But the unexpected tenderness pulled Lacey onto the bed, replacing the need to see Jocelyn off at the airport. These moments with Ashley were too precious and far too rare.

"What's the matter, Mom?" Ashley asked.

"You never say I love you," she replied honestly. "And I've heard it more than once, maybe more than twice, in the last few days."

"I'm sorry. Dad told me I should tell you more often."

Shit. That was not the motivating factor she wanted to hear. "That was…" *A tad manipulative.* "Nice of him."

"Yeah, he's nice. Why are you dressed? Where are you going?"

"The airport, I'm sad to say. Jocelyn has to go back to L.A."

"Oh, no." She sounded truly disappointed. "Will she be back?"

"I don't know, but would you like to come along for the ride? We can spend the day doing something fun on the mainland with Zoe and Tessa, if you like." Which might take care of some of the Mommy Guilt when Lacey stayed out late again with Clay tonight. Because she knew she would.

"Can't. Dad's taking me cave diving."

Cave diving? Lacey almost spat. She couldn't get out the "No!" fast enough. "Not—no! Do you know how *dangerous* cave diving is?"

Ashley squished up her face. "He said you'd say that and we should ease you into the idea."

God, she hated that they were talking about her, about how to *manage* her, while she was gone. *Then maybe you shouldn't be gone so much*, a nasty little voice in her head said.

"But he was going to tell you when you got home last night." Ashley gave Lacey a scrutinizing look. "You did sleep at home last night, didn't you?"

"Ashley!"

"I meant you didn't stay at the Ritz with your friends," she added quickly. Even though both of them knew that was so not what she meant.

"I wasn't out all night," she said. "I got home late, though."

"You were with him, weren't you?"

She swallowed, absolutely determined not to lie. "If by him, you mean Clay..."

"Mom, he's a sleazebag. When are you going to realize that? You called it the day he showed up on the beach trying to get your business by running around half naked."

Lacey dug for the right answer, the way to keep the connection alive but honest. "You've sure changed your tune, Ashley. You thought I was a b-word and he was the cutest thing you'd ever seen."

"Well, he's not. He's a slimebucket."

"Actually, he's not."

"You're going to defend him after what happened at the town meeting yesterday? Mom! What is wrong with you?"

"There are two sides to every story, Ash, and he has one that doesn't paint him as the devil, like Charity Grambling tried to do. He's going to do the job for me—"

"What?" Her eyes bugged out with exaggerated disbelief. "Mom." With disappointment in her voice, she plucked the uni from Lacey's hands, as if she couldn't stand for it to be on the wrong side of this argument. "I can't believe you *like* this guy."

Oh, she liked him, all right. Way too much. "I like his work."

"Yeah, right." She curled her lip. "What were you doing with him at the beach last night?"

"How do you know I was at the beach with him?"

"Because I got up to go to the bathroom in the middle of the night and walked on sand in the hall."

"Oh, boy. Now you're a detective."

"Am I right?"

She closed her eyes, wishing she could lie to her daughter. "We...talked. About what happened and how he was wrongfully accused of something, and cleared of it. Actually, he was helping someone out. He had a lot of explaining to do and I listened to him."

"Is that what you call it? Because if I did what you're doing, I'd be grounded for the rest of my life."

"First of all, I'm not doing what you think." Because

Ashley couldn't even imagine anything like what went on in the water last night, so that wasn't a lie. "And, secondly, I'm almost thirty-seven years old, Ashley."

"And he's twenty-nine! Don't you see how gross that is?"

Lacey almost smiled. "Depends on your perspective."

"It's gross."

"Look." Lacey reached for her daughter's hands, but Ashley pushed her away, glaring. "Honey, the point is I'm an adult and I can be with who I want to be with."

"But why can't you be with Dad?"

"I don't have feelings for—can you not call him that?"

"Why not? He's my dad. He's my *father.*" She said the word with so much pride it twisted Lacey's heart. "And I know, I *know*. He's been a craptastic father for all my life, but I've decided to forgive that and start over."

"As we've discussed, that's very mature of you, but—"

"Then why can't you?"

"Forgive him?" Lacey shook her head. "I'm not still mad at him. I have forgiven him," she said, picking her words like fragile flower petals. One poor choice, and the whole conversation could fall apart. Farther apart. "I understand why he made the decision he did, and went off to live his life instead of settling down." *Instead of taking responsibility for his child. The one he suggested she abort.*

But she loved Ashley too much to play that card.

"Then why can't you give him a chance? Why can't you be in love with him?" She whined the question. "Then my life would be perfect."

Oh, no it wouldn't be. "I can't make myself love a man I don't have any feelings for. And, I'm sorry, Ashley, I simply can't manufacture those kinds of feelings."

"You've been too wrapped up in Clay Walker, that's why."

Was that true? "I don't think that's it. And, Ashley, it would mean the world to me if you'd give Clay a chance. Talk to him and get to know him."

She folded her arms, narrowed her eyes, got into full adolescent-anger mode. "Only if you give Dad a chance."

"I *gave* him a chance fourteen years ago," she said softly.

Ashley didn't answer, thinking long enough to have another idea. "Why don't you go diving with us? He said we could drive up to this river, the Itcha-something."

"Ichetucknee. And, sorry, you're not going. I knew two UF students who died cave diving there."

"Not with a tether!" She threw back the covers and leaped from the bed toward her laptop. "Let me show you the YouTube videos. Dad's in one of them, Mom. It's so cool. He's done it all over the world, in Indonesia and Africa!"

Her head almost exploded. How dare he talk Ashley into things like this? Fisting her hands, Lacey shook her head. "No, you're not going. No arguments."

Ashley turned from the computer to fire a look of pure contempt, Princess Pot-Pie completely morphing into Nastina. "Why do you always say that? All you want to do is be with that stupid loser guy when Dad is right here trying to win you back!"

Lacey gathered every single bit of calm she could find, taking a breath and refusing to get dragged into this argument.

"That's not true," she said, purposely controlling her voice. "I'm offering to spend the day with you."

She curled her lip. "No thanks. Dad and I are going cave diving."

"No, you're not."

"You can't stop me!"

"Yes, she can." David stood in the door wearing nothing but sleep pants and a morning beard. "Your mom is your legal guardian, Ashley, and she has to sign a permission form for you to dive up there. So, if she says no, the answer is no."

Ashley looked stricken, blinking back tears. "You'd really say no? You'd really stop me from having the most amazing day of my entire life just so you can go off and... and... do it with that guy?"

"That's out of line." This time David's reprimand was welcome, because Lacey could hardly form the words as she stared at her daughter.

"Well, it's true."

Lacey stood, somehow holding it together. "What's true is that your comments are way beyond what's acceptable. You aren't going cave diving and you aren't leaving the house for the next three days."

"Mom!" Tears rolled over those cheeks, not so angelic now.

"Accept your punishment, Ashley," David said, stepping aside to let Lacey by. "You need to know there are consequences for your behavior."

Lacey walked down the hall, bracing for the tirade that would surely follow, but Ashley was uncharacteristically quiet. Had David's presence changed her daughter so much that she would accept punishment without a fight?

She stood in the kitchen pressing her fingertips to

her forehead as an Ashley-argument headache started to throb.

"You made the right call in there," David said.

Irritation and resentment coiled through her, making her want to lash out and remind him that she'd been making calls for years with no help from him.

Instead she just nodded. "Thanks for the backup."

"Hey, that's what parents do."

No, parents stay and raise their kids instead of going to Patagonia. "I'm sorry about wrecking your plans for cave diving."

"No biggie," he said. "We'll go when you're ready. I'd like you to come with us."

She turned to him. "I'm never going to be ready to go on family outings with you, David. I'm not going to change my mind and it has nothing to do with anything going on in my personal life. I'm not interested, okay? You can be her father and forge a relationship with her; I've never tried to deny you that. But let me make this perfectly clear: I am not getting back together with you. You have to stop painting that fantasy in her head because when it doesn't happen, *and it won't*, she is going to be heartbroken and it will be all my fault."

He stood completely still, regarding her. "If she's ever been heartbroken, Lacey, it's because I didn't take responsibility for her."

The admission stunned her, leaving her speechless despite the fact that she had plenty more to say.

"And the real epiphany isn't what happened down in Chile. The real eye-opener for me has been this time with an intelligent, beautiful, inquisitive, delightful—"

"I just told you, I'm not—"

"Daughter." He closed his eyes. "I care deeply for you, Lacey, but the person I love in this house is Ashley, and I only want a chance at being in her life to make up for the pitiful job I've done for the last fourteen years. That's all I want, I swear."

She believed him, she really did. And who was she to deny her daughter that kind of love?

Chapter Twenty-four

Lacey whipped open the bottom cabinet and prayed for a small miracle. And got one. She almost clapped her hands with relief.

"There is a God," she whispered. "And He has just provided a silver jelly-roll pan without a dent or a nonstick coating. Now if the chocolate in the fridge isn't ready, I can start a second pan."

From the living room she heard Clay laugh softly, a sound she'd been listening to and enjoying for almost ten days. And a lot of nights, when she could sneak out.

"Nothing is funny about chocolate ruffle cake," she called out, pushing herself up to a stand.

"You're funny when you bake," he replied. "Do you know how much you talk to yourself?"

"This cake is incredibly important, Clay." She set the pan on the counter and took a few steps to the left so she could see him in the living room. "The baby shower is being given by Julia Brewer, who is married to Scott Reddick, son of Paula Reddick, who sits on the town council. She's someone we have to impress."

She bit her lip to see if he'd reacted to the *we,* a word that had popped up between them an awful lot in the last ten days.

He didn't. Instead, he put down a coral-colored pencil and smiled at her, his grin like a bucket of sunshine in the cramped room. "I'm just laughing at how much you talk to yourself when you bake. I probably do the same thing here in my office."

And when had the rental-unit living room become his office? Again, things had just morphed in the last week and a half. Instead of an empty, badly decorated living area in a standard beachfront rental unit, the room had been transformed into Clay Walker's architectural studio.

A giant-screen computer design and drafting system and two other laptops stayed lit with bright green lines and angles and mathematical modelings of floor plans and rooflines and buttresses. Photos of Moroccan buildings were tacked to every available wall space, and a huge drafting table took up almost half the room.

"Well, I'm just happy this apartment came equipped with a decent jelly-roll pan because I don't feel like driving home to get mine and I've got to deliver this cake this afternoon."

He studied her, his head angled, his eyes bright. "C'mere."

And, just like that, she did. He was perched on his stool in front of the drafting table and she reached for him, wrapping her arms around his waist.

He flicked his finger on her cheek, then licked it. "Chocolate on strawberry. My favorite."

She snuggled closer, a familiar warmth folding through her like the satiny cocoa filling she'd just simmered on the stove. "What are you working on?" she asked, looking at the drawing in front of him. Rather than buildings or floor plans, this was a map of sorts.

"The traffic delivery system."

"The what?"

"Roads. To, from, and around Casa Blanca. But I really need to hear from my sister about those properties. She said she'd have information today about who bought them, and she's supposed to call me any minute. Knowing if we can have them really makes a difference in how I design the traffic pattern in and out of the resort."

"What if we don't know that, Clay? What do we present? Ideas with or without the other two properties included?"

"Definitely with," he said. "We'll find out who bought them and we'll figure out a way to get them. That's just an obstacle."

Which never bothered him. If she'd learned nothing else from Clay Walker, it was how to get over brick walls.

"So we are going to present as if we own the land. And we need to address traffic patterns in that meeting."

That meeting. The pressure of knowing that it was less than five days away almost made Lacey hustle back to her ruffle cake for some baking stress relief. But she stayed against Clay's warm body, and the anxiety magically lifted. Another small miracle. Who knew a man could be better than baking?

Not a man. *This* man.

"You look worried," he said, scrutinizing her face. "I can do this segment of the presentation, no fears."

She shook her head. "I'm just worried about everything. Including my ruffles. They can be tricky."

Nuzzling her, he worked his mouth into her neck for a kiss. "I like your ruffles." Sliding one hand over her breastbone, then lower, he caressed her nipple. "And your ridges."

"Very original," she laughed, arching into his touch because she couldn't stop herself. That's what he did to her every time. "And there can be no sex until I finish a second pan of chocolate, then make the ruffles, top the cake and—oh, shit!"

He eased his hand away. "What?"

"I forgot shelf liner to keep the chocolate against the sides. Damn, I shouldn't have agreed to a cake this complicated. No," she corrected herself, "I should have made it at home where I have everything. Except…"

"Except what?" he prodded, pulling her closer.

"Except that isn't home. It's my mother's house and she probably doesn't have shelf liner, either."

"There's a hardware store five minutes away."

Of course, he'd get right over the hurdle. He slid off the stool, wrapping her in both arms just as snugly as she planned to wrap that cake.

"Relax, Strawberry. It's all going to be okay. You'll finish the cake and we'll finish this presentation and we'll even get to sneak into bed later this afternoon and"—he tipped her chin—"we'll finish what we started when you walked in here this morning loaded down with bags of baking equipment."

She tried to swallow but couldn't, choked by desire and disappointment and happiness and hope and fear all at the same time. How was that particular mix of emotions even possible?

"I'm homesick." The admission popped out before she gave it a moment's thought, but the minute it did, all the emotions made sense.

She expected him to scoff, but he didn't, just looked at her with a very understanding expression.

"I miss having my own house. My own stuff. My own mess and special places to keep things. I want to bring you home, not to my parents' house where my ex is hovering like a helicopter and I don't even sleep in a room I can call mine." Her voice cracked again, and this time she couldn't fight the tear that spilled. "You can't imagine how hard it is not having your own place."

"Of course I can," he said. "Look around. You think I want to work like this? But you'll get there."

"Will I? I'm working so hard to build a business and this resort. But that's just a place for other people to have a vacation. Is that any kind of home? How will I raise Ashley there? How can I give her a—"

"Shhh." He put a finger over her lips. "I bet I know how to make you stop crying and start smiling. Come with me." He started walking toward the hallway, but Lacey stayed put.

"You can't take this feeling away with sex, Clay."

"Come on, Lace." He tugged at her hand. "I want to show you something."

"Oh, I know what you want to show me, and I'm telling you, that's not the answer to everything when your heart is breaking. And I need to finish my cake."

He turned, still holding her hand. "Please come in the bedroom with me."

"No."

He closed his eyes, almost fighting a smile. "Okay. Then wait here. This was going to be a surprise after the town council meeting, but I think this is a better time."

He dropped her hand and walked away, leaving her to stare after him. Then, burning with curiosity, she followed, peeking into the bedroom to see him on his knees, reaching under the bed.

He pulled out a few tubes of paper, folded back a corner to read something, then selected one of the rolls, shoving the others back under the bed.

For a moment she thought he was getting her shelf liner, since the paper looked thick enough to use. But then he unrolled the rubber band and spread a large blueprint over the bed. "This is something I've been working on for you."

The sketch of a building was similar in style to what he'd done for Casa Blanca, but this structure looked a little bigger than the villas yet still within the traditional Morocco-blended-with-old-Paris motif he'd captured for the resort.

But this was different, homey somehow. Intimate and inviting. This was like a...

"A house?"

"A home. For you and Ashley."

"Oh. Clay." She brought her hand to her mouth, as if she could contain the feeling welling up inside of her.

"You know that little corner, way at the end of the Tomlinson property line, just off the beach?" he asked. "I think we could build this right there, sort of at an angle facing southwest. You'd see Barefoot Bay and the resort, but be tucked away from the action of the business."

This was perfect. Too much. Too perfect. "How could I afford this?"

"Some creative financing," he said. "I've been talking to my sister about some mortgage options. In fact, that's another thing she's supposed to call me about today."

She looked up at him, a new waterfall of feeling cascading over her. "You talked to your sister about my house?"

"Of course I did. I'm close to her. She's the only family I have now."

"You have—" *Me*. She stopped herself before the word was out. "You have really blown me away with this," she finished, turning to the drawing, kneeling just to get closer to it. "This is just incredible."

"That's just the front elevation," he said, coming right down next to her to turn to the next blueprint. "Here's the back."

"It's even prettier. Is that a balcony?"

"I thought that would be Ashley's room. I gave her the whole upstairs, for, you know, teen privacy. But we could do anything to the floor plan." He flipped another page, and her heart went with it.

We could do anything. Yes, yes they could. Couldn't they? Her eyes filled again, making her vision too blurry to make out the clean lines of a kitchen and family room, a dining room and laundry. It was too much. He was too much.

"I thought we could—"

She cut off the suggestion with a kiss, hard and hot and as forceful as she could make it.

Under her lips, he laughed softly. "I take it that means you like it."

"I like it. I like it. I like *you*."

He chuckled again, the words having become a secret message between them. "I thought you said no sex until you do something to that cake."

"I need to do something to you first." She pressed herself into him, her fingers already grasping for more of him, dragging down his chest, over the delicious muscles, down to the zipper on his shorts.

Heat and desire pooled between her legs as she pushed him back to the floor and he tugged at her top to slide it up and get to her breasts. The instant his hand slipped under her bra her nipple budded in his hand, fireworks crackling through her, a molten ache building for more.

"Wait a second," he murmured, breaking their kiss. "I just heard my phone."

She clutched his hand and pulled him back to her. "Voice mail."

"It's Darcie," he said. "That's my sister's ring. She has a ten-minute window free today and this is going to take longer than that." He kissed her on the nose, pushing himself up. "Hold that thought, Strawberry. I'll be back in a minute, hopefully knowing who bought the land and how you can get a great mortgage on this house. Then we can celebrate all afternoon."

She smiled, watching him hurry to the other room, where he'd left his cell phone.

Sighing, she leaned against the bed and stared at the blueprints again. How did he know? How did he know what mattered so much to her? This wasn't part of the resort he had to build, this wasn't something she'd asked him for. This was just him *getting* her.

That was what caused a whirlwind of emotions every time she was with him. He got her. He understood. Overwhelmed, she let herself tumble back to the floor with a sigh of pure happiness. As she turned her head with a little giggle, she spied the other rolls of drawings tucked beneath the edge of the comforter.

Actually, that paper would make good shelf liner.

Reaching for the closest one, she drew it out, aware of Clay's monosyllabic answers on the phone. Were any of these blank? She uncurled one corner and saw a drawing of—*Ashley*?

Sitting up, she wiped away any guilt, rolling the rubber band low enough so she could see more of the drawing without actually opening it. Yep, it was a sketch of Ashley, looking up, laughing, a hammer in her hand.

Along the outside edge of the paper, in his square architect's printing, Clay had written the word *Family*.

Family? Did he see Ashley as—

No, that could mean anything. Maybe these were more sketches of the house. Should she look?

From the living room she heard Clay's baritone voice, a question, but she couldn't make out what he was saying. She was so, so tempted to open this drawing, but it wasn't her place. She'd ask him when he came back. He needed to explain why he'd referred to Ashley as family.

And then she'd show him just how happy that made her.

Chapter Twenty-five

⁓

Clay dropped onto the stool in front of the drafting table, picking up a pencil to shade a drawing instead of taking out his frustrations on his sister. "So, basically, all you've got is a Delaware-based corporation."

"And there are a million of those," Darcie agreed, equally frustrated. "This one has no more than a P.O. box, and a bunch of brick walls around that. And they paid cash, so there's no mortgage paper trail, or you know I'd be following it. I'm sorry, Clay. I really thought I got close to a name from a contact in D.C., but the flow of information shut off and now I can't get anything. Do you have a backup plan for the property?" she asked.

"A much smaller version of what we want," he said. And it wouldn't include that home he'd just showed Lacey, damn it. "But if we don't get those two properties, we have to compromise on everything."

"You're starting to sound French, big brother."

"Excuse me?"

"We, we, we. Or haven't you noticed that you never refer to 'the client,' only 'we' and 'us' and 'our'?"

He'd noticed.

"Now, do you want the information on the financing for the residence on the property?" she asked.

"Without knowing if we have those lots, it's moot. E-mail it to me."

"Okay, but…" She dragged out the last word, firing more frustration through him. He wanted to get back to Lacey.

"But what?"

"I have to tell you something." There was the tiniest note of desperation in her voice and it caught him.

"What?"

"Dad had a TIA."

His pencil froze as the words settled on his brain. "What the hell is that?"

"A transient ischemic attack, which, in English, is a mini-stroke. I wasn't going to tell you. Jayna told me not to tell."

A *stroke*? "What happened?" He got up and walked to the balcony, shoving open the sliding glass door and stepping outside into the humidity and sunshine.

"Nothing permanent, we think," she replied. "He just had this weird incident while he was driving."

"He was driving?"

"Yes, but no accident. Jayna helped him pull over and, oh, it was scary, Clay. Elliott was in the car and Dad just kind of blacked out. He couldn't even talk for a few minutes, an ambulance came and—"

"Is he in the hospital? Jesus, Darcie, why the hell didn't you call me?"

"Jayna said—"

He smacked the balcony railing hard enough to make it shake. "Damn it! He's my father I have a right to know if he's sick."

"I didn't think you'd care."

He didn't think he would, either. "Just let me know if anything else happens."

"The doctors are watching him. And Jayna's taking care of him."

"Checking all his bank accounts, no doubt." He regretted the words the minute they were out.

But Darcie just sighed into the phone as if she were so over the old wounds. Of course she was. He had the scars; his sister didn't. "I gotta go, Clay. If I find out anything at all about those properties, I'll call you."

He stood still for a long moment, staring at the Intracoastal Waterway shimmering in front of him, a lone skiff bouncing on the gentle waves. Nothing registered. Just emptiness.

Is this what he'd feel if his father . . .

Holy, holy shit. He couldn't even think the words. If Dad died with all this crap between them, well, that would be on his father's soul and take him right where he belonged, wouldn't it?

But Clay would carry it all around forever, like a bag of wet concrete hanging off his heart.

What the hell was he supposed to do? Forgive him? No way. No, no way.

"Hey, Clay, you coming back?"

"Yeah." Back to the comfort and warmth and escape he needed.

In the bedroom he found Lacey sitting cross-legged on

the bed, leaning over the blueprints, her hair falling into her face.

She didn't look up, mesmerized by the house he'd created. "You know what I love most about this floor plan?" she asked.

Right then, he didn't care. He didn't want to talk about floor plans or buildings or families or fathers he should forgive. Right now he wanted help. And the woman who could give it to him was on his bed.

He stood stone still next to her, his jaw clenched, his hands fisted.

"What's wrong?" she asked, finally looking up, her eyes as bright as sun-dappled whiskey and just as potent for the numbing he needed. "What did Darcie say?"

That my father is sick. "Nothing."

"Nothing? Doesn't look like nothing. Did you find out who bought the property? Oh, God, it's David, isn't it?"

He shook his head, snagging the blueprints and tossing them to the floor. "No, we don't know yet. C'mere." He dropped a knee onto the bed and reached for her.

"Clay, are you going all caveman on me?"

"Yeah." He practically knocked her back, climbing on top of her, kissing her hard on the mouth.

She managed to turn her head. "What the hell is up with you?"

He remained suspended just inches from her, blood already racing south, making him hard and needy.

"Lacey." His voice felt as rough as it sounded. "Don't take this the wrong way, honey, but I don't want to talk." He took her hand and very slowly brought it down to his erection, placing her palm on him.

"Oh. I see that."

Did she? Did she know that needing her physically helped erase the terror of how much he needed her in other ways? In all ways?

"That was a helluva conversation with your sister," she said with a wry smile. "It was your sister, wasn't it?"

"We don't have a buyer's name," he said, swallowing. "And..." *My father might be dying. Tell her. Tell her.* "And she's sending me information on your mortgage."

"And that got you this hot?"

"You got me this hot." He punctuated that with a slow kiss, rolling against her, taking it a little easier this time. "You started it," he said. "I just want to finish."

And then he'd share Darcie's news. When Lacey was naked and in his arms, when he'd given her everything and taken just as much.

"Okay." She kissed his throat, worked her way up his jaw until her lips found his mouth for another long, deep kiss. He slid under her shirt and up to her bra, thumbing her sweet, budded nipple, knowing that always numbed his brain.

She sighed, bowing her back to allow him to touch every inch. He pulsed against her, desperate and anxious, steaming with need. His head buzzed with the sudden loss of blood, his fingers ached to squeeze and touch, his balls tightening, ready for release.

Lifting his head, he bypassed another kiss, hungry to suck her breast and steal some comfort there.

"Clay." She pushed his forehead, forcing him to look at her.

He shook out of her touch, determined to get his mouth on her.

"Clay, what the hell is going on?"

He froze in the act of kissing her breast, realizing what was happening. Holy shit, he was crying.

Very, very slowly he lifted his head. She stared at him, neither saying a word.

He took a few slow, steadying breaths. "My..." He couldn't say the words.

"Your what?" she coaxed.

My dad might be sick. Why couldn't he just tell her? Why couldn't he share this intimate detail with a woman he was so, well, intimate with?

"Is it the resort? Your family? What?"

Your family. There, she'd opened the door wide and still he couldn't step through. Why the hell not? Rolling over, he fell onto his back on the bed, throwing his arm across his face. If he told her, he knew exactly what would happen. She'd tell him to get his ass to North Carolina, mend his broken bridges, forgive the old bastard, and move on. Move on and have a healthy, happy, loving relationship with a fantastic, smart, beautiful woman.

Wait a second. How had he gotten from point A to *love*? His mind, trained in every kind of geometry, couldn't even get around that.

"We could bake," she whispered softly.

"Pardon?"

"I do when something's really bugging me. I could show you how to make chocolate ribbons for the ruffle cake."

He actually laughed. "You want to teach me to bake. Now?"

"Hey, if you can master a Julia Child chocolate ribbon curl, you can master anything. Even whatever it is that's eating away at you right now."

Something warm and wonderful bubbled up in his chest as he looked at her. Something that felt complete. It wasn't what she suggested, it was how. With so much tenderness and caring and genuine concern.

And for some inexplicable reason, that turned him on more than anything.

"We can bake later." He eased his hand under her top again. "And the only thing eating away at me is all these clothes."

But she didn't cooperate with undressing, tracing a line over his face, tapping above his brows. "There's so much going on in here. If you let me in, I could help you."

"Please." He just closed his eyes and pulled her closer.

"Please what?" She leaned over him, her curls brushing his cheeks, her lips close to his. "You want sex?"

"I want you." It was a big admission, and he covered by working her top all the way up, concentrating on her body. "You."

The realization shocked him almost as much as the pressure of her kiss, the truth of it blinding him for a moment. He didn't need this; he needed *her*.

He unclasped her bra with one hand and started on her jeans with the other.

"You can have me," she whispered softly, a vixen with golden red hair and topaz glinting in her brown eyes. She fell on her back so he could suck the peak of one breast and caress the other.

Under him, she rocked her hips and they met in a natural, ancient, unstoppable rhythm, each time he groaned and she gasped, each breath triggering more sparks of arousal and need.

She wrapped her legs around him and he just rode

her, his hard-on so close to where it needed to be, his shorts and her jeans the only thing preventing their bodies from being exactly how they both wanted them to be: connected.

He kneeled up to get rid of those remaining barriers, his gaze locked on her slick nipples, taut and pink, still wet from his mouth. His brain went blissfully blank, his dick mercilessly rigid.

He freed himself while she wriggled out of her jeans, the scent of sex already filling the room and his head, her hands closing over his erection the moment she'd shed her pants.

Rocking into each stroke, he stayed on his knees, head back, eyes closed, pleasure shooting like fireworks up his back, down his legs, and straight through his balls. The world was forgotten, except right here in this room with this woman.

She took it all away.

She sat up, her lips inches from his shaft. He looked down at the very instant she looked up, their gazes locking as she opened her mouth and took one slow lick of his already moist tip. Then she slid him into her mouth. It was too much. A different kind of pleasure, a ripping sensation of closeness that electrified and terrified and stunned him.

"Lacey."

Still looking up, still holding him with her eyes and her mouth—and her heart—she took him even deeper. He wanted to be inside her, he wanted to make—

Pleasure jolted as she sucked, holding him like he was precious to her. Loving him with her mouth and kisses, giving everything just for his satisfaction. The act, as sexual and hot and mind-blowing as anything, suddenly felt like so much more.

Like she was giving him all the comfort he needed, with her mouth and hands and heart.

She licked again, closed her eyes, and slowly, lovingly, sweetly ministered her special brand of comfort. He relaxed into the sensation, letting the thrill of release build and grow and overpower every other thought or feeling.

He lost any shred of control, an orgasm kicking through him, squeezing him until he called out, torturing him while he grew stiffer and more helpless. Sweat tingled and blood pumped and raw, pure, intense pleasure punched through his body until he finally let go of everything. Everything but Lacey. He clung to her shoulders, her feathery silken curls, and spilled into her mouth.

Closing her eyes, she coaxed the very last drop out of him until they both fell back on the bed. He couldn't breathe, couldn't see straight, couldn't talk.

"Clay." She stroked his skin, her delicate touch like a firebrand over the sheen of sweat.

"Mmmm."

"I need to know something."

Of course she did. She needed to know why he had been upset on the phone. She needed to know how he really felt about her. She needed to know when this thing had gone from purely sexual to wildly emotional.

"I just don't know if I can tell you what you need to know, Lace," he said, his voice still raspy from the heavy breathing. But he had to. He had to be straight with her. "But I'll try."

"What are the drawings under your bed?"

He turned to face her. "You looked at them?"

She hesitated, then shook her head. "Not really, but I thought I could use the paper for shelf liner."

He didn't want her to see those sketches. "I have some extra paper like that you can use."

"But what are they?"

"Just ideas I have."

"For what?"

He waited for his heart to slow before he answered, carefully choosing his words. "They are ideas for things I might build in the future."

She studied his face, definitely not sold on that. "Things that include Ashley?"

So she *had* looked at them. "They're personal," he said, a little more gruffly than he meant.

She leaned up on one elbow. "If they include my daughter, they're not personal."

"I told you, I draw what I visualize. It's the curse of an overactive imagination."

"You visualize Ashley with a hammer?"

Was that all she'd seen? It had to be. If she'd seen the rest of those drawings, the one with Ashley hammering a two-by-four would be the least interesting to her. "I expect Ashley to have a role in building the resort and your house, don't you?"

"I hope so," she finally said.

"Well, that's all those pictures are. Memories of moments that haven't happened yet. You know, if I see something well enough to draw it, I can make it happen."

"What else do you see?" The question was tentative, a little scared, and full of hope.

"Right now I'm trying to visualize how you can

make ribbons out of chocolate. Why don't you show me and then we can come back in here and..." *Go ahead, man, say the thing you cannot say.* "Make love." He leaned in to whisper in her ear. "Can you visualize that, Strawberry?"

Because he could. He could visualize it all too clearly.

Chapter Twenty-six

Later that afternoon, when Clay pulled up to Julia Brewer's house, Lacey dipped her head to peer at the minivan in the driveway. "Well, it looks like we're a lot less than six degrees away from Paula Reddick, town council member." She gingerly shifted the chocolate ruffle cake on her lap. "She's inside. Want to come in and charm her?"

He shook his head, opening his door. "I have to call my sister back and ask her about something else while you take the cake in. But hang on. I'll help you get it out."

Lacey's heart slipped a little as he climbed from the truck. The afternoon had been amazing. They'd finished the cake, fallen into bed, and spent the last hour in the shower. And yet he still hadn't told her what had had upset him so much about the phone call with his sister, and she didn't want to whine or beg.

Maybe he didn't trust her, or maybe it wasn't that big

a deal. But, Lord, he'd *cried*. Something had upset him pretty badly.

Jayna?

She crushed the name when it popped into her head. There was no room for ex-girlfriend jealousy in her head or heart. For crying out loud, David was living with her and Clay wasn't acting jealous. But he had gotten off the phone pretty worked up for sex.

No. *Don't think that way.*

He popped open the door and reached in for the cake. "You did an amazing job on this, Lacey."

"I hope they like it. My business has come to a screeching halt since the storm." She stepped down from the running board and took the cake he held. "Be right back."

"Take your time."

So he could call...

Don't go there, Lacey. Don't make excuses where none exist. She headed up to the house gripping her ruffle cake with care, grateful when Julia opened the front door and she didn't have to knock.

"Hey, Lacey," Julia said. "How'd the cake come out?"

Lacey looked down at the nest of chocolate ribbons on the cake tucked in a topless box. "Pretty good, I think."

"Wow, would you look at that?"

Smiling at her creation, Lacey lifted it higher. "Yep, it's nice."

"I meant that guy outside."

Lacey followed Julia's gaze, catching a glimpse of Clay leaning against the truck, on the phone. "Oh." She laughed. "That's Clay. My..." *Lover. Boyfriend. Main squeeze.* "Architect."

"He can build me a house anytime."

"Lacey's not building a house," a woman around the corner said. Paula Reddick stepped into the entryway, as tiny and trim as she'd been when she'd taught PE at Mimosa High. "She's building a posh resort."

"It's not…" Yes, it was. Posh and a resort. "It's still in the planning stages, as you know. Hi, Paula."

Paula gave a quick smile. "Don't worry, Lace. I like the idea. Charity Grambling may kill me in my sleep, but you have my vote."

"Thanks," she said, handing the cake to Julia. "Keep it chilled until the shower tomorrow."

"Let me go get your check, Lacey."

When she left, Paula moved closer to the front door, peering over Lacey's shoulder. "Did you guys work out his shady past?"

"It's not that shady," Laccy replicd. "Hc's clean."

"Looks dirty." Paula grinned. "In a fun way."

Lacey just laughed softly. Oh, if Paula only knew how Lacey had spent her afternoon.

"What's your plan to counteract Charity's flyer campaign?"

Lacey drew back, surprised. "What flyer campaign?"

"Get thee into town, m'dear. You're up against a street team of people trying to stop you before you start. They're all under her wrinkled old thumb."

Lacey sighed as Julia returned with a check. "Thanks for the business, Julia. And for the warning, Paula. Guess I'll head into town and see how bad the damage is."

As she came out, Clay hung up the phone and opened the door for her. "All set?"

"Maybe not yet. We have to head into town now."

On the way there she explained what Paula had told

her, zeroing in on a bright yellow flyer with bold black letters as soon as they got to Ms. Icey's, an ice cream parlor on the outskirts of Mimosa Key's undersized downtown.

SAVE MIMOSA KEY!

Stop all zoning modifications!

Be heard at the Town Council meeting on September 15 at 10:00 AM!

Don't let progress replace pristine!

"Pull over, Clay. I'll grab it." She climbed out of the car, marching into the store to ask Bernadette Icey to take it down, barely noticing a group of teens at a corner table.

"Mom!" Ashley's voice broke through the laughter.

Lacey glanced at the group, all of their faces unfamiliar to her but one. "Ashley, what are you doing here?"

She popped up and threaded through a few empty tables to get to Lacey. "We just came in for ice cream. What are *you* doing here?" Her eyes were bright, her color high. She definitely hadn't been expecting Lacey to walk in.

Lacey looked at the kids again. "Who are they?"

"Just my new friends. Some of them live down south near us, so I'm getting to know some other people."

"Where's Meagan?"

"Oh, Mom, Meagan is turning into such a—"

"Is that Tiffany Osborne?"

Ashley hushed her, blocking the view. "Mom, you don't have to say her name like that. She's not some kind of pothead."

But Lacey wasn't sure of that. "I have to get that flyer in the window down. Is Bernadette here?"

"Miss Icey?" Ashley turned. "No, but that kid's the manager."

Behind the counter a sixteen-year-old was texting.

"Then he won't care if I do this." Lacey slipped behind the front table and ripped down the yellow flyer. "Go get your stuff, Ashley."

"What? Why can't I stay?"

"Because I don't know these kids." Weak argument, but Lacey had a bad feeling. And Ashley wasn't exactly dragging her over to meet them all.

"Hey, Ash!" A boy with swooping bangs and skinny shoulders called out. "Move your ash back here." The entire table hooted with laughter.

Ashley's cheeks flamed. "Shut up, Matt."

Lacey almost reprimanded her for saying shut up, mostly out of habit, but honestly, that felt like the least of her problems. "Get your stuff and let's go," she whispered. "Now."

"Mom, why?"

"Because..." *I said so* was just lame and this was not the time or place to make her point. She lifted the flyer. "I need your help getting rid of these. They're all over town."

"What are they?" Ashley took the flyer and read. "What the..."

"So get your bag and let's go," Lacey ordered with enough force that Ashley didn't argue.

"Gimme a sec. I'll meet you outside."

Lacey was waiting in the truck considering all the ways this could go when Ashley came out of Ms. Icey's and narrowed her eyes.

"Why is he here?" she asked, yanking open the door to the back cab. "I thought we were going alone."

Lacey ignored the question and whipped around to face her daughter. "I don't want you hanging out with those kids."

"Mom, they're fine. Honest."

"I don't like them."

"You don't know them."

"Then bring them home."

She snorted. "We don't have a home."

Lacey and Clay shared a silent look, and then Lacey let it drop.

They saw about fifteen more flyers on the way through the few streets that made up downtown Mimosa Key, taped to the locally owned storefronts and the old iron light posts that lined the main streets. Every time they spotted another one, either Lacey or Ashley got out to rip it down. With each sighting Ashley grew more indignant.

"This is so wrong!" she said when she climbed in after taking one off the railing by the harbor. "I knew Charity Grambling was a b-word, but this is so unfair!"

"Charity and her friends see our project as competition for their business, and it's a free country. They can fight us," Lacey said.

"Let them lose everything they have and see how they feel."

"You know what?" Clay said, taking an unexpected turn north. "I have an idea."

"Make our own street team and plaster some flyers all over town?" Ashley replied. "'Cause my friends would totally get behind me on this."

"I have the plans," he said quietly to Lacey. "They're under my seat."

The plans to the new house?

"I thought we might go up to Barefoot Bay and check it out," Clay said. "Let's take Ashley."

"Take me where?" Ashley asked.

"You'll see." Clay turned and smiled. "I think you're gonna like it."

At least she didn't argue. When they arrived at the property, Clay brought the rolled-up sketch and they walked north.

"What are we looking for up here?" Ashley asked. "More flyers?"

Clay slowed his step and got on her other side so that he and Lacey were flanking her. "What are *you* looking for?" he asked Ashley.

She scowled at him. "Is that a trick question?"

"Nope, I'm serious. What's missing in your life?"

"A boyfriend, and Mom probably just killed the deal by dragging me away from Ms. Icey's."

"If that Justin Bieber-y thing was your boyfriend—"

"Eww, Mom. Totally gross. Matt's so much cuter than Bieber."

"Answer his question, then. Something more important is missing in your life, isn't it?" Lacey couldn't keep the note of anticipation out of her voice.

She froze, horror on her face. "Oh my freaking God, you two are getting married."

This time Lacey's steps slowed as heat that had nothing to do with the late-day sun blasted her. But Clay laughed easily, seemingly not fazed by the question. Maybe it was so out of the realm of possible that he didn't take it seriously.

"Just answer the question," he said. "What don't you have that you wish you did?"

"Well, besides all my old clothes, my favorite Wii games, my collection of stuffed dogs, my yearbooks going back to kindergarten, and every Christmas ornament Mom ever got me, I guess my own room."

The list of missing treasures made Lacey's heart hitch. Clay must have felt the same way, because he put a gentle arm on Ashley's back and led her toward the far corner of the Tomlinson property line. "That's right, Ashley. You need a home."

"No sh—" She stopped again, looking from one to the other. "I thought you two wanted to build a resort."

"We do, and we will." Clay's confidence gave Lacey another thrill. "But we want to build something else, assuming we can get our zoning issues approved and get these two properties back." He looked at Lacey. "And I know we will."

"What?" Ashley asked, looking at Lacey for the answer. "What are you building?"

"This." Clay unrolled the blueprint and spread it on a patch of grass. "Your home."

"A house? For us?" Ashley's voice rose just enough to make Clay look up and smile.

"I hope you like it."

She dropped to her knees exactly as Lacey had when she'd seen the plans. "Ohmigawd, it's beautiful! Mom, did you see this? It's so awesome." She rocked back. "We could live there?"

"We're going to try," Lacey said, so completely hopeful about the idea that it scared her. What if it didn't happen? What if she couldn't afford it or the zoning didn't get approved or the property—

"That's my room?" Ashley shrieked as Clay turned the page and showed the floor plan, pointing to the space that said "Ashley's Room" in tiny, squared-off letters.

How did he know? she wondered again. How did he know just what mattered the most? "That whole thing is my room? With my own bathroom?" For a minute Lacey thought Ashley would throw her arms around Clay and kiss him.

Lacey knew exactly how that felt. "Isn't it amazing?" Lacey asked. But what she really wanted to say was *Isn't he amazing? Isn't he brilliant and special and thoughtful and don't you just love him?*

Because sometimes, like at this very moment, Lacey thought she could love Clay. Maybe she already did. Was that possible?

"Look at the kitchen, Mom! All that space for you to bake."

The comment touched Lacey enough to bring her down to her knees.

"She's quite a baker, too, your Mom."

More warmth crawled up her cheeks. Lacey didn't dare look at Clay because she didn't want to see the expression that went with that comment. The chocolate ribbons had gotten pretty sexy.

Wasn't that what he was thinking? While she was standing here dreaming about the L-word? She finally looked at him, self-consciously pushing a hair from her face

His gaze wasn't the least bit sexual. His gaze said he might be thinking the same thing.

"And my dad's a beast cook," Ashley said, crashing the moment with a dose of David. "He'd totally rock that kitchen. In fact, he texted me that he's making steak tonight. You should come over for dinner. Can he, Mom?" The note of hope in Ashley's voice must have surprised Clay as much as Lacey, as he suddenly stood, brushing some sand off his cargo shorts.

"Of course he can," Lacey said.

"Cool. Then we can we show Dad this house. He'll love it." Ashley smoothed down the curling edge of the blueprint. "It might be the kind of thing that would convince him to stay." There was even more hope in that statement. Just enough to break Lacey's heart.

David wasn't staying, but how could she convince Ashley of that? She looked up at Clay, who was gazing out to the Gulf, lost in thought.

And who was going to convince Lacey that Clay wasn't going to stay, either? "Do you want to come over, Clay?" Lacey asked.

"I'm going take a pass," he said. "I need to work through dinner tonight. That September fifteenth deadline looms right around the corner, Lacey."

"Another time, then," she said quietly. "Anyway, Zoe and Tessa are coming over." And maybe they'd talk Lacey off this love ledge before she fell right off and broke something. Like her heart.

Chapter Twenty-seven

After Clay took a long swim in the warm waters of the Gulf of Mexico, he headed over to the Super Min to buy some snacks to get him through the night of work. Instead of one of the older women he expected to see, Gloria Vail sat behind the counter. He could tell the G-cousins apart now, and Gloria was definitely more friend than foe, and he meant to thank her for tipping Lacey off to the secret meeting.

She sat on a stool, chatting with a man who stepped away from her the minute Clay walked in.

Not a man, though. *The* man. In a sharp sheriff's uniform, a Glock on his hip.

"Oh, hi," Gloria said to Clay, giving her bangs a quick fluff. "Nice to see you again."

Feeling the sheriff's attention on him, Clay gave her a nod, walking to the cooler to get a liter of soda. When he came back, the sheriff had moved to the candy display.

Clay grabbed some chips and his stomach rumbled, reminding him that he had next to nothing to eat in the apartment and he'd turned down a dinner invitation.

"How's it going?" Glo asked.

"Good." The smell of the hot dogs and burritos rolling out of a heated cooking unit drew him closer. "Starved."

"Well don't eat those," Gloria said quickly. "They're awful."

The sheriff chuckled as Clay took the rest of his purchases to the counter. "She's not lyin'," he said. "Charity sells the worst hot dogs on the island. Maybe in the state."

"Thanks for the tip." Clay slid the soda toward Gloria. "That's the second time you've given me good advice."

"Just remember, don't tell my aunt. I'll be disowned."

The sheriff took a step closer, tanned and sharp-eyed, a sizable dude who was no stranger to the gym. "You're too scared of her, Glo."

"I'm not..." She caught the other man's eye and shrugged. "Sometimes. Who wouldn't be, Slade?"

"She can be scary," Clay agreed.

"You two know each other?" the sheriff asked, eyeing Clay a little suspiciously.

"Clay Walker." He held out his hand.

"He's the architect I told you about, doing Lacey Armstrong's property up in Barefoot Bay."

"I'm Slade Garrison." He took Clay's hand and gave a tentative smile but a strong shake. "I heard you landed a few on Charity's chin recently."

"Not literally," he assured the lawman.

"Enough that you've become a little bit of a folk hero around here."

Clay almost choked. "I have?"

"Rumors and stories fly on Mimosa Key," Gloria told him. "By the time the tellin' was done, there were people saying you tore up the bylaw book and threw the paper shreds at Charity just for laughs."

"Wish I'da thought of that."

"I know," she said. "But people like the idea of someone taking her on. And congratulations for Lacey getting on the zoning meeting agenda."

"Any curveballs we should expect?" he asked.

Gloria rang up the soda and chips, shaking her head. "Not that I'm aware of."

The bell behind him dinged, followed by some conversation and laughter, both of which stopped almost instantly.

Clay turned to face the very woman they'd been discussing, Charity Grambling, accompanied by her daughter, Grace, and a heavyset man. Seriously heavyset.

"We get robbed or something, Slade?" the man asked as he headed to the back cooler.

The sheriff crossed his arms and stared the other guy down. "You better plan on walking if you pick up a Bud Light, Ron."

He got a laugh in response. "Like I'd drink piss-water beer. Anyway, Gracie's drivin' and she's sober as a judge."

Meanwhile, Charity leveled Clay with a hard look, moving toward the counter. "Hope you're not planning on hanging any more of these out there." She slammed a fistful of bright pink papers on the counter.

He frowned, looking closer at the words:

SAVE ASHLEY ARMSTRONG'S HOME!!! Vote Yes For Zoning Changes!!!

So Ashley had made her own street team, just like she'd mentioned.

"I had to stop those little hooligans from putting them up outside the Fourway," Grace said, scowling at him. "You should arrest them all, Slade."

"Is it against the law to hang a flyer?" Clay asked.

"Thought you had the local laws memorized," Grace shot back.

"Not against the law to hang flyers, but"—Charity flipped the back countertop and stepped to the register, practically shoving Gloria aside—"last time I checked *the use of marijuana* was illegal." She pointed a finger at the sheriff. "So maybe instead of hanging out in my fine establishment trying to work up the balls to ask Glo on a date, you should be rounding up some criminals down at the Mimosa High football field."

Shit. Was Ashley there?

"You certain about that, Charity?" Slade asked, his voice deeper and more authoritative than when he'd been hitting on Gloria.

Charity put a hand on her hip, snorting softly. "I'm sure. Those kids are hanging around the same place kids have been gettin' high since I was a freshman at that school." She gave him a slow, easy grin, turning her face into a web of creases. "No jokes about what year that was. Get down there now and you'll find 'em. Got all their stupid flyers up and now they're doing what kids do."

Clay grabbed the plastic bag with soda and chips, nodded to the others, and headed toward the door, mentally flipping through his options. Call Lacey and tell her? But could she get up to the football field in time to get Ashley out of there?

He slid behind the wheel of his truck, catching Slade and Gloria walking out in his rearview mirror. They talked for a minute, and Slade put a hand on the woman's shoulder.

Take your sweet time getting the phone number, Sheriff Garrison. Clay needed to get Ashley out of there.

He pulled out of the lot slowly, not wanting to draw Slade's attention, headed down to the first intersection, and then gunned it to the high school. When he reached the side street that ran along the football field, he parked the truck close enough to make a fast getaway and jogged toward the stands.

An impromptu party was well underway, about twenty kids messing around, laughing and standing in small groups. The bittersweet aroma of weed, the sound of teenage trouble, the thrum of a small-town summer night all hung under the bleachers that probably shook on Fridays in the fall.

"Have you seen Ashley Armstrong?" he asked a couple leaning against a post, arms around each other.

The guy shook his head, but the girl pointed to the other side of the field. "She's with Tiffany and Matt."

He had to hand it to Lacey: Her instincts were right on. He rounded the crowd, ignored the looks, and spotted Ashley standing apart from a few kids.

"C'mon, you guys," she said. "I want to hang the rest of these."

A skinny boy with a mop of hair threw a lit cigarette on the ground and stepped closer to Ashley, draping a way-too-familiar arm around her. "Chillax, AshPain. We got your stupid flyers up. Now it's time to party."

Ashley shook him off. "I'm serious. We didn't do half of town."

The boy slipped around behind her, sliding his grimy paws around her waist. "Ashley needs a toke, guys."

She jerked harder. "No, I don't, Matt. I need—get off me."

Instantly Clay launched forward, his fists already balled. "Hey!" he barked. "Let her go."

They all stared at him, and Mop Head let go.

"What are you doing here?" Ashley asked, color draining from her cheeks.

When Clay reached her, he resisted the urge to grab her elbow and muscle her away. The smell of pot was strong, but not on her, and she looked clear eyed and straight. Still, they had minutes until the sheriff showed.

"I'm taking you home. *Now*." She opened her mouth to protest, but instead slid an embarrassed look at the boy.

A girl next to Ashley wobbled a little on too-high platform shoes, long hair in her face, eyes red enough for him to take a guess that this was Tiffany the Troublemaker.

"You're dating Ashley's mom, aren't you?" she asked. "My mom and her friends were talking about you two."

"Want me to call the cops, Ash?" the boy asked. "'Cause this guy looks like trouble."

"No need to call them," Clay said quietly, leaning closer to Ashley. "They're on their way."

"Seriously?" The question came from Mop Head.

"Slade Garrison will be here in one minute."

"Is he really?" Ashley asked, her eyes wide with concern.

"Yes, he is. And you can leave now and I can take you home, or you can call your mom from the police station. Your choice, Ashley."

"He's full of shit, Ash."

But she ignored the boy, looking hard at Clay. "'Kay. I'll go."

She went with Clay, not even saying good-bye to her

friends. At his truck, just as he reached for the passenger-door handle, blue and white flashing lights cut through the darkness, sending the pack of kids scattering.

"Get in," Clay ordered, giving her a shove into the passenger seat before jogging around to climb in the driver's side.

He turned on the ignition and Ashley stared straight ahead until a loud bang on the truck bed made her jump. "Ashley! Help me get out of here."

"It's Matt," she said, turning to the back. "My... friend."

"Didn't act like a friend."

She gave Clay a pleading look. "Can you take him home?"

Clay nodded and Ashley opened her door to yell, "Climb in the back, Matt. Hurry!"

The boy yanked open the back door and slid into the crew cab behind Clay. In the rearview mirror Clay saw fear on the kid's face, and the first hint of whiskers like a dirty mark over his lip.

"Thanks, man," the boy said. "Some prick must have busted us."

"You want to ride in the truck, son? Tell me where you live and shut up until we're there."

Nobody spoke while Clay pulled out of the back of the school lot, easily missed by Slade Garrison. Except for giving directions to Matt's house, Ashley stayed silent until they arrived at a small house in south Mimosa Key, not too far from Lacey's parents'.

When Clay pulled into driveway, Matt threw open the back door. "Thanks for the ride."

"Wait a second." Clay was out as fast as the kid, blocking him. "I need to tell you something."

The boy looked up at him, a whole different kind of scared in his eyes. "What?" He tried for tough, but his voice cracked.

Clay leaned an inch closer, keeping his fists clenched but careful not to touch the boy. "You ever put a hand on Ashley Armstrong again and you'll be sorry."

"Yeah, I—"

"Seriously sorry."

The kid's protruding Adam's apple lifted and fell. "I don't even like her that much."

The little bastard. Clay moved one inch closer. "Then leave her alone."

"'Kay."

Clay didn't move, but Matt finally stepped to the side, giving a final worried look over his shoulder as he bolted into his house. When Clay heard the side door slam, he got back in the truck, braced for a teenage onslaught of fury.

But Ashley just gnawed on her bottom lip, reminding him very much of Lacey when something troubled her. "What a tool," she finally murmured.

"Yep." He threw the truck into Reverse but kept his foot on the brake, looking at her. "You deserve a whole lot better."

"I thought those kids were cool, but they're not." She turned to him, her eyes moist. "Are you going to tell my mom?"

"I have to."

"Please, please don't. She'll be so disappointed in me." Her voice cracked and she turned to hide her tears.

"Did you smoke pot?"

"No! Honest to God, Clay, I never have. I don't even want to. I was scared of what they were doing, and I was really kind of glad to see you."

The words squeezed his chest, tugging on a heartstring he didn't even know he had. "And you are never going to hang out with that idiot again, right?"

She laughed softly. "Right."

He picked up the flyers she'd left on the console. "Did you make these?"

She nodded.

"How 'bout we hang a few on the way back to your house?"

"Yeah." She smiled at him. "Good idea."

He parked near the Super Min, and Ashley produced a roll of tape she'd tucked into her pocket. They started on the west end of Center Street, slapping up flyers on every light post and storefront, and even the corner mailbox.

"Now that'll get you arrested," he said, ripping it off government property.

She laughed and taped one to the front post on the Fourway Motel sign. "And that'll get Grace Hartgrave's panties in a bunch."

"Damn straight. How about we put them on every car window?"

"Love it!" She grabbed more flyers while he lifted windshield wipers.

"I have to ask you a question, Clay."

"What's that?"

"You want kids?"

His hand stilled in the act of lifting the wiper blade on a Honda Civic. "Not really sure yet," he said slowly, searching her face to determine where she was going with that.

"'Cause, you know, my mom…she should have another baby before she's too old."

Going *there*. "Maybe she should," he said. "She's a darn good mother."

She smiled and pushed a hair out of her face, another gesture so like Lacey it kind of caught his heart. "Yeah, I know."

They tagged a few more cars. "My dad wants another kid," she said.

Of course he did, because he'd been so wonderful with the one he had. Clay just nodded.

"And, now don't take this the wrong way, but if you weren't around making my mom act like, well, all crazy and stuff, then she and my dad would get back together."

He came around the front of the last car in the row. "Do you really believe that?"

"I know it." She rolled her eyes. "I mean, she's all happy and sings and spends hours getting dressed when she's going to see you."

He almost smiled thinking about that. "What's wrong with her being happy, Ashley?"

"Nothing. What's wrong with her being married to my dad?"

Everything. "Hey, we're out of flyers," he said. "I'll take you home now."

"See?" she said as they walked toward his truck. "You don't even have an answer for that. 'Cause you know I'm right. You gave me that lecture about Matt. Well, how about taking one of your own? My mom thinks you're like, in love with her or something."

Or something.

"But all she ever tells me is how my dad is going to leave her, and that's exactly what you're going to do, isn't it?"

Eventually. Wasn't he?

"Isn't it?" she demanded.

He took a slow breath and exhaled it through clenched teeth. "We have to build this resort before—"

"I think she really wants another baby."

Did she? They'd never talked about it, but why would they? They'd known each other a few weeks and right now, it was all about sex. But Lacey was a nurturing woman, and young enough to have more kids. "And my dad wants one, too. I really like the idea of a little brother or sister. A bigger, you know, family."

He knew.

"And my dad, I know he hasn't been the world's best father, but he had an epi...efipan...a moment of knowing exactly what he should be doing."

An epiphany. "I had one of those once."

"Yeah? What did you decide to do?"

To stop trusting in the concept of *family*. "I, um, struck out on my own in business."

"Well, good for you." She put her hand on the truck's door handle. "I'm sorry for being such a, you know, opinionated kid. I just want you to know exactly what you're doing."

The problem was, he didn't have a clue what he was doing. Except feeling things for a woman who probably wanted more than he was equipped to give her.

"Let's get you home, Ash."

"That's not my home," she corrected. "But, thanks to you, I might have one soon. A home and a family."

Yeah. Well, he could help with only one of those.

Lacey, Zoe, and Tessa leaned over the coffee table, ooh-ing and awing over the house plans.

"I just can't believe he did this for you, Lace," Tessa said. "Talk about thoughtful."

"I know." Lacey sighed, stroking her hand over the edge of the blueprint. "I was so touched. I just love..." *Him.* "That he did this."

"Finish the sentence the real way," Zoe said. "You love *him.*"

She looked up, feeling warm blood rush to her cheeks. "Is it possible?"

"Anything's possible," Tessa said, putting a hand over Lacey's. "Only you know in your heart how you feel."

"I feel insanely happy when I'm with him. Completely capable and beautiful and sexy and—"

"Who needs a refill?" David marched in from the kitchen holding a wine bottle but killing the buzz.

The girls shared a look that said the conversation wasn't over but would have to wait.

Misinterpreting the look, David glanced at the bottle. "Unless you want to switch to red because the steak will be ready in a few minutes."

Tessa pushed up. "I'll set the table, then."

"I'll do it," Lacey said quickly.

"No, no. You keep decorating your palace. Fox and I have this covered."

"Thanks, and I'm fine on wine, David. Zoe?"

She shook her head, pointing to the master bathroom. "I'd go for a bigger tub, because I'm starting to think you're going to use it. A lot."

David and Tessa disappeared into the kitchen and Lacey dropped her chin on her folded arms. "Yeah," she said in a dreamy voice. "A tub for two."

"Shhh. Listen." Zoe leaned toward the kitchen, a hand to her ear. "Hear them laughing?"

"Yeah."

"Have you noticed how those two laugh *all* the time?"

Lacey scowled. "Tessa and David? She can't stand him."

Zoe lifted a very meaningful brow. "You know the definition of irony?" she asked in a soft whisper.

"Probably not the way you're about to describe it."

She grinned. "David gets this baby he says he wants from the person who openly longs for one. Tessa."

Lacey's jaw dropped so fast and far she actually knocked her elbows off the edge of the table. "Now that would be..."

"Ironic."

"Impossible. She can barely stand to be in the same room with him *and* she's infertile."

The ring of Tessa's laughter floated out from the kitchen.

"Yeah, that definitely sounds like it's killing her to be in there with him." Zoe rocked back on her heels, crossing her arms. "Did you see how she launched into table setting that puts her in the very same tiny kitchen with him and, by the way, for your information, infertility is often a two-way street."

"Billy's girlfriend is pregnant. He's obviously able to make a baby."

Zoe shrugged. "Sometimes it's the chemistry of two people. They can get pregnant with others, but there's something wrong with PH balance or whatever."

"And you know this, how?"

"Because I talked to my Aunt Pasha last night and she was reading her beer bubbles."

Lacey snorted a soft laugh. "Like tea leaves?"

"Exactly, only with hops."

"Okay, and what did the Budweiser say to the old aunt who thinks she's psychic?"

Zoe gave a put upon look. "First of all, she doesn't think she's psychic, she's full-blooded *Roma*." She dragged out the word as if that explained everything. "And second, she's not that old, somewhere between seventy and eighty; she won't say. And third, she prefers Blue Moon to Budweiser."

Lacey cracked up. "All right, and what did she predict?"

"She doesn't predict, she reads the clues."

"Zoe." Lacey was losing patience. "What?"

Zoe leaned very close to whisper. "She said Tessa's seed will grow in Barefoot Bay."

"And was this before or after you told her Tessa's moving here to run the gardens for the resort?"

Zoe just shook her head. "She wasn't talking about an organic mustard seed, honey."

"Okay, and David? Pasha's never even met David."

"Precisely." Zoe crossed her arms and smirked. "But the Blue Moon bubbles showed the face of a fox."

Lacey's eyes widened. "Are you sure it wasn't a wolf? Bubble art can be deceptive."

"Go ahead, make fun of her."

"Nah, it's too easy. Did you tell her about David?"

"Of course."

"Did you tell Tessa?"

She shook her head. "I'm filing it under one of those things we think is better kept secret."

Lacey took a drink from her almost-empty wineglass. "There's been a lot of those these past few—"

Headlights swept the driveway and a loud car-door slam pulled her attention and got her to her feet. "Oh, thank God, I bet that's Ashley. She went to hang her flyers in town with some friends and told me Meagan's mother would bring her home, but I was starting to—" She stopped cold at the front door, peering through the glass. "That's *Clay's* truck."

Why oh why did that send entire lightning bolts of happiness through her body? Because she was falling in love with him. She threw open the door, her smile faltering when Ashley climbed out of the passenger side.

"Hey, Mom," she called as Lacey stepped out on the patio to greet them.

"Hi. How did you two hook up?"

Clay threw a quick look at Ashley and ambled forward, his hands tucked in his jeans pockets. "I ran into Ashley in town, hanging some flyers, so I gave her a lift."

"Oh, good." She got a better look at Ashley's face, which was pale, and her expression was kind of worried. "Where's Meagan?"

"She, um, didn't go."

Clay reached her and Lacey waited for a quick hug or kiss; she'd gotten used to them over the past few weeks. But he seemed as uptight as Ashley.

"What's going on?"Lacey asked.

"Ashley was…" He gave her daughter another look, obviously opening the conversation for Ashley.

"Mom, I was with those kids you don't like and they got in trouble, but Clay knew about it and he got me home. I'm sorry."

Lacey didn't react, having trained for fourteen years not to be her own accusing mother but longing to know the whole story. "Are you all right?" she asked. "Did you get hurt?"

"Oh, no, not at all. And we did hang the rest of the fly-ers, so it wasn't a complete waste of a night."

Lacey nodded. "Go inside, Ashley. I want to talk to Clay."

"'Kay. G'night, Clay. And thanks a lot." She rushed up the walk and into the house.

"How bad was it?" she asked.

"Your instincts are right about those kids, but I think the night's events scared her enough that she won't hang out with them. You can get the details from her."

"I will." Her arms ached to reach out, but for some rea-son he wasn't coming to her, holding her, kissing her like always. "You okay?" she asked.

"Lacey, I..." He drew in a deep breath. "I have a lot of work to do before the presentation."

"I know."

"So, let me get focused on that. The minute I can, I'll call you and we'll start rehearsing."

Which was so not what she wanted him to say.

But how could she expect him to say anything when she was being just as coy and obtuse about her feelings? It was time to tell him the truth. But not here, not tonight.

"When can I..." Oh, God, she didn't want to sound desperate. But she was, at least a little. "When will you call?"

"Soon," he promised. He gave her a little smile, one that kicked her heart around in her chest until it felt a little black-and-blue. "You know I can't go too long with-out you."

Did she know that? "Same here." She couldn't help it; she took a step closer and put a hand on his chest, just to feel the strength and warmth of his body. She didn't expect to feel his heart hammering every bit as hard as hers.

"You sure you're okay?" she asked.

"I'm not sure of anything anymore, Strawberry." He gave her a tight smile and took one step back, denying her the chance to feel that beating heart. "But when I figure it out, you'll be the first to know."

Chapter Twenty-eight

A teenager would do this. A bad, out-of-control, irresponsible, consequences-be-damned teenager like Lacey hoped her daughter never would be. But Lacey was doing it anyway.

Tiptoeing out of the house at one-thirty in the morning, her sandals in hand to be sure she could escape in silence, Lacey turned the knob on the back door slowly to avoid the click. She kept one ear cocked in case Ashley or David sprang from the darkness and caught her sneaking out in the middle of the night to go have sex on the beach.

Outside, the still, silent night air, redolent with the hint of salt that permeated the whole island, sent a chill of anticipation over her skin. She pulled out her phone and texted Clay.

Made it—meet you in 5 min!

Okay, maybe the exclamation point was taking the teenager thing too far. But Lacey couldn't help it. She was *happy.*

He'd finally texted. After almost two days   two long, lonely, empty days—Clay had texted. Okay, it had been after midnight and probably a total booty call, but Lacey didn't care. She needed to see him. She needed to tell him how she felt and, damn it, she was going to do that before the presentation. No excuses.

Holding the straps of her sandals in one hand, she ran fast enough that the air lifted her hair and the breeze tickled right through the thin cotton sundress she wore with absolutely nothing underneath. Every cell in her body tingled in anticipation.

"Strawberry, you have it bad," she whispered to herself, holding the nickname close to her heart. She'd never taste a strawberry again in her life without thinking of him. She could certainly tell him *that* tonight, if not some of her more intense thoughts about him.

The thought sent a shiver through her, this time right down to her bare toes as she scampered over the sandy sidewalk. His truck was already parked in a shadowy section of the lot, the lights off. Even in the waning moonlight, she could see his profile as he leaned against the headrest, eyes closed. She slipped up to the passenger's side and lifted the handle.

"You asleep at the wheel, Clay?"

He looked at her, his eyes clear, his smile a little distant.

"Hey," he said simply, finally dropping his gaze to the open top buttons of her thin cotton dress, the angle, she was certain, making it clear she had no bra on. He lingered there for a minute, then reached to bring her all the way into the truck.

"You look…" He hesitated, and her heart hit triple time as she waited for what he would say. "Just like I imagined you."

"When were you imagining me?"

"Pretty much every minute I'm not with you." Still holding her hand, he pulled her closer and she fell right into him, leaning over the console, anxious to meet his mouth.

"I've missed you," she whispered.

"Yeah, me, too." He kissed her gently at first, but instantly reacted to her heat, opening his mouth, holding her head in just the right place, soft lips torturing and tempting and taking ownership of hers.

Already breathless, she broke the kiss. "How's the work going?"

"Done." He ran his thumb over her lip, studying it as though the shape of it fascinated him. "We can rehearse the presentation tomorrow and present the next day."

"Do you love it?" she asked.

"I love…"

Lacey held her breath, one word pounding in her head like a bass drum. You. You. *You*.

"I love a lot of things about it," he finished, sending a physical jolt of disappointment through her.

"But not everything?" she prodded.

"There are a few things I'd like to change. I'm nervous that we don't have those properties in hand but we're presenting as though we do."

"You thought that was the best way to go."

He nodded. "I still do. I'm just worried about a curveball being thrown at us."

"We'll handle it," she said, leaning in for another kiss. "Are we going to the beach?" she whispered, meaning, of course, the complete privacy of *their* beach on Barefoot Bay. That was where she wanted to tell him how she felt.

He shook his head. "Let's stay here."

More disappointment. But she covered it with a soft laugh. "Could get, um, steamy in this truck."

"Could." He fluttered some of her curls in his fingers, then dragged his hand down to the opening of her dress, his jaw slack as he slipped into the bodice and easily palmed her breast.

They both closed their eyes at the impact.

"I never stop wanting that," she murmured, arching her back so he knew how much she loved his hand on her.

He leaned over and kissed her again, taking his hand out and slipping it under the hem of her dress, up her bare thighs.

"Now I really feel like a teenager instead of the mother of one."

He didn't answer, but inched his hand back down, his eyes flickering with an expression she couldn't read. "Ever think about another one?"

The question threw her so completely she wasn't entirely sure she understood. "Another baby?"

"Yeah, do you ever think about having another one?"

Where had that come from? A low, slow warmth wound through her, completely different from the heat his hands and mouth had been causing. "Why?"

He shrugged, the gesture more casual than the look in his eye let on. "Just wondering. I mean, you're..."

"Getting older," she supplied with a quick laugh. "But not too old."

"That's not what I meant and you know it. I was thinking...."

Hope, unexpected and raw and real, clutched her chest. Did *he* want a baby? Had being with her, and being with Ashley, made him realize how wonderful family could be?

She simply couldn't fight the smile that pulled at her mouth. "If you want to know the truth, yes. I could see myself doing it all again. Maybe better next time."

"You're a great mother, Lacey."

"Better than my own, that much is true, but I could stand for some improvement. And maybe a little help from"—*the right man*—"a good father."

"David wants another, doesn't he?"

"He said so, but we don't really have any reason to discuss it. Who told you that?"

He hesitated, then shrugged. "I'm just observant."

He hadn't been around David that much, had he? "So what brought that question on?" Did she sound needy? Too bad. Maybe this was the opening she needed to tell him exactly how she felt.

I'm falling in love with you, Clay. Maybe he would say it first. Right now.

"I've been thinking about some things," he said, looking away toward the beach.

Her heart did a quick double-beat. "What kind of things?"

"Just things." He still wouldn't look at her, and she fought the urge to reach out for his chin and turn him, just to say *Look at me, damn it.*

But his attention was on the black horizon of the water. And he was silent just a second or two too long, and all that happiness and hope started slowly seeping away like her heart was a balloon and his silence the pin that pricked it.

"I think you'll like the final outcome of the plans," he finally said.

"The building plans." Because she had a feeling they were talking about two very different kinds of plans.

"Of course, the Casa Blanca plans."

She slowly dropped back to her seat as the rest of her air, and hope, slipped away. "I can't wait to see them. To present them."

"And after that..." He finally looked at her.

"After that we're building a resort," she said, a little too sharply. "A resort that you designed. With villas and a house." Right? *Right?*

Silence. Oh, God.

"*Aren't* we, Clay?" A bad, bad feeling slivered through her.

"Lacey, I think maybe you should take the project to another builder."

She just stared at him, any chance of taking a breath or firing back a response gone.

"I mean, you'll have what you need to get started and I'll have enough to sit for the exams. And I can consult from North Carolina if you—"

"Consult?" She practically choked the word. "You want to be a consultant?"

While she was sitting here rehearsing the first *I love you*? She grabbed the door, fighting the urge to flip the handle, shove it open, and run.

Instead she squeezed the metal and clenched her teeth. "If that's what you want to do, then fine."

"Lacey."

"What?" She turned on him. "What do you want me to say? Great idea, Clay! Be a consultant from a thousand miles away."

"I want you to have what you want."

"I want *you*." So much for subtle, perfectly timed, romantic admissions.

He took a slow breath. "I can't give you want you want."

"Meaning, what? You can't give me..." *Say it, say it, say it.* "Love."

The word hung like a cloying scent in the car. He swallowed and closed his eyes.

Shit. "I'm taking a walk," she said.

Without waiting for his response she slid onto the running board, then hit the asphalt, congratulating herself on not bolting away like a kid having a temper tantrum.

Instead she took long strides to the boardwalk, then down to the beach, making it about fifty feet before he reached her side and took her arm.

"Lacey, please. This is better for both of us."

"Is it? Well, sorry, I'll be the judge of what's better for me and I can tell you that your going back to North Carolina is not better for me. And David Fox is not better for me. No one is better for me than you."

"Are you sure?" He took her wrist to pull her closer, but she yanked herself out of his grip.

"What do I need to say to convince you? I'm not in love with him. I'm...I'm not interested in having another child with him, no matter what he says or anyone else says."

"I want you to be certain of that, because I can't give you that."

"I never said I wanted a child."

"I can't give you all the things you want. I can't give you the kind of love you deserve. I'm not—I don't have that in me. I have…"

"I know what you have," she said. "Issues. Pain. A hurtful breakup. Problems. It's called life, Clay. And you're using them as…" She laughed softly, the irony of it all hitting her so hard it might be funny if it weren't her heart that was breaking. "Excuses. You're just using your dad and your hurt as excuses not to fall in love, not to have a family, not to have a *life*."

He turned toward the water, away from her. "Maybe I am."

"Well, I'm not," she said, grabbing his arms to make him face her, the power of what she wanted to say and why she wanted to say it nearly rocking her backward. "I'm not afraid anymore. I'm not hiding behind excuses or old hurts." She took a slow, deep breath and squeezed his arms. "I'm falling in love with you."

"Lacey…" But his voice trailed off into silence.

"I'm waiting." She smiled. "And not for you to say the same thing. I'm waiting for some kind of pain to consume me because I know you're *not* going to say it."

Searching her face, he stayed silent. Miserably, woefully silent.

"But that's okay," she said, a weird brightness almost choking her. "That's okay because I feel the pain and the love and the need." She hammered her chest. "I *feel* it right here."

"Then you're really lucky." He took her fist and placed it on his chest. "You know what I feel there, Lacey?"

She shook her head.

"Numb."

Numb. Not the four-letter word she was hoping to hear. "Maybe you're just asleep," she said. "Maybe someone or something needs to shake your heart awake."

Without waiting for him to answer she walked away, the sand cold on her feet, vaguely aware of a buzzing in her head. No, that was his phone.

"Is someone texting you?" she asked. Now? At two in the morning?

He pulled it out, glanced at the screen, his eyes widening so slightly that someone who didn't know his every expression might not notice. But she noticed. He didn't read the text, just stuffed the phone back into his pocket.

When he looked up his entire expression had changed. His eyes were distant, and his brain somewhere else. Who had texted him? That wisp of jealousy she'd felt the other day wrapped around her chest. And squeezed.

Whoever it was had just taken him far, far away from a very important conversation. One she suddenly didn't want to have anymore.

She climbed into the truck, slipped on her shoes, and swallowed hard against the lump in her throat. She would not let him see her cry. When he didn't open the driver's door, she checked the side-view mirror to see what he was doing.

Reading the text. Standing frozen in the moonlight, reading the words someone had sent him, running a hand through his hair, looking up at the sky and closing his eyes like someone had just stabbed him. The way he'd looked when he'd gotten off the phone with Darcie the other day. When he'd teared up and wouldn't tell her why.

He stayed behind the truck for a good two minutes,

long enough for her to start to question everything she knew about him.

Who was texting? Why wouldn't he tell her? Was this text from...

Jayna. The name banged around her brain. Could he be talking to his ex? Still in love with her? Was that why he was numb? Unable to take the next step because maybe he thought there was still a chance with her?

Had he lied about talking to his sister that afternoon? Had he been talking to his ex?

He got in, his expression more frozen than before. They drove the two blocks to her parents' house in a thick silence, the echo of her ugly thoughts all she could hear in her head.

"Look, Clay," she said as he pulled the truck up to the curb. "The zoning presentation is in two days. Let's stay focused on that and when it's over we'll figure out where we go from here, whether it's to North Carolina or..."

"I'm going home." He muttered the words. "I have to."

She had no answer to that, and, honestly, it was obvious he didn't want an argument. He was going home after this presentation.

"I'll walk you to the door." He flipped his phone onto the console and got out.

Her gaze cut to the phone. Her finger itched. Her brain hummed. Her heart rolled around.

With a lightning-quick move she touched the screen, making it light up. Then she touched it again to read the list of texts, the top name the most recent.

Jayna Walker

Oh, *God.*

He opened her door and she turned guiltily from the

phone, inching forward so he wouldn't see the light of the screen in the car. She took a minute to gather her bag, and her wits, and slowly stepped down, certain she hadn't been caught.

Then she saw the moisture in his eyes. Apparently, there was a woman in this world who could make him cry. And it wasn't Lacey Armstrong.

"I want to do the presentation alone," she said.

"What?"

"Just let me make the presentation to the zoning committee on my own."

She waited for the argument, the "Why would you do that?" fight. She wouldn't admit she'd just peeked at who'd texted him, but—

"Okay."

Okay. *Okay*? Had two syllables ever stabbed so deeply? What could she say? *You're supposed to say no!*

"Okay," she repeated, grateful that the word even found its way through her pain-thickened throat.

He didn't respond, his eyes still distant. He was a million miles away—with Jayna.

"I'll get the materials tomorrow morning," she somehow managed to say. "Will you..."

"I'll leave the key behind the mailbox."

In other words, he'd be gone by tomorrow.

"Good-bye, Clay." She opened the kitchen door and stepped inside as fast as she could move, with no regard for waking David or Ashley.

When she closed the door and leaned her head against it, she took a deep breath, but all that came out of her was a low, slow, soul-cracking, heart-wrenching sob.

"Mom?"

She whipped around to see Ashley at the kitchen table drinking a glass of milk, waiting for her like a mother waits for a wayward teenager who's stolen away in the middle of the night. For a moment, Lacey braced herself for the inevitable disapproval, hearing her mother's voice in her head.

I told you he was scum.

I warned you about that boy.

You never pick the right ones.

"What's the matter, Mom?" Ashley stood slowly, her chair scraping over the tile floor, echoing loudly in the silent house.

"It's Clay. He's leaving."

Ashley's hand flew to her mouth. "Oh, no! I'm sorry!"

"It's not your fault, honey."

"But, Mom..." Her face looked stricken as she came around the table, reaching out. "You're crying!"

"I know you hate when I cry, Ash. I'm sorry. I-I just..." The sob caught in her throat, embarrassing her. "I feel so stupid."

"You're not stupid!"

She swiped her eyes, choking a dry laugh. "Honey, when you hand yourself over to a guy and give him everything and he dumps you, you are officially too stupid to deserve happiness."

Ashley hugged her close, squeezing harder than Lacey could remember. "You're not stupid, Mom. And you do deserve happiness."

"Yes, I do, baby. Yes, I do." The problem was she'd just thrown it away. And he hadn't even put up a fight.

Chapter Twenty-nine

Why are we waiting?" Tessa asked, leaning against the kitchen counter impatiently. "He said he was blowing out of town, so let's just go get the stuff and start helping you rehearse."

Lacey shook her head. "I don't want to run into him."

"I do," Zoe said. "I want to run *over* him with that big ol' Jeep, actually, then spit on his broken bones and tell him what I think of cheaters and liars."

"He didn't cheat," Lacey said quietly. "We weren't official. I let my imagination run away with me."

"Details," Zoe shot back.

"Excuses," Tessa added. "Where's David, by the way?"

"I let him take Ashley cave diving."

"You what?" Tessa slammed down her coffee cup hard enough to splash the granite. "I thought you were morally, ethically, and parentally opposed to that."

"They got me at a weak moment, and it's really a beginner's cave. I trust him, and I need the day to rehearse and prepare."

And lick my wounds.

"Honestly," she added, "I'm not afraid of him letting her swim tethered in a cave, but I'm scared to death she's going to tell him Clay had me in tears last night, and now David's going to drag the whole story out of her and think he has a chance with me."

"Does he?" Tessa asked.

"Not even a small one."

"Then come on, Lacey, let's go," Tessa insisted. "So what if you see Clay? You know where he stands now."

"He stands with his father's wife." Zoe made a face. "Eww."

Lacey grabbed her purse. "You're right. Let's go."

Zoe drove while Lacey sat in the front and tried not to summon memories from places she'd been with Clay. When they pulled into the parking lot of Hibiscus Court, she couldn't resist looking at his empty parking spot, remembering a few hot kisses in his truck before they stumbled into his apartment, and into his bed.

Memories, all bittersweet memories now.

"See? Coast is clear." Zoe took the space and turned off the ignition, patting Lacey's leg. "You feel better or worse knowing he's not here?"

"I just feel empty."

At his unit, no one answered the knock. She felt even emptier when she opened the door using the key he'd hidden and found exactly what he'd promised: the boards and 3-D model of the resort all neatly lined up on the kitchen table and counter. Everything else—the

CAD system, the laptops, even the drafting table—was gone.

But her stomach turned into a hollow pit when she walked down the hall to the bedroom and saw the open closet door with nothing but hangers inside. The bed was partially made, the comforter sliding off, the sheets pulled up like no one had slept there. In the bathroom a dry towel hung over the shower door, but there was no other evidence that a man had been living here for weeks.

Or that a couple had turned it into a love nest.

"Sucks, doesn't it?" Zoe said, standing in the doorway.

Lacey turned to her, aware that Tessa was already at work taking the first load of stuff to the car.

"What happened?" she asked Zoe.

"You fell in love with the wrong guy, Lace. Oldest story in the book."

"Is that what happened with you and Oliver?"

She paled slightly. "'Fraid so." Instantly Zoe turned back toward the living room. "I'll get the rest of these boards. You say your last good-byes to the fond memory of all those life-changing orgasms you had in that bed."

When she heard Zoe go out the front door, Lacey let out a long, pained breath and sat on the corner of the bed. "They did change my life," she said to herself. "You helped me realize what I was capable of, Clay Walker. So I'm eternally grateful."

She blew a kiss to the pillow and picked up the comforter out of habit. As she pulled it over the sheets, her foot tapped something tucked beneath the bed.

The drawings. Her heart practically launched into her throat.

He'd left the drawings behind.

Slowly she eased out a roll of paper, glancing over her shoulder to see if the others had come back yet. Still alone, she rolled the rubber band off and started to spread one of the drawings out on the bed.

Before it was fully open, her legs felt unnaturally heavy, like she'd had a half of bottle of wine and tried to stand suddenly. She flattened the paper, instantly recognizing his sure hand drawing their favorite beach, and the penciled outline of Lacey, lying back on the sand, a dress falling open, her breasts partially exposed.

Memories of things that haven't happened yet.

She slid the picture to the side and looked at the next one. "Oh my God," she whispered, stunned by the tableau of Lacey and Clay in the water. They were naked, entwined, her backside tucked into his front, her head thrown back as he captured the moment she'd had one of those *life-changing orgasms.*

That particular moment had most certainly happened. It was burned into her personal memory bank.

She was almost afraid to look at the next one.

It was the drawing of Ashley holding a hammer. But Clay was in this picture, too, holding the wood that Ashley nailed. Building the house together?

I expect her to help build the house, don't you?

"What are you looking at?" Zoe asked from the living room.

"I'm not sure."

"More stuff for the presentation?" Tessa walked into the room and stopped. "Hey, is that Ashley? That's good."

Lacey hesitated to slide the picture away, not sure she could take another unfulfilled fantasy of Clay's. "He told me once that he likes to visualize things, then draw them. That's how he gets them to happen."

Zoe came up next to her. "Whoa, who knew? He really *does* have a magic drafting tool."

"So he was hoping for a moment like that with Ashley?" Tessa asked. "That doesn't seem like a man who would jettison at the mention of a commitment."

"What else is there?" Zoe asked. "Let's see the rest."

Lacey moved one picture and smoothed out the next.

Tessa gasped. Zoe let out a soft grunt of disbelief.

And Lacey felt her legs buckle enough to kneel down in front of the bed.

"That's quite the imagination he's got there," Zoe said.

"No kidding," Tessa agreed. "Looks an awful lot like a woman and man getting married at the water's edge to me."

"A woman with curly reddish blonde hair," Zoe noted. "And, oh my God, is that the mayor dude who is marrying you two?"

It was hard to tell because something had dripped right over Sam Lennox's face and smeared the pencil. A tear?

Had Clay *cried* when he'd drawn them getting married?

"And look at the three bridesmaids." Tessa pointed to the row of women Clay had drawn next to the bride and groom.

"Oh, I look so pretty!" Zoe dropped to her knees next to Lacey. "I knew I loved this guy."

"There's one more, Lace." Tessa said gently. "Let's see it."

She looked up. "I'm scared."

"Oh, come on," Zoe said, dragging the sheet away. "First comes love, then comes marriage, then comes—"

Lacey, nude, joyful, laughing—and at least eight months pregnant.

Another tear fell, but this time it was Lacey's. Tessa put her hand on Lacey's shoulder and squeezed. "Maybe we misjudged him."

She rolled the edge of the page, silently closing up the sketch that revealed what really was going on in Clay Walker's fruitful imagination.

But she only heard one word.

Okay.

"What are you going to do, Lace?" Zoe asked.

"I'll save these. I've lost a lot of very real memories in the past few months. It'll be nice to have some new ones, even if they never happened."

"I wonder why he left them," Tessa said.

"They weren't important enough for him to take." Lacey rolled up the wedding picture. "They were just meaningless drawings."

"Maybe he wanted you to find them," Zoe said. "Maybe they're not meaningless at all."

Lacey smiled at her friend, but she knew the truth. And, damn, it hurt.

Fourteen hours after he left Mimosa Key, Clay barreled into the parking lot of Duke Raleigh Hospital and headed straight to the ICU. Darcie was waiting with a quick hug and a soft push through the double doors, not giving him a chance to even brace for whatever waited on the other side. The last time he'd seen C-dub . . .

A man takes what a man wants. Didn't I teach you anything?

His father's words still echoed, and still stung. A man doesn't *take* his son's woman.

"Go ahead, Clay." Next to him Darcie gave his hand a squeeze, sensing his hesitation. "They won't let us both in there at the same time because there's a limit of two people."

So Jayna was in there. Of course. She'd been by his side since the stroke last night, texting updates to everyone, including Clay.

"He's in the first room on the right," Darcie added.

He nodded, then walked down the wide hall, assaulted by the bitter smell of antiseptic. Turning to the glass doors, he froze at the sight of his father, who looked blanched and—dead. Ice trickled through his veins, so cold it stole his breath.

Jayna looked up as he entered, her eyes red from sleeplessness and tears. She didn't speak or smile, just looked at him.

"He'll be happy you're here."

Clay doubted that, but he slowly approached the other side of the bed, aware of the monitors softly beeping to prove that his father was, indeed, still alive, and breathing through the tubes coming out of his nose. "Will he even know?"

"He knows," she said.

Clay leaned closer, examining the ashen pallor of his father's face and noticing that the left side seemed to droop.

"Is he conscious at all?" Clay asked.

"They're saying he's in a comatose state, but I know he hears us. Take his hand so he knows you're here."

Dad's right hand rested at his side, completely still, but Clay made no move to touch him.

For a moment he imagined Lacey here. Even the thought gave him a surprising comfort, and an ache. If she were here, she'd tell him to...

Take the old man's hand, of course.

Wasn't that why he hadn't told her his father had had a stroke last night? Because she would tell him he had to forgive him, and he refused?

Still, he closed his fingers over older, thicker ones. A hand that had never been raised in anger, he mused. No, this man had other ways to inflict pain.

"Talk to him, Clay," Jayna said. When he didn't immediately answer, she added, "See what happens."

He took a deep breath. "Hey, Dad."

Jayna looked pointedly at the hand Clay held. "I think it's really hard for him to react, but if you talk, I swear you'll feel him squeeze your hand. Right, C-dub?"

His father's hand remained still.

"See?" She brightened. "Did you feel that?"

Clay didn't have the heart to tell her he didn't feel a thing.

She wet her lips, looking down at the hand that held her husband's, then back to Clay. "This might be a good time to tell him something important. Anything."

Like what? *Hey, old man, you're forgiven for being the biggest asshole on the face of the earth. For being insecure and miserable, and jealous of your own son.*

"Like I told him that Elliott drank out of his sippy cup all by himself this morning." Jayna's singsong voice yanked Clay out of his mental musings, giving him a second of emotional whiplash.

"And he squeezed my hand when I mentioned Elliott's name."

Of course he did. He wasn't competing with Elliott—yet.

Clay cleared his throat, repositioned his hand, and leaned closer, no words ready.

"I told him what you did for me." Jayna whispered the confession. "He knows that you did that to help me, and to help him. And, Clay, he only continued to blame you because it made him feel less guilty. You know that, don't you?"

Clay shrugged, ignoring the desperation in her voice. "Kind of moot, now."

Jayna stood slowly, her eyes on her husband. "Why don't you talk to him privately?"

She leaned all the way over and kissed Dad's head, closing her eyes and gently stroking his white hair. Clay stared at the sight, struck by the profound tenderness of the gesture.

She loved the old man. Really, truly loved him.

While Clay, his own flesh and blood, just hated him.

"I'll be back, sweetheart," she whispered. "Listen to Clay. He wants to tell you something important."

What?

Jayna left the room, closing the door with a decisive click, leaving him with the steady beep of life support and his father's limp hand.

Still he didn't speak. The words were there, hovering in his head, on the proverbial tip of his tongue.

I forgive you, Dad.

Why couldn't he say it? Because he didn't forgive him. And if he didn't forgive him, then what did that make Clay? Pathetic, harboring a grudge over a woman who, in the scheme of things, didn't matter. It made him small and guarded and…unable to love, no matter how much he really wanted to.

Unable to love.

Was it possible that this man right here held the key to Clay's deadened heart? No, Clay held it. He just didn't want to turn that key and let Lacey in.

Lacey.

Suddenly he knew what he wanted to say to his father.

"I met a woman, Dad." He cleared his throat again, and powered on. "I met *the* woman." He closed his eyes and pictured Lacey in all the ways he remembered her, and all the ways he'd secretly fantasized about her. Lacey, his lover. Lacey, his partner. Lacey, his…wife.

"She's really something, too." What was it about her he most wanted to tell his father? "She's got a heart like no one I've ever met before. She's determined and kind and smart, and she has a teenage daughter who's a really good kid hidden in a really tough shell." He knew that kid. He'd *been* that kid. "Dad?"

Still no reaction. Dad wasn't hearing this, Clay thought. But that didn't stop him from wanting to say it all.

"I'm in love with her."

Great. He could tell his dad, but not Lacey. What the hell? But he'd fix that. First he had to fix this. No, first he had to fix *himself.*

"I designed something for her. A resort in this place called Mimosa Key. It's down in Flor—"

The slightest pressure squeezed his hand. Clay looked down at the thick fingers around his, stunned. Had his father just reacted, or was that merely an unconscious twitch?

"Dad?"

Nothing. Okay. A mistake. "Anyway, I designed a resort for her and it's going to be—"

This time the squeeze was real and one of the monitors kicked up in speed. Clay looked at the screens, pinpointing the one that had just changed its tune. The heart. His heart rate was up.

"Dad, can you hear me?"

Should he call someone? He inched closer, holding tight to his father's hand.

"So, this project," he said, sticking with the subject because that was what got the reaction. "We're calling it Casa Blanca, and I gave it a really strong Henri Post influence. You'd like it."

Another firm squeeze and the slightest flutter behind his lids. Dad was definitely awake, and reacting to the name of his favorite French architect.

"Do you want me to get the doc?" he asked.

Nothing.

"Do you want me to keep talking?"

Nothing.

"Should I get Jayna? Are you waking up?" Frustration mounted when there was no reaction. "Is there something you want to say, Dad?"

The beep jumped another notch and his hand constricted. Hard.

Clay waited, his breathing as measured and slow as his father's. "Dad?"

Nothing.

"Is it about the building?"

A squeeze. Seriously? At a time like this he wanted to dole out architectural advice? He didn't want to clear the air and put their messy past behind them?

Clay leaned on the bed rail and threaded his fingers through his father's hand.

"The project," he said, getting a squeeze in return. "Is a resort on the beach." Another squeeze. "I'll be perfectly honest: She was looking for you when she accidentally contacted me."

Squeeze. Squeeze. Squeeze. *Beeeeep.*

"Dad, are you familiar with this property?"

Under closed lids, his father's eyes flickered back and forth and Clay took it as a yes.

"Is there something you want to tell me?"

More flickering, squeezing, and beeping.

"Did you—"

The door flew open. "Clay, what's going on?" Behind Jayna a nurse ran in, pushing her aside, flying to the bed.

"Out! Everyone out!"

Clay dropped his father's hand and stepped away from the bed. "Is he okay?"

"He's having another stroke. We need a doctor. Everyone out of here!"

Jayna grabbed his arm and yanked him to the door, everything moving in slow motion. Clay's head felt thick with grief and guilt. Had he brought the stroke on? By talking about architecture and resorts and—

Then he knew. He knew exactly what had brought that on. Goddamn it, C-dub, *why*?

From the other side of the glass he stared at the old man and hoped to God he'd get a chance to ask him that question.

Chapter Thirty

⌒

Lacey finished the last section of the presentation with her voice loud and clear so Zoe could hear it from the kitchen, where she was already opening a celebratory bottle of wine.

"And that's why the Mimosa Key Town Council should vote to amend the zoning restrictions in Barefoot Bay and welcome the potential of Casa Blanca."

Tessa clapped, Zoe hooted, but Lacey just shook her head.

"What?" Tessa said. "You were awesome, confident, unstoppable."

"Thanks, but—"

"It's wine o'clock!" Zoe came in with a bottle and three glasses on a tray. "Well, four. But we can officially drink now."

"In a second," Lacey said. "I need a new name for this place."

"For the resort?" The question was asked in unison, and with matching disbelief.

"It's bothering me here," Lacey said, tapping her chest. "It's our name, mine and Clay's. And if..." It hurt to say it, but she had to be true to herself. "If he's not there, then I don't want to call it Casa Blanca. It's too personal."

"But it's perfect for the design."

"I know, Tessa, but..." She already had the eraser out and walked to the first easel to eliminate the words that were bothering her so much. "I'm just not going to call it anything. The right name will come to me."

Her cell phone jangled and she cursed the way her heart kicked up, forcing herself to act as if she wasn't even thinking it could be Clay.

Zoe snagged the phone from the end table and checked out the screen. "Sorry, it's just Ashley."

Lacey rolled her eyes. "Am I that obvious?"

"Brutally so," Zoe said. "Here. Find out how the cave adventure is going. Maybe David drowned."

"Zoe." Lacey laughed softly and took the phone. "Hey, honey. How's it going?"

"It's David."

Something in his voice. Something bad. "What's the matter?"

"There's been an accident, Lacey." His voice cracked, and so did Lacey's entire being.

"What kind of accident?" She could barely hear him; her pulse beat a deafening thump in her head. "David, what happened?"

Both of the girls were at her side instantly, squeezing her, trying to listen.

"She hit her head."

"What? Is she okay?"

"She's in the hospital, Lacey."

Blood rushed, limbs weakened, and her chest exploded in an agonizing burst of disbelief. Not Ashley. Please, God, not Ashley. Anyone but Ashley. Please. "Please tell me she's okay." *Please*.

"She's unconscious, but alive."

Alive? There was a chance she wouldn't be? "Oh my God, David."

Tessa grabbed the phone. "Where are you, David? Tell me exactly how to get there."

Words wouldn't form. Nothing could come out of Lacey's mouth except shuddering breaths while Zoe calmed her and Tessa got them all into the Jeep to drive wherever David had told Tessa to go.

Zoe swore softly, putting Lacey's seat belt on. "Wait. Your insurance forms. ID. You're going to need that stuff at the hospital."

"My handbag's on the kitchen table and the insurance card is in my wallet."

"Got it. Be right back."

She had started climbing out when Lacey grabbed her arm. "Wait, Zoe. In Ashley's room. Get her unicorn."

"Good thinking, Mom."

"What else did he say?" she asked Tessa when Zoe jogged away.

"Just that she's unconscious. She hit her head on a low ceiling in the cave, and she's breathing on her own, but unconscious."

Everything shook uncontrollably. Her body, her guts, her knees literally knocking as Zoe climbed back in and wrapped her arms around Lacey, cooing soft words to calm her.

"I've got the hospital programmed into the GPS," Tessa said. "Hang on, girls. We'll be there in a couple hours."

"A couple of hours!" Lacey wailed. "What if she—"

"Shhh." Zoe squeezed her. "Just hold on and let's get there."

She couldn't do anything but pray and cry and curse herself for backing down on the cave diving issue. They drove in silence up the interstate.

Tessa had barely reached the ER entrance when Lacey threw herself out of the Jeep and started running toward the doors. Zoe was next to her in a second, taking control, asking the questions Lacey couldn't, calmly following the orders to get them to Ashley.

She saw David first. He sat in a waiting room with his head in his hands, still wearing a bathing suit and a T-shirt and a look of red-eyed anguish, so miserable looking that the worst imaginable thought slammed into her head and she gave voice to it.

"Ashley's dead."

Before he answered a nurse whisked into the room. "Are you Ashley's mother?"

Blood thrummed and a low, guttural grunt of acknowledgment came from her chest.

"Come with me," the nurse said. "Are you related?" she asked Zoe, who shook her head. "Stay here with him, then."

"I'm her father," David said, coming with them.

"Actually"—Lacey held up a hand to stop him—"I want to see her alone."

The nurse pushed her through double doors.

"Please, tell me, is she—"

"Oh, yes, she's awake. Has been for a while. She hasn't sustained brain damage, and that's what we've been watching for. Definitely a concussion, though. She's woozy and on some pain meds. It was quite a serious blow, but we think a monstrous headache will be the worst of it. Here she is."

Lacey took a deep breath as she entered the room, letting it out as a soft cry at the sight of Ashley, pale and thin and tiny in a hospital bed with tubes in her arms, a bandage on her head, her eyes closed.

"Go easy, Mom," the nurse warned.

Lacey nodded, forcing herself to slow her steps as she approached the bed. She touched Ashley's shoulder and her eyes opened.

Thank you, God. Thank you.

"Hey, Princess Pot-Pie." Lacey managed not to sob, but the words were barely a whisper.

"Mommy."

Lacy sucked back tears, willing herself to be strong.

"Please don't be mad."

"I'm not mad, honey. I'm just so grateful you're alive. I won't even say I told you so. How do you feel?" she asked as she tucked the uni into bed beside her beautiful daughter. Ashley smiled and pulled the uni closer.

"I'm okay. My head hurts, but they told me I knew my name and my birthday and my favorite color."

"What is it?"

"Lime green. Mommy, I'm sorry." She started to cry.

"Shhh." Lacey stroked her cheek, her chin, her quivering lips. "You don't have to be sorry."

"I shouldn't have done it."

"I gave you permission to go, angel. It's not like you sneaked away."

"But it's my fault. God's punishing me."

Lacey put her hand on Ashley's head. She *wasn't* making sense. Could there be damage they hadn't diagnosed? "No, not now, baby. Save your strength. We have to get you home and get you all better."

Ashley closed her eyes. "I made Clay leave you."

Lacey leaned in, not at all sure she understood. "What are you talking about?"

"I told Clay. That night he got me at the football field I didn't tell you everything." Tears streamed down her face.

"You told him what, baby?"

"That we'd be a family if he'd just leave."

Lacey stared at her, processing the words, trying to understand. "That's not why he left, Ashley."

Jayna had texted him at two in the morning. He said he wanted to go back to North Carolina. Ashley couldn't take the blame for that, no matter what she'd told him.

"I basically told him to leave, and he was being so nice." She squeezed her eyes. "He's really nice, Mom."

"Whatever you did or said couldn't make him leave or stay," Lacey assured her. "All you need to worry about is getting better. That's all."

"But I think he really loves you."

Lacey stroked her head, determined not to let Ashley's innocent—and mistaken—ideas make her sicker. "Just close your eyes, Ash. We'll talk later."

"I told Dad and he said..."

Lacey waited, curious whether David was behind this confession. Maybe he was all too happy to get rid of the competition.

"Dad said he should leave now and let you have your life." Ashley's voice cracked. "I don't want him to leave, Mom, but I want you to be happy."

"I *will* be happy when the doctors say you are one hundred percent healed. Sleep." Lacey kissed Ashley's forehead, keeping her lips on her daughter's silky hair. "This is no time to deal with the heavy stuff. Rest." She curled her hands around Ashley's much narrower fingers. "I love you so much, Ashley."

"I love you, too, Mom. I'm so sorry I screwed up."

"Honey, you didn't screw up. Please, rest now."

Ashley closed her eyes and breathed the sigh of a child with a clear conscience. In a few minutes she slept, and Lacey returned to the waiting room to update Tessa and Zoe, then headed outside, where David was getting air.

He stood braced against a waist-high brick wall, his face to the sun, his eyes closed.

"Whatever you have to say, you're right," he said without looking at her. "I screwed up royally."

"This is not about you," she said. "She's going to be fine, and that's all that matters. I let her go and you had an accident. I can't hate you for that."

"But you hate me for other things."

She sighed. "David, I don't hate you at all."

"I got in the way of you and Clay."

"No, and neither did Ashley. I appreciate how you and Ashley want to take the blame, but there's none to go around." At least not with these two.

"What did the doctor tell you?" he asked.

"I haven't seen the doctor yet, but the nurse seems to think she'll be fine. We'll monitor her. And she'll have an excuse for every C in math for the whole first semester of high school."

He smiled, hope in his eyes. "Listen, Lacey, I have to tell you something."

"Ashley said you're leaving."

He angled his head in acknowledgment. "I'll be on a flight to Papua, New Guinea, in four hours."

"Really? That's so..." *Far. Soon.* "Not a surprise," she said flatly.

"A few weeks ago I would have taken that response as hope that we could have a future."

"We don't. At least not like you first painted it when you got here."

"I'm trying to tell you I owe you an apology," David said.

She acknowledged his words with a nod. "Accepted, but I'm not going to hold this or the last fourteen years against you. Honestly."

"What I'm sorry for is not just the last fourteen years, because I've told you I regret them every minute I get to know Ashley more. And the way she's accepted me, when any other kid would resent me..." He sighed heavily. "She's amazing."

Lacey smiled, pride welling up in her chest. "Yes, she is, David, and I'm glad you finally know that."

He took a step closer, his eyes moist, struggling to swallow. "What I'm sorry for is how I reacted when you told me you were pregnant."

She didn't respond, leaning against the sun warmed bricks, the adrenaline and fear dumping out of her, leaving her muscles weak. Including her heart. That might be the weakest muscle of all.

Because she'd never planned to forgive David for that.

For not marrying her, for disappearing, even for showing up now and upsetting an already shaky apple cart, yes. Forgiven. But for pressing to terminate the pregnancy? That seemed unforgivable.

He searched her face as if he could read her thoughts.

"I have no excuse," he finally said. "I mean, I was pretty young, but you were younger. I was restless and unsettled, but you hadn't even graduated. I was scared to be a parent, and you were the one who had to carry and raise her." His voice cracked. "Please, Lace. Forgive me."

She managed to blink without shedding the tears that welled. "It's history."

His expression softened with relief. "Thank you." He reached out for her hand, squeezing it. "Thank you."

All she could do was nod, and wait for the pressure on her chest to ease. Surprisingly, the weight lifted quickly. Forgiveness weighed less than blame.

"You are always welcome in Ashley's life, David," she said.

"Good," he replied. "Because I have an idea how I can help you."

She frowned. "Help how?"

"I'd like to invest in your resort. No ownership, no ties. Just an investment that you can pay back when the resort starts making money."

"I-I don't know what to say, but thank you."

"And, Lacey, I don't know who has this kind of pull, but I can't find out who bought those properties, and God knows I've tried to grease some palms. But eventually the identity of the buyer will be revealed and you need to buy it back. That'll be my investment; I'll pay for those lots no matter what they ask."

"Oh, David, really. Thank you." She accepted the embrace he offered, leaning on his shoulder for a moment. "Thank you."

"And one more thing." He put his hands on her shoulders. "I've been a lousy father, but you are a remarkable mother."

"Thanks." She leaned back to look at him. "Did Ashley tell you she said something to Clay? Something she thinks made him leave?"

"She did, but—"

"But what?"

He gave her shoulders a squeeze. "I think he'll be back."

She cursed the hope that coiled through her. "I don't."

"Well, I saw the way he looked at you, Lace. And that man might not know it, but he's in love."

Maybe he was, but not with her. Still, when David left to say good-bye to Ashley, Lacey checked her phone messages, just in case David was right.

Nothing.

So the right guy didn't get the girl, and neither did the wrong guy.

Chapter Thirty-one

M rs. Walker?"

Clay looked up when the neurologist pushed open the waiting-room doors and scanned the small group on the other side, no doubt looking for an older woman. Sorry, doc. Meet the Dysfunctionals.

Jayna stood. "I'm his wife."

To his credit, the doctor didn't show any reaction. "And which one of you is Clay?"

Clay lifted a hand but didn't jump out of his seat. The doctor turned to him and gestured. "Your father would like to speak with you."

"He can talk?" Jayna exclaimed.

"A bit. The second stroke, which wasn't nearly as severe as the first, actually stimulated some activity and brought him out of the coma. I'm going to explain all that to you in a moment, ma'am, but your husband is quite forceful, even after two strokes. He was adamant about talking to Clay, and I see no reason to deny him that."

Clay finally stood. "I'll talk to him." Because the son of a bitch had a lot of explaining to do.

"Clay." Darcie gave him a harsh look, fully aware of what was going on. She'd already used her laptop to confirm what Clay suspected, and they'd been hard at work trying to fix things while the docs tried to fix their father. "Be gentle."

That earned an angry flash from the neurologist. "If you have any other intentions, son, don't you dare go into that room."

"I have no intentions other than to listen to what he has to say." And get his shaky signature. But the doc didn't need to know that.

He headed down the hall with slow, deliberate steps, not in any huge rush now that he'd gotten up here and found out what the old man was really made of. Not that he hadn't already known, but this latest stunt?

Unbelievable.

So C-dub wanted to confess, beg forgiveness, remind Clay that everything he'd ever done was out of fatherly love and driving ambition to build a business. Blah, blah, blah. *Just sign the papers and I'm out.*

The ICU room was quiet again, the beeping machines tapping out a softer, more stable rhythm, and his father's eyes were open. Not focused, but open.

For a moment Clay thought he might be dead. But the easy rise of his chest proved him wrong.

Clay approached the bed slowly, leaning over so C-dub could see him.

"Two strokes," Dad said through clenched teeth, his lips not even moving.

"One more and you're out," Clay said gently. "So take it easy, old guy."

Dark blue eyes shifted toward Clay, but his father's head didn't move. "I'm not going to die."

"I don't think anyone's worried about that. Just how nasty you're going to be when you get home is the real concern."

"Not going to be nasty anymore."

Clay snorted. "Then why'd you buy those two properties in Barefoot Bay?"

"I liked the land."

What the *hell*? "That gave you the right to undermine the whole project?" Clay worked to modulate his voice and keep the nurses at bay.

"I didn't know I was undermining you," his father said through a stiff jaw. "My office got a call about the project and I sent someone down to look at it. Standard procedure."

Lacey had mentioned that she'd called Walker Architecture after he'd left her on the beach the day they met. Of course that phone call would have set some exploratory wheels in process.

"The land looked good," his father said. "And my pre-project guys said there were two lots available for purchase. I bought 'em. You know we'd never put the name of a company on a purchase like that. It's a red flag to others."

The angry fist in his chest loosened its grip. "You didn't know I was involved?"

"I didn't, Clay. But I found out later you were competing

for the project and…" He closed his eyes, a soft grunt of pain drawing Clay closer.

"And what?"

"That's when I had that damn TIA that started all this."

The first mini-stroke? "Never knew you to suffer from guilt pangs."

"I was driving home to call you when it happened. I wanted to tell you, but"—a hint of a smile crossed his lips—"I got scared, Clay."

"Scared of what?"

"I knew you'd never believe me. You'd think I was out to screw you again. You'd hate me more."

Clay couldn't deny that, so he just stayed silent, the sound of his father's steady heartbeat on a monitor the only noise in the room.

"I have to tell you, son, Jayna has taught me about what it means to be a parent."

Clay gave a dry laugh. "The irony in that statement is damn near incalculable."

"Don't I know it. But I'm afraid I'll never have a chance to make it up to you," Dad admitted on a sad sigh.

"Darcie drew up an ad hoc contract to give me the land. Sign it and we're good."

"I will." He blinked back some moisture that on any other man might have been a tear. But this was C-dub, so Clay would bet it was just a bit of garden-variety watery eyes. "But, son, I don't want to die knowing you still hate me."

"You aren't dying." *God, I hope not.* "So don't sweat it."

"Clay, hold my hand."

He took the old man's hand and got a gentle squeeze.

"Only one thing matters, son."

What? Winning the game? Having the most toys? The youngest, prettiest wife, the biggest bank account, the most famous name? He knew what mattered to C-dub, but he came closer anyway. "What's that, Dad?"

"I love you, Clayton Walker." A single tear rolled slowly down his father's cheek, meandering to the side until it fell on the hospital pillow. "I love you."

Dad's heart monitor sped up just a little, eerily matching what was going on in Clay's chest. He couldn't remember the last time his father had said those words.

"Bring me those papers," C-dub ordered. "So I can prove it to you."

Clay stepped away, toward the door, turning before he left. *Say it, say it, say it.*

"I hope you get better, Dad."

Dad managed to look at him. "Three little words, Clay. Can't you say them to me?"

He tried to swallow, but something closed his throat. Those unspoken words, of course, balled up inside of him and keeping him from breathing, talking, or loving.

"Please?" The request was barely a whisper from his father's lips, so soft he may not have wanted Clay to hear him beg.

Clay turned away. "I ... can't."

Behind him he heard the old man sigh. A sad, resigned, pathetic sound of regret. Clay knew if he released his father, he could release himself.

And about seven hundred miles away, on an island bathed in sunshine and happiness, there was a woman who needed Clay to be free.

"Dad," he said as he slowly turned around. "I forgive you."

"Oh. Thank you."

For the first time in years, they smiled at each other.

Lacey blinked through a haze of sleep, aware that everything hurt as she tried to turn in bed. No, no, she wasn't in bed. She was on a window seat on a piece of foam rubber that doubled as a guest bed in a hospital.

The dawn's earliest light peeked through the blinds, and with it came the harsh memory that the doctors had insisted on keeping Ashley overnight for observation.

She blinked at the sight of someone standing next to Ashley's bed, then gasped when she realized who it was.

"Oh my God, you're here."

Jocelyn smiled and came around the bed to the window, holding out her hands. "Of course I'm here. I got on a red-eye when Tessa called. See? I have the red eyes to prove it."

Of course she didn't have red eyes or bed head or morning breath, unlike Lacey, who no doubt had them all.

"My cavalry comes again."

"The other two-thirds of your cavalry is asleep in the waiting room."

"Oh." Lacey sighed. "Where would I be without you guys?"

"You'll never have to know." She glanced at the bed. "Please tell me it looks worse than it is."

"It does," Lacey confirmed. "She has a concussion, but nothing permanent. We're lucky."

Jocelyn put both hands on Lacey's cheeks. "And how's Mom?"

"A wreck."

"What about the big meeting?"

"It starts in..." She looked around the room for a clock. Naturally, Jocelyn wore a watch, which was already set to local time. Lacey took her wrist and did a quick calculation. "Less than three hours. And I'm two hours away. Shit."

"Is that your excuse?"

"No, I have a better one. I'm not leaving Ashley. She's been through enough."

"Poor thing." Jocelyn reached out and touched the blanket but not the sleeping girl. "We'll stay with her. You go and fight the good fight, Lace."

Not a chance. "The meeting's at ten, Joss. I'd have to leave in the next hour to even get down to Mimosa Key in time, let alone shower, dress, and get my act together." She glanced at her sleep-worn T-shirt and jeans, the flip-flops on her feet, and—no, she didn't even want to think about her hair.

"We can go." Zoe stood in the doorway, looking a lot like Lacey felt. "You can stay here with Ashley."

"We can be down there with time to spare," Tessa said, coming up behind her with a sleepy yawn. "We're co-investors. We'll fight the old-school bastards."

Ashley stirred, stopping the conversation as Lacey practically leaped to her side.

"Hey, Princess Pot-Pie. How ya feelin'?"

"'Kay."

"Did she just call her Princess Pot-Pie?" Zoe nearly choked. "Did I hear that right?"

"That's what she calls me." Ashley smiled and brought her stuffed unicorn up to her chin, then her eyes flew open. "Oh! Aunt Jocelyn's back."

Jocelyn reached over and hugged her. "Hey, kiddo."

"Are they going to let me go home, Mom? I really want to go home."

"Not for a few hours, honey."

"Long enough for us to get back to Mimosa Key in the rental car I got at the Tampa airport," Jocelyn said. "We can handle the meeting, or at least start it. When you're done here, you follow. By then we could have the whole zoning issue resolved."

"You can't present," Lacey said, digging for her phone to check for a message she knew wasn't going to be there. "You have to be a resident of Mimosa Key." Nothing on the phone.

How long would she keep checking and hoping for word from Clay?

"Then let's do what Zoe suggested," Jocelyn said. "We'll stay with Ashley and you go."

"Yeah, Mom, that's the best plan."

"No." Lacey shook her head. "I have to sign you out, honey. You're a minor."

"We'll spring her," Zoe said. "Throw her on a gurney and sneak her out the back like they do in the movies."

Ashley giggled. "Fun!"

"C'mon, Lace," Tessa prodded.

"Well, let me talk to the nurse and find out if I can pre-sign or something, then if I leave now ... but I—"

"Lacey!" They all said her name in perfect unison. "Quit making excuses!"

"Okay, okay." She rounded the bed, kissed Jocelyn on the cheek, gave high fives to Zoe and Tessa, then leaned over and gently hugged her baby. "God, I love the four of you."

She'd made it out the door and down the hall a few steps when Ashley called out, "Mommy! I love you!"

"I love you, too, Pot-Pie!"

The nurse complied with the discharge paperwork, and in less than twenty minutes Lacey was powering the big Rubicon down I-75. By nine-fifteen she was in gridlock Fort Myers morning traffic, swearing as she watched the digital numbers on the dashboard clock click closer to ten.

Running out of time would *not* be her excuse for missing this presentation, damn it.

By nine-forty she crossed the causeway to Mimosa Key, flew across Center and whipped right on Palm, minutes from the house. She could do this. Hell, she might even have time to throw on some makeup and brush her hair.

She could *do* this!

She pulled into the driveway, ran up the walk, and stopped dead in her tracks when the front door opened.

No, no. This wasn't *possible*. Anybody, anybody, but—

"Mother, what are you doing here?"

"I live here." Marie Armstrong reached out to yank Lacey closer. Not hug, really, because Lacey's mother didn't actually *embrace* others. She squeezed them into submission.

"We got a call from David that Ashley had an accident. Where is she?"

"You know about Ashley?"

Her mother scowled. "Of course I know. We flew down last evening after David called us. He said not to bother you at the hospital but wanted us to know about Ashley. And David!" She said the name with nothing less than reverence. "It was such a thrill to hear from him, Lacey. He sounded wonderful."

She managed to get inside, brushing by her mother,

hoping for her dad, and scanning the living room for the . . .

The presentation materials were gone. "What did you do?"

"Lacey, you left an open bottle of wine here. I hope you and your friends weren't drinking and driving, and all those—"

"Where is everything?" Lacey demanded. "The boards? The model? The papers?"

"That mess? I had Dad put it all away in a guest room closet, and that room was not exactly tidy either, I have to say."

White lights practically popped in Lacey's head. "Mother, I'm presenting to the town council in ten minutes!" She started toward the hall, but her mother grabbed her arm.

"Where is Ashley?"

"She's still in the hospital."

"And you *left* her? What kind of mother leaves her child in the hospital for a—a garden club meeting?"

"There's my girl!" Dad came bounding out of the hallway, all bright and white-haired, big and happy. Exactly the opposite of the woman he'd married. But Lacey couldn't even sacrifice one precious minute to throw her arms around him.

"Dad, I need all the materials you just—"

"Paul, Ashley's alone in a hospital somewhere!" Mother cried. "Lacey left her there! We have to go to her right this minute."

"She's not alone," Lacey said through a clenched jaw. "She's with my friends. Tessa and Jocelyn and Zoe are with her."

"Zoe? That wild one? I don't think—"

"Mother!" Lacey snapped the word like a whip in the air, and Marie reared back, penciled eyebrows raised high into her forehead.

"Excuse me, young lady."

"No," Lacey said, her voice low and quiet now. "I won't excuse you. I won't listen to you insult my friends or tell me I'm not a good mother because I left my daughter in their care. In a hospital, I might add."

"But David said—"

"David's gone," Lacey replied, using the shot of adrenaline from her rebellious speech to ease her father out of her way. "Now, you guys could really help me or you can just get out of my way. Right now I'm on a mission to change my life and I'm not going to argue with you about it, Mother."

"We are not going to help you," her mother said. "We are going to the hospital to take care of Ashley."

"She's taken care of. In fact, she might already be on her way here. Dad, please."

"What's going on, Lacey?" he asked. "Are you sure Ashley's okay?"

"I'm positive. And what's going on is too complicated to explain right now. I just need your help."

"Of course. You know what I always say."

As she walked down the hall, she smiled. "There's a reason God gives you two parents?"

He chuckled. "I say that tough things make you tougher. And that granddaughter of mine is one tough cookie."

"Yep, she's going to be fine. I wouldn't have left her if I didn't believe that."

"And what about her mom?" Dad put a hand on her shoulder, a loving, strong, guiding hand that had always been there for her.

"Going to be fine," Lacey said. "If I don't get derailed by disapproval."

Almost instantly Mother was in the room, glowering at them as if her very presence could break the father-daughter bond. But it couldn't; that was one thing Marie Armstrong never could control.

"Her *mom* is very busy instructing *me* to back off," Mother said in response to Dad's question.

"Then maybe you should listen, Marie."

That got him a vile look. "Forgive me for doing my job and giving her advice. I'll never stop, no matter how old I am or how old she is. She doesn't have to listen, do you, Lacey? You never have, anyway."

That was the problem: She'd been listening for far too long. At any other time in her life, this would be the point where she would say something to make her mother feel better and back away from the conversation. Instead, she looked up at her father.

"Dad, I wonder if you would do me a huge favor?"

"Anything, sweetheart."

"Come with me and charm the town council."

"Is that hag Charity going to be there?"

Mother choked. "Charity Grambling is my friend."

"On Facebook," Dad shot back, then winked at Lacey. "I never accepted her friendship. She doesn't floss, you know."

Lacey laughed. Only Dr. Armstrong, Mimosa Key's only dentist for three decades, would know that.

"You are *not* going to confront her in the town hall," Mother said. "Especially looking like that."

"Like what?" She hoisted the 3-D model. "I think I look just fine."

Mother sputtered. "Your hair looks like you combed it with a rake."

"Marie, she looks fine," Dad said.

"And, Lacey, have you put on weight since this hurricane?"

She rolled her eyes and tilted her head toward the front of the house. "Grab the boards, Dad."

He marched right past her mother, who stood with her hands on her hips. "Paul, where are you going?"

"To help our daughter, Marie."

It was going to be okay. Lacey really could do this. She might not have Clay, but she had a little backup and— backbone. Now it was time to use it.

Chapter Thirty-two

In the hallway outside the community room Lacey could hear Sam Lennox's gavel slam, his booming voice calling the meeting to order. She shared a quick look with her dad, who, during just the short car ride there, had become so fully invested in Lacey's resort concept that he'd parked illegally right in front of the town hall. Good thing Mother hadn't come.

"Go, Lace," he said, nudging her toward the door.

Inside, the buzz grew louder as a few people called her name, some in support and some not. Sam rapped his gavel again, which did little to quiet the noise.

Of course Charity and Company had taken over the front row on the right side, a group that included her daughter Grace and her sister Patience. Standing next to their row, Lacey spotted Gloria chatting with Sheriff Slade

Garrison, who adroitly divided his attention between Glo and the rowdy crowd.

"I think our team's on the left," Lacey whispered to Dad, noticing him nodding to many friends and familiar faces on both sides of the aisle.

But some folks weren't smiling; not everyone wanted change and progress to come to Mimosa Key.

"Thanks for the support, Dad," Lacey whispered as they walked down the center aisle together. "I know you'll catch hell from Mother, but I really appreciate you doing this for me."

"I'm proud of you, Lacey, and I know my parents would approve of this resort. I'm just glad we could stay gone long enough for you to find your nerve and stand up to your mother. What happened while we were gone?"

She smiled. "A hurricane?"

"Looks to me like that wind swept away all your baggage and left you some confidence." He gave her a squeeze. "Good girl."

"It wasn't the wind." And she hadn't exactly been a *good* girl, but Dad didn't need to know everything.

They found two empty seats but had to climb over a few people, including Will Palmer, who stood to let them go by.

As she passed him he whispered, "Go get 'em, Lacey."

She gave him a quick smile and thought about Jocelyn, but there was no time to pursue that now. Instead she took her seat and scanned the town council table, trying to psych out who'd be on her side.

Paula Reddick, yes. Rocco Cardinale and Nora Alvarez, maybe. George Masterson and Sam Lennox, no way. Well, maybe Sam.

"Call to order!" Sam shouted, smacking his gavel again, to no avail. "Can I please have quiet?"

Finally the murmurs died down.

"We will be hearing four presentations for proposed land use and new structures," Sam said, adjusting his glasses as he read the papers in front of him.

"Alphabetical will put us first," Lacey told him. "As soon as he says the order, let's go get the stuff from the car."

Sam continued reading from notes. "The bylaws state that we hear presentations in geographical order, south to north."

They did? Or was that one of Charity's unofficial edits? Not for the first time Lacey wished she had Clay and his bylaw-memorizing talent with her.

"That'll put us last," Lacey said. "Which is fine."

"More time to gauge the mood of the panel," Dad replied with an encouraging nod.

Sam leaned into the mike to talk. "Up first is John McSweeny seeking to replace signage lost during the hurricane for the bowling alley at 4623 Palm Avenue."

Signage. That wouldn't take long.

"Next will be Barbara Pennick requesting all new windows and a new entry to Beachside Beauty."

From the sidelines Gloria beamed at her boss.

"Third presentation is Lacey Armstrong, Barefoot Bay property owner."

Lacey sat straighter. Wait, how could she be next? She had to have the northernmost property. Unless whoever had bought Tomlinsons' land decided to show.

Her heart jumped at the thought. Was someone proposing to build on that lot? Wiping damp palms on her jeans, she waited for Sam to describe her proposal.

"Ms. Armstrong is proposing a change in"—Sam paused, frowning down at the paper—"town codes, development standards, transportation flow…" His voice trailed off as he looked at the crowd. "That one will take a while."

The reaction was a mix of mumbles and nervous laughter, some throat clearing, and a lot of eyes on Lacey, who still didn't know how she could be third out of four presentations.

"What's the matter?" Dad asked.

"There's no one north of me," she said. "Who is presenting fourth?"

Just then she spotted Ira Howell, the banker who represented the anonymous property buyer, leaning against the back wall, a scowl pulling the skin of his bald head.

She gripped her father's hand tighter as Sam started reading again.

"Our final presentation addresses another lot in Barefoot Bay and another change in town codes, development standards, and transportation flow, given by Mr. Ira Howell of Wells Fargo."

No. *No.* Whatever they were building, however they'd gotten on the agenda, she had to stop it. At the very least she had to know *who* she was up against. "This is a nightmare," she mumbled.

Will Palmer leaned over. "You know, Lacey, code changes and development standards could mean they're hard-line environmentalists. It doesn't automatically mean the buyer is building something."

But she needed that land. Tomlinsons' and Everham's properties were north and south of her. They'd close her in. And her house, Clay's house, was supposed to go on the Tomlinson land. She couldn't let go of that dream. And with David's offer of an investment to buy those properties, she'd been certain she could make that dream a reality.

Dad patted her leg. "You can't find a solution until you know the problem, Lace. Let's find out what's going on."

What was going on were fried nerves and bad feelings in her gut.

Charity shot up. "I'm sorry, but Mimosa Key bylaws clearly state that the only speakers at a town council meeting must be current residents of the island. No representative can speak for them. Mr. Howell is not a resident of Mimosa Key."

For once she could have kissed Charity and her damn rules.

Ira Howell pushed off the wall to respond. "I have complete power of attorney for the property owner, Mayor Lennox. I have the paperwork to prove that I can speak on behalf of this individual who owns the land, and is therefore a resident of Mimosa Key."

"That's not good enough," Charity said, getting a loud reaction and a few boos from the crowd.

Ira shook his head. "There's actually a proviso in the bylaws regarding power of attorney if the individual is unable to appear before the council. If it pleases you, Mr. Mayor, I'd like to present that reason exclusively to the town council."

Despite the outcry of the crowd, Sam hit the gavel with authority. "We'll take a short break to discuss this behind closed doors," Sam announced. "Presenters, please get ready."

Lacey exhaled, but then nudged her father. "Let's go get the materials from the car, Dad."

"I'll help you, Lacey," Will offered.

"Oh, that would be great, Will. The car's illegally parked and if I chance it much longer, Slade'll slam me with a parking ticket."

As Ira Howell left with the five members of the council to a private chamber, Lacey, her father, and Will headed out.

"Good luck, Lacey!" A woman who'd had Lacey bake her wedding cake called out.

"You're our hero, Lace!" another said.

She was? She gave a little wave to some friends and a few baking customers, buoyed by their belief in her.

Lacey dashed through the hall and to the main entrance, where Will held the door for her.

She pointed to the big Jeep Rubicon. "That's my car."

Will slowed as the approached the vehicle. "I hoped, er, figured I'd see your friends with you today."

Lacey hesitated. Jocelyn. He meant Jocelyn. "They're out of town now, but they'll be back this afternoon. Jocelyn, too," she couldn't help but add.

"Is she going to stay?" Something in his voice said that mattered to him.

"I only talked to her for a few minutes this morning, so I don't know." Lacey opened the back of the Jeep and reached for the 3-D model. The sight of the mini version of villas made her miss Clay with a physical ache.

His work was genius. He deserved to get the credit today, but something, *someone,* was a more powerful draw.

Will took the model, glancing down at structures that stood on a miniature replica of the beaches of Barefoot Bay. "Wow, looks like north Africa."

"Inspired by the architecture of Morocco." *By a very inspiring architect.*

"Very cool. They'd be nuts not to let you build it." He examined it closely, looking from side to side. "Where's Clay?"

"Oh, he's not here."

"Really? Isn't he the architect?"

"Not…" *Anymore.* "Officially. We haven't signed a formal contract, yet. He did this as a favor to me." Good Lord, had she just boiled the past few weeks of life-changing *feelings* into a favor? How sad was that?

"Oh, that's too bad," Will said. "He offered me a job working for him on the resort. And he's obviously great."

Obviously. "Well, if we get approval you can have that job." Except Jocelyn might not like that. "That is, if all the investors agree."

She pulled out the rest of the presentation boards and gave them to her dad. "You guys take that stuff in and I'll move the car and bring the handouts."

With the car legally parked and her arms full of the documents that explained all the financial benefits of her project, Lacey hustled back into the town hall, doubts pressing down like the unforgiving sun overhead, a whole choir of excuses hitting high notes in her head.

Without Clay she should ask for an extension.

Without a chance to talk to Ira Howell about what he was presenting she could be completely blindsided.

And without five minutes to change her clothes, comb her hair, or put on a drop of makeup, she looked a little like a homeless person. Which, come to think of it, she was at the moment.

Still, she felt a smile pull across her face as she mentally squashed every excuse. She wasn't going to let anyone or anything hold her back now.

"Somebody looks happy."

She stopped so suddenly that the papers almost flew out of her hands. The heat and humidity evaporated, leaving nothing but a chill straight to her heart.

Clay.

Chapter Thirty-three

Lacey managed a shaky breath when he stepped closer, his hair as disheveled as hers, his eyes a little red-rimmed. Had he been crying or hadn't he slept since the last time she'd seen him?

"Lacey, I have to explain something to you. It's important—"

"Lacey Armstrong!" Grace Hartgrave smacked open both doors in a dramatic, noisy interruption. "Get your tush in here, now. They changed the order of presentations."

Clay nearly lunged to stop Lacey from moving. "No, I have to talk to you."

"Later," Grace answered for her. "The council wants to do the site-development plans first, so that's you and then that guy from the bank who's here because his client has a medical emergency."

"He really is presenting site-development plans?"

Lacey asked. That meant someone was *building* on the land they'd taken out from under her.

"I have to talk to Ira Howell," Clay insisted. "Right now. Right this minute."

Grace physically pushed him away. "Not now." She reached for Lacey. "Hurry up, 'cause right now you just became the lesser of two evils."

"Why?" Lacey asked, her voice as shaky as her legs, her head buzzing with shock and confusion.

Clay turned to her. "It's not what you—"

"Looks like your boyfriend screwed you in more ways than one, Lace." Grace pulled Lacey into the air-conditioning, right past Clay. "My mom got the inside scoop. Clay Walker's building a big-ass resort and spa right smack-dab next to you." She gave Clay a sly smile. "Looks like you've been playing both sides against the middle, Mr. Walker."

Lacey choked as Grace yanked her away and Clay took the other elbow. "No, Lacey, you don't understand."

Dad appeared behind Grace. "Lacey, in here now or you're off the agenda!"

Without even looking at Clay, without taking a minute to figure exactly what he'd done to screw her out of that land and the hopes for her resort, she ran inside.

"Lacey!" Clay called.

"Sorry, pal," Grace said harshly. "Residents only unless you get special dispensation from the mayor or sleep with the right people. You didn't." She slammed the door loud enough to shake the town hall rafters.

Lacey's dad guided her down the wide hallway. "Looks like someone wants to compete with you, kiddo."

Did he? Or was it his dad? *The* Clayton Walker.

God, she didn't know. She didn't know if she could believe him anymore. Her brain flashed to the drawings she'd found in his apartment. Didn't they tell her a lot about him?

Maybe. But he needed to say it. And show her, not just draw her.

Inside the community room, her father kept her marching straight ahead.

She tried to turn. "No backing out or dreaming up reasons to run."

"But Dad—"

"Lacey," he said softly as their steps fell into a matching rhythm and heads on both sides of the aisle turned to look at them. "What does this feel like to you?"

"Hell?"

He smiled and patted her hand. "A walk up the aisle with my little girl."

Her heart dropped so hard it practically rolled out onto the floor. "Dad, please."

"It's okay, Lacey. Unconventional, but okay." He beamed at her, pausing as they reached the front. "Now, you go up there and change your life, young lady. Doesn't take a man to do that for you."

"But Dad, that guy back there—"

"Is not important."

But he *was*. He could have been. He'd changed her and loved her and made her feel strong, smart, sexy, and powerful. How could that not be important?

"What's important is your future." Dad gave her a nudge. "Now go get what you always dreamed of."

What she'd always dreamed of was a guy like Clay. A partner, a friend, a father to her children, a lover for life.

Sam Lennox cleared his throat, making no effort to hide his impatience. "We're waiting, Ms. Armstrong."

So was she—for Clay. For him to run in and explain that this was all a mistake, and, by the way, he loved her and would she mar—

"Are you changing your mind?" Sam asked.

"Thinking about backing out?" George Masterson added.

"Afraid you'll lose?" Charity had to shoot her two cents in.

It would be so easy to quit now.

"No," Lacey said quietly, walking forward. "I'm ready."

At the podium she blew out a breath and looked at the back of the room as the doors opened again. She braced for Clay, but instead a woman she didn't recognize rushed in, hair pulled back under a red baseball cap, sunglasses covering her face.

And then Clay came in and put his arm around the woman's shoulders, speaking softly into her ear.

Jayna?

Instantly Ira Howell lunged out from his chair in the middle, nearly jogging back to Clay to shake his hand. Like they were *business partners*. Could he have secretly planned to buy that land and build on it without telling her?

Why?

Why not? After all, what did she really know about Clay Walker? But those drawings; they were from his heart, weren't they?

He still didn't look at her, didn't even glance in her direction. Instead he put his arms around the woman and squeezed her into his chest, lifting the brim of her baseball cap to give her a smile.

That smile. That heart-stopping smile. Then he leaned

over and kissed her on the cheek. A kiss that, even from here, she could tell was full of love.

"Your microphone is on," Sam said, giving Lacey a start as she imagined that her dark and pained thoughts might somehow be broadcast to the town.

But no one knew what she was thinking. Not even the man she was thinking it about. In fact, he hadn't even glanced her way. Instead Ira had his full attention, and the two men walked right out the back, deep in conversation.

He was gone, but the woman who'd come in with him took a seat in the last row, crossed her arms, and looked at Lacey with profound interest.

Interest in the competition, no doubt.

"Lacey, please." Sam's voice grew irritated. "You have the floor."

She cleared her throat, looked out into the crowd, and found her dad. What had he said to her earlier?

Looks to me like that wind swept away all of your baggage and left some confidence.

And right at that moment she found her voice.

"Ladies and gentlemen, members of the council, honored guests, and my lifelong friends and neighbors. I'm here to present an idea that I believe will change Mimosa Key for the better, will improve our lives, increase our revenue, and ensure that this island remains vital for many generations to come. I present to you Windswept at Barefoot Bay."

It had actually hurt not to look at her. Hurt not to hold Lacey's stunned and devastated gaze and give her some kind of sign that everything would be okay. But Clay couldn't look her in the eye until it *was* okay.

First he had to deal with Ira Howell, who'd promised late last night that he'd honor the change in ownership if Clay made it to Mimosa Key with the official paperwork before the town council meeting.

That had been thirteen hours and seven hundred hard miles ago. And at least six cups of gas-station coffee, all of which burned in his belly right now. Clay had driven to and from North Carolina without sleeping and he felt every mile on his body. But he couldn't rest now. Not yet.

"Do you have everything?" he demanded of Ira as they powered through the lobby and into the lot.

"Do you?" Ira shot back.

Clay guided him to the van with the lettering "Clayton Walker Architecture and Design, Inc." on the side. The van Darcie had snagged the keys to, and warned him that it tended to shimmy when it hit seventy-five so he needed to go easy on the gas. It shimmied at seventy-five all right, and felt like it would implode at ninety.

But he and Darcie had made it from Raleigh to Mimosa Key alive, with the paperwork intact.

"Right here," he said, grabbing the power of attorney forms they'd had notarized at the Raleigh hospital by a person probably more used to signing death certificates than property transactions.

"Because as much as I want to help you," Ira said, "there are some tricky legal issues doing it this way, according to the lawyer at Wells Fargo."

"I have what your lawyer needs. Trust me." Clay handed him the form.

Standing in a strip of shade, Ira opened the letter and read it. "I have to tell you, first of all, I'm very sorry about your father's stroke."

Clay nodded his thanks.

"How is he?"

"He's alive." Why lie? He might not be long for the world, and if he made it, he wasn't ever going to run a business or design a building again. "The second stroke was actually a blessing because it pulled him out of the coma and he could communicate."

Ira used the paper to fan himself, beads of sweat dampening his lip. "He didn't know you were involved when his company bought the land; you know that, don't you?"

"That's what he said." Although part of Clay suspected nefariousness on his father's part, he and Darcie had been able to put the pieces together, and it looked like Dad really had had no idea of Clay's involvement when he'd sent the scout who'd determined that the properties made a great purchase.

"After that last meeting," Ira continued, "I was confused. I couldn't understand why Walker Architecture was staying anonymous when someone with the same name was already involved."

"You told him?" Clay asked.

"I struggled with it; I'll be honest." Ira took out a white handkerchief and dabbed his damp forehead. "I figured it was a family feud and I oughta back out. So I didn't say anything for a while, but then I got wind of some of the stuff going on over here and I contacted the company."

"Why didn't he just terminate the deal?"

"Well, I don't want to make you feel guilty, son, but that day he had a medical, uh, situation."

So C-dub hadn't lied about that at least.

"I guess his health became his focus then." Ira dug into his bag and produced a massive amount of paper that would take at least twenty minutes to sign. Even though it meant he'd miss Lacey's presentation, he took the time because when he walked in there he wanted this deal done. No lies, no promises, no more misunderstandings.

When he put his last signature on the bottom line, Clayton Walker—the *younger* Clayton Walker—owned both parcels of land and he could do whatever he wanted on them. And, God, he knew what he wanted to do.

They shook hands and Clay couldn't resist giving the man a quick pat on the back. "You went above and beyond, Mr. Howell. All that work last night and early this morning to prepare this paperwork was outstanding. Thank you."

"Use my bank for this resort you're planning."

Clay grinned. "We will." The word "we" sounded so right and natural. Now all he had to do was make it so.

He walked inside, where Lacey stood beside the 3-D model of their resort, the main-building front-elevation board propped up next to her.

"Right here you can see how we..." She hesitated when her gaze landed on Clay, color rising to her cheeks. "How *I* propose to handle that."

So she rightly suspected the worst. And judging from the way she looked, she'd had a rough night. Guilt punched, but he knew it was just a matter of a few more minutes. He could wait that long.

He'd waited his whole life for her, so what was a few more minutes?

"How's she doing?" he whispered to Darcie when he sat down.

"Really well. You get 'er done out there?" Darcie asked.

He held up the packet of papers. "I'm the proud owner of ten acres of Barefoot Bay."

"And Dad paid for them."

"In more ways than one," he said. "Has she been through the feasibility and due diligence research yet?"

"Easily. She's just covering the physical buildings now."

Lacey spoke with confidence and pride when she described the villas, the spa, the greenhouse that Tessa wanted so much, even though they weren't sure they could fit it without the other properties.

Now they could. Now they could do so many things, including pick up where they'd left off. Just the thought of Lacey in his arms, in his bed, in his life, made Clay smile.

"Somebody's in love," Darcie sang into his ear.

Clay just grinned more broadly. Somebody *was* in love.

Around him the audience was as riveted on Lacey as he was, even those who looked unfriendly to change. But where was Ashley? And Tessa and Zoe? And David?

Why weren't they here to support her?

"And that," Lacey concluded, turning to the long table of council members, "is why we believe that Mimosa Key can benefit from the world-class, wholly environmentally friendly, revenue-producing, state-of -the-art resort known as Windswept at Barefoot Bay."

Windswept at Barefoot Bay?

Stunned at the name change, he felt his jaw, and his heart, drop with a thud. Only then did she look directly at him, and that expression said everything. An expression that said: *I don't need you, Clay Walker.*

"Hold all questions, please!" George Masterson shouted. "Our next presenter is from Clayton Walker Architecture and Design, and his plans will make all of these null and void."

Lacey closed her eyes as if George's words had kicked

her right in the teeth, but Clay was the one who felt kicked. Now she thought he *represented* his old man. He had to fix this, and fix it fast.

Clay made his way up the aisle with nothing but the packet of property papers in his hands. Lacey stepped away from the podium, turning her back on him to gather her presentation boards.

He stopped behind her, leaning a little too close, feeling her stiffen. But he had no time to set her straight now. Instead he put a hand on her tense shoulder.

"Pay attention, Strawberry. I mean everything I'm about to say."

As long as she didn't leave the room, Lacey Armstrong was about to find out exactly how he felt about her.

Chapter Thirty-four

With control she didn't even know she possessed, Lacey turned away from her presentation boards and walked toward the back of the room. She wanted to leave, of course. Wanted to run into the bathroom and howl in pain or possibly throw up.

But she refused to give him that satisfaction.

Her father was in the back row clapping for her. She gave him a smile and was about to sit next to him when the back doors opened.

"Mom!"

Zoe and Tessa each had one of Ashley's hands, and all three wore huge smiles. Ashley's head was still bandaged, but her eyes looked clear and her smile lit up the room.

"Did we miss it?" she asked as Lacey hugged her and led them all to the back wall.

"I'm done. But brace yourself. Things are about to get ugly."

"What's he doing up there?" they asked in unison.

"I'm not entirely sure, but he might be breaking my heart."

They all leaned against the back wall to listen.

"Jeez, he looks worse than you do," Zoe whispered. "And that's saying a lot."

"He does," Tessa agreed. "He looks like he hasn't slept for days."

He looked good to Lacey. Disheveled, unshaven, and was that a coffee stain on his T-shirt? None of it mattered. He was a gorgeous man, who loved...

She glanced at the woman in a baseball cap, who turned and looked right at Lacey. Then she slid off her glasses very slowly to reveal eyes as bloodshot as Clay's and also as blue.

The other woman nodded, and winked. Was that a bitchy move or what? Except it didn't seem as though she was trying to be bitchy.

More confused than ever, Lacey turned back to Clay, her head buzzing like a thousand cicadas invading the beach.

"Ladies and gentlemen of Mimosa Key. My name is Clay Walker and I'm delighted to be addressing you as the newest resident of your fine community." He held up a handful of legal-sized papers and Lacey tried to concentrate on what he was saying, not the baritone of his voice or the music of his North Carolina drawl. "These are the deeds to the properties formerly owned by Mr. and Mrs. Andrew Tomlinson and Mr. Ross Everham. They are now in my name, free and clear."

He owned the lots. *He* did. The betrayal stung like hot needles inside her chest. But she forced herself to listen.

"What do you plan to build?" Charity called out.

Good question, Char, Lacey thought. What *did* he plan to build?

"Something extraordinary."

The whole room went eerily silent, except for maybe Lacey's heartbeat, which surely everyone could hear.

"What kind of something, Mr. Walker?" Mayor Lennox asked, obviously not amused by Clay's obtuse response.

Clay never looked away from Lacey, pinning her to the wall with a dead-serious gaze. "Something everyone wants but not everyone gets."

Lacey's legs weakened and she used the wall to hold her steady. What was he talking about? He was looking at her, but...

Sam Lennox spoke into his microphone because the murmurs and comments and frustrations of the crowd were getting louder. "Mr. Walker, we have given you the floor, and if you can't make a serious and thoughtful presentation, your request for zoning changes will be denied."

"I am making a serious presentation. This land"—he held up the papers again—"will be part of the resort and spa that Lacey Armstrong just presented. With one minor stipulation."

Lacy held her breath.

"The resort is called *Casa Blanca*." He leveled her with a gaze. "Not *Windswept*."

Oh. She dropped an inch against the wall, bracing harder.

"What difference does it make?" Charity barked. "Just tell us what you want."

"What I want..." He inhaled deeply and finally smiled. "Is to spend every day and night with Lacey Armstrong, building..."

She absolutely couldn't breathe, holding his gaze, squeezing Ashley's hand, fighting the burn behind her eyelids.

"A life together."

"Oh my God," Zoe practically cooed in Lacey's ear. "I love him!"

"So do I," Lacey whispered, aware of the tears filling her eyes. "So do I."

"And if she would just come up here and join me"—Clay held out his hand in invitation—"we will answer any questions the good people of Mimosa Key might have so we can assure you that we want to make this island a destination that remains true to its roots but looks forward to the future."

"Amen!"

"Hear! Hear!"

"Go kiss him, Lacey!" The loud suggestion came from the woman in the baseball cap.

Clay leaned very close to the microphone and lowered his voice to dead sexy. "I think my sister just had a very good idea."

His sister? That was Darcie?

Ashley grinned, turning to her. "He likes you, Mom. A lot."

She looked at her daughter, putting a hand under her chin, holding her gaze. "You know that no man, ever, will come between us."

"Mom, don't be weird. Go kiss the guy. Listen to this place. They're going nuts."

The entire room clapped in unison, a chorus of female "Oohs" and "Aahs" adding to the cacophony.

She started up the aisle, and Clay left the podium to meet her halfway.

There, he put his arms around her and pulled her into a deep, dreamy, delicious kiss. The whole audience hooted so loudly she could barely hear when he whispered in her ear.

"Windswept at Barefoot Bay? Are you kidding me?"

She looked up at him. "Only because in *Casablanca*, the wrong guy gets the girl."

"Let's change the ending, Strawberry."

When the last of the council members had cleared out after the vote and a noisy victory celebration, Clay shook hands with many townspeople and promised more than a few job interviews for construction-crew candidates. Even Ashley congratulated him and told him about her own scary trip to the hospital.

Lacey was always nearby with a hand on her daughter's shoulder, giving instructions to her friends as they packed up the car, accepting congratulations as people milled about the meeting hall and eventually left.

He saw her talking to Darcie for a few minutes and then end that conversation with a quick hug.

Finally he made his way over to her, hands outstretched. "Hey, Strawberry. I missed you."

She came right to him, folding into his embrace and offering one of her own. "Oh, Clay, I'm so sorry I thought the worst of you."

"I can't believe you'd really think I'd buy those lots and build on them," he said. "What made you think that?"

"I didn't. I mean, that's not..." She closed her eyes as if just saying the words hurt her. "I looked at your phone the night we went to the beach. I thought you were going back to Jayna."

He let out a sigh, finally understanding. "And I should have told you why she texted. In fact, I should have told you my dad was sick before that, but I really thought you'd preach to me about forgiving him, and I wasn't ready."

"Did you?" she asked.

"Done and done." He held her closer and put his lips on her hair and inhaled, the smell of strawberry mixed with sun and maybe a little antiseptic reminding him that she'd had her own trip to the hospital. "How's Ashley doing?"

"She's fine and very apologetic for whatever it was she said to you that she thinks made you leave. But it was a hellish night, I'll tell you."

He held her again, hoping the hug could express how sorry he was that the last twenty-four hours had happened the way they had.

"I thought I'd lost you," she whispered.

"Not going to happen."

"Even after"—she fought to finish her thought—"even after we're done building the resort?"

"Did you not listen to my big speech?" He slammed a hand to his chest, only partially feigning pain. "I bared it all up there for you, woman."

"That wasn't just to win votes?"

"Maybe a few." He winked, but then his expression grew serious. "I've had a lot of time to think, Lace."

"Thirteen hours, Darcie said."

He sighed, shaking his head, looking into her eyes. "Maybe more than that. But when I talked to my dad in the hospital yesterday, I realized something. I realized that he can be a complete jerk, selfish as hell, and willing to do almost anything for what he wants. A man who hates the word *can't*."

"You're not like him, if that's where you're going with this, Clay."

But he could be. "I let him go. I let go of all the anger and hate. I forgave him because there's something—someone—I want to focus my attention on. You."

She sank deeper into his arms with a happy sigh. "Oh. I like that."

"I like *you*." No. This time she deserved more than their inside joke. "In fact..." He lowered his mouth to hers, brushed his lips against hers, and whispered, "I—"

"*Ahem*."

They separated, turning to face a woman who looked vaguely like Lacey, only older, thinner, colder, and nowhere near as happy.

"Mother."

"I heard you got what you wanted, Lacey. That's good."

Sure didn't sound good. Not in that tone.

"*We* got what we wanted," Lacey corrected her, slowly standing straighter, dividing her attention between her mother and him. "Have you met my ... Clay?"

The older woman marched a few steps closer, an amber brown gaze leveled at Clay, the same color as Lacey's but completely flat.

"I've been with Ashley in the parking lot," she said. "I don't think she should be in the sun with that injury. So I let her go off with that Zoe, but—"

"Clay Walker is the architect who is going to build the business I've always wanted to run. Clay, this is my mother, Marie Armstrong."

The woman sniffed, reaching out one hand to shake his, the other smoothing hair he'd never call "strawberry" blonde, although maybe a distant, dull cousin. "Then I guess congratulations are in order," she conceded with a nod.

"For Lacey," he said. "She's the owner, manager, lead investor, brain trust, and inspiration for the whole Casa Blanca concept."

A reddish brown eyebrow launched north. "I'm sure there are a lot of smart people behind her on this. Lacey's a follower. Her brother Adam's the leader in our family."

"Not anymore," he said.

Her mother ignored the comment. "Could I speak with you privately, Lacey?"

"Later," Lacey said. "Clay and I have to get that last model in the car and get—"

"Now."

Lacey froze and a few fireworks of fury sparked inside Clay, but he kept his mouth shut.

"What is it, Mother?"

"Privately."

They faced each other like gunslingers while Clay debated if he should offer to leave. Before he could, Lacey put a hand on his shoulder.

"Anything you have to say to me you can say in front of Clay," she said. "He's my . . . he's my . . ."

"I'm her partner," he supplied, suddenly wishing he could use a term with far more impact and emotion attached.

"I know what he is," Marie said, cutting a cool glance his way. "And, Lacey, I think you're entirely too old for this."

"For what?" Lacey asked with a soft cough of disbelief. "For a man? For a lover? For a business? For a *life*?"

"For a boy." She gestured toward Clay. "And you should be ashamed of yourself, taking advantage of a lonely older woman."

Clay started to laugh. A chuckle at first, then a full, sharp, from-the-gut laugh. "You're funny, Mrs. Armstrong."

But Lacey wasn't even smiling.

"C'mon, Lace." He reached for her hand. "Let's go."

"No." She pulled her hand away from him. "I don't want to go, Clay."

No? Was she going to give in and let this cold, cruel woman do what she'd obviously been doing to Lacey her whole life? "Lacey?"

"Very smart of you, honey." The first bit of softness formed around Marie's eyes, and a spark of satisfaction. "I knew you'd come to your senses."

"I have," Lacey said softly.

Disappointment curled through him, landing low and hard in his gut. Was she this weak? Had he misjudged her that much? A woman he was a breath away from loving?

"You can leave, Clay," Lacey said.

He stood speechless. What power did Marie Armstrong have over her? "Leave?"

"Just go."

Marie wore a smug smile and tipped her head to the door. He opened his mouth to argue but closed it again, taking the few steps to the back door. Pulling it open, he waited for Lacey to change her mind, but she didn't.

Without turning, he stepped outside into the hallway. Behind him the door started to close with the hiss of a pneumatic hinge, slowly enough that he heard Lacey's next words.

"Mother, listen to me."

He slid a hand in the frame to keep the door ajar.

"I don't need to hear your excuses, Lacey. Everyone makes mistakes and he, well, he was a doozy."

"I'm not making excuses, Mother. I want to say something to you. One time and one time only."

Clay inched closer. He had to hear. Had to know.

"Say it fast and then let's go. I can't stand the thought of Ashley with that Zoe woman."

He heard Lacey's intake of breath, as though she were about to start a speech. Then silence.

"What?" her mother demanded.

"I don't know why you have so much anger in you, Mother, or why you are so disappointed in me."

"I'm not—"

"It doesn't matter," Lacey insisted. "Because I forgive you."

Clay closed his eyes at the echo of his own words to his father. He knew exactly how liberating that was.

"I don't need your forgiveness. I don't need—"

"Anything or anyone. I know. But I do." Lacey's voice cracked, making Clay squeeze the door. "I need love and I need that man out there. I need him like I need my next breath."

"You're confusing sex with need."

"I'm not confused about anything." Her voice rose with conviction and clarity. "I love him and I want to spend every possible minute next to him."

Yes. Yes, Strawberry, *yes*.

"Well, you do that," her mother said. "And I'll be there to pick up the pieces when he dumps you for the next girl who gives him what he needs."

"There won't be a next girl." Confidence oozed from every word. "I'm all he needs and all he wants and all he will ever have to have."

He braced for Marie's cutting reply, but there was nothing but silence. And footsteps to the door, fast enough for him to realize she was running. To him.

"Clay!" Lacey called, pushing the door so hard he had to jump back to keep from getting nailed. "Clay! Oh. You're here."

"I'm here."

"You heard."

"Every word."

"And..."

He reached for her, pride and love and something he couldn't even name welling up inside of him.

Completion. That was what it was. Like the final stroke on a drawing that was just waiting for completion. He could see the whole picture ahead and, man, it looked good.

"And I think you are right about everything," he said. "Especially the part about how you are all I need and all I want and all I ever have to have."

Lacey leaned into Clay. "You know what I want to do now, Clay?"

He lifted an eyebrow. "Thank me properly?"

"After that, I'd like to make some of your drawings come to life. And I don't mean the floor plans."

He reached down to kiss her. "Told you, Strawberry. If

I can see it clear enough to draw it, I can make it happen. Let's make it happen...together."

"I like that."

He grinned. "I like *you*."

"I—"

He placed one finger over her lips. "Let me say it first. I love you."

Epilogue

⌇

Six Months Later

"Why is everyone whispering?" Lacey approached Zoe and Jocelyn a few minutes after the formal ground-breaking ceremony had ended.

They both shut up instantly.

"Secrets," Lacey said, shaking her head. "Why must we have any secrets? We're best friends."

"No secrets," Jocelyn said. "We're just talking about what a lovely ceremony it was."

"Especially the part where you and Clay did the first big dig." Zoe mimed scooping dirt. "Because nothing says romance like a shovel."

"Who said anything about romance?" Tessa joined them, her fingers wrapped around a small cluster of bright pink mimosa flowers that she'd insisted on planting months ago in honor of the island's name.

"Can't say much else when Lacey and Clay are together," Jocelyn said. "You two are the definition of bliss."

"Speaking of bliss, this afternoon kind of reminds me of a wedding." Zoe slid her arm around Lacey to turn her toward the beach, but Lacey caught Jocelyn and Tessa's sharp look of warning.

"It's okay, guys," Lacey assured them. "When it happens, it happens. We'll know when it's the right time. We have a resort to build, you know."

Again they shared a look that could only be interpreted as—what? Pity? Understanding? Concern?

"You guys, stop," Lacey insisted. "Clay and I don't need a piece of paper. We've never needed that, not even to build Casa Blanca together. It's always been sealed with a kiss."

Which really should be enough when a person is this much in love, right?

"Here, Lace," Tessa said, handing her the flowers. "A gift for you to celebrate this glorious day of new beginnings."

She took the bouquet and smiled, surprised when tears stung her lids. She wasn't disappointed that Clay hadn't proposed yet, was she? No, these were tears of joy and anticipation. They had so much ahead.

"And just look at those two," Jocelyn said, indicating Clay and Lacey's father deep in conversation at the water's edge, silhouetted against the first golden streaks of a magnificent sunset.

"They're like father and son," Lacey mused. They'd formed a strong bond almost instantly and, for the first time since he'd retired from dentistry, her father seemed truly happy. Even her mother...

Well, she was coming around. She'd joined the party today, at least. And Ashley, now halfway through her first year of high school, had managed to forge much better friendships and an improved attitude. Right now she was talking excitedly to Clay's sister, no doubt telling her all about the upcoming spring-break trip to the Caribbean to go snorkeling with her father.

David had been true to his word: He'd invested heavily in Casa Blanca. No word on when he'd be back to visit, but Ashley seemed content with their regular texting and Facebook exchanges, and the promise of at least one adventurous vacation with him a year.

"Hey, Lace." Zoe gestured toward the water. "Your hotter half is waving you down to the beach."

As her father walked up the sand, Clay stayed in the shallow waves giving Lacey a two-fingered come-hither beckoning. "Like I could resist that. See ya," she said, using the flowers to wave over her shoulder.

"Shoes off," he called, already barefoot himself.

She kicked off her sandals and headed into the warm water, letting the froth bubble around her ankles. Clay reached out to her and she slipped into his arms, the warm water of Barefoot Bay tickling her toes just as his first sweet kiss landed on her mouth.

"We did it, Strawberry."

"We sure did." She leaned back, secure in his arms, giving in to the sheer bliss of being held by him. He bent over and kissed her neck, getting some crowd reaction.

"We're drawing attention, Clay."

"Get used to it. We're going to draw a lot more." He smiled at her, a sly, sneaking smile that crinkled his eyes and kind of crushed her chest. "You know, Lacey, your dad reminded me we've forgotten an awfully big step in this project."

"We have?" She frowned. "What is it?"

"Our contract."

"A business contract?" She laughed at the idea, mostly because the notion seemed ridiculous when they'd done this much without one. Or maybe she laughed because, for one crazy second, she thought he might mean another kind of contract.

"I don't think it's smart to go much farther along without one, and your dad agrees."

"Of course. He wants to protect me."

He curled his arm around her shoulder as if protecting her was his job, pulling her into him so she had to put her arm around his waist as they turned to the sunset, their backs to the beach. "You have to admit a contract makes sense."

"If it's important to you…" She let her voice trail off as her eyes drank in the peachy pool of sunlight over the horizon and the violet-tinged sky above it. Beautiful. But she'd rather look up at the man she loved. "I don't think we need one."

"I do. This is a huge commitment, years of work, lots of decisions to make, people who will depend on us to stick together when times get tough, and, of course, there are always complicated legal issues to iron out in case of a dispute."

"I never want to have a dispute." She put her head on his shoulder, trying to just drink up the peacefulness of the moment.

"Just in case, I think it would be smart to have a formal, binding, stamped-by-the-mayor kind of contract that says this partnership is permanent."

She squinted up at him, blinking against the late

afternoon sunshine that washed him in gold. "Let's just seal it with a kiss, Clay, and agree to trust each other."

He stared at her. "A kiss?"

"Is just a kiss." She stood on her tiptoes to peck his cheek. "That's what our song says."

He turned so she hit his mouth and suddenly it wasn't a peck at all, but slower, longer, deeper, and warmer. "Unless it's a kiss like that."

"I'll say," she agreed. "That was pretty binding."

"But not good enough." He angled them both toward the sunset again, the sand squishing in between her toes. "I want legal."

"Okay. On Monday you call the lawyers."

"I don't want to wait until Monday. We have everyone we need here right now."

"Here for..." Deep inside, in the part of her chest that always ached a little when she looked at him, something twisted. "Here for us to sign a contract?"

"If that's what you want to call it." Very slowly, he eased her around, away from the sunset, toward the beach.

Every single person there gathered in a tight group, facing them. Except for Zoe, Tessa, and Jocelyn, who stood off to the side in a row.

"What's going on, Clay?"

"One more ceremony today," he said.

Then the crowd parted down the middle, as if choreographed, and Ashley stepped into the open area, more mimosa flowers in her hands. She looked at Lacey, smiled, and slowly began to walk toward the water, dropping the pink stems as she did.

Tears blurred her vision and a lump formed in her throat. "Clay. Is this..."

"This is it, Lacey."

She let out a little breath of air, suddenly strangled with happiness. "Now?"

"No chance to make a single excuse why we *can't*."

"As if I'd even dream of that."

Laughing, he stroked her windblown hair off her face, then held her cheeks. "That's why I didn't propose."

"Better do it fast."

He got down on one knee, earning a big cheer from the crowd.

"Lacey Armstrong, this beach is where I found you and fell in love with you and built a life with you. So this is where I want to make you my wife, the best friend and forever lover I will cherish, honor, adore, and love for all the days and nights we have together. Will you marry me?"

"Yes, Clay Walker. I will marry you right here and now. I love you, too."

Behind her, Zoe squealed just as Ashley reached them.

"Congratulations, Mom. I love you." She kissed Lacey and hugged Clay. "Welcome to the family, Clay."

She stepped to the side to join the girls, all three with tears that matched Lacey's and smiles that rivaled the beauty of the sunset.

Lacey's parents came next, and, miracle of miracles, her mother was smiling. And Dad was bawling like a baby.

Last was Mayor Lennox, carrying a single piece of paper.

Their contract. Their future.

"Please join hands," the mayor said.

Lacey looked down at her mimosa bouquet, then turned to her friends. Which one of them should get this? Should the bouquet go to Zoe, whose mischievous grin almost hid her long-ago heartache, or Tessa, with her nurturing spirit that couldn't be fulfilled in the garden no matter how hard she tried? Or Jocelyn, who tried to control everything by turning her back on the past?

She wished a lifetime of love for all three of her best friends, but only one could take the bouquet.

"Just a minute," Lacey whispered to Clay. "I need to give these to someone."

Turning, she hesitated, still trying to decide.

"Just throw them," he said. "Let the wind decide."

She tossed the bouquet toward the women. Tessa froze and Zoe reached out with a squeal, but the breeze caught the flowers and took them straight to Jocelyn. She snagged the stems right before they hit the sand, getting a huge cheer from the crowd as she held the flowers with tentative fingers.

"You're next," Lacey mouthed, then sidled closer to Clay.

As the mayor started the second official ceremony of the day, Lacey took a slow, deep inhalation of the salt air of Barefoot Bay. The tangy scent reminded her of the morning of the hurricane, when hope and anticipation and change had beckoned her.

And then love found her.

She joined hands with the man she loved and hung on for dear life. Because life, as it turned out, really was dear.

Barefoot in the Rain

For Louisa Edwards and Kristen Painter . . .
My besties who hand me the umbrella (drink)
every time it rains.

Prologue

*A*ugust 1997

"I know why they call this a comforter." Jocelyn pulled the tattered cotton all the way up to her nose, taking a sniff right over the Los Angeles Dodgers logo.

Will didn't look up from stuffing socks into the corners of his suitcase. "Why's that, Joss?"

"Because..." She took a noisy, deep inhale. "It smells like Will Palmer."

Slowly, he lifted his head, a sweet smile pulling at his face, a lock of dark hair falling to his brow. Lucky hair. Jocelyn's fingers itched to brush it back and linger in the silky strands.

"Don't tell me," he said. "It stinks of sweat, grass, and a hint of reliability?"

"No." She sniffed again. "It smells like comfort."

He straightened, rounding the suitcase to take a few steps closer to the bed, leveling her with eyes the same color as the Dodger-blue blanket. "You're welcome to take it to Gainesville. My mom bought me a whole new set of that stuff for the apartment."

"I'm sure it would be the envy of my roommates." Girls she didn't even know, except as names on a piece of paper sent to her by a resident adviser named Lacey Armstrong. Would Zoe Tamarin and Tessa Galloway be her friends? Would they make fun of her for bringing the next-door neighbor's comforter to her dorm room next week?

"Do you want it?" he asked, the question touchingly sincere.

"No, I don't need it," she replied. "I need..." The word stuck. Why couldn't she just say it, tell him, be honest with her best friend in the whole world who was leaving for college—a *different* college—tomorrow morning? "You."

He did a double take like he wasn't sure he'd caught that one-syllable whisper. "That's a very un-Jocelyn-Bloom-like admission."

"I'm practicing to be the new me."

"I hope you don't change *too* much up there at UF. I like you just the way you are."

I like you. *I like you.*

Lately, those three words were being tossed around like his baseballs during practice. It was almost as if she and Will wanted to say more. But they couldn't. That would change everything in the delicate tightrope of friendship and attraction they'd walked for all these years.

"Anyway," she said quickly, "you're the one who's going

to change. Living off campus, traveling with the University of Miami baseball team, fending off those pro offers."

"Please, you sound like my dad now."

"I'm serious. No one will recognize the golden boy of Mimosa Key when he comes home at Thanksgiving."

"You're the one with a full academic ride and so many scholarships you're *making* money going to school, Miss Four-Point-Six Smartypants."

"You're the one who's going to be on a box of Wheaties someday, Mr. MVP of State Championships."

He rolled his eyes. "Shit, now you really sound like my dad." Shaking his hair back, he came a little closer and propped on the side of the bed, the mattress shifting under his weight. "So what about Thanksgiving?"

"What about it?"

"You coming back home, Bloomerang?"

Her heart did a little roll and dive at the nickname he'd given her years ago.

Jocelyn Bloom-erang, he called her. Because you always come back to me, he'd say after she'd been MIA for a few days. But the truth was, she had no real reason to come back to this barrier island hugging the coast of Florida. Except him, and he was headed for bigger and better things.

In answer to his question she just shrugged, not wanting to lie and really not wanting to ask a question of her own: Would he ever consider taking her with him on his journey to fame and fortune?

"You're not coming back, are you?" he asked.

"I...might." She locked her elbow and let her head fall on her shoulder, hiding behind the hair falling over her face. "You know how things are."

He stroked her cheek and smoothed that fallen hair over her shoulder. "I know how things are."

They didn't have to say more than that. Ever since the Palmers had built this addition to their house so their star-athlete son could have a gym attached to his bedroom, he'd also had a front-row, second-story seat to the drama unfolding at the Bloom house next door. The windows behind his power-lifting station let in light—and noise.

He'd heard enough to know what happened next door. That was why he left the door at the bottom of the steps open, so Jocelyn could slip up to the safety and comfort of her best friend's loft.

And she had, so many, many times.

"Your mom will miss you," he said, his voice surprisingly tight.

"My mom..." She wanted to say mom would be fine, but they both knew better. "Was born without a spine."

"Which means she'll miss you even more."

"I'm not the parent-pleaser you are, Will. Well, I can't please him, obviously, and I don't need to please her. She refuses to leave him and, you know, half the time I think she feels like she *deserves* what she gets."

He didn't respond; what could he possibly say? Jocelyn's dad was a ticking time bomb and no one ever knew when the fuse would blow. All they knew was that her mother would end up bruised. Or worse. And, honestly, it was only a matter of time until that fist made contact with Jocelyn.

"But I *do* have a spine," Jocelyn said, lifting her chin. "And next week can't come fast enough for me."

Something flickered in his eyes. Sadness? Pity? Longing? "I wish Miami didn't start a week earlier than Florida."

"You're ready," she said. "You've outgrown the shrine."

He laughed at her favorite name for his loft. Did he know that when she said that, she meant a different kind of shrine—a sanctuary? That was what it was for her. This second-story suite might be his workout room and bedroom, but it was her safe harbor; the sight of his gazillion trophies and framed newspaper articles always made her feel safe and secure from the mess next door that was her home.

Or maybe it was just the broad, strong shoulders of a boy who always let her lean on him that made her feel so safe and secure here.

She realized he was looking directly at her, his expression serious, his hand still resting against her neck.

"What?" she asked.

Without answering, he tunneled his fingers into her hair, inching her closer. "It's our last night, Jossie," he whispered. "And I'm going to miss the hell out of you."

Warmth curled through her, unholy and unfamiliar—no, it was familiar enough, especially in the last few months They'd been dancing around this all summer, both too scared to tear the safety net of their friendship and do what they were thinking about constantly.

They'd almost talked about it. Almost kissed. Frequently touched. And every time they parted, Jocelyn felt twisted and tortured and achy in places that had never ached.

His Adam's apple rose and fell as he tried to swallow. Unable to resist, she touched that masculine lump on his throat.

"When I met you, Will, you didn't have one of these."

A smile threatened. "I didn't have a lot of things I have now."

"Like this manly stubble." She brushed her hand along the line of his jaw, his soft teenage whiskers ticking her knuckles.

"Or these massive guns." He grinned and lifted his arm, flexing to show off a very impressive catcher's bicep.

Then his eyes dropped from her face to her chest. "Speaking of things someone didn't have."

She felt her color rise and, oh, Lord, her nipples puckered. There was the ache again.

"Will…" She looked down, directly at the sight of a shockingly big tent in his jeans. He hadn't had *that* when he'd moved in seven years ago.

She stared at the bulge, her throat dry, her chest tight, her hands itchy. Dear God, she wanted to touch him.

"Jossie," he whispered, trailing a finger up her throat and across her bottom lip, sending fireworks from her scalp to her toes and a whole lot of precious places in between. "I don't want to leave without…"

She looked up at him, his face so near now she could count his sinfully long black lashes. "You think it's time…" She took a slow breath. "That we…"

"It's not about *time*," he said, a hitch in his voice nearly undoing her. "You have to know how I feel about you."

"I know."

"No, you don't."

"I'm your best friend," she said quickly. "The girl next door. The only person in town who doesn't swoon at the sight of your number thirty-one on the cover of the *Mimosa Gazette*."

She thought he'd smile, but he didn't. Instead, he closed his eyes. "You're so much more than that."

Was she? God, she wanted to be. She really, really wanted to be. But if this friendship was ruined, then what? They'd hugged a million times. They'd kissed on the cheek. They even made out a few times when they were fifteen, but then he started dating some dimwit cheerleader. Everything physical had stopped, but their friendship and his unspoken offer of an escape from the hell of her home kept on going.

But this summer, with college looming and the clock ticking and hormones raging and—

He kissed her. One soft, sweet, gentle kiss and everything in her body just melted.

"Joss," he murmured into her mouth. "I have to ask you something."

She backed away, the seriousness of the question scaring her. "What?"

"I need to know how you feel about me."

She almost laughed. "How I feel about you?" Didn't he know? Couldn't he tell? He was *everything* to her—her rock, her crutch, her soft place to fall. Her hero, her fantasy, her one and only. "Will, I...I..."

"I love you, Joss." His eyes welled up with the words, making them twenty times more sweet and perfect.

She cupped his jaw, searching eyes the color and depth of the Gulf of Mexico they'd spent so many hours swimming in over the last seven years. The words were on her lips, as warm and sweet as his kiss. But something stopped her. Something deep inside held on to those words and wouldn't let them out.

"I love you," he repeated, having no such problem.

Did he? Did he really love her? Love was so tenuous. Hadn't she heard those very words spoken to her mother and, ten minutes later, the smack of a palm against flesh?

His hand slipped out of her hair, down the column of her neck, over her breastbone. "Jocelyn, I'm dying here."

For love or...

He eased her back on the bed, covering her with his body.

Sex.

Was he dying for her to say I love you or...

He nuzzled into her neck, kissing her lightly, each touch of his lips like a little firebrand on her skin that made everything tight and hot and needy. The comforter balled up between them, lumpy but not thick enough to block out the pressure of his body.

He rocked his hips slowly first, then a little faster. Colors flashed behind her eyes at the intensity of the pleasure. Fiery ribbons of need and heat curled between her legs as she met each beat of his hips.

Grabbing the comforter, he yanked it away, throwing it to the side so he could get closer to her. All she could hear was the loud huffs of breath, both of them panting already as they found a rhythm. A rhythm of kissing, touching, rubbing, riding.

"Will..."

"Is it okay, Joss? Tell me it's okay." He nearly growled the words into her throat, kissing her as one hand—one shaking, large, masculine, beloved hand—slid over her cotton tank and settled on her breast.

She gasped at the shock of the sensation, making him lift his head. "You all right?"

"Yes. That feels good." She barely mouthed the words, her eyes damn near rolling back into her head it felt so amazing. His hand was so big he covered her whole breast, palming her until her nipple felt like it would pop.

His other hand went under her top, over her stomach, into her bra, touching, touching, *touching.*

"Oh my God," he moaned, pumping harder against her. "I can't believe how amazing you feel."

She couldn't answer, too lost in the newness, the strangeness, the complete wonder of Will's calloused, strong hand on her skin. His whole body quivered, and she knew he was as overcome as she was.

"Take it off," he pleaded, struggling with the top. "Take it off."

He pulled the T-shirt over her head, pushing up the bra without bothering to unsnap it, her breasts so small they popped right out.

He stared at her, searing her skin with the intensity of his focus. "Just like I imagined."

"You imagined?"

"Jocelyn, seriously? Do you not think I—"

"Don't." She put her hand on his mouth. "Don't tell me. Just...keep going."

"Are you sure?"

She nodded, driven by the need that burned low in her belly and deep in her chest.

This was inevitable, really.

All these hours in this room, together. She'd go home and kiss her pillow, touch herself, imagine Will's fingers and mouth and his...

She slid her hand between them, closing over the hard shaft in his jeans, making him grunt with surprise and pleasure. He kissed her chest again, moving from one breast to the other, fumbling with her shorts.

"I have a condom," he whispered between ragged breaths. "Want me to get it?"

"In a minute, yeah." She wrapped her arms around his neck. "Are you a virgin, Will?"

Still for a second, he finally admitted, "Um, not exactly."

"I am."

She heard him swallow hard. "I figured that. I won't hurt you, Jocelyn. I love you."

He *loved* her.

"Tell me," he urged, tugging at her zipper. "Tell me you love me."

"I will." When he was inside her. When they were one. Then she would tell him. "Just don't stop."

"Not a chance." He slipped his hand into her panties and she almost screamed when his finger touched her. "I love you so much, Jossie." Inside. "I love you." Deeper. "I love you. You have no idea how much...oh, damn, you feel good."

Heat coursed through her as she rolled into his palm, lost in his words, his hands, his beautiful, beautiful—

"You goddamn fucking bastard!"

The whole room vibrated with the shout as Jocelyn screamed and Will leaped off her, both turning to meet the blazing gray eyes of Guy Bloom.

"Get off her!" Guy's barrel chest heaved with fury, stretching his sheriff's uniform as he marched closer, already lifting his arm to a position she knew all too well.

"No, Dad, no!" Jocelyn screamed, jumping up, grabbing at her bra to pull it down.

But it was too late. Her father glowered at her, his face red, spittle at the corners of his mouth. "I'm going to fucking kill you."

"No!" She got the cups over her breasts just as Will stepped in front of her, arms outstretched.

"Deputy Bloom, please, I'm really sorry—"

Guy shoved him to the side to get to Jocelyn. "You whore! You cheap, trashy whore!"

"No, Dad, I'm not—" The crack of his palm snapped her head back.

"Stop it!" Will pushed him, hard enough to make the older man stumble.

He dropped his head, nostrils flaring like a bull as he stared at Will. "You touching an officer of the law, young man?"

"Don't hit her."

Guy wiped some sweat from his upper lip, his attention fully on Will now as they stared each other down. Will's fists pumped, his jaw clenched.

Oh, God. Oh, *God.* "Don't, Will, please."

He never even looked at her. "Don't you touch her." Will's voice was little more than a growl.

"You want to take me, boy?"

Will just stared.

Guy took a step closer, highlighting the fact that he was a good four inches shorter and thirty years older than his enemy. Will could kill him.

"Please, Will." She started to stand and Guy shoved her back on the bed.

It was all Will needed. He lunged at Guy, who ducked fast and whipped out his pistol.

Jocelyn screamed. "No, no!"

Thick fingers curled around the trigger of a gun she'd seen a million times on the counter. A gun even *he* never had the nerve to pull out when he lost his temper.

Will froze.

"There will be no skin off my back if I shoot the boy who attacked my daughter."

"He didn't—"

"Shut up, you little whore!" The words echoed through the loft, so wrong in this place of safety, like a curse screamed in a church.

"Or better yet, why don't I just put an end to that superstar baseball career of yours? One phone call." He snorted as if he liked the idea. "One phone call from the sheriff's office to the University of Miami and you can hang up your cleats, you little prick." Guy broke into an evil, ugly smile. "Rapists don't get scholarships. Rapists don't get drafted to the big leagues. Rapists go to jail."

Will still didn't move. Not even his eyes. Only his chest rose and fell with slow, pained breaths as he surely realized who had the real power in this room.

That was something Jocelyn had known since the first time her dad had what she and her mother called "an episode." But they learned that the only thing to do, the *only* thing, was to stay calm until it ended. And take what he dished out.

"Get out, Joss," her father ordered.

She looked down for her T-shirt and suddenly his big hand was on her arm.

"Never mind clothes, just get out." He yanked her off the bed.

"Hey!" Will stepped closer, inches from the gun still aimed at her. "Don't hurt her."

"I could say the same thing to you, Palmer." He gave Jocelyn a solid push, still looking at Will. "And believe me, nothing would give me more pleasure than to take you off the fucking pedestal this town has you on and see you rot in jail for raping my daughter."

"He didn't rape me!"

The back of Guy's hand cracked across Jocelyn's face, his wedding ring making contact with her tooth.

Jocelyn slammed her hand over her mouth to fight a sob.

"Stop it!" Will cried. "You're a goddamn animal!"

Guy shoved the gun right into Will's gut, making him double forward with a grunt, his eyes popping in horror.

"No one's gonna blame a sheriff for killing the kid who dragged his daughter into his room and forced himself on her!"

Another sob escaped Jocelyn's mouth. "Dad, please, please." She wept the words, her whole body trembling. "Don't hurt him. Please don't hurt him."

Guy's shoulders slumped a little as he angled his head to the door. "Go. I'll take care of you at home."

"Please," she cried, grabbing his arm, her near nakedness forgotten. "Don't shoot him."

"Go!" he bellowed.

Frightened, she stumbled to the door, turning to take one look at Will when she reached the top of the stairs. His eyes were red-rimmed in fear, his face white, his big, healthy, athletic body at the mercy of a gun six inches from his heart.

She'd done this to him. Her father could destroy Will's life, everything he'd worked for, all his plans, his future. She loved Will—really, truly loved him—far too much for this.

"I'm sorry..." she whispered before running down the stairs, pausing halfway to grip the railing and listen.

"If you ever, *ever* go within five feet of my daughter again, I will ruin your name, your face, and your precious fucking arm. You get that?"

Silence.

Squeezing the rail until her knuckles turned white, Jocelyn waited, bracing for a shot, a word, anything.

But there was just silence. Of course Will couldn't fight for her. Couldn't risk his life for her. No girl was worth that kind of love.

As long as Guy Bloom was alive, he had the power to ruin Will's life. The mean, miserable bastard always had the power. So there was only one thing she could do. Let Will go, forever.

She heard Guy's footsteps and she scrambled to beat him outside, wanting to run across the lawn to their house, hoping to lock herself in the—

He caught up with her at the pool.

"Get in the goddamn house."

What would he do to her? What did it matter? Nothing could hurt as much as the decision she'd just made. Nothing could hurt as much as losing Will, but she had no other choice. She loved him that much.

Chapter One

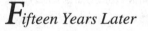

*F**ifteen Years Later*

The situation had gone way past dire.

Will stood in the living room of his next-door neighbor's house and surveyed the mess, the low, dull throbbing that had pounded at the base of his skull since he'd stopped by at lunchtime rapidly escalating into a screaming mother humper of a headache.

Son of a bitch, it was like a pack of wild dogs lived here instead of one confused, pathetic, and forgotten old man who couldn't remember his own name.

"William!"

But he knew Will's name and used it often, in that shaky, feeble voice that threaded down the hall right now.

"William, is that you?"

"It's me, Guy." On a sigh that shuddered through his

whole body, Will stepped over a pile of magazines that had been torn into a million pieces—the new scrapbooking project, no doubt—and picked up a basket of yarn with threads and spools stuffed inside. He put it on a table next to the remnants of the sandwich Will had made Guy for lunch, then headed down the hall.

"I decided to clean out this old closet," Guy called from one of the extra bedrooms.

This couldn't be good.

Shit. Clothes were strewn everywhere: men's suit jackets, women's dresses, kids' shorts, and a small mountain of worn shoes. Where the hell did he get all this crap? His wife had been dead ten years now. Hadn't he cleaned out anything?

"Guy, what are you doing?" Will fought to keep any anger out of his tone. If he so much as raised his voice by one decibel, Guy cried like a baby, and that ripped Will's heart into pieces.

"I saw a show called *Clean House* and got this idea." Guy stood in a walk-in closet holding a pile of what looked to be old blue jeans. His glasses were crooked, his white hair tufted and messy, his blue knit pullover stained from something red. Punch or Red Zinger tea, probably.

He'd made tea? "Did you remember to turn the stove off?"

"I might have. I was really enjoying this show on that decorating channel. A woman gettin' all in your face about cleaning up stuff." He grinned, his lemony teeth a testament to years of stinking up the local sheriff's office with the stench of Marlboros. And yet he lived while his wife had been the one buried by cancer. And his daughter...

Will pushed that thought out of his head.

"I think she was named Nicey. Smart lady."

Will just stared at him. "Who are you talking about?

"The lady on TV," Guy said. "She says the secret to happiness is a clean house."

Will glanced around at the piles of crap. "Looks like you're a long way from happiness in this house."

"That's the thing, Will! That's the thing about the show. This crew comes in and takes your house apart, sells your stuff in a yard sale, and cleans it so everything is perfect."

"Everything *was* perfect," Will said, picking up a bright-yellow dress sized for a young girl. Had he ever even seen Jocelyn in this dress? "Why do you still have this stuff?"

Guy gave him his blankest stare, and God knew he had a shitload of different blank stares. "I don't know, son."

Son.

Will had long ago stopped trying to convince the old man that was a misnomer. "C'mon, bud. Let's make you some dinner and get you situated for the night."

But Guy didn't move, just kept looking into the closet wistfully. "Funny, I couldn't find any of your old clothes. Just girl stuff. Your mother must have thrown them out before she died."

His mother had moved to Bend, Oregon, with his dad. "Yeah, she must have," he agreed.

"Do you think they'd come here, Will?"

"Who?"

"The *Clean House* people. They say if you want to be on the show, you just have to call them and tell them you want *a clean house.*" He dragged out the words, mimicking an announcer. "Would you do that for me?"

"I'll look into it," he said vaguely, reaching to guide Guy away from the mess. "How 'bout I heat up that leftover spaghetti for you?"

"Will you call them?"

"Like I said—"

"Will you?" Eyes the steel gray of a cloudy sky narrowed behind crooked glasses on a bulbous nose.

"Why is it so important?"

"Because." Guy let out a long, sad sigh. "It's like starting over, and when I look through this stuff it just... makes me feel sad."

"Some memories do that," he said.

"Oh, William, I don't have any memories. I don't know what half this stuff is." He picked up a rose-patterned sweater that Will remembered seeing Mary Jo Bloom wear many years ago. "It all just reminds me that I don't remember. I want a fresh start. A clean house."

"I understand." He managed to get Guy down the hall with a gentle nudge.

As he sat down in his favorite recliner, Guy reached for Will's hand. "You'll call those people."

"Sure, buddy."

In the fridge Will found the Tupperware container of spaghetti, but his mind went back to the yellow dress upstairs.

The thought of Jocelyn pulled at his heart, making him twist the burner knob too hard. He dumped the lump of cold noodles into a pan, splattering the Ragu on his T-shirt.

"Where's the clicker?" Guy called, panic making his voice rise. "I can't find the clicker, William! What did you do with it?"

Will pulled open the dishwasher and rolled out the top rack, spying the remote instantly. At least it wasn't at the bottom of the trash, like last week.

"I've got it." He checked the pan of noodles and took the remote out to Guy, who'd given up and turned on the TV manually, stabbing at the volume button so the strains of *Entertainment Tonight* blared through the living room.

Again with the crap TV? Alzheimer's didn't just rob him of his memories, it changed every aspect of his personality. The bastard county sheriff had turned into a little old lady obsessed with celebrities and home crafts.

Will gently set the remote on Guy's armrest, getting a grateful smile and a pat on his hand.

"You're a good son, Will." Guy thumbed up the volume and the announcer's voice shook the speaker.

"...with more on this shocking breakup of Hollywood's happiest couple."

God help him, couldn't they watch ESPN for just one lousy dinner? But the trash TV blared with an excited announcer's voice, hammering at his headache.

"*TMZ* has identified the 'other woman' in the stunning divorce of Miles Thayer and Coco Kirkman as a life coach by the name of Jocelyn Bloom."

Will froze, then spun around to see the TV, with a "What the hell?" of disbelief trapped in his throat.

"Known as a 'life coach to the stars,' Jocelyn Bloom has been working for Coco Kirkman for over a year, giving her daily access and, evidently, much more, to Coco's movie-star husband, Miles Thayer."

Will just stared, blinked, then took a step closer. The picture was grainy, taken by a powerful lens at a long distance, but not blurry enough to cast any doubt that he was looking at the woman he'd been thinking about a few seconds ago. Ebony hair pulled tight off her delicate features, giant dark eyes, narrow shoulders taut and stiff.

Jocelyn broke up a marriage?

"*TMZ* has published a series of texts sent between Jocelyn Bloom and Miles Thayer," the announcer continued, his voice full of barely restrained joy. "The most salacious texts detailed sexual acts—"

Will lurched toward the chair, grabbing the remote to thumb the Mute button.

Guy looked stunned. "That's the good part!"

Will opened his mouth to argue, but a change in the screen snagged his attention. This shot was closer and clearer and, holy shit, she looked good. Better than ever, in fact. "You know who they're talking about?" he asked Guy.

"Some movie stars. Who cares? I like that stuff."

"Some movie stars and..." *Your daughter.* "No one you recognized?"

Guy snorted. "I don't know those people's names, Will. I barely know my own. What does salacious mean, anyway?" He tried to get the remote.

"It means..." Things he didn't want to think about Jocelyn doing with anyone. "Sexy."

"I can take the dirty stuff, pal. I'm too old for it to have any effect." Guy managed to grab the remote and get the sound right back. Unable to help himself, Will turned back to the TV.

"Jocelyn Bloom has yet to talk to the media," the reporter said. "Or issue a statement to deny the accusations. Right now all we know about this woman is that she is a certified life coach and counts Coco Kirkman among a long list of wealthy and well-known clients."

Will looked hard at Guy once more, but the older man just stared at the TV without so much as a flicker of recognition.

"What the hell's a life coach, anyway?" Guy asked with a soft harrumph. "Sounds like an excuse to pick rich people's pockets and bust up their marriages." He punched up the volume.

Was that who Jocelyn Bloom had become?

"According to an attorney for Coco Kirkman, Ms. Bloom has been a close confidante for well over a year, and during that time, she has been frequently an overnight guest of the couple."

Will's stomach tightened as he forced himself to leave the room.

"Fuck!" Smoke and the smell of charred food filled the kitchen, and he lunged for the pot handle to slide the scorched spaghetti off the burner. "God damn it *all!*"

As he shook his hand more out of sheer rage than any real pain, a string of new curses fell from his lips. Pulling it together, he stirred the spaghetti and folded the bits of black into the noodles. Guy'd never notice a burned dinner. Hell, Guy would probably never notice *dinner.*

Forcing the image of a girl he once loved out of his head, Will put the food on a plate and carried it into the living room, where, thank Christ, Guy had switched to a game show.

"Where's yours?" Guy asked as he straightened his chair so he could reach the TV table. "Come and spin the wheel of fortune with me."

When Will had returned to Mimosa Key, he'd *tried* to hate the old coot, he really had. But over time, well, shit, how can you hate a guy who had no memory of what a nasty prick he'd ever been? The worst thing Guy Bloom did now was start and never finish a shit-ton of craft projects.

"Not tonight, Guy. I have some work to do."

"You worked all day." There was a tinge of sadness in his voice, enough to tweak Will's guilt. Guy was lonely, plain and simple, and Will was all he had.

"Just have to check my e-mail and pay some bills." Because who else was going to pay Guy's bills? He glanced at the TV, his mind's eye still seeing Jocelyn's beautiful features instead of a game-show hostess the screen.

"I'll check on you later, Guy." Meaning he'd be sure the old man got in bed and had a light on and didn't mistake his own reflection for a burglar.

Before Guy could ask him to stay, Will slipped out, crossing the patio and the small lawn that separated the houses. Inside, he dropped into a kitchen chair and stared at the pile of Guy's mail. Doctors' bills, insurance bills, pharmacy bills, and more doctors' bills. All to keep Guy relatively stable. A losing battle, on every front.

And the cost of private nursing? Astronomical.

Will knew exactly how much money Guy had; he wrote out the checks every month. The account just got smaller and smaller. Stabbing his hair, he blew out a breath, imagining just how much money Jocelyn charged as a life coach. How much she'd get for selling her story about sex with Miles Thayer to some tabloid.

Didn't matter. As far as anyone knew, Jocelyn had been home exactly three times in fifteen years after . . . that night. He'd heard she came home for her mother's funeral almost ten years ago and once, about a year ago, after the hurricane wiped out Barefoot Bay, Will had seen her at a

Mimosa Key town council meeting. But the minute she'd laid eyes on him she disappeared again. And although he wasn't there, he'd heard she'd made it to Lacey and Clay Walker's beach wedding.

Now she lived in another world, three thousand miles away, breaking up movie-star marriages. Funny, he was the one who was supposed to have become rich and famous, while she'd wanted to live in a comfy house in the country, if he recalled her childhood dreams correctly.

Fifteen years and a lot of water had passed under that burned bridge. And he couldn't exactly blame her. Or call her for help. Or even, as much as he tried, forget her.

And God knows he'd tried.

Chapter Two

Jocelyn did everything she could to get comfortable, but it just wasn't going to happen on a cross-country flight. She shifted in the plane seat, her back and bottom numb, her head on fire from the itchy wig, her hand throbbing from filling three notebooks for a grand total of... too many lists to count.

The lists gave her some measure of peace, but not much. Each had a title and a theme, a strategy with potential action items, and those all had priority ratings, a deadline, and, of course, her very favorite form of punctuation: the check mark.

So far, only one action item was checked, although it was more of a survival technique than anything strategic: *Get out of L.A. and hide.*

Nor was her destination exactly her first choice on a list of possible hiding places, but all her wealthy friends and clients—owners of multiple chalets in Aspen and getaways in Italy—had been conveniently unavailable. No surprise, really.

But Lacey had come through, of course, as the truest of true friends. When she'd suggested that Jocelyn take refuge at Casa Blanca, Lacey's partially built resort in Barefoot Bay, there'd been no hesitation. Jocelyn needed sanctuary from this personal storm, a place to avoid the media and figure out just where to take her life from here.

Funny that such a decision had to be made on the island of Mimosa Key, but beggars and homewreckers couldn't afford to be choosy.

Except that Jocelyn was neither.

Two seats away, a young woman skimmed the pages of *People* magazine, blind to the fact that the "other woman" in Miles Thayer's broken marriage was sitting a foot away, sipping water and wishing it was something stronger.

Jocelyn stole a few glances at the pages as she closed her notebooks and tucked them into her bag, narrowing her eyes at the image of Coco Kirkman on the cover of the magazine.

That defenseless shadow in her eyes had served her well in front of the camera, making her an empathetic character no matter who she played. That vulnerability had attracted Jocelyn, too, reminding her of another woman who needed a little help developing a spine. Coco was a young, talented, still-fixable version of Mary Jo Bloom, but, once again, Jocelyn had failed to make that fix.

Leaning against the glass, Jocelyn peered down at the swampy Everglades of Florida's southwest coast, the lush, tropical wetlands so different from what was now her home state. California was brown most of the year, horribly overpopulated and packed with people who *thought* they were rare birds, not *real* rare birds.

But this? This little corner on the Gulf of Mexico was home. A shitty home full of heartaches and bad memories, but it was home. And if her dear friend from college hadn't also lived on this island, she'd never, ever have come back here again.

And that might be sad, because Mimosa Key, for all its dark memories, was a pretty place. Especially Barefoot Bay. The picturesque inlet on the north end of the island was far away enough from those memories that Jocelyn could feel safe and secure. Relatively.

As the plane came to a stop and the deboarding announcements were made, the woman flipped the magazine onto the empty seat between them. "Feel free to take it," she said to Jocelyn, giving her a quick look.

For a moment, Jocelyn tensed, expecting shocked recognition. *Oh my God, you're the chick who had an affair with Miles Thayer!*

But there was only a cool smile, and Jocelyn's gaze dropped to the blaring, glaring lies across the cover.

Coco Is Crushed! Sexy Life Coach Steals an American Angel's Husband!

"No, thanks," Jocelyn replied, turning away.

At the medley of snapping seat belts and clattering overhead bins, Jocelyn tugged the long blonde wig and adjusted her sunglasses, not caring that the sun had already set here on the East Coast. If she could fit a hat over the stupid wig, she'd have worn that, too.

The regional airport was small, and she spotted Lacey and Tessa right past Security, standing close and peering over heads to find her. Lacey looked as radiant as she had the day Casa Blanca's groundbreaking ceremony had turned into her impromptu wedding to Clay Walker. Her reddish-blond curls framed her freckled face, a slight frown pulling as she scanned the crowd.

Next to her, Tessa looked relaxed if not radiant, tanned from hours in the gardens, toned from her uber-healthy lifestyle. Her deep brown eyes passed right over Jocelyn.

Only when Jocelyn dragged her carry-on in front of them and slowly raised her glasses did they gasp with recognition.

"Oh my God," Tessa said.

"Joce—"

Jocelyn put her hand over Lacey's mouth. "Shhh. Let's cut out of here, stat."

"I didn't even recognize you." Tessa reached for a strand of wig hair, but Jocelyn ducked.

"Exactly. C'mon, move it."

Lacey put her arm around Jocelyn and Tessa grabbed the rolling bag, both of them flanking her like bodyguards.

"There are no paparazzi in the airport," Lacey assured her, moving so slowly that Jocelyn wanted to scream. "And certainly none in Mimosa Key."

"Which is why I'm here," Jocelyn said. "We can skip Baggage. I've got everything here. Let's go."

"Can't." Tessa moved even more slowly, nudging them all away from the exit.

"*Must*," Jocelyn shot back. "I gotta get this wig off."

"Over here," Lacey said. "She's already landed."

"Who's already landed?" The airport wasn't that big, but it felt like she was crossing the Sahara from one gate to the next.

"You really think Zoe Tamarin could stand for the three of us to be together and *not* get in on it?" Tessa asked, her expression changing as she pointed to more people deplaning a few gates away. "There she is. Spent a fortune she doesn't have to fly direct from Phoenix and time her arrival with yours."

Instantly Jocelyn spotted Zoe, with her wild blonde waves and sunny smile, weaving through the crowd, waving madly. As much as Jocelyn feared Zoe would suddenly scream her name, the fact that the four of them were together sent a shudder of sheer joy through her. She'd pay Zoe for the plane ticket, and it would be well worth the cost.

"Woo-hoo! I made it!" Zoe practically danced through the crowds, her jade green eyes sparkling as she locked on Tessa and Lacey. Thankfully, she didn't even notice or recognize Jocelyn.

Lacey moved ahead, reaching Zoe first, hugging her and whispering in her ear. Instantly, Zoe's head popped up and she zeroed in on Jocelyn.

She stared, raised one eyebrow, then just shook her head as she approached Jocelyn and Tessa. Reaching out for a hug, she folded Jocelyn in her arms.

"That wig is so fake I can't even joke about it," she murmured in Jocelyn's ear.

"But you will." She hugged her friend. "Thanks, Zoe. I'm glad you're here."

Zoe fluffed some strands of Jocelyn's wig and rolled her eyes. "As if I'd miss this." She turned her attention to Tessa; once again there was a shower of squeals and hugs. "I'm glad you called me," Zoe said to Tessa, wrapping them all into a group hug. "We come together when there's trouble, right? That's what we did for Lace after the shit storm. Now that's what we do for you...*during* the shit storm." She leaned in and whispered, "Seriously, Miles Thayer, Joss? He's so not your type."

Jocelyn just closed her eyes. "For the love of God, can we please get in the car so I can get this thing off my head."

A man passed and took a long look at Jocelyn, making her cringe and drag the sunglasses down for coverage. "Did you see him stare at me?"

"That's how all men look at blondes," Zoe assured her, linking arms and nudging Jocelyn forward. "Especially fake ones."

Jocelyn kept the sunglasses on until they were in Lacey's car. Then she ripped off the wig and scratched her scalp, yanking at the clip that held her long hair in a tight knot. "Oh my God, that feels good."

Lacey grinned into the rearview mirror. "There's our Joss again."

"Give me this thing." Next to her, Tessa snagged the wig. "You don't need this here, okay? No reporters, no paparazzi, no one to hide from."

Well, there was at least one person to hide from. "Depends. Where did you decide I'm staying, Lace?" Last year when she'd come to help Lacey rebuild her life, she'd stayed at the Ritz Carlton in Naples and while her friends didn't exactly understand her adamant decision not to go to certain parts of Mimosa Key, they'd abided by it. She couldn't do that now; the media would be all over her in a hotel that public.

"Zoe's staying with me in the house I rent in Pleasure Pointe," Tessa said.

Too close for comfort. "I'm not staying there," Jocelyn replied quickly.

"We know," Lacey assured her. "You're staying in Barefoot Bay."

"So speaketh the former dormitory resident adviser and elder statesmen of the group," Zoe said.

"Two years. Not that elder," Lacey shot back.

"One year married to the younger man and she's a teenager again. All right, woman." Zoe turned in the passenger seat to face Jocelyn in the back. "Dish."

Where she was staying was an easy topic compared to this one. They'd want the truth, and it would be tricky. But she was ready. "There's nothing to dish."

Again, Zoe gave a signature eye roll. "Come on, Joss. Miles Thayer? He's like the hottest human on earth. I want gory details, including size, stamina, and any kinky shit."

"Zoe," the other two said.

But Jocelyn just shook her head. "All right, ladies. Listen to me. I'm going to say this once and once only. I did *not* sleep with Miles Thayer. I barely speak to Miles Thayer, and when I do, there's not the remotest molecule of affection or attraction between us. I hate Miles Thayer and, if you want to know the truth, so does Coco Kirkman."

They all just stared at her.

"Why?" Tessa asked.

"I'm not going to say," Jocelyn said, her voice taut. "And if I can't count on you three not to believe the crap in the tabloids, then turn around and take me back to the airport. I'll hide somewhere else."

Tessa put her hand on Jocelyn's arm. "You can count

on us," she said. "You can also count on Zoe being crass and thinking exclusively about sex."

"There was no sex. Sorry to disappoint you, Zoe. And none of this leaves the car, got it?"

"I'm not disappointed," Zoe assured her. "I'm proud of you for resisting his hotness. But if there was no sex, really, *why* is Coco claiming you broke up her marriage?"

Jocelyn dropped back on the seat, letting out a long, slow breath. "It's complicated," she said, the vague tone getting a quick, suspicious look from Tessa. "But Coco wants out of the marriage and this... is her way."

"Her way?" Lacey's voice rose with incredulity. "Why not just file for divorce? It's Hollywood, for heaven's sake. Why throw it all on you?"

Because Coco's shoulders weren't strong enough to handle the repercussions. And this was the only way.

"She needs to put the blame on someone other than herself," Jocelyn said, conjuring up her best shrink-like tone.

"Okay, but that doesn't explain why you don't publicly deny every word," Tessa demanded.

"Really publicly," Zoe added. "Like a billboard on Sunset Boulevard." She boxed her hands as if she were reading the headline. "*I Am not a Marriage-Wrecker.*"

"But I *am* a life coach," Jocelyn said. "And billboards on Sunset Boulevard are as fake and cheesy as the rest of that town. But with my job comes certain ethics about privacy. I know *stuff.*"

"So she makes you her fall guy?" Tessa asked. "I don't get it."

And they wouldn't, until they understood what "stuff" Jocelyn knew. And if they knew that, then...

"Look, guys, I don't want to talk about it. I just need to breathe and think and hide."

Tessa snorted. "Which, knowing you, will make you batshit crazy in two days."

Jocelyn smiled at her, not denying the truth of that. But every single client had put her on hold—or fired her last week. "Anything for me to do at Casa Blanca?"

"The resort's barely built," Lacey said. "So unless you're handy with a hammer, you're going to have to work in the food gardens with Tess."

She held up her thumb. "Totally brown. Unless your plants need life management."

"You know, Joss," Lacey said. "I've been doing all this research on high-end resorts and some of the best ones offer life coaching to their clients. Do you think you could help me figure out how I can incorporate that into my menu of services?"

"I'd love to." She leaned forward and put a hand on Lacey's shoulders. "By the way, marriage really suits you, girl. You are quite literally glowing."

She laughed. "That's because when Clay kicks me out of the construction trailer, I get to 'research' spas and their treatments. Doesn't suck."

"Don't listen to her," Tessa said. "She's madly in love and it shows."

Lacey grinned. "He's awesome, as you guys know. How can I ever thank you all enough for talking me into the hot young architect?"

"Like we had to do a lot of convincing," Zoe said with a laugh.

All the way over the causeway and up to Barefoot Bay, they chattered about Lacey's first year of happy marriage, her challenges with a teenage daughter, and the resort they'd all invested in financially and emotionally.

For the first time in over a week, Jocelyn felt certain this trip had been a very good idea. Even when they passed Center Street and she glanced to the south and memories threatened, she ignored them.

There would be absolutely no reason to see her father while she was here, none at all. So she didn't bother to bring him up and, being the friends they were, neither did the girls.

How long would that last?

Chapter Three

⌐

Something was different at Casa Blanca. Will could practically smell a change in the salty air of Barefoot Bay the minute he climbed out of his truck in front of the resort's construction trailer. The Gulf of Mexico was dead calm, the water a deep cobalt blue as the sun made its first appearance over the foliage along the eastern border of the resort's property line. The construction parking lot was empty, of course, and the structures stood silent in various degrees of completion.

Still, the air pressed, heavy with change. Funny how he could sense that. Like when the wind would pick up in the outfield, a signal that the game's momentum was about to shift.

Scanning the main building, he noticed a few additions since he'd last been to the job site. Clay and Lacey Walker ran a tight schedule, determined to get Mimosa Key's first exclusive resort up and running within the year, so it was no surprise that the subs had been hard at work on Friday while he'd driven to Tampa to pick up the flooring for one of the villas.

There were definitely more roof tiles on the main structure, the creamy barrels adding to the many textures of Clay's Moroccan-inspired architecture. And the window contractor had been busy, too, having left at least a dozen giant sheets of plate glass propped along the side and front of the curved entry, ready to be installed when the roof was completed.

But the main building of Casa Blanca was of no real interest to Will. His work centered on the six private villas the resort's most well-heeled guests would rent. He'd spent the better part of the last year building those smaller structures, including all of the finishing carpentry in Rockrose, the first completed villa at the north end of the main path.

He peered through the palm fronds and elephant-ear leaves that had grown lush since a hurricane stripped the trees over a year ago. He studied the unpaved road that led to the villas. Deep, fresh wheel grooves cut through the dew-dampened dirt. Had someone driven up there on a Sunday?

Even if there had been a sub here on a Sunday—which was really unlikely—the construction crew was primarily focused on Bay Laurel, the villa closest to where he stood now and the destination of the African wood flooring he'd loaded in his truck.

Why would someone drive up the path? Lacey and Clay's new house stood at the very far north end of the property, but you couldn't drive all the way up there from here; they'd take the back road around the property.

He paused at the passenger door, pulling it open to grab the cup of coffee he'd picked up at the Super Min on his way to the site. As he unwedged the cup from the holder, a drop of hot black liquid splashed through the plastic top, dribbling onto the seat.

Well, not the seat. Onto the newspaper he'd left there. And not exactly a newspaper, either, unless the *National Enquirer* qualified.

The headline taunted him.

Coco Cries on Set: "I Was Blind to the Affair!"

Why the hell did he buy that shit, anyway? To revel in someone else's misery? To get the dirt on a woman he'd once thought was perfect?

Well, hell, people change. Who knew that better than Will?

Holding the coffee in his right hand, he used the other to lift the front page to see the blurry shot of a woman with long dark hair, big brown eyes, and features so burned in his memory that he didn't need a wide-angle lens to capture them.

She had only changed for the better, at least physically. The years had been kind, even if the media wasn't. The memory that had haunted him for almost half his life nearly swallowed him whole when he looked at her picture.

Then don't look, you idiot.

Closing the page, he nudged the door closed with his hip and finished his coffee, intrigued enough by the tire prints to follow them after he tossed the empty cup in the trash. He strode along what would eventually be the resort's scenic walkway, canopied by green and lined with exotic flowers from Africa. Each villa was named for a different bloom found on this path.

He passed the partially built villas, mentally reviewing each construction schedule, but his thoughts stopped the instant he rounded the foliage that blocked Rockrose, the only fully finished villa

That's what was different.

He squinted into the sun that backlit the vanilla-colored structure, highlighting the fact that the french doors along the side were wide open, the sheer curtains Lacey had installed fluttering like ghosts. There was no breeze, so someone had to have the overhead fan on in there.

Shit. Vandals? Squatters? Maybe Lacey's teenage daughter or one of her friends taking advantage of the place?

There was no other explanation. Rockrose had been given a CO two weeks ago. But a certificate of occupancy didn't mean *actual* occupancy, and Lacey kept the secluded villa locked tight so that none of the construction workers traipsed through or decided to use the facilities.

He took a few steps closer, instinctively flexing his muscles, ready to fight for the turf of a building that somehow had become "his."

He took cover behind an oleander bush, slipping around to get a better view into the bedroom. He could see the sheer film of netting Lacey had hung from the bed's canopy, the decor as romantic as Morocco itself.

If anyone defiled one inch of that villa there'd be hell to pay. He'd laid the marble in the bath, shaved the oak wood crown molding, and hand-carved the columns on the fireplace mantel from one solid piece of rosewood. The whole job had given him more satisfaction than picking off a runner trying to steal second ever had.

Irritation pushed him closer to the deck, another damn thing he'd made with his own two hands. If some stupid kid had—

The filmy gauze around the bed quivered, then suddenly whisked open. Holy hell, someone was *sleeping* in that bed. He bounded closer, sucking in a breath to yell, then one long, bare, shapely leg emerged from the clouds of white.

His voice trapped in his throat and his steps slammed to a stop. The sun beamed on pale skin, spotlighting pink-tipped toes that flexed and stretched like a ballerina preparing to hit the barre.

The other leg slid into view, followed by an audible yawn and sigh that drifted over the tropical air to make the hairs on the back of his neck stand up. He took a few stealthy steps, wanting to keep the advantage of surprise but, man, he didn't want to miss what came out of that bed next.

The feet touched the floor and a woman emerged from the netting, naked from head to toe, dark hair falling over most of her face. Not that he'd have looked at her face.

No, his gaze was locked on long limbs, a narrow waist, and subtle curves that begged to be handled. Her breasts were small, budded with rose-colored nipples, her womanhood a simple sliver of ebony that matched her sexy, messy hair.

She stretched, widening her arms, yawning again, giving him a centerfold-worthy view as her breasts lifted higher. Every functioning blood cell careened south, leaving his brain a total blank and his cock well on its way to being as hard as the planks of African wood in his truck.

Son of a bitch. He backed up, ducking behind the oleander and cursing himself for being some kind of pervie Peeping Tom. He had to get back down the path and come back later—noisily, in his truck—to find out who the hell she was.

A footstep hit the wood deck and Will inched to the side, unable to stop himself from looking. At least she had on a thin white top now, and panties. With both hands, she gathered her hair up to—

His heart stopped for at least four beats, then slammed into quadruple time.

Jocelyn.

Was it possible? Was he imagining things? Was this a mirage spurred by a couple of lousy pictures in the paper and three days of fantasies and frustration?

She let go of her hair, shaking her head so that a thick, black mane tumbled over her shoulders like an inky waterfall. Then she closed her eyes and turned her face to the rising sun.

Any doubt disappeared. Along with common sense and years of rationalization and a decade and a half of telling himself he had no choice—even though he knew differently.

Everything suddenly changed at the sight of Jocelyn Mary Bloom. The sun was warmer. The air was cleaner. And his heart squeezed in a way it hadn't for fifteen years.

She turned, rubbing her arm as if a sixth sense had sent a chill over her. "Is someone there?"

Make a joke. Say something funny. Walk, smile, talk. C'mon, William Palmer, don't just stand here and gawk like you've never seen a female before.

"It's me."

She squinted into the bushes, then reared back in shock as he stepped out and revealed himself. Her lips moved, mouthing his name, but no real sound came out.

"Will," he said for her. "I thought someone was trespassing."

She just stared, jaw loose, eyes wide, every muscle frozen like she'd been carved out of ice.

He fought the urge to launch forward, take the three stairs up to the deck in one bound and...thaw her. But, whoa, he knew better with Jocelyn Bloom. One false move and *poof.* Out at the plate.

"What are you doing here?" They spoke the words in perfect unison, then both let out awkward laughs.

"Lacey brought you here?" he guessed.

She nodded, reaching up to run a hand through that mass of midnight hair, then, as if she suddenly realized how little she had on, she stepped back into the shadows of the villa, but he could still see her face.

"How about you?" she asked.

He cleared his throat. "I work here."

She looked completely baffled. "You play baseball."

"Not at the moment. I work for the builder. You?"

"I'm staying here."

Hiding here, more like. The pieces slid together like tongue in groove. She'd run away from the mess in L.A., and her best friend had cloistered her in a place that wouldn't even show up on a GPS yet, let alone at the other end of a reporter's camera.

Then another thought hit him like a fastball to the brain. "You alone?" He must have had a little accusation in his voice, because she raised an eyebrow and looked disappointed.

"Yes," she said quietly, sadness in her eyes and a softness in her posture.

Shit. He'd hurt her. He regretted the question the

instant it had popped out. She was hiding from prying eyes and personal questions and what had he done? Pried and questioned.

He held up a hand as though that could deliver his apology and took a few steps closer. "How long are you here? I'd love to..." *Talk to you. Kiss you until you can't breathe. Spend every night in your bed.* "Get caught up."

"I shouldn't be here that long."

In other words, no. "Too bad," he said, hiding the impact of disappointment. "Maybe I'll see you on the south end when you go home."

"I won't go there." The statement was firm, clear, and unequivocal. *Don't argue with me,* dripped the subtext.

She wouldn't even *see* her dad? A spark flared, pushing him closer, up the stairs. She wouldn't even do a drive-by to see if her old man was dead or alive? Because he'd bet his next paycheck she didn't know...anything.

Something hammered at him, and this time it wasn't his heart reacting to the sight of a beautiful, not entirely dressed woman. No, this was the physical jolt of a whole different kind of frustration.

"So, what exactly do you do for the builder?" she asked, apparently unaware she'd hit a hot button.

But her casual question barely registered, her astounding near nakedness practically forgotten despite God's professional lighting that gave him a perfect view of her body under those slips of white silk.

"Carpentry," he said through gritted teeth, a little surprised at how much emotion rocked him. He had to remember what she'd gone through, what her father was in her eyes, but right now all he could think about was a harmless, helpless old man who had no one to call family.

Even though he had a perfectly good daughter standing right here.

"A carpenter just like your father," she said, nodding. "I remember he was quite talented."

"Speaking of fathers." He dragged the word out, long enough to see her expression shift to blank. "I'm back in my parents' house. They moved out to Oregon to be closer to my sister and her kids."

In other words, I live next door to your father. He waited for the reaction, but she just raised her hand, halting him. "I really have to go, Will. Nice to see you again."

Seriously? She wouldn't even hear him out?

She backed into the opening of the french doors, hidden from view now. "I'm sure I'll see you around, though," she called, one hand reaching for the knob to close him out.

He grabbed the wood frame and held it as tightly as he had when he'd installed the very door she was about to slam in his face. "Jocelyn."

"Please, Will."

"Listen to me."

"I'm sure our paths will cross." But her voice contradicted that cliché. And so did history. One wrong word and Jocelyn would find another hiding place in another corner of the world.

Was he willing to risk that? If he so much as spoke the name Guy Bloom, she'd be on a plane headed back to California. But, damn it, shouldn't she *know*?

He let go of the door and she pushed it closed. He thrust his boot in the jamb to keep the door from closing.

"Will, I have to—"

"Your father has Alzheimer's." He had enough

strength in his foot to nudge the opening wider and see the shocked look that drained all the color from her cheeks. "I take care of him."

He slipped his boot out and the door slammed shut.

Well, he was right about the winds of change. And maybe that change was simply that after half a lifetime, he could finally get over Jocelyn Bloom.

Keep telling yourself that, buddy. Someday you might believe it.

Chapter Four

Mimosa Key curved exactly like a question mark, forming the perfect metaphor for the childhood Jocelyn Bloom had spent there. As she took the curve around Barefoot Bay in the car she'd borrowed from Lacey—with the excuse that she had to go shopping for clothes—and headed to the south end of the island, Jocelyn considered the eternal question that loomed for the seventeen and three-quarters years she'd lived on this barrier island.

What would happen next?

With Guy Bloom, no one was ever sure. When she was very young, nothing had been terribly out of the ordinary. But then, overnight it seemed to her childish perception, he'd changed. He'd go weeks, even months, on an even keel—hot tempered, but under control, before he'd snap. Dishes and books could sail across the room, vicious words in their wake. And then he had to hit someone.

More specifically, he had to hit Mary Jo Bloom, who took those beatings like she'd deserved them. Of course, with maturity, perspective, and the benefit of a psychology degree, Jocelyn now knew that *no one* deserved that. No one.

Your father has Alzheimer's.

Not for the first time that morning, she had to ask the obvious: Were his episodes some kind of early sign of the disease? When she'd been home for Mom's funeral he seemed fine. But maybe the signs were there all along and she'd missed them.

Guilt mixed with hate and anger, the whole cocktail knotting her stomach even more than it had been since she'd seen Will Palmer.

Will.

She closed her eyes, not wanting to think about him. About how good he looked. How hours on the baseball field had honed him into a tanned, muscular specimen who still had see-straight-through-you Wedgwood blue eyes, a shock of unexpected color against his suntanned skin and shaggy black hair.

God, she'd missed him all these years. All these years that she gave him up so he didn't have to be saddled with a girl who had a monster for a father and now—

She banged the heel of her hand on the steering wheel.

He *took care* of the bastard? It didn't seem possible or right or reasonable in any way she could imagine.

Like it or not, Guy was her parent. If he had to be put in a home, she'd do it. But before she could tackle this problem with a list of possible solutions, she had to figure out exactly how bad the situation was and how far gone he was with dementia.

The word settled hard on her heart. She knew a little about Alzheimer's—knew the disease could make a person cranky and mean. Wow, Guy must be a joy to take care of, considering he'd already been a ten on the cranky-and-mean scale. Why would Will volunteer for the job?

Because Will had one weakness: the softest, sweetest, most tender of hearts. And wasn't that what she'd once loved about him?

That and those shoulders.

She pressed her foot against the accelerator, glancing at the ranch houses and palm trees, the bicycles in driveways, the flowers around the mailboxes. This was a lovely residential neighborhood where normal families lived normal lives.

Right. Where dysfunctional families made a mockery of normal. Where—

Oh, Lord. Guy was on the porch.

He was sitting on the front porch swing, hunched over a newspaper, his mighty shoulders looking narrow, his giant chest hollowed as if it had been emptied of all that hot air.

Looking at him was like looking at something you remember as a child, only as an adult, that something doesn't seem nearly as big or daunting or dangerous.

Mom had bought that swing, Jocelyn recalled, with high hopes that the family would sit out there on warm evenings, counting the stars and watching the moon.

Fat chance, Mary Jo.

There were no such things as family nights in the Bloom household. And right there, in a faded plaid shirt and dusty gray trousers and a pair of bedroom slippers, was the reason why.

As Jocelyn slowed the car alongside the curb, Guy looked up, a sheet of newspaper fluttering to the ground. He looked right at her, icy fingers of awareness prickling her whole body

She waited for his reaction, some emotional jolt of recognition by him, but there was none.

Okay, then. He wasn't going to acknowledge her. Fine. That would make the whole thing easier. It was entirely possible he didn't recognize her, if what Will said was true.

But her knowledge of Alzheimer's said he'd be able to remember things that happened long ago but not what he had for breakfast. If so, he must be wallowing in some unhappy memories.

Good. That's what he deserved.

He stood slowly, frowning now, angling his head, and even from this far she could see his gray eyes looked more like rain clouds than sharp steel, and his hands shook with age, not rage.

"Can I help you?" The question came out hoarse, as though he hadn't spoken to anyone all day.

She turned off the ignition and opened the door. "You don't recognize me?"

He shook his head. What was he? Sixty-five? Sixty-six? He looked ninety.

"What do you want?" He sounded *scared*. Was that even possible? Nothing scared the former deputy sheriff.

"It's me, Jocelyn." She stepped onto the lawn, her heels digging into the grass like little spikes into her heart.

"Whatever you're selling, I'm not buying."

"Guy, it's me." She wasn't about to call him Dad; he'd relinquished that title on a hot summer night in 1997 when he threatened to ruin the life of a young man. The same young man who now *took care* of him.

Injustice rocked her, but she kept a steady path toward him.

"Do I know you?"

"You did," she said.

"You do look familiar." He rubbed a face that hadn't seen a razor in quite some time, frowning. "Pretty, too. What's your name, young lady?"

Had he ever called her pretty? She couldn't remember. Maybe when she was little, before his violent streaks became the norm rather than the occasional nightmare.

She ran her tongue under her front teeth, a tiny chip on the right front tooth her sacred reminder of just what this man could do.

"I'm Jocelyn. I'm your daughter."

He laughed, a hearty sound, and another thing she had no memory of him doing. "I don't have a daughter. I have a son." He reached out his hand, the gesture almost costing him his balance. "I bet you're looking for him. He's out now, but never stays gone too long."

"You don't have a son."

"Don't I?" He shrugged and gave her playful smile. "I have a sister, though."

No, he didn't. He didn't have a son or a sister—or a *memory*. But suddenly his jaw dropped and his silvery eyes lit with recognition. "Oh my word, I know who you are."

"Yep, figured you would." She reached the cement walk and crossed her arms, just in case he had some notion of hugging her or shaking her hand.

"You're the lady from TV! I saw you on TV!"

His voice rose with crazy excitement, but her heart

dropped. So the Hollywood gossip machine had been making noise on Mimosa Key.

"Didn't I see you on TV?" He screwed up his face into a tapestry of wrinkles, pointing at her, digging deep for whatever thread of a memory his broken synapse was offering. "Yes, I'm certain of it! I saw you on TV."

"You probably did," she said with resignation.

"You work for Nicey!"

Nicey? She slowly shook her head. "No, I'm Jocelyn."

"Oh, you can't fool me." He slapped his thigh like a rodeo rider. "That William. He is the most remarkable young man, isn't he? How'd he get you here? Did he call? Send pictures? What'd he say that finally convinced you to come and help me?"

"He told me about your situation."

"So he did write a letter." He chuckled again, shaking his head. "That boy is something else." He reached for her arm, but she jerked away before he could touch her. "All right, all right," he said. "Let's just start with a little chat before we go in. Because, I hate to tell you, young lady, you have got a lot of work to do."

"Work?" She didn't have a clue what he was talking about.

"Well, you'd like to talk first before you, uh, get to gettin'?" He bared his teeth in a stained but self-satisfied smile. "See? I'm a fan."

A fan?

"Sit down here," he said, indicating the porch swing. "We'll have a nice talk." He inched from side to side, trying to look over her shoulder. "No hidden cameras?"

"I hope not."

He laughed again. Had he ever laughed that much

before? Could Alzheimer's make a person happier? "You never know, those camera folks can be foxy."

"Yes, I do know that," she agreed, following him to perch on the edge of the swing.

Okay, fine. They could play this little game while she assessed just how bad he was and then she'd do what she surely had to do. Put him away somewhere. He probably wouldn't like hearing that.

Face your issues and solve your problems, life coach. You have an old man who needs to go into a home. You owe him nothing but...

Nothing, actually. Still, she wasn't entirely heartless.

"Would you like some lemonade?" Guy asked.

"No." She tugged her crossed arms deeper into her chest.

"Will there be a yard sale?" he asked.

She blinked at him. "A yard sale?"

"To get rid of all my junk."

Maybe he *wanted* to go into assisted living and just didn't know how to ask, or how to pay for it. In that case, he wouldn't give her a hard time. Everything would be nice and easy.

"Well, I guess that's a reasonable question," she said, mentally ticking off what needed to be done while she was here. "I suppose we could have a yard sale, although it would be easier just to throw everything away."

"Everything? Aren't they sometimes allowed to keep the things they treasure most?"

They? Patients in homes? "I suppose, yes." She bit back a dry laugh at the very thought that he'd ever treasured anything. He certainly hadn't treasured his wife and daughter. "What would you like to keep, Guy?"

"Well..." He rubbed his hands over his worn pants, thinking. "I guess my needlepoint and knitting."

The deputy sheriff of Mimosa Key did needlepoint and knitting? When did that happen? After his early retirement or his wife's death? "Sure, you can hang on to that stuff."

"And my recliner?"

Oh, he had loved that throne. Although by now he probably had a new one. "I guess it depends on space."

"You'll handle everything or what? You bring in a team?"

"I'm pretty efficient," she said. "I'll need a few weeks, I imagine, to get all the paperwork together, but I'll start the preliminary work tomorrow." God, this was going to be simple. He wanted to leave. No fight.

And with Guy, that was saying a lot.

"It won't be hard because I'm all alone," he said, sounding unbelievably pathetic.

Yeah, and whose fault was that? "That's... good," she said.

"Don't have a wife," he said sadly, adding a slightly wobbly smile. "I mean, I did, but I can't remember her."

Words eluded her. He *forgot*? What he'd done? How much misery he'd inflicted? Did he forget the time he threw an encyclopedia at his wife's head or poured her favorite cologne in the toilet or—

"If you're ready to go in, I can make tea," he said, clearly on a whole different wavelength than she was.

Tea? Since when did he make tea? Oh, he could certainly fling a pot of it at someone who pissed him off.

She would *not* forget, even if he had.

He pushed up. "Come on, then, um... what'd you say your name was again?"

"Jocelyn." Did she really have to go in? No, she didn't have to put herself through that. Not yet. She'd go back to the villa, make some action lists and phone calls. That would be so much better than touring her childhood home with the man who ran her out of it.

"Actually, Guy, my work here is done."

"Done?" He laughed heartily, the strangest sound Jocelyn could ever remember hearing. A real laugh, from the gut. "I don't think so, Missy. I kind of knew you were coming, so I started cleaning everything out for you."

He knew she was coming? "Did Will call and tell you?"

"Nah, William would never ruin the surprise." He pulled open the screen door, then pushed the wooden front door, which was no longer the chipped dark green stained wood she remembered from the last time she was here. This door had been refinished and painted a glossy white.

Will?

Another ribbon of guilt twisted through her, followed instantly by a squeeze of fury. How could Will be so nice to him? After what had happened?

"Come on, come on," Guy urged, waving an age-spotted hand.

She'd have to go in sometime.

She followed him into the front entry, instantly accosted by the dark punch of miserable memories. The linoleum was the same, yellow and white blocks that covered the entry and led into the kitchen that was oddly placed in the front of the house. That weird exposed brick wall, painted white now, still stood, separating the entrance from the kitchen and living room around the corner.

Without thinking, she touched the shiny paint of the bricks, her hand slipping through one of the decorative openings. He'd thrown her mother against this wall once. She jerked her hand back and took a good look around, into the kitchen, past the dining room, down the hall to the bedrooms.

Holy, *holy* crap.

The entire house was one giant hot mess. Kitchen cabinets were open, vomiting dishes, glasses, cookware, and utensils. In the dining room, the buffet doors gaped wide to reveal empty shelves, but stacks of china and vases and a few tea sets covered the dining room table.

This was what Will called "taking care of him"?

"I know, I know," Guy said, shaking his head. "I got a little ahead of myself, but it was that marathon they ran this morning."

Jocelyn finally looked at him, trying to make sense of his words. But nothing made sense.

"Who ran a marathon?"

"On TV! I don't remember seeing you, though." He put a hand to his forehead, pressing hard as if he could somehow force his brain to cooperate. "Doesn't matter. You're here now and...and..." His features softened into a smile, raw appreciation and affection filling his expression. "Oh, Missy. I can't tell you how glad I am that you're going to help me."

"You are?" She still couldn't believe he wasn't going to give her an argument about moving, even if he didn't have a clue who she was.

"Of course I am." He reached for her again, this time snagging her hand. He squeezed it between his two fists, all the strength of those thick hands gone now, just weak, gnarled fingers that didn't seem capable of the fury they'd unleashed so many times. "I've been waiting for you ever since I saw you on TV."

She blinked, shocked. "You have?"

"Well, I think it was you." He squirreled up his face again.

"The pictures were blurry, but it was me," she admitted. "There's more to it than you see on TV, believe me."

"Oh, I bet there is." He laughed and squeezed her hand. "But just so you know, you're not making a mistake. I need this so much. It's all I've thought about since I saw you on TV."

A wave of pity washed over her, watering down a lifetime of old feelings. Well, at least this would go smoothly. Then she wouldn't have to feel guilty about locking him in some home. And maybe she could let go of some of that hate. Maybe.

"So, what happens first?" He asked brightly. "When do the camera people get here? And, when do I get to meet that bossy lady with the flower in her hair?"

"What are you—"

Behind her the screen door whipped open and Jocelyn turned to see Will frozen in the doorway, looking at her with almost the same degree of shock he'd had this morning outside the villa.

"William!" Guy practically lunged toward him, arms outstretched. "You are the best son in the world. How can I thank you for getting her here?"

The older man reached up and grabbed Will in a bear hug, flattening his gray-haired head against Will's chest.

Over his head, Will stared at Jocelyn, his mouth open but nothing coming out.

"You did it," Guy said, finally leaning back to beam up at Will. "You got *Clean House* here and this pretty girl is going to make my life perfect. I love you, son, you know that?"

Jocelyn put a hand on the cool brick wall to steady herself. Not because the old man misunderstood why she was there. Not because he thought she was there to make his life perfect. Not even because he thought Will Palmer was his son and she was a stranger.

He'd just never, ever said the words *I love you* unless he was weeping in apology for having hurt someone or broken something. The words had always been meaningless to him.

But not now. Guy really did love Will. And as Will patted Guy's back, comforting the old man, it was clear that Will loved Guy, too.

And the irony of that was one bitter pill on her tongue.

Chapter Five

⌇

Jocelyn looked more real, more beautiful, and even more stunned standing in the entry of her own home than she had when Will had accidentally discovered her at Casa Blanca.

With one more gentle pat on Guy's back, Will gave Jocelyn a pleading look, hoping she'd just go along with this.

"He thinks I'm from a TV show called *Clean House*?" she asked, obviously still confused by what had unfolded. "Why don't you tell him—"

"I'm so glad you're here," he said, a little forcefully as he eased Guy away from him. "Why don't we go talk privately about…" His gaze moved beyond her to the kitchen. "Holy shit, Guy, what the hell happened here?"

"Now there's no need to cuss, son. I just got a little ahead of the game. This lady, this…uh, uh…what was your name again?"

"Jocelyn," she said with barely restrained patience. "Jocelyn *Bloom*."

Guy didn't even blink at his own name. "This Jocelyn is going to straighten it all out and set things right for me. That's what she does, right? Isn't that what you do, Missy?"

Will held his breath, watching a series of emotions play over her refined features. Dismay drew her dark brows together and doubt made her lower lip quiver slightly. But she finally lifted that deceptively delicate chin and nodded.

"Yes, actually, that is what I do."

Will exhaled slowly, fighting the urge to give Jocelyn a hug of gratitude. "Why don't we go somewhere and talk about the details," he suggested. "Guy, you take a load off in the living room and I'll show Jocelyn around."

"Is this the part where they do a tour?" Guy asked. "The 'before' tour?"

"Yes," Will said, stepping closer to Jocelyn. "But you have to sit down and let me take Jocelyn on the tour."

"Why?" he asked. "I want to show her everything."

Will gave another look, practically begging for help.

"He's right. I have to see everything without you. Go sit and we'll be back after I've looked around."

Oh, man. He could kiss her. "C'mon. We'll start out in the..." He looked around at the chaos. "Garage. It's through the laundry room over—"

"I know where it is." She rounded the brick wall and made her escape through the unused—and just as messy—office that led to the laundry room.

"Will." Guy grabbed his arm. "Thank you." He reached up for another hug. "I don't deserve you, you know that? You're such a good son."

"It's okay, Guy. Let me talk to her." Will inched him aside, knowing Jocelyn was damn near liquid mercury when it came to disappearing between a man's fingers. She could well be gone when he got into the garage.

He found her standing at the door to the garage, listening to the exchange. Shit.

"Hey, thanks," he whispered, coming closer. "Let's go out there and talk."

She slipped into the garage and he followed, closing the door and gathering his wits. He'd thought of nothing, absolutely nothing, all morning but the impact of seeing Jocelyn Bloom.

He'd talked to Lacey and found out that Jocelyn was here for an "indefinite visit"—and he supposed he knew why—but after how she acted this morning, he didn't imagine she'd come to see Guy on her own. At least not this soon.

"I'd been hoping to bring you down here myself," he said, giving voice to his thoughts. "I thought I'd ease you into what to expect."

She arched a dubious brow. "Then why did you make that closing shot about you taking care of him? I mean, what was that if not a way to get me here?"

"Desperation, I guess. Look, Jocelyn, I—"

"I'm sure there's plenty of desperation in this situation. But I'll take care of it for you and you'll be free. I'll take care of the problem."

He blew out a breath, his hands aching to hold her, his heart still not settled from the unnaturally wild beat that had started when he saw Lacey's car in front of the house. "It's really not a problem," he said slowly.

"Caring for an infirm old man who—"

"He's not exactly infirm."

"—is living like a pig and—"

"That mess just happened."

"—once threatened to kill you and now thinks you're his son."

He stared at her. Of course that night would be right under the surface, waiting to bubble up, waiting to rip him apart, waiting to suffocate him in guilt because Will had been able to forgive, if not forget.

"He's changed, Jocelyn."

She gave a mirthless, dry cough. "I see that."

"No, I mean, he's really a different man."

"He has no idea who I am," she said, still cool and controlled and pretending to be unaffected by something that *had* to affect her. "But he certainly has a fondness for you."

"He's confused." He attempted a smile. "I guess that's obvious."

She folded her arms tightly against herself, defensive and still defiant. "I guess I should say thank you for what you've done."

But, whoa, she sure didn't sound like she meant it. "Look, I came back here a year and a half ago to fix up my parents' house and get it on the market and I had no intention of speaking to the man." He stuffed his hands in his pockets as if that could stop the need that still made them ache. All these years and he *still* wanted to touch her.

"So why did you?"

"Because I'm…human. And he was in sorry shape." Alone, pitiful, and, god damn it, a really nice guy. "I started just by taking his trash to the front on pickup day and then cutting his grass when it got to be a mess.

Normal, neighborly things. I fixed a few things, like his broken sink and the back screen door that didn't close and—what?"

With each word she'd grown paler, smaller, more constricted in her posture. "What? You're asking me *what*, Will? Do you know why the screen door was broken?"

He swallowed hard. "I can guess."

"Then why would you do *anything* for him?"

He took a slow breath. "Because he's sick, Jocelyn."

"Then you should have called me."

Guilt slammed him. He *should* have called her. Not just when he realized how bad Guy was, but fifteen years earlier when she disappeared from Mimosa Key without saying good-bye. He knew she was up at UF, but he didn't call. He just let time go by, and then too much time went by.

"I saw you last year for thirty seconds and you bolted."

She swallowed guiltily. "I had a..."

"Phone call, I remember. But how could I call you then when it was obvious how you felt?" He recognized his own rationalization and swiped a hand through his hair in frustration.

"I'll get the house cleaned up and get him squared away," she said quietly. "I hope that can be done with a minimum amount of fuss or, to be honest, interaction with him."

He tried to focus on her words, the efficient tone snapping him to attention. "You mean, you'd go along with this? You'd pretend to be on that show? Because that would be great. You know, when he doesn't get his way, he—"

"I *know* what happens when he doesn't get his way." Her voice was icy, and he could have kicked himself. Of course she thought she knew what happened when he didn't get his way, except she didn't know this Guy; she knew a different Guy. "And like I said, I do this for a living. You'd be surprised how many people are willing to pay for a life coach to do nothing more than organize closets and files. Then we'll get him situated somewhere."

He tilted his head, trying to understand. "What do you mean?" Except, deep in his heart, he knew exactly what she meant.

"In a home somewhere."

Yep. Exactly. "He's in a home. *His* home."

She raised her chin, looking remarkably strong for such a petite woman. But she'd always been strong. Even at her weakest, most broken moments, Jocelyn had a backbone of pure titanium. It was one of the things he'd once loved about her. One of many.

"He can't stay here," she said simply. "And you can't be expected to care for someone who isn't your father, no matter how much he thinks he ... likes you."

Did she think he couldn't still read every nuance in her tone and delivery? They'd known each other since they were ten. "He said he loved me."

"Yes, well, I imagine he says a lot of strange things." She bit her lip and crossed her arms so tight he could see each tendon straining in her hand. Man, she was wired for sound.

"That probably hurt your feelings, since he doesn't even recognize you."

She let out a dry laugh. "You're assuming I *have* feelings where he's concerned, Will. Or did you forget what kind of man he was?"

"I didn't," he said softly. "But he did."

"And that makes everything okay?" Her voice rose with incredulity.

"I understand how you feel because I felt the same way when I first got here. But over time, shit, he kind of grows on you."

Her eyes grew wide in shocked disbelief.

"Maybe you could..." *Give him a chance.* Was that even possible? "Think about this a little more."

"I've thought about it enough." She turned as if she were looking for something—or just couldn't face him anymore.

"I just don't think he needs to be put away like some kind of criminal."

She whipped back around to flatten him with a dark glare. "He *is* a criminal and you might have gone all soft at the sight of him, but I didn't. I won't. I never will."

"Maybe there's another way," Will said. "He's old and out of it. He's sick and demented. But this is his home. It would be cruel to—"

"Cruel?" She threw the word back in his face like a ninety-five-mile-an-hour fastball. "Are you serious? He wrote the book on cruel. He hit my mother, Will. He threatened to shoot you. He...he..." She clenched her jaw and drew in a shaky breath. "He is a very bad man."

What was she about to tell him? What happened that last night? By the next day Jocelyn had left Mimosa Key; he never knew how she got away. And, shit, he'd been too scared to find out. Scared to lose his scholarship. Scared to lose everything he'd promised his own father. Scared of the recriminations of pursuing a girl he thought he—no, a girl he really *did* love.

He hadn't been willing to pay the price, and he'd had to live with that. Had to pay it now, in a different way.

"Jocelyn." He took one step closer, slowly taking his

hands out of his pockets, that need to reach for her still strong. Instead he cracked his knuckles like he had a million times in the dugout during a tense inning. "I understand your position. Maybe you could...*we* could...find someone to live with him. Or stay with him during the day."

"That's—"

"Expensive, I know. God, I know exactly what it costs and he doesn't have that much money left and neither do I, or I'd—"

She waved him quiet. "I would never expect you to pay for his care. He's my problem and I'll have a solution. That's what I do, really. This is right in my wheelhouse."

"In your *wheelhouse*?" He almost choked on a batting term he'd heard a hundred times on the field, the expression wrong right here in so many ways.

"Yes, this is what I do. I'm a life coach, Will. I put people's lives back together. I help them find solutions to the problems of life. I organize, structure, prioritize, and master their everyday lives. Usually I teach them how to do that for themselves, but in this case, I'll just skip that step."

She sounded so *clinical*. "Actually," she continued, slowing down as if a thought had just occurred to her. "If it's going to make things easier for him to believe that I'm from some TV show, then fine, I can play that game, as long as we can get him away somewhere."

"Where?"

"I don't know. I'll find a facility."

A facility. "You can't just lock him up. He's a person," he said stiffly.

"He's an anim—"

"Not anymore he's not!" His exclamation echoed through the garage, making Jocelyn's eyes pop wide and her cheeks pale. Son of a bitch, that was the wrong thing to do. "The disease has changed him," he added softly.

"Alzheimer's doesn't affect your soul." She hissed the last word, then closed her eyes to turn away. "Does the car run?" She gestured toward Guy's old Toyota.

He cleared his throat and jammed one more knuckle that refused to crack. "Yeah, I start it up every week or so to make sure the battery doesn't drain."

"Good, then I won't have to rent one to go to the mainland. You don't have to worry about him anymore, Will."

He put a hand on her shoulder and slowly turned her toward him. "It's not him I'm worried about."

She held his gaze, inches away, the first glimmer of vulnerability in her eyes. Shaking him off, she slipped out of his touch. "I better get to work."

"Now?" He practically spit the word. "Today? This minute?"

"Of course. There's no reason to wait." She put her hands on her hips as she looked around the garage and up to the loft, where more boxes were piled. "Are any of those empty cartons? I'll need them. And these." She snagged a box of Hefty bags from the worktable, yanking out a sheet of thick black plastic. "I'm sure there's plenty of trash around here."

He just stared at her. Who was this woman? Where was the tender, vulnerable, soft young girl he'd been so madly in love with when he was seventeen?

She snapped the bag with a satisfying crack. "Don't you have to go back to work?"

He took a step backward. "Yeah, I do. I'll be back here later."

"Why?"

"To make him dinner."

She lifted an eyebrow. "I'll handle it."

On a soft exhale, he just nodded like he understood. But, shit, he didn't really understand anything about her anymore.

Chapter Six

The show's on!" Guy came bounding into the dining room where Jocelyn had made stacks of three different china patterns, not enough of any one to make a complete set. "You have to come and watch it with me," he insisted.

"I don't have time for TV," she said, scooping up one pile of plates to fit them in a box she'd found in the garage.

"Not the blue roses!" Guy said, slapping his hands on his cheeks in horror. "I love them."

She looked up at him, still completely unused to every word that came out of his mouth. "Since when?" she asked.

"Since..." His shoulders slumped. "I don't know, I just do. They have sentimental value."

She almost choked. Her only memory of this wretched china pattern was when a bowl had gone sailing across the table one night because Mom had made mushroom soup.

"They have no value," she said, tamping down the memory.

"But I really like flowers."

She looked up, the memory worming its way into her heart anyway, stunning her that same man who *hated fucking mushrooms* could *really like flowers*.

"I'm sure you do," she said. "But there aren't enough to sell as a set, so I'm pitching these."

He shook his head like he just didn't get that as he lifted one of the blue rose teacups off a saucer, dangling it precariously from his finger.

She tensed, squaring her shoulders, her breath caught in her throat as she stared at the delicate china hooked to a thick forefinger. Any second. Any second and...*wham!* Whatever was in his hand would get pitched in the direction of the closest wall to make the loudest crash.

But he just moved the cup left and right like a pendulum, a smile pulling at his face. "You gotta gift me." He practically sang the words, his voice lifting playfully.

For a second, she couldn't speak. Just couldn't wrap her head around this man. "Gift you?"

"You know. I give up something precious and you gift me with something in return. A sofa. New carpet." He sucked in a breath and dropped his mouth in complete joy. "One of those fancy flat TVs!"

"I'm not going to—"

Gingerly, he set the cup back on its saucer, making the tiniest ding of china against china. Then he held out his hand to her. "You need a little refresher on your own show, little miss."

"My own..." *Clean House.*

"I've seen most of them before, 'cause they keep

running the same ones over and over." He closed his hand around her arms, his thick fingers lacking in strength but not determination. "But I don't mind the repeats. Come on, let's get to gettin', as they say."

"As who say?"

He clapped his hands and let out a laugh. "Very funny."

She followed him into the living room, where the TV blared a commercial. He gestured for her to sit on the sofa and settled into his recliner, waving the remote like a magic wand.

"I'm holding on for dear life to this thing. The way you're tossing stuff away you're likely to hide it."

She sat on the edge of a heinous plaid sofa that she didn't remember, something her parents—or Guy—must have bought after she left. Would Mom pick anything this ugly?

"Relax," Guy said, using the remote to gesture toward the sofa back. "It's the fastest hour on TV. But you know that."

She didn't relax, dividing her attention between a home improvement show hosted by a soulful, insightful, no-nonsense woman named Niecy—that must be who Guy called Nicey—and the man next to her.

She really had to do more research on Alzheimer's. Didn't the disease turn its victims nasty and cranky? Or did it just change a person completely? Because this man was...

No, she refused to go there. Leopards, spots, and all that.

"Watch the show," he insisted when he caught her studying him. "This is what you're going to do for me."

Niecy Nash went about her business of taking control

of a family's mess, tossing the junk, selling what could be salvaged, then redecorating their homes, all the while helping her "clients" see what was wrong with their lives. Kind of like what Jocelyn did, only funnier.

Was *that* what she was going to do for her father?

Absolutely not. She already knew what was wrong with him—then and now. She wasn't redecorating anything, just researching assisted-living facilities and solving this problem. It gave her something to do while she was here, anyway.

"Cute show," Jocelyn said, pushing up from the sofa following the big reveal at the end.

"It's more than cute," Guy insisted. "It's all about what makes people tick. You like that, don't you?"

"Made a whole career around it," she said casually. "I better get back to the china."

"You gotta gift me for it."

"No, no." She headed back into the dining room, armed with a little more knowledge of how to play his game. "She 'gifts' for things that have huge sentimental value. Half of a chipped china set has no sentimental value. No gifting."

"How do you know what has sentimental value to me?" he demanded, right on her heels.

She stopped cold and he almost crashed into her. Very slowly she turned, just about eye to eye with a man who had once seemed larger than life, but gravity had shaved off a few inches, and surely guilt weighed on his shoulders.

"I'm willing to bet," she said without looking away, "that you can't go through this house and find a single item that means anything at all to you."

She didn't intend for the challenge to come out quite that cruel, but tears sprang from his eyes, surprisingly sudden and strong. "That's just the problem," he said, his voice cracking.

She took a step back, speechless at the sight. Not that she hadn't seen him cry; he could turn on the tears after an incident. He could throw out the apologies and promises and swear he'd never hit his wife again.

And Mom fell for it every time.

"What's the problem?" she asked, using the same gentle voice she'd use on a client who was deluding herself over something. "Why are you crying?"

He swiped his eyes, knocking his glasses even more crooked. "You don't get it, do you?"

Evidently not.

"You don't understand how some things matter," he said.

"Yes, I do," she said, as ultra-patient as one of the crew on *Clean House* dealing with a stubborn homeowner. "Why don't you answer a question for me first, Guy?"

"Anything."

"Did you really live in this house?" Or did he just make it a living hell for the people who did? "Did you love anyone here? Make anyone happy? Build anything lasting?"

"I might have."

"Did you?" she challenged, resentment and righteousness zinging right down to her toes. It was bad enough that he didn't remember the misery he'd inflicted, but to twist the past into something happy? Well, that was too much. That went beyond the symptoms of a sad, debilitating disease and right into unfair on every level.

Forget the past if that's nature's cruel punishment, but, damn it, don't *change* the past.

"I think I did," he said weakly.

"You think you did?" She swallowed her emotions, gathering up the sharp bits that stung her heart, determined not to let them hurt quite this much.

"I don't know," he finally said, defeat emanating from every cell in his body. "I just don't know. That's why I've been so scared to throw anything away. I thought it might help me remember."

A wave of pity rose up, a natural, normal reaction to the sight of a helpless old man sobbing. Pity? She stomped it down, searching wildly for a mental compartment where she could lock away any chance of *pity*.

She had no room in her heart for sympathy or compassion. Not for this man who had made her childhood miserable and stolen any hope of her having a normal life. *With Will*. With that big, strong, safe, handsome man who still made her knees weak and her heart swell.

"Well, you have to give up that hope," she said harshly, talking to herself as much as the old man in front of her. Without waiting to see his pained reaction, she turned to walk to the table, ready to finish this task, make order, and accomplish her very simple goal. She had to take charge of this situation, not let the situation take charge of her.

"Why?" he asked, right on her heels. "Why do I have to give up that hope?"

She ignored the question, scooping up the teacup and saucer.

"Why should I give up hope?" he insisted, falling into a chair. "Is this like, you know, the part of the show where they make the person look inside their soul?"

Oh, don't go there, Guy. You won't like what you see.
"This isn't a show," she said stiffly. This is real life.

"Is this like a pre-show? Where they get the people ready before the cameras come?"

She could feel the threads of patience pulling, fraying, threatening to snap. God, was she as bad as her father? She'd always feared that horrible blackness was hereditary, but years of psych classes taught her she could overcome whatever ugliness she may have inherited from Guy.

She took another calming breath and continued packing the china.

"What should I do?" he asked.

She looked up, mentally searching for a way to get through to him. "You should start to make new memories." She slid four salad plates into the carton on the table and turned back to the buffet. "This will be a good change for you. You can replace the old stuff with new and better stuff."

In a home somewhere with people just like you.

But she couldn't say the words. Behind her, he was silent, no sniffling, no breathing. Oh, God. Was he about to blow? He was too, too quiet.

Very slowly, she turned. His head rested on the table, his shoulders shuddering with silent sobs. "I want to remember," he blubbered.

Automatically, she reached for him, then jerked her hand away like she'd almost touched a hot surface. "Maybe you don't," she said simply. *Maybe nature is doing you a favor, old man.*

"I really, really do." He lifted his head, and his glasses slid down to the bottom of his teary nose, his eyes red, his lips quivering. "It's all I want in the whole world, Missy.

A single memory. One crystal-clear story of my past that doesn't flash and fade before I can hold on to it and enjoy it."

She stared at him. "I...can't help you." Only that was a lie. She had so many memories, enough to fill up this house. She could tell him a lifetime of stories. Once upon a time there was a nasty man who had no control, a weak woman who'd given up control, and a scared little girl who lived for any shred of control she could muster.

"Then make one up," he said.

"What do you mean?"

"That can be your gift, you know?" He sat up a little, an idea taking hold. "In exchange for throwing away my china, you gift me with a memory."

"But it wouldn't be...real." Or nice.

He just lifted one brow, and, for a single, crazy second, she thought he knew exactly who he was talking to. Was that possible? She swallowed hard. Could he really know her, and he'd lied all this time? "Guy?"

He nodded, excited, sniffing a little. "You have one? A memory?"

"How could I?" she asked. "If I just met you?"

"You're so smart and kind," he said. "And you've been through half my stuff. You did the whole kitchen. The drawers are very neat now, even that junky one with the batteries. Surely you know enough to gift me with one memory."

"Okay," she agreed, looking around, taking in the remnants of their lives: a teapot her mother's friend brought from England, a salt and pepper shaker set painted as Santa and Mrs. Claus, a set of yellowed lace doilies her mother had loved.

The doily.

Somewhere, in her head, a little gold lock turned on, an imaginary safety box where she'd tucked away the bad stuff, never to be pulled out and examined again.

Until she had to.

The box opened and there she saw the crystal vase perched on that very doily, stuffed with a vibrant bunch of gladiolas that Mary Jo Bloom had bought at Publix for just $3.99.

"Four bucks," she'd said with a giggle in her voice to her little girl. "He can't get too mad about four dollars, can he?"

Her mother had placed the vase on the kitchen table, foot-long stems popping with life and happiness.

"Everyone should have fresh flowers in their life, don't you think, Joss?"

Jocelyn opened her eyes, barely aware she'd closed them, and stared at the man across the table from her, ignoring the expectant excitement in his eyes and seeing only the anger, the disgust, the self-loathing that he transferred to his family.

"Do you remember the day you came home from work and your wife had fresh flowers on the table, Guy?"

He shook his head slowly. "I'm sorry. What did they look like?"

"They were gladiolas."

He lifted one of his hunched shoulders. "Don't know what that is, Missy."

"They're long-stemmed, bright flowers," she explained. "They come in long bunches and they spread out like flowery arms reaching up to the sky, a bunch of ruffles for petals, in the prettiest reds and oranges you've ever seen."

He gasped, eyes wide, jaw dropped. A memory tweaked?
"You came into the house and saw the flowers…"
"All red and orange? Like long sticks of flowers?" He
nodded, excitement growing with each word.
"You wanted to know how much they cost."
"In a glass vase?" He hadn't heard her, she could tell,
as he pushed back the chair. "I know these flowers. I
remember them!"
"Do you remember what happened, Guy?"
He almost toppled the chair getting up, making Joce-
lyn grip the table in fear. What was he going to do? Reen-
act the whole scene?
"Wait here," he said, lumbering out of the room.
Did he want the memory or not? Didn't he want to
know about how he'd picked up that vase, screamed about
wasting money, and thrown that bad boy across the lino-
leum floor, scattering water and flowers and one terrified
child who tore under her bed and covered her ears?
You have no right to be happy!
Those were the precise words he'd said to her mother.
She could still hear his voice echoing in her head.
"I found it! I found it!"
Just like that little girl, Jocelyn slapped her hands over
her ears, squeezing her eyes shut, drowning out the sound
of that man hollering. *God damn you, Mary Jo, God
damn you.*
Why did he hate her so much?
"Look, Missy!"
He slapped a half-finished needlepoint pattern
clamped into a round embroidery ring on the table.
"Those are gladiolas," he said proudly.
The work was awful, no two stitches the same size,

loose and knotted threads, but the shape of a tangerine-and peach-colored gladiola was clear, the wide-hole netting made for beginners bearing the design of a bouquet in a glass vase.

"I never could finish it," he said glumly. "It made me sad."

"That's the memory making you sad."

"It is? What happened?"

She looked at the craft, each little row of stitches so clearly the work of someone who'd labored to pull that silky yarn and follow the simple pattern.

"Does it really matter, Guy?" she asked.

His shoulders slumped, tears forming again. "I just want to know why this makes me so damn sad. Every time I look at these flowers, I want to cry." A fat drop rolled down his cheek. "Do you know why, Missy?"

Of course she did. "No," she lied. "I don't know why they make you sad."

" 'Sokay," he said, patting her hand with thick, liver-spotted fingers, a fresh smile on his face. "Maybe that Nicey lady will help me figure it out when they do the show."

"Yeah. Maybe she will."

Chapter Seven

"Nice work, Palmer."

Will didn't look up at the sound of a female voice, barely audible over the scream of his mitre saw. He recognized the voice, though. "Just a sec, Tessa." Cutting wood this costly required a steady hand and a completely focused brain, and, shit, he'd been fighting for both of those since he'd left Guy's house a few hours ago.

When he finished cutting the plank, he shut off the saw and shoved his safety goggles onto his head, meeting his visitor's gaze as she stood in the doorway of Casa Blanca's largest villa, Bay Laurel.

"You like?" he asked, gesturing to the one-quarter of the living-area floor he'd managed to nail down.

"I do." She raised her bright red sports water bottle in a mock toast. "This must be the astronomically expensive

African wood that Clay's been talking about for two months, right?"

He grinned. "I picked it up on Friday." Grabbing his own water and a bandanna to wipe the sweat from his forehead, he paused to admire the wood he'd laid so far. Scary thing was, he didn't remember leveling or nailing half those planks. His head was not in the game. But the wood was gorgeous, perfectly grained and beautifully stained. "Bay Laurel's going to be spectacular when it's done."

"As nice as Rockrose?" Tessa asked. "I saw it last night all finished for the first time."

"Yeah, I understand we have our first guest." He picked up the freshly cut plank, dusted off the sawed edge, and rounded his cutting table to return to the floor.

She nodded. "Small world, isn't it?"

He threw her a look as he passed, trying—and failing—to read the expression on a face he'd gotten to know pretty well in the months they'd both worked at Casa Blanca.

"Sure seems that way," he said, laying the board so he could get the blind nailer on top of it and start hammering.

Tessa stepped over the new wood, getting her footing on the underlayment that hadn't been covered yet, and settled into a corner of the room like she was ready to chat.

Not that unusual; they'd had plenty of conversations about the resort, her gardens, the other construction workers when someone irritated them. But he knew that she knew—no, he didn't know what she knew.

And that made everything awkward.

He kneed the nailer against the board and waited to let her set the direction and tone of the conversation.

"So you and Jocelyn were next-door neighbors."

So *that* would be the direction and tone.

"Moved in next door when we were both ten," he confirmed, scooping up the soft-headed dead-blow hammer to start nailing the flooring. This was a critical plank, part of a decorative band of darker wood that offset the shape of the room, an idea he'd had and really wanted to make perfect to impress Clay.

He'd have a better shot at perfection if he wasn't nailing at the same time he was having this conversation.

But Tessa sipped her water and watched, not going anywhere.

He raised his hammer just as she asked, "Were you two close?"

He swung and missed the fucker completely.

"Sorry," she said sheepishly. "I didn't know it was like batting."

"It's nothing like batting," he said, shifting his knee on the pad and looking over at her. "And, yeah, we were good friends." The next question burned, and he couldn't help himself. "She never mentioned me?"

Tessa looked at him for a beat too long, a lock of wavy brown hair falling from her bright-yellow work bandanna, her soft brown eyes narrowed on him. She never wore makeup, he'd noticed, not even for employee parties or barbecues at Lacey and Clay's place. But her eyes were always bright and clear, probably from all those vitamins and organic crap she ate.

"No," she said simply. "Not once."

He nodded and raised the hammer again. This time he hit it direct and hard, a satisfying vibration shooting up his arm. *Not once.*

Why would she mention him? He'd never even called to find out where she was, if she made it to college, how she made it to college. *Not once.* And she'd never called him, either. He'd stopped waiting sometime around the middle of his first baseball season, a mix of relief and loss dogging him like a yearlong dry spell at the plate.

"I remember when Lacey was fighting for the permits to build Casa Blanca last year, I saw Jocelyn," he said, remembering how he'd practically jumped her before she'd shot out of the town hall. "And another girl was there with you, a blonde."

"That was Zoe Tamarin. The three of us were in a triple dorm room. Lacey was the resident adviser. Zoe's here, too, by the way. She flew in last night and is staying at my house."

"Really? College reunion or something?"

She screwed up her face like he was clueless. "Jocelyn's in trouble," she said, the words sending a weird punch in his chest. "The four of us are really tight. When someone has a problem, like Lacey did last year or Jocelyn does now, we rally."

"That's . . . nice." So she'd found another safety net when he was out of the picture. He wasn't sure how that made him feel, but the next hammer swing was even harder.

"How close were you two?" she asked.

"Maybe you should ask her."

She snorted softly. "You don't know her very well, do you?"

"Funny, I was just thinking that. I don't really know her much at all anymore."

"Well, she's not the most, uh, forthcoming person. She's very private."

She'd always played things close to the vest, but not with him. She had been open with him. But that was so long ago. He slid the nailer along the wood plank and nestled it into place, then raised the dead-blow hammer again.

"You don't think she had an affair with that Thayer guy, do you?" she asked just as he swung.

God damn it, he missed again.

"Sorry, Will."

He closed his eyes, silently accepting the apology and delaying his response.

"Do you?" she asked again.

"I haven't thought much about it." Which was pretty much an out-and-out lie. He'd thought plenty about it when he heard it on TV and still had the damn tabloid in his truck.

"Well, she didn't," she said. "It's all lies."

"Then why doesn't she say something to shut up all these yapping reporters?"

She took a sip of water. "In true Jocelyn fashion, she won't say. But I know her and I can assure you, she's caught in the middle of something that is unfair and untrue."

"That's a shame." And he meant it. She'd had enough crap in her life. "Good that she can ride it out here in Barefoot Bay."

"Well, she does have her dad here, but…" Her voice trailed off. "Do you know him?"

That one came in like a curveball, low and slow and totally unexpected. Good thing he caught curveballs for a living once.

He hammered a few times, thinking. How much had

Jocelyn told her friends? Any other woman, he'd guess everything. Jocelyn wasn't any other woman, though. And how much did she want known? Probably nothing.

"I live in my parents' old house, right next door to him, so, yeah, I know Guy Bloom."

Tessa inched forward, interest sparking in her eyes. "What's he like?" When he didn't answer, she added, "I'm not prying or anything, it's just that she doesn't talk about him much. At all, really."

He slammed the last nail and leaned back on his haunches to survey the board before pulling out his level.

"He's old," he said, doubting that he was giving away any state secrets. "Not real healthy. I, you know, keep an eye on him now and then." Like every morning, afternoon, and night.

"Nice of you."

He shot her a look. "Decent and humane. I'd do it for anyone, any old man living next door."

"Whoa." She held up a hand and smiled. "I just said it's nice, Will."

Puffing out a breath, he let his backside fall onto the underlayment, shaking his head, words bubbling that he just had to fight.

"What is it?" she asked.

"Look, she's private, you just said so. I don't want to speak out of school."

"Will, we all want to help her," she said, leaning forward. "We love her. But last time she was here and probably this time, too, she won't go anywhere near that part of Mimosa Key. She refuses to go south of Center."

"Well, she's south of Center right this minute."

"What's she doing there? I thought she was shopping."

He cracked his knuckles and looked at his fresh-laid floor. This woman was one of Jocelyn's best friends, a replacement for him all those years ago. Maybe they could help her—and help Guy.

He wouldn't reveal old secrets, just new ones. "He has dementia," he said softly. "I think she's down there trying to figure out what to do with him."

With a soft gasp, she lifted her hand to her mouth, eyes wide. "I had no idea."

"Neither did she."

"Oh my God, poor Joss. What's she going to do?"

It was a rhetorical question, he knew, but he answered anyway. "Let's see, she's going to organize his life, catalog his stuff, research facilities, pack him up, sell his house, move him out and anything else she can put on some kind of to-do list."

"Oh." She almost smiled. "That's our girl. So she was always a control freak?"

"Not as much as she seems to be now." He dragged his hands through sweaty hair, committed to the truth now. "I don't think it's the absolute right way to go. I'd just like her to think it through. He's not..." He blew out a breath. "He's changed from when she last saw him."

She thought about that for a moment, maybe struggling with how much *she* should reveal. "I don't know... details, but my guess is a change in her father's personality can only be an improvement. That's just conjecture on my part, but I did spend four years in college with her and I picked up a little here and there."

He just nodded, carefully choosing his words. "He wasn't the nicest guy in the world. But now, well, I'd just like to see him comfortable."

"Well, one thing about Jocelyn," Tessa said. "She's fair. And she's a really good life coach with a track record for helping people find balance and joy."

Then maybe she needed to work on her own life and not Guy's. And, hell, Will could use a little balance and joy, too. "Then maybe she just needs time to figure out the best way to help him. I'm just not sure how to convince her of that."

Tessa smiled. "My advice? Whatever you want, let her think it's her idea and she's in charge. Otherwise, wham, she'll—"

"Be gone." He heard the hurt in his voice and, from her look, so did Tessa.

"She has mastered the disappearing act."

You can say that again.

Tessa pushed up, gnawing on her lower lip with worry. "I wonder if she needs help down there."

"No, no," he said quickly. "Honestly, Tess, don't. She's fine and I'm going back really soon. I don't think she'd want—"

She waved her hand. "Don't worry, Will. I've been her friend for a long time. I figured out how to deal with her secretive nature ages ago, and I won't tell her you shared this. I'll wait to see how much she tells us."

"Thanks." He grabbed his bottle to take a gulp of water, wiping his mouth, realizing how glad he was to have someone to talk to about this. "You know, I'm just still getting used to the idea that she's here."

She gave him a slow smile. "Like her, do you?"

Jeez, was it that obvious? "I've always liked her." Understatement alert. "I've always...really liked her."

She cocked her head, thinking. "So you must be the one."

"The one?"

She let out a little sigh, like puzzle pieces just snapped into place as she nodded at him. "Wow, I'd never have put you two together."

"We weren't, not really. Why?"

"She got drunk once." She laughed softly. "*Exactly* once, as this is Jocelyn we're talking about. Zoe took her to a frat party one night and brought her home totally toasted." She was looking at him, but remembering something else.

"And?"

"Zoe was with her when she was, uh, you know, puking her guts out. Then Zoe left—probably went back to the party if I know her—and I had the privilege of getting Jocelyn in bed."

He tried to imagine her drunk, sick, helpless like that. Tried and failed. "What happened?" he asked.

"She told me..." She caught herself, shaking her head. "Never mind. File it under too much information for an ex."

"I'm not an ex; we were just friends."

"But she said she—" She cut herself off, firing total frustration through him.

"C'mon, Tess. I just told you more than I should have. Can't we have a little quid pro quo here?"

She considered that, no doubt balancing her fairly new friendship with him and her much longer, deeper friendship with Jocelyn.

"She said she was in love with someone back home but..."

In love. "But what?"

"But it didn't work out."

Because he'd been a coward and an idiot. "We had some...obstacles."

"You didn't hear that from me," she said, stepping back over the wood to get to the door. "I gotta go talk to Lacey."

He stood, brushing sawdust off his pants, his brain whirring like his mitre saw, howling just as loud, telling him what he had to do. "When you see Lacey, tell her I had to take off early. And I might not be here tomorrow. Personal day."

She just smiled. "*Very* personal, I'd say."

Chapter Eight

The front door popped open, startling Jocelyn. She and Guy turned to find Will in the entry, a red bandanna wrapped around his head, a smudge of dirt on his white T-shirt, a look of horror on his face as he stared at Guy.

"Why are you crying?" he asked. He shifted his gaze to Jocelyn and she could read the question: *Did you tell him where you're sending him?*

"Of course I'm crying, son!" Guy stood and ambled to William, arms outstretched. "You've seen the show! They don't get the ratings if they can't get the old farts to cry."

Will looked at her. "So the whole *Clean House* thing is still going well?"

"It's . . . going," Jocelyn said.

"She's gifting me with memories," Guy said.

"She is?"

"And you know what she deserves, William?"

A whisper of a smile pulled at Will's mouth, an old smile she recognized, one that always took her heart for a ride. He held up a bag. "Enchiladas from South of the Border. There's beer in my fridge, too. Can you stay, Joss?"

A strange pressure squeezed Jocelyn's chest. A longing to say yes, so real and strong and natural it nearly took her breath away. She really, really wanted to curl up and eat enchiladas with Will and Guy.

How insane and wrong was that? Wrong, on every level. "I promised Lacey I'd go over to her house tonight," she said quickly, standing up. "But thank you."

"Will you be back tomorrow?" Guy asked anxiously.

"I have some, uh, calls to make in the morning." To assisted-living facilities. "Maybe later or the day after. Don't make any messes while I'm gone, Guy."

"I promise, Missy." He broke away from Will and held out both arms. "Let me give you a hug."

She froze. "That's okay."

"Come here." He threw both arms around her and squeezed, moving his face to one side to give her a clear shot of Will, who just drank in the scene, clearly unsure what to make of it.

"Thank you," Guy whispered in her ear, still loud enough for Will to hear and react with a raised eyebrow of surprise.

"Okay," she said stiffly, backing away without returning the hug. She had her limits. "Bye, now."

She headed for the door, snagging her bag from the planter where she'd set it out of years of habit.

"Let me walk you out," Will said quickly.

"That's okay."

But he had one hand on the front door and one hand

on the knob, enclosing her in the space between. He felt warm from sunshine and work, a smell that reminded her so much of when he'd come home from practice to find her holed up in his room, seeking shelter

Softening, she looked up at him, fighting the urge to brush aside the lock of hair that had fallen over his eye.

"I need to talk to you," he said, in barely more than a whisper and far too close to her ear.

She started to shake her head, but he was so close, so strong, so familiar. She nodded instead. "Let's talk outside."

They headed down the narrow front walk in silence as Jocelyn dug for the keys in her purse.

"Lacey's probably wondering where I've been all this time," she said. "Or did you tell her?"

Behind her, she heard him blow out a breath, making her turn as they reached the driver's door of Jocelyn's borrowed car.

"You did, didn't you?"

"I told Tessa—"

"Oh, great."

"Very little, Joss. Nothing about...history. I told her you were here and that your dad is sick and that you're figuring out what to do."

She nodded. "I'd have to tell her that much, anyway," she said.

"You keep a lot of secrets, don't you?"

"Yep, you've been talking to Tessa. She who hates secrets."

"Well, she said she's your best friend."

"One of them, but even best friends don't need to know everything."

He took a step closer, heat rolling off his big body and the car right behind her, the Florida sun baking everything under it, even in November.

"You're lucky," he said after a minute.

"How's that?"

"To have so many best friends."

She smiled. "I know. I have three great ones."

"Four."

She frowned, not following. "Are you counting Clay as the husband of a best friend?"

"I'm counting me."

The statement stole her breath for a second, leaving her without a quick reply.

"I was your best friend once."

Was. Once. *So much more.*

"What happened, Jossie?"

Again, her breath got trapped, squeezing her chest. "You know what happened. I just had to..." *Let you be free of me.* "Move on."

"What happened...after you left that night?"

"What happened?" He sure as hell really didn't want to know, did he? This man who'd made every decision in his life based on loyalty and love, including the decision to help and care for a man who had once threatened to kill him?

No, he surely didn't mean *that*. He meant why did she cut him out of her life. "College happened, Will."

He put a hand on the roof of the car behind her, trapping her completely. "We have to talk."

This close, she could see every detail, in living, sun-washed color. The navy rim around the lighter blue of his eyes, the reddish tips of his thick black lashes, even the thread-thin crow's feet from all those years of squinting at a pitcher sixty feet away.

Without thinking, she reached up and brushed a few grains of sand and dirt from his cheeks, his skin warm and taut to the touch. "You get dirty at your job."

"Always liked a job like that."

She could actually feel herself falling into the blue of his eyes, like the Gulf, swirling around her, warm and inviting and gentle. "Do you like being a carpenter, Will?"

"When are we going to talk?" His voice was low, direct, as unwavering as his gaze.

"I'll be back in the next few days," she said, purposefully vague even though it was obvious he wanted to be anything but.

"Cancel tonight. Have dinner with me."

She tried to back away, but the car was right behind her. "I can't. I promised—"

"Lacey, I know. But you've known me longer."

She swallowed, surprised by his determination and so fundamentally drawn to it. He still made her feel like her skin was on fire and her head was a little too light. Still.

But surely he didn't still feel that way, not after all these years. Because if he did, he sure as hell wouldn't be taking care of the person who had torn them apart. So his loyalty—the steadfast, unwavering loyalty that thrummed through his veins—must be directed at Guy now.

And then she knew what he wanted from her: to change her mind. "You want to talk me out of this, don't you?"

"No."

She absolutely didn't believe him. "Are you sure? Because five hours ago you were pretty dead set against putting him in a home."

He closed his eyes. "I still am, but I want to talk to you."

"There's nothing to say."

His eyes flashed. "After fifteen years? There's a lot to say. A lot to catch up on." He leaned closer, his face inches away. Too close. Too warm. Too attractive. "Please, Jocelyn. We go too far back, we shared too much to just act like casual acquaintances with a"—he gestured toward the house—"issue. We have to discuss... everything."

"Like what?"

"Like your life and mine, like where you've been, who you've...." His voice trailed off, uncomfortable. "If you've ever thought about me."

She almost laughed. Almost told him the truth.

Just every damn night and most days, Will.

"Of course I've thought of you. I—"

"So have I." He got closer, too close. The magnetic force field between them sparked and arced and drew her to him. Instead of giving in, she put her hand on his chest, ready to push, stunned to feel his heart slam like a jackhammer. His chest was damp, hard, and so, so warm under the thin cotton T-shirt.

Before she could take her hand away from the heat, he pressed his on top of hers. "Don't shut me out." *Again.* He didn't say the final word, but she could hear it, unspoken but deafening.

"I...I..." It was like the earth was shifting under her, a terrifying tilt that made her feel like she was losing control. She tried to snap her hand away, but he pressed harder. "I won't shut you out. I'm sure I'll see you a lot while I'm here getting Guy's things in order." She slid her gaze toward the house. "We'll catch up."

Very slowly, he closed his fist over hers, slipping his hand around hers so that their fingers entwined. "I just want to know who you've become."

"Why?"

His eyes flickered in surprise. "Why? Because I cared about you. I ... wondered about you."

Not enough to hunt her down, though. She swallowed the thought; leaving Will without saying good-bye and never calling him had been her decision. He just went along with it.

She took a deep, shuddering breath. "Okay, but you might not like everything I have to say."

"I'm willing to take that chance." He pulled their fisted hands up to his mouth, searing her knuckles with his warm breath. "Because ... seeing you again, well ..." He lowered his head, touched her cheek with his, and whispered in her ear. "Not a single day has passed where I didn't think about you."

Her heart stuttered and she closed her eyes, letting the words settle over her.

"That's understandable," she said with as much cool as she could muster. Which, under the circumstances, wasn't much. "You see my father every day."

"That's not why."

She looked up at him, almost ready to confess that she'd thought about him, too, a million times, a thousand nights, and every morning when she woke up alone.

"William! I can't find my glasses!"

He blew out a soft exhale of frustration, sending unintended chills down her overheated skin. Leaning away, he turned to the front door. "Check the dishwasher, Guy."

"I did! Found my favorite cup with the birds on—hey, are you two kissing?"

Will stepped away. "I'll be right there, Guy." He fought a smile. "I'll never hear the end of this."

But she just looked at him, baffled. Didn't he realize that the very reason they'd lost fifteen years was standing in the doorway teasing them?

So was he trying to woo her with memories or did he have an agenda where Guy was concerned? Did he think he could get her to change her mind?

She wanted to find out. "I'll talk to you, Will. Not tonight, but soon."

"I can't wait."

Damn it, neither could she.

"I'll get a bottle of wine, stat." From her front door, Lacey deadpanned her opening salvo, and made Jocelyn laugh for the first time all day.

"Is my stress that obvious?" she asked as she entered Lacey's brand-new home tucked away in the north corner of the Casa Blanca property.

"No. Tessa had a nice long talk with Will today."

"Really." Was that why he all of a sudden seemed interested in what she'd been doing for the past fifteen years? He hadn't asked about the scandal. Had Tessa told him anything?

"Really." Tessa came out from the large country-style kitchen, two goblets of something red and inviting in hand. "You don't have to look at me like I read your diary," she said, handing a glass to Jocelyn. "It's just time to talk to your friends, hon."

"One of whom is already in here drinking and waiting for you," Zoe called from the family room.

"Come on in." Lacey put a gentle arm on Jocelyn's

shoulder, already in her role as nurturer and peacemaker, as she had been since the first week they'd all met at Tolbert Hall. The worst of Jocelyn's bruises had healed by then, thanks to the most unlikely of guardian angels, and she'd managed to hide the rest.

Still raw from the day's events despite the fact that she'd stopped in her villa and showered off the memories that had rained on her all day, Jocelyn let Lacey guide her toward the high-ceilinged great room. The scent of tomato and basil wafted from the adjacent kitchen, and a batch of fudgy brownies tempted from the granite island.

Jocelyn inhaled it all, giving Lacey a hug. "You've been baking. Lucky for us."

"Brownies? Hardly taxing my baking capabilities. But you smell those herbs? Homegrown by our very own Tessa Galloway."

Tessa gave a little bow of acknowledgment. "It's only going to get better when I finally learn how to work this sandy soil. But the herbs are doing nicely, so I put them in a lovely whole-wheat vegetable lasagna for us tonight. Completely organic and healthy."

Jocelyn tapped her wineglass with Tessa's, eyeing her warily. "All that gardening, and still time to chat with the construction workers."

Tessa smiled. "Come on and sit down. We'll talk."

Jocelyn took a second to look around, since her first tour had been so quick when she'd arrived. True to his word, Clay had made building this home the first priority at Casa Blanca, and already the signs of a happy family could be seen. A framed picture of Clay, Lacey, and her daughter, Ashley, taken last Christmas, hung in a place of honor near a fireplace. A soft fleecy throw over the back of the sofa looked like it was probably getting plenty of cuddle time, and the pool outside the wide-open sliding glass doors was dotted with a beach ball and inner tube, no doubt the setting for some relaxing family hours.

"I'm not getting up," Zoe said, sprawled on some cushions on the floor with a wineglass in front of her. "I may never walk again."

"What's the matter?"

"I took her to my hot yoga class," Tessa said.

"Also known as the second level of hell," Zoe said, trying to work out her neck. "But the instructor was almost as hot as the room temperature."

"He certainly liked you."

Zoe laughed. "Who doesn't? Sit down, Joss, and buckle in for the Spanish Inquisition."

Oh boy. She fell back into the corner of an overstuffed sofa. "I've had a tough day." In other words, *Take it easy, gang.*

They didn't respond as Tessa curled up in a big chair across the table and Lacey brought in a tray of veggies and dips, setting it on the table, then taking the seat next to Jocelyn.

"Is Clay here?" Jocelyn asked when the awkward silence went on one second too long.

"He went to Ashley's soccer practice and they're going out to dinner together afterwards," Lacey said. "Stepfather and -daughter bonding time."

"They're doing well, then?" Jocelyn reached for a carrot, knowing the small talk wouldn't last long.

Lacey nodded and patted Jocelyn's arm. "C'mon, kiddo. We know you weren't shopping all afternoon."

Jocelyn put the carrot on a cocktail napkin without

eating it, choosing instead to hold up her glass to the group. "How about we start with a toast?"

"Great idea." Tessa raised her glass. "To honesty among lifelong friends."

"To knowing you are loved and safe in this room," Lacey added.

"To a rocking game of truth or dare." Zoe grinned and raised her glass. "What do you want to drink to, Joss?"

She took a deep breath, looking from one to the other. "To not talking about me behind my back."

They shared a guilty look and all drank, except Lacey, who squeezed Jocelyn's arm. "We would never say anything bad, you know that. We love you." She set her glass down without taking a sip and scooted closer. "And you don't ever have to talk about anything you don't want to talk about."

Tessa exhaled softly. "Except you know how I feel. I hate when we have secrets."

"Then tell me what Will told you today," Jocelyn challenged.

She shrugged. "Not much, but he told me you went down to see your father, which we all know is weird because you are..." She hesitated, looking for a word.

"Estranged," Lacey supplied.

"And he said your father is sick," Tessa continued. "That's all. Well, pretty much all."

Jocelyn gave her a hard look.

"I mean, I think he...kind of has the hots for you," Tessa added. "But that's just conjecture. He didn't say."

Zoe sat up, yoga pain gone. "You *so* forgot to tell us that part."

"Honestly, I already knew that," Lacey said, plucking a

zucchini disk and nibbling on it with a sly smile. "Remember the big town council meeting when I presented the Casa Blanca plans and Clay..." She made a gooey face. "You know, practically proposed?"

"We remember!" Zoe made a kissing sound. "So does the rest of this island."

"We got there late," Jocelyn said, remembering the wild ride from a hospital hours away. That day had been crazy, and she had no recollection of seeing Will that time, although she had seen him at the previous town meeting. "Was he there?" she asked.

Lacey nodded. "When I first got there with my dad, I saw Will, and the very first thing he asked about was you. And not in a casual way."

"In what kind of way?"

"An interested way."

"When were you going to tell me this?"

Lacey exhaled, searching her friend's face. "Honestly, Joss, I thought it was Will keeping you from going south of Center when you visited. That maybe you had a history. I mean, I know your relationship with your dad is—"

"I have no relationship with my dad."

"I knew that, but I just thought there must be something important between you and Will. Wasn't there?"

She sipped wine. "Define 'important.' "

On her knees, Zoe crawled closer to the table. "S-E-X."

"No, we never..." Almost. Nearly. Wanted to. Still wanted to.

That last thought shot through her, surprising her with its intensity. "We were really close when we were young, really good friends. He was a great source of..." *Fantasies.* "Comfort for me."

"What kind of comfort?"

"Why didn't you tell us about him at school?" Lacey asked.

Jocelyn ignored Zoe's question but answered Lacey's "We just went our separate ways," she said. "He went to the University of Miami and had a big baseball career. I went to UF and met…" She lifted her glass, the early effects of the wine helping to dull the edges of her nerves. "The three best friends a girl ever had."

"Aww," Zoe said, coming around the table on her knees to curl her fingers around Jocelyn's hand. "That's so sweet." She tightened her grip. "But don't deflect. Did he hit you?"

"What?" She reared back at the question, so unexpected, especially from Zoe.

"Zoe!" the other two said in unison.

But Zoe didn't take her eyes off Jocelyn. "On the first or second night at school, you were changing in the room, and I saw some bruises on you."

Her blood chilled. "Will didn't hit me, no. Will has never ever hurt me. On the contrary, he…" *Tried to defend me. Was willing to take a bullet for me. Wasn't he?* Thank God they never had to find out.

"He what?" Zoe urged.

"He was exactly what I needed at the time."

No one spoke, the only sound the soft hum from the pool motor just outside.

"Jocelyn," Lacey finally said. "We know your dad is really sick. And we know you have a rocky relationship with him. You need us, honey, and you can trust us with anything. Even things you've never told anyone else."

Perspiration tingled despite the cool evening air that

tumbled in from the patio. All three of them looked at her with concern and love.

Which just made guilt smash at her heart. If they knew that she'd told Coco—a client and, yes, a friend—and not them? Lacey would be hurt. Tessa would be furious. And Zoe would remind her every chance she got.

But she'd told Coco for a reason, and these three women didn't have any reason to know except that they were more like sisters than friends. They could be trusted, and tender. Plus, with Will doing a full-court press to keep her from putting Guy in a home, they could be her allies.

"I hate my father," she said simply.

Yes, it was kind of hard to hate that weepy old man she'd spent the afternoon with, a man who couldn't remember her name, but she still hated who he was and who he'd been.

No one spoke, giving her time to sift through her emotions to find the right words. "He..." *Beat my mother. Kicked me so hard he broke a rib. Made me the control freak I am today.* "Was physically abusive."

"Oh, baby."

"Jeez."

"Shoot the em-effer."

Jocelyn smiled at Zoe. "Don't think the thought hadn't occurred to me. But I did the next best thing. I left home and never looked back. Until today, it was my intention to never speak to him, look at him, or think about him until the day his death notice arrived in my mailbox."

That silenced all of them.

"I know I sound harsh," she said. "Especially now, when you look at the guy. He's like a little old lady, doing needlepoint and watching HGTV. But I know what he is... what he *was*." Her voice cracked and Zoe handed her the wineglass.

She half smiled, accepting it with a slight tremble in her hands, then taking a deep drink.

Tessa leaned closer, pain clouding her eyes. "Some people should not be allowed to be parents."

"No kidding." One more drink and her limbs finally felt a little heavy, while the weight on her heart felt a little lighter. "Before I left for school, I...he..." Shit. "There was a pretty bad night." Her voice cracked, which she tried to cover with a fake cough. "Will was there."

"Did he hit Will?" Tessa asked.

She shook her head. "He was more mad at me than he was at Will, but he did have a gun." When Zoe gasped, Jocelyn added, "He was the deputy county sheriff on Mimosa Key at the time, so he was, you know, law and judge and jury. And my father. So I basically decided at that moment that Will, who was on a direct trajectory to huge success, would be better off if we didn't ever see each other again."

"And he agreed?" Zoe asked.

"He must have. He never tried to track me down at UF and our friendship ended."

"And now he's taking care of the guy you hate," Tessa said.

Zoe grunted softly. "That's gotta hurt."

"But that's Will," Lacey said. "He'll always do the right thing. That's his nature."

"I don't think it's the right thing," Jocelyn said. "I know that's cold, but I don't. And he's my father, not his. Despite what Guy thinks."

"Guy thinks Will is his son?" Zoe choked on that.

"He's pretty confused." She put the glass down hard enough to splash a little wine on the napkin. "Is the intervention over yet? I'm starving."

"Not an intervention." Lacey sidled up closer and put her arm around Jocelyn. "And, really, we've all suspected it was something like this. Honestly, Joss, Will's keeping your father's condition pretty quiet. I knew he checked on him once in a while, but he's been mum on how bad Guy is or, honestly, I'd have told you so you didn't get blindsided when you arrived."

"I wasn't really blindsided. I saw Will this morning and he told me how me how sick Guy was, so I went down there today and..." Another mirthless, dry laugh. "He doesn't remember me, he doesn't remember the past, and he sure as hell doesn't remember..." *That night.* "Anything he did to his wife or daughter."

They all sighed, a collective exhale of dismay and disbelief. All except Zoe, who narrowed her eyes with a question. "Maybe Will didn't know how bad it was with your dad for you."

"He lived next door. He had a front-row seat."

Tessa leaned forward. "You know what you need, Joss? You need to work this out. You need to get past this."

Jocelyn frowned at her. "I *am* past it. Why do you think I took all those psych classes? Why do you think I'm a life coach?"

"I don't think you're past it," Tessa said. "Or you could talk about it."

"I am freaking talking about it! What do you want, Tess? Pictures? Scars? Details?"

Tessa dropped to her knees so that only the coffee

table separated them. "I'm sorry, Joss. I don't want to upset you, really. We just want to help you."

"Then change the subject. I've never talked about it this much."

"Even in therapy?" Tessa asked. "Didn't you have to go through therapy to get your degree?"

"Nothing...deep." She'd been quite adept at avoiding the topics she didn't want to discuss.

"Not even to get certified as a life coach?"

She lifted a brow. "In California? Hang a shingle, baby, and get some bigmouth clients." She waved her hand to erase any wrong impression that might leave. "I am certified by several organizations." She reached for some grapes, plucking them from the stems, hating the hot and cold sensations that rolled through her.

Lacey put her hand on Jocelyn's leg. "You know we just want to help you and support you."

She nodded, taking a bite of a giant green grape. "Then help me find an assisted-living facility for him."

Tessa leaned her elbows on the table. "You sure that's what you want to do?"

"Yes, I'm sure. I'm not taking care of him."

"*Will* is," Tessa said.

"Which is...kind."

"How did he handle it?" Tessa asked. "I mean, everything that went on with your dad when you were young? Did Will ever try to stop him? He seems like he would have."

She shot a look at Tessa, surprised by the little jolt of jealousy that Tessa—and Lacey—had gotten to know Will Palmer when he was so lost to Jocelyn.

"My dad was the law back then. No, no. He was so far

above the law it could give you a nosebleed. And Will had a big-time career to worry about."

"As if he'd put his career before something like that," Tessa said.

"He is loyal to a fault," Lacey agreed. "Definitely our best and most reliable subcontractor, who just seems to work and live with all his heart."

"He was always that way," she said, feeling an unnatural sense of propriety. After all, she'd known—and loved—Will before they did. "And still is that way because he doesn't want to put Guy in a home, or at least wants me to think about alternatives."

"Would you think about alternatives?" Tessa asked.

Before she could answer the oven beeped and Lacey stood slowly, waiting to hear Jocelyn's answer before leaving the room.

Jocelyn shrugged. "I have a lot of work to do down there first. And he…" She smiled, knowing they'd laugh. "He thinks I'm with *Clean House* and I'm going to put him on TV after I straighten things up and have a yard sale."

Zoe popped up and gave her head a shake. "So you better git to gittin', uh-huh!"

Jocelyn cracked up at the spot-on Niecy Nash impression, welcoming the levity and a chance to get up and help Lacey in the kitchen. But as she did Tessa was up, too, taking Jocelyn's hand to hold her back.

"Hey," she whispered. "You know we just want to help you."

Jocelyn nodded, not trusting her voice.

"And so does Will."

One more nod and Tessa pulled her a little closer.

"He's been hurt, too."

Jocelyn just looked at her. "I read somewhere he was married." Not that she'd Googled him on one particularly lonely night back in L.A. or anything.

"He was divorced before he got here. I always thought that was what put the little bit of, I don't know, sadness in his eyes. Or maybe being so far away from baseball and not having a coaching job offer."

More inside information that Tessa had and Jocelyn didn't. Who could she blame? She'd never called Will, had never kept in touch, and, of course, neither had he.

"But today I thought maybe..." She waited a few seconds until Jocelyn nudged her.

"Maybe what?"

"I think it's you who hurt him."

"*Me*?"

"I don't know. Maybe it was his ex-wife. Short marriage—he never talks about it. You should find out."

She intended to. When they had that "catch-up" conversation he wanted so much.

The thing was, she wanted it, too.

Chapter Nine

Will turned his truck into the Super Min, as he did every day on his way up to Barefoot Bay, to shell out a few bucks for Charity Grambling's coffee. Like the owner of the convenience store, the coffee was bitter and a little past its prime. But it was usually served with a side of opinion or gossip, which Will filed away or shared with Clay if it had anything to do with Casa Blanca.

And her gossip often did focus on the resort, since Charity, along with a few of her family members, considered herself the last word on everything related to Mimosa Key. The building of Casa Blanca, the island's first true resort, was pretty much the biggest thing happening in Charity's world.

The bell dinged as Will pushed open the door, a charming reminder of earlier days when this was just a corner store and not the Shell Gas Station and Super Mini

Mart Convenience Store. Without looking up, Charity whipped the magazine she was reading out of sight, shoving it under the counter before she leveled a beady brown gaze at her customer.

"Morning, Will."

"Charity." He nodded and headed toward the back to grab a couple Gatorades for the job, pulling open the cooler door to check out the abysmal selection. Fruit punch and the blue shit. He let out a loud exhale.

"Sorry, I can't sell enough of it to get you that original flavor, Will," Charity called back. "You'll have to go back to the big leagues for that. Gonna happen anytime soon?"

He grabbed two sixteen-ounce reds and carried them back to the counter. "You'll be the first to know if the Yankees call, Charity."

She gave him a smile that didn't reach her eyes or make her leathery old face any more attractive. Scooting around on her stool, Charity held her bloodred fingernail over the cash register. "Will that be all?"

He gave her a look. "And coffee." Like he hadn't been getting a medium black every day since they'd broken ground at the resort.

" 'Kay." She tapped the register but didn't complete the transaction. "How're things up at the white elephant?" She never failed to make a dig, still stinging over the loss of her fight to stop Lacey and Clay from building a resort that might steal some business from the dumpy motel her daughter owned.

"Moving along real well," he said. Or they would be if he could get his head around Bay Laurel's floor today.

"Taking any guests yet?" she asked pointedly.

"Nope." Not unless he counted Jocelyn. Still,

something about the way she asked gave him pause; Charity had an uncanny knowledge of what was going on anywhere and everywhere on Mimosa Key. It wouldn't surprise him if she'd somehow sniffed out the return of one of their most infamous residents.

"I heard that one of those teeny little houses is all done and Lacey spent a fortune decorating it to look like something out of a Humphrey Bogart movie."

How did she *know* this stuff?

"We're a long way from taking guests," he said.

"Even just one?"

He gave her a hard look. How could she know? From the magazines she sold? Had one of them leaked Jocelyn's flight information or something? They were capable of anything.

He turned to the rack of tabloids, ready to grab them all and clear them out if he had to. It would only help locally, of course.

The entire top rack was empty.

He peered closer, glancing at the other monthly titles below. *Maxim* and *Cosmopolitan*, some fishing rags and a stack of *USA Today* next to the *Mimosa Gazette* on the bottom. Nothing that would have word about Jocelyn. But those cheesy tabloids, like the *National Enquirer* he'd picked up the other day, were all gone.

Shit. Had the entire town sucked up the news because she was a local girl?

"What are you looking for?" Charity asked sharply.

"The magazines."

"Sold out."

"Completely?"

She shrugged. "Is that going to be all, then, Will?"

"When do the new tabloids come in, usually?" he asked. She narrowed her eyes at him then hit the register key with an officious snap. "You taking a sudden interest in the latest on the movie stars in rehab, Will?"

"Something like that." He glanced at the empty rack again, pulling out his wallet. "It's Tuesday," he said, thinking out loud. "Will more magazines come in this week?" He'd buy every one of them if he had to, just to keep the locals from drinking that stupid Kool-Aid and somehow changing—or forming—their opinions about Jocelyn.

"Varies." She took his money and started to make change, faster than usual, he noticed.

The bell rang and they both glanced at the door, seeing Deputy Slade Garrison with two other men, one holding a small video camera.

"Charity, can I talk to you a minute?" Tough enough to be respected but still young enough to be respectful, Slade's tone was deferential toward Charity.

"What do you want, Slade?" Her gaze zeroed in on the camera, a touch of color draining from her face. "Something the matter?"

Standing near the coffee station, Will set up a cup, listening to the exchange while he poured.

"These gentlemen are from an Internet Web site and TV show known as *TMZ*."

The coffee splashed as Will missed the edge of the cup.

"What the hell is that?" Charity asked, setting Will's change on the edge of the counter with a loud slap.

TMZ? Holy shit. Will knew what it was. He knew exactly what it was—*thanks, Guy*—and why they'd be here. Son of a bitch, if Charity had given away the fact that Jocelyn was in town, he'd kill her.

"They stopped into my office," Slade said, not answering her question. "They are looking for some information on a former resident who I don't personally know, but I told them if anything is going on here in Mimosa Key, you'd know about it."

Only in a town the size of Mimosa Key would visiting reporters get an escort from the sheriff's department.

Charity stood, pushing back her stool and lifting the countertop so she could step out. When she did, a couple of Will's coins dropped but she ignored them, her unwavering focus on the men.

Of course. Charity would be in her element now. The most gossip-crazed busybody in the state of Florida with a chance to be on *TMZ*? Her head would explode.

And if she so much as uttered the name Jocelyn Bloom, Will would break their fucking camera and run them over with his truck. Right in front of Slade.

Will eyed the two men, one stepping forward and handing a card to Charity.

"Bobby Picalo," he said, flashing a fake-white smile and running a hand through hair that had spent too much time in the sun or maybe a salon. "Reporter-at-large for TMZ.com." Slimeball freelancer, in other words. "We're a news-gathering organization."

Will almost groaned out loud. *News*? They call this news? And, shit, this bastard would have Charity plastered all over TV tonight——or all over the Internet in an hour—and sixty more slimeballs just like him would be barreling over the causeway by tomorrow morning.

He had to stop her.

"What brings you to Mimosa Key?" Charity asked.

"We're tracking a big story out of Los Angeles and we

think it's possible a source we'd like to talk to is on this island. A young woman by the name of Jocelyn Bloom."

Despite the fire that shot through him, Will stayed perfectly still, not reacting, not breathing, just waiting, the coffeepot poised in the air.

Charity said absolutely nothing.

"Do you know her?" the reporter asked.

Charity glanced at Deputy Garrison, who didn't respond, then she lifted a skeletal-thin shoulder. "I've heard of her."

Maybe she wanted them to beg so she could negotiate for more airtime. That'd be just like her.

"From the papers or do you know her personally, ma'am?" Picalo asked.

"She used to live here years ago. Maybe came back now and again, but I think she's on to much bigger and better things than a little town like this."

Will gently set the coffeepot back on the burner. Was this Charity Grambling? Not attacking the opportunity to be in the middle of a national scandal? Something was not right.

"Does she still have family living here?"

Another look at the officer and then a sideways look at Will. If he didn't know Charity better, he'd have sworn she'd sent something like a warning. To him?

Because if these pricks went anywhere near Guy, he'd—

"Her mother passed 'bout a decade ago," she said. "And her father took an early retirement from the sheriff's office. Right, Slade?"

"That's right," Slade agreed. Will waited for him to mention that the retired sheriff lived a few miles south, but he stayed silent.

"No other family?" the man asked, looking from Charity to the sheriff.

"No." Charity locked her hands on her hips. "No one."

Will couldn't believe what he was witnessing. Charity missing out on the chance to gossip to a reporter? Why? Money, of course. She must want to have her palms greased thoroughly before she parted with any information.

"But if someone knew her or saw her here, how would—"

"I'd know about it, young man," she said, bouncing on her sneakers and crossing her arms with a remarkable amount of moxie considering that she was well north of sixty, at least. "I know every damn thing that happens on this island, and every person who lives here. She's not here, hasn't been for years, and won't be probably ever again. I suggest you head back to Hollywood for your story."

"Well, I—"

"You heard the lady," Slade said.

Charity flicked her fingers toward the door. "Good-bye now, gentlemen."

They backed out and Charity went with them, as if she didn't trust them to hang out in the Super Min parking lot.

No money, no airtime, no nothing.

What was *wrong* with this picture?

Holding his coffee, Will went back to the counter to grab the bills she'd left there for him, noticing the two quarters that had fallen to the floor. He set the coffee on the counter to crouch down and scoop up his change.

As he did, he happened to look at Charity's four-legged stool, and the pile of newspapers and magazines behind it.

Not just any newspapers and magazines. Tabloids.

He leaned closer, getting a better look. On top of the

stack, Jocelyn's face was as clear as it had been in his fitful sleep last night.

A stack of tabloids nearly six inches high. They weren't sold out; she'd taken them off the racks.

Why?

He'd known Charity Grambling since he was a kid, bought gas for his first car at the Super Min, and snacks on his way home from baseball practice. As long as he'd known her, she'd never veered off track from what she was: a know-it-all, greedy, meddling, opinionated troublemaker who considered herself the law and last word on Mimosa Key.

So something wasn't right. And that couldn't be good. Not if Charity Grambling was involved.

She came back in, a sour puss deepening the lines on her face.

"Not like you to hide from the spotlight," he said, pocketing his change.

"That's not the spotlight," she said gruffly, heading back to her counter. "Those idiots are just...liars." She slipped behind the counter and closed the top, securing herself—and her stash of tabloids—again. "What are you looking at?" she demanded.

"I'm just wondering about those magazines, Charity."

He could have sworn she swallowed. "What magazines?"

He indicated the empty rack. "The ones that are, you know, sold out."

"Why are you so doggone interested?"

"I'd like to buy one. When will you have some to sell?"

" 'Bout the same time I get your precious original-flavored Gatorade," she growled, waving to the door.

"You better get to work, Will. The Eyesore on the Beach isn't going to build itself."

"Charity, I—"

"I'm not in a talking mood, Will, or didn't you notice?"

"I noticed. I noticed plenty. Like what you said to those men."

"Don't you be talking to them," she warned, pointing one of her crimson talons at him. "We don't need those busybodies sniffin' all over Mimosa Key."

"No, we don't," he agreed. "We have our own busybodies, thank you very much."

She had the good humor to laugh. "Hell, yeah. This town ain't big enough for more than one busybody, don't you forget it."

"Not about to, ma'am. And, uh, thank you."

She just nodded, her mouth uncharacteristically closed.

Outside, the men had driven away but Slade stood next to his sheriff's car talking to a young woman Will recognized as Gloria Vail, Charity's niece.

For a minute, Will considered enlisting the deputy's help to protect Jocelyn, but after what he'd just witnessed, he wasn't sure whom he should trust or why.

Either way, Jocelyn needed to know the enemy was on the island.

The mosquito netting around the bed wasn't really necessary on a cool November morning, but Jocelyn drew it closed anyway, cloistering herself in the white gauze while she tapped her laptop and researched her options for assisted-living facilities.

She focused her search on the neighboring mainland

towns of Naples and Fort Myers, resulting in a number of options. Just as she clicked through to the second Web site, she heard a man clear his throat.

"You decent in there?"

Will. Just the sound of his voice made a quick electrical current shoot through her.

"Define decent. I'm dressed."

She could have sworn she heard him *tsk* in disappointment. "You taking visitors?"

Outside the netting, she could see him leaning on the jamb of one of the french doors, his familiar, masculine scent suddenly so out of place among the lingering aroma of herbal incense Tessa had sworn would make her sleep better.

Tessa had been wrong.

"You can come in," she said, leaning across the bed to push the sheer curtain open. "I'm working."

He smiled and, damn, if all the sunshine outside didn't pour right into the room. His eyes looked as blue as the sky behind him, his sizeable body suddenly taking up all the space in the room. "Nice office."

"Isn't it?"

He drew the curtain back a little farther, that soapy, sunny Will scent crazy-close now. He wore a white T-shirt that wouldn't be as clean by the end of the day and ancient khaki cargo shorts, and held a work belt in one hand, a cup of coffee in the other.

"You better have two of those," she said, eyeing the coffee. "I can't get an answer at room service to save my life."

He laughed at the joke and held the cup out to her. "Lacey's in a roofing meeting, I'm afraid."

She took the coffee and sipped, raising her eyebrows. "Whoa." She swallowed and made a face. "Super Min?"

"Some things never change."

"Come on." She patted the bed in invitation. "You're going to find out what I'm doing on this computer sooner or later."

Setting his tool belt on the floor, he sat on the edge of the bed to check out the computer screen. "I hope to God you're not at the TMZ Web site."

She almost choked. "I'm not a masochist, Will. Why, have you been there today? Is there new dirt online?"

He took a slow breath as if he wanted to tell her something, then shook his head, indicating the computer. "What's that?"

She turned the screen. "The Cottages at Naples Bay." She clicked to the next site. "Summer's Landing." And the next. "Palm Court Manor." And the last. "Esther's Comfort."

He held up his hand to stop the next click.

"I like the sound of that one," she said. "But I can get into one called Autumn House later today."

"Into one today? You're moving him today?" He couldn't keep the dismay out of his voice.

"No, I meant into one for an interview. Placement is much harder and most of these homes have a waiting list." Which she'd bet some cash could shorten.

He pushed down the laptop screen and gave her a direct look. "Why are you in such a hurry?"

"Because I long ago found that if you do the most distasteful tasks the very first thing in the day, they're done. I've extended that strategy to my everyday life. The longer I sit on this—"

"The more chance you might change your mind."

She just shook her head. "I'm not going to argue with you, Will. I'm going to Autumn House today."

"Then I'm going with you."

Not a chance. "No, thank you."

"You can't go alone."

She frowned at him. "I most certainly can, but if I need company, I'll get one of my friends."

"I am one of your friends," he said. "I'll go with you."

"You have to work."

"I'll . . . call in sick."

And he would, too, she just knew it. Then she'd be with him all day, too close for comfort as he launched his campaign against her plan. No, that would never work. "Will, you can't go with me and that's that."

"Why not?"

"Because you'll distract me."

He lifted his eyebrows as if that amused and didn't surprise him.

"And you'll try to talk me out of my plan."

"You need me there and I'm not backing down."

Damn the little thrill that went through her. Did he want to be with her that much? Did the idea of that have to feel so good? "I do not need you there."

"Anyway, you need a bodyguard." His serious, even ominous expression erased any little thrills.

"Oh, Lord. The media found me."

He put a hand over hers. "Not yet, but they're looking."

"They've been to Guy's house?" For some reason, that terrified her more than if they'd found her.

"No, I don't think so, but we should get down there and warn him not to open the door to anyone."

"Then how do you know?"

"They came into the Super Min."

She gasped softly. "Was Charity there?"

"Yeah, and she not only didn't talk to them, she kicked them out on their asses and made sure Slade Garrison knew not to give them any information. So Charity's either overdosed on her nice meds or something is up."

Neither one. But she wasn't about to tell Will the real reason behind Charity's behavior. Some secrets would last forever.

"Not only that," he continued, "she hid the tabloids." He shook his head, baffled. "I've never known her to not exploit every possible opportunity to gossip, and this was on a national scale."

Of course he'd think that. Most people would. But most people didn't know Charity Grambling like she did. "Who was it, TMZ?"

He nodded.

"Bottom-feeders," she said, lifting the computer screen. "Let me call these places and make appointments with every one of them."

"Let's just start with one, Joss," he said. "Let's go see one. Together. Let's find out if it's the right thing to do. And I can tell Lacey I won't be gone all day, which will make her happy."

"And I can work on Guy's mess this afternoon," she agreed.

"And we can have dinner together tonight."

She drew back. "Why?"

"We still need to talk."

"We'll have all afternoon to talk."

He put his hand over hers, so warm and big and

familiar. She couldn't help looking at it, at how his fingers eclipsed hers, at how strong and capable that hand was.

"We have fifteen years to catch up on," he said. "That's going to take longer than a trip to Naples and back."

She opened her mouth to argue, to turn him down, to put up the wall she had first erected on that horrible night in his loft and promised herself she'd never, ever tear down.

But nothing came out.

And then she nodded.

"Is that a yes?" he asked, his eyes dark blue with hope.

Another nod, still not completely sure what she'd say if she opened her mouth.

"I just want you to forgive me," he said.

For a second, she wasn't sure she understood. "Forgive you?"

"For never calling, for never finding you, for never making sure fifteen years didn't pass without... us..."

His voice trailed off but it didn't matter; her pulse was thumping so loud she could hardly hear him.

"Will," she whispered, "I'm the one who made sure all that time passed. I wouldn't have returned your call and I figured... this was better."

"Better?" He gripped her hand, picking it up, bringing it to his lips and holding her gaze. "Better for who?"

"For you."

He closed his eyes and kissed her fingertips. "It wasn't better for me."

Her heart folded in half, smashed by regret and, damn, hope. Maybe an afternoon with him would squash that for good.

Or maybe it would make her hope for more. There was only one way to find out.

Chapter Ten

⌒

Why did that dang thread always get stuck on the up-loop? Guy pushed his glasses up his nose and angled the hooped plastic mesh toward the window to get a good look. Not that the artwork could look *good*. No, this was one messy piece of needlepoint.

Maybe William would show him that little movie on the computer again with the lady who explained this needling to children. That had really helped.

With a sigh he studied the whole project again, letting his eyes unfocus so he could appreciate the shape and colors of the flowers and not the bumps and lumps of his mistakes. He'd gotten half a petal done since yesterday and then he'd lost interest. Why couldn't he stay with one thing long enough to finish it?

Same thing with his memory. Stuff disappeared as quickly as it showed up, always with those flashing lights like on a Christmas tree, teasing him in color so bright and bold then fading to black and white, before they disappeared altogether into gray nothingness.

But ever since that girl landed on his front porch, a few lights were coming on. And staying on. Threads of memories wrapped around his broken brain like it was this plastic embroidery net, then the colors almost caught, and, boom, they were knotted in shadows again.

Still, when he looked at her something deep in his gut stirred.

He knew her. And not just from the TV.

That was the thought that kept getting tangled just like this silky orange yarn.

He *knew* her. Was that possible? He had carefully lined up the needle and was ready to push it through the hole when the doorbell startled him and the needle jumped out of the spot.

"Son of a gun!" No Girl Scouts sold cookies at this time of day, so he hoped it wasn't some salesperson, 'cause he wasn't buying. He had enough junk in this place.

He pushed up, setting down the whole frame and embroidery panel on his chair, then rounded the decorative brick divider to get to the front door. Standing on his tiptoes, he squinted at two men, not recognizing either of them.

"Yeah, what is it?" he called.

"Mr. Bloom? Mr. Guy Bloom? Former deputy sheriff of Mimosa Key?" He was the former sheriff, he knew that for a fact. Didn't remember a blasted thing about it, but William had told him, so it must be true.

"What can I do for you?" he asked. Wait a second! Could these be people from the show? Where was Missy?

Shouldn't she be here? Dang, she might get in trouble for showing up so late, and he didn't want that to happen. "You with the TV show?" he asked.

He saw them look at each other, one with kind of thinning hair holding something black in his hand, the other with those horn-rimmed glasses and hair that women used to call "frosted." Which looked kind of ridiculous on a man, if you asked him.

"Yes, and the Web site."

Did *Clean House* have a Web site? *Of course, you old coot.* Everybody and his cousin was on the stinkin' computer.

"Can we talk to you a minute, Mr. Bloom?"

"About the show?"

After a beat, the man said. "About Jocelyn."

That was her name, even though Guy could never remember it. He'd heard William call her "Joss." But he didn't know where she was, and what if they came in here and didn't like him as much as she did? What if they looked around and didn't see the potential or had someone with a messier house and kids? They loved kids on that show.

The only thing he could do was play dumb. A little smile lifted his lips. Like *playing dumb* would be any challenge.

"I don't know anyone named Jocelyn," he said, his hand on the dead bolt, holding it firmly in the lock position. "Sorry."

"Your daughter, Jocelyn," he said.

Something stabbed his heart, not too hard, not as sharp as that embroidery needle he'd just been holding, but he felt the jab just the same.

"I don't have a daughter. I have a son."

He lifted up on his toes to catch the two men giving each other confused looks.

"You aren't Guy Bloom, father of Jocelyn Bloom? The sheriff said you lived here."

Wait a second, he *was* the sheriff. Well, not anymore.

A thin trickle of sweat, surprisingly cold, meandered under his collar, finding its way down his back.

"You got the wrong man. My son is named William and he's not here. I don't have a daughter."

"Are you sure?" Frosty asked.

"What kind of a question is that?" he fired back even though, heck, it was a darn good question. He wasn't sure what day it was, what street he lived on, or who was the president of the United States. But he kept that mostly to himself, so he didn't wind up in some nuthouse somewhere.

"Are you positive you don't have a daughter?" the man demanded, his tone making it clear he didn't believe Guy.

"I do not have a daughter," Guy confirmed. Suddenly the mail slot opened and a little white card tumbled in.

"That's my number, Mr. Bloom. If you change your mind, I can make it worth your while to talk. Extremely worth your while." He waited a moment, then added, "Like fifty thousand dollars worth your while."

Fifty thousand dollars! Is that how the show worked? "For remodeling?" he asked, imagining just how much money they spent on all that paint and furniture and the pretty blonde girl who reorganized all the shelves and closets.

"You can use it for whatever you want if you give us access to or information about Jocelyn."

"Why do you want it?"

"No one can find her, sir. And a lot of people want to talk to your daughter."

"I don't have..." He picked up the card. *Robert Picalo, TMZ.* Shaking his head, he slipped the card into one of the open spaces between the bricks, where he used to keep his keys when he could drive.

What a funny thing to remember. For a moment he put his hand on the cool bricks, remembering his keys so distinctly it shocked him. And...a woman. The color in his head was soft and peachy, light and—

"Call me if you change your mind, Mr. Bloom."

Who was he talking to?

He turned and looked out the little window again at two men. Who were they? Before he could ask, the men headed down the walk, talking and looking around.

Oh, that's right, he remembered with relief. They're with *Clean House.* He grabbed the memory and squeezed so it wouldn't go away, just as the bald guy picked up the black thing he was holding—was that a camera?

Oh, now they're taking pictures of the place! Video pictures.

"It's gonna be fine," he said to himself, turning around when they got in a van parked on the street. "Missy'll know what to do.

Are you positive you don't have a daughter?

The words echoed in his head, making him unsure whether he'd just heard them or made them up.

Maybe he did have a daughter.

On an instinct that he didn't understand, he ambled down the hall to his bedroom and, in just that space and time, those dang Christmas lights flashed again, burst of yellow. Orange. Red. Green.

Gone.

He shook his head, standing in the bedroom. What had he come in here for?

Pressing his fingers to his temples with a low growl of frustration, he tried to push the thoughts from the outskirts into the middle of his brain, imagining those little lines and valleys opening to tell him what the hell he had come into this room to get.

"God damn it!" He punched the doorjamb.

He couldn't remember. Couldn't remember what he was doing, watching, thinking. Everything was shrouded in fog.

Frustration popping in every vein, he opened the closet door, hoping to remember. A sweater? Shoes? Something to eat?

No, no, not here.

And then he remembered the box.

In the closet, he pushed the clothes to the side, determined to find his secret box. William didn't know about this box. The pretty TV girl didn't know about the box. No one knew about the box he kept inside the safe at the back of his closet. The "safe" was really a door built into the wall, painted over, and almost impossible to see. Good thing, because if it were a real safe, he sure as hell wouldn't be able to remember the combination. But in that hole in the wall was the big pink box.

The top was curved and had an embroidered rose glued to it. On the front, a key with a ragged silver tassel rested in the lock, but the lock didn't work anymore. He lifted the lid and peered inside.

Two rings. One tarnished necklace. He lifted out the top section and found what he wanted underneath. The picture. Of a man and a girl, sitting in a rowboat.

The girl was maybe six or seven? He didn't know. But she was deep inside a shiny silver boat not much wider than a canoe, oars in her hands, long dark hair blowing in the wind as she looked at the camera and smiled, front teeth missing. A man sat behind her, grinning from ear to ear.

There was a wisp of a memory. The girl's laughter, her head turning around, a word on her lips.

Daddy.

For a long time he just stared at the girl, and something inside him broke off in little pieces.

Daddy. *Daddy.*

"Guy? Are you here?"

William! He snapped the box closed, shoved it into its hiding place, and pushed himself up, shaking like a kid who'd been caught smoking in the boys' room.

"Guy? Where are you?"

Missy was there, too! A smile shot through him as he pushed his way out of the closet. Wait till she saw how far he got on those flowers.

"I'm back here in my room, you two."

You two. They made a heck of a nice couple, didn't they?

"Oh, I'm so glad." She came in, her long hair pulled back in a ponytail. Lord, the girl was a feast for the eyes, even ones as bad as his.

"We just came to check on you," she said.

"I'm fine. Could use a little lunch, though."

"I'll make him a sandwich, Will. You talk to him."

As she headed back down the hall, William came into the room, putting one of his big hands on Guy's shoulder in that way that made Guy feel so safe. There was just no one like his William.

"You okay, Guy?"

"Fine, fine, yeah. Why?"

Will looked at him funny. "You looked flushed."

"Me?" He touched his cheek. "I was just, you know, thinking about things."

Will guided him to sit on the bed, always so gentle for a big kid. Always so kind. "God, I love you, William."

He smiled. "I know, buddy. Listen, I want to talk to you about not letting—"

"What is this?" Missy stood in the doorway, eyes wide, face pale, a little white card in her hand. "They were *here*?"

She held out the card and William took it, looking just as stunned. "Did you talk to this man, Guy?" he asked.

Did he?

"What man?"

"Oh, God." Missy put both hands to her mouth, a look of panic making her big brown eyes look like giant saucers. "Please tell me you didn't tell them I'm here."

A flash of light popped in his head and he grabbed that thought, standing up, determined to hold on before the clouds came back. "I told them I didn't know who they were talking about."

"You did?" she asked. "You're sure?"

Was he? Son of a gun, he wasn't sure about anything. "I didn't let them in, I swear."

"It's okay, Guy." William eased him back to the bed. "You didn't do anything wrong."

But the girl looked horror-stricken. "You better stay here, Will. I'm going to—"

"Not alone, you're not."

"But you have to stay with him."

A little anger boiled through Guy, firing some synapses that were mostly dead. "Stop talking about me like I'm not here!" he boomed, pretty loud, because Missy gasped again and took a quick step backwards.

Then her face kind of froze. "I'm going, Will." She turned like a soldier and marched down the hall.

Oh, no! He'd made her mad! "Missy!" he called, jumping up to follow her, a wave of remorse strangling him. "No, don't get mad! I'm so sorry. I'm sorry!" He choked on the last words, hating that he was about to cry, turning to William for help.

"Just stay here, Guy. Let me handle this, please." Will gave him a quick squeeze on the shoulders. "Just wait here and let me talk to her. Please."

"She's upset, William. I hurt her feelings. I yelled at her." A light flashed in his head again, a pale baby blue this time. A familiar color that reminded him of sadness. "Talk to her, William. Don't let her leave. I like her. I like her so much."

William gave him a tight smile, nodding. "So do I, buddy. Just trust me on this."

Alone, Guy counted to ten. Again. And again, and so many times he had to have made a hundred. Then he stood and slowly walked down the hall, where he could hear them whispering in the kitchen.

Oh, he didn't want to hear what she was saying. He could just imagine her words: *I hate him. I have to leave. I can't stay with him.*

Where had he heard that before? He squeezed his temples, hard enough to make his head ache.

But when he walked into the kitchen William was standing next to her, his hand on her shoulder, and she held a phone to her ear.

"Is she calling someone from her show?" Guy asked.

William held up one finger, signaling for him to be quiet and wait.

"Zoe?" she said. "I need you to do me a huge favor, hon. I mean, major *huge*. Can you come over to my father's house and, um, hang out with him for a while?" Babysit, was what she meant, but Guy knew better than to argue.

After a pause, she nodded. "I knew I could count on you."

William breathed a sigh of relief and, back in the recesses of Guy's brain, the blue light faded, replaced by a familiar fog.

Chapter Eleven

Déjà vu teased Jocelyn as Will's truck rumbled up to the causeway. She closed her eyes, giving in to the peculiar sensation of knowing this wasn't the first time all these same internal chemicals and external forces synergized into this distinct moment.

"You okay?" Will asked, reaching over the console to put his hand over hers, his fingertips brushing her thigh.

She didn't yank her hand out from under his, but she didn't turn her palm to hold his hand, either. Even though she wanted to, just for the sheer pleasure and comfort of holding Will's hand, his blunt, clean fingertips still one of her favorite things to grasp.

That was part of her déjà vu, too. A big part. After the fear and anger, there was always Will. She looked down at his fingers, the massive width and length of them, the dusting of dark hair, the power of his wrist. Will had gorgeous, masculine hands. And huge. He used to say he didn't need a catcher's mitt.

"Joss?"

"I was just thinking I've done this before."

"Ridden over the causeway?"

Yes, with a desperate determination to escape the thunderous voice and threat of violence ringing in her ears. "Run away from him, wishing I could do something to change... him."

"Nature did that for you."

She shot him a look. "The old Guy is there, Will, right under the surface. You saw how he yelled at me."

"For one little second, Joss."

She snapped her hand away. "Don't defend him. I can take anything but that."

He left his hand on her leg. "This really could have waited a day or two," he said. "I feel like we should have stayed with him instead of calling Zoe."

"You could have."

"As if I'd let you come over here alone. I just don't know why we couldn't wait a few days."

"First of all, procrastination is for losers." She could have sworn she saw him cringe ever so slightly, but she was too focused on making her many points. "Second, the media is going to find me. It's only a matter of time un—"

"No, no. That's not true. We'll talk to Slade Garrison— he's got a good crew of deputies—and set him straight. He needs to know you're in town so he can divert any reporters that try to find you. And he can put an unmarked car or two at Guy's house and you'll be completely safe at Casa Blanca."

She didn't say anything, turning to look out at the

water instead. Sun danced off the waves and a giant cabin cruiser cut under the bridge, leaving a bright-white wake. Bet it was nice on that boat, lost in the air and salt water. Away from it all. Alone.

Or maybe with Will.

"Can I ask you a question, Joss?"

"Mmmm." The answer was noncommittal, but she knew him well enough to know he'd ask anyway.

"You didn't have an affair with that guy, did you?"

Oh. She hadn't been expecting that question— although it was natural and normal and should had been expected. Deep inside, she wanted Will to know she hadn't. She didn't answer.

"I wish you'd say no," he said softly. "Real fast and vehement, too."

"I did not have any kind of relationship with Miles Thayer. But any aspect of my client relationship with Coco is confidential, and I won't talk about it."

He choked softly. "She doesn't give a shit about protecting your reputation. Why should you care about hers?"

She turned to him, a question of her own burning. "Did you think it was true?"

He hesitated long enough for her to know the answer. Damn it. Maybe she hadn't thought this through enough. She'd sacrificed so much for Coco.

"I hadn't seen you for more than fifteen seconds in fifteen years," he finally said. "I didn't know what to believe."

That was fair, she guessed. "Do you believe it now?"

"Not if you tell me it's a lie. I believe you. And honestly . . ." He captured her hand again, this time holding so tight she couldn't let go. "You don't like overrated skinny blond guys who can't act their way out of a paper bag."

She laughed softly. "True."

"And nobody can change that much. You wouldn't sleep with a married guy."

"No, I would not, so thanks for that vote of confidence. I wish my clients felt the same way." Since she'd lost two more that morning.

"They probably do, but Coco is the one they have to side with because she's more powerful in the industry."

She sighed. Of course Will got it; he always *got* it. "Yep."

He turned his hand and threaded their fingers. "I still don't see what it would hurt to at least make a statement."

"It would hurt her," she said simply.

"That's what's stopping you? Did you sign some kind of confidentiality agreement?" He turned as he reached a light on the mainland, his eyes flashing blue. "Because a good lawyer could—"

"No, Will, stop. Respect and professional ethics are stopping me. You need to go right at the next light, I think."

"I know how to get there."

"You've been to Autumn House?"

"I looked into a couple of places when I first got here."

For some reason, that shocked her. Why hadn't he told her that? "And?"

"Besides being crazy-ass expensive, they didn't seem that great to me."

"You've visited this place already?"

He shook his head. "Not this one, but others. I did call here, but reconsidered."

"I can afford it," she said quietly.

"Even if your business is in trouble?"

There was that. "I've saved a lot of money."

"What about new business?"

She shrugged. "I'll get it."

"Could be challenging in L.A. after all this."

"I've faced bigger challenges."

He smiled, shaking his head a little.

"What? I have."

"I know you have. But do you have to be so damn tough about everything? It's like you have a hard shell around you."

She did. "I've had that for so long I can't imagine what it's like not to have that kind of protection. I've had it for…since…a long time."

He closed his eyes as if she'd punched him. She leaned forward to grab her bag so she didn't have to look at him or feel his referred pain. Pulling out the address, she tried to read, but the words danced in front of her eyes.

"It's not too far," she said, forcing herself to read and think about where they were and where they were going. Literally, on this street—not emotionally, in her head.

"Jocelyn."

She ignored the tenderness in his voice, the warmth of that big hand, the comfort it always gave her. "Two more lights," she said, her voice tight.

"I know."

She cleared her throat as if that could just wipe clean the conversation about protection and hurt and shells she stayed inside of. "So why didn't you look at this place again?" she asked, grasping at small-talk straws.

"I decided he needed to be home."

The words jolted her. The caring. The concern for a person who had threatened to ruin his life or end it.

"I can see you don't like that."

"Am I supposed to, Will?"

He blew out a breath, letting go of her hand to turn the wheel. "I know he's your dad, not mine, and you resent that I take care of him."

Was that what he thought bothered her? That *he* took care of *her* father? He didn't even remember what took them apart. What had left *a hard shell around her*?

She had to remember that he didn't know everything.

"I just couldn't sit at my house and ignore the fact that he needed help," he said.

Well, they had that in common. Wasn't that the reason she was in this situation in the first place, with Coco? "You should have just picked up the phone and called me. I'd have taken care of the situation."

"Well, I didn't."

"Why not?"

He threw her a look. "Maybe because I felt like I owed you something."

Her? What could he owe her? "Me? Why?"

"Because if it weren't for me, that...night would have never happened. You wouldn't have left or you would have come home." He swallowed, his voice thick with regret and remorse. "I blame myself for what happened that night."

"You shouldn't," she said simply. "You should put the blame where it belongs."

"On you?" He sounded incredulous.

"No, Will. On Guy Bloom." She pointed to a large white stucco building set back on a lawn, a simple sign at the parking lot's edge. "We're here."

When he pulled into the lot and parked, she started to open the door, but he took her hand and pulled her closer.

"What's it going to take?" he asked.

The question and the intense look in his eyes stunned her. "To decide he shouldn't go into a home?"

"No." He reached over and grazed her jaw with his knuckles, his touch fiery and unexpected and chill inducing. "To break that shell?"

"I'm sorry, Will. It's unbreakable."

But he just leaned in and breathed his last few words, the closest thing to a kiss without actually touching. "There's no such thing."

"Doesn't your husband want to come in, too?"

Outside the director's office door, Will turned to catch Jocelyn's slightly surprised look and the color that rose to her cheeks. It was a natural assumption on the woman's part. They'd never said they weren't married during the tour, just that they were there for Jocelyn's father.

"I'll wait out here while you talk," he said, gesturing toward the lobby.

Jocelyn's dark eyes searched his, but then she nodded and stepped into the office of the admissions director. Admissions. Like it was a freaking college instead of an old folks' home with the patently ridiculous name of Autumn House.

Should be *Dead of Winter End of Days House*.

Will had seen enough of their rainbows and happy-face bullshit in the past twenty minutes of walking through the special areas where visitors could go. Nothing he wanted to know would be visible during that surface skim. And the truth wasn't going to come out behind that director's door when Jocelyn asked more hollow questions like "How often are they fed?"

For Christ's sake. This wasn't a kennel.

Or was it?

But he had swallowed all those comments while Bernadette Bowers, director of admissions and patient relations, spewed the party line.

A year ago he'd visited two similar facilities. Neither one had been as upscale as this place, he had to admit as he cruised through the softly lit lobby of the main house and nodded to the receptionist hidden behind a plastic palm tree. But they were the same beasts: God's waiting room. With fake plants.

Maybe this wasn't the kind of place where they let someone hang in a wheelchair for eight hours, forgotten. Maybe this wasn't where an old man could rot in bed, forgotten. Maybe this wasn't a place where someone with virtually no training but a good heart forgot some meds and the results were dire. He got the feeling that Autumn House was better than most of these homes.

But it wasn't Guy's *home*.

He pushed open the front door and stepped out to the patio, scanning the manicured grounds, the perfectly placed hibiscus trees, the carefully situated tables and chairs.

All empty.

Okay, maybe it was too hot for old folks to come outside. Or maybe no one took them. Or maybe they were short-staffed.

The door opened behind him, and he turned, expecting Jocelyn, but another woman came out, fifty-ish, mouth drawn in sadness, eyes damp.

" 'Scuse me," she mumbled, passing him.

"Can I ask you a question?" The request was out before he gave himself time to think about it and change his mind. But wasn't part of the "tour" talking to the customers?

The woman hesitated, inching back a bit. "Yes?"

"Do you have a…" He almost said "loved one," but corrected himself. "A relative living here?"

She nodded, absently dabbing an eye and biting her lip.

"How is it?" he asked. "We're considering this for my… we're looking at the facility."

She didn't answer right away, clearly choosing her words and wrestling with her emotions. "It's expensive, but one of the better facilities."

"How's the care?"

She shrugged. "You know."

No, he didn't. "Doctors?"

After a second, she let out a breath. "Some are better than others."

"Staff?"

"Good, but no place is perfect." She tried to sound upbeat, but he could read between the lines, especially the two drawn deep in her forehead.

"Would you make the same decision again?" he asked her, knowing he'd way overstepped the boundaries of two strangers sharing a casual conversation.

"I really had no choice," she said. "My mother's not able to be at home."

He nodded, understanding.

"If she was or if I could be with her twenty-four-seven, of course that's what I'd do. But you have to be realistic. You have to compromise." She tilted her head and gave a smile. "Your parent?"

"No, my friend." He wasn't exactly sure when Guy Bloom had become his friend, but he had. And the word felt right on his lips.

Just then, the door opened and Jocelyn stepped into the

sunshine, looking cool and crisp and not nearly as defeated as the sallow-skinned woman he'd been talking to.

"We're all set," she said quietly.

"You *enrolled* him?" He couldn't think of a better word, not when a flash of white hot anger burst behind his eyes.

"Not yet. Of course I have to see another place or two, but, overall, I'm quite satisfied."

With what? The chilly cafeteria? The dreary halls? The single room for a man who was used to living in an entire house?

Jocelyn glanced at the other woman and gave her a quick smile, not warm enough to invite conversation.

"Listen," the lady said, turning to Will, keeping that tenuous connection they'd somehow found in a moment's time. "I don't know your situation, but if you have any option at all for home care, any possible way to keep from taking this step, do it."

Jocelyn stepped forward, her back ramrod straight. "You're right."

Hope danced in him.

"You *don't* know our situation," Jocelyn said. "But thank you for the advice. Let's go, Will."

He stood stone still as she walked by and headed toward the parking lot.

"Thank you," he said softly to the woman. "Good luck."

Jocelyn was almost to his truck by the time he caught up with her.

"Don't reprimand me for being a bitch to her," she said as he reached for her door. "This isn't your decision to make."

"You weren't a bitch," he replied. "It's a tense situation." And, damn it, she was right, it wasn't his decision. But that didn't stop him from caring about the outcome.

She climbed into the truck and yanked her seat belt. "Yes, it is tense. Were you talking to her?"

"Briefly." He closed the door and started around the back of the truck.

"Wait, sir. Wait!" The woman from the porch was jogging toward him, a hand outstretched. "I just want to tell you one thing."

Jocelyn stayed in the car, but he knew she was watching in her side-view mirror, possibly hearing the conversation even though her door was closed.

"What's that?"

The woman put a hand on his arm, her fingers covered with veins and age spots, making him revise his age estimate. "They're fine with the new ones. The ones that haven't gone too far...away. But the really bad ones?" She shook her head, eyes welling. "They are lost and forgotten."

Forgotten. Exactly as he suspected. He patted her hand. "Your mother's not forgotten. She has you."

She smiled and stepped away.

He waited for a minute, then climbed behind the wheel of the truck. He shot Jocelyn a glance, his mind whirring through his options. Her father was her responsibility, that was true. He couldn't demand that she change her mind about this, but maybe he could get her to think a little more about it.

"Hungry?" he asked.

"Not in the least."

Damn. " 'Cause we're not that far from Kaplan's."

Her eyes widened and she smiled. "Oh my God, those Reubens."

It wouldn't be their first trip down to Marco Island; they'd gone often after baseball games when he'd be plagued with late-night teenage boy starvation and she just wanted to get out. Especially that last summer, they'd probably driven down to the deli near the marina a dozen times.

"With extra Thousand Island and no ketchup on the fries," he said, smiling. "The lady does not like wet fries."

"Aww, you remember that."

He remembered so much more than that it wasn't funny. "So, yes?"

She considered it for a minute, then nodded. "But I have to wear this hat." She reached into her bag for the baseball cap she'd brought. "I don't want anyone to recognize me."

"They won't recognize you."

"Don't be so sure," she said, tugging the cap on.

He pulled the brim a little. "I hardly recognize you, Joss."

She paused, looking up at him, her eyes so brown and soulful it damn near cut him in half. "What's that supposed to mean?"

"You've changed, is all."

"So have you," she shot back.

"True." He shrugged. "I've been through a lot."

"Why don't you tell me everything over Reubens?"

"Everything?"

"Everything."

That wasn't why he wanted to go to Kaplan's. He wanted to talk her out of rash decisions, but instead he made one himself. " 'Kay."

Chapter Twelve

The closer they got to Kaplan's, the more Jocelyn felt her mood improve. Maybe she was hungry, after all. Or maybe she felt relaxed for the first time since they'd left Mimosa Key, on a familiar road that reminded her of late nights and long talks and a wonderful boy she once loved.

She slid a sideways glance at him, her gaze lingering on his shoulders, which were even broader than they'd been back then. In fact, everything about Will was stronger now. His profile, his muscles, his personality. He still had a heart as big as his hands, but he moved like a man in complete control.

And, damn, she liked watching him. He took her breath away when he smiled, something he'd done more and more on the short ride to Kaplan's down the beach road.

"Place has changed a lot, don't you think?" he asked,

indicating the behemoth skyscraper condos that now entirely blocked the view of the water.

"Exactly what they're trying to avoid on Mimosa Key."

"We *are* avoiding it," he said. "Clay's architecture is the polar opposite of this heinous-looking stuff. Casa Blanca is going to be one in a million."

She heard the pride in his voice. "You love working there." It was a statement, not a question, and filled with a little wonder when she realized how true it was.

"I like it," he admitted. "Way more than I thought I would. It's amazing to be part of something like that from the ground up." He angled his head toward her. "You know, you're an investor."

"I am, which is why I'm surprised Lacey never mentioned you were working there."

"Did you ask?"

Honestly, no. "I had no idea you were a permanent resident of Mimosa Key. When I saw you last year at that town meeting, I figured you were there on behalf of your parents or something."

He sighed. "Or something."

"What does that mean?"

"I never planned to stay this long," he admitted, pulling into the strip center. They were long enough past the lunch crowd to get a space close to the deli. "Let's go in. I'll tell you about it inside."

She kept her hat pulled low and sunglasses on, but she shouldn't have worried. The waitress who greeted them and walked them to a booth by the front window never even noticed her. She only had eyes for Will.

He put a hand on Jocelyn's back to guide her, staying close until she slid into the booth, and then he sat across from her, taking the menus and ordering iced tea for both of them.

After a minute, feeling more ridiculous than disguised, she took off the sunglasses and glanced around to see what had changed in fifteen years. Not much, but Will leveled his eyes directly at her. The power of his stare warmed every corner of her body.

"Does it look different?" he asked.

She met his gaze, grabbed for a moment by the deep blue of his eyes. She'd never gotten used to how unexpectedly blue they were against his sun-burnished skin. "The kid across from me does."

His lips curved in that slow, sweet, soul-melting smile that used to take her from heartache to happy in ten seconds. "He's not a kid anymore."

"I noticed."

He lifted a brow, silently asking for more.

"You have a couple of crow's-feet."

He squinted, exaggerating the crinkles at the sides of his eyes. "What else?"

She didn't answer right away, loving the excuse to examine every inch of his face, and the little roller-coaster ride her insides took as she and Will focused on nothing but each other.

"You let your hair grow out longer."

"No annoying coach insisting on a trim."

"And that's what's most different of all," she said, leaning back as the waitress delivered two iced teas. When she left, Jocelyn finished the thought. "You don't play baseball."

He touched his stomach and feigned hurt. "You think I'm getting soft?"

Hardly. "I've never known you not to be on your way to a game, coming from a game, talking about the game, pissed off 'cause you lost a game, or whistling 'We Are the Champions' because you kicked the holy hell out of the Collier High Blue Devils."

She thought he'd grin because she'd remembered the rival high mascot, but he just looked down at the tea, turning the glass and revolving the paper napkin with it.

"My career is . . . on hold." He snorted softly and added, "He said optimistically."

She just waited, knowing Will well enough to expect more. But he picked up his tea and took a long drink. She watched his eyes shutter closed and his throat rise and fall with each gulp.

Then he thunked the glass on the table and exhaled softly. "Speaking of baseball, we should get you a Marlins hat instead of that designer thing."

"Speaking of putting walls and shells around yourself, you should tell me what the heck is going on with your career."

A smile teased. "Good comeback, Jossie. Lose the hat and I will."

"Why?"

He reached over and tapped at the brim, pulling it off and making her hair fall around her shoulders when the strands slipped through the hole in the back. "Because I like your hair and I can't see your pretty face when you have that thing on."

"That's the idea," she said, cutting a glance toward the empty booth across from them.

He lifted the hat and looked inside at the stitching. "Dolce and Gabbana? What the hell is that?"

"Expensive. Why are you being optimistic when you say your career is on hold?"

"Because, my friend who buys expensive hats..." He twirled the red-and-blue cap on his finger, a cocky move that belied the thick emotion in his voice. "Will Palmer, number thirty-one, holder of a few obscure and meaningless winning stats in the annals of minor league baseball, is finished playing."

He tried the hat on and, of course, it barely covered the top of his head.

"Finished forever?" she asked.

Setting the cap on the table, he avoided her eyes. "Unless I can score a coaching job and, man, they are hard to come by in the majors or minors. My agent's looking, and I'm trying to remain hopeful."

"You don't think you'll get a coaching job?"

"I don't know," he said honestly. "Every day the hope thread gets a little more frayed."

"What about carpentry? Do you like what you're doing? I mean you're so good at it."

"You know, I do like it, but it's so..." He shook his head as if what he was about to say amazed him. "Meaningless?"

The use of a question surprised her. "Building resorts and jaw-droppingly beautiful villas that will bring hours of pleasure to the guests and mountains of money to the owners? What's meaningless about that?"

He laughed softly. "Touché, life coach."

"You always loved to work with your dad. I remember when he built the shrine—er, the addition."

He grinned. "It remains a shrine since I've moved into the master."

She tried not to think about the room and all the memories wrapped up in that loft. "So you don't... use it?"

"Just to work out."

"Is it weird, sleeping in your parents' old room?"

"I redid the whole thing, knocked down a wall, built out the closet, remodeled the bath. The whole house is practically new. The place is way more ready to sell this way."

"But you haven't put it on the market yet."

He shrugged. "I'm... waiting."

"For what?"

Before he answered, the waitress stepped up to the booth, blinded him with a smile, and asked for their order.

"Two Reubens with fries." He closed his menu and handed them both to her but winked at Jocelyn. "Hold the ketchup on the the lady's order."

She smiled, the memory of the time he'd accidentally put ketchup on her fries during the midnight meal they'd shared still vividly clear. They'd fought and laughed and felt so damn comfortable.

That was just a month or so before—

She snapped her napkin on her lap and straightened the silverware until they were alone again.

"So why haven't you sold their house? What are you waiting for?" she asked, grabbing at the conversation before he could read her expression. He'd been so good at that.

"Well, a coaching job, obviously. That's the next natural step in my career."

"And if that doesn't materialize?"

He leaned all the way back, hooking his arms behind his head, a move that emphasized the biceps she was trying so hard not to stare at. "Guess I'll have to figure out what I want to do with my life."

"Better get on that, Will. You're thirty-four."

"Yep. Know any good life coaches who can help me?"

She grinned. "I sure do, but she's expensive."

"Of course she is." Relaxing, he picked up the hat and popped it up, landing it perfectly on the sugar carousel. "Not cheap to buy Something-and-Cabana hats."

She automatically righted the hat and neatly piled the Splenda packets back in order. "She has been known to work for a discount if she really likes you."

"Do you really like me, Joss?"

She tapped the sugar into place, then restraightened the whole pile. Her heart slipped around in her chest a little, the feeling so intense and sweet it almost took her breath away.

"I've always liked you, Will," she said carefully, searching for a way to keep this light. "And that means you may have the special-friend discount."

"Which is?"

"My services for only a Reuben and fries. Buy lunch and we'll fix up your life."

"If only it were that easy." His voice had a surprising sadness to it that pulled at her.

"Is it that bad?"

"Let's see, I'm not on the run from the *National Enquirer*, wrongly accused of adultery, and being forced to play *Clean House*, so I guess it could be worse."

She had to laugh. "All right, let's start coaching."

"Right now?"

"I loathe procrastination. You want life coaching, let's go. What are you prepared to die for?"

He just stared at her. Blinked, then frowned. "What did you say?"

"What are you prepared to die for? That's the first question I ask in the initial interview," she explained. "I have to know what's the most important thing to a client, and then we take it from there in bite-size pieces."

"Do you know what *you're* prepared to die for?" he asked.

"This is not my interview."

He took another sip of tea, definitely a delay tactic. "It's a stupid trick question," he finally said after he swallowed. "The answer's the same for everyone. Love, family, friendship, truth, honor, justice, and a grand slam in the World Series." He paused, then grinned. "Okay, that might not be on your list."

"None of those things are on my list, Will." Not a single one.

He looked stunned, enough that she was a little embarrassed.

"Well, I might die for one of my friends, if I had to, but I don't really have a family, and I can't honestly say I'd die for honor or justice, though I value it, and I doubt I'll ever go to a World Series."

"You skipped the first one."

Love. She'd skipped it on purpose. Still she frowned, as if she couldn't remember the first thing on his list of things to die for.

"Love," he reminded her.

"Oh, so I did," she said. "Well, I've never..." Oh, yes she had. "I haven't been married, but you have." Thank God for that question-flip technique she'd learned in training. "Why don't you tell me about her?"

"Does my marriage and divorce have to be part of the life-coaching interview?"

"Understanding your marriage might help us get a better picture of your..." *Heart.* "Problems."

"Then my problems would be blonde, crazy, insecure, and camera-happy." He angled his head and looked a little puzzled. "And that's kind of interesting, isn't it?"

That his wife was blonde, crazy, insecure, and camera-happy? Zoe would eat that gossip with a spoon. "How so?"

"That my ex was everything you're not."

His ex had a name. Nina Martinez. And she might have been blonde and crazy, but she was also drop-dead gorgeous. "See?" she said with false brightness. "A breakthrough already. Life coaching works."

The waitress sidled up to the table with steaming platters, the delectable smoky tang of corned beef wafting along with her. As the woman set Jocelyn's plate down, she glanced at her. And then did a double take.

Instantly, Jocelyn cast down her eyes, staring at the plate, but the grill marks on the sandwich swam in front of her eyes. Shit. *Shit.*

"Do I know you?" the waitress asked, forcing Jocelyn to look up and meet an unrelenting frown, the face of a woman digging through recent memory and about to come up with celebrity gossip.

"We used to be regulars here," Will said quickly. "And that's all we need, thanks."

"Ohhh." She drew out the word and looked from one to the other, but settled her attention on Jocelyn. "Well, I just started here, so, that's not it."

"Thank you." Jocelyn said sharply, picking up her fork

and knife despite the fact that she wouldn't use either one on this meal.

The waitress got the message and left.

"Eesh," Jocelyn said on a sigh. "How long will I have to hide like this?"

"Until you tell the truth."

Which would be never. "You don't understand."

"I understand you're protecting a person who has no compunction about throwing you under a bus."

She set the silverware back down, lining it up perfectly, gathering a lot of possible responses and discarding most. "We all do what we feel is right regardless of what other people think."

"More life-coach bullshit," he said, picking up his sandwich and making it look petite in his giant hands.

"Is it?" she fired back. "I'm doing what I feel is right even though you don't agree with it just like you're doing what you think is right with my father even though I don't agree with it. How are the two things so different?"

He just shook his head and took a bite. After he swallowed, he said, "There was one other thing about my ex-wife that's different from you."

Jealousy made a quick sting at her heart. "What's that?"

"She'd have never let the issue of another woman drop. Don't you want to know more about my marriage?"

She knew enough, actually. "Of course. How did you meet? How long were you married? Why did it end?"

He looked up just before taking his next bite. "Not 'Was she pretty'? That's what most girls want to know."

Except this girl already knew his wife was on the

cover of *Fitness* magazine once. "Last I looked, I was a woman, not a girl."

"Sorry." He looked at her and smiled, slow and bad and good all at the same time. The kind of smile that made Jocelyn's whole insides rise and flutter and sigh. "You are a woman. A beautiful one."

And flutter again.

She picked up a fry and nibbled the end. "We were talking about your wife."

"Ex."

"Semantics."

"Incredibly important semantics." He took a slow, careful bite, wiping his mouth with a napkin, drawing out the silence for a few seconds. "Well, let's see. We met at the baseball field, we were married for three seasons, and it ended when it became painfully clear I wasn't headed to the majors or a career in any kind of limelight, which was all that mattered to her."

She smiled. "Most people count their anniversaries in years, not seasons."

"She was my manager's niece," he said with a shrug, searching out his own fry. "It was definitely a baseball-centric marriage."

"She was Latina, right?"

He whipped his head up at the question. "How do you know that?"

Damn it *all*. Why had she revealed that? "I saw something in the paper."

"In Los Angeles?" Obviously, he didn't believe her. "Sorry, but I didn't make any papers outside of Florida." He pointed a ketchupy fry at her, unable to hid the happiness that had just hit him. "You Googled me."

She felt her cheeks warm, ate instead of answering.

But he laughed, a satisfied, bone-deep laugh. "You did. When? Recently? Yesterday? After you saw me last year?"

"A couple of years ago. And, really, this is supposed to be *your* life-coaching session, not mine."

"Why?"

"Because you don't know what you want to be when you grow up and I do."

"I meant why did you Google me?"

She blinked, hovering between the truth and a lie. She slid in between. "I was curious how you'd been."

He nodded slowly, searching her face. "Never thought about calling, though, did you? Or an e-mail?"

She shook her head just as the waitress walked by again, slowly, looking at Jocelyn, who lowered her head and let her hair cover her cheek. "I think I've been busted."

"I'll say. Who knew you'd Google me?"

"I meant by the waitress, Will."

He nodded. "I know." She turned toward the wall as Will gave the woman a sharp look and she scooted away. He reached over the table and put his hand over Jocelyn's.

"It's okay, Jossie."

Déjà vu rolled over her again, much stronger this time, a whole-body memory that didn't just hint of the past but lifted her from today and dropped her right back into every feeling she ever had for Will.

Respect. Appreciation. Admiration. And something so much more, so much deeper. "But if you want to leave, we can," he said.

"No, let's work on your career. What exactly are you doing in order to get that coaching job?"

"Waiting to hear from my agent."

"Then you mustn't want it very much."

He shook his head vehemently. "That's where you're wrong. I want it very much."

"Then the first word you use for your 'action' wouldn't be 'waiting,'" she shot back. "You'd be calling, meeting, searching, networking, applying, fighting, clawing, interview—"

He held up his hand. "I get the picture."

"Do you?" She propped her elbows on the table and rested her chin on her knuckles. "Prove it."

"What's to prove? When you finish in the minors, you get a coaching job in the minors."

"Are you passionate about coaching?"

"I'm passionate about..." When he hesitated, her whole body tightened in anticipation. What was Will passionate about? She wanted it to be—

"Baseball."

"Of course."

"Surely you didn't forget that about me."

"I didn't forget anything about you." Lord, why had she told him that? Because he had that gift: He made her so comfortable she forgot to maintain control.

The admission made him smile, not cockily like when he found out she'd Googled him, just—well, she couldn't quite read those dozen different emotions flickering in his dark blue eyes. "Then we're even. And you know that from the time I was five, I've lived, breathed, and slept the game. You know I love baseball. It's all I know, all I've ever known."

"You know," she said, "I have a choice right now."

Lifting his eyebrows in question, he waited for more

explanation. "You do? I thought this was about my choices."

"It is. But I have to make a choice." She sipped her drink and chose her words carefully. "When I am coaching a client and I believe they are self-delusional, I have two choices. I can either let them off easy because they don't really want to face the truth and they'd rather write a check and believe they found their answers, or..."

He didn't respond, scratching his neck a little, as if he wasn't quite sure where she was going with this. And might not like it when he was.

"I can challenge them to face the truth head-on and deal with what that means."

"You think I'm self-delusional?"

"I think you're not that passionate about baseball."

"Are you nuts? If I'm not, what the hell have I been doing for the last, Jesus, thirty years since my dad bought the first tee and put a bat in my hand?"

She just stared at him. "Precisely."

"Precisely *what*?"

"Will, baseball has always been your father's passion. Good God, I can remember him talking about you playing for his beloved L.A. Dodgers since the day you guys moved in."

"He always hated that I couldn't get into that franchise," Will admitted. "But we shared the passion, Joss. You can't get as far as I did without it."

She wasn't sure about that. "With your natural talent, you could get very, very far. And you did. But—"

"But what?" He damn near growled the demand. "But if I had been more devoted, I *could* have gotten into the majors? I *could* have played for the fucking Dodgers?"

She flinched and his hand shot across the table to take hers. "Sorry, I didn't mean to get mad like that."

"No problem," she lied. "That's exactly why I let some clients take easy street. It's easier for me, too." She slipped her hand out from under his. "And I'm not saying if you were more devoted your career would have gone differently because, frankly, the past doesn't matter anymore, unless it helps you see your own patterns."

He nodded, but she could tell agreeing with anything she was saying wasn't easy.

"I'm suggesting," she said, "and quite seriously, that if you were truly, madly, and deeply passionate and in love with the idea of doing something with your baseball career, you would be doing it and not 'waiting for someone to call.'" She air-quoted the phrase.

Picking up a fry, he swiped it through his ketchup and shook off the extra. "My name's out there," he said, working to keep the defensiveness out of his tone, and failing. "My agent has me in with every minor league team in the sport, and the first bullpen or base-coaching job available, I'll be considered."

"Is that the kind of coaching job you want?"

"That's where you start."

She pushed a little harder. "I don't know, it seems to me that you could manage a whole team if you wanted to. You've always been the captain, always the leader."

He took in a slow breath, obviously uncomfortable with the subject.

"Hey, you volunteered to be my client," she said. "It's not always easy. But when you dig deep and force yourself to think about what puts a bounce in your step and joy in your soul, then you might adjust your career goals."

He didn't answer right away, then said, "I know this is going to sound crazy, but my parents lived their entire lives and gave everything they have for my success. I still feel like I can't let them down, you know?" He hesitated a minute, the wheels turning as he worked it out. "Maybe I don't want to be a minor league coach, but that would somehow be a slap in the face to my dad, who did everything so that my career—my *whole* career—would go the right way. And, shit, my *liking* to be a carpenter? That's like my ignoring everything he ever told me. A carpenter was a failure to him, somehow. Blue-collar and...*ordinary*."

She nodded, truly understanding and recognizing his predicament. "But you can't make lifelong decisions because of sacrifices your parents made when you were a kid, Will."

"I know that." He smiled. "That's why I'm waiting. And you want to know something else? I think your standard life-coach question is meaningless, completely rhetorical, and tells you nothing about the person."

"About what you're prepared to die for?"

"A stupid question, if you ask me."

She leaned forward, more interested than insulted. "But the answer tells me everything about a person. It tells me what matters to them."

"Nope, it tells you what they think should matter to them, not what really does. I'm more interested in what someone has sacrificed for in the past."

"What do you mean?"

"Like for me, I sacrificed my life for baseball. College was a joke. I never went to a party, didn't join a fraternity or a club or anything. I just practiced, played, traveled, and studied. I sacrificed everything for baseball, so I think you're whole theory is bogus."

She shrugged but couldn't help smiling. "I still think you had a breakthrough."

"You just want me to pay for lunch." He grinned and put a hand on the check the waitress had left on her last trip by, one of at least five in the last ten minutes. "So what about you, Joss? What have you sacrificed?"

She looked him right in the eye, so drawn to him, so certain of him, it slammed her right back into the past.

"Ah, speaking of a breakthrough," he said. "I can see it on your face." He leaned so close she could see every lash now, every fleck of navy in his eyes, every hint of whisker stubble, even the tiniest bit of ketchup in the corner of his mouth.

Her whole being ached to kiss it off. And she hated ketchup.

"No breakthrough," she said. "This was your life-coaching session."

"Answer my question. What have you sacrificed to achieve your passion?"

She swallowed, but even that couldn't keep down the truth. "I sacrificed everything for love."

His jaw loosened as the waitress zoomed over and scooped up the check and money. "Keep the change," he said without taking his eyes from Jocelyn. "You did?"

"Everything," she assured him. Everything that mattered, given up one summer evening in a stairwell outside his bedroom.

"I gotta tell you, Joss, whoever he is—or was—I hate his fucking guts."

He wouldn't if he knew the truth. "Why?"

"Because I'm jealous of someone you loved," he said simply. "It should have been me."

The food thunked to the bottom of her stomach and she actually felt a little sick.

It was you.

"If you felt that way, why didn't you call me when we went to college?" she asked.

He closed his eyes. "I was waiting for you."

She tried to smile, but her mouth trembled a little. "I think I see a pattern here, Will Palmer."

He laughed, tipping her chin with his knuckle. "Damn, life coach, you're good."

"Only if you break your pattern, Will."

"Yeah. Well, I intend to." The low, sweet promise in his voice reached right into her chest and squeezed her heart.

Chapter Thirteen

Guy slapped the jack of spades on the table and gave Zoe the dearest look she'd seen in—well, since she'd left her great-aunt in Flagstaff, Arizona.

"You old coot," she said, dropping her remaining card on the pile and shaking her head. "You beat the pants off me in Egyptian Rat Screws. That is not easy to do."

"I'm really good at cards," he said, fighting a smug smile.

She leaned on one elbow and pointed at him. "You like older women?"

"I might be dumb but I'm not blind, Blondie. You're not older than me."

"Not me." She laughed, waving her hand. "My great-aunt. She's pretty hot for eighty...ish. How old are you?"

He angled his head, thinking. "I don't have a clue."

She didn't know whether to laugh or cry, he was so

damn sweet. "Well, you're not her age, I can assure you of that. I'll go with sixty-five. Still, you'd like Pasha."

"Who's Pasha?"

"My hot great aunt who is, I might add, almost as good as you at the game I just taught you an hour ago." She marveled at that; for a man suffering from Alzheimer's, there were still a few sharp cells at work up there.

The doorbell rang and his eyes widened. "Who's that?"

She pushed up. "No way to know until I answer it. But I hope to hell it's a reporter."

"Why?"

She grinned. "So I can channel my inner Meryl Streep." She peeked through the window in the door and smiled. "They're back," she called out. "Stay in the kitchen, Pops. I'll handle this. Oh!" She turned to him. "What's your real name? Is Guy short for something?"

"Alexander." Then he gasped. "Where the heck did that come from?"

She laughed. "Your memory, smarty-pants. Now stay there." She shook her hair and arms, took a deep breath, and opened the door. "Yes?"

The little bald eagle stepped forward. "We're looking for Mr. Bloom. For his daughter, actually."

"Daughter-in-law," she said. "You found her."

He frowned. "His daughter, Jocelyn Bloom."

She let out a full-body put-upon sigh, leaning on the doorjamb and shaking her head. "When are you nitwits going to get it through your head? This is not the man you want, no Jocelyn Bloom lives here, and anything you're reading in the paper is not true."

None of that was, technically, a lie.

Baldie wasn't buying. "We have proof that this is the childhood home of Jocelyn Bloom who lived here with her parents, Guy and Mary Jo." He lifted up an official-looking paper, and Zoe curled her lip.

"They did live here, like, eons ago. This is the home of Mr. Alexander."

Again, not a lie. But distrusting eyes narrowed at her; he was no doubt familiar with the runaround. "Where's Jocelyn?"

"Beats me, but you guys are barking up the wrong address."

"She used to live here."

Zoe leaned forward and flicked a finger at the paper he held. "Your info is wrong. Buzz off and don't come back or you'll be facing the sheriff himself. We're sick of you all."

"There've been other reporters?" A note of worry cracked his voice.

"A few. They're gone, and so are you."

She closed the door and instantly another white card slipped through the mailbox hole. Zoe ripped it into tiny pieces and shoved it right back out.

"That ought to keep the creeps at bay for a while," she said, brushing her hands like she was good and finished and heading back to the living room, where Guy was shuffling the deck for the next game.

"What's she look like?" he asked.

"Oh, it was a he. Bald and ugly."

He grinned. "I meant your aunt."

"Great-aunt. And, trust me, she is—great, I mean." Zoe dropped onto the sofa across from Guy, giving him raised eyebrows. "So you do like older women?"

"I figure if she's anything like you, yeah."

"Aw, you sweet thing." She started collecting her cards as he dealt slowly and with great precision. "She's funkalicious for an octogenarian."

He laughed. "I don't know what that means, but I think I like it."

"It means she spikes her gray hair, has too many earrings, and has a weakness for beer."

"At eighty?"

She shrugged. "Youth is wasted on the young, you know."

"I'd like to meet her." He scooped up his cards and tapped the half-deck carefully. "What happens when you put down an ace, again?"

"The other person has four tries to beat it."

His shoulders sagged a little, a gesture she recognized as one Pasha made when she was just a little overwhelmed at the moment. "Let's take a break," she suggested, setting down her cards. "I think I'd rather just talk for a little while. You want more of that delicious tea?"

"Nope, makes me have to pee."

She laughed again. "I love that you say what you're thinking. It's always been a problem for me."

"It bothers my son."

His son. "Will?"

He nodded.

"Did it always bother him? You know, like when he was little?"

He considered that, chewing on his bottom lip. "I'd like to work on my needlepoint now."

Either he couldn't remember or didn't want to say. Or didn't want to lie. Because a thought kept niggling at her: Was it possible Guy really *did* remember the past?

"Sure," she said, getting up to gather the cross-stitching he'd shown her earlier.

Maybe he did remember who Jocelyn was and maybe he did know Will wasn't his son. Because what better way to wipe your personal slate clean—especially if it was messy—than to conveniently forget everything you ever did? It was that or just run away when people got suspicious; God knows she knew that trick well enough.

He didn't strike her as that cunning, but who knew?

She handed him the frame with the thick "training mesh" that a kid would use to learn needlepoint, along with some pearl cotton thread and a needle. "How'd you learn this?" she asked, wondering just how hard it would be to trap him.

"Will taught me."

"Really? How'd he learn?"

"Computer videos. That tube thing."

"YouTube." She watched his hand shake ever so slightly as he pulled the thread through to execute the most basic half cross-stitch. "Will's good to you," she said, carefully watching his reaction.

He looked up, his gray eyes suddenly clear. "I love that boy more'n life itself."

More than his own daughter? "What was he like as a kid? A baseball player, I understand."

Guy's eyes clouded up again and he cast his gaze downward. "I don't recall."

"You don't recall or you didn't really know him that well?"

He refused to look up. "You know, my mind."

"No, actually, I don't know your mind. Surely you have a picture of him? His trophies? Where are they?"

"In his house, next door." He stabbed the needle. "I don't go over there."

"Why not?"

He shrugged. "I just don't."

"Why not?"

The needle stuck in a hole and he tried to force it, pulling some of the thread and making an unsightly lump. "Let's go back to talking about your beer-drinking old aunt."

She leaned forward. "Why don't you ever go to your son's house?"

He looked up. "I did once."

"And?"

"It made me cry." His voice cracked and his eyes filled and Zoe felt like a heel.

"I'm sorry," she said, taking the frame from his hands so she could try to undo the tangled stitch. "I shouldn't have made you talk about it."

He just shook his head, swallowing hard. "I can't remember," he said, wiping at his eyes under his glasses. "But..."

She got the thread through, saving him from that one little mistake on the needlepoint anyway. "But what?" she prompted, handing it back to him.

"But you wouldn't be the first person to try to prove I'm lying."

"I'm..." Her voice trailed off as he lifted his eyebrow. Then she just started to laugh. "Shit."

He grinned. "Shit what?"

"Shit, you and my aunt would really hit it off."

Smiling, he leaned back and worked on his flowers in silence.

• • •

"There's a marina around the corner, remember?" Will asked as they stepped outside the deli. "Want to go down there? It's too pretty to—" *Go look at more old-age homes.* "Do anything indoors."

"Sure." She slipped the sunglasses on again and tugged at the brim of her red cap. "And we can finish your life-coaching session. You want to?"

"I want…" He reached under the cap and pulled the shades down her nose. "You to take off these stupid things. I can't see your eyes, Jossie."

A smile threatened but she shook it off. "I have to."

"No." He slid the glasses off and slipped them into his pocket, reaching to put his arm over her shoulders. "I'll protect you from the roving paparazzi."

She laughed. "You like playing bodyguard."

"Who's playing?" He squinted into the parking lot, then pressed an imaginary earpiece. "The coast is clear. Let's get Bloomerang to her yacht."

She smiled up at him, the prettiest, widest, sweetest smile he'd seen from her yet. "You used to call me that."

"Because you always came back to me," he reminded her with a squeeze.

She held his gaze for the longest time, the magic that used to connect them so real at that moment he could feel the physical presence of it. "I liked it," she admitted. "I liked being your Bloomerang."

"I liked it, too." His voice was gruff, even to his ears, and he covered the emotion by pulling her into him. She slid her arm around his waist, the most natural, and wonderful, move in the world. She felt small and compact next to him, and he could have sworn she actually relaxed a little.

He led her along the walkway of the strip mall, past a consignment store and a frame shop, his eye on the entrance to the marina at the other end.

"You always were good at protecting me," she said softly.

The words slowed his step—imperceptibly, he hoped. "Not good enough," he murmured.

She looked up at him. "Maybe 'protect' is the wrong word. You always gave me…security. Safety. Sanctuary."

He tucked her tighter against his torso. God, he'd tried.

"Safety and sanctuary," she said, "were what I said I'd be prepared to die for when I was first asked that question in my therapy."

He wanted to respond to that, to mull it over, but another question popped out instead. "You were in therapy?"

"It's part of getting a psych degree. Oh, Will, look." At the marina's grand arched entrance, she stopped. "It's like a different place."

The quaint little neighborhood dock, with its hand-painted sign, weathered bait-and-tackle stand, and rotten boathouse, was completely gone. In its place was an expanse of four individual mooring peninsulas, each chock full of million-dollar yachts, cabin cruisers, and high-tech fishing boats. Along one side, a bustling yacht club blocked the view with giant columns and bright orange Spanish tile. A sleek marble marker announced they'd reached *Marco Harbor.*

"Kind of sad to see the little neighborhood marina turned into this," Jocelyn said as she slipped out of Will's arm and walked along an asphalt drive that led to the boats.

They headed down the first maze of docks between

boats so big they cast a shadow over them. As Will took Jocelyn's hand, the squawk of a heron and the rhythmic splash of water against hulls were the only sounds. Some rigging hit a mast, the clang like a musical bell over the quiet harbor, and, in the distance, the steady thump of—

They both looked at each other as the sound of running feet registered at the same instant.

"There she is! Right there!"

They whipped around at the woman's voice, seeing their waitress jogging toward them holding up a cell phone, a man next to her with a more professional camera.

"That's Miles Thayer's lover!"

Jocelyn froze in shock, but Will instantly nudged her forward. "Run."

They did, taking off down the next hundred-yard mooring, ducking behind a massive trawler, then scooting around a corner to hide.

"Damn it," she whispered, her breath already tight.

"They went this way!" the woman yelled.

Will turned one way, then the other. They could run out into the open toward the storage unit, jump in the water, or climb onto an empty boat.

He nudged her toward the back of the trawler. "Climb up!"

Without arguing, she grabbed the railing and scrambled up to the deck, and he followed, leading her around the cabin to the opposite side, away from the dock.

"Get down." He pushed her to the fiberglass deck, flattening her and covering her so they could both fit in the narrow space of the portside walkway. Under him, she struggled for quiet breaths, every muscle taut.

"Oh, God, this is a nightmare," she whispered.

"Shhh." He kissed her hair and put a finger over her lips. "We're completely out of sight. They'd have to get in every single boat to find us. Just stay still and quiet."

They heard footsteps and voices on the next dock and Jocelyn turned to him, her face inches from his, their eyes locked on each other. They both held their breath, and he clutched her a little tighter, his legs wrapped around her, her backside tucked into his stomach.

The footsteps on their dock were like thunder, loud enough to feel right through the fiberglass.

"They found us," she mouthed, her eyes wide.

He just shook his head a little and put his finger over her lips.

God, she was pretty. Her curves fit right into him, her hair tickling his face, her lips, curving in a secret smile, warm on his fingertip.

He wanted his mouth there, not his fingertip. Wanted their lips to touch so badly it made his mouth ache, and his muscles hurt from fighting the urge to close that one whisper of an inch that separated them from a kiss.

"They must be on one of the boats." The woman's voice carried over the water, as clear as if she were five feet away. They heard a splash as someone climbed onboard a boat nearby.

"Well, find them, damn it," the man said. "Do you have any idea how much a picture of her is worth to the tabloids? Jesus, Helen, we could retire."

"I'll find them," she said, determined. "I'll climb in every boat in this marina and I will find you, you fucking homewrecker!"

Jocelyn cringed at the last three words, hollered into the wind.

"You could tell her," he whispered. "You could tell her the truth."

She shook her head and somehow inched even deeper under him, sparking every powerful, protective need. And, man, he had many needs where Jocelyn was concerned, but protecting her was always at the top of his list.

"Excuse me? Can I help you?" A new voice called out, one of male authority. "That's not your boat, ma'am."

"I'm looking for someone," the woman said. "They're..." Her voice trailed off and the other man spoke to her, too far away for Will to make out the words.

"You cannot get onboard a boat you don't own. Sorry." More footsteps. "You're going to have to leave, ma'am."

Under him, he felt Jocelyn relax ever so slightly.

"But there's a woman hiding on one of these boats! She's wanted by the...people."

"Why don't you two just come with me, please?"

Their footsteps retreated, the voices faded, and after a minute it was silent but for the lapping waves and the soft chime of sail rigging in the breeze.

"Should we try to get out of here?" Jocelyn asked.

He closed his eyes, picturing the layout of the harbor they'd just run through. If they could slip off this boat and travel over one row, they could get behind the storage unit. But more likely, marina management would be all over them and their pursuers would be ready to pounce outside the marina.

"Let's just wait," he said.

"Like this?"

He smiled. "You got a better idea?"

She shifted a little and squished up her face. "My hip bones are smashed."

He lifted up an inch, hating the loss of warmth. "Scooch around. But don't rock the boat. Literally."

She carefully slipped out from under him, rolling to press her back against the side of the cabin. He turned on his side, making them body-to-body and face-to-face. And damn near mouth-to-mouth.

She slid her hand between their chests, reaching up to touch his face tenderly. "Thank you, Will. Thank you for cooperating. I know you don't agree with or understand what I'm doing, but I really appreciate this."

" 'Sokay," he assured her. "Are you comfortable?"

"I'm always comfortable with you, Will. You *are* comfort to me."

The compliment touched him. "You say that now. Wait until your right arm, backside, and both feet fall asleep." He leaned his face closer to hers, so close he lost focus. So close their noses touched. So close he could feel her warm breath on his lips. "Unless, of course, you keep the blood flowing."

"I suppose you have an idea for how to do that."

"Plenty of them." He added just a hint of pressure, and instantly everything came rushing back, all those old achy needs.

He always, always wanted her.

"Guess what I'm about to do?" he asked.

"Rock the boat?"

"For once, I'm not going to...*wait*." He closed the space and easily, softly, barely let their lips brush, the contact sparking tiny explosions of white lights behind his eyes.

How could she still do this to him? Fifteen years, three thousand miles, and their whole adulthood they'd been separated and just this much of a kiss and every feeling came thundering home.

But he held back. Their mouths weren't completely opened, and their tongues stayed poised for that first encounter, hands still but already heavy with the desire to touch.

And way down low, he started to grow hard.

Her mouth was sweet and supple, and pliable as she finally relaxed and offered her tongue. He took it, curling it with his own, tasting mint tea and sweet memories and—her.

A tiny whimper made him need to touch her throat, just for the pure pleasure of feeling that tender skin pulse under his fingertip. He closed one hand around the narrow column of her neck and, with the other on her shoulder, inched her closer.

She didn't stiffen or fight him, but leaned into the kiss and pressed her palm on his chest. Right over his thumping heart.

They broke the kiss but stayed a hair apart, opening their eyes at the same time.

"What are we doing, Will?"

"Hiding from the cameras." He kissed her again, and she added some pressure of her own, so he slid his hand down her throat, over the slightly damp, completely soft skin just under the dip of her collarbones.

Her hips rocked slightly, enough to fire more blood to his already overcharged erection, his breath tight as he worked his mouth over her jaw and back to her ear.

She moaned softly.

It was all he needed to hear to kiss her again, to delve his tongue deeper and slip his hand into her silky hair.

She smelled like the sun, tasted like magic, and felt like—

Like nothing he'd felt for fifteen years.

Dragging his hand through her hair, he took his palm lower, over her shoulder, over her breastbone, just to the rise of her body where he could count the heartbeats, as rapid as his. One more kiss, one more breath, and he slowly caressed her breast.

Her whole body shuddered instantly.

"Did I find your weak spot?" he murmured into her mouth.

She sighed. "It appears you *are* my weak spot."

Something about the way she said it, the catch in her voice, slammed into his chest. "I'm lucky that way."

Their lips brushed again, a soft groan of satisfaction rumbling in Will's chest as he intensified the kiss, melting their mouths together and sliding his leg up enough to tuck her deeper into him.

"I can't just kiss you," he admitted, fondling her breast, already itching to touch her bare skin. "I want it all."

She froze for a second, leaning back.

"Not here, obviously," he added at the look of panic on her face.

"Then we better slow down," she said, her voice husky.

"Is that what you want?"

She closed her eyes. "I don't know what I want, Will."

"Then let me give you options. We could just kiss…" He took her mouth again, finishing the suggestion with a long, wet, completely well-received kiss. "And I could touch you." He thumbed over her nipple, loving the way it responded. "And we could, you know…" He rocked his erection into hers.

So far, she just kept her eyes closed, saying nothing.

"Or we could..." He slid his other hand over her shorts, dipping between her legs, and her eyes snapped open. "Don't worry, honey. Nothing you don't want."

"I don't want...to do this...out here."

"Think we could break into the cabin?"

She laughed a little. "No. Just..." She was already having a hard time breathing evenly; her pupils were dilated, her heart hammering. "Just kiss me some more. That's safe."

Safety and security were so important to her. He had to remember that. Had to.

"Why don't we just talk?" he suggested.

She gave him a smile. "Sure. What do you want to talk about?"

"You."

"What about me?"

"Back in the restaurant you said you sacrificed everything for love. Who was this clown who hurt you?"

The strangest look darkened her eyes. "He didn't hurt me. It was my choice."

"What happened?"

She shook her head. "I don't want to talk about it."

"I do. Were you in love with him?"

She just smiled, and, damn, that kicked him. Of course Jocelyn would meet other men, fall in love, but he didn't have to like it.

"But you've never been married, right?"

"Not even close."

"Then who was he? How'd you meet him? How long were you together? You said you sacrificed for love. What did you sacrifice?"

"Why does it matter to you?"

"I told you, I hate the guy. He hurt you."

"He didn't do anything to me," she assured him.

"He's the reason for your shell, isn't he?" The shell he was going to crack if it was the last thing he ever did. "You don't trust men because some joker broke your heart."

She caressed his face again, the look in her eyes unreadable. "He didn't hurt me and he's not the reason I protect myself. You know the reason, Will."

Guilt kicked him harder than ten tons of lust, and it hurt. Guy was the reason.

"And that's why it's killing me that you've forgiven him."

It was worse than forgiveness. He loved Guy Bloom when, really, he should hate him. But he couldn't. Would that cost him any chance he might have with Jocelyn?

"Will." She touched his face with soft, gentle hands. "I think we can try to make a run for it now."

"I think we should wait."

She lifted one brow. "The only thing worse than a procrastinator is a paralyzed procrastinator."

Shit. That was his whole life in a nutshell: the paralyzed procrastinator trapped in a holding pattern.

But he was holding a woman who wanted a man of action. And he didn't ever want to let go of her again.

"All right, then, Bloomerang. Let's go."

Chapter Fourteen

An hour after Will had easily hustled them through the marina and safely around the back of the strip mall, Jocelyn finally felt back in control.

Barely.

Her body still hummed from his touch, and the certainty that she could look up and see a camera lens at any minute had her just as on edge. She took deep breaths and studied the intersection where they were stopped, known as "the Fourway" for as long as she could remember.

It was right on this very spot that she'd been picked up and taken away, bruised, battered, and broken. If Will knew that...

"Did Lacey tell you Clay's promised Charity a free front-elevation re-do for the Super Min when Casa Blanca is finished?" he asked, the question eerily mirroring her deepest thoughts.

"No." She studied the old wooden sign and tried to imagine something more modern. And failed. "It's been that way forever. Is it some kind of peace offering?"

"More or less. There's still a lot of bad feelings, but Clay's a charmer, you know."

She laughed. "I watched him charm Lacey."

"He's determined to win over every businessperson in Mimosa Key, because he thinks they'll be important for sending new business. Plus, the Super Min's an eyesore and it's one of the first things you see when you come over the causeway. This island has to attract big bucks, not shrimp fishermen."

"That's exactly what Charity and her sister, Patti, didn't want."

"They'll come around," Will said confidently. "I've seen Charity back down in the face of Clay's devilish smile."

Jocelyn eyed the convenience store. "Then maybe I should go in there and at least say hello." At his surprised look, she added, "To help the cause and my investment in Casa Blanca."

"If you want. Like I told you, she did surprise me by not selling you out and hiding those magazines."

It didn't surprise Jocelyn, not one bit. Mimosa Key might think Charity Grambling was a sixty-year-old Mean Girl, but Jocelyn knew better.

"Hey, look, there's Slade Garrison." Will veered into the next lane to pull into the parking lot of the Fourway Motel, across the street. "We should talk to him."

A uniformed deputy Jocelyn didn't recognized stood by the car, talking to a woman with dark hair, who looked up and laughed at something he said.

But she did recognized the woman. "That's Charity's

niece, Gloria." She'd changed a lot in fifteen years, but Glo still had a pretty smile and a youthful, fit figure. Unlike her cousin, Grace, Charity's daughter, Gloria never seemed to have a self-serving agenda. She didn't work at the Super Min or the Fourway Motel, but styled hair at Beachside Beauty a few blocks away.

"Is she still single?" Jocelyn asked, and just as she did, the young officer put a hand on her shoulder, the gesture both intimate and familiar.

"Slade's been after her a while but something's keeping them apart." Will smiled. "Not that I follow too much of the Mimosa Key gossip."

She laughed. "Can't really live here and not know it."

Will pulled into a parking spot right between the Super Min and the Fourway. "I'm going to talk to Slade when he's alone," he said.

Just then, the deputy sheriff leaned closer to Gloria and she glanced left and right as if to see if anyone was watching. Then she stood on her tiptoes and kissed Slade lightly on the mouth.

"They make a nice couple," she mused. "Is he a good guy?"

"Yeah." He cut a glance at her. "Were you friends with Gloria?"

"Not really." She hadn't been close friends with anyone, except Will. It was too risky to bring any friends home, in case Guy had an episode. But Gloria had been in the car that night. "But I know her well enough."

Gloria and Slade separated and Will put his hand on the door handle. "You want to wait here?"

"I want to..." Did she really want to do this? *Yes.* Last year when she'd been here Charity and Lacey had been so wrapped up in legal maneuverings that she'd stayed away from the Super Min. "I want to go in and see what's up with Charity."

"Really? You want to tell the town crier that you're here? That might be pushing it, Joss."

"You go talk to Slade." She put her hand on his arm. "I'll handle the other voice of authority on this island."

As she started to pull away, he took her hand, keeping her in the truck. "You okay?" he asked.

"I'm fine."

"Not freaked out about what just happened?"

Did he mean making out on the boat or running from the cameras? Because both of them freaked her out more than she'd like to admit. "No," she lied. "Not freaked out."

"Good." He tightened his grip and leaned toward her. "Because I'm not done, Jocelyn. I want..." He closed his eyes and blew out a breath, giving her the impression he'd been thinking a lot about this while they'd driven over here. "I want a chance with you."

"A chance?"

"A chance. For us. Again."

She just looked at him, then nodded. "I'll be here a while," she said. "We can talk while I figure things out with Guy."

He smiled. "I might not want to wait for *everything*, you know."

She wasn't quite sure how to interpret that, but a slow burn low in her belly told her exactly how her body interpreted his words.

And, honestly, could she spend that much time with Will and not think about sex? Not want it?

She should put a stop to that right away, shouldn't she?

But instead she stroked his hand and slipped out of the truck without answering, trying to think about Charity but in her mind hearing Will's words instead.

I might not want to wait for everything, you know.

But she had. And what would he think of that?

She looked over her shoulder in time to catch him crossing the parking lot, moving economically and smoothly, like the strong athlete he'd always been. A whole new wave of longing swept over her, almost as powerful as it had been on that boat. All she could think about was how that body felt pressed against her, his mouth against her throat, his hands—almost everywhere.

Talk about losing control. Just giving up everything she held on to with two tight fists—if she let herself feel or fall—it could hurt so much more to have to walk away from him this time.

Pushing back the emotions, she pulled open the door of the Super Min and when the little bell dinged she smiled at the woman behind the counter. "Hello, Charity."

Sharp brown eyes squinted into the sunlight of the doorway, and then Charity's normally sour expression softened, a network of wrinkles breaking into a tentative smile.

"I hoped you might have the nerve to come and see me this time."

Jocelyn took a few steps closer, glancing around the store. Two men with work belts and hard hats were in the back, probably construction crew from Casa Blanca. The rest of the convenience store was empty.

And so were, she noticed as she walked closer, the tabloid racks.

"I wasn't here very long last year," Jocelyn said as she reached the counter and paused. "But I heard what you did with those reporters and I wanted to come in and thank you."

Charity lifted a bony shoulder as if an act of kindness on her part was an everyday occurrence instead of the rarity they both knew it was. "We don't need that kind of crap on this island."

"They might come back."

"And my position hasn't changed. They're not welcome and I haven't seen you."

Jocelyn put her hands on the counter. "Not the first time you've covered for me, is it?"

Another shrug. "Heard he's sick," she said.

She nodded. "He is."

"Good. I worked too damn hard to get him out of a sheriff's uniform to ever let him get back in one."

Jocelyn shook her head. "He's not capable of doing the job anymore."

"He wasn't back then, neither." Charity reached across the counter and patted Jocelyn's hand. "You got nothing to worry about, honey. No stinkin' reporters'll get to you if they have to get through me."

"Thanks, Charity. For everything."

She rolled her eyes. "Honey, you thanked me enough with that loan when Patti got so sick and needed that heart valve replacement."

"It didn't have to be a loan," Jocelyn said quietly. "I wanted it to be a gift."

"Twenty thousand dollars? You gotta be kidding."

"I owe you that and more, Charity."

She waved. "Keep that to yourself or you'll ruin my reputation as the Wicked Witch. You think I don't know what people call me? I live for that shit."

The back door popped open and Gloria stepped out of the ladies' room on the other side of the candy rack, her eyes so bright she might have been crying, except she looked absolutely radiantly happy. At the sight of Jocelyn, her jaw dropped.

Charity held up her hand. "Don't say her name, Glo. She's our little secret."

Gloria smiled. "You're back." Then she inched back, giving Jocelyn the once-over. "Truth or lies?"

Jocelyn sighed. She had a special bond with these two women. She trusted them. "It's not true."

"Oh, too bad. My cousin Grace has the hots so bad for Miles Thayer. She'd want every detail."

"My daughter Grace has the hots for everyone, that's her problem."

"No," Gloria shot back. "That's her husband, Ron's, problem." She winked at Jocelyn. "See? Some things never change on this island. I'd love to talk, Jocelyn, but Slade's off work and we're going out."

"Did you tell your mother you're going to be out tonight?" Charity asked, referring, of course, to her sister, Patience Vail, Gloria's mother and the recipient of Jocelyn's secret loan a few years ago.

Gloria bit her lip. "Aunt Charity, I'm in my thirties."

"Not too old to tell my poor sister when you'll be home."

"Later," she said, slipping past Jocelyn, giving her a smile. "Nice to see you again, Jocelyn."

As the bell rang with Gloria's exit, the two construction workers came up with armloads of soda and chips.

"I better go," Jocelyn said.

"Just you wait," Charity ordered, ringing up the men first. "I have to tell you something."

Jocelyn turned, not wanting to make eye contact with the strangers, picking up a copy of the *Mimosa Gazette*, her gaze on the headline. *New Roads to Be Approved for Barefoot Bay.*

So Lacey was making headlines in the *Mimosa Gazette*, she thought with a smile. Good for her. When the men left, Charity pointed at the paper.

"I was going to fight that resort, you know."

"Of course you were."

"But that damn Clay Walker came up with a way for that road to have another Shell station that we can get the franchise rights to. We'd have two gas stations in north Mimosa Key and I'd own them both." She grinned. "How could I fight that?"

"You're going to be very glad when Casa Blanca is finished," Jocelyn told her.

Charity looked skyward, like she hated to admit it. Then she crooked a finger to get Jocelyn closer, lowering her voice even though the convenience store was empty.

"How sick is he?" she asked.

"Pretty bad. I'm going to put him...somewhere. Not sure where, though."

"Check hell. I heard there's plenty of vacancies."

Jocelyn smiled.

"He meets the criteria," Charity insisted. "And if the devil needs a referral"—she leaned even closer to whisper—"I still got them pictures."

"You do?"

" 'Course. They're in a safe-deposit box down at the credit union. They're yours if you want them. I'm keeping them just in case, you know."

"Just in case of what?" The thought of those pictures still being around made Jocelyn a little nauseous.

"You know, if he ever tries anything again."

She shook her head. "He won't. He's freakishly changed. Nice, even."

"I heard a rumor to that effect. And you can bet those pretty diamond earrings you're wearing that I didn't repeat that rumor, 'cause I spread the truth."

"It's true he's sick and—nice."

She snorted noisily. "You know what they say about a rat-bastard wifebeater and his spots."

"Shhh." Jocelyn closed her eyes.

"Well, it's a fact. And I don't regret for one minute what I did, young lady. Call it blackmail if you want, but that man was a disgrace to the uniform and a terror to his family."

There was no way to argue that.

"But the pictures are yours if you want 'em."

Did she? She could destroy them. Or use them to remind her of why she couldn't get all soft inside where Guy was concerned. "Yes, I do," she said. "I want them."

Charity nodded. "Fine. I'll get them for you. And in the meantime, I haven't seen you, and I doubt you'd ever come back here. Oh, and I stopped carrying the tabloids."

"Bet that's hitting your bottom line."

Charity huffed out a breath and waved her bright-red nails like a flea was in front of her. "I don't give a hoot what's hitting my bottom line, long as no man is hitting me." She reached her hand out for a formal shake, the gesture striking Jocelyn as odd, but she took the older woman's weathered hand. "We stick togeth—"

The bell rang and Will caught them shaking hands. Jocelyn knew from his expression there'd be some explaining to do. Just as she knew that she'd never give him the full explanation.

"Bye, Charity." Jocelyn let go of the other woman's hand and stepped away.

"You ready?" Will asked, holding the door open.

With a nod to Charity, she followed Will back into the warm sunshine.

"What the hell was that all about, Joss? I had no idea you were such good buddies with her."

She just shrugged. "Not everybody hates Charity Grambling."

"Well, she might be acting really nice to you now, but, believe me, she lives and breathes on gossip, so I'd be careful how much you tell her."

The irony of that statement made Jocelyn smile. If it weren't for Charity Grambling, she'd never have been able to escape Mimosa Key. If she'd stayed, Will would have seen the evidence of Guy's fury that night.

His career would have been spent in jail because he wouldn't have let Guy Bloom live.

Yeah, plenty of irony there. Irony she didn't want to share.

"I briefed Slade," he said. "He'll keep an eye out for more reporters and send a cruiser around my neighborhood."

She nodded, grateful for the assist but tired from the whole ordeal. "You know, Will, I'm going to pass on dinner tonight. I'm wiped out. I think I should just go up to Barefoot Bay."

He glanced over his shoulder at the Super Min, as if he blamed Charity for Jocelyn's change of heart. " 'Kay." As he opened the truck door, he leaned in, "But I'm still not done with you."

Chapter Fifteen

⌒

Will hadn't slept more than two hours, maybe three, hot and hard and miserable for most of the night. By five, he'd abandoned his sweaty bed and headed upstairs to his old workout room to pump iron and punch out the frustrations.

Which hadn't helped a bit since all he'd done was stare at his old bed and remember all the hours he and Jocelyn had spent there. On the bed, not in it. Either way, it was some one hundred and eighty fucking months later, and he was still imagining what he wanted to do to her on *or* in that bed.

After an icy shower, he packed up what he needed for the day and made his usual trek across the backyard to the Bloom house, tapping on the back kitchen door before using his key to go inside.

Most mornings he found Guy in front of the TV or working on some craft. Sometimes the old boy was still asleep and Will made sure he was up and knew more or less what day it was.

And some days, like today, Guy was busy in the kitchen, making his own breakfast, whistling a tune and acting like nothing—absolutely nothing—was wrong with him.

These days baffled Will, of course, but right now it just infuriated him because Jocelyn wasn't here, seeing just how *normal* Guy was.

Sometimes.

"Good morning, William!" He looked up from the small center island, where he was measuring milk for his oatmeal. "Can I interest you in a heart-healthy breakfast? That Doctor Oz is always yapping about the power of the oat."

"I'm good, buddy. Just stopping by to see how you're doing."

Guy beamed at him. "You are the best son in the world."

Was he "normal" enough this morning to handle the truth? "I'm not your son," Will said quietly. "And you know that."

He braced for waterworks, but Guy's smile never wavered. "Does the blood matter that much? You're as much a son as I could dream of having."

Oh, yeah, he was in good shape today. "Thanks." Will jutted his chin toward the oatmeal. "And, you know what? I'll have a bowl of that if you're pouring."

The days like this were so rare, and Will didn't really feel like rushing out of here, leaving Guy alone.

"I was just wondering," Guy said as he reached for another cereal bowl. "You think that *Clean House* gal's comin' back here today?"

"Jocelyn?" Will took a seat at the kitchen table, eyeing the other man. When he was this lucid, Will had to wonder. Didn't he recognize his own daughter? Didn't Guy remember Will and the night he'd threatened to end his career or his life?

Didn't he remember anything?

"Yeah. Do you think, William? I really like her."

"Me, too," he admitted.

Guy turned from the microwave before he punched the numbers to warm his oatmeal. "I can tell."

"That obvious, huh?"

"She's a looker."

Will blew out a breath and stabbed his fingers in his hair, the thoughts that kept him awake all night plaguing him. Of course he was still attracted to her. Still lost in pools of brown eyes tinged with vulnerability and a fight for control. Still wanted to take away that control with his mouth, open her up with his hands, get inside her with his—

"Well, would you?"

Will shook his head clear. "Sorry. Would I what?"

Guy chuckled. "Oh, she's got you good. You don't even know what day or time it is."

Will skewered him with a look. "You should talk."

That made Guy laugh more, smiling as he went about the business of serving them both oatmeal, smug with his ability to be the one to handle the chores today.

After he had his first taste, Will put his spoon down and looked at Guy. "C'mon. What did you just ask me before?"

Guy gave him a look of sheer incredulity. "You expect me to remember that?" His shoulders shook with more laughter. "I'm funny today."

"Were you always funny?" Will asked, knowing the

answer but wondering what the hell this old man thought
he used to be. He didn't know his own daughter, he didn't
know his own neighbor; did he know himself?

"Can't say." Guy slurped his oatmeal. "But what the
hell difference does it make? I'm funny now."

Really, what the hell difference *did* it make? Why
couldn't he get Jocelyn to see that? Not just because she
might change her mind about putting the old guy away but
because she could forgive him.

And if she forgave him, if she could take that monumental, impossible, unbelievably hard step and forgive this
man who didn't even remember who he'd been, then she
could let go.

Because right now she couldn't let go of a penny if her
fingers were greased, let alone a lifelong hate match she
was determined to win.

Until she let go, she couldn't do anything that he had
been thinking about doing all night.

"You look mighty serious, William."

"I'm just thinking."

" 'Bout Missy?"

He smiled. "Yeah."

"You got it bad, boy. Oh, I know what I was going to
ask you!" His whole face brightened.

"What?"

"Why aren't you married?"

He flinched a little at the question, thrown like an
unexpected knuckleball that bounced off the plate and
into the dirt. "I was," he said. "I'm divorced."

Guy nodded, scraping his spoon around a nearly
empty bowl. "I was married."

Will stayed very still. "I know."

"Her name was Mary...Beth."

"Jo," he corrected, and Guy looked up with a shocked expression. "Mary Jo," Will added. "Not Mary Beth."

"Really? Are you sure?"

"Yes." Will stood slowly, picking up his bowl, watching for signs that Guy was about to lose it. Some conversations just sent him over the edge of frustration because he wanted to remember and couldn't.

"Bet she was pretty," he said softly. "That Mary Jo."

"She was." He rinsed the bowl and opened the dishwasher. "Do you want to know something about her?"

When he didn't answer, Will turned to see Guy very slowly shredding his paper napkin into long strips, concentrating with everything he had, his thick fingers shaking a little.

"Do you, Guy?"

He looked over the napkin at Will. "I saw a show about *papier mâché*. Did you know that's a French word?"

"I guess." But how did Guy know that and not his own wife's name?

"I think I'm going to try that."

"Do you want to know about Mary Jo?" Will insisted, a burn of frustration stinging his gut.

"Don't know any Mary Jo," he said, then he balled up the napkin pieces and squeezed so hard his knuckles turned white. "And I don't want to."

And, just like that, Guy's moment of clarity was over.

"I gotta go, buddy," Will said, crossing the kitchen to take Guy's bowl. "I've got to run a few errands in town before I head to work. You going to be okay?"

"Who, me? I'm fine, William. Just fine. I'll see you at lunchtime."

"There might be a sheriff's cruiser in the neighborhood," Will warned.

He pushed up. "Yeah, yeah, I know. I'm a celebrity now because of that television show." He chuckled. "Hope that Missy comes by later to see me."

He shuffled away, his bedroom slippers tapping against the linoleum, a sound as heartbreaking as anything Will had ever heard.

Serenity hung over Barefoot Bay like the lone pelican that hovered over the still Gulf waters looking for breakfast. Morning on this beach was beyond divine, silent but for the soft breaking of the surf and the occasional cry of a gull, perfect for an hour of yoga before a day of— whatever the day would hold.

Jocelyn dug her toes into the morning-cool sand and tried to conjure up a mental to-do list. There was little she hated as much as an open day.

Okay, she could visit more homes. Or she could pack more of Guy's boxes. She could always help Tessa garden or go find Zoe for some shopping or—an unwanted chill danced over her. She could find Will.

Which was all she really wanted to do.

A bolt of frustration pushed her across the beach, closer to the hard-packed sand where she could begin her stretching exercises. Find the source of frustration and eliminate it, the inner life coach demanded.

Will, of course. He made her frustrated and needy and out of control. A few stolen kisses and Jocelyn's much-ignored libido had kicked into overdrive, torturing her with thoughts of his hands and his body and his—hands.

But it wasn't just Will. She felt lost, somehow.

Disconnected from a business that had occupied her brain every waking minute, distant from a city she mostly loathed but had managed to call home.

It was no wonder she felt out of sorts and lost.

As she approached the water's edge, two sets of footprints pulled her attention. Fresh, deep, one large, one much smaller.

The footprints of a couple walking side by side down the beach.

Jocelyn placed her bare foot in the smaller set and followed the steps, headed south, with the lapping waves on her right. The footprints continued for about a hundred feet, then turned toward the water.

This couple had gone for a morning swim together.

For a moment she stood and stared at the horizon, imagining what it would be like to be that free, that much in love. The smell of salt and sea hanging heavy in the morning air, in the arms of a trusted man, giving yourself so completely.

The ache that took hold of her engulfed her full body, and it was not just sexual.

Jocelyn ached for love.

She let the next wave wash that thought away, following the footsteps when they continued about forty feet away, knowing exactly whose footsteps she was walking in. Of course they took her right to the construction trailer.

She stepped up to the door of the trailer and tapped lightly. "Any owners in here?" She pushed the door just enough to get a peek of Lacey and Clay, kissing at the coffee machine in the front reception area. They turned, both sporting soaking wet hair and satisfied smiles.

And Jocelyn ached some more.

"Joss!" Lacey said, a flush on her cheeks. "You're up early."

"Not as early as some of our resident swimmers."

They laughed and shared a look. "We take a dip every morning on the way to work," Clay told her. "Probably won't be able to do that soon, so we're taking advantage of it."

"You know, when the guests come it'll be awkward," Lacey said quickly.

"You don't wear suits?" Jocelyn asked, fighting a smile.

"They're optional." Clay winked at her. "Want some coffee?"

"I was going to do a little yoga on the beach, but I could stand a cup. Black, please."

Clay grabbed a mug from the makeshift shelves by the coffee station. "Lacey was just saying the other day that we should have morning yoga on the beach," he said. "Our guests would love that."

"Or suit-optional swimming," Jocelyn teased, taking her coffee and giving a mock toast to Clay. "They'd love that, too."

"Here's what they're going to love," Lacey said, waving Jocelyn to the wobbly card table where she unfurled a set of blueprints. "Wait until you see these, Joss."

A few minutes later, Jocelyn was still studying the plans and still speechless with admiration.

"Isn't my husband talented?" Lacey asked, the question directed to Jocelyn but her smile beaming to Clay.

"It's a team effort," he said humbly.

But it was a fact. He may be attentive and sweet and

attractive, but the man was a stunningly gifted architect, and the plans Jocelyn had just perused proved that.

"This spa and treatment center is unbelievable," Jocelyn agreed. "Mimosa Key has never even dreamed of anything this glorious. I love how high-end it is but how natural and even simple it feels."

"That's the whole goal of Casa Blanca," Lacey said. "Simple luxury in the arms of mother nature."

"Hey." Jocelyn snapped her fingers. "Nice tagline."

Clay ambled over to glance at the plans, still sipping coffee. "We have buildings to finish, roads to lay, and a whole hell of a lot of details before we can get to the fun stuff like taglines and holistic spa centers."

"You'll get it done," Lacey said, pride and certainty in her voice.

Jocelyn looked up from the blueprints. "Oh, the confidence of true love."

"I know, right?" Clay laughed, rounding the desk where he worked. "It worries me, though. The higher they go, the harder they fall."

"You're not going to fall," Lacey said before turning to Jocelyn. "He's got the financing figured out and he's found these amazing deals on everything we need. The subs love him."

Clay lifted his booted feet and dropped them on his desk, grinning at Jocelyn. "My wife forgot the walking-on-water part," he said with a self-deprecating eye roll. "And speaking of the subs, I missed my villa carpenter yesterday. Is he going to be back or are you two off gallivanting around Naples again today?"

"They weren't *gallivanting*," Lacey corrected. "Were you?"

"We looked at an assisted-living facility for my father."
And then there was a wee bit of gallivanting. "I can go on
my own if you need him. I really don't want to be the one
to slow down progress on this." She gestured toward the
plans, but Lacey moved the blueprints away.

"If you need him, take him," she said. "We'll be fine."

Clay made a face that said they wouldn't be fine at all.
"You're really getting soft, Lace," he said with a smile.

Lacey smiled back. Jocelyn had the distinct feeling
that there was a serious silent conversation going on and
she definitely did not speak the secret language.

"I'll do some more work down at my father's house
today," Jocelyn said. "I can go visit some of the other
places tomorrow. It's just that Will wants to go. He's
so..." She shook her head. "Invested."

"He cares about your dad," Clay said. "I've picked that
up in things he's said."

Jocelyn cast her eyes toward the plans, not wanting to
respond to that statement. She didn't have to look up to
know Lacey and Clay were silently communicating again.

Let them. They didn't understand; they didn't know
the whole story. Nobody did.

Well, a few people did. Unlikely people. Charity
Grambling. Coco Kirkman.

"The thing I like about Will," Clay said slowly, taking his feet off the desk so he could lean forward to make
his point, or maybe just to get Jocelyn to meet his piercing blue gaze. "Besides the fact that he is one of the most
meticulous and talented carpenters I've ever met, is that
he's, you know, full of heart."

The words, for some reason, stabbed at Jocelyn's own
heart. That was just so true—and so scary. Jocelyn wasn't

full of heart. Her heart was closed, firm and tight, and Will's was wide open and giving.

He deserved someone who could love him the way he loved, and that would never, ever be her.

"Was he always that way?" Lacey asked Jocelyn. "I mean, when I knew him as a teenager, he was just that superstar baseball player who was going to be the next Derek Jeter."

Jocelyn smiled. "I guess he's always been an emotional guy. Played baseball with heart and now he builds villas with heart." And kisses with heart.

"And now," Clay added as he stood. "He does adult day care with heart."

But that was wrong. That adult hadn't *earned* Will's heart.

"You headed out?" Lacey asked, looking up at Clay with warmth in her golden brown eyes.

"The DOT guys are coming at seven-thirty to do the embankment inspections. When the Department of Transportation shows, I'm there." He came around the back of the table, placing his hands on Lacey's shoulders to lean over and look at the plans. "So, Jocelyn, you like this high-end superorganic over-the-top-expensive spa and wellness center?"

Jocelyn laughed at the hint of sarcasm in his tone. "I think it's amazing and, as an investor, I think it's going to be quite profitable."

"It could be," he agreed. "But expensive as hell to build."

"The spa isn't important to Clay," Lacey explained. "He's all about the structures and design."

He bent over and kissed her head. "Take it easy today, okay?" he whispered.

She shot him a look and nodded. "Easy as I can considering…" Her voice trailed off and they shared one more look. "Considering what we're building here," she finished

"Just don't get stressed out." One more kiss and he straightened, giving Jocelyn a wink. "She's the one who's going to need a spa treatment."

Lacey flicked away the idea with a disdainful fingertip. "I've had enough while I did research. I just want to get this thing done, fast. Go get the roads approved, Clay, so we can pour the asphalt and start building the privacy wall."

He gave her shoulder a squeeze but looked at Jocelyn. "She's a slave driver."

"*She's* in a hurry," Lacey corrected. "And *we* want to stay on schedule."

He saluted her. "Got it, boss. See ya, ladies."

He poured another cup of coffee and left them alone in the trailer.

"You're so happy," Jocelyn observed.

Lacey's eyes moistened a little. "You have no idea."

"No, I don't," she said on a sigh.

Lacey reached over the plans and gave Jocelyn's hand a squeeze. "You okay?"

"I'm fine. Rough night."

"Were you with Will?" she asked.

"No, of course not. Why would I be with Will?"

Lacey shrugged. "Just wondering. You didn't come over for dinner last night and Tessa and Zoe said you didn't go out for Mexican with them. So we thought—"

"Don't think. I spent the evening alone."

"You do like your solitude," Lacey said. "Zoe says being alone is like air to you."

"Zoe's smarter than she acts. I made a sandwich with all that lovely food you stocked in my fridge. I was really tired."

"Tell me about it," Lacey said. "I crashed around nine, so it's fine." She searched Jocelyn's face again. "You sure you don't want to talk about Will?"

"Yes, I'm sure." She tapped the plans. "So how are you going to fit a life coach into all of this and what do you need from me?"

Lacey took the cue, shifting her attention to the plans. "Well, I'll have to hire, of course. People to run the spa and treatment centers, obviously, and a fitness expert, and a few trainers. I'll need an aesthetician and beauty specialists, and a masseuse. " Lacey sighed slowly. "It's going to be a lot."

"You haven't taken on more than you can handle, have you?" Because she sounded utterly overwhelmed by the work.

"Yeah, but if I knew I had a really great spa manager, someone with incredible organization and people skills..." She leaned forward. "Maybe with a little life-coaching experience and knowledge of this community..."

The implication couldn't be ignored. "Me? I'm..." For one flash of a second, Jocelyn imagined herself running a state-of-the-art spa, surrounded by beauty, peace, and people trying to improve themselves. It would be crisp, clean, pure—and safe. "I'm not your girl."

"Why not?"

She tried to laugh it off. "Um, because I have a business and a life in Los Angeles."

Lacey just lifted a brow. "You don't love living in L.A."

She didn't argue that.

"And that business is in the tank at the moment."

Deep.

"And if Zoe were here, she'd probably ask, 'What life?' "

Jocelyn laughed. "So true. But you need someone trained in spa management and hospitality."

"I'm trained in hospitality, remember? I almost have a degree in it."

"Well, then because you need someone who..." She couldn't think of another reason, damn it. "Who lives here. Or close by."

Lacey dropped her elbows on the table. "I got Tessa here, didn't I?"

"Are you serious about this?"

"Why not?"

"Aren't *you* going to run the spa?" Jocelyn asked.

"I'm going to run the resort, or at least hire the right management, and I'm going to run..." She leaned back and shook her head a little, a hint of sleeplessness suddenly evident under her eyes. "Owning this place is a huge job. Clay wants to be an architect, not a resort manager. I'm looking to farm out whatever I can and I want those people to be trusted friends. I want to surround myself with people I love and who'll love my kids and husband, so I'm starting early recruitment. Would you even think—"

"Did you say kids? Plural?"

Lacey's jaw dropped and she slapped a hand over her mouth. "Shit," she muttered. "I did."

For a second, they just stared at each other as a slow smile curved Lacey's lips. "I suck at secrets."

Jocelyn jumped up and let out a little scream. "Oh my God, Lacey!"

They hugged awkwardly over the table, nearly knocking it over, and then, laughing, they both scooted around for a proper embrace.

"Can you believe it?" Lacey squeaked, her eyes good and teary now.

"How far?"

"Six weeks."

Jocelyn leaned back, still holding her shoulders, looking at Lacey with new eyes. *That's* what was radiating off her. Not just love, but motherhood. And a damn understandable reason for exhaustion. "You want this." It wasn't a question.

"So bad."

"Does Ashley know she's going to be a sister?"

"We haven't told a soul," she said. "Not my parents, not Ashley, not Tessa." She made a face. "Which is not going to be fun."

"Why? She'll be thrilled."

"Doubtful. You know how badly she wanted a baby. All those years trying with Billy, and his new girlfriend gets pregnant before the ink was dry on the divorce settlement."

Jocelyn waved that off. "Tessa loves you and she's going to be the proudest aunt of all. Why are you waiting?"

"Just keeping it to ourselves, making sure everything's okay. But I'm getting so used to the idea, and, God, how do you keep secrets so well?"

"It's an art," she said drily. "So you don't have to worry about me. I won't tell anyone until you're ready."

Lacey dropped back in her seat, still looking worried. "I guess I'm ready, once we tell Ashley. But I am starting to stress out big time about running this place and having a baby."

"You're going to be fine," Jocelyn assured her. "You'll do it the same way every working mother does. With lists and help and sleep-deprivation and wine. Wine! You had wine the other night."

"I fake-drank." She grinned. "My plants are pretty looped, though."

Jocelyn laughed. "You are a sneak!"

But Lacey leaned in again, reaching a hand to Jocelyn. "My offer is legit and now you know just how much I need someone like you. Maybe not immediately, but after this baby is born, we'll be close to opening and I want this place to run so smoothly. But I also want to be a good mom." She touched her belly, rubbing. "So, think about it, okay? Come and run my spa for me. You'll have plenty of time to close up your business."

She rolled her eyes. "My business is closing for me."

"It would be so wonderful, Joss—"

The door popped open with a resounding bang followed by an equally loud, "I'm pissed!"

Tessa bounded inside, her boots hitting the floorboards so hard the whole trailer shook.

"What's wrong?" Jocelyn and Lacey asked in perfect unison.

Tessa waved her cell phone. "The son of a bitch did it again!" She marched across the small space and slammed the phone between them, nearly collapsing the card table. "His girlfriend is pregnant again! And he had the audacity to text me. Their first kid isn't even a year old, they still haven't gotten married, and now he has another one on the way."

Jocelyn and Lacey were stone silent, both blinking like they'd been caught in headlights, but Tessa was too worked up to notice. She grabbed a folding chair and practically threw it next to the table, plopping down with a soft curse.

"How can he text me like I'm supposed to be happy for him? Who does that, anyway—texts their ex-wife when their new girlfriend is pregnant? What the hell does he think I'm made of?"

They still couldn't quite talk. Lacey swallowed hard and Jocelyn dug for the right thing to say, coming up with nothing.

Tessa looked from one to the other, then down at the plans. "What are you two discussing, anyway?"

"M-my..." Lacey stuttered, obviously unable to come up with anything.

"Job offer," Jocelyn supplied. "She wants me to work here."

Tessa gasped and grinned and gave a solid clap. "A capital idea!"

And just like that, they managed to steer the conversation away from babies and onto business.

Chapter Sixteen

⌒

Will climbed out of his truck at the Mimosa Community Credit Union a few minutes after the bank opened, the last of the stops he had to make that morning. Just as he reached for the handle of the charcoal-tinted glass door, it popped open, pushed by someone inside.

" 'Scuse me," he murmured, stepping to the side and nearly getting run over by Charity Grambling, who had her head down, her nose in the open end of a manila envelope.

With a soft gasp, she looked up, jerking the envelope away. Then she shot him a vile look, her features arranged in a way that screamed anger. Brows drawn, lips down, nothing but fury carved into the deep lines on her face.

Man, she'd been poorly named.

"Everything okay, Charity?"

Her dark eyes tapered as the wind lifted her frizzy caramel-colored hair, revealing a band of gray roots underneath. "No, Will. Some things are just not okay."

He hesitated, stepping farther to the side but still holding the door for her. "Sorry to hear that," he said, expecting her to fire a retort and stomp away.

But she just sucked in a breath so deep it made her narrow nostrils quiver.

Oh, boy. Charity was in a mood to gossip. "Hope your day gets better," he said quickly, trying to zip by her into the air-conditioned lobby of the credit union.

But she stood stone still, five feet two inches of granite and grit. "Where's Jocelyn?"

The question threw him enough to make him stop. Charity may be playing the good cop this week, but he'd known this woman too long to trust her. "Is someone looking for her?" he asked, purposely not answering.

"Yes, for cryin' out loud. I am. Where is she?"

He just shook his head.

"I need to see her. I have something for her. I promised it to her."

She had? Curiosity tweaked, but he tamped it down. "I can give her whatever you have, Charity."

"No way. This is eyes only. Her eyes only."

"I won't look at it."

She practically hooted with disbelief. "Like I'd believe a man."

"You can believe me."

She shook her head. "Where is she?"

"I'm sorry, Charity. I'm sworn to secrecy and my word is good. Whatever you have, give it to me. Does it have to do with her situation?"

"I'll say it does." She tapped the manila envelope against her hands.

"I know everything," he said earnestly. "I know the truth and she trusts me. Is that what you want to give her?"

She clutched the envelope tighter, scrutinizing his face like she could eyeball whether or not he was a liar.

"You can trust me." He held out his hand.

"Have her call me and come to the store."

"She might not," he said. "She's keeping a very low profile. But suit yourself. I'll tell her I saw you." He tried to slip by her, but she inched to the side.

"I can trust you for sure?"

"You have my word."

She shoved the envelope into his hands. "Give this to her. And if you even think about opening it, God'll strike you down dead. And if He doesn't, I will."

What the hell could it be? He didn't make the mistake of looking remotely curious, but took the envelope with a solemn nod and tucked it under his arm. "You want her to call you or anything?"

"Just…" She drew in another breath. "Be there if she falls."

Coming from anyone else, it would have been a cliché. Coming from Charity, who hadn't spoken five kind words in her life, the expression damn near blew him away.

And piqued his curiosity, but he kept the envelope under his arm the whole time he made his transaction at the teller window and returned to his truck. Feeling a little like he had contraband, he set the envelope on the passenger seat with his bandanna, Gatorades, and a box of protein bars that kept him going all day. After glancing around for wayward reporters who might jump or follow him, he headed up to Barefoot Bay.

How did Charity fit into the whole Miles Thayer–Coco Kirkman scandal? What could she have? Copies of those texts he'd heard about on TV? An affidavit? The confidentiality agreement? News stories? Why the hell would Charity Grambling have anything like that?

Why would she tell him to be there if Jocelyn falls?

As if he needed someone to suggest that. But maybe there was more news about to break and—

As he came around the bend near the bay, he slammed on the brakes, screeching to a stop a few feet from a roadblock of bright-orange drums and two DOT trucks.

Everything on the passenger seat went sailing forward, the Gatorades thumping, the protein bars flying, and Charity's envelope shooting to the floor.

Shit, he'd totally forgotten the transportation inspection was today.

Clay and another man stepped out from behind the truck and waved.

"Hang on, Will," Clay called. "We'll get you through in a second."

Will waved back, holding the brake with his left foot and reaching down to the floor to retrieve the lost bars and juice.

And the contents of the envelope, which had slipped out and lay on the floor.

Pictures.

Will froze halfway to the floor, absolutely unable to keep his gaze from going where he'd given his word it wouldn't go. But his gaze had a will of its own and he glanced at pictures of—

He blinked, his head buzzing at the image that scarred his brain.

Pictures of Jocelyn.

Nothing on earth—no promise, no word of honor, no guarantee that he wouldn't look—could stop him from staring at the sight. His breath stopped, his heart leaped into overdrive, and he picked up a photograph with a shaky hand.

He stared at it, only half aware that his throat had closed up and out of his mouth came an inhuman whimper of pain.

He jumped when Clay pounded on the hood of the truck. "Hey, wake up, Palmer. You can go through now."

Trying to swallow, trying to breath, he just stared at Clay, not sure if he could drive or even keep himself from opening the door and puking his guts out.

Clay banged again and made a grand gesture for Will to drive.

Somehow, he did, still holding a picture that changed *everything*.

Damn it all, she couldn't even concentrate on a simple garland pose. Jocelyn's heels sank into the wet sand the same way the conversation she'd just had with Lacey pressed into her heart.

Lacey was pregnant; that was, quite honestly, not a surprise. From the moment Lacey and Clay had stopped fighting the battle and given in to their feelings, Lacey had wanted to beat the biological clock and squeeze in another child. Even with a fifteen-year-old from her long-ago college love affair, Lacey had always wanted a second child.

But that wasn't what made Jocelyn's slow rise to a chair pose so unsteady.

The equilibrium problems came from deep inside her gut, the origin of all balance. Because way in her innermost core, Jocelyn was actually considering Lacey's offer. Lacey needed her and she needed—

"Hey!"

The single word, shot like a bullet across the beach, knocked her right on her ass. Landing in the sand, she turned to see Will marching across the beach, the first flutter of happiness instantly erased by the sense that something was very, very wrong.

He carried a paper or card of some kind in one hand, his arms swinging as though he could propel himself forward faster. His face was dark with a scowl, his muscles bunched, his jaw set.

Was Guy hurt?

She pushed up, brushing sand from her yoga pants, not sure why Guy would be her first thought or why that thought would tighten her stomach with worry.

Something was wrong.

At a distance of about twenty feet, she could practically see Will's nostrils flare.

"What's the matter?" she asked, her words carrying over the breeze but eliciting no response as he marched off the remaining space and stopped right in front of her.

"Will?" She tried and failed to read his expression.

He took a slow breath, his chest rising and falling as he stared at her, the silence so unnerving she bit her lip and took a step backwards.

"Why didn't you tell me?" The question was low and husky, almost drowned out by the squawk of a gull.

"Tell you..." Her gaze fell to the large envelope he was holding. And her heart stopped.

"I ran into Charity at the credit union," he said.

Oh, no. *No.*

"She gave me something for you."

Finally, she dragged her gaze from the envelope to his face, simply unable to put words to the tornado of emotions twisting through her. "And you looked at it."

"Not intentionally. But I saw—" He closed his eyes, a shudder rolling through him. "Why didn't I know this? Why didn't you come to me? Why?"

She took another step back, the impact of the words— and him knowing the truth—too much for her to handle.

"He gave you a black eye."

Agony stretched across her chest, pressing so hard she couldn't breathe.

"He beat you." His voice cracked and he swallowed, his Adam's apple quivering. "He left marks all... over...you."

She shivered, running he hands over goose-bump-covered arms, blood rushing so noisily through her head she couldn't hear her own thoughts.

"And you never told me." The last sentence was spoken on a sigh, all the anger gone, only sadness there.

She finally exhaled. "You'd have gotten yourself killed or ended up in jail. It would have cost you everything."

"Who cares? He *beat* you because of me."

No, he beat her because he was a heartless animal. "You shouldn't have looked at those."

"Kind of a moot point now, Jocelyn. You should have told me. You should have come to *me*, not Charity Grambling."

"I didn't go to Charity. She picked me up on the street."

He grunted like she'd punched him. "You left that night and didn't walk fifty feet to *me*?"

"So you could do what? Ruin your life and your dreams and your career?"

"Jocelyn." He could barely say her name. "He deserved to die."

Stepping closer, she reached for the envelope. "But he wouldn't have. And you might have. Give it to me."

He just gripped it tighter. "He could have killed you."

"He almost did." She snagged the envelope from his hands, the paper still warm from his touch. "Now you know why I never contacted you."

He tunneled his fingers in his hair, dragging them through like he could yank out the facts. "God, I hate him."

"Welcome to my world."

He opened his mouth to say something, then closed it. Jocelyn looked down at the envelope, part of her almost wanting to open it, but she couldn't stand to see those images again. She wasn't even sure why she'd asked Charity to give them to her, except for the joy of burning them.

And now they were burned into Will's brain. Where she'd never, ever wanted them.

"This can't come as a surprise to you," she said softly, tucking the pictures under her arm.

"I didn't think he'd actually hit you. Fuck, why didn't he hit me? I was the one on top of you when he found us."

"Because he's a *wife*beater, Will." She spat the word. "That kind of sick human doesn't go after other men who are bigger and stronger. They go after weak females who are dependent on them."

She started up the beach, but he was right next to her.

"What are you going to do?" he asked.

She froze and let out a dry laugh. "Do? I'm not filing charges, if that's what you mean. I did what I needed to do, Will, fifteen years ago. I left. I gave up the only thing in the whole world that mattered to me and I ran away, put myself through college, and started a life three thousand miles away. It's too late to do anything else, now."

She kicked some sand as she took off toward her villa, absolutely unable to stand the way he was looking at her. She could never look at Will Palmer again without knowing he was seeing those pictures, her pummeled, helpless body.

Pictures that Charity insisted on taking and using to get Guy to resign from the sheriff's department and hole up in his house for fear of having those images on the cover of the *Mimosa Gazette.*

Will was next to her in three steps. "What did you give up?" he asked.

She slowed again, kind of unable to believe he didn't know. "What do you think?"

He frowned and then everything just fell. His shoulders, his mouth, his heart.

"I gave up you," she said, confirming what he'd obviously just figured out.

"It was me." He almost choked on the realization. She could see the moment it dawned and all the pieces of the puzzle fit. "I was the person you sacrificed for love."

She didn't have to confirm or deny; the sucker punch contorted his expression.

"You walked away from me, to protect me, when I should have protected..." He closed his eyes, unable even to voice the last word. "Oh, God, Jocelyn."

This was exactly what she didn't want. His hate and guilt, his regret and anger, his inability to look at her without feeling inadequate.

"This is why I didn't tell you."

"But I never went after you. I was...*waiting*." His lip curled in self-loathing as he said the word.

"I didn't expect you to," she replied quickly, aching to take that look off his face. "In fact, I was relieved you didn't. I didn't want you saddled with Guy Bloom any more than you..." Her voice faded away as she realized what she'd just said. "I guess I failed and you're saddled with him after all."

"Like hell I am."

She drew back, surprised by his vehemence.

"If we can't get that son of a bitch in jail, then the old-age home is the next best thing."

"*Now* you want to put him in a home?"

"Now I want to put him in a grave."

"Well, I'd prefer you didn't, since I gave up an awful lot a long time ago to make sure you didn't commit murder." She kept on walking, her eye on the villa in the distance. If she could get there, she could survive this. She could get through this moment of hell.

"Where are you going?" he demanded.

"Away." She finally turned and looked at him. "I'm going away."

"Damn it, why? Why do you always do that? You run and you hide and you disappear. You can't do that again, Jocelyn."

Oh yes, she could. "That's how I survived the first eighteen years of my life, Will. I'm not about to change. Even for you."

His face registered the hit, and while he stood stone still, she made her escape.

And, just like the last time, he let her go.

Chapter Seventeen

Will Palmer, man of fucking inaction. Protected by the very woman he was supposed to protect. Hatred—for himself, for Guy, for the messy cards they'd been dealt—constricted his chest so hard he could barely breathe through the pain.

He could have gone his whole damn life and not have known that because of him, the only woman he'd ever really loved got the crap kicked out of her.

Because of him.

Shoving his hand in his pocket, he pulled out his bandanna and wiped the sweat from his face, starting the trek across the beach to the path.

This time he was not waiting for an invitation. He was not waiting for a goddamn thing ever again. Not this woman, not permission, not a decision, not the truth. Thrumming with focus and raw with emotion, he approached the villa quietly, noticing that the side french doors were closed tight. His heart finally slowing to a steady, if miserable, thump, he walked up to the door, turned the handle, and pushed it open.

"Joss?"

From the back, he heard the soft hiss of water. The shower.

"Joss?" he called, a little louder so he didn't scare her when he went back there.

She didn't answer, so he rounded the galley kitchen and poked his head into the bedroom. The bed was made like housekeeping had just left, pillows propped, the mosquito netting neatly pulled back.

Except there was no housekeeping at Casa Blanca yet.

In fact, everything in the room was pristine, like it was when Lacey decorated it to shoot pictures for her first brochures. If he hadn't heard the shower in the bathroom, he'd swear no one was staying here.

He walked to the bathroom door and put his hand on the brass lever and pushed, half expecting it to be locked but relieved when it opened a few inches.

In spite of the hiss of the shower, he heard her sniff.

She was crying, of course. The thought ripped him.

I bet she cried that night Guy beat her.

On the floor, he saw paper. Pages of it, strewn around like someone had opened a package of loose leaf and used it as confetti. Pushing the door open, he looked toward the curved glass doors that had been such a bitch to install. The water was pouring, but the stall was empty.

"Are you in here, Joss?"

This time, the sniff was accompanied by a shudder, and the sound of paper tearing.

He stepped inside and found her sitting against the wall next to the shower, wearing a bra and panties, the floor littered with handwritten pages, some with just a word or two, some with more.

She didn't look up from the notebook in front of her.

"What are you doing, Bloomerang?" he asked with every drop of gentleness he could muster.

"I was about to take a shower, but decided to make some lists."

At any other time, that would have made him smile. But nothing about her pain-ravaged face was amusing. He went in a little farther. "What's on them?"

She finally looked up, her eyes red-rimmed. "Things to do."

"What things?"

She stared at him for a second, then, without looking down, she stripped a sheet of paper off the spiral, the tearing sound echoing through the bathroom. "Goals, plans, strategies, tactics, time lines, action items."

"Of what?"

She just let out a little puff of air. "That's just the problem. I can't come up with the right theme, the right word."

He closed the space and got right next to her, slowly dropping to a catcher's crouch until they were nearly eye level. "Maybe I can help."

In response she smoothed her hand over the white page, silent.

His bad knee throbbed, so he relaxed onto the floor next to her, bracing himself on the marble countertop on his way down. He remembered the day he'd set that counter. Never dreamed he'd be in here with Jocelyn nearly naked, making lists while the shower ran.

"How do you come up with this theme?" he asked.

She clutched a pen so tightly her fingers were turning white. "It usually just comes to me. A word or phrase will resonate and then I know what's troubling me and what I need to fix."

"With a list?"

"Don't knock what you haven't tried."

He glanced at the pages on the floor, most containing a few crossed-out words. "Maybe you're trying too hard," he suggested, reaching to relieve her of the pen before she snapped it in two. "When I was in a slump at the plate or made a bunch of errors, it was always because I was trying too hard not to."

She relaxed enough to let him take the pen. "What did you do?" she asked, her voice a reedy whisper.

"Tried to psych myself into thinking nothing was wrong. Would walk up to the plate and pretend I was batting .450 instead of, you know, .110. Or I'd get behind the plate and just pretend it was practice instead of a play-off game. Stuff like that."

"Lot of pretending," she said. "Did you notice that's what you did both times? Pretend."

"Worked."

"It's stupid to pretend."

"Not if it gets you out of a slump. Try it on your list: pretend."

"Okay, let's see," she said, loading up for a shot of sarcasm. "I could *pretend* you never saw those pictures."

But he had.

"I could *pretend* you didn't know that happened."

But he did.

"I could *pretend* my childhood was completely normal."

But it wasn't.

"I could *pretend* I don't care about what you think."

"Stop right there," he said, reaching for her. "What I think doesn't make a damn bit of difference."

She took a slow, ragged breath, searching his eyes, her brows drawing closer and closer together as she fought a sob. "That's where you're wrong, Will."

She lost the battle and choked on a lump in her throat, cringing in embarrassment. "I don't want you to... know... about that."

He gripped her, careful not to squeeze, not to break. "It doesn't change anything."

"It changes everything!" Her eyes flashed and filled. "I can't stand to even look at you now."

"No, no. Don't ever say that. Never."

"I can't." A tear escaped and rolled down her cheek. "It was better before," she said, giving in to the sob and letting him pull her closer. "It was better with you not knowing."

"Maybe it was," he agreed, stroking her hair. "But it wasn't right. You and me separating because of Guy was never right. We were just getting started." He eased her away so he could look into her eyes when he said the rest. "We were just falling in love."

A soft whimper caught in her throat. "Were we?"

He traced her wet cheek, wiping the tear. "You know we were."

"I was."

"Me, too."

She leaned against his forehead. "He stole that."

"We let him," he said, his voice as rough as the nine-inch nail that felt like it was sliding through his breastbone and into his heart. "Jocelyn." He cupped her chin and held her face steady. "I'm so sorry he hurt you. It was my fault."

"No, it—"

"Yes, it was."

"You can't blame yourself for his violence."

"I should have taken him that night." Memories flashed in his mind: the gun, the look on Guy's face, the gut-deep certainty that he was about to die. And even after Guy left, all he could do was stand there like a complete idiot and stare at his shrine, paralyzed with fear.

While Jocelyn was taking what was meant for him. "I was chickenshit," he admitted. "Not going after you was chickenshit."

"He had a gun, so chickenshit was a smart call."

"Even...after. When I went to school. I knew why you didn't call me and I...was too scared of...losing everything." His throat was thick with disgust and regret, the emotions choking him. "And I did lose everything. I lost you."

She shuddered softly, as if the words electrified her.

He held her face, spreading his hands and then burying his fingers in her hair. "Everything," he whispered. "You were everything and I didn't even know it."

Closing her eyes, she exhaled slow and long, as if she'd held that breath for years.

"But, it's too late, Will."

"Is it?" He tried to pull her closer, but she froze and inched back, away from him. "Is it?" he asked again, somehow feeling her slip away emotionally as well as physically.

"Of course it is," she said brusquely. "But thank you."

"Thank—for what?"

She gave him a gentle nudge, pushing him completely away, driving him crazy. "That's exactly what I needed."

"What is?"

"The word for my list. I just couldn't figure out what I was looking to organize and now I know." She grabbed the notebook, took back the pen, and scratched the word *everything* on the top of the page as she stood up.

"Everything? What kind of list theme is that?"

"Everything I have to do to get out of here." She wrote *Guy.* "Get him moved." *Stuff.* "Pack his trash." *House.* "Sell his house." *Business.* "Get new clients." She took a few more steps, entirely focused on her list. "Oh and I have to help Lacey find a spa manager, and..." Her voice faded as she walked out the bathroom door.

"Where am I on that list of everything?" he called.

"You're not."

Why the fuck not?

"That's not acceptable." Will's hands landed on Jocelyn's shoulders, his grip far less tender than it had been in the bathroom. He turned her from the closet before she had a chance to grab a sundress so she could sit outside and breathe fresh air.

She didn't bother to ask what wasn't acceptable; it was clear by the look on his face, the fire in his eyes, and set of his strong jaw.

"I want to be on that list."

No, that would never work. Not now that he knew the truth. And she knew Will; he'd make room in his big old heart for Guy. And that history would always be there, haunting them. Or, worse, he'd forgive Guy and expect her to do the same. *No.* "There's no room for you on my list." *Or in my orderly, controlled, emotionally safe life.*

"Make room."

"There's no time for you."

"Make time."

"There's no..." She shook her head. "Please, Will. The same thing that's always been between us is still between us."

"Guy? I thought we had a..." He gestured toward the notebook on the bed. "A strategy for him."

"We?" She almost smiled.

"Everything's changed, now, Joss. We're in this together. Everything's changed."

"Yes, it has. You know and I...I can't stand that you know."

"I can't stand that I did nothing to stop it. That you ran away so that I could have a life and gave up everything—"

"I didn't give up everything, Will." She turned back to the closet, trying to think, digging wildly for control of the chaos in her heart. And failing.

"How did you...how did it all unfold?"

Did he really have to know this? She pushed some hangers, hard, like they were the memories she didn't want. "Charity and Gloria found me on the street. Charity took me in and respected that I didn't want to file charges."

"Why the hell not?"

She closed her eyes and exhaled.

"Because of me," he assumed, correctly.

"I didn't want you dragged in as some kind of witness the week you were off to college and your baseball career."

Behind her, he swore softly. "Then what?"

"Then Charity fixed me up, got all my stuff, got me to college. And she made damn sure my father knew she had proof of what he'd done, and forced him to resign from his job. She used to come by and check on my mother periodically, too, and let me know that everything was okay."

"So I was replaced by Charity Grambling."

"Will!" She whirled around, patience gone. "This isn't about you."

He held up both hands to stave off her anger. "I know, Joss, I know. But I can't fucking stand that I let you down like that." His hands relaxed and came down on her bare shoulders. "I want to make it up to you."

She lifted her eyes to meet his, knowing the pain and regret she saw there mirrored her own. "You have. You took care of Guy."

He grunted softly. "If I'd have known…"

"You'd have killed him."

"Then everything worked out like it was supposed to, because he's alive and I'm…and you're…and we're… together."

She lifted a brow. "Not exactly."

"I want to be. I want to be with you. I want to—"

He pulled her into him and met her mouth with his, hard and fast and unexpected. His arms tightened and he pressed hard, with no finesse but so, so much emotion.

"Give me a chance, Joss." He ground the words into her mouth. "Give me a goddamn chance to show you that."

Her fingers closed on his arms, the power in them emanating through her whole body. Everything in her responded, head to toe, heart to soul. She fought for a moment, her hands fisted, pushing and then pulling.

But she had to stop. *Had* to.

Couldn't.

Instead, she opened her mouth and let him in, bowing her back and pressing her body into his, dizzy with the thrill just that much contact gave her. He dragged his hands over her bare back, letting them slide on to her backside, adding pressure and pleasure and pain all at the same time.

She burrowed her fingers into his hair, holding his head, taking, taking, taking the kiss.

But she had to stop. Otherwise, they'd—

With superhuman effort, she finally pulled herself away, the separation actually making her ache.

"Will." She exhaled. "You are completely controlled by emotions."

And she shouldn't be. Couldn't afford to lose control and trust a man. Even Will. *Especially* Will.

His lips curved up in a half smile. "Yeah, I am."

"You can't live that way." At least she couldn't. It was too scary and made her much too vulnerable.

"That's what you don't understand, Joss. You can't live any other way; you can only exist."

She shuttered her eyes and leaned into him, shaking uncontrollably. Whole-body terror gripped her. "I don't want to lose control," she whispered.

"I noticed." He kissed her cheek, her neck, along the line of her shoulder. She could feel his erection growing, his heart pounding. "But I'm going to do whatever it takes to get on your damn list."

She dropped her head on his shoulder, the sheer bliss of it weakening her knees. "You don't want to be on my list, Will."

"That's where you're wrong. We're in this together now. Fifteen years to make up for, and I'm going to do that. I am." He tilted her chin up, stealing the strength of his shoulder but replacing it with the power of his eyes. "I am."

Deep down inside her, everything boiled and brewed and bubbled up, threatening...everything. Her legs nearly buckled under her and, sensing that, he backed her right into the bed and eased her down.

Oh, God. Was this it?

Every kiss was so hot his mouth burned her skin, one hand on her bra, the other sliding over her belly to touch her.

She let out a soft cry, pushing him with her arms while she pulled him with her legs.

What the hell was wrong with her? "Stop, Will, stop."

He did, instantly. Lifting his head to look into her eyes, his hand frozen on top of her breast. "You don't want to?"

Oh, yes, she did. She wanted to with every white-hot nerve in her body. But she—how could she tell him the truth?

Hadn't he had enough life-changing revelations? "Tell me what you're thinking, Joss. Just tell me. We're starting over, square one, new game, first inning. Tell me what you're thinking."

How could she? "I'm really, really scared." Of what was inevitable: sex. Every time, those old fears bubbled up, memories of that night when they'd been so close to losing control. And what it had cost her. "I'm scared of that feeling of not being in control."

"Tell me something I don't know."

Maybe she should. Maybe she should just tell him that because of that night—

From her dresser, the soft ring of her cell phone saved her from any confessions. She nudged him off her, getting a moan of frustration when she left his arms to get the phone.

"Hey, Zoe, what's up?" she asked after glancing at the caller ID.

"I'm at your dad's house." It wasn't the words but the utter lack of humor in Zoe's voice that made Jocelyn straighten and listen, placing her hand on the dresser for a little support.

"You are?"

"Tessa had to go to work and I was, you know, just thinking about the old dude after all the fun I had babysitting yesterday, so I thought I'd check on him."

"That was thoughtful." Which seemed to be what Guy elicited from *everyone* these days. "And?"

"You need to get down here, Joss."

She tried to swallow, but it wasn't easy. "Why?"

"Just get here. Fast."

"Okay. I'll be there soon." She tapped the screen and turned to Will, a thousand possible ways to go with this at war in her brain.

Something was wrong with Guy. How would Will react to that? The way he reacted to everything: emotionally. She couldn't deal with that now. She couldn't *control* that now. Or ever.

"What's wrong?" he asked.

"That was Zoe." She slipped by him to grab something to wear from the closet. "She . . . needs me."

"Is she okay?" He blocked her, reaching to her face. "You look so pale."

"Yeah, fine. She's just Zoe. Everything's a crisis. It's

nothing. She's a drama queen, but I'm going down to, um, to Tessa's to see her. So..."

"So I should get lost."

She smiled. "Not in so many words."

"Then use real words and tell me what you want."

All she ever wanted: space, solitude, and security. Except—she glanced to the messy bedspread, imagining what had almost happened there.

Space, solitude, security—and, now, *sex*.

She wanted that so much she didn't trust herself to be alone with Will. "I just need some time and space," she said vaguely.

"I'll give you a little," he agreed, reaching for her waist to pull her into him. "And I'll give you a warning."

Her eyes widened at the tone in his voice.

"We're just getting started, Jocelyn Bloom. I screwed up, bad. But I have fifteen years to make up for and I'm going to. No matter what it takes, I'm going to make it up to you and I'm going to *be* your goddamn action item at the top of your goddamn list. And you know what the theme is going to be?"

Sex? Healing? Love? "What?"

"Everything." He pulled her into him and ground out the word. "I want it all."

She just blinked at him. "I've never given anyone... my all."

"There's a first time for everything." He trailed his finger down her throat until he landed on the soft swell of breast over her heart. "I'm going to crack that shell, Joss. I am. I'm the one."

She could have fainted the words hit her so hard.

"Will, I'm afraid."

"Of what?"

Of everything. "You crack the shell, you break my heart."

"I won't," he swore, his voice strained with the power of his promise. "I won't."

She just dropped her head to his chest, wanting to believe him so much it hurt. But that would mean letting go of all her control, and she just wasn't sure she could survive that.

Chapter Eighteen

Jocelyn's heart stopped when she turned onto Sea Breeze, the sight before her so completely surreal she had to brake and blink to accept what she was seeing.

Guy was halfway across the street, dragging their old aluminum rowboat behind him. And Zoe was *helping*.

"What are you doing?" Jocelyn asked as she climbed out of the car.

"Oh, shit," Guy said, dropping the rope. "Now we're busted."

Jocelyn slammed the car door and marched closer, dividing her attention between Guy, who looked a bit sheepish, and Zoe, who hooked a hand on her hip and flattened him with an I-told-you-so look.

"Where are you going with that thing?" Jocelyn demanded, not even sure how they'd gotten it down from the garage loft.

"We're hiding it," Guy said.

"Where? Why?"

He looked at Zoe for help, but she just waved an innocent hand at him. "It's your gig, hot stuff. You do the 'fessing up."

"We're hiding it in the river," Guy finally said, shuffling on old sneakers. It was the first time Jocelyn had seen him out of bedroom slippers. "You probably don't know this, but there's one behind those houses," he added.

It wasn't exactly a river, but a series of crisscrossing canals that cut into the western border of Pleasure Pointe. The waterways were dotted with tiny mangrove hammocks generously referred to as "islands" even though they were little more than mounds of muck and home to gators and snakes. Locals kayaked and fished in there, just as Guy had many years ago.

In *that* boat.

"I know what's back there," she said, shifting her attention to the boat just as a sudden and unexpected memory surged up. A snapshot, really, of a moment in that rowboat, holding a paddle, smiling up at Mom, who held a camera, laughing, calling out *Say Happy Birthday, Jossie.*

She put her hand to her mouth as the impact washed over her senses, so crisp and clear she could practically smell the brackish water and feel the warm wood of a paddle in her hand.

"Why are you doing this?" She directed the question to Zoe, who really should know better.

"So you don't sell it in the yard sale," Zoe said, obviously parroting Guy.

When Jocelyn opened her mouth to respond, her father held up his hand. "Don't try to gift me, girlie, there is nothing you can buy me that will equal what this boat means to me."

"It *means* something to you?" How was that possible? He had no memory of, let alone, attachment to, this boat.

"Darn right it does."

"What?" Jocelyn got close enough to see two bright spots of color on his cheeks, along with a light sheen of perspiration from the exertion. "What does it mean to you, Guy?"

He took a deep breath, his eyes darting back and forth the way they did when he was trying to mine for a memory and came up with nothing. He finally gave a look of sheer desperation to Zoe. "Help me out, Blondie. You know I'm not good with details."

Zoe wiped a stray curl from her face, her skin also pink, either from sun or strain or mischievousness. "He was pretty dead set on the idea." She pushed up her sunglasses to add a look. "I guess stubbornness is hereditary," she said, a little too softly for Guy to catch.

"Well stupid isn't, and this is just—" Frustration zinged at the mere sight of the damn boat, little more than a tin canoe with boards and oars. But still, it had been their *boat*. "But you can't just take this to the canal and leave it there."

"Why not?" They asked in perfect unison and, worse, perfect harmony.

"It'll get stolen," Jocelyn said.

Zoe snorted. "Have you looked closely at this vessel?"

In the sunlight, the thirty-year-old aluminum looked more like aged pewter, all the shine it ever had long gone. The three wooden "pews" across the middle were faded and chipped, and the old marine numbers along one side were illegible now.

"No one'll take it, Missy." Guy reached down to pick up the rope and hoist it again, the aluminum hull making a scraping sound on the asphalt.

"You're supposed to carry it," Jocelyn said, automatically reaching toward the boat to stem the damage and stop the painful screech.

"It weighs ninety-seven pounds!" he said.

How did he remember that and not his own daughter? "I'll help you." She grabbed the side. "It's supposed to be carried upside down, overhead. Three of us can do it. Let's get it back in the garage."

"No!" he barked, making Jocelyn jump.

"Guy—"

"Missy," he whined. "Let's just take it for a ride on the river. Please?" He sounded more like six than sixty-four. "I want to show my new friend the islands and all the wildlife."

Jocelyn looked at Zoe for some backup.

"Well," Zoe said, "we do have it all the way out here and it's a really pretty day."

Not *that* kind of backup. "No, we're taking it back—"

"Jocelyn!"

"Missy!"

Again with the unison and harmony. Whatever had made her think putting these two together was a good idea?

"Really, Joss," Zoe added. "Why not?"

"Because…" She stepped in front of Zoe, her back to Guy, lowering her voice to make her point through gritted teeth. "You said there was some kind of emergency."

"There was, but I solved it."

"By dragging a canoe across the street?"

"It calmed him down. When I got there, he was in his

closet crying like a baby and blubbering about a canoe. The only way I could talk him off the ledge was if he showed it to me. Once we saw it..." She shrugged. "Well, shoot, I like boat rides. I thought it would be fun."

"What about this is fun?"

"Holy hell, Joss, lighten up. He's got nothing. He's lonely and bored. Let's take him out on the water. What can it hurt?"

"It could hurt..." *Me.* "Without sunscreen."

Zoe tilted her head. "Say *what*?"

How could she tell Zoe that a trip down those canals in this rowboat could hurt Jocelyn's heart, and her head, and force her to unlock boxes of lovely memories and perfect afternoons that should never, ever be set loose?

It was bad enough that the only version of Guy that Zoe knew was a sweet old man who loved needlepoint and reruns of home-improvement shows. If she knew there was actually a time when he was—

Daddy.

"I'm melting," Zoe singsonged.

"It's nice and cool in the canals," Guy said. "Shady, too."

"I..." Jocelyn looked from one to the other, then down at the ancient boat.

She really ought to be able to go out there, take a nice little relaxing row, and move the hell on. Wasn't that what she'd tell a client? *Physician, heal thyself.*

"Okay," she said softly, bending down to get a grip on the boat. "Go get the paddles, Zoe. Can't exactly go up a creek without one, right?"

Zoe threw an arm around Jocelyn's neck while Guy shouted, "Hooray!"

"Good girl," Zoe whispered in Jocelyn's ear.

Jocelyn pulled away and gave her a withering look. "This was so not on my to-do list today."

"Ah, spontaneity." Zoe looked up at the sky. "My work here is done."

"Like hell it is," Jocelyn said. "You're paddling."

The subcontractor meeting was coming to an end and Will had no idea what they'd discussed for the last hour. Clay had run the weekly meeting, as always, and since most of the time-line discussions were about the main building, Will had zoned out.

Because all he could think about were those pictures. And the way Jocelyn had felt in his arms, how much she still got to him, all these years later. He was torn, confused, hurt, and, most of all, so full of anger and hate that he wanted to punch a wall instead of build one.

"Are you, Will?"

He did a double take at Clay's question, clueless how to answer.

"The marble inlay for Bay Laurel's master bath. Are you laying it next week?"

Was he? Who the fuck knew what he was doing next week? Or if there'd be any laying involved. "I'll let you know," he said.

Clay gave a dry laugh. "That'd be good, Will, since I'm running the show."

"Sorry," Will said, turning to leave the trailer. "Lot on my mind."

"No kidding. Come on." Clay gave him a nudge. "I'll walk over to Bay Laurel and check out your progress."

"I'm almost done," he said. "No need to check."

Clay smiled. "I think we need to talk."

Okay. Either he was getting shit-canned from this job or Clay had something on his mind. Some*one* on his mind

They walked in silence around the other workers, taking the path to Bay Laurel, the largest villa on the property.

"So how's it going with Jocelyn here?"

That hadn't taken long. "Fine."

"You two go way back, I understand."

Will threw him a sideways look. "Yep."

"And now she's planning to put her father in a home."

Which would be too good for him. "That's the word on the street, which, obviously, you're getting."

Clay laughed. "Lacey tells me everything."

A surprising little twinge of jealousy pinched his chest. "Must be nice," he said, giving voice to it.

"We went way past nice a long time ago." At the villa, Will went inside first, while Clay lingered on the front porch to look up at the second-story soffits that had been hung by the roof sub last week.

"I'm down to the baseboards," Will said, grateful he'd taken out all his frustrations on the dead blows that morning. "A few finishing boards, some putty on the nails, and we're done."

Clay let out a low, appreciative whistle as he stepped over the threshold, a grin growing as he looked around. "Damn. That's nice wood. Worth every penny."

The dark grains gleamed in the afternoon light, even with the slight dusting of wood shavings. "Might be the nicest floor I've ever seen," Will agreed.

Clay crouched down to examine a seam and the

invisible nailing while Will waited for the verdict. "Might be the nicest floor *job* I've ever seen."

Will nodded his thanks. "So I'm not fired."

Laughing, Clay pushed up. "Why the hell would I fire you?"

Will scratched his head and looked at the floor. "Because I don't have a clue what went on in that meeting," he admitted. "And my head's not in the game."

Clay crossed his arms and walked along the side of the room, appearing to study the floor, but Will knew he was thinking. "First of all, do you have any idea what I'd have to go through to find someone of your caliber to come out to this island and work?"

"Thanks, man."

"I mean it. I wake up in a cold sweat worrying about you getting a call from some baseball team, and then where would I be?"

Will shrugged, not sure how to answer that one.

"But I have noticed you've got a lot going on the past few days. Our schedule's good, if you need some time off."

"I'm okay," he said. "I'll let you know if I need it."

Clay gave him a long look. "What happened in the car this morning?"

Shit. Clay had seen him the very minute he had found the pictures. "Nothing."

"Nothing? You looked like you saw a ghost and damn near ran over the DOT inspector's boots."

"Did I?" He made a face. "Hope we passed anyway."

Clay laughed softly, propping on a stool Will used when he sawed. "You really weren't paying attention in that meeting. Yeah, we passed, and I chalked your driving up to morning fog. But do you know how many times you spoke in our sub meeting?"

"I'm more worried about what I said."

"No need. Because you didn't say a word, but that's the thing about you, Will. You don't have to."

Will met Clay's sharp blue gaze, quite used to the younger man's longer hair, earring, and tattoo. Clay might not look like a hard-core professional, but he was one. And wise beyond his barely thirty-one years.

"What are you saying?" Will asked.

"Not saying anything, just offering an ear. I know you've got some things going on with Jocelyn and her dad. Thought maybe you'd want to talk."

Did he? Did he want to tell Clay about Jocelyn being beaten? Hell, no. About her keeping it from him and him wearing blinders to protect himself? Not particularly.

But feelings bubbled up, and the words that had tormented him all day were right at the surface. "I just found out that the one time in my life I should have done something even if it cost me everything, I did nothing." He cleared his throat, looking away. "Now I have to do something and it might be too late." He paused, the echo of his vague confession hanging in the air. "Did that make sense?"

Clay laughed. "Enough. I know what it's like to feel like you should have done something years ago and didn't. I don't want to pry, so I won't ask specifics, but I'll tell you this. Jocelyn and Lacey have been friends for a long time, so I suspect they're made of the same basic stuff. Which includes the ability to forgive someone who's acted like a moron, or an asshole, or a stubborn bonehead."

Will laughed. "Why do I think that's the voice of experience?"

"It sure as shit is. But the thing is, Lacey made it all worthwhile."

"So you fucked up and groveled back to her good graces?"

"More than once," he said with mock pride. "You have to know how important she is to you."

Will just nodded, unwilling to admit that even the thought of Jocelyn made him soft in the gut and hard in other places. He'd worn his heart on his sleeve enough for one day.

"So take the time you need." Clay pushed off the chair. "But get that marble inlay done soon."

"Will do, boss." Will grabbed his hammer. "I'll be done here before the end of the day and then I'll start the bathroom marble job."

As Clay walked out of the villa, he stopped in the doorway. "What happens if you get that call?"

Will frowned, not following.

"From a baseball team. You *are* still waiting for a coaching job, right?"

"Oh, yeah. But don't worry, Clay. The pickings are slim and that call isn't coming soon. Even if it did, I wouldn't leave you in the lurch. I'd help you find carpenters to replace me."

"I meant what happens to you and Jocelyn?"

Inside, his chest squeezed. "There is no me and Jocelyn." Yet.

This time Clay frowned, confused. "Oh, then I misunderstood. I could have sworn Lacey said that was one of the reasons Jocelyn is thinking about moving here to manage the spa. Geographic desirability and all, so I just thought..." His voice faded, probably due to the look of disbelief and hope and utter shock on Will's face. "Never mind. I'll check in with you later."

Clay turned and left before Will could ask any questions. Jocelyn was thinking about staying here?

Hope nearly strangled him. And then everything was crystal clear: He'd do anything and everything to get her to stay. What was that whole life-coaching business about, anyway? Finding your passion. The thing that gives you joy.

Well, he'd found his passion. And he'd do anything to make her stay.

Chapter Nineteen

⌒

Is that what I think it is?" Tucked into the pew at the helm, Zoe gripped the sides of the boat and stared at the charcoal-colored gator sunning along the side of a grassy hammock, not ten feet away.

Jocelyn just smiled. "Stay in the boat, Zoe. You can't wrestle him."

"I just want a picture," Zoe said, patting her pockets.

From her perch in the center seat, controlling the oars despite her threats to Zoe, Jocelyn threw a glance at Guy, who sat on the aft bench, his face tilted toward the sunshine like a prisoner who'd just gotten an hour of freedom.

She tried to squash the guilt that image brought on, and the mess of memories churned up like the muck under the oars. Back in the earliest days of her childhood, long before his first "episode" ever turned Guy Bloom into a monster, Jocelyn and her father had spent entire days together on these canals, fishing, talking, spotting gators just like the one they'd just passed.

"I don't have my phone," Zoe said, reaching toward Jocelyn. "Give me yours, quick, I have to get a picture for Aunt Pasha! She's never seen a gator, I don't think."

"Zoe, you went to the University of Florida. That's our mascot and they were all over the lakes up there."

"But my great-aunt hasn't seen one. She may never get the chance. Phone, please."

Jocelyn fished the phone from her pocket and handed it over, using the paddle to slow them down and turn so Zoe could get a good shot.

"You know you have your phone on silent?" Zoe asked as she looked at the screen to figure out the camera.

Because she didn't want Will to call and find out where she was, and come after them. For all she knew he'd throw Guy to the gators. "Too peaceful out here for phone calls."

"You missed a text."

"Henry! Look, it's Henry!" Guy called excitedly, leaning far enough to rock the boat slightly. "Henry the Heron!"

Jocelyn sucked in a gasp and Zoe laughed, automatically counterbalancing the weight by tilting to the port side to straighten them out. "Don't worry, Joss. We're not going to capsize."

The boat wasn't, but her heart had just tipped over and sunk.

Very slowly, as if she were afraid of what she'd see, she turned to look over her shoulder at Guy.

"Henry?" she asked, her voice thick with emotion. "You...remember him?"

He grinned, crinkling up his whole face, his eyes dancing behind his glasses. "Isn't that a miracle?" He slapped his hands on his thighs and then tapped his temples. "Every once in a while, the old popcorn popper comes through with a kernel of goodness."

"See?" Zoe said, wildly snapping pictures. "Fresh air and wildlife is good for him."

"Darn right it is! Look at that big blue fellow. I've always loved him."

Jocelyn stabbed both paddles into the water, digging deep.

How could he remember a blue heron they'd adopted on a fishing excursion—and this was probably the great-great-grandson of that heron—and not remember *his own daughter*?

Or what he'd done to her?

She stole another look at him. Maybe he did remember. Maybe this was all an act, so she'd forgive him. Oh, she hated that thought, but every once in a while it sneaked into her head.

"C'mere, Henry," Guy called, making clicking noises that would no doubt spook the bird, who balanced on one long, skinny leg, his bright-orange beak aimed skyward in a regal pose. "Wish we had some bread crumbs. He loves those."

And he remembered *that*? Pain squeezed her throat, making it almost impossible to breathe. Why did this disease work so randomly? Why did he conveniently remember the nickname of a bird, yet not remember his wife or child?

Because he never *beat* the bird.

"Hey," Zoe said softly, balancing herself on two knees right in front of Jocelyn. "You okay, hon?"

She managed to nod. "I'm fine. It's hot out here."

"You want me to row for a little while? I think I could handle it."

She shook her head. "Who was the text from?" *Will.* Say Will. Please, please say Will.

Zoe tapped the screen and read. "La Vista d'Or."

An assisted-living facility in Naples. "What does it say?"

"Unexpected opening." She spoke in a whisper, even though Jocelyn's position in the middle of the boat blocked the conversation from Guy. "An unexpected opening is never good at those places."

Someone had died, and made room for Guy. Guy and his superselective memory. Guy who really did deserve to go to jail and not some high-end home. Guy who—

"Good-bye, Henry!" he called out. "Next time we'll bring bread, won't we, uh...Missy?"

Guy who couldn't remember her name.

Zoe leaned closer and read. "They want you to come for a tour today. You're next on the waiting list, but if they don't see you today, they give it to someone else." She looked expectantly at Jocelyn. "Want me to text back that you can't?"

She closed her eyes, trying to imagine what she wanted. Will. She'd always had Will when she needed to escape from her father. But it was fifteen years later, and she had to fix this problem herself. Now. This text was a sign, and she should follow it.

"No," she said. "I'll go this afternoon."

"You will?"

But she couldn't do it alone. And she couldn't call Will. "Can you come with me?" she asked.

For a second she thought Zoe would say no because it looked as though everything in her expression was gearing up for an argument.

"Guy'll be fine," Jocelyn assured her. "We'll tell him not to answer the door."

"All right," Zoe agreed, reluctant. "But I promised him we'd have a barbecue at his house tonight."

Jocelyn gave a look of total disbelief. "You did what?"

"C'mon, Joss..." She peeked over Jocelyn's shoulder, but Jocelyn didn't turn to look at Guy. "Have a heart."

That was just the problem. She did, and it was all torn up instead of nicely encased in its usual protective covering.

"Let's go," Jocelyn said loudly, digging the paddle in. "Party's over. I have work to do this afternoon."

"Me, too," Guy said from the back.

"What are you going to do?" Zoe asked brightly, leaning around Jocelyn to smile at Guy.

"I'm going to clean out this boat and give 'er a paint job."

"You are?" Zoe asked.

"I want to bring my boy William fishing like we did when he was little."

Jocelyn felt her jaw drop, but Zoe grabbed her knee and shook her head. "Let it go," she whispered. "Just let it go."

The problem was Jocelyn had never let anything go in her whole life. Except the one thing she should have held on to.

An hour later, with Guy happily ensconced in front of a *House Hunters International* marathon, Jocelyn and Zoe climbed into the hefty Jeep Rubicon Zoe had rented.

Zoe tapped the steering wheel with love. "I am so glad Hertz had my baby available. Remember how much fun we had in this thing when we were here last year?"

"Fun?" Jocelyn choked. "I don't remember any fun."

"That's 'cause you don't know how to have it. God, I really need to work on you."

"I had fun today," she admitted, the words tasting like sand in her mouth. "Until Henry came along."

"You know what you need, Joss?"

Oh, boy. "Ah, Dr. Zoe Tamarin doles out advice. I know this prescription. Sex, travel, and a cocktail."

"God, I hate when I'm predictable. So just to throw you off, I'll tell you I was going to say you need a life coach."

"Very funny."

Zoe wove her way through the light traffic and crossed over to the causeway, hitting the accelerator so more wind whipped through the open top.

"You do."

"Stop it." Jocelyn tugged her baseball cap and shades, holding them in place. "I'm fine."

"Really? Let's review, shall we?"

"No."

Zoe settled deeper into the driver's seat, one hand on the wheel, one tangled in her mess of hair that flew like a curly platinum flag behind her. "First, you have been falsely accused of single-handedly breaking up one of the most famous marriages in the world, and yet you refuse to clear your name."

Jocelyn shifted in her seat. "I have my reasons."

"So you are forced into hiding or wearing a disguise. That's totally normal."

"Extenuating circumstances."

"Second, you hate your father—"

"For good reason."

"And yet, you care enough to find him the right place to live, make sure he's not alone for too long while you do so, and you kissed him good-bye when we left."

Ugh. She'd hoped Zoe hadn't noticed. "He kissed me. He does that now. Trust me, it's a result of his disease."

"His disease that makes him kind and affectionate, despite the fact that Alzheimer's famously makes people nastier, not nicer."

Damn it, she hated when Zoe got deep. Couldn't she just stick to sex and booze jokes? "His case is unusual, I suppose. But I still hate how he treated my mother." *And me. And Will.* "It was...bad."

"But he's forgotten it."

"Has he? I don't know. I certainly haven't."

"You think he's faking it?" She stole a glance at Jocelyn. " 'Cause I have to tell you, the thought occurred to me, too."

"Would be convenient, don't you think?"

Zoe puffed out a breath of disgust. "It would be so fucked up there are no words. But kind of brilliant, too."

Jocelyn squeezed her hat brim against the wind. "I don't know how sick you'd have to be to forget you took your wife's favorite perfume and dumped it down the toilet because she forgot to call the plumber."

"What kind of perfume?"

Jocelyn choked. "Chanel Number Five."

"Ouch. The good stuff. But, seriously, you think the old guy is faking this?"

Jocelyn pulled the seat belt away from her chest; the

pressure on her heart was making it hard to breathe. "I wouldn't put anything past him. How could he remember Henry the Heron and not his own daughter?"

"I read somewhere that Alzheimer's patients remember the most random things, like what shoes they wore in 1940 but not what underwear they put on that morning."

"When were you reading about Alzheimer's?"

"I read a lot of stuff about old people, Joss. The woman who raised me is damn near eighty. Maybe older, maybe younger, she won't say."

"Pasha is healthy as a horse."

Zoe just looked out over the deep blue water of the Intracoastal. "So, what if this is all an act and he finds out his shenanigans are landing him in an old-age home? That would blow."

"It'd blow his cover, is what it would blow."

Zoe tapped on the brakes as the car in front of them slowed, using the chance to give Jocelyn a hard look. "Do you really think he's faking it?"

"I don't know. Maybe at times he is, maybe not. It wouldn't change my decision either way."

"But if he can take care of himself, why don't you just let him be?"

"Because he can't take care of himself," she said, ire and frustration rising. "Will has to take care of him and that's wrong. Will's not his son, regardless of what Guy thinks. So he's going, whether he wants it, knows it, or has an opinion about it."

"That's right," Zoe said. "Plus you love shit like this. Organizing, managing, shoving bad people into their proper boxes."

Jocelyn just closed her eyes and let the powerful gusts

partially drown out the words she didn't want to hear. Was she shoving Guy in a box? Well, what the hell, why not? He shoved her mother into a closet once.

"So where were we?" Zoe asked.

"On our way to Vista d'Or."

"I mean where were we on the Jocelyn Bloom Life Management Track."

"We came to the end." She folded her arms and turned away, hoping that would end the conversation.

"Without taking a trip down Will Palmer Road?" Zoe asked.

"Dead end. Take a left at the next light."

Zoe took the turn down a wide boulevard in the middle of Naples, taking in the designer stores and upscale restaurants as they passed. "Are we in the medical district?" she asked.

"I think the hospital is nearby."

"Always is near those assisted-living facilities, isn't it? And then the graveyard."

"Nice, Zoe."

"Don't tell me you wouldn't be good and happy if Guy dropped dead and made this simple for you."

Jocelyn closed her mouth, unwilling to lie. Instead she squinted at the GPS on her phone. "Just keep going a few more blocks."

"Okay, back to Will-I-Am. Did he pop your cherry?"

Oh, God. Jocelyn tsked. " Remind me again why I'm friends with you."

"Easy." Zoe grinned. "I held your head when you got drunk and threw up after the Alabama game. Remember?"

Actually, she remembered next to nothing, but Zoe

loved to remind her of that night their freshman year at Florida. "First, last, and only time I've ever been that drunk. And yet you will lord it over me forever."

"That's what friends are for. And for sharing secrets. Tell me about Will. I want to know if—" Zoe slammed on the brakes so hard Jocelyn smashed into her seat belt. Jocelyn scanned the road; no car or pedestrian or errant dog in sight.

"What the heck, Zoe?"

Zoe stared to her left, her jaw open.

Leaning forward, Jocelyn tried to see who or what had caused Zoe to nearly kill them. Dream shoes? A hot guy? No, a simple Spanish-style office building next to a frozen yogurt shop.

Following Zoe's stunned gaze, Jocelyn read the elegant gold lettering on the undertstated building.

Dr. Oliver Bradbury
Oncology

For a long, silent moment, Jocelyn just stared at the words.

"He doesn't need an oncologist," Jocelyn said. "And, whether you want to believe it or not, I'm grateful for that."

Very slowly, Jocelyn looked straight ahead, all color drained from her cheeks. "He must live here," she whispered.

"Who?" Jocelyn looked at the name again and instantly a memory flashed. "That's the same guy we saw in front of the Ritz in Naples last year, isn't it? The one who freaked you out."

"I didn't freak out," she said. Behind them, a car honked impatiently. Jocelyn expected a typical Zoe response, which could be anything from a friendly wave to the finger, but she just gently put her foot on the accelerator and drove about five miles an hour.

"You freaked out," Jocelyn said. "You dove onto the floor of this very car—or one a lot like it from the same rental company—and..." Jocelyn snapped her fingers, the whole thing coming back now. "It was an oncology conference at the Ritz. And that guy, Oliver, was there with his wi—" She let the word fall away.

Zoe was biting a damn hole in the bottom of her lip.

"You okay?" Jocelyn asked gently.

"Fine," she croaked. "Where's my next turn?"

"Zoe, who is this guy? What happened?" Other than the obvious. Only, God, she hoped Zoe wasn't stupid enough to get involved with a married man.

"Nothing. Ancient history."

It was so tempting to tease, if for no other reason than to make Zoe laugh. But something about this Oliver wasn't funny. Not to Zoe.

"Straight ahead, just a few more blocks," Jocelyn said instead, and they drove in silence until they reached a two-story stucco building with meager landscaping and, oh Lord, bars on the windows.

"I thought you said this place was in high demand."

"I got that impression from the marketing materials," Jocelyn said. "Maybe it's nicer in the back. Plus, the octogenarians probably don't notice."

"He's in his sixties, Joss," Zoe said as she threw open her door. "Not eighty, which, correct me if I'm wrong, is what an octogenarian is."

Jocelyn didn't answer, but came around the car and headed to the front door. As they got closer she saw chipped paint, a flowerless trellis, and rust on the giant doorknob.

Inside, the reception area was dim, just two beige sofas and a plastic panel hiding the top of a woman's head. Jocelyn approached her and waited. The woman didn't look up.

"Excuse me," Jocelyn said.

"Hang on." The woman continued to write something. Finally, cold gray eyes met Jocelyn's. "Yes?"

"I was contacted about an opening and came for the tour."

"Patient's name?"

"Um...well, I just really wanted to look around first."

"Insurance?"

"Some, but I really don't—"

"Hang on." She pressed an earpiece Jocelyn hadn't noticed earlier. "What is it, Mrs. Golgrath?" She closed her eyes and let out an impatient sigh. "Well, that's the only channel you pay for, so you have to watch *Singing in the Rain* one more time, dear." She paused, biting off the last word. "No, an aide cannot get to your room for at least two hours. So watch the movie. I'm sure it'll seem like brand-new every time. Good-bye, now...What?" She shook her head, still focused on the voice in her ear, impatience rolling off her like body odor. "Mrs. Golgrath, you will get your lunch when you get your lunch. Have we ever forgotten? Ever since you've been here?" She waited a second, then looked back up to address Jocelyn. "We can have someone walk you around after lunch. Maybe three o'clock. We're seriously shorthanded today."

Jocelyn swallowed. "No, that's all right."

"We have a video you can watch in the waiting room."

Jocelyn backed away, bumping into Zoe, who was right behind her. "I don't..." *Want to put even my worst enemy in this hellhole.* "...have the time."

The woman shrugged and returned to her work.

"Let's get out of here," she whispered to Zoe, practically dragging her back outside. "It looked a lot better on the Internet."

"Most things do," Zoe said drily.

They couldn't get outside fast enough, both of them sucking in the fresh air after all that stale, miserable sadness.

"I'll cross that one off the list," Jocelyn said as they reached the parking lot.

She waited for a Zoe quip, but none came. Zoe just adjusted her sunglasses and Jocelyn could have sworn she reached behind one lens to wipe her eye.

"Maybe this is a bad idea," Jocelyn said. "I should have come alone."

"No, no. It's just..."

"You're thinking about your Aunt Pasha?" Or... Oliver Bradbury.

"No, that poor Mrs. Golgrath." Her voice cracked. "I hate that stupid movie."

Jocelyn sighed and nodded. "The first place I saw was better."

"Really?"

"I swear it was."

Zoe stopped in the middle of the parking lot and took off her sunglasses, looking right at Jocelyn, not hiding the moisture in her eyes. "Do you remember that night you got drunk?"

Seriously? "Jeez, how often are we going to relive it?"

"Do you remember it?" she insisted.

"Well, since I was pretty much pickled on Southern Comfort and orange juice, I'm going to say no, I don't remember the details, just the fact that I never wanted to be that drunk again. And I haven't been."

"Then you probably don't remember what you said to me. You told me that the only thing in the world that mattered was seeing your father go to hell."

Jocelyn swallowed. "Did I?"

Zoe gave her a squeeze. "Guess some dreams die hard, don't they?"

Chapter Twenty

Will didn't trust himself to stop at Guy's house when he got home from work. No, he'd be too tempted to give the old bastard a taste of what a fist in the face felt like.

For the first time in months, probably in well over a year, Will bypassed 543 Sea Breeze Drive and pulled into his own garage next door. He didn't bother with the mail, threw his tools on the kitchen table, and didn't waste his time opening up his laptop looking for an e-mail from his agent that wouldn't be there anyway.

Restless, tense, and itching for a fight, he stripped off his work clothes, yanked on a threadbare pair of jeans, and took the stairs up to his old room two at a time.

Halfway there, he paused, closing his eyes.

He'd been in this room a thousand times since that dark evening fifteen years ago. Somewhere along the way, it had stopped reminding him of Jocelyn and even of Guy.

But now he'd have to remember. Remember how the early-evening light had cast Jocelyn in shades of gold as she curled up on his bed and sniffed his comforter. He'd have to remember the way they'd kissed and touched, the sheer breathlessness of knowing it was finally going to happen. He'd have to remember how far they'd gone: He'd had his fingers inside her and she was begging for more, rolling against him and—

"Hey."

He spun around so fast he nearly lost his balance, grabbing the handrail and barking out, "What are you doing here?" at the sight of Guy standing at the bottom of the stairs. "You never come over here."

"Thought I'd change that." Guy drew back, out of the shadows of the landing, into the fading light. "Something wrong, son?"

"I'm not your son." He spoke through clenched teeth, squeezing the handrail like it was a bat—and he wanted to use it on Guy's head. "What do you want?"

The words felt foreign and ugly on his tongue. Will didn't speak like that to Guy; he hadn't said a harsh word, except for the occasional reprimand when Guy didn't follow instructions or tossed the remote in the trash.

Guy was too helpless, too old, too lost to be spoken to like that.

Will closed his eyes and let his brain see the purple bruises on Jocelyn's thin teenage arms and the eggplant-colored shiner that had closed her eye to a slit.

"What do you mean, what do I want?" Guy came up the first few stairs, reaching for the railing.

"Don't come up here," Will said.

The older man frowned, then adjusted his crooked glasses. "I just wanted to know if you like what I'm wearing."

What? What the hell was he wearing, anyway? Bright-yellow pants and an orange sweater.

"You look like a Creamsicle."

Guy tried to laugh, but it came out more of a cough. "That good or bad?"

"Why are you dressed up?" he asked, wishing he didn't care or even want to know.

"For the party!"

"What?"

"They're having a party at my house tonight," he said, his voice implying that everyone who was anyone would know this. "The whole *Clean House* crew will be there, is what Blondie told me."

"Blondie?" Zoe, of course.

"And you know who will be there." He wiggled his finger and sang the sentence like a second-grade tease.

He knew who.

"C'mon, William." Guy took a few more steps, each one an effort, but he was clearly driven by happiness. That was what really irked.

He looked like a great big orange-and-yellow splash of happiness.

Wonder how happy he'd be when he found out what the *"Clean House"* crew was really planning? How happy he'd be to take a good long look at those pictures of "Missy" and be told flat-out that it was his hands that had battered her?

How happy would the old fucker be then?

Will waited for the words to form, the accusations to

fly, but he stood stone silent, his whole body itching and sweating.

"You do like her, don't you?" Guy asked. "I mean I might be old and have more holes in my brain than a sponge, but I can see what I can see, and you two like each other."

"It's none of your business," Will said brusquely.

That earned him a flicker of surprise as Guy held up his hands and then wobbled as he lost his balance.

"Jesus," Will muttered, lunging to make sure the old man didn't fall.

"Oh, oh! I'm okay." Guy stabbed in the air, finally finding the railing and righting himself. "Not the first time I nearly went down today."

"It's not? You fell today?" Why, oh Good Christ, *why* did he care?

"Capsized, I mean." He grinned, his teeth nearly the color of his pants. "In the boat, William. My old rowboat! We took it out today!"

"Who did?"

"The girls and me." He shrugged both shoulders in a fake giggle. "I bet we're not supposed to call 'em girls anymore, but that's what they'll always be to—"

"What girls?" Surely Jocelyn hadn't gone out in a boat with him today? Surely she hadn't left Will—kissing her and holding her and making all kinds of emotional breakthroughs—to take Guy out on a boat ride? After—

"Blondie and Missy, of course." He clapped his hands. "And we saw Henry the Heron, William! Oh, I'm going to have a surprise for you soon. Not yet, but soon. I'm starting a new project."

Exhaustion pressed and forced him up the stairs

backwards, still facing Guy so he could be sure the old man didn't follow.

"I can't come to your party," he said gruffly. "I have too much work to do."

"Work?" Guy whined. "You worked all day, son. You have to learn to have a little fun. To..." He made fists and a pathetic attempt at some kind of dance. "Let loose once in a while."

Will inhaled slowly, and then shook his head. "Can't, sorry." Why was he apologizing?

"What work?" Guy challenged.

"Your bills, for one thing," he shot back. "Your insurance forms and Medicare. Your mortgage and your utilities. You're a full-time job, Guy!"

Guy's happy face fell like whipped cream thrown against a wall. "Oh," he said. "I see."

No he didn't, but Will didn't feel a damn bit better after that outburst. He felt like shit on the bottom of a heel, which he was.

The pictures. The bruises. The pain.

"Just let me get a workout and a run in, Guy," he said quickly. "I'll check on you later."

"Zoe actually doesn't know how to throw a bad party." Tessa sidled up next to Jocelyn on the cracked vinyl cushion, setting the swing in motion and looking up at almost threatening skies. "Even if it rains, she'll figure out a way to take this thing inside, bring out the games, and have your father playing Truth or Dare before nine o'clock."

Jocelyn smiled as she watched Guy claw his way through a game of Egyptian Rat Screws with Lacey's teenage daughter, Ashley. "I can't believe she still loves to play that game and keeps teaching it to people. It's like she's spreading a sickness."

"I refuse to play it with her," Tessa said. "And let me tell you, when I lived out there in Flagstaff with Zoe and her great-aunt, they'd play four-hour Rat Screws marathons."

"I have a feeling this card game is Guy's favorite new pastime."

Tessa looked around. "Then Will ought to learn the game. Where is he, anyway?"

"I have no idea," Jocelyn said, but of course she knew exactly why Will wasn't here. He was too angry with Guy to come to the impromptu party. But that wouldn't last. He'd forgive and forget, too warmhearted to hang on to hate.

But she could, and would. Even if that meant she never had a chance to explore her feelings for Will or wallow in the sweetness of the confessions he'd made this morning.

He'd been her everything.

She stared at her father, the thief of her happiness.

Across the patio, Clay and Lacey stood arm in arm by the barbecue, laughing as they flipped burgers, punctuating almost every sentence with a kiss, a touch, a shared look of affection. No one had stolen their happiness, she thought glumly.

"You want to go try and find Will?" Tessa asked. "You'd think the aroma of cooking meat alone would get a bachelor out of his house and onto the lawn."

Jocelyn attempted a careless shrug.

"Hey." Tessa put her hand on Jocelyn's arm. "Go find him. You're staring at his house."

She looked away. "I am not."

Puffing out a breath, Tessa popped off the swing and nearly knocked Jocelyn on her butt.

"Excuse me," Tessa said, walking over to the table. "Guy, have you seen Will?"

Jocelyn watched her father, expecting his usual blank stare, his big bear shrug. But, instead, emotion flashed in his eyes, so fast probably no one else saw it. Only a person who'd spent every minute of her childhood watching that face for a clue to when it would happen would see it.

They'd talked. Jocelyn knew it instantly. What had Will said to him? And was that why he was conspicuously absent?

"He was in his house last time I saw him," Guy said.

"When was that?" Tessa asked.

Now he went blank and lifted a shoulder.

"In the last hour or so?" Tessa prodded.

"I saw him out jogging," Ashley said, her next card poised over the playing table. "He was running up toward the high school when we got here. Okay, you ready? Slap!"

Ashley threw down a card and Guy was right there with her, the conversation forgotten as Tessa came back to the swing.

"It's going to rain in the next half hour," Tessa said. "Probably when we're eating, so I better see about setting a table inside."

Jocelyn stood. "I'll help you."

"No, you won't."

"I don't want to just sit here, Tess."

Tessa gave her a look. "Go find him. Tell him whatever it is that has you sighing and staring upstairs at what I can only assume was once his bedroom."

"I—"

"I'll cover for you. Go, quick before it rains." She held out her hand to help Jocelyn up, adding a knowing smile. "I saw you two arguing on the beach this morning," she added softly. "He's probably waiting for you to invite him to our little party."

Jocelyn just laughed softly. "Secrets are so overrated around here."

"They are with me." She bent over to the cooler of drinks that Clay and Lacey had brought, snagging a beer. "Take him this as a peace offering."

"We're not at war."

Tessa just lifted her brow and gestured for Jocelyn to go.

A few minutes later, Jocelyn had escaped out the front, unnoticed. Tucking the beer in the pocket of her white cargo pants, she traced her old familiar route toward the high school.

If she knew Will—and she did—she knew exactly where he was.

Twilight hung over the Mimosa High baseball field, and the clouds that had rolled in from the east made it even darker.

But Jocelyn didn't need the field lights. She just followed the familiar ping of a baseball knocking against a metal bat. Rhythmic, steady, a whoosh of wind, a ding of noise, and the soft plop of a ball hitting the outfield.

Was he batting alone?

She walked behind the home dugout, pausing as she always did at the numbers painted on the back wall, each circled with a baseball and a year. The Mimosa Scorpions' most valuable players.

And there was none more valuable than the superstar of 1997, number thirty-one, team captain William Palmer. *Whoosh*, *ping*—that was a long ball—*thud*.

She trailed her fingers over the red paint of his name, then walked around the dugout, staying far enough from the chain-link fence to see him but not be in his field of vision.

Speaking of visions.

He wore nothing but hundred-year-old jeans, hanging so low she could practically see his hipbones and the dusting of dark hair from his naval down to his—

She forced her eyes up, only to stop on his chest, bare, damp with sweat, every muscle cut and corded as he took his swings.

Low, deep, and inside her belly, desire fisted and pulled.

He held the bat on his right shoulder and tossed a ball up—she spied a white plastic bucket full of baseballs next to him—then, in one smooth move, he'd grip the bat and take a swing, sending the ball high in the air or straight down the middle. There was a name for this practice. Fun something? She couldn't remember, but the sight of him swinging took her back in time, when the same sensations of need and want had rocked her young body.

She'd nearly given in to them. What would have happened if Guy hadn't walked in on them that night? How different would their lives be? Would they have made it in the long haul? Or would she still be living in L.A. and so, so alone?

Foolish even to think about it, she chided herself. The past couldn't be changed.

Still, it could be remembered. For at least ten swings

of the bat, she just stood next to the dugout and drank in the sight of Will at the plate, his swing a little different now, a little slower, a little less confident than when he'd been a cocky high school superstar. So much was different about Will now.

His hair had curled at the ends from sweat despite the black bandanna he'd wrapped around his head. His body had lost that sinewy look of youth, but had grown into broader planes, more mature muscles, even better shoulders to lean on.

Without thinking, she took a step forward, closed her fingers over the cool metal of the chain-links, and—

Instantly got his attention.

For about as long as it took a fly ball to reach the fence, they stared at each other.

"I brought you a peace offering," she finally said, holding up the beer bottle.

He leaned over and picked up another ball, tossed it left-handed, then took a powerful swing. "That'll go down nice after hitting infield fungoes."

Fungoes. That was the word. "Haven't heard that term for fifteen years."

He smiled and slammed another, far and long, the ball bouncing along the ground until it came to a stop deep in center field.

That was no *infield* fungo. "Hitting 'em a little hard tonight, aren't you?"

"There's a glove in the dugout if you want to field," he said.

A smile pulled. "You think I can catch those fungoes?"

"I'll hit puff balls for you, Bloomerang." He grinned and used the bat to gesture to the dugout.

Bloomerang. *The girl who always comes back.*

She stepped down into the dugout, set the beer on the bench, and grabbed the brown baseball glove. "They just leave this stuff out here?" she asked.

"My key still works the equipment room."

That made her laugh. "Seriously? They haven't changed the locks in fifteen years?"

"They haven't changed a lot in fifteen years."

As she stepped out onto the field, she slipped the mitt on her left hand. "But you have, Will."

"We all have, Jossie."

She trotted out to center field, her thin, flat sandals all wrong for baseball. "Hang on," she said, kicking them off. "Okay, batter."

She got into position behind second base, hands on knees, butt stuck out. "Bring it."

He popped her a slow and easy grounder, rolling the ball so gently she had to walk forward to get it before it stopped. "You can do better than that, Palmer."

"Let's see your arm."

Grabbing the ball, she straightened, held it up, and threw it straight into the dirt.

"Ah, the perfection of the female throw."

"Screw you."

From forty feet away, she could see him grin.

"Is this what you'll do as a coach?" she asked.

"At fielding practice." He hit another one, a little harder down the middle, and she managed to stop it.

"Ugly," he said. "But you got the job done."

She threw it back. "What about all those balls all over the outfield?"

"I'll clean up when I'm done."

"When are you going to be done?"

He slammed a fly ball. "Go back, go back," he called, and she did, wanting to be that woman who just turned the mitt and caught it and not the one who cowered behind the glove hoping it didn't bop her in the head.

She stuck out the glove and missed the catch.

"Oh, man," he said, disgusted. "Run the bases, scrub."

"What?"

"You heard me. Run the bases. Complain and you do it twice."

She put her hands on her hips and opened her mouth to—

"Three times around."

"Hit the ball, Palmer."

"Catch the next three and I'll let you go."

She laughed, spreading her feet for balance, the grass soft and cool on her toes, so utterly grateful for this moment of pure pleasure. The air was thick with the rain that would surely come and the unspoken truce that they were just here to play.

"Fun job you have," she said just as he was ready to toss a ball and hit it.

"Throwing balls in the air?"

"Playing. Just relaxing."

"Well, I don't actually have it at the moment." He tapped another softie right to her. "That's one," he said.

She threw it in the general vicinity of home base and he jumped to the side and snagged the ball before it hit the dirt.

"Still a great catcher," she said.

"Passable and my knees are screaming at me. Ready?"

He hit this one a little harder, but she dove for it and went sailing on the grass and caught it, holding up the ball with far more drama than the situation called for.

"Uh, you have to throw a grounder to a base or you didn't make an out."

She waved the mitt. "Details."

He had the next ball, but instead of tossing and hitting it, he stood very still, looking at the field. It was so dark she couldn't quite read his expression, but she knew Will's body language.

"You're not mad anymore," she observed.

"That's not what I was thinking."

"What are you thinking?" she asked, a funny, unholy tendril of anticipation curling up through her chest at the intimacy in his tone.

"I was thinking that…" He hooked the bat on his shoulder and held out the ball. "You're even prettier than you were when you were a teenager."

Her heart hitched.

"And you were really pretty then."

She smiled, knowing he couldn't see her in the dark but giving him thanks for the compliment anyway. "You're prettier now, too," she said.

Laughing, he threw the ball in the air, flipped the bat down, and whacked that ball long and high and all the way to the fence.

She didn't even try to get it. Instead, she just turned and watched it bounce off the centerfield fence.

"First one there gets the beer!" he said, throwing the bat and starting to run.

The instant she realized it was a race, she took off, but he caught up to her in seconds, slowing down so they reached the ball at the same time, both of them diving for it, both of them hitting the grass.

And because it took no thought to do the most natural thing in the world, Jocelyn reached for Will and he pulled her close and kissed her with the same power he'd used to hit that ball.

Chapter Twenty-one

Oh, man. The only thing better than the tangy, fresh smell of outfield grass was the bone-deep pleasure of rolling in it with Jocelyn Bloom.

The instant their mouths connected, Will tried to ease her down and get above her, over her, on her. The need was swift and desperate and so pent-up he let out a groan.

She pushed him on his back and leaned over him instead. "My white pants are going to get grass stains," she murmured into the kiss.

"You're right," he said with mock concern. "Better take them off."

She laughed, still kissing him but maintaining all the control, on top, hands on his face, her every muscle taut. "One of us half undressed is enough."

No it wasn't. He flipped her firmly on the grass,

looming over her, liking it so much better up here. "Every once in a while, you've got to let go of control."

"Who said?"

"I said. What are you doing here, anyway?"

Her lips curved up as she placed one finger in the dead center of his bare chest. "Came to see you half undressed."

"You can do that anytime," he said. "Just ask."

She walked her fingers up his chest, up his throat, settling on his Adam's apple, one of her favorite spots in the world.

Déjà vu sparkled behind his eyes for a second, then was gone as quickly as it had come. Trailing her finger higher, she traced the line of his jaw, then his mouth, finally looking into his eyes.

"We never finished," she said softly.

"This morning?"

"That night. This morning. This whole life. Everything with you is like... unfinished business." She managed a shaky smile. "You know that kind of thing drives me almost as crazy as the permanent grass stains I'm getting on my favorite cargo pants right now."

"It's good for you," he said. "You need to be driven crazy, Joss. Let go and let me..."

She didn't move, the only sound their evenly matched, and slightly intensified, breathing. "Let you what?"

"Drive you crazy."

She barely nodded and he lowered his face to hers, starting soft and sweet, which lasted about four seconds, then everything intensified to—more. Her breath caught in her throat, and her leg curled around his, her bare foot grazing his thigh and sending a heat flare straight to his balls.

Instantly, he was hard for her.

The second she felt his erection she put both hands on his shoulders and started to push him away, but he kept kissing, kept torturing her tongue and nibbling on her lips and grazing her front teeth until her fingers relaxed. For a long, long kiss, he felt her suspended between surrender and second thoughts.

"Will," she whispered. "I'm not sure I can do this."

"We're just here for practice, Jossie," he assured her. "Nobody's going to hit a home run, I promise."

"Promise?"

He nodded. "We're just hitting fungoes." He kissed a path from her lips to the opening of her collar, easing the material back to expose more skin. "Emphasis on fun."

She laughed softly, arching her back just enough for all her pressure points to hit his, sending a surge of blood from his brain right down to the most pressure-filled point of all.

As hard as the bat he'd just tossed to the clay, he rocked slightly, his erection right over her pelvic bone, making her suck in a quick, sweet breath.

"See?" he said. "Just make a little contact."

"Is this entire makeout session going to be baseball puns?"

He chuckled into the next kiss. "Yeah, it might be. First base is this, right?" He opened his mouth and gave her his tongue, which she sucked and licked and shared with a sweet moan of pleasure.

"You like first base?"

She sighed, angling her head to offer her throat. "It's safe. I can handle first base."

They kissed some more, but he couldn't control his

hand. Couldn't resist sliding around her ribs and stealing a touch. Her only response was a sharp intake of breath, so he flipped the first button and then the next.

"We appear to have a runner headed to second," she teased, making him laugh.

"The catcher's busy. This guy's got the base."

She moaned her yes and he finished the next two buttons, delighted to find a front-clasp bra that he could unsnap before her next breath. At the same time, she kissed him some more, wrapping one hand around his neck and doing a little caressing of her own on his pecs.

"Not fair," he whispered. "I don't have a shirt on."

"I noticed." She kissed him again. "And noticed." Another kiss. "And noticed some more."

He chuckled at the compliments, then began a slow rock of his hips against hers.

God, they fit. Her fingers tightened their grip on his hair, angling his head, deepening the kiss, giving him all kinds of silent permission. He pushed the shirt over her shoulders, taking the bra with it, and finally pressing their bare chests against each other.

"Will, we're outside."

He laughed. "We're on my home field, honey. I know what I'm doing."

She gasped when his hand touched her breast, the nipple budding against his palm. Blood slammed harder into his erection and he let out another groan.

She tensed enough that he could feel all her muscles clench. Was she that scared of him?

No, her dark eyes told him to go on. Shuttered, lost, falling into a place he'd never seen her go. He took a moment to drink in the shape of her breasts, the feminine slope, the deep pink nipples. Only a minute. He had to taste.

Still holding his head, she guided him there, both of their hips moving in perfect rhythm. Engorged now, his hard-on found the sweet spot between her legs, thread-bare denim and thin white cotton all that separated their bodies.

Murmuring his name, her head fell from side to side as he suckled one breast and thumbed the other.

"Oh my God, Will."

Noisily, he let go of her and headed back up to kiss her. Only then did he realize her face was wet.

The sight hit him like someone had slammed a fastball into his gut. "Are you crying? No." He wiped her face. "Don't—"

"It's rain, Will. Don't you feel it?"

The second she said it, a drop splattered on his back. "Oh, thank God. I thought I made you cry. Jocelyn, I never want to make you cry. Ever."

She bit her lip. "I'm not going to cry, but…"

"What? What is it?"

Closing her eyes, she let out a soft groan of helpless-ness, moving her hips against him, riding his erection. "This feels so good.…I never…" Each breath was work as she rocked harder. "I never…felt anything…like this. Oh, God, Will, I can't stop."

She rammed against him, her eyes shuttered in ecstasy as an orgasm washed over her. "I can't stop," she mur-mured over and over again, holding him with everything she had, battering his poor, engorged cock, damn near making him come, too.

But he held on as the rain picked up, splattering over

them, so cool he was surprised it didn't sizzle when it touched their heated bodies.

"I don't believe that just happened," she managed to say, still shaking, "I just...you know...on the Mimosa High baseball field."

He grinned. "Which just became my best memory on this grass in a lifetime of many."

She finally opened her eyes, unfocused and lost. "I can't believe I lost—"

"Believe it." He quieted her with a kiss. "In the pouring rain, too."

She wrapped her arms around him, biting back a smile. "I liked it."

"No shit."

Still smiling, her eyes sparking with arousal, her cheeks flushed with a climax and wet from the rain, she wrapped her legs all the way around him. "What *is* your best memory of this field?" she asked.

"Prior to the last five minutes? Um, let me think."

"The championship game against Collier?" she asked. "No, I bet it was that grand slam junior year."

He didn't respond, but a slow chill of disbelief walked over his bare skin.

"Or maybe it was the night you got MVP as a freshman. That was big."

Holy, holy hell. "You remember all that?"

"Of course. You were..." She swallowed and gave him the rueful smile of a shared joke. "You were everything to me." Her words echoed his of that morning, as sweet as a fastball snapping into his catcher's mitt.

Except for the past tense. He wanted to be everything to her *now*.

Cupping her breast, her heart pulsing into his palm as if her blood were pumping right into him, he looked into her eyes. Around them, the world lay silent except for the gentle tap of raindrops on the grass and his back.

"Jocelyn, what's it going to take?"

"To get me in bed?"

He smiled. "I think we're on our way to that. To get you to say those words you never got a chance to tell me that night?"

For at least five, six, maybe seven beats of the heart he could feel under his palm, she just looked at him.

"You want me to say..."

"I lo—"

"No." She put her hand over his mouth. "Not yet. Not here. Not half naked in the grass."

"I can't think of a better time or place."

She shook her head. "No."

Disappointment thudded in his stomach, but he just nodded.

"Hey," she whispered, lifting her hips. "We gonna leave a runner on second?"

"Not if I'm calling the plays." He kissed her again, dragging his hand over her bare body, loving every curve, every moan, every sensory overload. The rain intensified, no drizzle now, but a pounding, pouring wash over everything. He slipped his hand between her legs, massaging gently, then flipping the snap and pulling the zipper of what were surely some grass-stained white pants.

"Jossie?"

"Mmmm."

"I think I'm getting to third."

He eased his hand over her lower abdomen, into her

satiny panties, onto her sweet mound. She arched up to meet his touch, giving him entrance to her slippery womanhood.

There. There. There was the everything he wanted. White lights exploded behind his eyes, blinding and—

"Shit!" They both jumped at the same time, the near simultaneous thunder warning just how close that lightning had struck.

"Off the field!" He scooped up her fallen clothes, grabbed her hands to yank her up, and tore across the field just as another jagged white line split the blackened sky and a rumble rolled over the stadium.

Her hand slipped out of his, and he whipped around to see her standing in the rain, naked from the waist up, barefoot, bedraggled, and so fucking beautiful it ripped his heart right out of his chest.

"Joss, come on," he urged. "This storm is close."

She didn't move, her expression stricken with shock and fear.

He grabbed for her hand, knowing the next strike was seconds away. He'd seen lightning hit the right field pole; he knew how dangerous this was. "Come *on*."

She relented, letting him pull her, sliding when they hit the muddy clay so he had to put his arm around her to help her keep her footing. Just as the next bolt flashed, he threw them both into the dugout, which still wasn't safe enough.

"Holy shit, that storm came fast." He stood in front of her, protecting her, giving her the wet shirt, which she bunched in front of her bare breasts.

On the bench, she looked up at him, sopping strands of hair falling in her face, the whisper of makeup smudged under her eyes.

Breathless, she nodded.

"Why did you freeze?" he asked. "Panic?"

She nodded again, sliding her lower lip under her front teeth.

"Don't worry," he said, reaching into his pocket. "We can squeeze into the equipment closet." He pulled out a set of keys and grinned. "And finish."

But she looked every bit as panicked by that as she had been by the lightning.

Chapter Twenty-two

Panic? Let him think that. It beat the truth.

Jocelyn followed Will around the dugout to the clubhouse, staying close to the concrete of the structure, one wary eye on the sky, the other on the man who led the way.

It was one thing to treasure her childhood feelings and teenage crush. It was one thing to let go of her initial anger that he was caring for Guy and see Will for the remarkable, attractive man he'd grown to be.

But the feelings that had just rocked her down to her bare toes?

No. Those were something altogether different, and those feelings *had* to stop. Now. Because those feelings belonged to a person who had no control. Or at least they belonged to a deluded dreamer who thought love was something good and grand and lasting.

Not Jocelyn Bloom. She wasn't deluded and she sure as hell didn't harbor those dreams.

"Wish we could get into the clubhouse." Will jiggled the rusted knob of the small baseball clubhouse on the other side of the dugout. "But they changed those locks." A few feet to the left, he stabbed the key into the metal door of a stand-alone structure she'd seen a hundred times but never imagined she'd walk into.

As he opened the door and guided her in, he ran his hand along the jamb. "Good. Rubber stripping. At least we won't fry if we get hit by lightning. Just..." He smiled as he pulled the door closed and trapped them in darkness. "Fry another way."

"How long do you think we have to wait it out in here?" How long would she be locked in a dark closet with Will, her new, raw, frightening feelings so close to the surface they could bubble up at the first clap of thunder—or with the first heated kiss?

"As long as you want to."

"They're going to get worried about me," Jocelyn said, blinking to get her night vision, but it was still nearly pitch black.

And then it wasn't, as Will hit the switch and the little room was washed in yellow light, revealing a five-foot-square mess of bats, buckets of balls, lost gloves, batting helmets, and giant catcher's vests hanging like dead men from hooks along the wall.

He stared at her, intense and direct. She tightened her grip on the shirt bundled against her chest and met his gaze. Could he read the vulnerability that coursed through her?

"Nothing is going to happen in here if you don't want it to, Joss. Lights can stay on."

But all the light did was highlight the set of his jaw, the burn in his eyes, and the rise and fall of his stunning chest. Against her will, her gaze dropped over that sight, down to his jeans, and—

She looked back up. "Too bright. Turn them off."

Immediately they were back in black, surrounded by the echo of thunder and the rain on the roof. The dizzying smell of leather and clay, familiar scents that transported her back a decade and a half to a time when the mere scrape of metal cleats on concrete made her knees go weak.

"What's the matter?" he asked, reading her, of course.

"Nothing, I..."

"Something's the matter."

"I..." *Think, Joss.* "I don't want the first time to be in a closet," she whispered, only a little surprised by the actual truth of that admission.

"Well, that's some good news."

It was? "What is?"

"That there's going to be a first time for us." His seductive tone, like the evaporating rain, left a fine chill on her skin. And yet she let her hands fall to her sides, the shirt still hooked to her fingertips, her bare breasts completely exposed to him.

He stood about six inches away, making no move.

"Jocelyn?"

"Mmmm?"

"Are you over that moment of panic?"

Not even close. "I am." God, she wanted to touch him. Just make this about fulfilling her need and taking that crazy ride of complete abandon again. Why did he have to mention *love* out there on the field?

She was just getting used to the idea of sex and he'd brought up the only thing scarier, the only thing that stole any shred of control.

He took one step forward and they touched. His bare chest to her bare chest. His legs against her legs. His—

Oh *God*. He was so hard.

He pressed a huge, daunting, mighty erection against her stomach and all she could do was drop her shirt with a soft *whoompf.*

"So, what happened out there?" he asked. "Are you scared of lightning?"

"I'm scared of..." *Love.* "This."

"Of being with me?"

Define *being*. "Maybe."

He tipped her chin with his thumb, then cupped her jaw, forcing her to look up at him. The air vent above the door let in a whisper of ambient light, enough to see how serious he was. "Are you scared of sex?"

"It always reminds me of...that night," she admitted. "And what happened."

"Oh," he angled his head, sympathy all over his expression, agony in the single syllable. "Then all the more reason for us to try to make new memories."

She closed her eyes. "You always know the right thing to say."

"And do." He pressed against her, making her nipples pucker against his warm, wet chest. Between her legs, the twisting coil of need tightened again. Her fingers grew heavy and numb. Her head buzzed.

This was like being drunk. Like being helpless. God, she hated helplessness. More than anything.

"It's also scary to lose control." Maybe it was both.

Loss of control, loss of sanity, equaled pain and misery. Was that the equation that added up in her head every time she felt like this?

Not that anyone other than Will had ever made her feel *quite* like this.

"I can give you control," he said softly, kissing her first on the forehead. "You want to call the shots?"

She nodded, slack-jawed at how much need coursed through her.

"What do you want to do?"

"I want to...not lose control."

"Then you take charge," he said, gently sliding his hands over her bare arms. "You call the game, Coach."

She wet her lips, but it didn't help her parched mouth. She put her hands on his shoulders. God, she loved those shoulders. Big, strong, reliable, sexy shoulders.

She splayed her hands over the muscles, dragging her fingers down, closer to what she wanted. Over his abs, closing her eyes so that every sense was focused on the masculine ripples of each perfectly formed muscle.

She could do this. She could do this and not hear the accusations and feel the punches, not relive the night when letting loose had caused her so much pain.

Forcing the memory away, she continued down to her knees, unbuttoning his jeans on the way, scraping the zipper.

He was naked under there, erect and pulsing and as big as she'd always imagined.

And, oh, Lord almighty, she had imagined.

"Joss." His fingers tangled in her hair. His skin smelled like salt and something sexy she couldn't identify. Not sweat. Just man.

A stone stabbed her knee and sweat stung her skin. Through the slotted vent above the door, lightning flashed, one second of near-illumination that let her see his swollen, wet, smooth tip as she freed him.

He pushed the jeans down and guided her mouth to him, murmuring, "Please."

She had control. Complete, utter, blissful control. And she took it, sucking gently at first, then using her hand to fondle and stroke him.

His knees buckled and he swore and begged and plunged in and out of her mouth, over and over again, slow then fast, deep then shallow, long strokes then quick ones. Her hands moved, her tongue licked, and her mouth took him all the way until he lost all the control she held so tightly. With a low, long, helpless growl of release, he spurted into her mouth, grasping her head with two hands and almost crying with each squeeze of pure relief.

Her head thrummed with the thrill of it. The sheer blissful wonder of making Will come with just her hands and mouth. Finally, she released his shaft and looked up at him.

His face was still wet from the—

No, that wasn't rain. Very slowly she stood, not at all sure her legs could do their job.

"Will?"

He just closed his eyes and shook his head, unable to speak.

"Oh, Will." She put her hands on his face. "Don't."

"I'm so sorry, Jocelyn." He barely whispered the words. "For not being there when you needed me."

Suddenly she was cold. In this tiny, airless room that was probably ninety degrees and a hundred percent

humidity, she was cold. The chill came from inside, from
her chest—from her heart. Icy, empty coldness. "Will,
if you can't forget what you saw in those pictures, then I
can't be with you."

He nodded, as if he understood. "I will." He pulled her
into a hug, holding her close, his body still quivering from
his orgasm. "I promise I will."

But could he?

When she shivered, Will bent down and grabbed her
blouse, shaking it out and handing it to her. She slipped
her arms into the sleeves, but it was wet and made her
even colder.

"The storm's moving away. Let's go home, babe," he
whispered. "I want you in bed with me tonight."

Now. She had to explain. Had to tell him the truth.

"You know that moment when...you realize that..."
She fought for a breath and the right words. "You want
something you can never have?"

"Yeah." He puffed out a soft laugh. "I know that
moment."

"Well, that's why I froze."

"What do you want that you can never have?"

Love. Trust. Sex. A complete and total loss of control.
"Um, Will, there are things about me you don't know.
Things you might not believe even if I told you."

"Oh." It was no more than a soft moan. "Honey." Like
he'd lost a battle, he reached for her, pulling her into him,
pressing them together, squeezing so hard she almost
couldn't breathe. "I don't care about your past. I don't
even care if...if..."

She stilled, waiting for him to finish. "If what?" she
prompted when he didn't.

"Whatever happened in California, I don't care."

It was more like what *didn't* happen, but if he wanted to go there, it was easier for her.

"Well, I'm not ready to... spend the night with you," she admitted.

With a soft sigh, he buttoned her blouse, all the way to the very top. "I can wait. I'm pretty good at that, as you know." Holding her hand, he led her back out into the soft evening rain.

Chapter Twenty-three

Guy looked around at the strangers in his living room, all piled in there after the rainstorm started.

Who *were* these people? A thread of fear wrapped around his chest as he glanced from one to another, trying—and failing—to put names with the faces. There was the lady with wavy copper hair holding hands with the young man who made her laugh a lot.

A teenager who never shut the heck up and couldn't say a sentence without the word "like" in it, but she'd been very kind to him when they'd played cards and he kept forgetting how many you had to put down for all the royal cards and aces.

Then there was Blondie, who blew in and out of the room like a breath of fresh air, kind of pretending she owned the place, the way she doled out drinks and jokes.

But *where was William?*

Good Lord in heaven, that's who was missing. He hadn't lost William again, had he? Not his son. Not like the other time.

An old dull ache he'd long ago learned to ignore pressed on his heart, like a mallet on the inside, throbbing and reminding him of things he wanted to forget.

His son.

"Where's William?" he called out, silencing the soft buzz of conversation as everyone turned to him at once. He felt a flush of shame for yelling and adjusted his glasses and cleared his throat. "I haven't seen him," he added sheepishly.

A woman he'd barely talked to came out of the kitchen. "Jocelyn went to find him, and then it started raining. I assume they ran into a restaurant or something."

"You assume?" Guy didn't mean to boom the question or make the teenager across from him flinch in surprise. "What if something happened to him?"

Where the heck would that leave Guy? William was *everything*.

"I'm sure they're fine," the woman said, tucking dishwater-brown hair behind her ear and giving him a quick smile that didn't quite meet her eyes.

She was lying.

"How can you be sure?" He pushed up from the recliner so fast he wobbled the table next to him and the lamp on top of it started to fall.

Blondie dove in and grabbed the tumbling shade just in time. "Easy there, big guy. He'll be home. I'll text Jocelyn now and find out where they are."

"Who the hell is Jocelyn?" He didn't care that he was yelling. These were a bunch of damn strangers. Strangers

scared him. "And who the hell are all of you? I never saw
any of you on that show!" He threw the remote on the floor
so hard the batteries popped out and skittered everywhere.

And that very moment, William walked in the front
door. Missy, looking like a drowned rat, was right beside
him, eyes wide, hand over her mouth.

"What going on?" William demanded, marching
toward Guy, his eyes fierce and furious.

That just made Guy madder, damn it. "You tell me,
son! You disappear and leave me with a house full of
strangers."

"Guy." The blonde stepped closer and he waved her
off, his hand flying too close, making her duck.

"Stop it!" William lunged at him, way past furious
now. His tone turned Guy's innards into water and his
legs into Jell-O.

"What the hell are you going to do, Guy? Hit her?"

Guy cringed and cowered back, stunned by this William he didn't even know.

"It's okay," Blondie said, coming closer. "It was—"

"No!" William shouted. "It's not okay. It's not okay
to take a swing at a woman or at anyone, for that matter,
Guy. Do you know that? Do you *know* that?"

"Will." Missy slipped into the room, curling her arm
around Will's, her jaw quivering. "Don't."

"Don't?" He spun on her. "I *didn't* last time, Joss, and
look how great that turned out for us."

What was he talking about? Tears welled in Guy's eyes
and he tried to wipe them, but that just sent his glasses
tumbling to the floor. Missy immediately bent to pick
them up for him.

"Here." She straightened the arms and gave them

back, and then she turned to William. "This isn't the time or place for this conversation. And it's too late, anyway."

"What are you two talking about?" Guy demanded, his mix of anger and sadness and fear all balling up in his belly. "William, you left me with all these people, and I... I was scared." He looked at the blonde, her name suddenly popping into his head like a gift from the memory gods. "Zoe was very nice and taught me how to play cards and... and..." He waved toward the couple with the teenager. "And they were nice, too, but... William."

Shoot, he was crying and there was no way in heaven or hell he could stop. "You left me and I thought... I thought..." He blubbered and Missy grabbed a tissue from a box on the table. Taking it, he blew his nose, realizing that the entire room was dead silent.

They were all looking at him. The strangers, expectantly. The girl from *Clean House*, pitifully. And William. How had it happened that William would look at him with such hatred? "Are you mad at me, William?" He could barely say the words.

William just swallowed and took one of those long breaths that he always took when Guy had left the stove on or misplaced his needlework or come out of his room hollering that there was a stranger in the mirror.

There was *always* a stranger in the mirror, and, right this minute, he couldn't stand that anymore.

"Don't hate me, William!" he cried. "That would be like losing a child all over again. I... can't."

Missy's eyes widened, but William stepped closer. "Stop crying, Guy," he said, but not in his normal voice. Not the kind voice that always made Guy feel like he really could stop crying.

"I can't stop crying," he said.

"Yes, you can." Missy came next to him. Closer, in fact, than she'd ever come on her own since he'd met her. She was a cool one, always keeping an invisible fence around her, scrunching up her face when he tried to touch her, giving him icy looks like she knew something he didn't. But right now she wasn't so chilly. She was as kind as William used to be. "Just sit down, Guy."

But he didn't move. Instead he stared at William, who stared right back. What was going on in that young man's head?

"Son, I don't want to lose you again."

William's eyes closed, but he didn't answer.

"Because when you came back to me after all those years..." Damn, Guy's voice cracked and they were all staring at him. Even the teenager. He hated to be on display like this, but if this was what it took for William to know the truth, then he'd do it. "I thought I'd lost you forever and ever. They told me you were gone."

Confusion pulled at William's brow. "I don't know what you're talking about."

"You do, though, William," Guy insisted. "You know what I'm talking about."

"Actually, I don't." He stooped over and picked up the clicker and batteries, avoiding Guy's eyes as he put the thing back together again. "But just calm down—"

"I don't want to calm down!" Guy yelled.

Missy jumped back with a soft gasp.

"Sorry," he said quickly, reaching for her, but she stepped away from him, holding up a hand.

"Don't." William was between them in a second, as if he were guarding her or something.

"I'm not...going to..." One of his loose threads tugged at his brain. An old, frayed bit he rarely thought about, but he could just imagine what was happening in his head as that thread curled into one of the many holes in his brain and tried to tie something together.

William...and this girl.

William...and...someone.

But no matter how hard he tugged, he couldn't pull the memory. "Please don't be mad at me," he said instead, to both of them. "And, William, understand how scared I get when you're gone. I lost you once, I really thought I'd never ever see you again, and all I had was my daugh—" The thread plucked and, suddenly, he could remember.

Both of them stared at him, jaws open. Oh dear, what had he done now?

"Your what?" Missy asked.

He closed his eyes. "I had a daughter."

Nobody in the room said a word; not a single person so much as breathed.

"But she died when she was really, really young." Guy reached toward William. "That's why you're everything to me, son. Everything."

" 'Kay, Guy. Let's call it a night then, buddy."

"Oh, thank you." Guy felt the waterworks, but he didn't care as he reached out to hug Will. "I love you, son. I love you so much."

Will didn't hug him back, but that was okay. He was here. His son was here.

Jocelyn managed to snag a ride back to Barefoot Bay with Lacey and Clay, even if Will wasn't happy about that. He walked her to the car and promised to talk to her tomorrow, but she'd had enough revelations, enough emotion, enough Guy, enough close calls, enough of everything.

Solitude screamed for her.

She rode in the back cab of Clay's truck with Ashley, who, while texting, sent wayward glances at Jocelyn.

"Yes, Ash, the thing with my father is a tough situation," Jocelyn finally said. "You can ask me about it, honey."

Lacey looked over her shoulder to give Jocelyn a grateful smile.

"I was really wondering why you came home all wet."

"We got caught in the rain."

She leaned close and whispered, "Aunt Zoe said you totally don't have your bra on."

Jocelyn's jaw dropped but, damn it, Clay heard and laughed.

"Listen to your iPod until we get home," Lacey said sternly, fighting a smile. "But if you want to talk about your dad, Joss, I'll come up to your villa and Clay can take Ashley home."

"Thanks," Jocelyn said. Solitude might be calling, but she really needed to talk to Lacey, too. For a minute. "I'd like that."

Ashley gave her another sideways look and Jocelyn gave her thigh a friendly punch.

"Hey, what's that for?" Ashley asked.

"For Zoe. Give it to her next time you see her."

When Jocelyn and Lacey stepped into the dimly lit villa, Lacey was the one to drop onto the sofa with a huge sigh. "Well, you missed all the drama."

"I got enough, thank you very much." She turned on the softest light in the living area and looked down at her shirt. "Why does Zoe have to notice everything?"

"Where is it?" Lacey asked, curling a long stawberry-blonde strand and giving a sheepish, teasing smile.

"Somewhere in right field."

"At Mimosa High?" She practically choked.

"Don't be scandalized. I'm sure it's not the first bra to be left at that field. Hell, there's probably an entire Victoria's Secret catalog buried under the bleachers." Jocelyn headed to the back. "I'm going to change. Help yourself to some water or . . . milk."

After she changed into sleep pants and a tank top, brushed the rain out of her hair, and clipped it up, Jocelyn returned to the living room to find Lacey flat out on the couch, sound asleep.

"Whoa, mama. Somebody's tired."

Lacey blinked, sighed, and rolled over, grabbing a pillow with a soft moan. "Oh, I'm so glad I went for the expensive fabric on these pillows."

"So your drool won't stain?"

She smiled, eyes closed. "This babymaking job is tiring."

" 'Specially when you're building a resort in your spare time, raising a teenager, and attending family drama performances."

She opened her eyes. "He's really messed up, isn't he?"

"Confused, I believe, is the proper term." Jocelyn opened a water bottle. "I kinda wish this were wine."

"There's some in there," Lacey said. "I stocked your fridge."

"No wonder you're exhausted."

"So . . ." Lacey dragged herself up. "You want to tell me what happened with Will or would you like to hear how Tessa took the news?"

Jocelyn slammed the bottle on the table hard enough to spill a little water. "You told her?"

"We told everyone. Well, we told Ashley at home first. Then we told the gang tonight."

Guilt squeezed. "Damn, what was I doing? I should have been there for Tessa."

"Zoe was there. You were leaving underwear on the baseball field. Did you do it?"

"No." She rolled her eyes. "Nothing is sacred, is it?"

"Is it?" Lacey sat up a little higher. "Is sex with Will Palmer sacred?"

What a damn good question. "It's not…meaningless, let's put it that way." The need to share her fears rose up a little, but she tamped it down. She shared judiciously. And so, so rarely. And this subject? Totally off limits. "How did Tessa take the news?"

"She was fine. I think she already knew."

"Really?" Wouldn't she have said something to Jocelyn? They'd talked so much about infertility in the past eight or ten years. "God, I hate how we're always keeping things from each other."

"From the Queen Secret Keeper."

Jocelyn shrugged. "My secrets are out," she said. "My dad's mean and badly…"

"Confused."

"Yes. And I came home from a walk with my old next-door neighbor missing some clothes. I have no secrets left." Just one.

"Coco Kirkman."

Okay, two. "No word from those reporters?" she asked.

"Clay talked to Slade Garrison and he said some are sniffing around asking questions. Don't take this personally, but most of the people on this island barely remember you. Of course Slade knows who your dad is, since he was the former sheriff, but he retired so early, even before your mom died. But since then, Guy's been off the radar, and really, those reporters are getting nowhere. Charity is your only real danger."

Charity was no danger. "I need to go see her tomorrow."

"You're safe up here," Lacey said.

"I know." A rush of affection rolled through her, making Jocelyn reach over and give Lacey's ankles a squeeze. "Thank you for this sanctuary. You have no idea how much this means to me."

Lacey smiled. "You can pay me back."

"Anything. Name it."

"Take the job."

Jocelyn laughed softly. "I walked right into that one."

"I'm serious."

"Lacey...I don't know."

Lacey sat up completely, awake and alert. And, oh God, on a mission. "You could be close to Will."

"What makes you think that's a plus?"

"The bra in the outfield."

She'd never live that down. "A little trip around the bases does not a relationship make."

Lacey looked skyward. "You are so into him, why are you lying to yourself? And he's like...wow. He adores you. It's all over his face. He couldn't even string a noun and a verb together to make a sentence in the sub meeting yesterday."

"That's not because of me." That was because of what Guy did.

"Bull."

"It's not, but listen, taking your job offer is not about Will. Or any man. Not that there really is any other man to consider, but—"

"Of course there is."

"No." She gave Lacey a serious look. "I'm not seeing anyone in L.A. Not even clients," she added with a rueful laugh.

"That's not the man I meant. I meant your father."

"Oh. Him. I'm putting him in a home." Wasn't she?

Lacey's look was sheer compassion and possibly a little mind reading. "Are you certain about that?"

Maybe she should go get the pictures hidden in her bureau and put the whole conversation to bed. "Relatively certain."

"Because Zoe said…"

"What?"

She shrugged, sliding her feet to the floor and slipping them into flip-flops. "Nothing. She was mistaken."

"What did Zoe say, Lace?"

"She thought you might be changing your mind, is all. I think she's developing a soft spot for the old guy." Lacey stood, smoothed her wrinkled top, and pulled out her phone to glance at a text. "Clay's going to meet me and walk home with me," she said.

"Okay." Jocelyn stood to hug her friend, holding her tighter and longer than she held most people. "I'm honored that you think I have this job in me."

"Are you kidding? The place would be run like a German U-boat. But it's more than that," she said, reaching up to cup Jocelyn's face. "You need to take risks, Joss. You need to take chances. If you don't, you're always going to be protected."

"And you think this new job is the risk I need to take?"

"This new job and..." Lacey pulled her closer to give her a kiss on the cheek. "Will Palmer."

"I'll think about it," she promised. Then, after a second, she smiled. "I'll make some lists."

Lacey laughed. "Excellent sign." Her phone vibrated. "There's my man. See you tomorrow."

Jocelyn let her out the front door and waved to Clay, who walked down the path with a tiny flashlight beam bouncing with each step. She watched them greet each other with a kiss, then waved good night.

When she closed the door, she stood for a long time leaning against it, her hands pressed on the gleaming wood, imagining the hands that had made that wood.

On her.

Yes, if she took the job, she'd be near Will. *And* Guy.

She'd certainly never expected this when she came here for refuge. She might have been safer staying in L.A. and dodging the media.

Still hungry for air, she opened the front door again, frowning when she saw that little light moving down toward the beach. She stepped outside and peered toward the moving light, seeing Clay and Lacey's silhouettes in the cloud-covered moonlight, strolling the beach, stopping to kiss.

That was love and yet there was no fear, no impending doom, no sense that love was a lie. Couldn't Jocelyn look to her best friend as an example instead of her own parents?

Longing squeezed her, stinging her eyes, burning her stomach. Envy, flat out and so real, grabbed hold and took complete ownership.

What would it be like to trust a man like that? What would it be like to believe in that kind of love? What would it be like...with Will?

Good God, she never wanted anything so much in her life. What was stopping her, except Guy?

On every level, it was her father who had stolen that kind of happiness from her. Would putting him away in one of those places free her? Would taking him out of the picture open her heart to possibilities?

No. She'd have to forgive and forget. One she couldn't and the other she wouldn't.

The soft ring of Lacey's laughter floated over the sand, like music in the moonlight, a reminder of what Jocelyn could never, ever have but wanted more than she'd ever realized.

Chapter Twenty-four

Jocelyn had risen at 4:00 a.m. and launched into the mother of all lists, feeling a little less burdened by the time the sun came up. Sitting on the front patio watching the water and sky change from the deep violet of night to shades of morning peach, she smoothed her hands over the pages, satisfied with every action item, priority rating, deadline, and the lovely little boxes reserved for check marks.

She had a plan. Several of them, as a matter of fact, with various strategies dependent on the rollout of different tactics for every one of her pending issues.

She closed her eyes, dropped her head against the cushion, and smiled.

In other words, anything could happen, but she would be ready for whatever it was. Maybe the first thing that should happen was some sleep. Or at least coffee.

"Hey. Wake up."

She popped up with a soft gasp, the sight of Tessa holding two large paper cups as welcome as just about anything she could have imagined.

"My supreme sacrifice for you," Tessa said, climbing the two steps to join Jocelyn and hand her a cup. "I'm drinking nonorganic Lipton from the Super Min instead of my usual Nepalese black tea brewed exclusively in the Himalayas. You, however, get Charity Grambling's finest."

"You could be carrying motor oil and I'd drink it right now," Jocelyn said, scooting over to make room on the patio seat. "Bless you, child. There's a coffeemaker in there, but I think I need to grind beans." She sipped, closing her eyes in pleasure. "Call me crazy, but I like Charity's coffee. This is early even for you organic farmers, isn't it?"

"Mmm. I didn't sleep well."

"That makes two of us," Jocelyn said, but added a gentle pat on Tessa's leg, so tanned and toned under her work shorts. "I make lists when I can't sleep." She angled her head toward the stack of paper she'd placed on the end table.

"I know that," Tessa said. "I was your roommate in college, remember?"

"What do you do when you can't sleep?" Jocelyn frowned. "Not that I remember you ever having a problem with that."

Tessa shrugged. "I go dig in the dirt, of course, which is where I am headed. Want to come and help me plant the next cycle of bok choy and kale or just take a walk on the beach?"

Jocelyn heard the subtext: *I need to talk to a friend.*
"I'll walk the beach with you."

Taking their cups, they crossed the path and maneuvered through the sea oats. The tide was low, leaving a huge expanse of untouched cool, cream-colored sand peppered with a colorful array of shells.

"Good day for collecting shells," Tessa mused.

"Perfect." The coral reef and sandbar hidden under the calm waters of Barefoot Bay offered up plentiful and exquisite shells with each high tide, and when the waters receded, collectors could score.

"I bet every single person who stays here takes home a few as souvenirs."

"Can't blame them." The thought left a little impression on Jocelyn's heart, the slightest longing to be here when those guests discovered all the secrets of Barefoot Bay.

"I'm so grateful Lacey got to keep all this land and do the right thing with it," Tessa mused. "I mean, I know development was inevitable after that hurricane, but at least Casa Blanca is going to be natural and built to respect the environment, not destroy it."

"It's going to be a great place," Jocelyn agreed. "One of a kind."

Tessa gave her a sideways look. "Great enough to lure you here?"

Jocelyn laughed softly. "It seems Lacey's suggestion has turned into the talk of the town."

"Don't worry. I didn't tell Charity or it would be. Are you even tempted to consider it, Joss?"

Why lie? "A little." A lot. "It's complicated."

"Moving from L.A., leaving your business, and

starting a whole new job?" Tessa asked. "Complicated would be an understatement. But I'm so happy to hear you're considering it."

"I wouldn't go as far as 'considering,' but, well, let's put it this way, it merited a few lines on my morning lists."

"Cool." Tess waited a few beats, then gave Jocelyn a sideways look. "Who's going to bring this up first?"

"About Lacey?"

Tessa nodded. "I'm only a little mad that she told you first."

Jocelyn sipped her coffee with one hand and put her free arm around Tessa. "She didn't tell me. It kind of slipped out."

Tessa didn't answer, looking down as though she were interested in the shells and letting her hair cover her face. Jocelyn dipped a little so she could get a good look at her friend. "Is that all you're mad about?"

Tessa paused, sipping her tea and making a face when the offensive taste hit her tongue. "God, I'm not mad. I'm just, you know..."

"I do know," Jocelyn assured her. "You feel like crap and, worse, you feel guilty about it. You know you should be all kinds of happy for Lacey—and you are—but you hear the clock ticking and you're not quite ready to accept the fact that you may never have your own baby."

Tessa slid her a look. "Do you have to be so raw and honest?"

"Am I right?"

No answer.

"You want euphemisms and platitudes?" Jocelyn asked. "You want me to dance around the truth? Or do you want to solve your problems?"

"Just my luck to pick the hard-ass control-freak life coach to talk to in my time of need."

"It's not like this is the first time we've talked about it, Tess. And I'm not a hard ass."

"You're tough."

Was she? "I don't feel so tough right now, but I am a life coach, so making someone look at the truth is usually my default mode. And a list," she added with a smile.

"What would be on my list?"

"Your problems."

Tessa shook her head, a soft breeze lifting one of her golden-oak colored waves. "I don't have any problems, Joss. I love my new job, I love living here on Mimosa Key."

"Your ex-husband is a baby-making machine and you want one more than you want your next breath and your closest friend and co-worker just announced she's pregnant at thirty-six."

"Seven. Which should give me hope; Lacey's a few years older than we are."

"You don't need hope, honey—you need an action plan."

"I need a new uterus."

Jocelyn puffed out some air, not quite sure how to respond to that, because Tessa was so dead set on having her own baby, not someone else's.

"And I could use a husband."

"So traditional for an organic tea-drinking hippie like you."

"I'm not a hippie!" Tessa leaned her shoulder into Jocelyn to nudge her hard. "My parents were, but I'm just…"

Jocelyn waited, knowing the next word would be the closest thing to the truth.

"Desperate," Tessa admitted on a sigh.

"Aw, Tess." Desperation was the worst. "You know you have options."

"I don't want to do it alone, and honestly, I had a husband, remember? I can't get pregnant for love or money. We tried both."

"Seriously, Tess, why won't you consider adoption?"

She shook her head. "It's not what I want." She stopped, looking down at a grouping of shells, then she bent over to pick one up. "Look at this. Pure perfection."

"Throw it away," Jocelyn said.

"Why?"

"Just toss it as far as you can."

"I like it. I want to keep it." She stuffed her hand into her pocket. "Since I moved here, I've been collecting them. I met a local artist who's kind of a shell expert, and he makes—"

"He? Interesting."

"Shut up. He makes these amazing pieces and I thought I might try my hand—"

"Throw it away," Jocelyn ordered.

Tessa stared at her, their gazes locked. "Fine." Yanking it back out of her pocket, she whipped the shell over her shoulder and angled her head. "And your point is?"

"That could be your baby."

"Oh, please."

"I'm serious. Some perfect baby is being...let go today. Somewhere, someone is having a baby that needs a good mother. That child is out there, like one of these shells, waiting for you."

Tessa started to argue, then closed her mouth, shaking her head. "I've heard the argument and I'm not going to change my mind. If you think that makes me some kind of selfish monster, then—"

"Of course it doesn't. It makes you a liar. You don't want *a* baby. You want *your* baby. Your body won't cooperate. So let go of the dream or adopt a baby."

"You should talk about being a liar."

Jocelyn almost spewed her sip of coffee. "Excuse me?"

"Telling your father you're with *Clean House.*"

"I tried to tell him who I was and it didn't sink in. Don't try to make that whole charade my fault. I'm just going along with what Will wants. For now, anyway."

"Will wants you."

"Oh, Tess. Will knows too much about me."

"And that's a problem?" She choked, incredulous. "Look at it another way. He knows everything you've been through and he still cares about you. Maybe more because of it. That's a gift, Joss. That's a rare and wonderful—Oh my God, look. A fighting conch."

Tessa loped away, scooping a shell from the ground.

"What is it?" Jocelyn asked.

"A rare beauty." She flipped the shell on its back, still studying it. "This type of shell is found almost exclusively in the southern U.S. Barefoot Bay has some of the most exquisite conchs in the country."

"I didn't know that."

She held it up to the sun. "That orange iridescence means the animal that lived in this shell was hearty and maybe got into a few scrapes down at the bottom of the sea."

"Whoa. Sounds like someone's been spending an awful lot of time with the local shell expert."

"Who's about fifty-five. Can it."

Jocelyn smiled and reached for the shell. "Let me see. This is a keeper, huh?"

Tessa pulled away. "Not a chance I'm going to give you this so you can toss it and make some life-coaching point."

Laughing, Jocelyn reached for it. "I just want to see it. I swear."

"You do?" Tessa's soft brown eyes glinted. "Fine. Open your hand."

She was up to something. Still, Jocelyn obliged, palm up, and Tessa set the shell right in the middle of her hand.

"This, my friend, is a keeper." Tessa was so serious and quiet that her voice made the fine hairs on the back of Jocelyn's neck rise. "Maybe a little flawed, but still great looking." Tessa traced the soft rim of the shell. "The edges are just worn enough to know this one's been in the sea for a long time, but it's still beautiful and will last for several thousand more days before time and sand and wind break it down."

Jocelyn looked at her, sensing exactly where this was going. "Will?"

Tessa lifted one shoulder. "You can throw it back in the sea, if you like. But it is being offered to you to keep."

Jocelyn rolled her eyes. "You've gone from coaching to melodrama."

"I'm making a point using a seashell, just like you did."

"Are you giving this to me?" Jocelyn asked.

"Yeah. I am."

She leaned in and gave Tessa a kiss on the cheek. "Then I won't throw it away. And, Tess? For a gardener, you're not a bad life coach."

She laughed. "Speaking of gardens, you want to walk up there with me?"

Jocelyn shook her head. "I think I'll stay down here until the sun rises and then get to my list."

" 'Kay. Thanks for the advice."

"Same here."

They gave a quick hug and Tessa took off, but Jocelyn stood for a long time looking at the Gulf, holding her shell and thinking.

She wanted Will. She wanted him in every imaginable way.

What was stopping her? Looking down at her hand, she studied the shell. Damn it, she was so sick of shells. Especially the one around her heart.

Chapter Twenty-five

⌒

The garage was done and the sun was up.

Amazing.

Will stepped out into the morning light of the drive-way, surveying his work, satisfied with the results of six hours of hard labor. The attic was cleaned out. The garage was empty except for some boxes and a half dozen bags of trash. And Guy hadn't even gotten up yet.

At the sound of an engine slowing he turned, surprised to see the Lee County sheriff's car pulling into Guy's driveway with Deputy Slade Garrison at the wheel.

"Morning, Will," Slade said as he rolled down the window.

"Slade. What's up?"

"Just checking in, making sure you haven't had any problem with the media."

"Why? Have they been around again?" Not that he

needed any more reason to accelerate his plan, but those guys would certainly give him one.

"Charity said they stopped in again, and I heard a couple of guys were in the Toasted Pelican last night asking about Jocelyn."

"Shit," he mumbled, putting a hand on the car roof to block the sun from Slade's face. "Anyone say anything?"

"Very few people know she's here."

"Charity does." And that would normally be like putting it on the front page of the *Mimosa Gazette*.

"Well, she's keeping this secret," Slade said. "For whatever reason."

Will knew the reason. Charity had been the one to pick up the pieces when Will had let them all fall apart. Guilt kicked him, as sure and strong as it had all night while he'd packed up Guy's house.

"How is the old guy?" Slade asked, his gaze following Will's to the garage.

"Moving into assisted living very soon."

Slade nodded. "Guess it's true, then, what I heard."

Will gave him a questioning look.

"So many rumors why 'Big Guy' left the force so young, even before his pension kicked in," Slade explained, air-quoting the former sheriff's nickname.

Will didn't react; now he knew why "Big Guy" had left the force: Charity's blackmail pictures. "Some of the older guys said he had trouble and started mentally slipping on the job," Slade continued.

"Must have," Will said, not interested in sharing the truth with the young man. "I really appreciate you keeping an eye out on things, Slade."

"Not a problem. Plus, it seems to make Charity happy and I'm trying to get in good with that whole family."

"Looks to me like you're in good with her niece."

Slade grinned. "Workin' on it, buddy. How about you and Jocelyn?"

Was it that obvious? "Workin' on it, buddy."

"Even though she had an affair with that movie star?"

Irritation rocked him. "She didn't. It's all a lie."

Slade's brows lifted. "Sure going to a lot of trouble to hide from the media if that actress is lying. And the guy? Miles? He's kind of letting on that it's true."

His fists balled like he was going to give a good punch to his catcher's mitt. "He is?"

"Don't you read these rags you're so busy hiding from?" Slade turned to the passenger seat and grabbed a paper, shoving it at Will. "You ought to."

"Thought Charity wasn't selling these."

"Gloria gave it to me."

Will took the tabloid but didn't look at it. "I'll use this to wrap Guy's dishes," he said. " 'Cause I don't have a dog who could shit on it."

Laughing, Slade put the car in Reverse. "Do whatever you want with it, Will. But you should know things are only getting worse for her. I'll watch this street as long as I can, but those guys..." He nodded toward the paper. "They're going to be relentless until she makes some kind of statement. Maybe you could convince her to do that."

Maybe he'd be playing in the World Series next year, too. "I'll try," he said, backing away just as another car came down Sea Breeze.

Slade used his side-view mirror to check the car. "There she is now. Perfect timing."

He pulled out and Jocelyn drove into the empty drive-way, her window down, her hair blown, her expression oddly happy.

Will rolled the tabloid and ignored a jolt of pleasure as he opened her door. "Good morning, gorgeous."

She smiled, stepping out, then tilted her head to get a good look at him. "I wish I could say the same thing."

"Ouch."

"Tough night, Will?"

He dragged his hand through his hair and rubbed his unshaven cheeks. Yeah, he probably looked like hell. "I will show you exactly how tough. Brace yourself, Ms. Bloom. I have a surprise."

With the hand that held the paper, he put his arm around her and walked her toward the garage. "Never let it be said that I'm not a man of action, or one who can't make a decision."

Inside the garage, he waved a hand to the boxes and bags, everything but the very top of the loft empty. "I emptied the attic, too. And you did the kitchen and dining room. All that's left is a few closets in the house. Oh, and I signed up for two more tours at assisted-living places, so I figure we can have him settled somewhere by next week."

She stilled, turning toward him. "This is quite a one-eighty you've done. You're a life coach's dream." She took a step closer, tentatively reaching for his face. If she touched him it'd all be over. Her fingers barely grazed his unshaven cheek.

"I'd like to be a life coach's dream," he said. "If you're the life coach."

Her eyes widened, and her whole body kind of stilled. "Will, I…"

"Listen, Joss." He stopped her by taking her shoulders and holding tight. "Last night at the baseball field was…" *Life-changing.* "Really nice with you. And when we came home, and found Guy throwing that little temper tantrum, I knew I couldn't drag my heels on this anymore."

She searched his face, taking in each word. "This change of heart isn't just because of—of the pictures? Of what happened that night?"

"Partially," he admitted. "I'm pissed beyond words and I kind of feel duped by him."

"He can't help that he doesn't remember."

He inched back, trying to process that statement. "Look who's had a change of heart."

"No, no." She shook her head. "I really don't have a choice where he's concerned, but I agree." She slipped out of his grasp and walked toward the garage storage loft, pointing to the boxes up there. "So that stuff is all that's left out here?"

Behind her, he tossed the newspaper on top of an open carton, unwilling to change the direction of this encounter by talking about the media and Miles Thayer. The sooner they got Guy moved out, the sooner they could get past him and on to the next problem.

Action felt good, he realized, watching her grab the ladder rails and hoist herself up, looking over her shoulder as she climbed.

"Why are you smiling?" she asked.

"Nice view," he said, nodding toward her backside.

She made a face and climbed and he followed, both of them crouching over so they didn't hit the ceiling as they made their way to the two cartons he'd left in the back corner.

"I have no idea what those are," he said. "I tried to lift them and they weigh a ton, so I figured I'd go through them and throw stuff away or sort."

Jocelyn made her way over, then settled next to the boxes, swiping at some cobwebs and brushing off a few that must have hit her face. "These came out of my mother's closet after she died."

"Oh." He sat next to her. "I didn't know."

She put a hand on top of one of the boxes but made no move to open it. "When I came home for her funeral, these boxes were all packed. I don't know if Guy did it or what, but I never looked through them."

"You want to now?" He put a hand on her back, sensing her hesitation. "We don't have to."

"I do have to," she said. "It's all I have of her."

"No it's not, Joss. You have your memories."

She sighed as if those didn't satisfy much. "All right. I'm ready. Open 'er up." She put her hand on his arm. "But be warned, I might need...comfort."

He leaned over and kissed her on the cheek. "You got it."

The soft scent of a spicy perfume mixed with the musky smell of old clothes when Will stripped the duct tape off the carton and opened the flap. He pulled out a stack of sweaters and gave her a questioning look.

"I doubt we can sell these," she said, taking the pastel-colored pile. "They're kind of dated."

"Oh," Will said, reaching deeper into the box. "This is what weighed so much."

Jocelyn got up on her knees, sneezing softly. "What is it?"

"Furniture. A small wooden cabinet." He reached in

and wedged his hands on either side of a large box. "Weird. Why put this in a carton? Have you seen it before?"

"I don't think so. Here. I'll hold the box, you pull it out."

With a little effort, they maneuvered out a stunning rosewood cabinet a couple of feet wide with two drawers.

"Wow, this is nice," Will said, grazing the polished wood. "Handmade by a pro. You've never seen this before?"

She shook her head.

Will tugged on the brass knob. "It's like an old fashioned..." He pulled the drawer out. "Baby's dresser."

Full of baby clothes. Tiny, newborn, brand-new *blue* baby clothes.

Jocelyn's fingers shook as she reached for the wee navy blue sleeper with a baseball bat on the front. "Are these yours, by some chance?" she asked.

"No clue. Why would they be in your garage?"

"I don't know," she said, taking out one precious piece after another. "Weird. The tags are still on them."

They'd been folded with love, neatly lined up and separated by tissue paper. The top drawer was all onesies and tiny sleepers with feet.

The bottom drawer had little-boy T-shirts with trucks and trains, tiny shorts no bigger than her hand, socks, and three little pairs of booties.

"I should give these to Lacey," Jocelyn said. "But I don't know whose they are."

"Are you sure this box was left when your mother died?"

She nodded. "I distinctly remember seeing it come out of my parents' bedroom, all taped up by my father." She lifted the last layer of clothes to find a blue satin baby book. "Oh. Maybe this'll tell us something."

The spine cracked when she opened it as if it had never been used. But there was handwriting on the first page. Her mother's distinctive sideways scrawl. The words tore a gasp from Jocelyn's throat.

Alexander Michael Bloom, Jr.

Laid to Rest January 19, 1986

She'd had a brother? The words swam in her vision. How was this possible? She tore her gaze from the book to Will's eyes, his expression as shocked and confused as hers must have been.

"You were, what, seven years old?" he asked.

She couldn't speak, just nodded.

"And they had a baby you didn't know about?"

That wasn't possible. Her throat felt like someone had a hand around her neck and wouldn't stop squeezing. Very slowly, she turned the pages of a book created with the express purpose of memorializing a baby's life.

Baby's Earliest Days! A grainy, faded sonogram print-out on yellowed paper, far blurrier than the kind they used nowadays, was taped to the page. In the corner the letters had almost disappeared with time, but Jocelyn could make out the words.

Bloom baby boy. December 9, 1985

"Oh my God, Will." The words came out like a rasp of pain as she turned the page.

Mommy's Growing Too! A list of months from August to January with a number and a pound sign had been inserted in her mother's writing. Chills blossomed over her whole body despite the heat of the garage. Will turned the next page for her, but every single line was empty.

Baby Arrives! But that page was empty. No date, no pictures, no words.

Baby's First Bath! Blank. *Baby's Sits Up!* Blank. *Baby Can Crawl!* Blank.

Page after page of the saddest story never told. Never told *to Jocelyn*. The thought slammed her. "He must have been stillborn. Why didn't they tell me? I never even knew she was pregnant."

"You were only seven, Joss. You couldn't handle it."

"But later? When I got older." She spread her hand on the blank page reserved for *Baby's Growth Chart*, digging back into her memory banks and coming up as blank as the page. "Why wouldn't my mother have told me she was carrying—and lost—a baby boy?"

"I don't know," he said, turning a page. "Too painful, I guess."

And then a memory teased. "She went to the hospital when I was in second grade," she said, staring ahead, digging for truth. "They told me she had appendicitis. She must have been"—she flipped back to the sonogram and squinted at the old computerized numbers, quickly doing math—"about five months pregnant and lost the baby. I vaguely recall my grandparents came down from up north and stayed for a few days until she came home."

"Do you remember how she handled it?"

"No, but that's when Guy's episodes started." She blinked away the tears, clarity and understanding dawning.

This was what had made him snap. This was why he'd grown violent and moody. And why—oh, God. Realization dawned. "This is why he thinks you are his son who he was told was gone forever."

He just closed his eyes at the direct hit.

She flipped to the last page, tucked in a pocket for

keepsakes marked *Baby's First Hair*, a piece of paper was folded in half.

With a glance at Will, she drew it out, her hands trembling as the meaning of this settled on her heart. As she opened the paper, she swallowed hard at the sight of her father's distinctive handwriting.

"He wrote this," she said, her voice as wobbly as the rest of her.

Will put his arm all the way around her, holding her tight. "Let's read it together."

To my son…

She closed her eyes and let out a soft whimper.

"It's a poem," Will said, tucking her closer and letting her rest against him.

After a minute, she opened her eyes and read.

> *Today we said goodbye to you*
> *A little man I never knew.*
> *I wanted you to be my friend*
> *But now those plans will have to end.*

Jocelyn covered her mouth to hold back the sob. Will stroked her arm until she could bear to read the rest.

> *Even though you were never here*
> *I love you, son, my little dear.*
> *There are no words for all this pain*
> *No way to stop the grief and rain.*
> *Goodbye. Goodbye. Good…*

That was it.

"Who knew he wrote bad poetry?" Will asked wistfully.

She almost smiled. "The man who loves needlepoint and decorating shows? He was always in there. Always." But then that man had changed. He became a wifebeater. "He must have blamed my mother," Jocelyn said as pieces fell into place. "He must have cracked and taken out all this agony on her." She choked back the tears, turning to Will. "I shouldn't have hated him so much."

"It's no excuse," Will said quietly. "Do you want to go talk to him?"

"What good would that do? He doesn't remember. He doesn't remember anything. Not this unborn child, not me, not my mother, not what he did. He sure as hell won't remember these clothes or this cabinet." Her voice rose with each word, squeezing her, choking her.

She pushed up, desperate for air. Without a word, she scrambled to the side of the loft.

"Where are you going?" he asked.

"I need to breathe. I need to think." *I need to reevaluate everything I thought was true.* "I just need..." Her words trailing off, she got to the bottom of the ladder and took off, aching to get out of the garage.

A stillborn baby boy. That could change a man and a marriage. It could transform a family from a happy one that went fishing in a rowboat to one that fought over fresh flowers.

Will was right. It was no excuse for what he'd done, but it was an explanation. And for some reason she didn't quite understand, she wanted to cling to it.

She hit the grass of the side yard, walking without thinking, picking up speed, not entirely sure where she was going until she found herself standing at the back door of the Palmers' house, the one that led up to Will's room.

He was next to her in seconds, wrapping his arms around her, cradling her with comfort, just like always.

She looked up at him. "I need to go back up there."

"In the garage?" he asked.

"Up there." She pointed to the room. "I need you to hold me."

Without a word, he opened the door and guided her up the narrow stairs where she'd long ago let him go and led her right to the comfort of his old Dodgers blanket.

Chapter Twenty-six

Judging by the sun pouring into the bedroom window, Jocelyn and Will had slept for at least a few hours. Her legs were wrapped around his, her face pressed against his shoulder. She woke with a funny feeling in her heart, a mix of bone-deep exhaustion and something like freedom.

Was she free now?

It sure felt like it. Her whole being felt lighter, despite the news that twenty-seven years ago she'd lost a baby brother. Guy must have cracked; maybe her mother had inadvertently caused the miscarriage and Guy just couldn't forgive her.

No, it wasn't an excuse, she realized that. Nothing got him a pass for what he'd inflicted on both of them, but somehow, some way, Jocelyn felt like a chain had been unlocked from around her chest and she could breathe again.

When they'd come up here, she'd babbled and sniffled

and sobbed like a fool, and Will did what Will did best: he'd held her. And then they fell asleep, in spite of the fact that they'd spent the night apart, restless and longing for each other. Or maybe because of it.

She sighed and nestled a little deeper into his side, her arm draped over his chest, her hair spilling over her cheeks. She couldn't see his face from this angle but didn't want to risk moving and waking him.

So instead of looking at him, she just let the musky, masculine scent of Will fill her head.

Stinks like sweat, grass, and a hint of reliability?

No. It smells like comfort.

The words were as clear as if the exchange that took place in this very room had been last night, not fifteen years ago. She'd loved him then and she—

What exactly did she feel now?

Come on, Joss. *You love him. You've* always *loved him.* Curling her fingers around the comforter, she pulled it higher, loving the softness of the old blue blanket, the symbol of his ultimate dream team.

Which was funny; he'd hate L.A. Just like she did.

She blinked at the thought. She'd always acknowledged her issues with the crowded, glitzy mess that was Los Angeles, but did she actually hate living there? Maybe she hadn't realized that until she came here, which was, for better or worse, her home.

So why go back? Why not just settle right here, in these arms, with this man, in a new job, with a new life, and even a new father?

Now that she knew the truth, could she possibly forgive Guy? Maybe not, but she could tiptoe past her pain and maybe get to a better place with him. Couldn't she?

Yes. Because she could do absolutely anything for Will. Even forgive Guy.

At the thought, an unfamiliar joy warmed her from the very deepest place. It felt radiant, real, and so unshakable.

Was this love? This sense of certainty? That desire to do anything for someone else? This feeling that life couldn't get any better, combined with the awareness that it would?

Yes. This was most definitely love.

The realization made her shift in Will's arms, stretching along his hard side, sliding her leg over his, positioning herself to watch this gorgeous man wake up and grow erect at the same time. Talk about watching the sun rise.

Under her thigh, his manhood twitched and throbbed. A low groan pulled at his chest and he turned to meet her gaze.

"Why is this woman smiling?"

She just rubbed her thigh over his erection, a zing of anticipation and nervousness fighting her own twitches of arousal. "Because she's happy."

He frowned a little. "You went to sleep crying."

She chafed his hard-on again. "You went to sleep flaccid."

He made a face. "That's an ugly word."

"There's nothing ugly about..." She lowered her hand and rubbed over his tented shorts. "This."

His features shifted from sleepy to sexy as he hissed in a breath. Her gaze drifted over his face, settling on his mouth, stirring everything in her low and deep. Her thighs tightened and her breasts seemed to swell and ache.

"I'm ready," she whispered.

He had no idea exactly what those words meant. And

right now, that was fine. Someday she'd tell him; maybe soon. But if she made a big announcement now, he'd get all weird.

She didn't want weird. She wanted him.

He shifted a little to accommodate the erection and when he did, she started to untangle their legs, but Will squeezed his together, pinning her calf between his.

"You're ready?"

"The long wait is over." So, so over. She couldn't help smiling. She'd made the right decision. There'd been plenty of near misses, plenty of pissed-off almost-boyfriends, plenty of nights when she wanted to lose control but couldn't or wouldn't or chickened out.

But she was finally ready.

"Oh, Jossie." He stroked her face, brushing her hair back. "My beautiful, sweet, strong, sexy Bloomerang. I knew you'd come back to me."

Time and space hung suspended like a curtain about to fall. Her heart slammed. Her breath caught. Her whole body tensed in anticipation.

No more waiting.

He kissed her so hard their teeth tapped, both of them sucking in the breath they'd been holding. Open-mouthed, their tongues touched and explored as they moved into the most natural position, body to body, almost instantly starting to rock in a heavenly rhythm.

"I can't wait anymore, Joss," he admitted with a rasp, already letting his hands begin to roam her body. "I can't wait."

"Don't." She kissed his neck and slid her hands over his chest, as desperate as he was. "Don't wait. Don't stop. Do whatever you want. Do . . . everything."

He rolled her onto her back, shifting on top of her so he could press his whole body into the kiss. He didn't bother getting under her shirt, but stripped it off in one satisfying move that she almost instantly mirrored with his T-shirt.

His hand quivered as he took off her bra and closed his palm over her breast, letting out a helpless groan as he lowered his head to take her nipple in his mouth.

Why had she waited for this?

Because it had to be Will. It *had* to be.

He licked her nipple until she budded under his tongue, then went back to her mouth, her cheeks, her throat, her ears. All the while they pumped against each other in an age-old beat of need and desire.

Desire that usually took her to a dark place. But this time all she felt was awe and relief and more desire. With a soft moan of joy, she let him roll her over again so she was on top, and her hair tumbled toward his face.

Sitting up, she straddled his hard-on and unzipped her shorts, staring at him, taking a million mental snapshots, wanting this extraordinary, perfect moment to last. Wanting so much to make up for the big black hole of longing and waiting that had consumed her for the last fifteen years.

She slid off him to slip out of her shorts, and he ripped off his, and then, for a span of about ten seconds, they lay naked, but not touching.

She smiled, touching his lips with her finger. "The wait is over, Will Palmer. Make love to me."

He kissed her finger and closed his eyes. "That's like...confetti at the World Series parade. Nothing could feel better than those words."

Laughing, she drew her finger in and out of his lips. "Something could."

"You're right." Very slowly, as tenderly as he could, he laid her back down, taking a moment to caress her breasts and slide his hand over her body and down one thigh.

She moaned with pleasure, lifting her hips to invite his touch.

"My Jocelyn," he whispered as he trailed his finger from her belly button down to her very center.

His Jocelyn.

"I am," she whispered, looking up at him, fighting not to completely lose control and buck wildly like she wanted to.

"My best friend." He touched the most tender part of her, making her suck in a breath, but still she maintained control. "My girl next door." He lowered his head and kissed her stomach while his finger slipped inside her a little deeper. "My lover."

"Finally." The word turned into a half-gasp when his tongue flicked over her.

"I love your body," he murmured, kissing and sucking gently.

Answering with another moan, she dug her fingers into his hair and held his head where she wanted it. Pleasure exploded through her, so different from the quick release she'd had last night. This was intense, alive, deep. Hot flames licked all over her skin and every cell sparked.

"I love..." Her stomach tightened in anticipation, knowing he would say it now. He'd said it all those years ago. Will had no problem professing his love.

But instead of saying anything more, he opened his mouth over her, slipped his tongue inside, and nearly detonated her with one stroke. Arousal punched so hard her head buzzed with the loss of blood. Control evaporated, leaving only shreds of awareness, everything so insanely focused *there.* With a long, desperate cry of pure pleasure, she bucked against him, coming mercilessly against his mouth.

Still clawing through each breath, she pulled him back up, letting him kiss every inch he could find until their lips met.

She tried to talk, but another little aftershock stole her voice, so she looked up at him, barely able to get the next strangled breath. "What are the chances, Will?"

Really, what were the chances that she could have waited all these years and they would finally find their way back to this room to make love for the first time? It was as if, in the back of her mind, she knew. She *knew.* For as many times as she had questioned her own sanity, made a hundred excuses, and even lied about her sex life, she *knew.*

It had to be Will.

"You mean what are the chances that there's a condom handy?"

No, she didn't mean that at all, but she wasn't ready to tell him yet. Knowing Will, it would completely throw the game, and she wanted him now. All of him, inside her.

He reached over to the side of the bed to lift his shorts from the floor. He shook them and his phone fell with a clunk, followed by his wallet. "After last night? My wallet is stocked."

He put on the condom, then got on top of her, holding her gaze as he slipped the tip against her still electrified womanhood.

And she knew: She should tell him. It was *wrong* not to tell him. He'd be happy. What guy wouldn't want to be the first?

She took a breath and said, "I have to tell you something."

A hint of frustration darkened his eyes as he throbbed against her. "*Now?*"

"Yes. Before I . . . we . . . before you're inside me, you have to know something." She reached up and touched his face. How would he take this?

"Joss, I'm showing more control and restraint than I even knew I had. Just say it, sweetheart. Say it. Tell me you love me."

She bit her lip and lifted her hips, the move so natural. Because this was the way it was supposed to be. She loved him. She *loved* him. And really, at this moment, this close to the brink, that was *all* he needed to know. "I love you, Will Palmer."

A slow, beautiful, completely heartfelt smile curled his lips. "Yeah?"

"Always have, always will."

"Now that was worth waiting for."

So was this.

Will gritted his teeth to keep from plowing forward, inch after mind-blowing inch of tightness wrapping around him, making him want to scream. She was so damn tight.

But he held back, watching her face, taking his cues, seeing her bite her lip to make him wonder if she felt more pain than pleasure at their coupling. Still, blind with need, braced on the bed, he went deeper until he was all the way inside her.

"Are you okay?" he asked.

She bit her lip again, nodding, working for each breath. He wanted to stop, or at least slow down, but each stroke was more incredible than the last, each plunge taking him closer to release.

"Will." She pulled at him, her legs wrapped around him as their bodies moved and met perfectly. "Come closer. Come closer."

His face nuzzled in her hair, her lips next to his ear. "Listen to me," she whispered, her voice as insanely sexy as the body he was lost inside.

He barely nodded, blood pumping and pulsing, his breathing so fast and hard he could hardly hear her.

"Will." She squeezed him harder, her movements slower and more controlled. "Listen to me," she said again. "I want to tell you something. I have to."

Let her talk. Say what she wanted. All he wanted was this insane pleasure that was about to—

"I've never..."

He shook his head, unable to hear her through the rushing blood. No words got through as sweet and silky morphed into fast and frenetic, the sounds of their breath and their bodies like a deafening whoosh that pulsed and screamed and finally spun out of control.

Completely lost in raw, relentless release, he spilled into her, stroke after stroke, pump after pump, a rush so intense he had to damn near howl.

He fell on her, exhausted, depleted, and so fucking happy he could cry. She loved him.

"What did you say, Joss?" he rasped.

"I said...I've never..." She closed her eyes. "Felt anything like that before."

"Me neither. God, you're like, oh..." Somewhere on the floor his phone vibrated. He couldn't move. He couldn't think about anything except how amazing that was. And that she loved him.

She *loved* him.

The phone vibrated again.

"You going to get that?" she asked.

He managed to move his eyes to look at her. "No."

One more time the phone vibrated, then the call moved to voice mail.

"Go ahead," she urged. "I understand."

"Nothing is more important than you." Than what she'd just given him.

"It might be Guy. Does he have any idea where you are?"

Somehow he found the strength to drop his arm to the floor, feel around, and find the phone, dragging it back to the bed to read the caller ID.

Scott Meyers, Sports Management of America.

His agent?

"Is it important?" she asked.

"It's not Guy." But it might have been important. He pressed the number for voice mail, turning to look at her while he put the phone to his ear. Listening to it ring, he traced her jaw with his finger, then her lips.

Lips that had just said she loved him.

Under his touch, she smiled. "I made a decision, Will."

"Hey, bud, where the hell are you? I have news."

Will blinked at her, the buzz saw of his hyperactive agent's voice feeling completely wrong while he was looking at Jocelyn.

"What is it?" He asked her the question, but Scott's message kept rolling.

"Oh, what the hell. I'll tell you. You got an offer, dude."

"I don't want to go back to L.A., Will. I'm taking Lacey's job offer."

"I . . . you don't?"

"The Los Angeles Dodgers, dude! Fuckin' Rancho Cucamonga needs a bull-pen coach. Interview is tomorrow in the AM. Get your ass on the next plane to southern California, Palmer. We did it, man!"

"I want to stay here in Mimosa Key, with you."

There . . . here . . . *what*? His head almost exploded with the conflicting announcements.

"So call me ASAP. They're desperate and we can swing a sweet deal. Congrats, buddy. This is the one you've been waiting for, right?"

Right.

"Will?" Jocelyn perched up on her elbow, searching his face. "Is something wrong?"

Yeah. Something was really wrong. He'd waited too long.

Chapter Twenty-seven

Not so fast with those rash decisions, Joss."

Something in Will's voice unraveled everything inside her, his face falling fast as she told him her plans and he listened to someone's message. All her words, promises, pledges, and heartfelt announcements about love just fizzled in the face of a man who just didn't look like he wanted to hear them.

Of course he didn't. What the hell had she been thinking?

Suddenly aware of how naked and open she was, she gathered up the old comforter, her fingers closing around the frayed edge. With the material almost to her nose she felt covered, but the old scent of Will's room made her dizzy, intensified by the unfamiliar, tangy scent of sex and the look of sheer bewilderment on his face.

She cleared her throat, not trusting her voice, but he spoke first. "That was my agent."

"Oh."

He deliberately set the phone on the pillow between them, straightening it like he was buying time.

"Looks like…" His lips twisted in a smile that was more bitter than bright. "The wait is over."

The wait. "For a new job?"

He nodded, slowly, his gaze moving over her face, looking for something, and maybe hiding something, too.

"Wow," she said on a whisper. "That's…" Incredibly bad timing. "Amazing. What is it?"

"Bull-pen coach, minor leagues."

"What you wanted, right?" Except, sometime in the last hour or day or maybe week, she'd decided she wanted him. "You know, everything I just said—"

"Joss." He touched her face again, cupping her jaw, inching his warm body next to hers. "The job's in L.A."

For a moment she wasn't sure she'd heard him right.

"Los Angeles," he confirmed.

"With the Dodgers?" Her fingers clutched the comforter, the Dodger-blue comforter. The physical-embodiment-of-a-childhood-dream comforter.

"The Rancho Cucamonga minor league team."

Holy hell. "That's half an hour drive from my house in Pasadena."

"So, about that decision to stay in Mimosa Key…" He stroked her cheek, curling hair around his finger.

"Yeah, you just complicated it."

"Complicated it? Decision's made." He eliminated whatever space was between them, wrapping a leg over her thigh to cuddle her closer. "We'll go together. We'll *be* together. We'll—"

She put a hand on his lips. "What about Guy?"

"What about him? Our plan is perfect. We'll have him in a ho—"

"It's *our* plan now? Up until Charity Grambling handed you some pictures you were doing your damnedest to convince me that it was a very bad idea, that Guy needed to be at home, with help, and—"

"Everything changed, Jocelyn." He sat up, too. "Everything changed in the last two days. I know what happened—"

"So do I." She backed away, still holding the blanket to cover her. "At least I have a pretty good idea. He snapped when that baby died. In fact, it makes perfect sense. Maybe he blamed my mother, maybe she had an accident, maybe—"

"No," he said sharply. "No. You can't just forgive him that quickly."

She drew back. "You've been asking me to do just that since I arrived. And it's not that quick. He's been different, he's so changed and—"

"No." He took a deep breath like he needed to gather strength to make his point. "This is too perfect. This is meant to be. A job in Los Angeles. With"—he gestured toward the blanket—"my dream team. And you live there. Jocelyn, this is perfect."

"But my father—"

"Kicked the holy crap out of you when you were young and defenseless," he shot back, pushing himself out of the bed now and grabbing a pair of shorts. "And then he threatened to kill me or at least ruin my career, so you made the decision to never speak to me again."

She started to respond, but he waved his hand to stop her. "And, I know, I went along with that, so I'm to blame,

too, but, Jesus, Jocelyn. Fate and the Los Angeles Dodgers baseball franchise may have just handed me everything I ever wanted professionally." He stepped into the
shorts, eyes blazing on her. "And five minutes before that,
you handed me everything I ever wanted personally. And,
damn it, I want both."

"What about what I want?" *One time in bed and he
got all the control?* Anger and resentment fired through
her sex-sated cells. No, it wasn't going to work that way.

He stared at her, as if the question made no sense.
"You said you loved me."

And he'd never said it back. "I was in the middle of a
climax."

He frowned. "Not exactly."

"Close enough." A lie, a complete lie. But he hadn't
said it back, so . . .

"And you said you made a decision not to leave." He
stabbed his hand in his hair, inching back, thinking. "But
you haven't told Laccy, have you? So, we'll just go to L.A."

"Will we?" She shot out the words much harder than
she'd intended.

"Jocelyn, listen to me."

"No." She shook her head. "You can't call the shots
in my life. I don't want to go back there with all that crap
hanging over my head. You can't . . ." *Not go to the Dodgers.* It was unthinkable.

She let out a long breath as the realization of what she
was doing dawned. Once again she held the keys to his
career. Last time she'd let him go have it. But this time?
If she asked him to stay he would, once he gave it some
thought. He was that noble, that loyal, that completely
rock solid and reliable.

And, once again, she knew that the right thing to do was going to hurt like hell.

"When are you going?"

"Right away," he said, reaching for the phone. "The interview is tomorrow morning. I have to call Scott now."

"And I have to..." *Figure out what the hell to do with my life—and with my father.* "Go see my dad."

His eyes flashed at that. "Since when do you call him anything but Guy?"

"Since I found out that he had a great tragedy."

"A miscarriage isn't exactly like he lost *you*."

"But he did lose me."

Will almost choked. "Because he damn near killed you! And he threatened to kill me."

"But before you knew that, you forgave him, Will. You took care of him. You worried about him. You valued him. You..." Did she dare say it? Yes. "You *loved* him."

He just sighed. "But now I know differently."

"So you actually stopped loving him?"

"It made me..." He held his head like it was going to explode. "Yeah, I did. Look, we'll figure it out. We'll put him somewhere. We'll make this work, Jocelyn. I don't want to wa—"

"So you can stop loving someone that easily?" The reality of that made her breathless. "Just because they did one thing you think is wrong? You just walk away?"

"No, I—"

"What if you found out I really *did* have an affair with Miles Thayer?"

His eyes widened almost imperceptibly, but she saw the impact of the question. She didn't care. She had to know. She had to know what he was made of. Because if he wasn't who she hoped he was, then he wasn't worthy of the risk.

When he didn't answer, she pushed harder. "Would you stop caring about me because I did something that was repugnant to you?"

He swallowed. "I don't know why you don't tell the truth."

She had. To him. Wasn't that enough? "You know what your problem is, Will?"

"Guess I'm about to, right?"

"It's all or nothing with you. What did you say you wanted with me? What was the word you used? The word I heard you whisper in the bushes the morning you saw me climbing out of bed in the villa?"

This time his reaction wasn't imperceptible at all. He drew back, frowning. "What did I say?"

"*Everything.* You whispered 'everything,' just like you did in bed half an hour ago. Just like you told me in my villa. You want everything because you are an all-or-nothing kind of guy. There's no gray area."

He crossed his arms and bobbed his head a little, no argument at all. "What the hell's wrong with that?"

"It scares me," she admitted.

"Why?"

"Because if you're willing to walk away from a man you've spent a year and a half nurturing because you found out something he did fifteen years ago, then..." Wasn't it obvious? Did she have to spell it out for him? She looked at him, her bottom lip trapped under her front teeth as she bit down to keep the emotion at bay. "An all-or-nothing man is the worst possible kind for a woman who was raised in a house built on fear."

"Jocelyn." He came closer, holding out his hands. "I would never hurt you."

She just stared at him. "But what if I did something to hurt you? Could you stop loving me that easily?" Like somehow managed not to mention that he'd just taken her virginity?

His expression changed as the wheels turned. "Did you? Is that what you were trying to tell me before?"

Her fingers dug a little deeper into the old comforter, words trapped in her chest.

"Did you sleep with Miles Thayer?" he asked, a hitch in his voice. "Did you have an affair with your client's husband?"

The words cracked with the same impact as her father's ring against her tooth, making her run her tongue along the old familiar chip. "Is that what you think I mean?" she asked.

"Well, did you?" he demanded. "Is that why you don't just get out there and deny it, hiding behind some code of professional ethics instead of defending yourself?"

Oh. She couldn't take this. Looking down, she blinked at the watery Dodgers logo that now mocked her with *comfort*.

"Will. I need to get dressed. Why don't you go downstairs and call your agent and..." *Go follow your Dodger dreams*. "I'll say good-bye before you leave."

"Jocelyn." He reached for her, but she backed away, too hurt to let him touch her. On a frustrated exhale, he dropped his hand.

"Just go, Will."

All the color drained from his face as he stared at her, processing what he assumed was the truth. Let him. It didn't matter that it wasn't the truth.

What mattered was that he thought it was true and, well, with an all-or-nothing kind of guy, that left her with nothing.

Nothing except a father who really needed her.

Jocelyn washed up in Will's bathroom, collected herself, and made a very short mental to-do list. On it was one thing: forgive. Maybe the joy of doing that would ease the ache of Will's obvious doubts about her and hers about him.

She didn't stop downstairs on the way out, but slipped out the back door and crossed their yards. But before she went in to see Guy, she walked around the front—and froze midstep when something flashed in the distance. Like glass catching the sunlight.

Like a camera lens.

She dodged behind the protection of the house, crouching down behind a hedge to see a car drive slowly down Sea Breeze, the back window partially open, a telephoto lens sticking out of the back.

When the car was out of sight, she ran into the garage and slammed the button to close the door. Damn it. They'd found her. She had to get Guy out of here and up to Barefoot Bay, where they'd be safe. Clay wouldn't let anyone on Casa Blanca property and they could wait this out up there.

But for how long? How long until she was yesterday's news? How long until people forgot? Will certainly hadn't forgotten.

The thought plagued her as she pulled herself back up to the loft and bent over to creep back to the box they'd opened.

She scooped up as many of the clothes as she could

hold, and the baby book with Guy's poem tucked inside. Maybe she'd very carefully get him to look at this; maybe it would jog a memory.

On her way back down, she scanned the garage for an empty box. Just inside the garage door she saw the perfect-sized carton with newspaper lying on top. That'd work, she thought, carrying the clothes to it.

And, once again, she stopped cold.

This time it wasn't the camera, but the headlines that sucker-punched. Headlines that Will had been reading while he packed.

Miles Misses His Life...Coach!

She blinked at the words, a little dizzy at the mental image of Will holding this paper, reading these words and letting the seeds of those ugly lies take root in his heart.

It made her dizzier still to think that the next thing he'd done was sleep with her and not say he loved her when she'd confessed those feelings.

Thank God she hadn't confessed everything.

But would he have even believed her? Maybe if she'd told him he was her first, she'd never have had to see that shadow of doubt in his eyes.

Because that shadow *hurt*.

Leaning closer, she tortured herself even more by reading the first line of the story.

Refusing to reveal the whereabouts of his mistress, Miles Thayer...

She closed her eyes, and a few of the baby clothes fluttered to the garage floor. A part of her newly forgiving heart wanted to run back across the grass, risk the reporters, and scream the truth to Will.

But she shouldn't have to, she thought as she stooped

over to gather up the tiny sleeper and bootie. He should believe her. If he wanted *everything*, didn't that include trust?

Ignoring the carton, she clutched the clothes, fumbled with the knob, and let herself inside. "Guy?"

When he didn't answer, she headed straight down the hall to the bedrooms.

"Guy, are you back here?"

She heard something thud in the closet, the sudden scrape of hangers over the bar, then the door popped open and he stepped out.

"Have you been crying?" she asked, dropping the whole armload of stuff on the bed to reach for him. "What's wrong?"

"Missy." He came right into her arms and embraced her, sending a strange set of chills all over her body. "There you are."

"What were you doing in there, Guy?" Her heart sort of rolled around and swelled up all at the same time.

"I was missing someone." He leaned back. "I forget her name."

She patted his shoulder, the gesture awkward but somehow natural. She'd have to get used to that feeling now. "It's okay. I'm here now and guess what we're going to do?"

"Pack and start pricing things for the yard sale?" His gray eyes lit up and his brows rose high into his crinkly forehead.

"Better. We're going on a trip."

His smile wavered. "Where you putting me, Missy?"

Oh, Lord. She almost *had* put him somewhere. She still could. Her gaze drifted to the baby clothes. No, she couldn't.

"I'm just taking you to a very nice villa for a little bit,"

she said. "It's a safe little house and I'll be right up the
road at my friend's house."

"Oh, I know what this is!" He clapped like a little kid.
"This is the part when you send the people away to a fancy
hotel so they can swim and make a plan for how they're
going to change their life and live in a *Clean House!*" He
shouted the last two words like an ad for the TV show.

"Kind of, yeah." That was actually a perfect way to get
him out of here. And with that car circling outside, they had
to move quickly.

"But we're not finished yet," he said. "Don't I get to be
here for the yard sale to see how much money it made and
how you're going to match it?"

God, was there no aspect of that show he didn't have
memorized? "We'll come back for that," she assured him.
"But let's pack up some clothes for a few days away."

He looked at the pile of blue-and-white baby clothes.
"What's all that stuff?"

Now wasn't the time to walk through his shrouded
memories. "Just some things I found that I want to give
to my friend who's having a baby. I'll go put all of that in
some bags and you find a suitcase." She gestured toward
the closet. "You want me to help you?"

"No!" he said quickly, moving to block her from the
closet. "You go." He flicked his hand. "Find your bag and
I'll take care of mine."

"Okay. But hurry."

"What's the rush?" he asked.

"Um, the cameras are going to be here soon. You're
not ready for—"

"The big reveal!" He beamed at her again. "I know
this game, Missy."

"You certainly do." She lifted her arms, almost reaching for him, and then she froze. It would be a long time before hugging him came naturally.

But it did for him. He stepped into her arms and patted her back softly. "You're a funny one, Missy."

Wasn't she, though?

"What was your real name again?"

She swallowed. "Jocelyn." With a deep, steadying breath, she added: "Bloom. Jocelyn Bloom."

She could have sworn he stiffened a little, then relaxed. "You're a good girl, Jocelyn."

"And you're a good man...Guy."

In the distance she heard a car door slam, making her jump away. "Hurry up, now. Pack. I'll be right back."

Hustling down the hall, she went right to the front door, carefully peering out to the driveway.

No strange cars, just hers and—

Will was standing next to her car, on the passenger side, looking at something. She couldn't see from this angle, so she walked around to the dining-room window and carefully separated the blinds, giving her a perfect shot of him in the driveway.

He was looking at her phone; she'd left it in the console when she'd gotten out to say hello to him.

What was he doing? Searching for texts from Miles Thayer?

The thought was like a sharp spike across her heart.

Carrying the phone, he rounded the car and headed toward the front door. On the way, he slowed his step and turned as a car came down the street. The same car, with the same telephoto lens.

The driver's window rolled down. "Hey, is Jocelyn Bloom in there?"

Will ignored them, marching to the front door and unlocking it before letting himself inside. She was waiting when he walked in.

He searched her face for a moment, then said, "They've been out there for a while."

"I know," she said. "I'm taking Guy up to Barefoot Bay."

He held out her phone. "You left this in your car." His eyes were wary, cold even. She took it from him, careful not to touch his hands and suffer the electrical shock. "I thought I'd get it so those assholes circling the house didn't try to steal it from you."

"Thanks."

"William!" Guy came bounding out of the hallway. "Look what Missy found! All your old baby clothes."

Will shot her a dark look, but she interceded instantly. "Those are for my friend Lacey, Guy." She reached to take the bundle from him. "They don't belong to Will."

"But they did." Guy managed to hold on to one little sleeper, waving it up like a baby-blue flag. "Can't believe you were ever this small, son."

"They're not mine, Guy."

"Then whose are they?" Guy asked, looking from one to the other, bewildered.

Neither said a word.

"They belong to a baby who's no longer around," Jocelyn said gently, taking the sleeper from him and putting a hand on his back. "Come on, Guy. You have to focus. We need to leave quickly."

He turned to look at Will. "This is the part where I

go to the fancy hotel. You know, William? In the show? They always send the people off to a nice place. Will you be there?"

"He's going to California," Jocelyn said, hating the ice in her voice but making no effort to warm it.

Guy froze, his eyes wide with horror. "What?"

"Just for a day," Will said quickly. "You'll be with Jocelyn."

That calmed him and he let her lead him back down the hall. "When are you leaving?" Guy called out.

"Well," he said. "I was going to leave now, but…"

Jocelyn turned to look at him. "But what?"

"I don't want to go with…" He pointed toward the street.

She gave Guy a nudge ahead then returned to the dining room. "I have this covered. We'll be at Casa Blanca and Clay won't let anyone on that property."

"I'll follow you to Barefoot Bay and make sure—"

"No!" She hadn't meant for it to come out like a bark. "Just do me a huge favor and go."

"I am," he said with sharp simplicity. "I am going to California, Jocelyn, and I'll tell you why."

"I know why."

"No, you don't." He leaned a little closer, smelling fresh, like he'd just taken a shower. And washed off her and her admissions of love. "You think you know everything. You think you can control everything. You think—"

"I get the idea." She waved him to the door. "I don't know anything, Will. I was certainly wrong about you."

He looked hard at her, brows drawn over pained eyes. "And I was wrong about you."

Ouch. She swallowed, closing her eyes to keep from reacting. "Do me a favor, Will. On your way out, pull my car into the garage, and then tell those reporters that you're going to pick me up at the airport. Let them follow you there as a decoy."

"You think they'll fall for that?"

"Yes, if you're convincing. Will you do that for me?"

"Actually, I'll do a lot more than that for you."

"Don't," she said quickly. "That'll be all I need. That'll be enough."

"All right," he agreed. "Do this your way. But I just want you to know one thing." He took her chin in his hand, holding too tight for her to wrench away, forcing her eyes onto him. "I know what I did wrong all those years ago. I know what I should have done and didn't do. And now I know the consequences of that decision and"—he worked hard to keep his voice from cracking, the effort appearing more painful than if he'd actually cried—"I'm going to make that up to you."

By demanding she go back to California? By believing gossip rags and not her? "You don't have to," she managed to say.

"But I'm going to. I'm going to do what I should have done back then."

He should have gone to California to chase his father's dreams of wearing Dodger blue? But she didn't have the heart to say that to him because, deep inside, she still loved Will Palmer. She always had and she always would.

But love wasn't enough. There had to be trust, too.

"Good luck to you, then, Will. Hope you find what you're looking for in California."

He rubbed his cheek, still unshaven, nodding to her. "I will. And I won't come back until I do."

Then I'll miss you. "Good-bye."

He went through the garage and pulled in the Toyota, closing the door. Then she saw him head out to the street to talk to the driver of the car with the photographer. After a few minutes, Will pulled out of his driveway and the media followed his truck.

Jocelyn just leaned against the window and, like she had so many times in this house, she cried because she only wanted one man to love her, and he didn't.

Chapter Twenty-eight

⌒

Just as Jocelyn pulled out to the empty street, Guy grabbed her arm with a sudden whimper.

"I forgot something!"

"What?"

"I..." He pressed his hands to his temples so hard he made dents. "I can't remember, darn it."

She looked up and down the street, expecting more reporters to jump out of the bushes at any time. "Whatever you forgot, I can come back and get it." Or someone could. "You need to stop worrying and relax."

He looked like he didn't know the meaning of "relax," leaning forward like he was about to jump out and run. "William is gone," he said. "That's what I forgot."

"William is on a quick business trip," she assured him, forcing lightness into her voice when the statement made her feel anything but. "He'll be back before you know it."

"Before the yard sale?"

"Yes," she lied. "Before the yard sale. Now put your seat belt on and let's get to this amazing hotel. You're going to love it."

She didn't see another car except for the UPS truck until they got closer to town. No one honked, cut her off, or sidled up next to her when she hit the Fourway and stopped at the intersection of Center and Harbor.

There, she spotted a sheriff's car in the parking lot of the Super Min. God willing, that was Deputy Slade Garrison and she could tell him what was going on.

As she pulled in, Guy grabbed her arm again. "I won't go in there."

"I just want to…" Did he remember Charity? "Why not?"

He shook his head hard. "No. I won't go in there."

Charity had made it her mission to force him to resign from his position as the local deputy sheriff and had essentially threatened to ruin him for what he'd done to Jocelyn. How would she react if Jocelyn said she'd forgiven her father?

Didn't matter. Now wasn't the time to worry about that; she had to talk to Slade and not sit here, out in the open.

"Stay in the car," she said, pulling into a spot along the side of the convenience store. "I'll only be a minute."

He gave her a dubious look, his mouth drawn, his shoulders slumped.

"Everything's going to be fine, Guy," she promised him.

But his eyes filled. "I miss William already."

"So do I," she admitted. "Give me one second, okay?"

As she started to climb out she heard him mumble, "Christ, I hate that woman," under his breath.

She froze, then turned back to Guy. "You *remember* Charity?"

"No," he said quickly. "I just remember I hate her."

Everything pressed on her as hard and hot as the Florida sun. "Wait here, Guy," she said, climbing out to rush into the Super Min.

Slade was leaning on the counter, talking to Gloria Vail behind the cash register.

"I have to talk to you, Deputy Garrison," she said quickly. "Privately." The deputy and Gloria shared a look that told Jocelyn Gloria knew everything that was going on. "Or not," Jocelyn added with a nod. "Just let me tell you both."

The back door popped open and Charity stepped out. "Are you okay?" she asked.

Absolutely nothing got by that woman. She was probably watching the store on closed circuit TVs in her office.

"I'm fine, but the media has definitely found me. They're at my old house, so I'm taking my father up to Barefoot Bay with me."

"You're taking him?" Charity's drawn-on brows shot up. "Why?"

She swallowed. "So he's protected."

The older woman choked, but Slade stepped into the conversation. "That's smart, Jocelyn. Did you happen to see what kind of car they're driving?"

She described it to the best of her ability and answered a few more questions, painfully aware of Charity's dark scowl of disapproval. When Slade stepped to the side to call another deputy, Charity came around the counter and took Jocelyn by the elbow.

"Come with me," she said harshly.

"I can't, Charity. I left him in the car."

"Let him rot!"

Jocelyn freed herself from the other woman's grip. "Please."

"Really, Aunt Charity," Gloria said. "Slade has this covered."

Charity flattened her niece with a glare and took Jocelyn's arm again. "This'll take one minute. Get back here. Might change your life."

"My life is changed," she said softly. "I want to forgive him, Charity."

"Oh, hell. C'mere." She gave Jocelyn a nudge to the back door and, fueled by curiosity more than anything, Jocelyn followed.

The office was tiny, cluttered, and smelled like the cardboard boxes of snack items stacked in the corner, but Charity seemed to know exactly what she wanted, going right to a filing cabinet to whip a drawer open.

"You want to forgive him, huh?"

"I want to move on." She hated the cliché, but it worked for the moment. What did Charity have in that drawer?

A thin manila file, it turned out, that Charity used to fan herself. "I've been keeping an eye on your old man."

"I know you have. At least until my mother died."

"And after." Charity slammed her hands on her bony hips. "Someone had to watch the old prick."

Someone had: Will. But she stayed very still, waiting for Charity to explain.

"After she died, he started to go downhill pretty fast," Charity said.

"I know."

She held out the file. "Or did he?" When Jocelyn didn't move to take it, Charity snapped the folder like a whip. "Don't you want to know?"

Maybe she didn't. "Whatever you have doesn't matter, Charity, because so much time—"

"It matters!" She shook the folder viciously. "You can't let someone get away with abuse!"

"The abuse is history." She had to hold on to that belief. It had taken so long to get to this point and it had cost her so much. She wasn't about to let this old busybody steal her forgiveness. Even if this old busybody nearly saved her life once. "Guy is suffering from dementia and doesn't even remember what he did."

Charity threw the file on an already overcrowded desk with a dramatic sigh. "Of course he wants you to think that, Jocelyn! What if you press charges?"

"I decided long ago I wouldn't."

"Even after your mother died?" The question was loaded with implications.

"Of brain cancer, Charity. He didn't kill her." Made her life a living hell, but didn't end it.

"Are you certain of that?"

"Absolutely. I spoke to the doctors."

"It was sudden, though, wasn't it?"

Jocelyn's gaze shifted to the file. She had no doubt her mother had died of natural causes—and possibly a broken heart. But Guy hadn't killed her.

"Just look at it, for crying out loud."

Very slowly, she reached for the file and opened it to

see a single piece of paper with *The Lee County Library System Serving Southwest Florida* scrolled across the top.

"That came courtesy of Marian Winstead."

"Marian the Librarian," Jocelyn said softly, the locals' nickname for Mimosa Key's keen-eyed librarian popping into her head.

"She doesn't like to be called that," Charity said. "As you may know, she's my lifelong dear friend and quite trustworthy."

Jocelyn read a list of books, authors, and Dewey Decimal numbers.

Elder Law: Financial and Legal Considerations for the Alzheimer's Patient

Alzheimer's and the Law

The Defense Rests: One Man's Acquittal and Dementia

"You'll notice that all of those books were checked out in a five-month period by Alexander Bloom."

Alexander. Like the baby boy. She shook her head, wishing she could throw away all of these thoughts and just start over. "What are you saying?"

"I'm not saying anything. I think that list says it all. Now, I'm not accusing him of anything that he's not already guilty of." She took a few steps farther. "It just makes a person wonder, doesn't it? Just how convenient it is for him to 'have Alzheimer's.'" She air-quoted and lowered her voice to a new level of sarcastic.

Jocelyn put down the file and met Charity's gaze. "If you're implying he's faking the dementia to cover up for anything he did or *didn't* do, you're wrong."

"You're letting him off the hook." Charity's nostrils flared at the thought. "Maybe you should take another look at those pictures I gave to Will Palmer. Count the bruises. Remember the pain. I was the one who put ice on you, you know. I was the one—"

"I know!" She shot her hands up in apology the minute the shout came out of her mouth. "I know," she repeated, softening her tone. "I just don't want to live with all this hate anymore. He's sick."

"Is he really? Are you absolutely certain of that, Jocelyn?"

She closed her eyes, picturing Guy and all he didn't know and couldn't remember.

I hate that woman.

She could still hear the echo of Guy's sly comment. "It's a very hard disease to understand."

Charity leaned so close Jocelyn could count her over-sized pores. "So's abuse. I know. I had my own broken ribs to help me *understand* it. And I got the hell out of there, and took my Gracie with me. Which is more than I can say for your poor, pathetic dead mother."

She couldn't take this. No matter what Charity had done for her, she couldn't stand here and listen to her accuse Guy of being a fake or a murderer or whatever. He was what he was—and Jocelyn had decided to get past that regardless of what Charity wanted her to do. "I've made up my mind, Charity. Thank you for the information."

As she turned to the door, Charity's hand landed on her arm. "Be a shame for that file to land in the hands of the wrong person."

Jocelyn froze and looked at her. "Yes, it would."

"You know, like the *National Enquirer.*"

Jocelyn opened the door and stepped into the store

without answering, nodding to Gloria and Slade. "Thanks again," she said softly. "If you need me, I'll be up at Lacey and Clay Walker's house."

Outside, the sun smacked her, blinding after the dreary, miserable back office of the Super Min. But it couldn't wash away the accusations and doubt. Maybe Guy had known he was forgetting things and needed to check up on his rights or insurance. Without Mom to help, and in the aftermath of her death, that would be a reasonable worry.

Maybe he was scared all the stuff he had done would come to the surface.

Maybe he—

Was gone.

Jocelyn stopped dead on the curb and stared at the empty front seat of the car and the wide-open passenger door.

"Guy!" She ran around the car, turning in a full circle, sweat already dribbling down her back. "Guy!"

She ran into the lot, looked up and down the intersection, over to the motel parking lot, everywhere, *everywhere.*

Guy was gone.

When Will landed in L.A., it was still light and fairly early, a blessing for a person who wanted to make a cross-country round trip in as little time as possible. If all went according to plan, he could be on a red-eye tonight, mission accomplished. If not, then his plan just sucked.

But he had to do something. He had to help Jocelyn—this time. And it couldn't be too little, too late. It *had* to work.

Scott hadn't been happy, of course, when Will had called him back to turn down the offer. But telling Jocelyn that he wasn't taking the job wouldn't have convinced her of anything; he had to show her he loved her. Plus, she'd have wallowed in guilt, assuming it was her decision to stay that had made his decision.

Not true at all. She loved him, and he was never going to lose her again. But until he made up for the wrongs he'd been carrying around for fifteen years, he hadn't earned her.

Well, he was about to. He hoped. Unless this stunt was an exercise in futility.

After he got situated in a rental car and figured out which freeway to take, he checked his phone, just in case. Jocelyn had called once, when he'd arrived at the airport, and, man, had she sounded miserable. A little terrified and a lot stressed out.

She'd asked him three times if he was certain the reporter followed him and he'd confirmed he had. But there must be more of them for her to be that tense. The damn reporters were probably crawling all over that island now, which made his mission even more imperative. Maybe she wasn't physically beaten this time, but she was being emotionally, professionally, and personally battered and he sure as hell wasn't going to sit back— again—and watch that happen.

Fueled by his focus, he navigated the mean, and sickeningly slow, streets of Los Angeles, threading his way through the Hollywood Hills and onto a canyon road off Sunset Boulevard. He found the address and drove up to an eight-foot-high gated entrance, then picked up his cell phone and called the number he'd taken from Jocelyn's phone. He knew he had the right number because it had worked that morning when he'd first texted and put his plan in motion.

"Bringing Jocelyn Bloom in," he said when the phone was answered. Just please don't ask to talk to her.

She didn't. In a moment, the gates slowly parted like opening arms, leading Will down a half mile of creamy white bricks to a sizable Tudor-styled house tucked into a wooded lot.

The front door opened and a woman stood in the entry, so small he thought for a moment it might be a teenage girl, not the superstar actress who thought Jocelyn was coming to see her. When he climbed out of the car, he could see her face and made a mental note never to fall for on-screen beauty again.

Coco Kirkman looked nothing like she did on TV.

"Hello." He nodded to her as he approached.

An oversized sweatshirt hung halfway down her legs, the sleeves so long they hid her hands. As he got closer, she hugged herself as if she were cold, despite the hoodie and the black scarf knotted around her neck. A few honey-colored strands of hair slipped out of a sloppy ponytail, and she brushed them away to train famously sky-blue eyes on him.

"Where's Jocelyn?" she demanded, leaning over to peek into the car as if he'd hidden her in there.

Time to come clean. "She's not here."

"Excuse me?" Her eyes flashed in horror. "Her text said she and a bodyguard would be here to talk to me. You have my private number?"

"She gave it to me." More or less.

She made no gesture to invite him in, but blocked the

door as much as her waif-like body could block anything, so he stopped at the bottom stone step, making them essentially eye to eye.

Behind her, a crystal chandelier lit an oversized entry and a sweeping marble staircase that he certainly wouldn't build in a Tudor house, but probably cost more than he ever made in a year.

"So..." She shifted from one bare foot to the other, shooting a quick glance behind her as if she expected someone to pop up any minute. "Why did she send you here?"

"She didn't," he said. "I sent you the text that you thought was from Jocelyn."

"Oh, fuck." She snorted the curse. "I can't believe I fell for that. Of course, no one in the world has that phone number but Jocelyn, so it's not like I'm a complete idiot. What do you want?"

"What do you think I want? To ask you to please, please reconsider what you're doing and tell the world it's a lie."

She lifted on eyebrow. "You think it's a lie?"

"I know it is. Jocelyn wouldn't break up a marriage any sooner than she'd jump off the Empire State Building. And she won't say why she's letting you do this, before you jump all over her for breaching life-coach ethics."

She smiled a little, a sad smile that barely reached her eyes. She leaned against the doorjamb, her arms still firmly wrapped around her middle. "You're that guy."

"What guy?"

"The baseball player."

He nodded, ignoring the little punch of happiness because Jocelyn had actually talked about him.

"So everything she said about you was true."

"Guess that depends," he said vaguely. "On what she told you."

"She told me you were... kind."

Was he? Or did she have that mixed up with *passive*? "I have my moments."

"And reliable."

"Enough."

"And..." She gave an approving nod. "Hot."

"I didn't come here to talk about me." He took one step closer, glancing into the house in a silent request for an invitation.

She shook her head, her eyes widening just a little. "Look, the only reason I said yes to the text is because I thought Jocelyn wanted to see me. Does she? Or does she have a message for me?"

"Yeah. Get your butt in front of a camera and tell the world you lied."

She bit her bottom lip so hard he thought she'd drawn blood. "She knows I can't do that." He barely heard the whisper.

Okay. He hadn't expected this to be easy. But he also hadn't expected to stand on her front porch and make a plea. "Are you really that selfish that you don't care about her reputation or her feelings?"

"She's the strongest person I've ever met."

"So that's why you picked her as your fall guy?"

She laughed softly. "That's why she volunteered for the job."

"She what?"

She wrapped herself up again, so small and vulnerable he wondered whatever made her decide to pursue a career that put her in the spotlight. "Guess she didn't tell you everything."

"Guess not." Jocelyn was *in* on this? "Why?"

"To protect me, of course."

"At the expense of her career?"

She shrugged. "It'll blow over and she'll..." She glanced to the side, into the house, then stepped a little farther out of the doorway. "She'll weather this storm much better than I will. It was her idea."

It was? Would she go her whole life sacrificing her own happiness for other people?

Yes, maybe she would. And wasn't that one of the things he loved about her?

He heard a noise from inside the house, and instantly she startled and flinched, throwing a wary look over her shoulder, but no one was there.

"Who was that?" he asked.

"My housekeeper," she said quickly. "And I have security here."

"Then you should feel comfortable letting me in. I'm not armed and I won't hurt you. I just want you to understand what Jocelyn is going through because of you."

"It's not..." She closed her eyes and fought for something—the right word, composure, maybe. Inner strength. She looked like a person who had none, inside or out. There was something helpless about her that reminded him of someone. Not Jocelyn, that was certain. "It's not because of me," she added.

"Miles?"

Her eyes flashed in warning, like a secret message to him.

"He threatened to... you know."

No, he didn't know. But he was starting to suspect. "Your husband threatened to hurt you?"

She nodded.

"And Jocelyn suggested you say he was having an affair with her so you could...what?"

She swallowed hard. "Try and leave him."

"Try?" he asked furiously.

"Shhh." Her eyes darted again, fear radiating off her.

"Why? Is he here?"

"No, just the housekeeper."

"Who's your friend, Coco?" The male voice boomed from inside, making her jump as a man appeared behind her.

How long had the son of a bitch been back there?

Unlike Coco, Miles Thayer looked every bit the movie star. Not very tall or broad, but he had the golden good looks and a phony smile that the camera loved. He held out a hand to Will. "I'm Miles. Have we met?"

Will ignored the hand. "I'm not here to talk to you."

"Funny, this is my house. You're on my property. You're talking to my wife. Who the fuck are you?"

"He's a friend of Jocelyn's."

Miles considered that, angling his head and scratching under long blond hair exactly the color of Coco's. They were like a matched set, only Coco was so tiny and defenseless and her husband had nasty all over him.

"And you're just leaving, I take it," Miles said.

"I'm not leaving until one of you calls a press conference and tells everyone the truth."

"The truth's out there, bud. I was boning the life coach."

Coco stared at the ground and Will's fists tightened like a runner just shot off first to steal. Every cell in his body wanted to act. To throw a fist if not a ball. To shut this asshole up.

"You got an issue with that?" Miles asked, using his shoulder to push Coco out of the way. " 'Cause that's our story. And we like it. Right, Co?"

Instantly she looked up at Will, a plea in her blue eyes. "Don't tell her he's here, please. Just go."

"Good advice," Miles said. "Get the hell out of here before I call the LAPD."

"Miles, plea—"

"Get inside." Miles grabbed her arm and practically dragged her into the house. "I'll deal with our—"

Will lunged, ripping the other man's hand away. "Don't you dare touch her."

They both froze and stared at him, Coco shaking her head a little but Miles breaking into a much more real grin. "Did you just *touch* me, dickhead?"

Memories jolted through him with the same force he wanted to use on this bastard.

You touching an officer of the law, young man?

Will took a steadying breath, sizing up the competition.

No gun this time and Will could take him. But to what end? Coco would run into the house and he'd lose any chance of getting her to help Jocelyn.

"Just leave her alone," Will said quietly. "I'd like to talk to her some more."

"Well, she doesn't want to talk to you."

He looked at Coco, tiny, scared, and so powerless. And then he realized who she reminded him of: Mary Jo Bloom. The same expectant look of fear in the eyes of a victim. The same helpless hunch to her shoulders and downward tilt to her chin.

Was that why Jocelyn had gone along with this idea, or even conceived it? Because she, too, wanted to make up for not helping someone in the past?

Coco brushed back her hair, the move shifting her neckline enough for Will to see a deep purple bruise cutting across her flesh.

His stomach lurched as the pictures of Jocelyn's bruises fought for space in his brain, fury firing through his veins.

"You son of a bitch," he murmured to Miles.

"Excuse me?" Miles stepped closer, giving his shoulders a shake. He wasn't six feet tall and sure as hell hadn't spent his life playing sports or swinging a dead-blow hammer. "What did you call me?"

"Please," Coco cried. "Please don't fight. It's my fault for taking him back. Will, just leave."

"Yeah, Will, just fucking leave or..." He lifted his hand but Will got the first swing in, a satisfying right hook that landed on the movie star's jaw and knocked his head back.

Coco screamed and lunged toward them just as Miles recovered from the blow. Miles spun around and shoved her into the house with so much force she fell backwards.

Will shot forward in full attack mode, seizing the man by the shoulder, yanking him around and slamming another fist in his face.

"You fucking—" Miles pushed back, barely getting decent force, but it was enough to knock Will off the step and make him stumble.

Miles leaped out and jumped on Will, getting his own swing into Will's face while the woman shrieked from the doorway. Using all his might, Will whipped Miles onto his back, thrust a knee into his chest, and pinned him down.

With a yell, Miles fought back, but he had nothing on Will. Easily in control of the fight, Will raised his right fist, let the blood surge through his arm—and froze.

Blood dribbled out of Miles's nose, and his eyes squeezed shut as he braced for the impact. When Will didn't swing, the other man whimpered like the coward he was.

Will looked up at Coco, who rocked herself with two arms, also whimpering. For a moment, they held each other's gaze as she, too, waited for his fist to make contact.

But that wouldn't make him any better than this asshole or Deputy Sheriff Guy Bloom or any other man who thought *this* was action.

He narrowed his eyes at Coco. "You want to help him? You want to help yourself?"

Biting her lip, she nodded. "Get in that car and let me get you out of here."

Under him, Miles squirmed. "Don't even think about it, Coco!" Will nailed him with a knee into the chest and jerked his head toward the car.

"Come on, Coco," Will urged. "You can do this."

She took a breath, hanging on the edge, then shook her head. "I can't," she practically mouthed the words. "Jocelyn understands."

"Then do it for you, not her," he insisted. "Get yourself out of jail. You don't have to live like this."

"Fuck you!" Miles shouted, his movie-star looks contorted with anger. "You get in that fucking car and I'll kill you, Coco. I am not kidding!"

"Don't give him the power," Will said quietly. "You

can stand up to him and you can make a difference to a whole lot of women."

She choked softly. "That's exactly what Jocelyn said."

"Then why don't you?"

"I'm scared." She shivered and backed away like a beaten dog.

"Don't be afraid," he said. "Get what you need and get in the car. He can't hurt you anymore."

"And then what?"

Will just smiled at her. "Then you'll be a real star."

"Move and you're dead, Coco," Miles growled.

She stabbed her hair, dragging it back, revealing another bruise by her ear.

"Stay and you're dead, Coco," Will said. "It's just a matter of time."

He held Miles down long enough for her to make her decision.

Chapter Twenty-nine

Jocelyn fingered the embroidery thread, resting the hoop on her lap, the buzz of activity in the house fading into the background as the weight of loss pressed on her chest.

The whole situation reminded her of the night of her mother's funeral. Except Guy wasn't dead. She hoped.

Please, God, don't let him be dead. I have to tell him—

Zoe came up behind her, putting her hands on Jocelyn's shoulders with a soft squeeze. "Nice gladiolas."

Jocelyn almost smiled and twisted the needle. "I want to finish this for him but I haven't a clue how to do this kind of thing."

"I do." Zoe reached over and took the needle, twirling it like a mini-baton. "I know, who would think I had a crafty bone in my body? But you need to go in the kitchen now, sweetie."

"Why?"

"Deputy Dawg wants to talk to you."

Jocelyn whipped around, the spool of embroidery thread tumbling to the floor. "Slade's here? Did they..." Blood drained from her head instantly.

"No news, I promise. He just wants to tell you what the plan is for the night."

The night. It had been dark for several hours now. After the initial scouring of town, then the streets that led out, the ragtag team of Lacey, Clay, Tessa, and Zoe, later joined by Lacey's daughter, Ashley, had gathered at the house so the professionals could take over.

But no one had seen him. A maid at the Fourway Motel thought she saw a man meeting his description wandering along the walkway behind the hotel, but a thorough search of the building turned up nothing. A tourist at the harbor was certain he saw an older man just like him fishing on the docks, but that lead took them nowhere as well.

And, the worst of all, the UPS guy said he thought he'd seen an old man crossing the causeway. What if he'd fallen off the bridge? What if he was...

Please, God, no.

The ache in her heart as heavy as a lead ball, Jocelyn handed the embroidery hoop to Zoe, refusing to give voice to her dark thoughts. "You can do needlepoint?" At Zoe's nod, Jocelyn just smiled. "You're full of surprises."

"Aren't I, though?" She pointed the needle toward the kitchen. "Go talk to the hot cop."

She started to walk out, but Zoe stopped her. "Speaking of hot, have you reached Will?"

She hadn't tried after that one call to verify that he'd gotten the reporter out of town, since Jocelyn had wondered if someone from the media had actually kidnapped

Guy to get to her. But she hadn't told Will they'd lost him. "He'd just be on the next plane back and miss his interview tomorrow morning. There's nothing he can do."

"He could comfort you," she said.

Not anymore. Jocelyn just shook her head and left Zoe, turning the corner to face a kitchen full of people.

Tessa and Lacey had coffee going and food on the table. Ashley was cleaning up. Clay and some other men were talking to Slade Garrison.

"Do you have any news?" she asked the deputy as he shifted his attention to her.

"We haven't turned up a single person who's seen him, except those I told you about. And, Jocelyn, time is critical. He has to be found in the first twenty-four hours or..."

She waved her hand. "I know the statistics."

He stepped closer, his expression softening. Lacey and Tessa also joined the conversation, flanking Jocelyn in support.

"Look, I realize your situation is a bit different than usual," Slade said. "And out of respect for your privacy and the fact that our island location makes it hard to get too far, I've held off on the next step. But I have to issue a Silver Alert, Jocelyn. I have to. I'm sorry."

"What exactly is that?" Tessa asked.

"It's like an Amber Alert for missing teens, but this is for elderly dementia patients."

"Why *wouldn't* you do that?" Lacey asked.

"Because," Jocelyn answered, "it'll have media crawling all over this place by morning."

Slade nodded. "It will, but there's no reason you have to be in the spotlight, Jocelyn. My office will handle media contact."

"But reporters will come here."

"Possibly," he said. "But just as likely someone watching the local TV station will have seen him. That's how it usually works, if we move fast. I normally wouldn't even talk to the family first, but considering the situation and all..."

"Do it," she said without hesitation. "Do whatever you have to do to find him."

He nodded. "I will, Jocelyn. Go get some rest. We'll be working all night."

"Please have your men consider this a base," Lacey said. "We'll keep coffee and food and whatever you need."

Lacey and Tessa's arms tightened around Jocelyn for a quick hug, just as the front door popped open without a knock. Everyone turned expectantly, only to see Charity Grambling march in like she owned the place.

"Did you find the old bastard yet?"

Instantly Lacey stiffened. "Charity, don't make this worse than it already is."

Charity ignored her and slid a gaze to Slade. "My niece told me you were here."

Slade didn't look happy about that. "The best way for you to help is to stay at the Super Min, Charity. You can talk to every single customer and, frankly, that's where he was last seen. We need you there, not here."

"Gloria's there, as you well know. I'm here to help Jocelyn."

Lacey bristled again. "She doesn't need you—"

"Yes, I do," Jocelyn said, stepping forward. Charity had saved her once and no matter what the woman thought of Jocelyn's recent change of heart, she was always welcome. "Thank you for coming, Charity."

Jocelyn could feel Lacey's glare on her, but she guided Charity toward the living room, where Zoe sat on the sofa doing needlepoint. Like bodyguards, Tessa and Lacey followed.

"Can I get you a cup of coffee, Charity?" Jocelyn asked.

The older woman stood in the middle of the room, her strawlike dye job sticking out in a few directions, a pair of khaki pants hanging loose on her hips. She stuffed her hands in her pockets and kept her gaze on Jocelyn. "I know you didn't like what I had to tell you today, but you have to consider the possibility that it's true."

"That what's true?" Zoe asked, either completely oblivious to the strange dynamics in the room or at least pretending to be.

"He's faking Alzheimer's," Charity said.

Tessa and Lacey sucked in a soft breath, but Zoe just pulled a long green strand of embroidery yarn through the pattern. "That's what I thought."

"You did?" Tessa asked.

"What do you think?" Lacey asked Jocelyn. "You know him better than anyone."

"I don't think he's faking it," she said. "He's always been...unstable."

Charity snorted. "He's a fucking criminal!"

The women stared at her, but Jocelyn held up her hands. "That's not true—"

"How can you say that?" Charity practically stomped her sneakered foot. "He damn near killed you."

"What?"

The question came from all three women at once. They stared at her with a mix of horror, shock, and genuine sadness. Jocelyn turned to the kitchen, catching Ashley in the doorway. "Honey, please. Don't."

"Give us a minute, Ash," Lacey said quickly to her daughter, who obeyed by pivoting and disappearing.

"Why didn't you tell us, Joss?" The crack in Tessa's question almost tore Jocelyn's heart out.

"You didn't need to know the details. And, honestly, he didn't…" Yes, he did. "It was a long…" That didn't matter. "I've tried to forget it."

"Well, I haven't." Charity practically spit the words. "And, frankly, if he fell off the causeway it wouldn't be good enough for him."

"Charity, please." Jocelyn reached for her. "I know how you feel. And I know you think that my forgiving him is some kind of personal affront, or not—not showing gratitude for what you did, but—"

"What did she do?" Lacey asked, unable to hide the disbelief in her voice. Of course, Lacey, like every lifetime resident of Mimosa Key, knew Charity as a nasty, mean-spirited gossipmonger. And last year, that mean spirit went to new and personal heights when she tried to stop Casa Blanca from ever getting built.

"I saved her life."

Again, every eye in the living room was on her. Zoe's needlepointing fingers stilled and Lacey just looked positively wretched at this turn of events. And Tessa, the woman who hated secrets the most, was clearly on the verge of tears.

Jocelyn dropped onto the edge of the sofa with a sigh. "I never wanted to tell you guys this."

Zoe put the needlepoint hoop on the table and reached for her. "We kinda knew."

"Not really." Jocelyn looked up at Charity. "Not the extent of it. Not how bad it was."

"I'll show them." Charity reached into her back pocket. "You don't think I was dumb enough to give you the only copies of the pictures, do you?"

"No!" Jocelyn jumped up, but Charity flung the pictures on the table like she was folding her poker cards, an array of bruises, blood, and brutality instantly spread before them.

Oh, God. She couldn't even look—not through the eyes of her friends. Sharp daggers of shame pierced her heart and stung her eyes as she choked on a sob. She had to get out of here. *She had to get out of here.*

"Holy hell," Zoe said. "He *did* almost kill you."

"Why are you doing this?" Jocelyn demanded of Charity. "Why betray me? I trusted you."

"Her?" Lacey almost spit. "Why would you trust her?"

"Because she picked me up off the street when I was running away." Charity had been the right person at the right time. "She helped me."

Charity waved her off. "I'm no Good Samaritan, believe me. I just hate abusers. I hate men who hit." She touched her face as if she could still feel the pain of a fist there. "And I hate Guy Bloom and couldn't care less if he is dead."

Jocelyn closed her eyes. "But I care." She put up her hands in surrender, needing the conversation and the pitiful looks and the hurt for not sharing to stop. As fast as she could without actually running, she left the room, headed down the hall, and darted into Guy's bedroom, fighting the urge to slam the door just to get rid of some of the emotion surging through her.

Dropping on the bed, she let the sobs escape.

Now they knew everything. Just like Will, they'd never look at her the same. They'd never look at Guy the same and, at one time, that wouldn't have mattered, but now it did.

Now she not only didn't hate him, she actually cared for him. She—

"Hey." The door popped open and Lacey's reddish-blonde curls edged in. "Can we come in?"

Everything in her wanted to scream no. *Go away. Leave me alone.*

Alone being her default and most preferred place to be. But alone was so—alone. And now she knew how much it sucked to be alone.

"Yeah."

In a split second, the three of them were in, surrounding her on the bed, cooing, sighing, laying their hands on her back with so much love and support she almost started crying again.

"I'm sorry, you guys," she murmured. "I should have told you."

"It's okay," Lacey said.

"We understand," Tessa added.

"You owe us for life," Zoe teased.

She looked at them, one after another, her heart swelling with love. "Obviously, I'm embarrassed."

"With us?" Tessa tapped her leg. "There's nothing about each other we don't know or haven't seen. We love you."

"And"—she took a deep breath—"I don't want you to hate him. Because when I find him—and I am going to find him—I'm going to forgive him and take care of him for as long as I'm able."

She braced for the onslaught of judgment and opinions, but got none.

"He's a different man now," Zoe finally said.

"He's forgotten," Tessa added. "So it's pretty damn wonderful of you to do the same."

Lacey rubbed her hand up and down Jocelyn's arm. "It's going to be tough, though. Charity's hellbent and might not keep your secret any longer. She's pissed that you're letting him off the hook. You'll need to face that."

"I'd face anything if that'll help find—" Suddenly a thought sparked in the back of her tear-soggy brain, forcing her up. "The media. The tabloids."

They stared at her.

"Forget a Silver Alert. If *I* called a press conference to talk about Coco, just imagine how far the message would go. Network TV, *Entertainment Tonight*, they'd all have to carry the story. And maybe someone saw him, maybe someone knows where he is. Even if"—she cringed at the thought—"even if he is faking it and hiding out or something. I don't know what's going on in his head. All I know is I have to find him. What better bullhorn to use than national media?"

They looked at each other, obviously unsure.

"I think those rags are more interested in your dirt than in your dad," Zoe said.

"There *is* no dirt," she said.

"Then you need to tell them the truth and let them know why you're the fall guy in a marriage you didn't break up."

Would she do that? Would she sell out Coco to find her dad? "Maybe I can just not address that." No, that would never fly.

"Just tell them the truth," Lacey said softly. "What's the worst that could happen?"

"Nothing to me. But Coco." She fell back on the pillow. She couldn't put Coco in that kind of danger. She couldn't hurt poor, sweet, weak Coco who was just so much like another poor, sweet, weak woman that she'd stolen a permanent place in Jocelyn's heart.

But maybe if Jocelyn had forced her mother's hand, she wouldn't have lived in fear.

"I'll decide in the morning," she finally said. "Maybe they'll find Guy overnight."

"Maybe," the others agreed.

But no one sounded very certain.

A nasty mosquito nibbled on his neck, but Guy was too tired and too scared to move and slap it. Where was Henry? Shouldn't he be here to flap his wings and ward off these horrible bugs?

Guy curled deeper into the tiny opening he'd found in the mangrove hammock, the cloying stink of rotten honey from those darn white flowers making him want to puke. The sharp smell of the pepper trees made him sneeze. He sniffed again, then started sniveling like a toddler.

Which he might as well be.

Turning from the stiff tree root that poked his back, he brushed some sand and dirt off the side of his face. Something crawled on his finger and pinched.

Fire ant. Shoot.

He shook it off and tried to get comfortable, back into the place where sometimes, when everything was really quiet, he could clear those cobwebs in his head.

Because some things really did stay in his memory.

They got mixed up, sure, and tangled like that cheap red yarn he'd used when he took up knitting. But the gist of the memory was there, so he could close his eyes and imagine the face on that picture.

Oh, that picture. That was what had gotten him into trouble in the first place. He'd wanted to go back and get it, and he didn't want Missy running after him, telling him to stop and go to some hotel.

If he didn't get that picture, the *Clean House* people would throw it away!

And then he'd die for sure because it was his only picture of the girl who called him "Daddy."

He couldn't remember her name. Maybe it was the same as her mother's. It seemed to him it was. But he could remember her face. Brown eyes and a big space where her front teeth would grow in.

But they never grew in, did they? No. Because she—

Tears stung. Jeez. Hadn't these old eyes dried out yet? Did he have to get all weepy like a woman every time he thought about the child he'd lost?

He didn't actually remember. He just knew there'd been a girl. A sweet little girl who went fishing with him.

And there'd been pain. A deep, aching, numbing, changing pain because he had lost a child. So...

What happened to her?

Another mosquito buzzed by his ear and something splashed in the water just a few feet away. Oh, boy. Hope the gators weren't hungry.

How the heck had he gotten out here? He squeezed his eyes shut and tried to remember what had happened. He'd been so careful not to be seen taking those old back streets.

He'd remembered the way, somehow. But then he got to the house and needed to get in the back door and there was the old boat leaning against the side and—

But now the boat was upside down and covered with water and Guy was all alone.

No William. No Missy. Not even Henry the Heron showed up to keep him company.

His stomach gurgled with hunger and all he could do was swallow some spit to wet his parched throat.

Another splash, only louder this time. Closer.

"Henry? Is that you?"

Maybe it was Missy. Maybe it was William! He sat up and listened, but only cicadas and crickets sang and mosquitoes buzzed.

Guy just covered his face with his hands and let the tears fall until they burned his cheeks. This was it, then. He was going to die tonight, for sure.

And somewhere, way in the back of that clouded up brain of his, he knew the truth. He was just getting what he deserved.

The splash was so loud Guy jumped and called out. "Go away, gator! Go away."

Nothing.

If only someone were here with him. If only Henry would fly over and lay his head next to Guy for his last night. Because surely this was Guy's last night, and after this he'd be headed to another place. He wasn't sure why, but he had a feeling it wasn't the *good* place.

He pulled up his legs and wrapped his arms around them, burying his head in the darkness. What had he done? What in God's name had he done?

He didn't know. All he knew was how he felt right

now. Slowly, he lifted his head and looked at the stars, as deeply into the darkness as he could, to speak to whoever might listen.

"I don't know what I did, but I know it was bad. And I'm sorry."

But he doubted very much that anyone heard his confession except the bugs and the gators and the birds that had flown away like his memories.

Chapter Thirty

Jocelyn sat straight up just as the clock radio next to Guy's bed clicked to 6:00 a.m., the light blanket one of the girls had covered her with shoved to the foot of the bed. Outside, the soft drizzle and pre-dawn darkness cloaked the room in a dreary shroud.

Sliding off the bed, she opened the door, but the house was completely quiet and dark. Where was everyone?

Asleep, she discovered after a quick walk through the house. Tessa and Zoe spooned on a twin bed in Jocelyn's old room. The sheriff's men had left. Clay and Lacey had taken Ashley home earlier and must have stayed there.

She went back to Guy's room, circling the bed and standing in front of the dresser that used to be her mother's. It was empty now, no perfume bottles or that pretty pink jewelry box with a big embroidered rose Jocelyn had loved as a little girl.

Was that jewelry box gone, too? She hadn't seen it in any of her cleaning and organizing, but they hadn't finished the closets. She turned to Guy's closet, opening the door. The moment she snapped on the light and looked down, she was rewarded with the very thing she'd been looking for. Not only had the jewelry box not been thrown away, it sat on the floor, wide open.

Kneeling down to examine the contents, she lifted an old not-really-gold chain that had turned black with time, and two tiny rings with blue stones, vaguely recalling that they were her mother's birthstone.

A top shelf lifted out to reveal more space at the bottom, empty but for a picture.

Oh. A piece of her heart cracked and left a jagged edge in her chest as she stared at the snapshot. The edges were worn from handling, the photo almost warm to the touch.

And the memory of the moment so clear in her mind, Jocelyn let out a little cry when she looked at it.

It was her seventh birthday, so January 4, 1986.

January of 1986? That was the same month—

She put her hand to her mouth as pieces fell together. This was the last time they'd gone out in the rowboat. After that, Guy had changed. Life had changed. Everything had changed.

Had Guy been looking at this photo when she'd come to drag him away to Barefoot Bay? Had he realized his "Missy" and this little girl were one and the same? Did he remember that day when they went out on the row—

With a soft gasp she shot to her feet. Had anyone looked for the boat? Had anyone thought to check the islands? She needed to call Slade. They had to search out there right now.

Clutching the photo, she ran down the hall, not bothering to wake the girls. She needed her phone. Turning in circles, she couldn't remember where she'd last seen it, a low-grade panic and certainty making her whole being tremble with the need to know if her hunch was correct.

She pushed open the garage door and looked around for the rowboat, but she and Zoe had left it outside to dry in the sunshine. Barefoot, she darted across the garage to open the door and run to the side of the house to find the—

"Holy shit," she mumbled, staring at the empty spot where they'd left the boat. "Is it possible?"

She squinted into the breaking dawn, wiping raindrops from her face.

Was Guy out there in the canals or on the islands *alone*?

Fueled by that fear, she started to run, slipping in the wet grass and ignoring the chilly breeze that came with the rainy cold front. She didn't bother to look when she ran across the street, but in her peripheral vision, she saw a car pull out of a parking space up the street.

A fine chill raised goose bumps on her arms. The Silver Alert had gone out hours ago, her name most certainly attached as the next of kin. The wolves waited for her with cameras and microphones.

Fine. If her suspicion was wrong—and, God, she prayed it was—then she'd do whatever was necessary to find her father. Even tell the truth if she had to.

She plowed through some shrubbery in the neighbor's yard, not bothering with the access path to the canals. How far could he have gotten? Was he out there rowing? Lost? Or—

She let out a soft cry as she reached the water's edge, the muck squishing through her bare toes. The canal wasn't deep, maybe four feet, and she could wade or even swim it, but not for long. And not safely.

She turned left and right, thinking hard and fast, spying a bright-yellow plastic kayak leaning against a dock two houses away. She took off for it, a million rationalizations spinning through her mind. But no one called out to stop her when she dragged the lightweight craft down a stone path, used the oar to push off, and hopped into the single seat.

Rain bounced off the water and made a popping sound on the plastic kayak, falling just hard enough to make the effort completely uncomfortable and the world wet and blurry.

Or maybe her vision was blurred by tears, because without her realizing it, they were pouring out of her eyes.

Just thinking about Guy lost out here, alone and terrified, ripped her heart to shreds. *Please, God, please let him be okay.*

Dragging the paddle through the water, she squinted at the little mounds of mangroves that made up the islands, a question nagging at her, as incessant as the rain.

When had he started to matter so much to her?

Why did she love a man who had made her life a living hell?

"Because that man is gone," she mumbled into the rain and breeze. And in his place was a new man who deserved a second chance.

Just like Will.

Maybe Will hadn't sacrificed his career for her, or come after her when they were separated, and maybe he'd opened his heart and life to a man Jocelyn thought she hated. Maybe Will needed her forgiveness, too.

Maybe Jocelyn needed to let go and love instead of holding on to hate.

There was no maybe about it. But first, she had to find her father.

A loud splash made her jump and almost drop the oar, but she clung to the slippery stick, her eyes darting as she expected to come face-to-face with an alligator. But it was a mighty blue heron who'd made the noise, a helpless fish hanging from its mouth.

"Henry," she whispered, a sob choking her. "Have you seen my daddy?"

He tipped his head back, devoured breakfast, and stretched his wings to take flight, heading south to disappear in the rain. Without a clue which way to go, she followed, staying close to the shore, her arms already burning from the effort of slicing the kayak through the water.

This was lunacy. He wasn't out here.

But who had taken the rowboat? a voice insisted.

How had he dragged it across the street and into the water all by—

The kayak hit something hard in the water, pulling another gasp from her throat. What the—

A narrow tip of aluminum stuck straight out of the water. The tip of a sunken rowboat. No, no. Not *a* rowboat. Their rowboat!

Shoving wet strands from her eyes and tamping down panic, she looked around, zeroing in on a mangrove hammock about twenty feet away. It was the closest island, the only place a person could swim to from here.

"Guy!" she called out, the words lost in the rain. "Guy!"

With every ounce of strength she had, she plowed the oar through the water, reaching the island in about fifteen burning strokes. He had to be here. He *had* to.

She climbed out of the kayak, stuffing the edge of the oar in the muck for balance, her foot landing on a sharp rock that made her grunt in pain. Dragging the kayak to dry land, she remembered the picture she'd taken from the house and found it pressed to the wet bottom of the kayak seat.

Wanting it with her, she unpeeled it from the plastic and turned to squint into the rain and through the mangroves that lined the island's edge.

"Guy! Are you here?"

Shoving branches out of her way, she headed toward the middle of a hammock that was not more than thirty feet in diameter. In the center there should be some clear space and—

She spotted him rolled up in a ball under a Brazilian pepper tree.

"Guy!" Ignoring the roots and rocks stabbing her bare feet, she ran to him, falling on his body as relief rocked her. "Oh my God, are you okay?"

He moaned, murmured, and turned slightly, his glasses completely bent from the weight of his head, his poor face marked with bug bites, his teeth as yellow as ever as he bared them in a smile.

"That you, Missy?"

He was alive. Relief rocked her. "Yes, Guy. It's me." She folded him in her arms and squeezed her eyes against the sting of fresh tears.

"Are you mad at me?" he asked, as contrite as a kid.

She sat up, tenderly holding his head while she slipped the ruined glasses off his face. "No." Her voice cracked. "Just tell me you're okay."

"I'm fine."

But she could tell by his gruff, hoarse voice that he wasn't. He was scared and suffering, and surely wouldn't have made it out here much longer.

"Did I miss the yard sale?"

She almost laughed, but shook her head, rocking back on the wet dirt and grass with him in her arms.

"We waited for you." She inched him away to search his face, so battered and bitten, so old and tired. He didn't even resemble the man of her childhood anymore. Not inside or out. "What happened, Guy? Why did you leave me?"

His eyes clouded as he shook his head. "I don't remember."

Really? Was he telling the truth? "You really don't remember anything, Guy? Not why you left or what your life used to be like or—"

"I wanted this! How did it get here?" He snapped up the wet picture that had fallen to the ground.

"I..." She slid the picture from his fingers, the image so water-damaged that it was almost impossible to make out any details. "It's mine," she said.

"You know that little girl?" His voice rose with a mix of fear and hope.

Jocelyn nodded, biting her lip, fighting more tears. Finally, she looked up to meet his gray gaze. "I am that little girl."

Something flickered in his eyes, a flash of recognition, a split second of awareness, then the fog came back.

"Do you know that, Guy?"

He closed his eyes and shook his head, abject misery in the tiny move. "I forget."

She cupped his face with her hand. "Then so will I." She leaned closer so her forehead touched his. "I forget and I forgive."

He heaved a great big sigh.

She lifted her head, pressed her lips to his wet forehead, and gave him a kiss. "Let's get you home, Daddy."

The tailwind that got the flight across country by dawn East Coast time turned out to be a cold front that left all of southwest Florida in a mist of cool rain, snarling up traffic even at this crazy early hour.

Was it Will's imagination or was the causeway just more crowded than usual?

Next to him Coco stirred, finally taking off the baseball cap and sunglasses she'd kept on since before he'd returned his rental car at LAX. Must be the standard L.A. disguise, he mused, thinking of Jocelyn and her designer cap.

Coco had slept almost the whole flight, stayed pretty quiet when she woke, and had been remarkably ignored by almost everyone.

Of course the way Will looked at anyone who came within five feet of her kept any curious celebrity hunters at bay.

"You sure she'll be here?" Coco asked as his truck rumbled over the causeway toward Mimosa Key. "Because I will *not* do this without Jocelyn."

He didn't respond, weaving through way more traffic than he'd have expected at this time of the morning.

"You are sure, aren't you?" she pressed.

"I'm not sure of anything," he said honestly.

"Except that you love her."

He shot a surprised look at her. "That obvious?"

For the first time, she laughed softly. "Maybe you should step back and review your behavior for the past day. Have you even slept? No, you've just flown cross-country—twice—and threw yourself at the mercy of a woman you've never met, sucker-punched a movie star, and kidnapped me to—"

"I didn't kidnap you," he shot back. "You were ready to leave him."

"I thought I had. Then I took him back. I'm done now."

"What finally changed your mind?"

She let out a dramatic sigh. "You."

"Because I beat up your husband?"

"Because you love Jocelyn enough to do what you did. I want that," she said simply. "I saw it in action and it wasn't in a movie script. It was real. I want that for me."

"Then you should go find it."

"This is the first step, big crazy lover boy."

He grinned at her. "You think I'm crazy?"

"I do, which makes you absolutely perfect for Jocelyn, in my opinion."

"Why, because her role in life is to fix crazy people and make them better?"

"No, because she's a nutcase herself."

He took his eyes from the road to glance at her. "Are we talking about the same woman? I've never met a person more sane than Jocelyn."

"With the compulsive list making?"

He laughed softly. "Yeah, she's a list maker, but that

doesn't make her crazy. It makes her organized and gives her a sense of control." And he loved that about her.

"And the neatness?"

"Like I said, control and organization. She's not OCD."

"Borderline. And, sorry, but there is nothing sane about hanging on to your virginity into your thirties."

He slammed on the brakes, getting a deafening horn from the poor guy behind him. "*What*?"

"You didn't know?"

A few white lights popped in the back of his head, blinding him momentarily.

Jocelyn had never slept with anyone?

That wasn't possible. That wasn't *normal*. And that wasn't true anymore, even if this woman had her facts straight, which he sincerely doubted she did. "I don't think she's the kind of woman to talk about that to her friends."

"Oh, we talked about it. She talked about everything with me."

Probably not everything, but he wouldn't be the one to share her secrets.

"I know about her dad."

Okay, maybe everything. He flipped the wipers up a notch as they passed through a band of heavy rain. "He only...only beat her once," he said, hearing the shame in his voice. Did she know Will's role in that spectacular night?

"Once was all it took to freeze her up in the sex department."

He slipped around a slow-moving van, spraying water as the end of the causeway beckoned. And, he hoped, the end of this conversation. "I don't think you know what you're talking about."

He prayed she didn't, anyway. Not that he didn't like the idea of being the only man who'd ever made love to her, but had he played a role in stealing *that* from her, too? Guilt pummeled his chest.

"I know what she said. Her old man damn near killed the guy she was fooling around with. Her dad—he's one for the books, isn't he? Anyway, she told me he caught her with the guy and beat the holy hell out of her. Called her a whore over and over again. With each punch, he said it again—"

"Stop it." He pounded the steering wheel, his eyes stinging. "Just...stop it."

"Oh my God, it was you." She reached over and grabbed his arm. "You were the guy she was with that night. She never told me it was Baseball Boy, just...a guy."

Of course not, because she was *still protecting him.* He shook off her hand, gritting his teeth in silence while new waves of hate rolled over him. Remorse and regret roiled through his stomach, making him sick.

"She never told me his name," Coco continued, on a roll now. "She was just, you know, trying like hell to convince me to leave Miles when the whole story came pouring out of her. And I...I couldn't just walk. I was chicken and so she came up with this fake affair for me. She let me save face and him, too. We hoped that would be enough to..."

"To what?"

"Keep him away from me."

He grunted. "That's what restraining orders are for."

She just shook her head and shifted in her seat. "Jocclyn's one in a million, you know?"

God, he knew. *Fifteen years.* That was a damn long time to be alone. Too long.

As if he could cut some of that time short, he smashed on the accelerator and fishtailed a little as he swerved through more traffic.

"Holy shit!" She dove down like someone had shot through the windshield, fighting to get her seat belt undone.

"What's the matter?" He looked at the car next to them, right into a telephoto lens. "What the hell?"

"Just drive. Fast!" She pushed onto the floor, scrambling for her hat and sunglasses. "How much farther?"

"We're almost there." But the dark van slid right behind them, on their tail, and stayed there until he turned onto Sea Breeze and hit the brakes one more time to stare at the spectacle that made absolutely no sense. Except that it did.

"Um, Coco."

She didn't move from her hiding place below the dashboard. "What?"

"About that press conference."

"What about it?"

"I think it started without you."

Chapter Thirty-one

They were drenched by the time Jocelyn managed to get Guy back to the dock where she'd found the kayak. The whole deal took well over an hour since the kayak was built for one. She managed to squeeze them both in, keeping him calm, getting him in and out of the water, tenderly helping his bug-bitten body make the short journey.

By now she'd have expected the kayak owners to be awake, but all of the houses seemed unnaturally empty. And quiet. Still, someone was making noise. She could hear voices—quite a few, in fact.

Jocelyn put her arm around Guy and guided him across the grass.

"You're going to be okay," she promised, leading him along a thick six-foot hedge of hibiscus trees that blocked the view of the street and his house. "We'll get some ointment on those—"

The voices suddenly grew even louder, almost like a crowd screaming in the stands at a game, making them both slow their step.

"What was that?" Guy asked, clinging tighter to her.

"I don't…" But deep inside, she did know. Deep inside, she knew exactly what they were going to find when they reached the street. Reporters. Cameras. Paparazzi.

"Guy, I have to tell you something."

He didn't answer as he navigated the wet grass and drizzle that smeared his glasses.

"I need you to brace yourself for when we get to the street."

"Why?"

"Because…" She took him a few steps farther, the crowd noise rising up as if they already saw her, the constant clicking of cameras like a serenade of crickets, a few voices shouting, the words impossible to make out. Neighbors she recognized gathered in small groups outside their houses, some still in bathrobes, some with cameras of their own.

"There she is!" someone yelled.

"With that man!"

Jocelyn turned left and right, confused. No one was pointing at her. No reporters came running at them. She took a few more steps and rounded the shrubbery to get a view of Guy's house.

"Oh, my word, Missy, look!" Guy practically stumbled as he pulled her forward and they saw the crowd covering her front lawn and driveway and spilling into the street.

"I know, Guy, I know."

He turned to her and threw his arms around her. "You did it, girl!" He knocked his glasses to the ground but didn't even notice, practically jumping up and down. "You got the crowds here for the yard sale! Look at all the cameras!"

She couldn't help laughing at his exuberance and the pure innocence of his assumption. "Guess we did, Guy." She dipped down to get his glasses, wiping them with the hem of her shirt, which didn't help at all but gave her a second to collect her thoughts as she peered past him at the pack of reporters.

Why were the cameras all pointed toward the street, where a truck slowly—

Not a truck. *Will's* truck. Chills exploded over her skin as she covered her mouth in shock. "Oh my God, he's back."

"William?" Guy greedily grabbed his glasses. "I knew it! I knew he'd come back to me. He always does. Like... like... like one of the Austrian toys."

"Australian."

"What are they called?"

She just smiled, an inexplicable happiness washing over her like the rain. "Boomerang." Or *Bloom*-erang.

You always come back to me.

"But his interview..." *Was today.* Her words were lost in the breeze and crowd noise as the truck slowed in front of the house, unable to get in the driveway.

"Come on." Guy tugged at her, running on pure adrenaline now. "We gotta get over there."

"Wait." The media rushed the truck, surrounding it, shouting questions, pounding on the hood. Did they think she was in there?

Will parked on the street just as the front door of the house opened and about a half dozen sheriff's deputies came marching out of Guy's house. They dispersed the crowd and stationed themselves in a protective pathway to the car.

All for *Will*?

Didn't the media realize the person they wanted was right behind them, standing out in the open? Obviously not, which gave her a chance to change her plan. She had Guy now; there was no reason to make her public plea.

Just then, the crowd roar erupted as Will got out of the truck, rounding to the other side, shouting at the cameramen. A few more deputies surrounded the truck, one opening the passenger door to help someone out.

Oh, not someone. Coco.

For a moment Jocelyn couldn't speak. Shock and disbelief stole her breath and crushed her lungs. Coco Kirkman was here? With Will?

Why?

The press shouted questions, but Will and one of the deputies flanked Coco, who held up her hand in a plea for space. Will shouted at the reporters, but Jocelyn couldn't catch the words over the noise. She'd make a statement? Was that what he said?

Next to her, Guy just shook his head, then patted her back lovingly. "Gotta hand it to you, Missy. I've never seen a yard sale like this one."

Neither had she. "Let's go through the neighbor's yard, Guy. Let's get around the back and into the house through the pool patio. No one will even notice us." Not with a superstar like Coco headed in the front door.

He blinked at her. "Why?"

"So we can..." She rooted around her brain for a reason that would get him to move. "Meet the hostess. That's who they're bringing inside."

"Nicey?"

She urged him across the street, ignoring the strange looks from the neighbors. "Not this time, Guy. Her name is Coco. And I cannot wait to hear what she has to say."

"She's gone. And so is her father."

Will blamed sleep deprivation on his brain's refusal to process what Lacey said when they got Coco inside the house.

Coco processed it, though, and instantly started to whine. "I can't make any statements without her!"

"Wait a minute. Wait." Will held up a hand to silence her, just as he caught Guy's picture in the middle of the TV screen with some reporter talking. What the *hell*?

A bad, bad feeling crept through his gut, but he tamped it down and stayed focused on Lacey and Clay. "Where are they?" he demanded.

"We don't know." Clay said, a protective arm around Lacey, who looked pale and as stressed out as Coco, only she was quieter about it.

"I have to talk to Jocelyn," Coco insisted. "I'm not going out there until I talk to her. I have to—"

Zoe swept in and practically scooped the actress away, and Tessa instantly leaped to Coco's other side.

"Let's get you in the back and calmed down, Ms. Kirkman," Tessa said.

"Yeah," Zoe added, leaning close to Coco. " 'Cause, honey, you could really use a little makeup before you get in front of any cameras."

Will shot them a grateful look and turned back to Lacey, Clay, and Slade. "Someone tell me what the hell is going on."

As they explained, only certain words really took hold. Guy had been missing since yesterday. Woke up and Jocelyn was gone. Silver Alert got the media here.

And they had plenty of questions of their own, but the need to find Jocelyn and Guy shot like liquid mercury through his veins.

"We have to find them," he said simply, marching to the door, ready to take on every damn reporter and an army of deputies to get his woman back. And her father.

Damn it, they all belonged together. They all—

"William!"

He froze at the sound, the punch of relief making his gut drop. He turned toward the patio to see Guy hobbling across the grass with Jocelyn next to him, both of them soaked, bedraggled, filthy, and absolutely the most beautiful sight Will had ever seen.

Ignoring the noisy reaction of the others in the room, Will strode to the sliding glass door and threw it open, running across the patio and practically tearing the screen door off its hinges to wrap these two people he loved so damn much in his arms.

Guy might have sobbed and Jocelyn let out a soft, sweet moan, but for the space of one breath of joy they all held each other and no one said a word. They just stood together in complete union.

Finally Guy pushed away. "Where's Nicey?"

"What the hell happened to your face?" Guy was covered with welts, his glasses damn near collapsed, his clothes filthy and wet.

Jocelyn was just as wet, her face streaked with dirt and tears. "He spent the night on an island in the canal," she said, her voice cracking. "He got...lost." She closed her eyes and dropped her head against Will's chest. "We have to take care of him. Please, Will. Please don't put him in a—"

"Shhh." He quieted her with a kiss on her wet head and a finger to her lips. "We won't. I promise. We won't."

"Where's this hostess?" Guy broke away from them and started toward the house. Will turned to follow, but Jocelyn grabbed him by the shoulders.

"Will, he isn't the same man."

"I know," he admitted. "And neither am I."

She frowned at him. "What do you mean?"

"No more waiting. From now on, I act. And don't be too surprised, but I brought someone back from L.A. with me. She wants to come clean, clear your name, and help other abused women. You don't have to live this lie for her anymore, Joss."

"Oh, Will." She leaned into him for another embrace. "I can't believe you did that. I can't believe . . ." She pulled away, searched his face, confusion making her frown. "What about the coaching job?"

He snorted. "I turned that down before I left Mimosa Key. I'm not going to L.A., I'm staying right here, building things that last. Like villas and houses and a life with you."

She put her hand on her mouth like she couldn't contain her happiness. "Here?"

"Right here." He pulled her closer, wrapping his arms around her. "Right here where you belong, Bloomerang."

She answered with a salty, sweet, straight-from-the-heart kiss on his lips.

Chapter Thirty-two

Will took over caring for Guy while the five women somehow squeezed into the hallway bathroom Jocelyn had often locked herself in during Guy's episodes, shaking with fear, hating her life, wishing him dead.

Coco was the one shaking with fear now, perched on the toilet seat so Lacey could fix her hair and Zoe could apply makeup. Tessa leaned against the counter, making notes for Coco's speech.

Jocelyn crouched on the floor, holding the actress's tiny hands.

"You don't have to do this, Coco."

Coco looked down. "Yes I do."

"But you do have to look at me," Zoe insisted. "Unless you are willing to settle for less-than-perfect makeup."

Coco complied. "And I want to do this, Joss," she added. "Not just for you, not just for me, but for every woman who's ever been trapped in an awful situation."

"Great opening line," Tessa said, scratching on paper.

"Thanks," Coco said. "I came up with that on the plane."

"You don't need lines." Jocelyn squeezed Coco's hands gently. "You just have to talk from the heart."

"I'm an actress. I need lines."

"You're a woman, just like us," Jocelyn told her. "And if you want to be heard, you will have to look at the camera and speak honestly. And, honey, you have to be prepared for backlash."

"Backlash?" Lacey asked, holding up a strand of Coco's hair as she combed through it. "What kind of backlash could there be for doing something so right?"

"Miles's fans, for one," Coco said. "They're rabid women who would die for him."

Zoe snorted. "Then maybe they should move in with him."

Coco smiled up at her. "I like you. Have you ever thought about acting?"

Surprising all of them, Zoe shook her head. "No lime-light for me, doll face. But I wouldn't mind the cash and cars. Close your eyes. I'm going all smoky on the creases."

Coco obliged and gave Jocelyn's fingers a squeeze back. "I'm going to be fine," she said. "As long as you're with me and you field the questions about why we did this."

"Gladly."

"And maybe that'll help you get some clients back," Coco added. "I'm really sorry that your business has crashed and burned."

Jocelyn shrugged. "I'm not. I'm moving on."

Lacey froze mid-comb. "You are?"

"I'm going to be the spa manager at Casa Blanca."

Zoe shrieked.

Tessa gasped.

And Lacey dropped the comb and fell to her knees. "Jocelyn! Thank you!"

"Why are you all surprised?" Coco asked. "She's got the stud ballplayer who'd do anything for her and great friends who rally. And a kind of quirky but very cute little old father."

Jocelyn smiled at her, so eternally grateful that Coco hadn't given her a fight when she'd explained her decision to forgive Guy. "Exactly," Jocelyn agreed. "Why are you all shocked?"

"But I thought..." Tessa put down the paper, frowning. "Will was interviewing for a job in L.A."

"He blew it off to stay in Mimosa Key and be the best damn carpenter this island's ever had." And the best damn *man* Jocelyn had ever known.

"The only job he's interviewing for is to be your main squeeze," Coco said. "That man loves your ass."

"Ahem," Tessa said pointedly.

"Amen," Lacey replied.

"I like this girl," Zoe said with a grin.

Jocelyn just beamed. "He might get that job."

"Great." Coco laughed. "It'll be awesome for you to finally let go of that pesky virginity you've been carting around for a lifetime."

That was met with stunned silence and Jocelyn felt heat creep up her neck.

Zoe's hands froze mid-eye-shadow-stroke. "You're a *virgin*?"

Jocelyn swallowed. "Not anymore."

"But...with Will...that was your *first*?"

She nodded, then looked up to Lacey and Tessa for help, but got nothing except open-mouthed, wide-eyed disbelief.

"You know I was never with anyone in college," Jocelyn said.

"But, we assumed...after...no one?" Zoe shook her head as if the thought just would not find a place in her brain. "At your age?"

"Zoe, not everyone is the sexual tigress you are."

"But not *anyone* is a virgin at your age."

"Well I was," Jocelyn said.

Zoe gave Jocelyn a look, then straightened to get back to work on Coco's face, still unable to process the unbelievable news.

"So," Tessa said, tapping her pen on the paper. "You don't tell your three best friends that you're a virgin, but you share that with a client."

"Coco's more than a client," Jocelyn said quickly. "She's my friend, too. And she is a sister in..." She closed her eyes. She'd have to talk about this now, so she might as well practice with the ones who loved her the most. "Abuse."

No one spoke for a few long seconds, but Jocelyn and Coco squeezed each other's hands, the shared experience always there between them.

"All right, Ms. Kirkman," Zoe said, grabbing a hand mirror. "Now you're ready to face your adoring fans."

"Yes, I am." But she didn't even look, standing slowly and pulling Jocelyn up with her. "You guys are all awesome and Jocelyn is lucky to have you."

"We know," Tessa said, reaching out to hug Jocelyn. "We love her even if we don't know her secrets."

"You know them all now," Jocelyn said. "And in a few minutes, so will the rest of the world."

"Except the Oldest Living Virgin part." Zoe grabbed Jocelyn to nudge her onto the toilet seat. "Uh, you need a little makeover, too, Joss. You don't want *the only man you ever slept with* to see you like this."

Ten minutes later, Coco and Jocelyn walked hand in hand to the front patio of 543 Sea Breeze Drive, the place of so many unhappy, violent moments in the past. The sun had finally slipped out from behind the clouds and the crowd of reporters had grown exponentially.

A cheer erupted at the sight of Coco, who walked up to a podium hastily erected by a media outlet after she'd requested one for the press conference.

She glanced nervously at Jocelyn. "Maybe you should, you know, introduce me."

"Maybe you should introduce yourself."

Coco nodded and headed toward the microphone, the papers Tessa had written fluttering on the stand. She tapped the mike, and that just elicited more of a roar and a cringe from Coco. Jocelyn walked up next to her and took her hand.

"C'mon, Coco, you can do this. You can do this for every woman just like us."

"Hello," she said into the mike. When the crowd quieted, she leaned closer and said, "I'm here to speak on behalf of every girl who's ever been hit, every woman who's ever been beaten, and every wife who's ever had to lie to get away from violence."

Complete silence fell over the crowd and a soft gust

of wind picked up one of the papers and floated it away. Coco ignored the loss, looking out to the crowd.

"I have a message to give to you, and I want you to deliver it to every corner of this earth because abuse *has to stop*."

Behind her, the screen door opened and Guy stepped out on the patio, his face the image of confusion. Instantly Jocelyn stepped away, but Coco kept talking.

Jocelyn reached him, turned him around, and guided him inside. Will was in the living room, leaning against the brick wall, dividing his attention between Coco live on TV and Jocelyn.

"He's not quite understanding what's going on," Will said. "I did my best to explain."

"It's just part of the show, Guy," she said, guiding him to his recliner.

"I never saw this part of the show." He slumped into the chair, automatically patting the arm for his remote. "Where's the gifting part? When do you gift me with something special?"

"Right now," she said, kneeling next to him.

Will walked in and handed her the remote. "It was in the—"

"Dishwasher, I know." She smiled up at him. "What do you think we should gift Guy with for all the trouble he's been through these past few weeks?"

Will reached for her. "Let's talk about it." Wrapping her in his arms, he took a few steps away from Guy. "You've forgiven him?"

She nodded. "Completely. I can't let the past ruin the present, Will. And I can't spend whatever time he has left hating him." The announcement felt so good and right on her lips.

"And me?"

"You? I could never hate you. I love—"

"Wait." He cupped her face with both hands. "Me first. Jocelyn, I love you. I want to live every day for you, with you, next to you. I trust you, I need you, and you have always been the only one for me. Always."

A happiness so bone-deep she could feel it down to her toes washed over her. "I love you too, Will."

"Am I on your list of everything now?"

The list that now included family and trust and forever love? "You're right at the top, where I intend to keep you for the rest of our—"

"Excuse me!" Guy called. "My gift, Missy?"

"—lives," Will finished for her, guiding her back to the recliner. "How's this, buddy? We're getting married."

Jocelyn sucked in a soft breath at the announcement, but Guy sat bolt upright. "Really?"

"Yup," Will continued. "We're going to live right next door and keep an eye on you." He threw Jocelyn a questioning glance, and she nodded happily. "And we're having kids."

Guy tried—and failed—to hide his smile. "Kids running around here calling me crazy?"

"No." Jocelyn put one hand on Guy's arm and the other on Will's strong shoulder, gratitude for the gift of forgiveness and love bursting in her chest. "They won't call you crazy. They'll call you . . . *Grandpa*."

Epilogue

Seven Months Later

Casa Blanca's parking lot was no longer a gravelly home to a construction trailer; it was a smooth asphalt expanse currently filled with shiny Mercedes, Beamers, and Jaguars. The new surface was so smooth that Jocelyn's high heels made a satisfying tap as Will opened the door of her Lexus and she climbed out.

As her silky skirt slipped way up her thigh, Will let out a low whistle of appreciation.

"Zoe picked this outfit," she said.

"A true believer in form over function." Will loosened the knot around his neck, taking his eyes off her only when the whine of a sports-car engine stole his attention. "What do you call this thing again?"

"A tie?"

Laughing, he took her hand as she stepped out. "I meant this shindig we're all dressed up for."

"A soft opening."

"I like the sound of that." He pulled her closer, inhaling deeply as if he couldn't get enough of her scent. "You know, Artemesia is the only villa not finished yet. I left the back door unlocked. Let's sneak up there and find your soft opening."

She added a little pressure to his embrace, their fit against each other so natural now they didn't even have to think about it. "Later, I promise. But now it's time to entertain the moneyed set from Naples, here for the VIP preview of the resort."

She turned when a candy-apple-red Porsche swung into a space a few feet away.

"Arriving in true style," he noted.

"Don't knock it. These ladies pay top dollar for luxury, and Lacey and I plan to deliver."

"Lacey plans to deliver any minute now, from the looks of her."

She gathered her wrap and bag, tucking her hand into his arm. "As of an hour ago, she was pretty sure she'd be here, but she's been having contractions all day. I have no such excuse and, as the spa manager, I need to make friends and charm potential customers."

A man climbed out of the Porsche looking like he'd been plucked from central casting for the event. Black hair with maybe a whisper of silver threads, jaw-droppingly handsome, dressed in Armani, a phone pressed to his ear.

"If she's not responding to the sandostatin, then we need to closely monitor her kidney function overnight," the man said with gruff authority as he walked around the car to the other side, reaching for the car door. Jocelyn thought there was something vaguely familiar about him. "Administer it with high-dose conditioning protocols for the next three hours and keep the patient sedated. If anything changes, call me."

He opened the passenger-side door and an exquisite brunette dressed in a strapless white dress climbed out, her expression as icy as the diamonds around her neck. "You said your partners were handling the calls tonight."

"This case has extenuating—"

"I don't care. You have to fake this for one more night."

Will put his arm around Jocelyn and guided her past the awkward exchange, keeping her tucked close to his side.

"Promise me we'll never fight," he said.

"Never? I make no such promises. But promise me you'll never drive a screaming-red Porsche."

"Never? I make no such promises."

They laughed, looking at each other and slowing just enough to share a kiss.

"C'mon, Joss," he murmured. "Let's blow this thing off and go hit fungoes at the field." He dragged his hand down her waist and over her backside. "I have a key to the clubhouse now."

"Ah, the powers of a volunteer high school coach," she teased. "Who needs a hundred-thousand-dollar sports car when you can do me against the varsity lockers?"

He grinned. "I love the way you think."

"Behave, Will Palmer," she warned as two uniformed porters welcomed them and opened the doors to Casa Blanca's creamy, dreamy lobby.

Will kept his hand on Jocelyn's back as they scanned

the crowd. There were mainly unfamiliar faces but a few were friendly, like Gloria Vail, who'd agreed to work in the salon against her aunt's wishes. The guests were busy checking out the elegant North African mosaic work along the registration desk and reading informational pamphlets about Casa Blanca's all-organic spa, which Lacey and Jocelyn had decided to call Eucalyptus.

The staff and subcontractors chatted in small groups wearing expressions of pure satisfaction. They'd done it. They'd made the deadline. Lacey's delivery date had become the de facto "end date" for the last six months, and the ever-growing crew of construction, hotel, restaurant, and spa staff had worked nonstop to get the resort ready before its owners brought baby boy Walker into the world.

"Where is everybody?" Jocelyn asked Will.

"And by everybody you mean Lacey, Tessa, and Zoe."

"And Clay." She glanced around, but none of the people she most wanted to see were there.

Suddenly the henna-glass spa doors shot open and Ashley burst out, looking more than a little panicked. When she spotted Jocelyn, Lacey's daughter looked like she'd cry with relief.

"Aunt Jocelyn! We have a problem." She grabbed Jocelyn's arm and pulled her close, her eyes moist with tears. "My mom's in labor. It's happening so fast. Clay took her into the spa and we called nine-one-one and they're headed over the causeway, but, oh my God, I think she's gonna have the baby any second!"

Will and Jocelyn looked at each other, a silent communication instantly exchanged.

"I'll get that doctor," Will said. "Go be with Lacey."

Will rushed off and Jocelyn wrapped an arm around a very shaken Ashley. "Don't worry. She's going to be fine."

"I don't know. She's in so much pain."

"She's having a baby, Ash. There's pain." They hustled through the doors, running as fast as feasible on the heels. Jocelyn barely noticed the Marrakesh silver mirror she'd hung that afternoon or the Moroccan berber rugs they'd just imported for the opening.

Eucalyptus was an exotic, inviting, luxurious spa, but not the ideal place for a baby to be born.

Jocelyn took a deep breath, fighting the old urge to control everything. She sure as heck couldn't control this.

Ashley pushed open the massage-room door, where the lights were as low as they would be for a client but the woman on the table was anything but relaxed. Tessa and Zoe's backs blocked her view of Lacey, but Jocelyn heard the long, low, harrowing cry of her friend's agony.

Ashley froze, then put her hand to her mouth. "Mom!"

"Shhh. Ash. Relax." Jocelyn came around the table to stand next to Clay, who looked as pale as his stepdaughter. He held Lacey's hand, and from the looks of it she was squeezing the living hell out of his fingers. Lacey's beautiful periwinkle silk dress was soaked with sweat, and something else. Her shoes were off, her legs up, her hair a wild coppery gold mess.

"There's a doctor coming," Jocelyn said, taking Clay's other hand. "He'll be in here in one second."

"He better hurry the hell up." Lacey ground out the words and slammed her other hand on the massage table, her distended belly heaving with each gasp. "Because I have to push. I have to push *now*!"

"Don't do that, Lacey," Zoe said.

"Why not?"

"Because in the movies they never want you to do that."

"I can't...help..."

The door shot open and the man from the parking lot barreled into the room, instantly taking over the small space with an aura of calm, commanding control.

"Clear the table," he ordered.

Everyone backed away, except Zoe, who stood stone still, ghost white, and speechless.

The doctor stood at the bottom of the makeshift bed and fired questions at Clay. How long, how many, how often, how bad.

Clay answered as Tessa put an arm around Ashley. "Let's get you out of here, hon."

"No, my mom needs me."

Her mom let out a howl of pain.

"Your mom needs you to leave," Tessa ordered with more force, ushering Ashley to the door.

"Can you deliver a baby?" Jocelyn asked the doctor, who was already getting into position to do just that.

"I went to medical school," he said dismissively. "Get me gloves and a sterilized pair of scissors." He put his hands on Lacey's knees while she endured the next contraction. "And towels."

"Help me get that," Jocelyn said to Zoe, relieved that the doctor seemed so competent.

But Zoe remained rooted in her spot, still staring at the man.

"C'mon, Zoe," Jocelyn urged.

At her name the doctor looked up from his patient, seeing Zoe for the first time. His eyes widened exactly like hers did and, in that second, Jocelyn knew where she'd seen him before.

Oliver. The doctor who'd had Zoe dodging for cover all those months ago. The one whose practice they'd passed in Naples.

"Zoe?" he asked, obviously as stunned as she. "What are you doing here?"

Lacey grunted and annihilated Clay's hand. "For the love of God, I have to push!"

Will appeared with the gloves and scissors, thankfully more focused than Jocelyn was. Jocelyn turned and opened a cabinet, yanking out a stack of fresh towels.

"You can leave now," the doctor said as he pulled on the latex gloves. "I only need the baby's father."

Will gathered both of the women and led them out, having to nudge Zoe a little harder than Jocelyn. In the small vestibule designed for clients to meditate before and after their massages, Tessa stood with both arms around Ashley.

"He's going to deliver the baby," Jocelyn assured them as much as herself. "He seems like a really good doctor."

Zoe snorted.

They all just looked at her, but Will said, "Actually, he's an oncologist. His wife just let me know in no uncertain terms that he wasn't here to work."

Zoe closed her eyes, turned, and walked down the hall away from the group while Tessa continued gentle words of assurance for Ashley.

"C'mere." Will took Jocelyn's hand and tugged her out of the vestibule.

She glanced over her shoulder at the closed massage-room door. "I want to wait here," she said. "It could be any minute."

"We'll be right around the corner. I need something."

At the serious tone in his voice, she followed him into the facial room, completely dark and cool and smelling vaguely of mint and lavender. In the center of the room, a simple bed with clean sheets awaited the first facial...or...

She smiled at him. "You're kidding, right?"

"I'm dead serious."

Laughing, she put a hand on his chest. "Let's take it to the villa later."

Will's eyes flashed dark blue as he came closer, wrapping his arms around her. "Don't worry, we will. To celebrate."

"The new baby?"

"Life's curveballs."

"So says the catcher."

"I'm serious." And he was. There was no smile on his face, no humor in his expression. "Shit happens, fast and unexpectedly."

"Yes, it does."

"So, Joss, let me ask you a question. What are you prepared to die for?"

She blinked at him. "Excuse me?"

"That's the question you asked me once, when you were life coaching. You said it told you what was important to someone."

"That was really just a rhetorical question I used to ask clients to get a conversation going."

"I know what I'm prepared to *live* for." He got closer, stealing her air and space and any last shred of sanity as he walked her toward the middle of the room. "You."

She kind of melted, letting him dip her back on the facial bed. "Likewise."

"So why are we waiting for the right time?"

"I know you hate to wait now," she teased, but it was hard to joke in the face of all this certainty. Determination. Focus.

"I don't want to wait another day or night or minute."

She closed her eyes and dropped backwards, the words and the man sweeping her right off her feet. "I've created a monster who refuses to wait for anything."

He laughed a little, kissing her throat. "So, when?"

"Right now, right here?" A shiver of anticipation and desire shot through her, control slipping away as he trailed his tongue along her jaw and settled her deeper onto the bed.

"Maybe next week."

She gave him a little nudge away, to see his face. "Next week?"

"We can't get everything together before then."

"You don't mean for sex."

"No, I mean for marriage." He cupped his hands over her face. "I love you so much, Jocelyn. I want to know we're in this together, forever, as one."

"Oh, Will, I love you, too. You know we're together."

"I don't know anything except I love you." He kissed her, still holding her face, tenderly like she was his prize. "I love your heart."

She put her hand on his chest. "You're the one with the big heart, Will. You're all heart."

He rocked against her. "Not all."

"Okay, and some soul."

He nestled against her, kissing his way to her ear. "Let's make this official then. Jocelyn Mary Bloom, love of my life, girl of my dreams, mother of my future—"

The door popped open and they froze as Zoe stood in stunned silence, taking in the scene. "Seriously, guys? Now?"

Will held Jocelyn firmly on the bed, ignoring the intrusion with an unwavering gaze. "I was just proposing," he said.

"Oh," Zoe whispered. "Well, what'd she say?"

"I don't know yet." Will gathered her a little tighter as more footsteps came toward the room and Tessa's happy laughter floated in.

"We have an audience," Jocelyn whispered.

"I don't care. Where was I?"

"Something about love, girl, dreams, motherhood..." She closed her eyes as happiness clutched her heart. "It was all good."

"Say yes, Bloomerang."

"Dying here," Zoe sang from the doorway. "Just say yes."

"Yeah, just say yes, Aunt Jocelyn," Ashley added.

Jocelyn looked into Will's eyes and called, "Tess, what's your vote?"

"Go for it, girl. Break that damn shell around your heart."

She took a deep breath, savoring the word she was about to say, the commitment she was about to make, and the life she was about to live.

At just that moment, Elijah Clayton Walker let out his very first cry and they all yelled out at the same time. "Yes!"

The women in the doorway instantly disappeared, leaving them alone for a better drama.

"You said yes," Will whispered.

"I screamed yes."

"Even better." He gave her that slow, sweet, sexy smile that turned her entire body to mush. "So guess what I finally have?"

"A fiancée?"

He kissed her forehead, her eyes, her cheeks, and put his lips against hers to whisper the answer. "I have... *everything.*"

In Barefoot Bay, you're guaranteed to find family, friendship, and romance—fall in love with more books in Roxanne St. Claire's *New York Times* bestselling series!

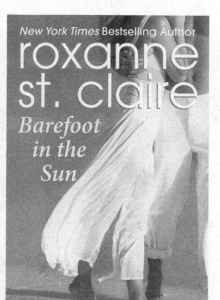

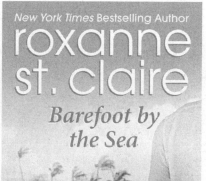

About the Author

Roxanne St. Claire is a *New York Times* and *USA Today* bestselling author of more than fifty novels of suspense and romance, including many popular series such as the Dogfather, Barefoot Bay, the Guardian Angelinos, and the Bullet Catchers. In addition, she has penned numerous standalone books and two young adult novels.

In addition to being a ten-time nominee and one-time winner of Romance Writers of America's prestigious RITA Award, Roxanne has won the National Reader's Choice Award for best romantic suspense four times, as well as the Daphne du Maurier Award, the HOLT Medallion, the Maggie, Booksellers Best, Book Buyers Best, the Award of Excellence, and many others. Her books have been translated into dozens of languages, and one has been optioned for film.

Roxanne lives in Florida with her husband and adorable dog, and still tries to run the lives of her twenty-something kids.